PRAISE FOR SCOTT T. BARNES

"This had me with the setup. The Ever-Guise series is fun, vivid and engaging, well written and described, with engaging characters and a creepy villain. Channeling the modern-day perils of social media, Barnes' fantasy features a protagonist whose coming of age revolves around an enchanted tangle of lies, half-truths and magical suggestions–some of which she herself has spun. The descriptions are great, the characters are very well-developed. We are off on a grand adventure and I am hooked and enjoying it."

— KEVIN J. ANDERSON,
NEW YORK TIMES BESTSELLING COAUTHOR
OF *DUNE: HOUSE ATREIDES*

Reviews sell books! Kevin J. Anderson was kind enough to review *Chaos Woods*. Please consider doing the same on Amazon, Barnes & Noble, Kobo, or wherever you normally shop for books. Thank you!

— SCOTT T. BARNES

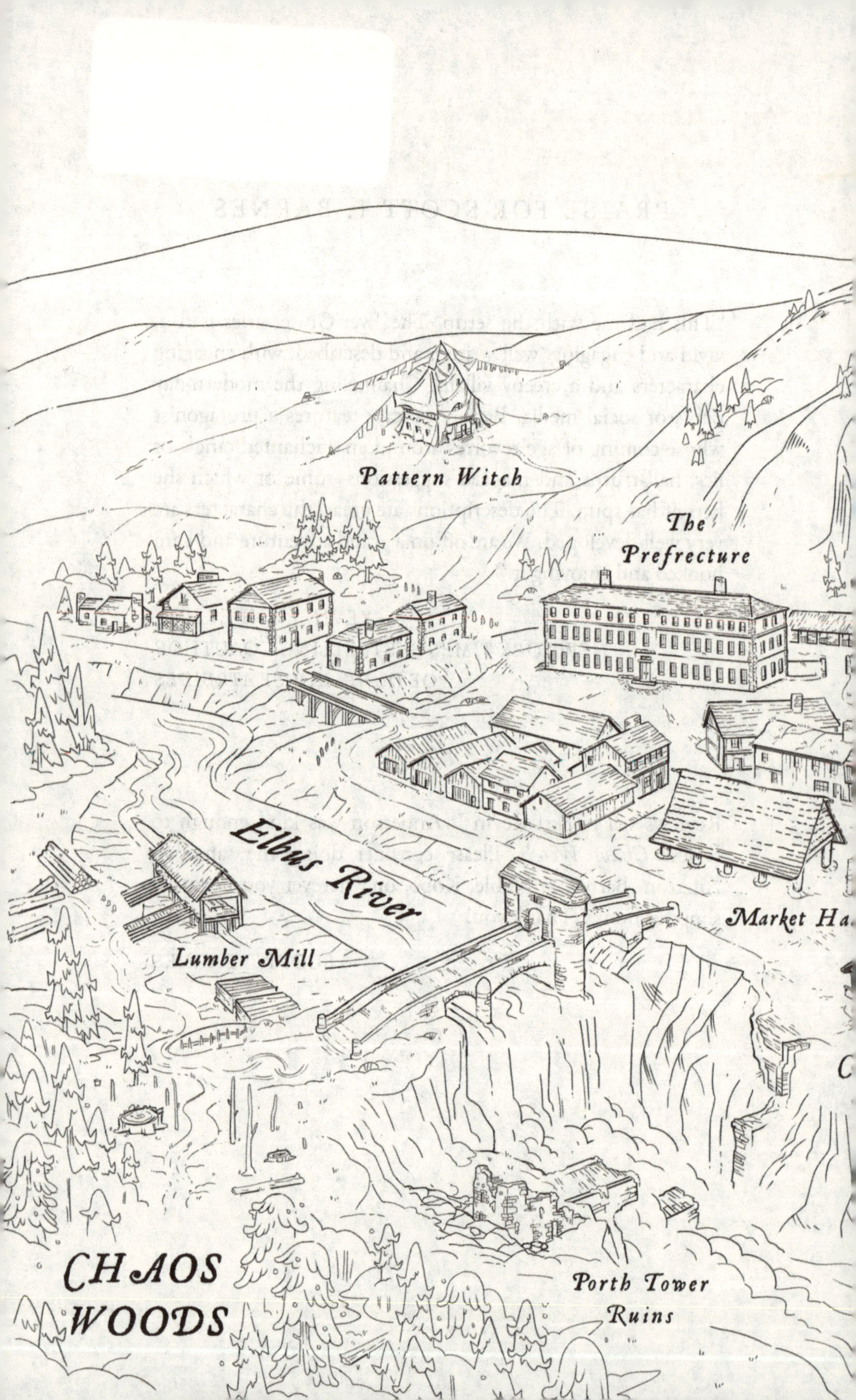

Pattern Witch
The Prefrecture
Elbus River
Lumber Mill
Market Ha
CHAOS WOODS
Porth Tower Ruins

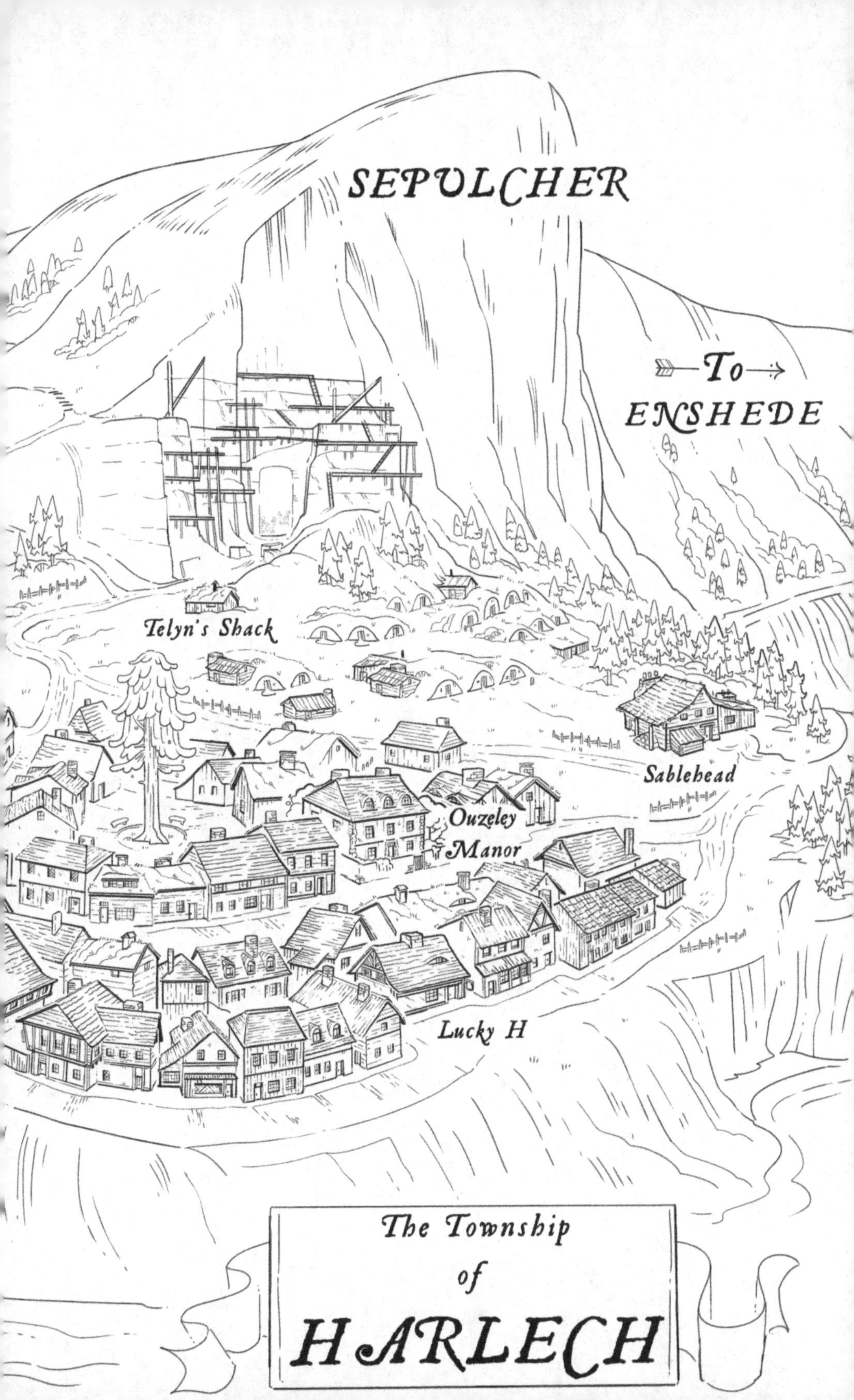

SEPULCHER
To ENSHEDE
Telyn's Shack
Sablehead
Ouzeley Manor
Lucky H
The Township of HARLECH

CHAOS
WOODS

CHAOS WOODS

CHRONICLES OF THE EVER-GUISE
BOOK ONE

SCOTT T. BARNES

NEW MYTHS
PUBLISHING

Chaos Woods

Copyright © 2025 by Scott T. Barnes

ISBN e-book 978-1-939354-35-8
ISBN Hardback, Case Laminate 978-1-939354-34-1
ISBN Trade Paperback 978-1-939354-33-4
ISBN Audio 978-1-939354-36-5

Cover and Interior Art © 2025 by Tom Tolman
Cover Design by Allyson Longueira, © 2025 by New Myths Publishing
Interior Design by Allyson Longueira, © 2025 by New Myths Publishing

*Dedicated to my wife Grace, my daughters Elizabeth and Kaylynn,
and to God, to whom I owe all.*

CHAPTER ONE

Telyn spit on her hand, placed her elbow on the greasy table, and leaned forward. A geometry lesson of a girl—tall, skinny, sharp-nosed, and pointy-chinned—she wore a stained apron over a long gray skirt and white blouse. She'd rather be wearing trousers, but in the mountain town of Harlech, trousers were frowned upon for women unless the specific activity demanded it, activities such as ice climbing or trapping.

Opposite her, the furry gray eehoo tilted her head and vibrated her purple nose—as if she didn't know the game. They'd been arm-wrestling for years, but now that Telyn was fifteen and rather strong, the marsupial's enthusiasm had waned.

"Come on, Tums. Raz will be here any second. 'Where's my stew?'" Telyn did a decent imitation of Razenbock's gravely voice. "Just give me the paw and we'll see how my new training routine compares to your animal biceps. *Lazy* animal biceps, I might add."

The creature hardly ever exercised—not really. She just hung from the walls by her sucker paws for hours on end. But Telyn climbed daily—trees, cliffs, the side of buildings, the frozen waterfall in winter, whatever, rain or snow, without fail.

Too bad you couldn't make a living climbing.

The two were in a kitchen made of so much wood—wood table, wood stools, wood shelves, ceiling and walls—it seemed to have been hewn from a single tree...excepting the stone fireplace, of course. Wicked orange light warmed them; a bubble popped in the stew-pot on the hearth.

Slowly, Tums placed her paw in Telyn's waiting hand.

"There you go, no cheating now."

The sucker paw felt rubbery until Tums activated it. Then it felt like the back of Telyn's hand was being sucked through the bones. Even though she'd been expecting it, she couldn't help grunting.

Telyn's sister swung into the kitchen, her lips parted in a wide grin, her floor-length, blue skirt swooshing. A clamor of voices followed her in, then quieted as the door closed. "Uh, Telyn," she said, putting her armload of dishes into the stone basin at the back of the room, "how long do you plan to go without actually working?"

Telyn made a point of not looking up. They were twins, but they were entirely different. Cressida followed rules—when she wasn't making them. Besides standing at an appropriate, shoulder-height to most men, she was blond and curvy, with a button nose and round, happy cheeks. Telyn was none of those things.

"On three," Telyn began. "One—"

The eehoo slammed Telyn's hand to the table faster than she could say *two*.

Cressida laughed.

Telyn straightened up slowly. "She hangs around all day like a pinecone picking yuck from her pouch...and yet—" Telyn sighed and began rubbing the hurt from her knuckles. "It isn't fair."

"Maybe pouch yuck is her secret weapon. You should try it."

"I have; didn't help." Telyn flicked a wooden spoon at her sister before plunging it back into the stew pot. "Tasted like stock, though —the flower, not the broth. Not bad."

Somehow, Cressida managed to look even prettier with a streak of grease across her forehead. That blue dress showed off her curves better than it should. She'd modified it, dropped the neckline, added lace around the seams. And when Cressida walked, the hint of pedicured toes beneath the embroidered hem drew an unfair number of eyeballs.

Both girls eschewed shoes until winter demanded them.

Telyn blew a curl of brown hair from her face and braced herself to stir. Skill with a needle was one of many things the two didn't share...along with pedicured toes.

"You'll never guess what I heard." Cressida idled up to her sister and bumped her with her hip. "Everyone's talking about it."

"You forgot to do your top button." Telyn soured at this reminder that Cressida got the plum serving job while Telyn was relegated to the kitchen.

"There's a new couple in the Dating Chart. You'll never guess."

"Oh, Aled's rump, not this again." The Dating Chart, what a load llama puckies! A load of busybodies tried to figure out who might get hitched—or unhitched—in the coming year and created a chart out of their data. Worse yet, the townsfolk of Harlech bet on the outcomes!

Telyn rubbed her nose vigorously. "See what you've done? You've gone and made my nose itch."

"Because you want to know—"

"'Cause the Chart gives me the hives."

The kitchen door burst open. "Stew ready yet?" A bearded man, his chest hair fighting its way out of his plaid shirt-collar, brushed past the two girls. He grabbed mitts from the mantle.

"Telyn forgot to put in the garlic." Cressida smiled prettily.

Of course, Cressida would notice that!

"I was just about to. Put in the garlic, I mean."

The man stared at her for a minute and Telyn anticipated a red-forehead tirade—one of Razenbock's specialties. Instead, the big man reached to scratch Tum's ears. "Good. No one 'll be complaining this evening, what with the flacks to keep them diverted. Garlic's expensive." Razenbock leaned in, as if the eehoo was his confidant. "We're closing early. Clean up in here and get home."

He scooped up the pot of stew and disappeared through the swinging door.

The girls whirled toward each other, mouthed, *'Closing early?'* and rushed to peek out. Telyn's chin rested on Cressida's head; her brunette waves spilled over Cressida's straight, blond hair; their bodies pressed together. It took a moment for their eyes to adjust to the public room's dim interior to discern more than smoky outlines. But when they did—

A shiver of interest spread from Telyn's lower back; she spotted at least five flacks. Five! In the Sable Head!

Flack was the catch-all term for non-humans, creatures with magical powers—those you'd best stay away from or likely you'd go missing, or get sold into slavery, or die. Flacks didn't call each other that, of course—they called each other the complimentary term *thaumas*.

Flacks never came into the Sable Head; there was too much chaos wood in the walls. Chaos wood disrupted magic and made spells go awry. An abundance of chaos wood made flacks nervous.

"Some mighty strange ones here tonight," Cressida commented.

"You think?"

Two small, chattering schmooks sat together on a bench near the fire. Telyn thought they looked like chipmunks beneath their brown hoods—if chipmunks had bright-orange mouths and eyes where their ears should have been. Despite sitting next to the fire, they had not removed their cloaks. They talked incessantly, leaning close together as though every word was a conspiracy. A third schmook sat on the other side of the room, all alone in the shadows. Now and then lantern-light glinted off his wide-spaced, emerald eyes.

Near the fire, quiet and mean-looking, sat a green-skinned, reptilian trogo. He stared around boldly and gabbed to himself in a guttural language as if chatting to an invisible friend. A bit of drool oozed its way down the trogo's ivory-like tusk and dripped to the table. He wore a stylish trench coat, currently unbuttoned, over black trousers and shirt. Several gold necklaces and bracelets jangled as he moved. Not a few humans sat near the beast, evidently hoping for some trouble. Telyn recognized Heath Robinson, a tough who frequented both the Sable Head and the Lazy H, and Tyre Flint, who'd had a tryst with Daisy Brooks at Dragon Tower.

It would take both of them to take down the brawny trogo, if Telyn was any judge. And she'd seen enough brawls to know.

Cressida exhaled audibly. "Get a load of that cereb. That's enough to give a brakdaw nightmares."

"What? Where?" Telyn's eyes scanned the room—then her nose honed in on him. The creature's skin gave off an odor like a dead man's boots—wet leather, ashes and foot fungus rolled unto one. She smelled it above the malt and smoke and body odor of all the other patrons, and it led her eyes to the nook furthest from the fireplace. The cereb—also called a mind wizard—wore a dark cloak with the hood thrown back. While rare, everyone had heard tell of this most powerful of non-humans. This one had a light blue complexion reminiscent of turquoise, complete with the black veins over his skull. Telyn peered with morbid fascination to see if she could make out— Yes!—the nest of the worm-like tentacles beneath his chin at the base of his neck, writhing like undersea algae.

Must be a 'he,' Telyn decided. *No female would let herself smell like that.*

"No cornics," Cressida said, a little breathlessly. The sheep-headed beings who controlled Harlech usually appeared wherever flacks congregated, sitting in the corners, watching. Somebody must have bribed them to stay away.

"Don't see none."

"Bound to show up sooner or later."

"Not if Raz closes early." That shiver of interest had spread all the way to her forearms, and Telyn's fingers twitched with anticipation. "Look, sis, we—"

Bustling across the public room, holding a bouquet of full mugs by the handles like foaming flowers, Razenbock's head swung toward the cracked door, and his glower caught Telyn square in the eyes, cutting her off mid-sentence.

"Er..." Telyn faltered.

"Not this time, Tey," Cressida said, as she pulled back into the kitchen. "That is a really, really bad idea. 'No ladies after supper!' You know the rule."

That was Raz's mantra. He believed the presence of ladies in the public room increased the likelihood of fights a hundredfold.

"At least we ain't no ladies." Telyn muttered their standard joke rotely.

Her fingertips tingled like crazy; she *had* to see what was up. She'd never get to sleep if she left now.

Cressida wriggled out from under Telyn and stepped back into the kitchen. "Tey. Tey, listen. He told us to clean up and go home."

"We can do this, Cressida. We'll just hide behind the winter stores." Telyn let the door close a smidgen further to fool Raz, then she turned sideways and squeezed into the public room.

"Tey, wait!"

"Come join me," Telyn said, over her shoulder. She smiled dismissively at a nearby trapper. "Not you, honey, my sister."

"Wait, Tey, the dishes—"

"Sorry, really. Tums 'll lick 'em clean." Telyn allowed the door to swing shut on her sister's protests.

Too bad Cressida was stuck with all those greasy pots and pans, but it'd look suspicious if they exited the kitchen together, and Telyn wouldn't get a better chance. Raz's back was to her as he spoke with the mind wizard; patrons jammed the public room to bursting. No one would notice her in the smoke, the flickering lamplight, the crowd. The jumble of winter stores took up a large section of floor against the side wall of the public room; they hadn't had time to carry them down to the cellar.

Wicked perfect, she thought, and glided forward. *Your loss, Cressida.*

CHAPTER TWO

The big fireplace ensured the public room remained warm and sweat-filled and smoky. The challenge became immediately obvious: Telyn had to cross the whole public room, in front of everyone, to reach the winter stores. And then maybe, just maybe, she could hide in there somewhere.

If no one noticed.

And everyone was watching her.

Or so it felt.

The Sable Head hadn't been so packed in...well, maybe ever. It was a drafty, run-down place and had been since Telyn started working there at the age of twelve, three years before. Telyn's cooking didn't help. Though, to be honest, if Razenbock bought proper pork speck instead of mystery meat (usually marmot) it might help matters. Or if he'd stop watering down his malt. Or a host of other "ifs."

If we'd planned a little better, she thought after promising to bring malt to the third impatient trapper on her way across the room, *I could have had Cressida make a distraction, drop some mugs or something. And scream, she's good at that. Course, then I'd have to listen to her worries...*

A hand slapped her backside. She whirled to find a grizzled trapper with a pockmarked, red nose.

"Why, ain't you a pretty one." He smiled with his three remaining teeth. "I seen your ankles."

"Why thank you," Telyn said shortly. "But I'm surprised you can see anything past your turnip—I mean nose."

This caused howls of laughter from the man's friends. The drunk sat at long table with at least eight bearded trappers who looked like hairy, pickled puppets.

"That ain't nice." He wiped his mouth with the back of his hand. "Maybe you should buy me a drink to soothe my hurt feelings." At least, that's what he might have said. His voice sounded like his tongue didn't quite remember how to form words properly.

"That's the malt talking." Telyn sidestepped another awkward attempt to slap her backside. "You'll pay for it with a headache next morning." This really wasn't going as planned.

"Three to one against, Galam," one of the trappers at the table offered.

"I'll take that," hiccupped another, passing a coin across the table.

Telyn lowered her voice. "Last warning, Pickle. I belong here, and I can have you thrown out—on your head."

Razenbock wasn't in sight. Heath was too far away to do anything, but he was standing up—it would be a good excuse for a fight. Telyn hoped the trapper's friends would stay out of it; a full-scale brawl would end the evening for everyone.

The drunk's chair whipped off its legs and he fell to his back. A tall man in a tan duster coat stood over him.

"Get out of here," said the tall man. Telyn saw eye-to-eye with the stranger, and she was six foot three. "I've no patience for dung like you."

The room pulled away from them, patrons knocking chairs and tables askew. A circle formed.

Mister Pickle wobbled to his feet. "You looking for trouble?"

"Not really."

"You found it!"

Wobbling with the effort, the drunk reared back to swing. The tall man easily sidestepped the blow, then moved behind his opponent. He trapped Pickle's arms then dragged him outside. Telyn had never seen anyone so graceful. One move flowed into another like a puma— or a snake.

A few seconds later the tall man returned to the public room alone. The noise that grew with the fight quickly subsided and everyone turned to stare into their earthenware mugs, except for the trogo. His throaty laughter exploded from the corner of the room, causing more than a few heads to turn. He seemed unable to control himself, and he laughed, spilled his drink, then laughed some more. Then Pickle's friends joined in the laughter, and the tension drained. In the commotion, Telyn was safely hidden behind sacks of flower and sugar, barrels of molasses, kegs of malt, bladders of angel water, and crates of salt.

A sticky spot on the floor pulled at Telyn's skirt when she shifted position to peer between the barrels.

Cressida had exited the kitchen and sidled around the room— apparently the only one who saw her hide, judging by the glances she shot in Telyn's direction.

The tall man looked around for a moment. His eyes rested on the stores. Telyn was dying to move out of sight. If she could see the man, then he could see her—if he knew where to look. But Telyn knew to never, ever move when you're hiding, unless you knew for sure you'd been spotted—then run like crazy. Redbeard taught Telyn that years ago, clustered with the town's children around a roaring winter fire. The crusty old trapper had a story for every hour of the day.

Apparently, though, the tall man did not spot her, for he crossed the room to talk with Razenbock alone. Telyn wondered if Raz was going to kick the man out. *Not much of a fight, really. Nothing got broken, no heads busted open.*

Only the glow from the large fireplace in the far corner and oil lamps hanging from opposite walls provided light, so the room was dim near the entrance. Even so, Telyn made out an exchange between the tall man and Raz—the glitter and jingle of a purse—and nodded approval.

Perhaps something was broken after all.

Then Razenbock shouted loud enough and long enough that the whole place stopped to listen. "Sable Head's closing early. Everyone clear out."

The patrons looked at each other in astonishment.

As Telyn scanned the room, she caught Cressida squinting worriedly at the stores. She motioned none-too-subtly for Telyn to come out of hiding.

Telyn gestured equally frantically that no way, no how was she moving. *Not for all the hurons in Ouzeley's fat purse would I miss this.* She gestured for Cressida to join her.

Razenbock hustled people out the door as fast as he could. The patrons were too surprised to cause trouble. Heath Robinson announced loudly that he was going to the Lucky H, where pansies didn't go to bed early and the stew didn't taste like earthworms. (*The nerve!* Telyn fumed. *I only put an earthworm in that one time—and only because Raz made me so angry I could just spit.*) Heath let himself be hustled out with all the rest.

The flacks didn't move. There were a lot of them—more than Telyn had noticed before. Then only the flacks remained, and the tall man. And her sister, who was slipping along the shadows near the stores.

"Cressida!" Razenbock called. "You can go home now. I'll clean up here."

Cressida stood before Telyn's hiding place, right in front of the crack between the barrels. Telyn could smell the lavender she kept in a sachet in her pocket.

"I just got a few things to do first," Cressida said.

Telyn's heart felt heavy in her chest. Was it still beating?

For all her bravado, she wanted her twin's company. They were a team, a pair, a turtle and shell. They belonged together.

"Nothing to do. Come on, I'm feeling extra generous tonight." Raz held out a stack of hurons.

Was that...their pay?

Their back pay?

Telyn counted on her fingers how many weeks it had been since

Raz had paid them in more than food—and ran out of fingers. Their mom would be so pleased! She could get new fabric...

"Just have to clean up this mess on the floor," Cressida said.

"Now, before I change my mind."

Cressida jerked forward, like her legs moved on their own. Her hands took the hurons, and she kept walking.

"Where's Telyn?" Razenbock called after her.

Telyn held her breath.

Cressida stopped, one foot out the door, thinking furiously. "She's gone home." And Cressida left without looking back.

Telyn sat, stunned, for a moment. And then, slowly, a grin spread across her angular face.

She was alone.

And she was going to witness everything.

CHAPTER THREE

The flacks moved three tables together. The tall man sat at its head, to Telyn's left, the cereb at the other end, to her right. The var, a long-necked, bird-like species with yellow plumage managed to squeeze his lower limbs under the table on the near side, along with a schmook and another unidentified creature, while on the far side of the table sat two hooded schmooks dwarfed by the lizard-like trogo. If she craned her neck, Telyn could see them all from the crack between the barrels.

Surely the flacks were up to no good. Maybe they were going to play a high-stakes game or hold some kind of covert meeting. Danger hummed in the smoke-laden air. Since no cornics were around, it could be some sort of empire-overthrowing conspiracy. It could be. Now that Razenbock had gone upstairs, if Telyn got caught out, she'd be in a heap of trouble—the kind of trouble a human girl might not survive.

Still, something about the tall man reassured her. His boots were polished reptile hide, and he kept them always on the floor, raised to the balls of his feet like a fencer ready to spring. The outline of a dagger showed underneath his shirt, the handle an easy reach over his shoulder. Oh yes, he was dangerous, not someone you'd wanted to cross. But he had protected her once, and he was human. That surely counted for something if Telyn got caught out, right?

Right?

The man tossed something on the table. "I believe one of you is missing this."

The object did a little flip, then jiggled and turned. It inched around the table like a worm.

The trogo jumped back in surprise, knocking over his stool with a crash. The two schmooks next to him yelped and dove under the table. Telyn couldn't make out what the thing was, flat and oval like a slice of potato, but with a golden sparkle on the end.

The var trilled, his beet-red tongue vibrating a foot from his mouth.

The object was blackened and shriveled-up dry. It flipped grotesquely on one end and spun. A golden hoop finally pulled itself free. That's when Telyn recognized it—an ear. The earring floated deliberately over to the mind wizard; he caught it with a wrinkled blue hand and plopped it into a breast pocket on his cloak.

The ear flopped down lifeless.

Bile rose in Telyn's throat. She'd seen plenty of nasty things in Harlech—frostbite, hunting accidents, infected animal bites, even flacks deformed from spells gone awry—but she'd never seen a severed ear. Thankfully, there wasn't any blood. Fresh, oozy, nasty crimson, the kind that spurts, sticky like the floorboards under her bum. Blood made Telyn's head lighter than fumes from angel water.

She tried really hard to think of something besides oozy red blood. She breathed in through her nose, out through her mouth.

No blood, no coppery smell.

Inhale.

Dry things: sand; dirt; cold, powdery snow.

Exhale.

"Thank you, my friend," the cereb nodded graciously. "I have been awaiting word from my associate. I will convey this to his next-of-kin."

The human then tossed the mind wizard a coin-purse. "And this. I found it on him as well," he added, with a hard smile, "a refund for a job left unfinished. You should have hired professionals, Yona. If I was not expecting treachery, I would have never showed up this evening. The auction would have been called off—and your name would not be on the invitation list for the next one."

"Such a harsh punishment," the cereb sneered.

Yona. The cereb has a name. Telyn tried using that solid piece of information to climb back from the verge of vomiting, or passing out, or some weird combination of the two she didn't want to imagine. She'd done weird things a few times when she saw blood.

Sticky, nasty, coppery—

Stop it!

The cereb named Yona gestured around the table. "You should thank me, Dagger. My associate eliminated three others for the privilege of dying at your hands. His competence, or lack of it, made things simple for you."

The tall man—Dagger—snorted.

"Enough of this," the trogo said, and flicked the ear off the table. It landed near the crack between the barrels, of course. "We came here for something."

Telyn half-expected the ear to drag itself across the floor to betray her hiding place. Its fleshy lobe pointed at her like an accusation. She looked at her own fingertips, tugged her own soft earlobes. Her ears withered in her imagination, fell limp, dropped to the floor, and splattered there like rotten pears.

Stop it!

"Why this place?" squeaked one of the schmooks, climbing out from under the table. "This town reeks of human. And this place— watered-down malt, food fit for swine. We feel you have asked much to hold the auction here."

Dagger held up his hands to stifle the murmured agreement.

"You all know why it has to be here. The forest shields us from clairvoyance. And the walls," he gestured around the public room, "are for my protection. We're all equal here. Your magic is lessened— even yours, Yona." He turned a steely gaze to the mind wizard. "If you use your magic within the walls of chaos wood, you will find it useless. And then you will find my blade in your gut."

"Chaos wood," the unknown flack said in a slithery voice, then turned to Yona. "You took a risk with your ear trick, mind wizard. If the chaos wood twisted your magic the wrong way, no telling what might have happened. I'll not be party to that again."

Telyn nearly gasped. What she'd taken as a hood was in fact the creature's billowy head. The flack was a conda, a strange creature with long, flappy extremities made for paddling, and a sort of lure sprouting from its forehead. The lure gave a faint glow in the dim public room.

Condas were said to inhabit an underwater kingdom far out to sea. This might be the first conda who'd ever traveled all the way to the Cairn Range. Ever.

The cereb shrugged. "Is everyone against me?"

None of the other flacks bothered to answer. After all, even if all of them opposed him oddsmakers would bet on the cereb in a fight—they were that powerful.

And then, Telyn forgot all about the blood and the ear, and even about her excitement and fear. The thief had pulled a box from under the table, and from the box he pulled a dazzlingly beautiful mask.

"Behold, the Ever-Guise," Dagger stated.

The var droned something with its long tongue.

The mask depicted a human female with voluptuous lips, almond eyes, thick eyebrows, a high forehead, a strong jawline, and a wide nose—the exact opposite of bony, angular Telyn. If that woman showed up at a dance, men would queue out the door for a spin. Just the sight of it made Telyn's breath catch.

"Let us examine it," the trogo rumbled. "Perhaps this is illusion and counterfeit."

"Properly used, the Ever-Guise wields a subtle magic—not something you can easily test," Dagger replied, passing the mask over to the trogo. "And besides, surrounded by chaos wood, it will not function properly here."

As it passed from human to nonhuman, lamplight bounced from the mask's surface, and Telyn noted that different sections comprised the whole, each seemingly fabricated from a different rare material. Gold, copper and bronze ceramic comprised the eyes, forehead, and crown—except for a turquoise iris in the middle of the forehead. The strong cheeks, perhaps of marble or jade, expanded to the side, a jeweler's rendition of frilled-neck lizards. The chin was pewter, while some flesh-colored material formed the nose. Somehow this hodge-podge meshed like a soul-filled puzzle, as if the craftsman had captured all the aspects of a personality in this single mask.

Mother of Squirrels, Telyn breathed.

"Stick with influence, Kulon," Dagger suggested, his lip curling in a smile, "you're less likely to make enemies that way."

"You think I care about enemies?" In the trogo's hands, the mask looked fragile as ribbon candy; placed on his over-sized face, it barely covered from mouth to eyeballs. But little by little, the mask stretched, took on the scaly green of Kulon's skin, and finally seemed to merge with his face. Telyn had never seen anything like it. The mask disappeared entirely.

The trogo stood slowly, bowed his head—and rainbow light burst in every direction. It reached toward the walls, toward the flacks, and toward Telyn like a spectacular, multicolored fist. She couldn't move out of the way fast enough. It slammed into her forehead. There was no mass to it, but it penetrated her skull and amplified her thoughts to a multitudinous scream. She found herself on her back, numb and drooling.

She groaned.

In the public room, the flacks moaned, groaned, cursed, and shoved furniture about—or so it sounded.

It felt like forever before Telyn managed to pull herself back into a sitting position, blink away her tears, and peer through the crack between the barrels.

Wobbling on his feet, Kulon pulled the mask away from his face. The Ever-Guise didn't seem to want to go; he struggled with it, and his cheeks and lips bulged as it finally came free. The schmooks and var righted their bench as the others returned to the table. Only the cereb seemed unfazed. He thrummed his fingers on the table. He didn't seem to have a proper number of fingers, though Telyn didn't trust her eyeballs at the moment.

"Very foolish," Dagger said, sheathing a blade. "I told you—the chaos wood."

"If we can't use it, then how can we test—?" the conda hissed.

"Yona can test it."

"And if we don't trust him?"

"Then shove off."

There was muttering all around, but finally, reluctantly, the trogo allowed Yona to don the mask. It melted into the wrinkles of that turquoise-colored face.

The cereb spread his four-fingered hands wide.

Immediately, Telyn felt off, as if her mind rode a toboggan over a patch of ice. She could steer in a general way, but her thoughts slipped and skidded—it felt delightfully terrifying—and things could get out of hand really fast. Bumps, jiggles, staticky shocks along her spine interrupted at irregular intervals, and Telyn thought the chaos wood must be challenging the magic.

That made Telyn angry. She wanted to be completely at ease on the sled. She wanted to please Yona.

Yona. The name felt comfortable on her tongue.

"I propose a spirit of complete frankness," the mind wizard said.

That sounds reasonable. Truth is always preferable to lies. Of course, why not?

"Let's start with an exercise in trust."

Yes, of course. How reasonable.

"What are your real names?" the mind wizard asked.

Telyn needn't respond, nothing compelled her to. But then again, why not? It felt like the proper thing to do, very much in the spirit of frankness. This cereb, this Yona, sharing with him made her happy. She trusted the mind wizard without knowing his background or anything about him. They had a sort of bond. And besides, if she happened to be mistaken, if this was the magic talking and not her own free will, the mind wizard didn't really know her, so even after giving her name she would remain anonymous. Completely anonymous.

Just another teenage girl in Harlech.

Still wrapped in comfy blankets on the sled.

"Telyn Lilith Brower," she offered her full name. A satisfied grin split her face.

Several of the flacks spoke also. She didn't catch their names—they all spoke at once. A few eyes drifted around the public room at the unusual echo, but no one left their seat, no one acknowledged Telyn Lilith Brower. She was disappointed that Yona hadn't heard her; she wanted so much to be his friend. Just a small nod of appreciation would do. Still, she was grateful the others hadn't noticed her, particularly that trogo. If he found her here, no telling how Kulon would react, all muscle, drool and reptilian violence.

Dagger leaned back on his stool. "Nice try, Yona. But you won't be learning my real name that easily."

The mind wizard bowed and pulled the mask from his face. He floated it across the table to Dagger and sat back down. "It is authentic." He sounded bored.

Telyn felt sad that Yona didn't like the Ever-Guise as much as she did.

The thief began to fit the mask into the traveling box.

"I haven't tried it," one of the schmooks complained, and the var trilled.

"If you still have doubts, the door is over there. Prattle is cheap; the mask is not." Dagger snapped the box closed.

"Ah, I would feel more comfortable with the mask visible to all," said Yona, "since we are dealing with a spirit of unusual frankness."

Dagger dropped his hand to his side beneath the table and Telyn saw a glint drop into it; a ceramic something. A piece of the mask? Dagger must have palmed one of the plates!

"Do you not trust me?" Dagger asked, his hand paused beneath the table.

"It is not a matter of trust. But—well, yes, it is." Yona's throat tentacles wiggled in a way Telyn couldn't read. "In all frankness."

Had the other flacks not seen? The slight-of-hand was so obvious from Telyn's vantage point.

The var trilled again, this time more insistent.

Telyn held her breath.

The thief reopened the box.

No reaction.

Dagger must have replaced the ceramic plate with another. The old switch-'em-up, oldest trick in the book. Telyn was dying to be on the other side of the tall man, to see the Ever-Guise, to see everyone's expression from his point of view. She was sure violence would explode when one of the flacks realized what had happened. Sorcerers, all. And with the chaos wood all around....

The severed ear seemed to twitch.

CHAPTER FOUR

I f Telyn added up all the money she had ever seen, even here in the tavern, it would not equal a single bid put forth for the Ever-Guise. There was a stack of gold and silver coins in front of each flack. The conda produced bags filled with gold dust, Telyn guessed. He passed these around for the others to inspect before adding them to his pile. Finally, after over half an hour, the var dropped out. He made some odd noises with his beak, and Dagger retorted something about weak currency and alloys—words Telyn only half understood. The bird-like creature did his best to purse his beak in consternation then put his coins back in his pouch. Without another word, with his chicken-like feet and matching gait, he strutted to the door and out.

The firelight flickered in the cold air that stole into the room.

That creature was in a hurry. He doesn't want the others to find him alone at night on the road, I'll bet.

The var's departure reminded Telyn of the slippery ice on the walk home. Fall had replaced summer. Most townsfolk had already started wearing shoes, but Telyn always waited until first snow. Tight leather boots—or worse yet, hard wooden clogs—felt like toe-prison to her.

"Anyone else ready to drop out?" Dagger asked.

The trogo struck with astounding speed. His arm whammed the

closest schmook in the neck, sending the small flack flying across the room. A left fist followed the first, catching the second retreating schmook a glancing blow that almost knocked him off his feet. The schmook chattered and gesticulated with his paw-like hands. Magic burst from his fingertips in all directions, a great orange wave of energy and smoke. The energy struck the walls of the tavern and vanished, leaving only the smell of peaches and a delightful tingle on Telyn's tongue. The third blow of the trogo knocked the schmook over his companion.

"I am combining our bids," said the trogo, bowing respectfully to the thief. "That is, if my friends have no objection."

The schmooks were moving toward the door, the choking one supported by the other, their cowled, rodent-faces drawn in defeat. They muttered gibberish at the trogo as they exited.

"That's right, tell your friends I have robbed you," challenged the trogo to their retreating forms.

Bully, thought Telyn. She had no use for bullies, whether they used fists, mind-games, or cutting words. Still, bullies generally got their just desserts, and she suspected the trogo would get his before the night was through. Those schmooks would figure out some way to ambush him.

Things were definitely getting interesting.

The third schmook, sitting across from the trogo, made no protest. From inside the many folds of his cloak he produced more golden coins until his stack matched the trogo's.

Wait until Cressida hears about this, Telyn thought, shifting around to remove the cramps in her back. *This must be the greatest, most incredible thing that has ever happened in Harlech.*

Her leg had fallen asleep and she pulled on it with both hands. *Careful, careful.* She almost succeeded when the pad of her foot squeaked against the floor. The flacks at the table stopped talking, listening, like mice when the owls stop hooting.

The flacks shifted in their chairs. Dagger got up from the table and moved out of sight. Any moment he would peep over the barrels and catch Telyn hiding there.

What would he do? Would he run Telyn through without a

second thought? Beat her up and throw her out to the night? Telyn, all scrunched up like a pretzel, was in no position to flee—

The man poked at the fire. There was a pop, and a log fell into place, making almost the same noise as Telyn's foot.

The trogo chuckled; the tension broke.

Telyn was able to breathe again. Her leg finally freed, she managed to lie on her back, her neck turned sideways so she could see through the crack and her legs resting on some sacks of flour. She squeezed her thighs together to still the pressure in her bladder. She tried not think about getting caught.

The severed ear kept reminding her about it.

The trogo growled, "Are you going to match this, or are you out?"

There were four flacks left: the trogo, strong and brutish; the conda with his built-in cowl, so alien as to be unreadable; the schmook, diminished since the surrender of the others, but not beaten; and the cereb, the most fearsome and always last to match the bid. The trogo was looking him squarely in the eyes—or under his hood, at least.

The cereb reached tentatively into his cloak. He pulled forth a small figurine, too dark for Telyn to see other than it was carved... something. Telyn had never seen anything so black. The light from the fireplace seemed to be sucked into the statuette, creating a shadow-like aura around it. The room dimmed even further, if that was possible.

"What have you brought me?" said Dagger. "A toy? I have no need for toys. The agreement was for coin or gold."

"Do not take the figurine so lightly. It is of a magic of similar quality to that of the Ever-Guise."

"If so, why do you part with it so easily?"

The folds of the conda's head twitched and warbled.

"I am well-protected outside of these walls. It is knowledge that interests me, knowledge that I hope to attain by careful use of the mask. But you—you have a long way to travel before you are truly safe. Remember who you are doing business with. And forget not who you stole the mask from."

"Where I got it is of no consequence."

"Not my concern, no, but surely a concern of yours. The hand of vengeance knows no limits of distance—or time."

"Knowledge is a valuable commodity, as is time," the schmook said. "Let us have time to consider this bid, and knowledge for the same purpose. Enlighten us as to this toy's worth."

"It is a penumbra daemon."

The trogo growled a deep rumbling in his throat. "Gold, or coin," he finally managed to spit out.

"The penumbra daemon. You have heard? The last known one killed the Emperor of Vool, and every last member of his personal guard. If our friend the var were still here, he would confirm this."

"I know the story," Dagger said, voice thick with consideration.

"I have managed to procure one of these daemons. Very much as powerful, I assure you."

The firelight flickered a long moment while the man thought. Finally, deliberately, he pulled the trogo's bid over. "It is the best," he said. "And no tricks in gold."

"I object—" the schmook began.

The figurine exploded into a spectral mass, black within black, a shadow-bear with tentacles of nothingness sprouting from its back. It stalked around the table, tentacles whipping.

In a blur, Dagger pulled his knife and hacked at the creature. Telyn heard a sucking sound like a boot drawn from wet mud. Steam poured from where the blade pierced the blackness. A shout. Dagger dropped his weapon. The blade was gone, the handle smoking. The room reeked of scalded metal.

"You decide too quickly," said Yona, calmly.

The daemon stopped advancing; its edges danced with the firelight. Telyn could just make out the knots in the wood behind it.

In a blink, the penumbra daemon transformed back into a statuette and clattered to the floor. The cereb retrieved it.

Eying the cereb warily, Dagger poured a mug of malt over the burns on his now-empty hand.

The conda gathered his coin and took his leave without a word. The others did not seem to notice.

"What's the catch?" Dagger asked skeptically, flexing his fingers.

"Just this. The daemon is bound by a code that you and I know nothing about, a bargain made by the sorcerer who created the statuette."

"Did you create it?"

"No."

The trogo walked over, picked up the dagger handle, and examined it with his slitted, black eyes. The blade had completely disappeared, along with part of the guard. He curled his fist around it experimentally. The heat didn't seem to bother him.

"You are trading a debt," the schmook said to Dagger. "It is like a money lender; you borrow one coin, you must pay back two. Master Yona is offering you a debt, and if my guess is correct, it is near time to collect."

"Is this true?" asked Dagger.

"Not a debt. A contract."

"And what does the daemon get out of this contract?"

"I do not know. Perhaps it got what it wanted long ago and is still paying its obligation. Perhaps, as Taito-Vaiana says, the debt will become due shortly. It may demand your very soul. Who knows?" Yona leaned forward. "I was led to believe you were a gambler. Was I mistaken?"

"He is baiting you," said the schmook.

The mind wizard pushed his bid slightly across the table. "Here is enough money to last a lifetime." He held out the figurine. "And here, the chance to live that lifetime. The Chaos Woods reek of gold and greed tonight."

"Who sent the assassin?" Taito-Vaiana, the schmook asked, turning to indicate the ear. Telyn shrank away from the crack. "You know you cannot trust Master Yona to keep his word."

"Who will make it out of Harlech alive?" The mind wizard used magic to float the figurine to the thief, who caught it deftly. "A chance."

"Treachery," the trogo growled.

"A penumbra daemon is valuable, yes, but risky," Taito-Vaiana said. "What kind of contract does this thing have? I would not take that gamble, myself. Now our friend, the trogo, would have a fine bid, except he stole it right before our eyes. How can you trust him? Only I have followed the letter of your invitation. Only I present a safe alternative." The schmook exhaled. "Nevertheless, to match Kulon's stolen coin, I am willing to raise my honest bid by—"

Dagger pushed the wooden box across the table to the mind wizard.

Taito-Vaiana snapped his orange mouth closed.

No! Telyn wanted to shout. *It's a trap; it's got to be. Can't you see it?*

"Bidding is over," Dagger said.

The cereb allowed a pasty smile to wrinkle his face. His neck tentacles practically vibrated themselves to a pink hue.

"A wise choice. The words to summon the daemon are inscribed on the bottom of the figurine. You need only to speak them." The mind wizard peeked into the box, closed it, and walked briskly to the exit. Taito-Vaiana collected his coins, mumbled good-bye, and followed on his heels.

"They were together," the trogo said when he and the thief were alone. "They played you like a puppet."

Dagger scraped his earnings into a pouch, which he then tied to his belt. "The hour is late, and I am tired."

"You know, don't you, that Yona took you?" the trogo insisted.

"You came out fine for your trouble, Kulon, borrowing the schmooks's gold the way you did." Dagger smiled at the trogo, and the two embraced like old friends. Despite the thief's height, the trogo towered above him.

"It will make no difference to the number of ambushes we have to evade." The trogo shrugged. "And the bidding was going too slowly."

"If the schmook's spell had worked, you might have regretted it."

"'Might, could, may;' mathematics have never been my strong suit. Only the mind wizard worries me, my friend. Let us hope the Ever-Guise satisfies him. An ambush by Yona, and we might find ourselves fighting each other."

"I will not hold it against you—not with the cereb controlling your mind."

"When are you ever going to share your true name with me, Dagger? It seems unfair, since you know mine."

"When you've earned it, my friend."

"Hmm. Tell me, is there anything written on the bottom of that statuette?"

"Do you think I'm fool enough to activate it?"

"It will sell for more if the command word is written there."

Telyn detected something amiss in Kulon's voice. Dagger didn't. He glanced down, just for an instant.

With the dagger handle curled in his fist, Kulon punched Dagger square in the jaw. The man flew several feet and landed on his back, dazed. His jaw slumped at an awkward angle. The contents of his coin pouch scattered across the floor, and the black figurine skittered across the wooden floorboards. Dagger saw it too, and reached for it, but the statuette skidded out of reach—straight toward the crack between the barrels.

CHAPTER FIVE

lood and drool trailed from Dagger's broken jaw. Limbs shaking and with a dazed expression, he managed to crawl after the statuette. His eyes widened when he saw Telyn crouched there, peeking between the barrels. Telyn put her finger to her lips so he wouldn't betray her.

"I am sorry, my old friend," Kulon said, grabbing Dagger's ankles and jerking him backwards. "There is just too much at stake. Glas Courier wants to make sure the forehead is properly taken care of. She just doesn't trust you anymore." From the way Dagger's forehead crinkled, it looked like this barb hurt as much as the physical blow.

Dagger managed to flip onto his back. Protecting his head with one arm, he reached for the knife on his back—but it was gone, the blade a melted slag on the floor.

Looming over him, the trogo began punching down with his massive fists, one of them still holding the knife's handle. "Can you—blame Glas—you have—poor taste—in friends," he said between breaths.

Dagger rolled side to side and blocked with his forearms, moving his head out of the way as best he could. Clearly, the effort cost him, and his jaw flopped unnaturally with each move. Pain caused deep furrows across his brow.

"The daemon—will be a—beautiful addition—to Glas's collection—don't you think?"

Telyn watched in stunned fascination. Dagger now knew she was there. What would happen if he won this fight—as unlikely as that seemed? Would he kill her for witnessing the auction? In a perverse twist of fate, should Telyn be rooting for the trogo?

But the trogo was a traitor. He already betrayed two schmooks—and now the human. The trogo and Dagger knew each other. In fact, the trogo had called him 'old friend.' Clearly the trogo was an honorless murderer. She couldn't root for him. No way. She'd take her chances on the human. If she saw any chance to help him, she would.

That settled in her mind, Telyn began watching for an opportunity.

Dagger lined up his feet and kicked hard, but the blow barely troubled the trogo. More massive fists rained down until the human took a glancing blow to the head and his struggles ceased. He moaned something between heaving breaths. Telyn caught the words *mask*, *Yona*, and *fool*.

The trogo listened with his head tilted. Then he smiled. "Not to worry, old friend. I have plans to deal with Yona, just as soon as I relieve you of the statuette...and your life. Nothing personal. I've enjoyed our games of senet."

What could Telyn do? She had no weapon and no illusions about her chances if she had. And Dagger was past fighting in any meaningful way. Telyn had seen enough barroom brawls to know he wouldn't recover quickly. His fighting will had been shattered by the overwhelming might of the trogo. Another punch or two would kill him.

"Ah, begging?" the trogo said, although Dagger had done no such thing. "Well, tell me who you planned to sell the forehead to. Who do you trust more than Glas Courier?" He turned an ear-hole at the thief's face. "Tell me and I'll leave you with broken legs."

Dagger muttered something.

"What's that?"

He muttered incoherently again, obviously stalling for time.

Kulon gestured with his fingers. "Last call..."

"Spring Sale," Dagger moaned. "The buyer...will be...Spring Sale. Hall of Magic."

"Ah, I could have guessed that. So sorry. I need a name."

"The name's—" Dagger said something rude about toads and Kulon's ancestor.

The daemon statuette beckoned. About the size of Telyn's fist, it resembled an obsidian bear. She didn't think she could wedge it through the crack between the barrels quickly; it'd probably get stuck sideways, and the trogo would notice if a pale hand suddenly reached to snatch up the treasure. But she couldn't sit by and just watch this man get murdered.

She *had* to do something.

So be it. Let her be noticed. She reached out—but the crack between barrels was too narrow for even her forearm to pass.

The trogo sat up tall, reared back, and prepared for the final blow. One direct hit from a massive lizard-fist would drive anyone's skull into the floorboards and would surely kill a human, even a man as tough as Dagger.

"My old friend, I will tell Glas you are worse than a traitor. I'll tell her you fought like a girl."

Telyn braced her feet against the sacks of flour and pushed against one barrel with her shoulder. It hardly budged. Again, she shoved, this time engaging her core, her back, her thighs. The barrel tipped onto its rim, rolled a bit, then toppled into the room, banging up a cloud of flour and dust from the floorboards. The trogo looked up in surprise. Telyn slithered forward and grasped the statuette with the tips of her fingers. Rather than the texture of stone, it had the slippery texture of a warm, peeled grape.

Dagger slid out from under the flack. Rolling to hands and knees, his mouth sagging open, he held his open hands toward Telyn.

From her position it was an awkward, impossible throw—especially for such a slippery, nasty thing—but Telyn cocked her elbow and tossed the statuette as far as she could. It made it about halfway, bouncing under a bench. Both man and trogo lunged for it. They tangled in a confusing, writhing mass of lizard skin, human hair, and splattered blood. Dagger wound up on the bottom again.

But he had the statuette.

The trogo punched him again and again. The thief rolled into a protective ball and began reading.

Ago—

Stunned by a glancing blow, he faltered...

...began again.

Agor...

With the broken jaw, Dagger's voice sounded more moan than enunciation, but it seemed to be working. The room around the fighters darkened, becoming slick with shadow. The trogo's fists crashed down on Dagger's curled form, now more desperate.

...rm...

The trogo abandoned the attack. He straightened, pivoted toward the exit.

...ic.

The daemon exploded into a shadowy outline. An appendage shot out and latched onto the fleeing trogo's ankle. The daemon used the captured momentum to slingshot itself to the trogo's back. Kulon bellowed a deep-throated scream; momentum carrying him forward, he managed to throw open the door.

The two became darkness and confusion. The trogo toppled, and with the sound of sucking mud, he dissolved into the body of the daemon. It was as if the daemon had dissolved the trogo into mist and then absorbed the mist itself.

On all fours, looking very much like a black bear with four tentacles sprouting from its back, the daemon blocked open the door without dissolving either door or frame. After a moment, during which Dagger managed to lift himself from the floor to hands and knees, the daemon padded back into the public room, bringing with it the aroma of sweet, burnt brioche crumbs. The delightful aroma, combined with the horrific scene, made Telyn want to gag.

The door swung closed, pushed by a blustery gust; the firelight flickered.

With long-fingered hands, Dagger gripped his jaw, pulled the bone downward, and twisted his head sharply. The jaw popped back into place with an audible crack that made Telyn wince. Dagger chewed a few times until satisfied. The penumbra daemon arrived at his side.

"Well, my ankle-baring friend," Dagger said, turning toward Telyn. His enunciation slurred from the swollen jaw muscles. "This puts us in an odd place."

Slowly, so as to not startle the daemon, Telyn stood up. She hoped the expression *a life for a life* meant something to the man. If Dagger had any honor, it would. "I won't tell the cornics anything," she said. Thinking it sounded a weak promise, she added, "Nor anyone else. That is, I won't tell if you give me three birds. You've got plenty there on the floor." When Dagger frowned, she added, "I'll even pick them up for you, if you right those stools you knocked down. That's extra work for me and my sister you made. I'm normally home in bed by now."

Everything was a negotiation in Harlech—this man surely understood that. A couple of hurons would buy her mom enough fabric for several dresses.

After a brief hesitation, Dagger dropped his head and began laughing.

"What's your name?" he managed. She noticed a big gap between his front teeth.

Sharing her name wouldn't be the wisest thing. On the other hand, anonymity in a town the size of Harlech would last all of ten minutes. She bit the inside of her cheek, considering.

"I like your spirit, girl. Tell you what, I think we can come to an arrangement...but I will need more from you than your word."

They had entered the negotiation after all—an affair Telyn knew exceedingly well, and she relaxed considerably. The trick would be to pretend she had some bargaining power when, in reality, she had none. Keeping Dagger's identity secret would certainly be worth something—but only while she was alive, alive with some capacity to transmit the knowledge to the cornics. Or to whomever Dagger had stolen the mask from in the first place. For the man before her was a thief, no doubt about it. She'd known many crooked people in her fifteen years, but to her knowledge, Dagger was the first professional thief she'd ever met.

He must be very good at it, considering the powerful bidders he'd brought to the auction in the middle of nowhere, and the piles of gold they'd laid on the table.

"I think we are missing the point here," Telyn said in her best market-day voice. "Humans are always one step ahead of slavery. And the mind wizard is sure to come back asking questions about the, ah, the forehead."

The thief raised his eyebrows. "The forehead?"

Nothing for it; she'd tilted the candle, and the wax would burn what it burned. "I saw it. In your boot."

Dagger reached down and pulled the mask piece from the boot. It didn't look like it would fit there; his boots laced up clear to his knees, but the mask had a surprising elasticity and only resumed its forehead-shape once he opened his hand.

It looked like it had been made with the finest ceramic, albeit with little sparkles, as if the craftsmen had added mica into the clay before firing it. And then plated that with gold, bronze, and copper. This piece comprised the forehead, the top half of the eye-holes. Upon closer inspection, there was an empty setting for the third eye in its center. Slightly translucent, golden lamplight shone through as the thief turned it over and over in his hands.

They remained that way for some time, Dagger rotating the forehead, Telyn staring, wondering. Finally, she could stand it no longer. "What *is* the Ever-Guise? Why does it look like a human face?"

Dagger looked up sharply.

"I mean, humans couldn't have made it. Only flacks have magic. Why would they have made it look like a human face?"

"It looks like a human because the Ever-Guise represents the Queen of Lies." Dagger passed his hand over the forehead, and it disappeared. "And humans are the biggest liars."

Telyn gasped.

"A bit of an illusionist," he said, and grinned. The blood coloring his teeth spoiled the effect to some degree.

Telyn swallowed. "And a showoff."

"We were talking about how I could trust you to keep your silence."

"We were talking about how many birds you would pay me."

"Ah. I believe you mentioned three?"

Telyn nodded. "Per month. You can pay in advance, if you don't plan on being in Harlech regular-like."

"A month!"

"Yes." Excitement built in Telyn's breast. Dagger hadn't killed her yet. He hadn't even said no—which meant they were still negotiating. She might get enough to buy her own cabin. Mother of Squirrels, she might be able to buy the Sable Head!

"For a lifetime of silence... You're what, sixteen—?"

"Fifteen, going on sixteen."

"Very well, you can expect to live another forty, fifty years." He tapped counted on his fingers. "At three birds per month, that would be approximately—" Dagger didn't get a chance to finish his speculation, for at that moment the daemon reached out its tentacles and embraced him.

It happened so fast. Telyn had just enough time to flinch, bite her cheek painfully, and then—

—and then—

She wanted to look away, but she couldn't.

She just couldn't.

It was too horrible.

The aroma of sweet, burnt crumb filled her nostrils, and the night was filled with the sound of sucking mud.

CHAPTER SIX

Smoke from the fireplace began to curl and swirl in quickened eddies. Everything felt off. Telyn's teeth tingled like she'd sunk them into an icicle—though the room hadn't changed temperature. Energy: the air hummed with it, probably a byproduct of the daemon, which now snuffled around the room like a raccoon exploring a garbage heap. At first, Telyn thought the daemon was looking for scraps, maybe a stray nose or something, or that severed ear...

No, the ear was still there. The daemon appeared uninterested in it. Likewise, it ignored her, though that might be a feint, the same way it had come to stand next to Dagger as if nothing was going to happen. The daemon traveled in a deliberate, thorough pattern across the floor, gathering the hurons. Telyn wasn't entirely sure if the daemon was picking them up, eating them, or absorbing them.

What a bizarre creature. Was everything it took in dissolved like powdered medicine, or could it absorb people whole and regurgitate them—unharmed—at some other place? Could the cereb himself travel inside the daemon's belly in a sort of extra-dimensional bladder, impervious to attack? The possibilities were endless. But right now, the certainty was that, sooner or later, the daemon would turn its attention to Telyn.

She looked around at the stores for ideas. Perhaps if she dropped a barrel of molasses on it, she could sprint for the door.

The fireplace smoke acted stranger and stranger, braiding into twin strands that crossed the room, slithered beneath tables, and snaked over the daemon. Telyn would have sworn the smoke wanted to strangle it. Simultaneously, pressure built on Telyn's brain, a pushing, pulsing sensation. Her ears wanted to pop; a rush of dream-speak tickled her eardrums, whispers and moans in a distinctly male voice. And then she felt something invite itself into her mind.

A desire to inhabit.

To share.

Her body.

The penumbra daemon's head swiveled back and forth. Its tentacles puffed out at the ends, tasting the air.

Saliva filled Telyn's mouth. The pressure on her mind increased.

"No, I won't," she said, crouching defensively. "Whatever you want, leave me out of it. I'd rather die."

The moans, the multitudinous voices formed a single word:

Revenge.

The penumbra daemon let out a low, throaty growl.

Floorboards rippled under Telyn's bare feet. The lanterns billowed sooty, black smoke that rose into rings...or mouths.

"Leave. Me. Alone," Telyn growled through gritted teeth. She'd started to guess what had happened. Dagger had been murdered; his ghost wanted to come back. Of course it did. Humans always came back as ghosts. And if that human had been betrayed and brutally murdered, it would bend all of its malevolence toward one goal: revenge.

And it needed a body.

Telyn wrapped her hands over her ears and fell into a crouch. "No! I don't want you."

Abruptly, the pressure on Telyn's mind evaporated; Dagger's ghost had abandoned the effort.

The penumbra daemon's ears flicked back and forth. It dropped its head and began absorbing coins again. Telyn had just enough time to breathe once, twice, when little sounds emerged from the kitchen. They sounded like the kisses of an over-exuberant and slightly drunk aunt. The swinging door pushed open.

Kiss.

Kiss.

Kiss.

Oh no, no, no, no., thought Telyn, perfectly aware of who was coming.

Tums.

That foolish, curious eehoo.

The suckers on the ends of its paws made that sound when it walked. Which it rarely did, the lazy thing. She preferred sticking to the wall like a fuzzy gargoyle—unless Telyn brought her down for arm-wrestling or snuggles.

No, no, Tums, stay away. No need for both of us to die.

Kiss by sucker-kiss, the eehoo crossed the floor, and although Telyn knew she should use the distraction to make a break for the exit...she couldn't take her eyes off the unfolding scene. The fire puffed twin braids of smoke; the lanterns spewed blacker-than-black mouths. The penumbra daemon turned to face the approaching eehoo.

Without fear, Tums advanced, her little gray body strolling possum-like, her eyes strangely intense, her purple nose quivering. Finally, the two were within arm-wrestling distance. One swipe, and the daemon could take her out. One step forward, and the eehoo would fall into nothingness.

Funny thing, the daemon looked...nervous. Its ears quivered. Its four tentacles, while poised in the air, pulled as far away from the eehoo as possible. It turned sideways like a cat cornered by a coyote. And it seemed to be—was it possible?—it seemed to be losing its coherence, as if someone shone a lantern into darkness.

Tums leaned forward, lips pulled back against her square teeth. As the daemon pulled even further away, a wail erupted from the eehoo such as Telyn had never heard—nor ever wanted to hear again. She covered her ears. She screamed to try to drown out that awful noise.

That sound pierced her hands and her skull and her very sinew. Electricity scampered up and down her teeth. Smoke filled the room such that Telyn's nose burned, and her eyes watered. The floorboards twisted; Telyn stumbled to one knee.

The keening began to ululate.

"If you stay any longer, that thing is going to get you," Telyn called above the cacophony of groaning wood and eehoo screams.

The daemon rumbled. It could have been words or a threatening growl. Frankly, Telyn didn't care, as what remained of the daemon—more charcoal sketch than three-dimensional creature—turned and bounded outside.

A moment later, Cressida appeared in the doorway and froze. "Telyn? Sis?" she called tentatively, as if disbelieving her own eyes.

"Here," Telyn answered.

The building groaned. The coals flared. The black smoke danced, forming castles, boulevards, trees, heads, mouths. It painted sooty pictures on the walls, tables, floor, ceiling.

Memories.

A lifetime of memories.

A lifetime that was coalescing here, through the floorboards and the fire and smoke and into poor Tums.

Frozen in a rictus of terror, Cressida's face could have broken a mirror. "Ah, Telyn, what's happening?"

Telyn stumbled around the edge of the public room, past the overturned stools and benches, giving that ululating eehoo a wide berth. The Sable Head was going to pull itself apart. She had to get Cressida out of here before she got hurt!

They had to get Razenbock. They had to get help, get the pattern witch, get as far away from here as possible.

"Telyn! I've been waiting outside," Cressida said breathlessly, beckoning her from the doorway. "I saw them all leave, the var, the conda, the schmooks, the mind wizard—he rode off in a coach with a schmook. I could see them from where I was hiding."

Step by shuffling, trembling step Telyn reached her sister, and they embraced in the doorway. Telyn buried her head in her sister's sandy blond hair. "Took you long enough."

"I didn't want to come in and give you away. I knew there was still a trogo, and that you would want to stay until the end."

Tums' wail trailed off, and Telyn's ears rang tinnily in the unexpected quiet of the cold night. Through that, she could just make out the eehoo's harsh panting as the poor creature tried to catch her breath. The chaos subsided. The Sable Head stopped groaning; now it popped and creaked as it settled.

"Telyn, the door opened; I thought I saw a trogo but it was like...like...an icicle melting. And then the screaming began and I couldn't wait any longer."

"It's okay. It's over now. I knew you wouldn't leave me." Telyn hugged her sister tighter, wetting Cressida's hair with some tears.

They held each other for a moment, then Cressida spoke. "What happened? What's the matter with Tums?"

Reluctantly, Telyn pulled back to an arm's distance. "We need help. You get Raz. I will get the pattern witch."

"Telyn, I'm not going anywhere until you tell me what happened."

Telyn took a second, trying to simplify it in her mind. So much had happened in the last hour or so. How could she explain it all?

Okay, just the basics. Cressida didn't need everything all at once. She gave her twin the barest outline.

Cressida nodded slowly. "I thought I saw the trogo in the doorway...."

"It's complicated. Even from where I hid...the shadow-creature...I just can't explain it. But it killed the trogo and the man, took the birds, and ran away. The thief's ghost came back and—and it wanted to possess me, but I refused, so it took Tums."

"Mother of Squirrels!" Cressida said.

"That shadow-thing that ran by you, well, it's too complicated. You go upstairs and get Raz. He must be completely sauced to have slept through this. I'll get the pattern witch."

"Sauced? He might be, but he's not here. Razenbock went to the Lucky H." Cressida gingerly stepped back inside the public room and looked around, taking in the soot drawings all over the walls and tables. That's what happened when a ghost appeared: it painted the area with its most vivid memories, though Telyn had never seen so many, and so vivid. "So much to clean—he's going to be furious."

Things had calmed considerably, though they were by no means still. Tums turned in circles, trying to bite its nubby tail. The fingers of braided smoke seemed content to layer soot over the images it had already painted—an artist layering over his initial sketches. Dagger's ghost must've been getting used to his new body.

"I'll just grab my cloak from the kitchen." Telyn darted past Tums, who didn't seem to notice her.

They had to get the pattern witch—had to make sure the ghost didn't get too comfortable. Telyn wanted her eehoo back.

CHAPTER SEVEN

The Sable Head sat a little east from downtown Harlech and the girls walked quickly along the dirt road in their bare feet, despite treading on the occasional sharp stone or llama dropping. The Elbus Canyon dropped away to their left. The river hid in the canyon depths, but Defiance Falls roared in the distance, and the mist rose from it to caress their ankles like icy fingertips.

Telyn kept thinking about the Ever-Guise. Did the daemon have the mask inside itself now, along with the remains of Kulon and Dagger—clothes, boots, and yucky, gray brains—and those coins it'd snuffled from the floor? Would it excrete all of that out for the mind wizard in a gooey mess, or did the daemon have its own agenda?

Or did it carry everything more-or-less intact like some bottomless satchel?

"Nearly shoe season." Cressida skipped over an icy patch of mud.

Telyn grunted.

To their right, Harlech's commercial district slumbered. Over shop doors or dangling from wooden awnings hung signs with pictures instead of words: a hammer and anvil; a hatchet over a pig; a twisted pretzel. Light peeped through the shutters on a few of the second-floor windows, but most folks had gone to bed. No wonder no one had come to investigate the boards creaking and the eehoo wailing.

A couple embraced on the porch outside the Lucky H. Through the door, they could hear a dulcimer and a few tired voices trying to sing along.

"Are you sure?" Cressida took Telyn's hands, stopping at the edge of the light pooling from the Lucky H's windows. "We could go to flacktown together. Raz can't do nothing about the ghost."

Telyn hesitated. She would rather dig a badger from its hole with her bare hands than wake the pattern witch at this hour. She'd been mulling this over during the walk, and decided she felt a certain sense of responsibility. Not for what happened; she didn't have much to do with the auction, the murder, and all of that. But, well, Tums needed her. If she had allowed Dagger inside her own head, the eehoo wouldn't be in its current predicament.

She nodded. "I'll be all right. We've got a perfect right fetching the pattern witch in the matter of ghosts. Besides, I'm the one that saw it. If she has questions...."

"If Raz knows you stayed after supper, you'll be in a heap of trouble."

"Yeah, I know." *A whole heap more than you imagine, sister.* Telyn hoped the witch didn't ask too many questions, like, "What were you doing there?" "What were the flacks doing there?" "What exactly did you see?" She didn't want to answer any of those questions. "I'm gonna say I forgot my cloak and came back for it. That's as close to the truth as I can go."

"See you at home." Cressida smiled lopsidedly and leaned forward for a hug.

The waterfall's thunder grew louder as Telyn hurried along, the air more humid. Harlech had maybe two thousand full-time residents. She crossed the little, arched bridge and creek that separated Harlech proper from the flack residences. In nothing flat, she found herself in front of the strangest home in Harlech—if the tent-like structure could even be a called a home. Silk, canvas, cotton, muslin, lace, linen, chenille, cotton, cashmere—she'd once spent half a morning with Cressida trying to name every fabric and weave on the exterior of the... er...house. The overlapping fabric ribboned into, around, and through, an explosion of colors and textures all woven together, enough material to stock a dozen haberdasheries.

The garish structure rose at least three stories and billowed in the slightest breeze. If Telyn stared at it too long, she got woozy.

Telyn's mother was a seamstress—when she was sober enough to hold a needle—and could have made her fortune out of that fabric. She could have dressed the whole town for a costume ball and half of Enshede besides.

The pattern witch's house was the sort of place children would stare at for hours, daring each other to poke a finger into the side. For if you did—so the children said—you might end up sewn into the fabric, or worse, made to wear dress clothes for all eternity.

It's just a tent—a big, billowing tent that breathes. Basically, a giant lung. Nothing to be scared of.

The pattern witch must've been home, for light shone from the inside through the various fabrics depending on thickness and material.

I'm happy about that, right?

Right?

Go on, then. Tums needs me.

Telyn approached reluctantly, swallowed, stepped again. Within touching distance. A fabric entryway ran ahead to a beaded doorway. She paused about halfway and then, remembering the childhood dares, poked the wall. The material to the left resisted like silk, soft and firm, pleasing.

She poked the right: more of a flannel-like material, also taut, warm, fabric to snuggle in on winter's nights.

Not so scary after all.

She was looking for a place to knock when the beads moved aside on their own. Telyn tiptoed through a foyer and pulled aside a length of green cloth covering a door, following quiet sounds into a sort of kitchen. A fire crackled inside a metal stove—a fire!—and while Telyn wondered why the place hadn't gone up in flames, she tripped on the edge of a rug and almost tumbled into the home's inhabitants.

"Mrs. de Galati, hi…"

Two flacks looked up as Telyn righted herself. The elder sat at a small table wearing a long dress tied with a green sash and a matching green headscarf—and the cross look of someone interrupted from deep concentration. The younger, her daughter, sat cross-legged atop a fabric cube, dressed in overalls without even a shirt underneath, showing an obscene amount of…fur. Both women rose. The younger smiled, or seemed to, although her lips hardly moved. It was all in the slow squint of her eyes and a slight lift of her whiskers.

Both females could have been human, except there was too much cat in them. Their feline heads sprouted thick fur in a mottled white, gray and brown pattern, whiskers, and triangular ears on top. Their hands sported nubby fingers, albeit furry, and Telyn had the distinct impression those finger-pads could extend claws. But their legs! No wonder all the men had secret crushes on them—they had curves in all the right places and moved with the grace of panthers.

"There is a break in the pattern," the mother announced. "Can you tell me what it is?"

Relief flooded through Telyn. She didn't know what she'd expected, but a smile and a question she could answer were a good start. "A ghost—in the Sable Head. It's inside of Tums, the eehoo."

The flacks exchanged a significant glance.

The mother sat down again. "I thought it must be more than that," she huffed, and resumed picking apart a doily with bone needles. A Sylvan scene had been woven into the cloth, but it was upside down, and many threads had been pulled loose. Telyn couldn't spot more than a doe and a couple of trees.

After several moments, Telyn said, "Er, it's sort of an emergency. I think it might be a poltergeist. Maybe even a vengeful spirit."

"Who died," the mother asked, one ear twitching, "and how?"

With a quiver of her whiskers, the daughter continued to grin. She stared at Telyn with striking, violet eyes—another reason the men all had crushes on her, no doubt.

"I, um, I don't know. A man."

Telyn repeated the made-up story of going back with Cressida for her cloak, hearing some ululating cry from inside, and going inside to discover the eehoo already possessed. The story sounded lame to her, but she stuck with it. She couldn't let on that she had seen Dagger auctioning off a magical mask called the...What was it?...the Ever-Guise. The cornics would question her to no end: Who died? Who killed whom? What were they selling? Who said what? What mask? What were you doing there? And while Telyn didn't know exactly which rules she'd broken, she knew from experience she must have broken at least a dozen.

The pattern witch picked a thread loose from the weave, examined it, and very carefully tightened it again. "Has it started speaking?"

"Tums? No," Telyn said, rocking from one foot to the other, irritation growing. Tums was in trouble and she was supposed to sit here and watch someone play with needle and thread? She could do that at home. "Razenbock keeps trying to teach the eehoo dirty words, so I expect it wouldn't be pleasant if she did."

The daughter giggled.

The witch fixed Telyn with her large eyes—violet like her daughter's—and Telyn decided her flippancy hadn't been such a good idea. "It just sort of moans," she added. "But the lamp smoke is making rings like mouths."

"What else?"

"I could feel the ghost pressing against me, trying to get in, as if it were knocking on the door of my mind. But I wouldn't let it in. It took Tums, instead."

"I thought you heard the ghost while you were still outside. You said Tums was already possessed when you entered the tavern."

"Er, I don't really remember. It is all a bit muddled." *I will not let my cheeks redden. Cool thoughts. Cool, innocent cheeks, pale as wind-driven snow.*

Briskly, the pattern witch swept the needles, scissors, doily, and thread into a bag, which she pulled tight with a drawstring. "What have you told the cornics?"

"Nothing. Cressida is at the Lucky H getting Razenbock—the owner of the Sable Head. I came straight here."

"Best get your stories straight before the cornics question you," the pattern witch said, tying the bag to her sash and throwing a cape over her shoulders. "My daughter, Rayvn, will keep you company. Stay here until I get back, both of you. There is more out there than ghosts this night."

Telyn knew that all too well, schmooks and var, conda, penumbra daemons, and mind wizards to name a few.

The door-flap pulled aside. The pattern witch paused there. "Rayvn, sharpen the chisel while I'm away."

"Yes, ma'am," Rayvn replied to her mom's receding form.

No one had told Telyn she could sit down. Accustomed to long hours in the kitchen, she didn't really mind, much. She rocked from foot to foot, unfocused her eyes, and daydreamed—a technique she'd perfected scrubbing pots. Her mind adrift, she recalled the eerie scene at the Sable Head: Tums' ululation, the ghost plastering the walls in soot. If she went back and studied the drawings the ghost had left, she would uncover Dagger's past. No wonder human mercenaries were so frightening. Imagine the chaos once they started to fall....

A sudden voice—practically in her ear—almost gave Telyn a heart attack. "Your button's torn," Rayvn said. She had approached so quietly Telyn hadn't noticed, and now she was reaching toward Telyn's chest.

Telyn looked down; her mother wouldn't let her leave the house with a torn button, but there it was, her top button dangling by a single thread.

"The ghost disrupted the pattern," Rayvn said, reading Telyn's confused expression. "You are lucky it is just one button." She reached out.

Telyn backed away. She did *not* want a flack touching her.

Rayvn stepped forward.

Telyn retreated until her back was pressed to the fabric-wall, and still Rayvn advanced. The flack touched the button with a single finger, and the threads rewove into a neat little knot. "The Sable Head must be a mess."

Telyn took the button in her hands and tugged, but it had been repaired perfectly.

"Don't ever touch me again," Telyn said, a little more forcefully than she'd intended—but the flack had scared her. Besides, flacks had no business touching humans.

Rayvn's smile didn't waver. "Would you like an infusion?"

Telyn moved to the other side of the room, still clutching her button. She found a spare puff-square and sat. She couldn't very well refuse an infusion, not in the flack's own home. "All right. That'd be grand." Her eyes roved everywhere except the other...girl.

Flack. She's not a girl, she's a flack. And she shouldn't have touched me.

Rayvn filled a kettle from a brass spigot by the stove and set it in the firebox on a hook. She placed some wood in and, by muttering a few words, began a fire. "Mom doesn't know I can do this, but patterns can be unwoven easier than woven, and fire is best for un-weaving." She set cups and saucers on the table, put dried herbs in small sachets, tied them off with magic, dropped them in the cups.

"So, you must be excited about the new Dating Chart."

The change of subject jolted Telyn back to the present. "What? No! Not at all."

"They've just cleared the board, so to speak. Brand-new matches."

"Well, yes. After eighth moon they wipe it clean and start over with new odds, new questionnaires..." Telyn squirmed, unable to find a comfortable spot on the overstuffed pouf. "Why are we talking about this?"

"Oh, I place a bet now and then." Rayvn's ears twitched, as if considering whether to say more. Presently, she wrapped a thick swatch of cotton around her hand and removed the now-boiling kettle from the firebox. Then she poured a steaming stream of water into each cup. "Do you take honey?"

Telyn reached for the frilly, ceramic cup. "No, thank you." Normally she loved honey, but the flack and her choice of conversa-tion made her feel contrary—even to her own detriment.

"I generally win my bets." Rayvn stirred a spoonful of honey into her own infusion and sat beside Telyn. "Being a pattern witch, I'm rather good at discerning patterns."

"Er...okay." The cup felt really good against her numb fingers, and

Telyn felt a little guilty for being so abrupt. "I'm called Telyn. Telyn Brower."

Rayvn nodded sagely. "You are the taller twin. Your sister is Cressida; your mother is Esther; and your father, Dorian Brower, died trapping. We are the same—without fathers, two-cord strands. My mother makes me study the names on the Sepulcher as part of my training, although my interest lies with interpersonal relationships."

"You mean the Dating Chart? Seriously?"

Rayvn sipped noisily. Her violet eyes sparkled like a silly, crush-besotted girl's.

Telyn stared, incredulous. "You want to date a human? Which one?"

I've got to get out of here. Dealing with ghosts must have driven the witch insane! But Mrs. de Galati might get angry, since she told me to wait here. Mother of Squirrels, what a barrel of pickle juice.

"I hadn't actually considered dating a human, but that *would* open up new areas of research."

Research? The Dating Chart? Does she think we're insects to pin to a board and dissect? Telyn dearly wanted to change the subject. "Have you lived here long?"

"Fifteen years. Not very long in the life of a stone, but my entire life."

"Same."

Well, that didn't go anywhere.

Searching her mind for a subject as far away from the Dating Chart as possible, Telyn hid her face behind the ceramic cup, sipped, and spit the light-green infusion out just as fast. It tasted like a cranky old boot.

"Horrible, isn't it?" Rayvn said, taking the cup out of Telyn's hands. "Mom gives me spinosa infusions when I have an owie. It freezes your cuticles so that you have something else to worry about. Tell me if it works."

Indeed, Telyn's fingers began to go numb again, starting at the nails and working deeper. Telyn checked herself just before berating Rayvn with some choice public room vocabulary. She had no power against a flack. Sure, she had a six-inch reach on the shorter girl, and she was probably stronger as well—unless Rayvn had cat strength to match her fur.

But magic, it always came down to that.

With the power of their magic, flacks could get away with just about any abuse. And if that failed, the cornics were always on their side. Always.

Telyn pushed her anger down as best she could. "Why would you do that?"

"You're thinking about something else, right?"

"I'm thinking about knocking your teeth in!"

"That so worked," Rayvn said happily, and plopped back down on her fabric cube.

"Oh, no, no, no, no. You are *not* getting away with that." Telyn shot to her feet, numbing fingers balled into—loose—fists. "I'm so out of here."

The pattern witches lived on the far side of Harlech with the other flacks—and a little apart even from them. No one wanted to live nearby if you worked with ghosts. Telyn had about a mile to walk home, a dark and frightening night to walk alone, time enough for her temper to cool. A few courageous stars tried to peek out from between the clouds, but the crescent moon remained in hiding.

That spinosa infusion affected more than her cuticles. Her toes were halfway numb. Her feet stumbled on the slightest ridge or stone. Just what she needed on a night like this.

She didn't believe for a minute that Rayvn had served it to *give her something else to worry about*. She did it because Telyn had flinched when Rayvn tried to repair her button. She'd been less than diplomatic, sure.

Well, why not? Flacks treated humans poorly enough.

She'd made it back to Harlech proper when approaching footfalls caused Telyn to duck into an alley. She didn't want to run into anyone. The flacks from the auction might still be in town. Humans up this late would probably have been drinking, their judgment left in the bottom of a mug. They might proposition her—or worse.

No, Telyn definitely didn't want to meet anyone on the roads tonight.

The footfalls carried on, and Telyn returned to the road. She might have just missed Mrs. de Galati returning home.

Three main roads ran parallel to the Elbus River canyon, Upper, Middle, and Main, with Harlech stretched along them. Telyn took Upper Road, that furthest from the canyon, where the trappers maintained temporary shacks and the poor people lived.

She amused herself wondering what she might do if she had the Ever-Guise. Maybe she'd put herself at the top of the Dating Chart. *Most eligible bachelorette in Harlech—Telyn Brower!*

Maybe she'd get Rayvn on the Chart just for kicks. *Wouldn't that teach those busybodies in the Dating Circle.*

At last, Telyn arrived at her one-room cabin. She tried the door and let out a sigh of relief when the latch moved. More than once, her mother had locked the twins out for coming home late, and sleeping in the Sable Head wasn't an option this evening.

Cressida, rising from a chair by the fireplace, rushed forward and gave her a hug. Telyn felt such emotion on feeling her sister's embrace that she spilled a couple of tears. Her sister loved her completely—crooked toes, slatted ribs, morning breath (afternoon, sometimes), snarky attitude, and all.

At last, Telyn drew enough courage to lift her head from Cressida's neck to look round at her mother. What she saw didn't reassure: Esther had swept her gray and black hair into an untidy bun; malt stained her nightshirt; her eyes didn't focus right.

Drinking. Again.

Telyn didn't need the spinosa infusion to feel cold disappointment.

Esther put down her needlework. "Let me guess, daughter. You stagger home in the middle of the night, hours after the Sable Head has closed. No explanation; didn't even leave word with your sister. Cressida has been worried sick." A pause. "What's his name?"

"Mother—" Cressida began.

"Let your twin speak for herself."

"There is no boy," Cressida said. "I would know if there was."

Esther rose and approached the twins shuffle by shuffle, far too feeble for her forty-two years. Too feeble, too old, and way too dour.

"You wouldn't believe what happened, Esther," Telyn whispered. She refused to call her "Mother" until Esther stopped drinking. She'd told Esther as much, in case she missed the point. She didn't want her thinking she called her Esther for spite. Telyn had a good reason for doing so. Spite had nothing to do with it.

Love—that's why Telyn called her Esther. Because she loved her mother. *This* woman, she barely recognized.

"You've been pinching malt," Esther said, sniffing.

"You smell your own smelly breath," Telyn retorted. Something about Esther sniffing her breath—sniffing!—rankled her nerves. She forgot all about the mental strain of the evening, the terror of the trogo and the penumbra daemon, and the cold in her fingers and her toes. Anger began to build from her belly outward—as it always did when Esther had drunk herself into a state.

"You'll lose yourself that job, and then you'll have nothing— nothing at all."

"Mother, Telyn doesn't drink."

"You stay out of this!" Esther demanded, and Cressida shrank away.

"Cressida is right." Telyn stepped around her sister to face her mother full on. Telyn towered a good eight inches taller, and she straightened to emphasize the point. "I don't drink because I don't want to end up like you—a smelly old hag."

"You see how you fare when your man leaves you to care for two thankless girls." Esther punctuated her words with a finger jab to Telyn's chest.

That's it, she brought up Dad.

Telyn wanted so badly to grab that finger and bend it backwards. Instead, she dug her freezing fingernails into the palms of her hands.

"That's the malt talking," Cressida warned. "Don't pay any attention to her, Tey. I think she was worried about you."

Fat chance of that.

Looking at her mother, at the bags under her eyes, the sagging skin of her throat, Telyn suddenly felt pity. Could it be that—like a small child—Esther provoked her simply to get attention? Or was it because Telyn reminded Esther of Dad? He had disappeared shortly after Telyn was born, lost to the Chaos Woods. Frozen to death, likely, or set upon by some beast. It happened all the time. Widows were as common as spit in Harlech.

"Did you tell her?" Telyn asked her sister.

Cressida shook her head.

"What? Tell me what?"

Telyn moved past her mother to the bed she shared with Cressida. She wiped her bruised feet with a rag from the pewter wash basin. "Best get some sleep, Esther. We have a funeral tomorrow."

"Funeral? Who is it? Who died?" Esther sounded quite flustered that the argument had ended so abruptly.

Telyn felt grim satisfaction at that. She pulled the blankets over her and turned toward the wall. "No one you knew. A stranger."

Esther started muttering about waking up early, ungrateful whelps, and other innumerable woes.

Cressida blew out the oil lamp and crawled into bed beside Telyn. Cressida's hand touched her leg moments later. She drew a line on the thigh, followed by a tap.

It was their own personal touch language. *I'm sorry.*

Telyn replied with a touch, a turn clockwise. *It's okay.*

Those were the first words they'd developed, at night, in this very same bed: *I'm sorry* and *It's okay*. Sorry for Esther. Sorry for the pain. Sorry for Dad dying. Sorry for this whole mess of a life. And *It's okay.* We'll make it. We have each other. Not your fault.

Nobody's fault.

They had developed the secret touch language in childhood as a defense against Esther's drunken anger.

Cressida began spelling letters: *P-A-T-T—*

Pattern witch, Telyn guessed. But Telyn didn't want to talk in front of Esther. Their mother had long ago guessed that the twins could somehow exchange secret information right underneath her very nose. She would make them pay if she discovered them doing it now.

Besides, the warm bed made Telyn realize just how exhausted she really was. She sighed to let Cressida know she was too tired to talk, and with her fingernail drew an arc on Cressida's thigh.

Tomorrow.

The warmth of the covers and her sister's body lulled her to sleep.

CHAPTER EIGHT

Τhe funeral bell sounded, slamming shut the town's doors and shutters. No one had to ask—that singular gong cut through silence and hubbub and told the citizens that someone had died, they'd better come, a soul had to be put to rest before the ghost started causing havoc.

Too late. Telyn bound a rather messy braid of Cressida's hair, which she then wrapped into a bun. *The havoc has been done, both by the ghost, and on Cressida's hair. Why does she keep asking me to do it? We both know there would be fewer stray hairs if she did it herself.*

The twins dressed in their funeral best, full skirts gathered at the waist by colorful sashes—blue for Telyn, yellow for Cressida, white blouses with lace at the wrists and necks, and tight, auburn vests. Telyn chose the fishtail braid to deal with her brunette frizz, Cressida two low, blond buns to show off her neck. And yes, both girls wore stockings and ankle-high shoes; neither rough stones nor salacious glances would bother them today, no matter how the wind blew.

Cressida kept throwing Telyn significant glances; she clearly wanted to talk about the night before. In reply, Telyn kept nodding toward Esther as if she didn't want to wake their mom, but both girls both knew that was a lie. Telyn didn't give a burnt tuber whether she woke Esther at the best of times. The woman shouldn't spend half the day in bed sleeping off a drunk. She just didn't feel like talking, too many thoughts and not enough answers.

The twins donned their long coats, shut the cabin door quietly, and joined their friends Hosh and Caitlin along Main Street. They were all fifteen years of age, and they'd been friends forever.

Over the summer, Hosh had grown several inches, catching up to the girls. Well, except for Telyn. He'd been on the pudgy side, which was adorable when he was smaller; now he simply looked awkward. His bum leg didn't help, though Telyn hardly noticed it. The four of them adjusted their pace to Hosh's, and that was that. He had an easy smile and ruffled, orange hair. Currently, he was attempting to grow a beard, a patchy thing that looked like the remains a wire brush left in the elements all winter. Telyn greeted him by tugging on the beard and tsking.

He responded with a grin.

Caitlin had wide lips and wide hips, and the men gawked at her, especially when she swayed deliberately, which was pretty much always. Telyn only rarely felt jealous at this; mostly she preferred anonymity to having to deflect unwanted attention. Caitlin's eyes were as dark brown as her hair, unusual in this village of light-eyed folks. Today her dress was pleated and pink with white lace around the collar and at the bottom.

Called there by the funeral bell, nearly all the town's inhabitants thronged Main Street, and most had already heard enough to be dangerous.

To their left, the scrawny owner of the pretzel shop elbowed a shorter man with a knit cap pulled low over his ears. "I heard two men were fighting because that Brower girl's ankles were showing, and one of them killed the other!"

"Small surprise, ain't enough material in Harlech to keep her legs covered."

"You know it. Like a tree, that one..."

To their right, one of the trappers Telyn recognized from the Sable Head conferred with a washerwoman. "Razenbock kicked out all the humans, nothing left but flacks. Small wonder they killed him. I always knew the barkeep had it comin'."

"He ain't dead; I seen 'im this mornin'."

"Ah, dang it."

Behind them, a woman's voice took on a haunted tone. "They say they never found the body... Nothing left but the nose."

She was answered by an unladylike snort. "Oh? Raz must have ground up the rest for stew and dumped the bile in the malt for color."

A young boy raced past them, forcing them to pause, and skidded to a halt in front of his father. "Heath Robinson said he'll show you where it happened for an egg. Claims he might 'a done it himself if he'd had a mind."

"Give Heath an egg and all he'll show you is the bottom of a mug, I say."

Enough townsfolk knew the twins worked the Sable Head that the friends huddled in a protective circle to deflect the questions as best they could. But that didn't stop nosy old Caitlin from asking questions of her own.

"They say you found the body," Caitlin prodded.

Telyn couldn't help starting a bit at this revelation. "Who said?"

"I knew it! You're always where trouble's to be found. Well, do tell."

"I left my coat and had to go back for it," Telyn said, annoyed at herself for falling for Caitlin's trick so easily. "It was cold."

"You left your cabin in the middle of the night because it was too cold—and walked all the way across town to get your coat?"

"Yeah," Telyn replied, scowling. She really *had* to get a better story before the cornics interrogated her, or at least a better gambling face.

"I believe her," Hosh said, chewing on a sweet ube dumpling. "I forget things all the time."

Caitlin tapped her chin with one finger. "They say some trappers were fighting over your bare ankles. What did they look like? Were they bearded?" She had a thing for long beards.

"No one was fighting over me. I told you, we went home with everyone else when Raz closed up."

"If you ask me," Hosh said, licking the purple filling from his fingers, "I think Telyn should flash her ankles anytime she chooses. If we were to go swimming, say—"

Caitlin smacked the back of his head.

"Ouch! How come men can show ankles and women can't?" Hosh complained

"Because when women see a sliver of skin, they don't slobber like bloodhounds."

"I don't slobber."

"You're slobbering now."

"Because I'm eating an ube dumpling!"

The only thing that saved Telyn from this embarrassing conversation was the clicker-clank of iron-rimmed wheels on the dirt road.

Hosh paused mid-sentence, tilted his head, and announced, "The death car."

"It's called the Conveyance to Celestial Etherealness," corrected a harried-looking woman clutching the hands of two toddlers who chose that moment to run in opposite directions.

Hosh snickered.

Pulled by four llamas, the death car started at the east side of town, the low side, and pulled past the Sable Head, the Lucky H, the Copcut Ash, and finally the Market Hall where the Spring Sale was always held. Then it turned right, moving uphill toward the giant stone mountain-face known as the Sepulcher.

In normal times, the flatbed would carry a simple wooden coffin. On each side of the coffin, an urn of incense would leave sweet smoke that pulled the humans along like trail ants—first the more prominent members of the town, then the lesser ones, with kids sauntering behind. In normal times, the driver would sing "Ode to the Departed," a dirge to pacify both the surviving and the dead. Only humans came, except for the pattern witch and her daughter. Flacks avoided funerals. Funerals reminded them humans *did* have magic of a sort—an uncontrollable, unpredictable magic which brought ghosts back from the dead.

Telyn suspected funerals would have been banned by the cornics if they weren't essential for preventing ghosts from coming back.

As the flatbed came into view, they could see that today was different. Instead of the usual wooden coffin, it carried a metal cage, and the cage held an eehoo. Tums' snarls and crazed eyes gave no doubt that two things must have happened:

First, a human had died, a human with unfinished business here on Earth. Second, that person's ghost had returned and possessed the eehoo.

Poor, lovable Tums.

Quid, wagon-driver and schoolmaster, whom many considered insane, hummed to himself as he drove. At times, during a funeral procession, he would belt out the funeral dirge at the top of his lungs, but today's event seemed to have subdued him.

The pattern witch and her wide-eyed daughter Rayvn sat crisscross on either side of the metal cage, muttering spells and waving incense urns. Taken by the ghost's magic, the smoke formed marvelous, terrifying shapes: creatures, humanoid figures, trees, alleyways bound by tall buildings—all in motion, all half formed.

"So, it's true," Hosh said, his voice a reverent whisper. "They haven't found the body."

As the wagon rolled past, Tums gripped the bars with both hands and stared at the teenagers. His snarls took on sounds nearing coherence. Telyn thought she could make out the words, "Yonaaaaaaaa daeeeeeeemon. Yonaaaaaa daeeeeeeeemon killlllllll meeeeee." The eehoo's wild eyes sought hers, but she refused to meet them. The shapes in the incense smoke seemed to form a wide-eyed girl emerging from behind an overturned barrel.

If a normal *celestial conveyance* caused a normal hubbub, this one put Harlech into an uproar.

Hosh babbled a few times once the wagon had passed, finally managing to say, "That. Was. Creepy."

"The ghost got Tums?" Caitlin asked, eyes wide. "The eehoo's possessed?"

Caitlin and Hosh rounded on the twins.

"Why was he staring at us like that?" Caitlin asked. "What was he trying to say?"

Several people who had been following the death car slowed their walk to listen. It was well-known the Brower twins worked at the Sable Head.

Telyn threw out her hands to the side in surrender. "You got me. I killed Raz. And ate him. That's why there's no body." She clutched her belly dramatically. "And I've got a tummy ache."

Cressida raised an eyebrow. Caitlin blew a strand of brown hair from her face, and Hosh began tapping his bum foot on the ground.

"Come on, guys. Would I hold out on you? You know as much as I do. I didn't even know they hadn't found the body."

"Because you ate it," Cressida said.

"Well, I didn't eat all of it." *I left an ear,* she almost said, but stopped herself. That would be too close to the truth, if the truth ever got out. She really needed practice on this lying bit. "The, ah, the feet. Raz's feet are too stinky by far."

Raz's gruff voice spoiled her charming tale. "Ya girls comin'?" He must have been among the folks trailing the death car.

"Um, girls?" Hosh protested.

"You're right, I should've said *ladies.* I forget how old y'all are getting'." Raz clapped Hosh on the back as he walked past, adding belatedly, "and gent. Y'all 're gonna be left behind if you don't move it."

CHAPTER NINE

The trek led to the foot of an immense rock called the Sepulcher. Nearly vertical, the rock's face rose a thousand feet and must have pierced to the heart of the mountains. Etched into the stone, crowded chaos like fish in a salt barrel, was the name of each person who had died in Harlech, most moss-filled and cracked beyond recognition. Near the base of the rock, a single name remained clear and bold, etched a span tall and shiny as if polished with oil: KABUZ, the Queen of Lies, the deity banished to Sheol with the demons and the dead.

What had Dagger said about the Queen of Lies and the Ever-Guise? Something about humans being the worst liars?

The names had been carved to keep ghosts in Sheol. Presumably, the Queen of Lies could be held back the same way. This happened many ages ago, but her name was preserved through the generations by humans and pattern witches alike. Rumor said the human names around her name dated from the same era—from when Harlech was called Gaer Rhaeadr and was a free human settlement.

Telyn doubted it, though. The magic-wielding races had always dominated the human population, in her estimation. In any case, Gaer Rhaeadr must not have had a proper pattern witch, for ancient ghosts still hung around, wispy things that could have been mist—if mist took on vaguely human form and sometimes followed you around.

When these ancient ghosts whispered in their dead language, it gave Telyn the willies.

People pointed and chattered like they did each time they came to the Sepulcher, claiming to have relatives where the sand piled along the base and fanned out in rain, and some particular claim to the Cairn Range because of it. Wooden scaffolding propped against the rock face rose eighty feet, past countless etched names, to where the granite awaited more tattoos. Nearby, the maroon vendors perfumed the event with smoke as they grilled the dark shells filled with wondrously sweet nuts that opened when heated slowly and exploded when heated quickly.

Telyn was surprised to see Minister Svemas standing at the bottom of the scaffolding in his dress uniform. His presence at the human funeral gave the murder some importance. Like all cornics, he had what could only be described as a ram's head. His horns curled a full two turns, indicating his prominence better than any emblem on his uniform. He wore his usual grin and nodded amiably to those he recognized. Most folks considered him something of a likable dunce—just the kind of administrator they liked in these parts.

Which made Telyn wonder how much of it was an act.

A most unwelcome person caught her eye: Tabbard, the local bully, surrounded by his usual thugs. "Hey Telyn," he said, stuffing a whole maroon nut into his cheek. "Looking a little pale. I hear the stiff died from seeing your fat ankles."

His buddies laughed appreciatively. "Maybe he died of Telyn's cooking," another boy added, earning him an affectionate arm-slug from Tabbard.

"What I think," Tabbard added, "is that no one died at all. That's just what happens when anyone sees Telyn's legs."

"That can't be true, Tabbard Ouzeley." Telyn put as much derision into his surname as she could. "'Cause we all know you *can't* think."

Tabbard's clean-shaven face reddened down to the neck. She'd clearly scored. In fact, it looked like the bully would storm over and start real trouble until another of his crew, Joram Lycargus, whispered something to calm him down. Tabbard threw his maroon shell down in anger but stayed his ground.

"You leave my sister alone." Cressida glared at Tabbard. Then, taking Telyn by the arm, she spoke softly. "Never mind them. They wish they knew enough to be interesting."

The pattern witches, mother and daughter, affixed the eehoo's cage to a block-and-pulley system, and two men hoisted the cage to the top of the scaffolding. Rayvn followed, climbing the rickety ladder with an ease that made Telyn frown. The two might end up competing in the climbing event at the Spring Sale, and Telyn didn't want a flack to beat her at her own game. Mrs. de Galati climbed next, holding a short plank in one arm. About ten feet up she wedged the plank in the scaffolding and stepped onto it, looking for all the world as if she were about to swan-dive into the crowd.

Hosh sucked his breath through his teeth, and he wasn't the only one. If it weren't for their thick fur, the witch's legs would be exposed for all to see—ankles, calves, even knees. Mrs. de Galeti's stockings didn't cover her thighs!

Caitlin smacked Hosh in the back of the head.

The pattern witch's voice carried easily. "The suffering you see in this eehoo, poor creature, reflects the suffering of a man's soul. It is a difficult thing to see such suffering. It can reflect torment in the man's life, or the violent way the man died, or an unhealthy division of the soul—an unresolved struggle of good versus ill."

As if in answer, Tums threw himself at the bars of his cage and snarled what sounded like swear words. Only Tabbard and a few others chuckled—though their laughter quickly died. Most people shuffled their feet and looked anywhere but directly at the eehoo.

The pattern witch continued. "The suffering soul thus casts part of itself—a ghost of itself, if you will—into this world. We are not here to exorcise the ghost from the eehoo. Such is beyond our power. The ghost has its own reasons for haunting our world, decisions made or unmade, vows made or broken, regrets, anger, pain... No magic spell can resolve those. The best we can do is to bind the ghost to this place, tie it to this great Sepulcher which touches not just our world, but also the next. By doing so, we affix the ghost within the pattern here, at this place, at this moment in time. Unable to affect this world anymore, the ghost will depart of its own accord. If we fail..." The pattern witch let the sentence hang.

"Fail?" Hosh asked. "Who's talking about failing?"

"The pattern witch, you sheep-brain," Caitlin said.

Telyn had never heard such a thorough explanation of what the pattern witch did. Funerals had always seemed straightforward before. A person died, the witches carved the name into the Sepulcher, took a little blood from a relative (at which point Telyn always had to look away), burned some incense, and the day resumed.

Today, Telyn leaned forward, eager to understand what was really happening.

The dawn seemed to crackle...but it was only Minister Svemas, who had stepped on a frozen puddle as he moved to stand beneath the pattern witch.

"What're they doin' here?" Hosh asked.

Telyn's heart lurched as two most unwelcome visitors joined the Minister: the schmook and the mind wizard from the Sable Head.

A cone atop one of the nearby chaos trees literally popped. One of the flacks had cast a spell. Immediately, Telyn felt like she had mounted that mental toboggan, as if she slid towards dumb complacency.

Oh, Mother of Squirrels, they're looking for witnesses, Telyn thought, stumbling against Cressida. *They're using the Ever-Guise.*

Cressida gripped her arm. "Tey, you okay?"

"No."

As if oblivious, the pattern witch continued. "We are in the rather unusual situation of knowing what tormented the ghost without knowing the deceased's true name. You see, the man stole something which belongs to the cereb below; a mask which, I'm told, has something to do with a dagger."

A dagger? That was his name. Dagger *stole the mask, a magical mask called the Ever-Guise. The schmook and the mind wizard, they've given the pattern witch partial information. They're trying to plant clues and pull the name to the surface.*

They want to trick me. I'm the one they want.

"Listen to Mrs. de Galati," Minister Svemas urged. "She has the interest of Harlech at heart."

After a brief pause, Mrs. de Galati spoke again. "It is difficult to control a ghost without proper identification, particularly one as unsettled as that which has possessed the eehoo called Tums. For the good of Harlech, if you know the name of the deceased, please come forward now. Minister Svemas has given me his word that nothing will be held against you."

Instead of the Minister, the mind wizard Yona spoke aloud.

"That's right. We are prepared to be completely reasonable. Complete amnesty will be given to anyone who comes forward with the thief's true name, or with the stolen *forehead-mask*." The words hissed through the air, charged and distorted with a potent burst of magic. "Return it to us and be relieved of the burden."

Minister Svemas nodded affably.

Telyn wanted to shout, *Dagger, that was his name. Dagger!*

But she resisted.

The mind wizard didn't want the thief's name; he wanted the mask—the Ever-Guise. But he had it, didn't he? He'd traded it for the pile of gold and the statuette of the penumbra daemon.

Her mind played over the scene, the auction, the box and the mask. Dagger had palmed a piece of the mask: Dagger, mask, auction, Ever-Guise. But even if Dagger had kept a piece of the mask, it had been absorbed into the penumbra daemon. It had dissolved like the bodies, the coins...

The penumbra daemon must have kept the ceramic forehead piece.

Yona's mental attention settled on her, a wet, gossamer blanket.

'I saw you in the Sable Head.'

Huh? Who are you? How are you in my head?

'What do you know, servant? What did you ssseeeee?

Nothing. Nothing. I work there.

"Telyn." Cressida's voice broke in, but it sounded so far away. Her fingers tightened on Telyn's arm.

Telyn clutched her sister's hand like a lifeline. "He's talking to me. He's in my mind."

"Don't answer him."

We don't know his name. We don't have a mask. We don't have a da—dagger. Telyn tried as hard as she could to keep the capital out of "Dagger." *That's my eehoo. That's my Tums up there, suffering.*

'You are hiding things. It is not wise to try to keep secrets from a mind wizard.'

Telyn gasped at the wave of magic that surged over her. *I saw Dagger die. I was hiding, and I saw it.* The cereb's gossamer spell tightened, and Telyn couldn't stop. *Oh, Mother of Squirrels, I did. A shadow ate him, like a bear with tentacles. Don't kill me, please don't kill me. It was an accident. I didn't mean to see nothing.* She couldn't feel her legs. She no longer knew if she stood or knelt. She felt like a little girl in the face of a room full of disapproving adults. *Minister Svemas promised amnesty... He promised.*

'Do you have what I'm seeking?'

No. No! I don't have nothin', I swear it. I swear it on my life.

'I see your truth, Telyn Brower. I will remember.' A pause. 'Daemons are dangerous beasts, Miss Brower. You never know when they will lash out.'

The spell lifted. Telyn and Cressida found themselves leaning together, checks pressed one to another, holding onto each other's arms to keep from falling.

Minister Svemas addressed the crowd. "Well, humans, as you all can see, we have a possession on our hands. This incident is unusual in that—as you have undoubtedly already heard—the body is missing. If any of your friends or relatives don't make it to breakfast this morning, please drop by the Prefecture and let us know." He tilted his head this way and that, as if thinking. "As Mrs. de Galati said—may my horns crack if I'm lying—if you come forward with information—or the stolen mask—before the end of this ceremony, you will receive complete amnesty, regardless of circumstances."

Tums responded by swinging her paws through the bars of her cage and snarling.

"After the ceremony," Minister Svemas added, "I promise nothing."

At this, Mrs. de Galati scaled the rest of the way to the catwalk. Rayvn showed her a place in the Sepulcher to chisel the name, but the pattern witch didn't seem satisfied. Together, mother and daughter scoured the granite face while the humans below grew quieter—until the only sounds were the rustle of the wind in evergreen needles and the crackle of the maroon vendors' coals. Even Tabbard and his buddies stopped chattering.

Finally, the witches chose the most unlikely of places: across a deep crack than ran for several feet above and below the platform, they chalked UNKNOWN in tall letters. No other names had been engraved within a yard of the crack. Finally, with a great racket, Ravyn began chipping into the rock. Beneath her thick mottled fur, her triceps bulged with each swing. *Unknown.* The weakest incantation. That *Unknown* is not me, the ghost could think, and storm free to wreak havoc. Maybe Dagger would possess a human instead of Tums this time.

Telyn remembered how the ghost had probed her mind. If she had accepted the Dagger's advances, if she'd been a little weaker, Telyn would be in that cage, snarling, instead of Tums.

Lost in her musings, Telyn hardly noticed that Mrs. de Galati had descended the platform again and was beckoning her forward.

"Ah, Telyn, I think she wants you," said Caitlin.

Telyn hesitated. "Can't be."

Cressida looked as stunned as she.

"Um, yes, pretty sure it is." Caitlin helped her along with a little nudge.

"Go on, you can do it," a gruff voice said behind her. She didn't need to see Razenbock to know who had spoken.

Step by reluctant step, as if in a dream, her legs brought her to the base of the scaffolding, right next to the mind wizard. His sodden-leather smell wafted over her.

Mrs. de Galati held out a bronze bowl with pestle. She addressed the crowd. "Chiseling a name into a stone will not keep a ghost in the otherworld. The stone must be properly prepared, spells must be cast, and a paste must be applied, one which fuses the anchor of the Sepulcher with the soul of the deceased. A chief ingredient is pitch from a chaos tree. And the other must be—"

The people answered, "Blood."

Sticky, spurting, crimson...

Mrs. de Galati nodded. "Blood. Ideally from a close relative, a son or daughter. If not that, a friend or acquaintance can work, someone who touched deeply by the deceased. But since we cannot identity of the victim—" *Dagger,* thought Telyn. "—we must make due with a friend of the eehoo. Do you know the eehoo's name, my dear?"

Telyn managed to reply. "Tums."

"Friend of Tums, please hold out your hand."

Behind her, Cressida gasped.

That's not why they want my blood. This has nothing to do with Tums. Mrs. de Galati examined the Sable Head; she spoke to Razenbock. She must have guessed I'd seen the thief, at least in passing—which makes me the human in Harlech closest to Dagger.

Numbly, Telyn presented her right hand. The pattern witch grabbed her wrist tightly, twisted it upright, and then, with her free hand, drove a glass needle into the center of Telyn's palm.

Telyn grunted in pain.

The needle was about six inches long, thin, and hollow. Blood seemed to be drawn up it of its own accord. Swiftly, the glass turned a deep shade of red. When it reached the end, the flack withdrew the needle, put it over the bowl, and blew into the fat end, sending a thick red drizzle into the mortar bowl.

The flack released her wrist, and Telyn staggered back into Cressida's arms. In growing horror, her gaze went from her throbbing palm, to the concoction in the mortar, to the staring throng. The hole in her hand filled her palm with blood. The sun shone pale and made the staring faces ashen.

"Squeeze your fist," Raz encouraged.

"Why did she have to poke you so hard?" Caitlin said. "I thought the spike might come out the back of your hand."

Her friends' voices swirled around her. Even with her fist closed tightly, blood pulsed between her fingers. Telyn's head grew light; her ears started to ring. The maroon vendors stared blankly, mouths slumped open. The smell from the toasting shells was sweet and oily, and the smoke reeked like...like burning bodies. They sizzled and popped and as Telyn watched one tore open and an ear flipped out onto the grill.

Eyes rolling to white, Telyn pitched forward onto the damp earth.

CHAPTER TEN

"**W**ow, Telyn, on a scale of embarrassment to humiliation, I'd say you set a new standard." Hosh snorted with amusement. "Passing out your own eehoo's funeral!"

"Tums didn't die, bone-head," Cressida said, scowling. "The funeral was for the, ah, unknown human."

Telyn pulled her legs up cross-legged and buried her face in her hands. The crowd had begun to disperse—and none too soon from Telyn's perspective. Yes, everybody saw that Brower girl pass out. Everybody was talking about how far off the Dating Chart this would set Telyn's name—even though she sat right in front of them!

Shut up and move on already!

As least Yona and Taito-Vaiana had departed right after the funeral. They didn't seem concerned that Telyn had watched the auction, only that she didn't possess the missing piece of the Ever-Guise.

She and her friends remained at the base of the Sepulcher. In a couple of hours, it would cast a shadow over half the town, but for now they had the sun.

"You okay, Tey?" Cressida asked. She'd been hovering like a mother hen ever since Telyn woke up.

"Sure, fine. Never better." Telyn rubbed her eyes in hopes the ground would stop spinning. "Just feeling a little dizzy. That maroon smoke is thick." She didn't want to tell her sister she'd seen a hallucination of an ear popping out of a maroon shell. Cressida would call an herbalist and try to make Telyn stay in bed for a few days, which would mean spending time in the cabin with Esther.

No thanks.

Cressida said, "That mind wizard, you feel it, too?"

"Yeah."

"We weren't the only ones. I think he talked in everyone's mind at once—all at the same time. Imagine having that kind of power! He's really agitated about something."

"I don't know what he was talking about. Really."

"Someone stole something that belongs to him."

"I swear it; I don't know what he's missing. If I did I...I would have told him."

Cressida's scrunched-up face expressed doubt, but she said, "Okay, Tey. Okay."

Furry, calico calves entered Telyn's field of vision. She looked up into the wide, surprised face of Rayvn and her intense mother.

"Are you well, Miss Brower?" Mrs. de Galati asked.

Telyn smiled falsely. "Never better. Just a little dizzy. I have a thing about...blood." She avoided Rayvn's owlish eyes. Couldn't the girl have the decency to blink?

"Ah, yes. I thought the cereb may have done something to you. I am relieved." Mrs. de Galati held Tums out to Cressida. "Your eehoo will be fine. I find no trace of the ghost within him. It seems that, even without the body or the name, the incantation held. It helped that we had part of the body."

Telyn tried very hard to keep her expression neutral.

Mrs. de Galati's head tilted. "Miss Brower, did you notice the ear when you were in the Sable Head?"

"An ear!" Cressida exclaimed, just as Telyn said, "I, ah, wasn't paying a lot of attention. Mostly, I was avoiding the—" Telyn gestured toward Tums. "It frightened me."

"Of course it did. Perfectly natural." Mrs. de Galati's tone, however, said it wasn't natural at all. She either knew—or guessed—more than she was letting on.

Telyn took a deep breath. "Mrs. de Galati, is it really over? Is there any chance the ghost will come back since, ah, you only had an ear?" *And the wrong ear, at that.*

The pattern witch opened her hands in a gesture of uncertainty, but the black tip of her tail whisked against the hem of her dress impatiently. "Who can tell what the pattern weaves? A thread can snap without notice...or support surprising weight."

As the older flack strolled away, Rayvn rocked forward and back on the balls of her feet. "Mom's spells almost always work. But if the ghost comes back—" She tapped the side of her furry head. "—don't let it in." She winked as if she had said something reassuring then hurried to catch her mother.

Telyn turned to see Tabbard and his friends, five or six in all, mime rolling their eyes back into their heads and swooning. Joram was particularly good at it, getting his eyes entirely white before wobbling.

Telyn picked up a nearby stone and threw it at Joram's mullet-head, but she couldn't get much power from where she sat on the ground, and he ducked it with ease.

CHAPTER ELEVEN

The sun smiled gleefully as the friends made their way back to town. Tums hung happily on Cressida's back, winding her sandy-brown hair around its black paws. Occasionally, the eehoo would reach toward Telyn in askance.

Telyn shied away.

Harlech would be abuzz for the rest of the day. Not much work would get done, and not much would be discussed aside from the funeral and the possessed eehoo—and Telyn fainting. Telyn and her friends got more than a few stares, and a gaggle of children started following along, the more daring ones dashing up to touch the eehoo. Cressida suffered all this with a smile.

Tums cooed.

"Oh, she's a prima donna," Caitlin remarked.

Telyn scowled. She liked kids fine—from a distance.

Why had the mind wizard returned to Harlech? Why did he asked me what I had seen instead of simply eliminating me, the witness? It doesn't make sense!

Something must have gone wrong with Yona's plan. He— through his daemon—had killed both Dagger and the trogo named Kulon. He had won the auction, so he had the Ever-Guise. He'd recovered all that gold, thousands of hurons worth, plus the two bodies and everything on them. She didn't suppose the penumbra daemon actually ate what it absorbed. It absorbed it, yes, but she was sure it could regurgitate it elsewhere just as easily. Else, why bother with the gold?

What demonly things it did with the bodies she didn't want to think about—not even a little bit.

What had Yona missed that he would risk exposing himself to Minister Svemas that way? The Minister wouldn't countenance murder, even by a mind wizard.

They passed the cornic stable and the stone-built Prefecture where Minister Svemas held court. They passed the Copcut Ash, Harlech's best tavern, owned by Tabbard's dad Wulstan Ouzeley.

"I know what will cheer everyone up." Caitlin bounded forward, skipping a little. "A nice, hot infusion."

"I don't know," Hosh said.

"Is it too girly in there for you, Hosh?" Caitlin teased.

"Nah, I'm just not thirsty."

"The kids won't follow us in there. Come on...my treat."

Hosh brightened instantly. "I'll probably be thirsty by the time we get there."

Telyn almost smiled. Hosh would accept a snowball in winter as long as someone else was buying.

What Telyn could use was a good climb. She relaxed by climbing—the higher the better—but an infusion made a decent substitute.

They reached the Rusty Shackles by taking the alley beside the Copcut Ash to the middle road and turning right. A cozy, stone-built place with a sod roof, women had been meeting there, or dragging reluctant boyfriends there, for ages. The name came from a set of manacles and fetters hanging from the wall near the back. Rumor said the building used to be part of a lord's private dungeon, and if you tore out the stone wall in the back you would find a tunnel leading to extensive catacombs. Telyn hadn't yet figured out how to confirm the rumors without breaking into the place and tearing out the wall with a pickax, which was a half-step beyond what she was willing to do.

These days, the shop's owner hung bouquets of dried lavender from the installation.

Sure enough, the trailing children dispersed when they heaved open the heavy door. The Shackles' windows received direct sunlight for about three hours a day, and the four friends sat at a table near the door to soak in that coveted warmth, Cressida sideways in her chair because Tums refused to descend from her back.

The owner bustled over. Probably a dozen years older than Telyn, Heledd Glines kept her hair in a neat bun except for one strand that curved over her nose. She presented a tray with a ceramic bowl in the middle. The bowl held grayish water, and pinned into that water was a struggling insect.

"Welcome, welcome ladies...and Hosh. Spicy wigglum—caught it this morning. That one is special, it is, guaranteed to put hair on your chins. See, it has a golden spot on its belly."

Telyn frowned at the struggling thing. It looked a lot like a water-strider with a lime-green body. A long pin held it underwater, affixing its middle to a cloth at the bottom of the bowl. The pin reminded her way too much of the glass needle Mrs. de Galati had used to draw blood from her hand.

"What's it taste like?" Hosh asked.

"A bit of a bite, as you might expect. No one's grumbled. Only two birds, and you get him on the day he was caught. It's not near the same after they drown."

Hosh looked permission at Caitlin, who, after all, was buying. She nodded as if the price made no difference.

"You keep him alive, hear? It's worth a huron if you don't."

"I'll be careful."

The girls ordered creamy veela-hair infusions. And then a thought came to Telyn. "Do you have spinosa?" The owner tilted her head. Although Heledd was a relative of some kind of the Ouzeleys, Teyln considered her decent enough. "Put a little of that in mine as well."

"That's usually reserved for Leutric Quid at the school, or for parents who want to punish their children."

"I know. I've felt it." Telyn displayed her wounded hand. "I think it might help numb this."

Heledd gave a considering look, as if considering a new sales ploy. She withdrew with a nod. "Right away."

An older woman with over-sized ears and hoop earrings grabbed her arm and hauled her to a stop. "Heledd, who you bettin' on?"

"You lookin' for a refill, Vicky?" Heledd said, vexed.

"A tip—for all the times I shoulda paddled your bottom 'n didn't."

"Oh, for all those times?" Heledd shrugged free. "For those times you can bet on the moon marrying its own reflection—in a yellow puddle!"

Vicky cackled as Heledd strode off.

"Worth a try," Vicky lamented over her steaming cup. She turned her head to speak directly to Telyn and her friends. "Watch what you jaw in here, young-uns. Heledd listens real close to all what's said— real close, see—and she never bets wrong on the Dating Chart. She'll know you're canoodling before you and your lover's lips cross!" She cackled again.

The kids drew their chairs closer together.

Making sure that Vicky had turned away first, Caitlin leaned forward. "Okay, Tey, you've been holding out long enough. Tell us what happened."

Telyn kept her voice low. "Where do you want me to start?"

"I heard Raz closed the whole place down. Is that true?"

Telyn nodded. "It's true. All the humans had to leave, including me and Cressida." She exchanged a significant look with her twin. "But I hid behind the winter stores..."

Telyn told the story of the auction all the way through the daemon killing the thief and disappearing into the night.

"Dagger," Hosh breathed. "What a name! He must have survived all kinds of things."

Cressida folded her arms across her chest. "Telyn, you should have told the pattern witch the thief's name. *Unknown* is the weakest incantation. The spell could have failed; the ghost might have escaped the Sepulcher."

"The pattern witch said the spell took. Tums is fine."

Tums cooed.

"So that little statue-thing, that's what killed Dagger?" Hosh asked. "What kind of ghost do you reckon it was, anyway?"

Cressida brought Tums around to her front so she could more comfortably recline in her chair. "A vengeful spirit," she said, darkly. "The worst kind. Like, the 'everybody dies—the end' kind."

Unseen by Hosh, the spicy wigglum had managed to loosen the pin through its belly and climb to the edge of the cup. It leapt from cup to tabletop and began scuttling away.

"Hey!" Hosh knocked the ceramic cup over in his scramble to snatch the pin; warm infusion spilled everywhere. He stabbed the table several times, but the insect jumped to Caitlin and crawled into her hair. Hosh likely would have tried stabbing it there—he raised the pin to strike—but for Caitlin's warning glare.

She managed to extract the insect from her curls without damaging it and considered the creature pinched between her fingers. "This little guy has earned his freedom."

"That'll cost you a huron!" Hosh said.

Against Hosh's protests, Caitlin took the insect outside to set it free. When she returned, Hosh had resorted to licking the deepest puddle on the table, which he announced was delicious.

Cressida bumped Telyn's elbow to get her attention, which had wandered. "You don't look so good, sis. Everything all right?"

"Just need some fresh air." Telyn pulled Tums into her arms. "I, eh, I've got to go. See you at the Sable Head?"

"Sure." Cressida raised her cup. "I'll just finish this and check on Mother."

Telyn found the Sable Head's front door locked; Raz must still be out. She scaled one of the poles holding up the front porch, then moved to the window they left unlatched for this purpose. She slid it open, climbed inside, and made her way downstairs.

Drawings of awesome buildings, menacing faces, weapons, treasure, monsters, battles, and more covered the public room. When a ghost manifested, it always painted its memories with dust or soot, ash or snow—whatever was available—though Telyn had never seen any so vivid. If a living person had drawn them, these would win an art show, hands-down.

What a life Dagger must have led!

But she had neither the time nor inclination to admire the art. Raz would return any minute. With the funeral-goers, Harlech was packed, and he'd want to make as much money as possible—and Telyn wanted to test out a hunch.

Pacifying Tums with a bidy tuber and leaving her in the kitchen, Telyn returned to the public room, squatted behind the winter stores, and recreated the auction in her mind: the bidding, the explosion when the chaos wood caused the trogo's magic to misfire, the fight between trogo and the two schmooks, the mind wizard testing the Ever-Guise, and Dagger returning the mask to the box.

She slowed her recall.

When Dagger's hand had dropped to his side, he'd substituted a false forehead for the real one: *The old switch-em-up, oldest trick in the book.*

What if Dagger didn't palm the piece? What if he'd hidden it here? That would explain why the penumbra daemon hadn't absorbed it, and why Yona and the schmook returned to Harlech.

They were missing a piece.

It can't be far from Dagger's seat, roughly the length of his reach.

She peered under the table. Nothing, not a thing out of place, neither under the table Dagger's bench, nor any of the other benches, for that matter. She hiked up her long skirt and crawled around until her knees hurt. She'd almost given up when she remembered how the mask had molded itself to the flacks' faces.

What if—?

She made herself close her eyes and rely on her sense of touch. She found several crusty biscuits, some dried mystery meat, and one pile of gloop that made her exclaim *eww* and wipe her hands fretfully on her dress.

She swallowed bile and made herself continue, groping around the bench's cross-braces until her reticent fingers touched something not-wood and not-gloop—something rather slippery-sticky, like the layer of fascia just under an animal hide.

That didn't bother her the way blood did; she lived in a town full of trappers, after all.

She peeled the false forehead from under the bench, took a second to admire the almond-shaped eye-holes, the mica-sparkles in the ceramic-like material, and scrunched it into her belt sash.

CHAPTER TWELVE

With as little fanfare as possible, Telyn exited through the upstairs window, tiptoed across the shingles to the far side of the roof, and dropped onto Middle Street. There she stood, indecisive. She wanted to rejoin her friends at the Rusty Shackles; she wanted to tell them about the forehead piece!

She wanted to keep this secret all to herself.

Magic: she'd actually discovered a magical object. This could change their fortunes! They wouldn't have to worry about their places on the Dating Chart (not that she'd paid a lot of attention to that, not really). Esther could drink herself into oblivion, and it wouldn't matter. A hundredth part of what Dagger got for the full mask would be more than she could earn at the Sable Head in a lifetime.

They'd be rich.

She'd share the money with her friends, of course—some of it. Enough to keep them quiet. If they spoke out, she'd be sunk. Keeping magic was against Cornic Empire Rules—for humans. Flacks could do what they liked.

But she could trust her best friends, couldn't she?

Her breath came in little gasps. The angle of sun and shadow on

Middle Street said they'd passed eleven a.m. She needed to think things through, consider whom to trust.

An hour to herself, to climb and to think; that's what she needed, in that order. Climbing cleared Telyn's mind, quieted the confusion of her brain, and allowed her to focus on the problem at hand or to forget it—whichever she needed in the moment.

The four-hundred-foot trees grew across the Elbus River in the Chaos Woods, but going there would take too much time. Instead, she headed for the small park in the middle of town, a park surrounding a single chaos tree. The red-barked evergreen was already a hundred feet tall, enough of a challenge to break a sweat, and the climb wouldn't keep Cressida waiting long. Besides, Telyn always loved the view from up there: the roofs of Harlech, sod, shingle, and slate, spreading in all directions like a three-dimensional quilt; the majestic Sepulcher at the town's back, the Elbus River Canyon to its front; and across that, the awesome Chaos Woods and the ever-white peaks of the Cairn Range.

She never made it to the tree.

A voice hailed her by name as she emerged from the alley into the park. She turned, and a young cornic soldier waved at her. He wore the standard solid metal breastplate and chain mail skirt over a cream-colored cotton uniform, which was embroidered with gold thread at the cuffs and collar. His free hand held a pole with a loop of rope around the end—a slave catcher. With this, soldiers could hook a slave by the neck and keep them at a distance, choking them as needed, or snag a fleeing slave by the ankle.

Telyn's throat went dry. She hated to see this implement of flack dominance, but she smoothed the creases from her dress, stilled, and awaited the soldier. What else could she do? The forehead's pliable ceramic felt heavy against her belly.

"Yes, sir?" she said, with as steady a voice as she could muster.

The soldier closed the distance and looked up at her, planting the butt of his tool in the dirt. At least he didn't loop her neck immediately. "You're wanted in the minister's office."

"What for?"

He turned Telyn toward the Prefecture and gave her a shove. Like all cornics, he had the girth of a barrel and the strength of a mule, and when he pushed, Telyn stumbled forward. She considered it a small victory not to have landed on her face. She straightened her back and used her long legs to set a pace just faster than comfortable for the cornic.

If she was to be interrogated, she would go there with dignity.

How to play it? Confess everything and beg for mercy? It might just work. Telyn had a load of information about the auction she could trade for amnesty—the buyers, that mind wizard Yona, the thief, the trogo, the schmooks, an anaconda....

Minister Svemas had promised amnesty, after all; he'd promised just this morning.

Or try to distract this young soldier and drop the forehead piece someplace? He didn't look too bright; it might just work. The mask grew cold against her belly, as if loath to be parted with her. Or, she thought, as if it were warning her. The odds of the guard seeing the drop was high...it wasn't like Telyn knew slight-of-hand. And if the guard didn't notice, some kid would almost surely happen by and find the mask.

No, trying to ditch it during this walk was a stupid risk.

The minister probably wanted to ask her a few questions about the Sable Head and the dead man. Whom had she seen? Did she know why Raz closed the place early? As long as she didn't act suspicious, she would be fine.

They weren't going to search her, were they?

Were they?

The guard started humming "Hey, Ho, the Gallows Tall" as they walked.

He'd doing that on purpose to intimidate me. Well, it won't work.

They entered through the side entrance meant for humans. Good, she'd attracted enough gossip by fainting at the funeral. If they had gone in through the main entrance, she would have died.

They quickly passed through the familiar area. Down a long corridor, they passed cornic soldiers and functionaries who either ignored Telyn or stared with open interest. She didn't see a single human.

The austerity of this part of the Prefecture surprised her. The human area was built to impress: great paintings of battles and troop movements; ornate chandeliers; weapons, shields, crests above the doors. Here, lit by sunlight from windows every twenty feet or so, the thick, stone walls stood bare.

The solder opened a nondescript door to reveal a narrow staircase. Telyn felt a pang of relief when he took the flight up rather than the one leading toward the dungeon. They exited into a corridor all bustle and business where important-looking flacks carried important-looking scrolls, some sealed with red wax.

At the corridor's end sat a door carved with a basket weave pattern guarded by two sentries. They saluted Telyn's soldier, who knocked and entered without waiting for an answer. They stepped into a reception room, and through an open door (plain this time) on the opposite wall, Minister Kenelm Svemas leaned over a wide desk. The soldier stood at attention, and control seemed to pass to the other cornic in the reception room, an officer with many medals pinned to his black vest.

Telyn regretted that she had never learned cornic ranks. Officer medals traded frequently on the black market; why hadn't she bothered to learn what they meant?

"Wait," the officer said, as Telyn was about to seat herself in one of the red velvet upholstered chairs along the wall. "Remove your coat."

Slowly, Telyn complied, handing the garment over to the soldier, who hung it on a peg. The soldier was but inches away from the mask. If her sash drooped, if the outline of the forehead protruded even a tad, she would be sunk.

Telyn felt that peculiar combination of fear and exhilaration which spiked during a particularly hard climb, where you had to release both handholds to stretch as high as you could, bracing on your toes, to grab the next ledge. One wrong move, and you would plunge a hundred, two hundred feet.

This wouldn't be much different.

Humans were not allowed to possess magic. It was one of the Rules. Breaking it would send you to slavery or death, depending on the severity of the crime…or the whim of the minister.

"Hands up," the officer commanded. "Search her."

Telyn slowly raised her hands above her head, and the soldier started patting down her shoulders, her armpits...

Minister Svemas came around his desk. "Come now, Second Gajos, no need for that. No one is under arrest here."

The soldier looked to the officer for directions. He gestured for the soldier to continue.

Quietly, the soldier broke into "The Secret Places of My Heart" and kept patting, though with less diligence: hips, thighs, ankles, obvious places to conceal a weapon. He didn't bother with her belly, where the mask was hidden, and Telyn sent a silent thank you to the High Father for small favors.

After shooting the officer a displeased look, Minister Svemas led Telyn into his office, returned to the far side of his desk, and sat. "Second Gajos views me as a scholar, you see, incapable of looking after my own safety. Too interested in human affairs for my own good, which puts my sanity into question. Have a seat."

Not understanding cornic etiquette, Telyn curtsied as best she knew how, then sat on the hard wooden chair in front of the desk. Its legs were not level; she wobbled back and forth without finding a balance point.

They gave me this wobbly chair on purpose.

She remembered the red-velvet chairs in the reception room and considered whether she dared drag one in to sit more comfortably. The minister might admire her cheekiness—or he might decide she needed a lesson.

She stayed put.

"You know why you're here?"

"I, ah, think so."

A hinged wooden box sat prominently on the minister's desk along with an ink pot, quill, and sheet of blank paper over which he folded his hands. "I've been advised to drop this investigation." Minister Svemas nodded toward the officer in the other room. "It's a human problem. The ghost has been laid to rest. But some things have been bothering me. I am, as I said, a cornic of letters. Poems, in particular. The ones you call epic, with heroes, damsels, and daring-do." He

97

gestured to the wall on Telyn's right from which hung a coat of arms depicting an Otter holding a flute to its lips. Surrounding this were the words *Academy of Enshede.*

So, the minister went to the Academy. I'd better act impressed.

"This story feels like what we call *in medias res*. Do you know what that means?"

Telyn had no idea where this was going. She might have heard of 'inmedares' in school, but she didn't like to be called out if she couldn't define something. "No." She widened her eyes in what she hoped was the expected reaction.

"It means we've come in the middle of things," Minister Svemas explained with the relish of a teacher on his favorite subject. "We missed the proper beginning. Oh, I'm confident it will be revealed in the end. That's part of the fun, puzzling out how the story started from the clues peppered in the middle."

"It's probably a boring poem anyway."

Minister Svemas laughed. "Not much of a reader?"

"More of a climber."

"Yes, I remember. Third place in the ice wall competition last year. Have you been training?"

"I guess."

"Then you understand the importance of not giving up just because you have a setback. Setbacks, they say, are the fuel for progress —for training harder, training different. Do you understand?"

"Not really."

In the other room, the cornic officer burped and began chewing his cud.

"No, I've read too much poetry to say things clearly. This missing body, that is a setback. If we had a body, we would have a cause of death. If we had a cause of death, we could rule out murder. But since we don't have a body, we have to assume the worst. I have another name for setbacks. Do you know what that is?"

She realized the minister didn't really expect an answer, just an acknowledgment to go on, so she grunted.

"Clues. Something happened in the Sable Head different from

anything I have ever seen before. If the story were just about humans, I might have let it drop. But it wasn't, was it?"

"Er, no sir?" She made it a question.

"Tell me what you saw in the Sable Head."

A pause. She wondered whom Minister Svemas had interrogated before her. *Raz? Yes. The pattern witch? Certainly. Maybe Cressida also; it's possible the cornics picked up my sister at the Rusty Shackles.*

Cressida wouldn't have blabbed. She would have said as little as possible.

That means only two people could rat me out: Hosh and Caitlin. I wish I hadn't told them about staying in the Sable Head and witnessing the murder. If only I had kept my mouth shut a little longer.

"I didn't see anything," she said, tentatively. "Nothing important, least ways."

Minister Svemas eyed her a moment, then pulled a sheaf of stiff paper from his desk drawer—charcoal sketches, twenty or thirty of them—and began leafing through them. "Mighty peculiar, a body disappearing like that. If there hadn't been a ghost, we would never have known someone died. Not many people could arrange that. Some people are saying Razenbock chopped the man up and served him in his stew."

Telyn cringed.

"The most likely explanation, of course, is that a wild animal killed the man and dragged the body into the woods—except a cereb and schmook came to me claiming someone stole something from them. A most unusual pair, don't you think? They've been rather cagey about what, exactly, they lost, but it has to do with a mask and a dagger, of all things."

Telyn shifted, and the seat wobbled so hard she nearly fell over backwards.

The minister looked up from the sketches. "Your father disappeared, didn't he?"

Even at a distance of years, Telyn's throat caught. She swallowed into a dry, tight lump. "Lots of people disappear in the Chaos Woods. It's a...a dangerous place."

She'd been telling herself that for years, trying to make herself feel better about it happening to her dad, to her and Cressida, to her whole family. Dad's disappearance was the seminal event driving Esther to slowly drown herself in malt.

The minister rotated the sketches so Telyn could see. The first showed Telyn herself emerging from behind the winter stores, firelight reflecting in her eyes.

"At times, I think there must be a city of ghosts out there in the woods with all the humans disappearing every season. I hope they all end up in one place, sort of a ghost city. We wouldn't want your dad to be lonely out there." The minister slid another drawing forward. This one showed a closeup of a human hand flinging the daemon statue. "The smoke wrote the most interesting narrative on the Sable Head walls, a story unlike anything I've seen in my life-time. I would have liked to postpone the funeral until the ghost fully possessed the eehoo so we could interrogate it properly, but according to Mrs. de Galati, it was imperative we get it laid to rest right away. Leave them out too long, and it gets difficult—especially if you don't have the name. And this ghost was particularly destruc-tive. Nearly chaosed the Sable Head to ruin. She said it was likely a vengeful spirit."

Telyn took a deep breath. The minister was trying to keep her off-balance. He probably mentioned her dad on purpose. She didn't like the low blow, but she understood his reasoning. The minister was looking for a murderer, after all. She wished she could just admit that Yona's daemon killed the thief—but that would never do, not with the forehead in her sash at this very moment. "I was working in the kitchen last night, making the stew. There weren't no bodies in it. Cressida, my twin sister, she serves the tables. She told me there were flacks in the public room." She cringed a little bit at her own choice of words; one shouldn't call a flack a flack to his face, not if you wanted to keep your teeth, but the minister motioned for her to continue. "So, when I finished cooking, I came out and took a look."

"And who did you see?"

"The usual people—my sister, Raz, Heath Robinson, and Tyre Flint. And some non-humans: a few schmooks; a giant lizard; a var.

Then two I'd never seen before, not even at the Spring Sale—a conda, I think, with a light sprouting from his head, and a mind wizard, the one at the funeral."

"Seven in all?"

"I didn't count."

"Anyone else?"

"There was a fight. I was going to get something from the winter stores, and a fight broke out after someone slapped me where I shouldn't be slapped." The minister frowned in askance, she clarified. "He slapped my bottom. It happens when people get too much malt in 'em." She shrugged. "No one got hurt, least that I saw."

Telyn always increased the grammar mistakes when she spoke with flacks—at least flacks in authority. They seemed to expect it, and it helped them underestimate her.

The minister leaned forward. "Do you think someone could have gotten hurt that you didn't see? We *are* talking about a ghost. Maybe someone fell down, hit their head on the floor?"

"Um, could be. They took the fight outside. It could have happened out there, where no one seen it." Mother of Squirrels, Telyn wished she'd thought of that story herself!

"Go on."

"After that, well, Raz has a rule: *No ladies after supper.* So, I had to leave. Cressida went home, and I—I went climbing."

"Overcoming setbacks."

Telyn shrugged, relaxing a bit. "It's what I do. Day, night—if you can't find me, I'm climbing. When I walked by the Sable Head later in the night, there was this weird keening, and I went inside to investigate."

"And then you went to get the pattern witch."

"Well, first I found Cressida, and I told her, and she went to get Raz from the Lucky H while I went to get Mrs. de Galati."

"You usually climb the tree in Elin Llyweln Park," Minister Svemas said, and Telyn nodded. "Or in the chaos trees across the river —" She nodded again. "—or near the Sepulcher."

How in the world does the Minister know all that?

"The Sable Head is a long way away from where you usually

climb. You have to go clear across town, past your own cabin to get there."

"I don't much like spending time at home," Telyn allowed.

Minister Svemas rubbed his goat-like beard. Telyn had the impression he looked right through her. He might seem an affable innocent —some would say a dunce—but his questions were keener than most. "You look anxious, Telyn Brower. Anything the matter?"

"No. I just, ah, I should be getting to work."

"Well, then, you have no reason to be anxious. The Sable Head will be closed until the investigation is over. Which could be a long time—with no body." He put his hands out in a helpless gesture. "Unless there's anything you want to add."

Sensing a dismissal, Telyn stood.

The Sable Head closed? That means no jobs, no income, no food. No income for Raz, either. We'll have to open the jars meant for winter...or go without.

Telyn didn't have to hide the worried pinch to her temples; Minister Svemas knew perfectly well how much pressure he'd just applied.

The soldier returned bearing her long coat.

"Miss Brower," the minister said, as she shrugged into her sleeves, "this is not going to go away, not with a missing artifact of some kind, a murder, and seven thaumas involved."

"What if fla—er, thaumas—weren't involved?"

"Now, Miss Brower, that would be the first time a human didn't want to turn blame onto non-humans when they had the chance." He sat back in his chair and considered her.

"Oh, and one more thing, I just remembered." Minister Svemas pulled a small, soft-sided leather bag from under his desk and set it beside the stack of sketches. He undid the knot on the drawstring, loosening it, but leaving the opening mostly closed so that Telyn couldn't see what was inside. He pushed the bag across the desktop. "We found something on the floor in the Sable Head that might be related to the man's disappearance. Do you want to tell me what it is?"

The ear.

Telyn tried to speak, tried to say she had no idea what they might have found. Would the minister believe she'd only heard about it from the pattern witch?

A little croak came out. Her mind went to blood and maroons and sickly maroon smoke at the funeral. That horrible ringing started in her ears.

"You can either reach inside the bag and try to identify the object by touch—" Minister Svemas held Telyn still with the force of his topaz stare. "—or you can tell me now what it is."

Telyn's breaths came in rapid bursts. *It isn't blood. Not sticky blood, nor dry, crusty blood...just a shriveled, old ear. Cartilage. No biggie. I eat it all the time.*

"Will—Will it hurt me?"

He tapped the bag, urging her to reach in.

She reached forward tentatively.

"Go on, a few more inches. Yes, that's it. Put your whole hand inside; don't be frightened."

The cornic soldier came to stand behind her like a menacing shadow. Her own coat brushed her arm, making her shiver.

The interior of the bag was fuzzy and wrinkled. As her fingers delved further and widened the opening, the scent of leather increased. Leather, dead cow-skin. Telyn felt between the folds, pressed her fingers to the corners. At any moment, she would find the rubbery, rotten ear...

And...

Nothing. The bag was empty.

Those topaz eyes appraised her. The minister didn't need a confession; he already knew she'd been lying, and she'd witnessed more than she let on.

Telyn had stopped breathing altogether. She couldn't hide it; she released her breath with an audible gasp. Her face must have been three shades paler than pale.

I will never underestimate the minister again.

Never again.

Minister Svemas pulled the bag back to his side of the desk and dropped it into a drawer. That affable grin grew on his wooly sheep-face. "If you think of anything you want to tell me, Miss Brower, tell Corporal Velky downstairs." He nodded to the soldier behind her. "He will bring you right up to my office. Or Second Gajos, if you happen to see him. They have my strictest confidence."

"Yes...yes, sir."

CHAPTER THIRTEEN

Across the Elbus River, Telyn could readily find trees several hundred feet tall, but crossing the bridge felt so final. If everything went south—the cornics caught her with the forehead; the mind wizard came after her; the Dating Chart paired her with Tabbard Ouzeley—she would have to flee that way, never to return. Her life expectancy in the Chaos Woods would be short, but the woods offered the only escape for humans on the run.

Humans cannot own magic.

If she crossed the bridge with the forehead in her sash, it would be a bad omen. Therefore, she ascended the slope between her cabin and the Sepulcher and picked a chaos tree at random. This one had low, friendly branches that spiraled to a height of around thirty feet. From the scuff marks and names carved into the reddish bark, it was obvious she wasn't the first to notice the way the branches practically begged to be climbed.

All the better.

Minister Svemas's threat hung over her like a thunderhead. He'd shuttered the Sable Head, destroyed her livelihood, and sent his soldier to spy on her. The past few days, Telyn had kept running into —what was his name? Corporal Velky, that was it. Ever since Minister

Svemas had interrogated her, the corporal appeared at random times —by their cabin, at the human well, outside the bakery.

Always he greeted her with a cheery tune, like "Weeping at the Gallows" or "Thief's Curse." The corporal seemed to have music for blood.

So Telyn had begun climbing even more than usual, getting the corporal used to it. *This is Telyn's thing; this is normal.* He'd have a hard time Good luck to the Corporal following her to the top; cornics were too heavy, too short, and too inflexible. Grinning, Telyn lifted her bare foot nearly to her ribs, snagged a toe-hold, and pulled herself up.

Beyond the first thirty feet, hand- and footholds became scarce. Here, Telyn's pot-washing fingers came to life, and her six-foot three height actually served her rather than simply marking her as an oddball.

She spiraled around the trunk once, peering at the needle-carpeted slope. No one in sight.

The first difficult move required her to leap up about a foot and grab a fist-sized branch. On the ground, no one would think twice about such a feat. Here, fifty feet in the air, few would dare. Cressida might have; they used to climb together, racing each other to the top. The risks they took! Cressida gave that up when Esther's drinking got too much for her to run her dress shop, Meander and Mohair, properly—when Cressida decided she had to play mom.

Telyn jumped, grabbed the little branch, and used the swing to press her belly onto the branch. A laugh burst from her lungs. She loved when timed coordination did the work for her.

Then she felt a touch of panic—she'd pressed her weight square on the Ever-Guise.

She scooted to the trunk and felt around her midsection. Yes, the mask was still secure; it hadn't broken. In fact, it had softened to better absorb the impact.

The mask had a thing for self-preservation, it seemed.

Telyn rested a minute, legs dangling over either side of the branch. *It's magical, after all. I probably couldn't break it if I tried. Nothing to worry about.* A trickle of sweat meandered from her eyebrow to her cheek. *That pickled trapper would see more than my ankles now, the way my dress bunches up to my knees. What a bother! Too bad I can't climb in stockings alone.*

Well, why not? No one will see me here, and it'll make the climb a lot safer.

With just a second's hesitation, she stripped off the skirt and tucked it into the crook of a small branch.

Without any branches for about twenty feet, the thick, knobby bark offered the only way up. Telyn breathed deeply a few times, slipped her hand into a wide crack between layers of bark, made a fist to wedge it tight, and went for it. An invigorating, clove-like odor came from where her fists squished a resinous pitch.

With luck, her fingers wouldn't tickle a centipede.

Life would have been so much simpler if she hadn't hidden behind the winter stores, hadn't watched the flacks and their stupid auction, hadn't recovered the forehead piece. No finger-freezing tea with Rayvn, no blood-letting glass needles, no passing out in front of the whole world.

As with many chaos trees, a cluster of branches grew near the top. Telyn disappeared into them and pushed past the itchy needles until the tree offered its views. To the south and west were Harlech's rooftops, mist from Defiance Falls, the canyon bridge, and the Chaos Woods proper. To the north, the towering Sepulcher stood. To the east, the long road wound through Gopher Pass to Enshede and the sea.

Telyn reclined against the tree and removed the forehead piece. It stiffened under her fingers, changing from a leathery texture to one resembling ceramic. Eyelashes had been carved into the material, and fine, dark eyebrows were painted on hair by hair. The smooth forehead looked somehow feminine. Most striking, painted in the middle of the forehead lay a third eye with white gold prongs to hold a missing gem.

She hadn't noticed the prongs before. They must be set (she placed her thumb in the divot to measure) an inch-and-a-half wide and an inch tall.

What a gem this must hold!

Telyn ran her thumb around the perimeter. The lower right had a jade edge; the left a wooden edge.

How much is the Ever-Guise worth? Well, this small part of it.

A hundred birds?

A thousand?

My life?

Telyn began to consider what must have happened after the auction. The other flacks must have left Harlech lickety-split. Three roads led out of Harlech. The Upper Road led past the Sepulcher and Mirror Lake and dead-ended at the lime pit; the west road crossed the Elbus River and into the Chaos Woods; but the flacks would have taken the south road. In the capital of Cornic Empire, they could disappear, take a ship back home, or simply deposit their treasure in a bank for safekeeping.

She turned the forehead over and over in her hands.

No one else knew about it yet—not Cressida, not Caitlin, not Hosh. Telyn and her friends hadn't had time to meet, though she was dying to tell them...and try it out.

Even though she thought about using it daily, hourly, she'd stayed cautious, lulled Corporal Velky into her routine. *Really, I should wait to tell anyone until winter closed the mountain passes and the mind wizard could not possibly return, but come on. No one could wait that long.*

Carrying a blackened maroon nut, a squirrel scurried to the top of the tree. Squatting far out on a branch with one eye on Telyn, the rodent worried the shell into pieces and began munching. At this height, even the weight of a squirrel caused the tree to sway.

Telyn closed her eyes, letting the dappled sunshine warm her face and chest. She inhaled the chaos tree's resinous aroma.

The safe thing to do would be to lose this thing forever. That's what Cressida would tell me.

That thought rankled her. She put the forehead to her face. Without hesitation, it molded to her skin. She ran her fingers from cheekbones to scalp. Yes, it felt a little thicker than normal, almost like a callus. By moving the tips of her fingertips along the ridge of her eyes, she could feel where her skin ended and the mask began. The gem prongs had melted.

She wished she had remembered a mirror!

Time to experiment.

"Give me a hundred birds."

Nothing.

"A thousand birds."

She didn't think it would work that way, but it was worth a shot—until she thought about it a little more. What if the mask thought she was talking about real birds? A vision came of a hundred raptors swarming her as she tried to climb down....

Better be more careful about wording.

Telyn sighed.

The Sable Head was closed until Minister Svemas concluded the investigation—until they found a body, he'd said. That would be a *long* time. Like, eternity. Most of Harlech's population would be heading out as soon as the List was posted in two weeks' time. Two weeks for Raz to make a profit. Two weeks for Telyn and Cressida to make enough tips to last the winter.

I have to do something. Now.

What had Dagger said...something about influencing? Could she *influence* the Minister into opening the Sable Head again?

Probably not. But the trappers could. All the trappers together.

Telyn took a deep breath. "I propose that the Sable Head is the coolest place in Harlech. Even eehoos want to hang out here. Even ghosts!" The forest seemed to wobble just a little, as though a bent piece of glass slid between her eyes and the trees. "While you're there, arm wrestle Tums the eehoo." Another wobble. "And don't forget to tip well. The twins work really hard. Especially the taller one."

CHAPTER FOURTEEN

"Get up."

Telyn awoke as the blankets were jerked off her. She rolled over, still half-dreaming. She tried feebly to find the warmth given off by Cressida's body, then retracted; an icicle had slept beside her. She balled up tighter, her hands touching the callus-like ridge where the mask rested on her forehead, making sure nothing had slipped overnight. Finally, after an eternity or so, the cold air got the best of her, and she opened her eyes.

Esther, standing before the stone fireplace, her hair long and uncombed, wearing her pink flannel nightshirt—the one with the chickamee stains—glared at her over handful of twigs. "You have chores to do," Esther said, snapping the twigs, her expression making it clear that if she could have snapped Telyn the same way, she would have, "or do you plan to let Cressida do everything?"

"Where is Cressida?" asked Telyn. The chill floor stung her feet. She jumped up to dress on the bed and bumped her head on the ceiling.

Esther scowled.

"Come on, get up," mimicked Cressida from the doorway,

113

hooking a second bucket to the yoke across her shoulders. "I'm getting the water. That means you get the chamber pots."

Telyn rubbed her eyes again.

When Cressida opened the door, the twins gasped in delight. The first real snow of winter, several weeks early. It was barely enough to call a snow—only an inch or so—but the air that swirled through the doorway was cold, colder than usual for an early snow, and Telyn hoped it wouldn't melt too quickly.

"Close the door before we freeze," Esther grouched.

As soon as door closed, Esther pulled the bolt into place, locking Cressida out.

Telyn paused in the process of tying off her belt-sash. "You're not locking her out, Esther," she warned.

"Just making sure you and I have time for a little talk."

Telyn bit her cheek to restrain one of a dozen retorts she could have made and continued layering on clothes.

"The cornics've been asking 'bout you," Esther said. "They've been wonderin' where you spend your time." She sauntered over, chin thrust out. "Wonderin', same as me."

"Was it that Corporal Velky?" Telyn didn't like that one bit. *Where else has he been poking his sheep's snout into?*

"You might've fooled your sister, but I know you're up to no good. If it ain't a man—"

"If it ain't a man" —Telyn glared—"then what do you think I've been doing?" Considering she wore forbidden magic on her face at that very moment, Telyn was proud of her cheekiness.

Esther shrank back a little. She cleared her throat, picked up her favorite mug, and slurped noisily.

A feeling of power swelled inside of Telyn, much like the charge of adrenaline from a good climb.

She'd been right to take the Ever-Guise down from the tree. Corporal Velky had been dogging her, and it took too much effort to ditch him every time she wanted to climb the dang tree. What better place to hide it than her own face?

Besides, she couldn't wait to tell her friends about it.

"I've always known you ain't right," Esther said from behind the mug. "I heard what happened at the funeral, the way you fainted clean out. Angel water's warped your little brain, or one of them magic critters from the woods."

"Like Cressida said the other evening, Esther, I don't drink." She grabbed a pair of logs and laid them over the kindling in the fireplace. "I don't drink 'cause I don't want to end up a disgusting old hag like you."

A thunk against the door indicated that Cressida had arrived.

"If it weren't for your father's memory, I'd throw your ungrateful hide out. I still might."

"Well, I'll..." Telyn didn't really know what she'd do. Except, well, she *was* wearing the mask. "I'll, ah..."

The door rattled. Cressida called her name.

Telyn moved slowly to the door, taking her time, trying to get her thoughts straight. Use the mask on her mother? Why not? It couldn't hurt. Nothing could be worse than waking up with this drunken hag every morning. A little suggestion could do no harm. "I want to help you, Esther. I propose that you don't like malt anymore."

Esther scoffed, said something about Telyn going soft in the nut, and toed the half-full chamber pot from under her spinning wheel. "Enjoy your chores while you're proposing."

"I propose—" Telyn threw back the bolt on the door. "—that when you taste malt, Esther, it tastes like...like the back-end of a brak-daw." She named one of the biggest, most disgusting creatures in the Chaos Woods. Brakdaws made grizzly bears look like princesses: skinny princesses who bathed thrice daily.

With a gigantic pop, sparks jumped from Telyn's face to the walls.

Esther shrieked.

The forehead became heavy as lead, and its weight pulled Telyn forward. She fell into Cressida as the door opened, and bucket-water sloshed all over place.

"Wha—?" Cressida said, barely able to keep her footing.

"The fireplace," Telyn blurted, trying to untangle herself from her sister. She slipped on the spilled water and landed on her hip in the doorway. "Pitch, sparks, um, sap caught fire, loud. Must have put in some green wood." She shot to her feet. "I'll clean this up. Sorry."

What happened? Did the chaos lumber of their cabin made the mask misfire? Thank goodness for the fire, and for having my back turned to Esther when I made that wish. Mother of Squirrels, that was close.

"You okay?" Cressida asked, steadying her.

"Fine. Never better."

"Fool girl can't even stoke a fire properly," Esther complained, pulling her snarled hair into a ponytail.

Their shack sat in a grove of trees near the Sepulcher which the locals called "Uptown," where the trappers had their temporary dwellings and the poor people theirs. Five or six shacks stood within a stone's throw, each about as shabby as the other. One had no door. A bear had broken in last spring, and someone had salvaged the door for the wood. If the owner didn't come back soon, the whole thing would be chopped up.

But Telyn thought they could do worse. They lived on a corner of the trail leading up and over a small ridge. People had to go around the house to climb the trail, and the twins always knew who came and went. Just on the other side of the ridge, and the reason for all this traffic, was one of the town's necessaries. People used it when it was too cold to water the woods, and they dumped their chamber pots in it. When the Marrow Wind blew from the north, the smell would meander through Uptown, whispering through the cracks in the walls and doors, wiping the tang off apple tarts and siphoning the butter warmth from freshly-baked bread. Living so close, the Brower family had grown used to it.

We're lucky on that account, Telyn thought, grinning as she and Cressida descended toward town.

They'd managed to sort out the rest of the chores, and Cressida had finished a fancy Dead-Winter dress for Ms. Madge. The green, off-the-shoulder dress might represent the last income they saw until the Sable Head opened again; thank goodness Cressida had talent with the needle.

Hand in hand, they walked the length of the Upper Road so they could get a view of the snow-capped Cairn Range, then they dropped down the stairs in the little alley behind Ouzeley manor to Main Street.

Starting at the Sable Head, you came to three taverns, two mercantiles, numerous eateries and other businesses, an apothecary, a bakery, the market hall—each beating to the pulse of Defiance Falls—then Steamy Betty's and attached stores, none of which the twins could afford.

With the Sable Head closed, they were in no hurry to deliver Ms. Madge's dress; Cressida carried it over her shoulder like a stole. A few clouds scudded across a brilliant, blue sky. The air was still; their feet scrunched the fresh snow deliciously. It was the kind of morning that made Telyn love being outdoors.

The entire way, Telyn debated whether or not to tell Cressida about the mask. She wanted to; she really did. But Cressida was such a rule-sie. She knew just what her sister'd say: "You got to turn that in this instant! The longer you keep it, the worse it'll be. Where do you think you're gonna sell it? If they don't put you in irons, they'll knock out your teeth and take it, and nothing you'll be able to do but cry. And who will marry someone without teeth? You'll be off the Dating Chart for life!"

If Cressida didn't make her turn it in to Minister Svemas, she'd heft it into the middle of Defiance Falls—and good riddance!

Expectancy greeted them everywhere. Trappers bustled around purchasing grain or salted meat, oiling skins to cache food, oiling saddles for smoother riding, oiling leggings and jerkins to waterproof them. With so much lanolin, Harlech smelled like regular sheep-herd.

A hundred or more trappers had gathered before the Prefecture, keeping slightly less than a respectful distance away from the doors and the line of cornic soldiers before them. Most of the trappers polished metal or oiled leather, and two blade sharpeners did a steady business, but others muttered together in angry knots, some using llamas as screens. Occasionally, one gathered enough courage to shout at the soldiers, although they always ducked quickly back into the crowd.

With a wrinkle to her nose and a hand on Telyn's elbow to hurry her along, Cressida complained that the trappers must have spent the night drinking. "Looks like a riot about to start. Best be getting along before things get out of control—fool men."

They'd nearly passed the square when Telyn paused. She thought she'd heard two little words...

Yes, there they were again: *Sable Head*.

The tavern's name peppered the conversations.

Food vendors had set up, mingling the cook-fire smells with the smell of lanolin, and Telyn steered her sister that way. "Just a minute. No harm in listening," she said to Cressida's protests.

They found a place near a cook fire.

"...have little superstition, but fact is that we have seen a divine apparition, a ghost come from nothing, no body. And that ghost chose the Sable Head to appear in. Now why is that?"

"Because Raz served the body in his stew."

They'd stopped at a baker's brazier, complete with red-hot coals, a grill, and billycans filled with—Telyn sniffed—gooseberry acorn dough, slowly rising.

"I know that ain't so; Raz was nowhere there. I seen him in the Lucky H."

"Then one of his girls done it. That bean-pole—"

A shout from a man in a plaid sweater interrupted this conversation: "I demand the doors of the Sable Head be opened so that we can read the signs on the walls—"

"And drink lots of angel water!" another man shouted, to raucous laughter.

Both fellows disappeared behind the screen of llamas and people.

The crowd seemed about equally divided between people who earnestly wanted the Sable Head opened, and those determined to laugh at anything and everything.

Mother of Squirrels, the Ever-Guise did this, I know it did. Just the little forehead by itself! So much power in such a small thing. I made this happen—me, a human with magic. Wow. If just one of five Ever-Guise pieces contains this much power, what might whole mask accomplish?

"I see faces in the windows," Cressida said, nodding at the Prefecture. "Mark my words, they're noting who shouts. We should be getting this dress to Ms. Madge before the dam breaks."

"A minute more."

Cressida tsked. "Trouble's afoot, Telyn."

"Just a minute more, promise. You know you're curious."

"I ain't leaving Harlech without Tums seeing me off with a good luck handshake," promised one of the fellows around their fire.

"That's right. Every time I leave without scratching the eehoo's chin, I lose a toe to the Aumerhem Devil. Tums is good luck, I say."

The Cairn Range's tallest mountain, Aumerhem Peak, was synonymous with cold weather calamity.

Cressida screwed up her face. "Tums, good luck? Since when?"

Smiling inwardly, Telyn shrugged.

A trapper with a handlebar mustache climbed the bottom steps of the Prefecture and began taunting the soldiers, calling them "goat face" and "hoof-head." He'd just finished dissing their armpits—he hadn't a whole lot of imagination—when one of the soldiers brought the butt-end of his spear down on the man's skull. The trapper collapsed and rolled away.

The crowd's muttering swelled.

One of the pastry sellers tugged on Cressida's sleeve. "You work there at the Sable Head, don't ya?"

"I think I would remember you if we met," Cressida said, putting on her serving smile.

He didn't look familiar to Telyn. A little on the grubby side, he had wiry, red hair like many seasonal workers that came to Harlech in the fall as the trappers gathered for the List, and then again for the Spring Sale. Where they spent the rest of the year, Telyn had no idea.

"I've seen you there waiting tables, beautiful. You're friends with the famous eehoo, eh? Tough luck with the Sable being closed and all. You hungry? Have an acorn." With a heavy glove he removed a billycan from the fire, ran a knife around the inner edge, and popped out the jelly pastry. He blew it cool before handing it to Cressida.

"Thank you, sir."

Telyn frowned a little. Since Cressida served in the public room, she got all the attention. In the kitchen, Telyn got nothing but smelly hair and greasy feet—but she took half the acorn when Cressida offered it. It was hot to touch, but not too hot, with the pleasant smell of charcoal in the crust. The twins never bought themselves treats like this; times were tough for the Brower family, and a single acorn cost as much as a banger at the Lucky H, a bath at Steamy Betty's, or two yards of coarse cotton fabric.

A niggle of worry tried to work its way into Telyn's belly, but she had better things to put there than worry. She closed her eyes and bit deeply into the delicious bread and sugar frosting; a squirt of fiery-hot gooseberry jumped into her mouth. The heat added to the fun. She had to balance the mouthful on her teeth, being careful not to touch it for too long with her tongue while she breathed in and out rapidly. Finally, she swallowed, and the gooseberry warmth spread from her stomach like a dollop of happiness.

She ate some more, playing the game each time, taking small bites to make it last longer. She didn't care if people stared; eating was one of life's greatest pleasures. She separated the flavors in her mind: sugar, bread, and even the filling she separated into seeds, sour, jelly, and best of all, gooseberry.

The red-haired worker chuckled. "Was a time I enjoyed eating that much."

"Thank you, sir," Cressida said.

Telyn couldn't speak with her full mouth.

Another man poked his scowling, bearded face into their midst— this one most unwelcome: Archie Todd, the town baker. For some reason, he'd hated the twins for as long as Telyn could remember. Beady, green eyes flashed from the empty billycan to the twins and back.

"That'll be four eggs."

Telyn stopped mid-bite, her eyes seeking Cressida's.

Her twin took her hand and signed. *What?*

They hadn't assigned swear words to their finger-talk, so Telyn had to content herself with, *Unfair!*

Cressida put on her sweetest smile. "Your man told us to take one."

The baker crossed his arms, revealing tattoos on either forearm. "Nothing's for free, darlin'. You want me to call the cornics down from their posts? They don't take kindly to thieves, and they're looking nervous, what with all these people—"

Telyn hated when the baker called them "darlin'," but now wasn't the time for semantics. Against Cressida's palm, she signed. *Run-hide!*

What?

Now. Run-hide!

"—protesting about the Sable Head being closed—"

Telyn bent down, scooped up a handful of mud, and held it over the billycans. "Your man gave that acorn to us fair and square, so admit it or I'll destroy the whole lot."

"Now listen—"

"I give you three seconds. One—"

Coming to his senses, the red-haired worker tried to pull the tray out of the way, but the crowd hampered him, and Telyn skinned around the fire so the dirt remained over the cans.

The baker snapped his gaping mouth closed and came at her from the other side.

"Two—"

Cressida bolted, Ms. Madge's dress billowing as she weaved between trappers, llamas, and gear. Before counting "three," Telyn threw the mud straight up and dashed the other way. The red-haired man tried to spin the tray out of the way before the dirt rained down.

Archie Todd followed Telyn.

Telyn sprinted across the slush-covered square as fast as her long legs would carry her. From behind, footfalls pounded closer. She ducked into the labyrinth behind Steamy Betty's, cornering every fifth step or so.

Snap! A belt lashed behind her. The air split next to her skin.

Missed.

She slowed just a tad. If he got too close, he'd catch her, but if she could lure him in...

She whipped around behind the apothecary and to the other side. The belt landed this time, smarting her hip and ripping the hem of her shirt. He was close now, just about close enough. They emerged from the alley labyrinth onto Main. The baker would have a clear shot here—

Telyn turned her head left, grabbed the hitching post, and spun her body the other way. The baker tried to grab her and missed—his legs slipped out from under him. She heard a crash and a series of curses.

Telyn turned to face the man sprawled face-first in the slush. Jogging backwards at a measured clip, she licked the gooseberry jelly off her fingers one at a time.

The look Archie Todd returned could have melted glass.

CHAPTER FIFTEEN

The nice thing about all of that, Telyn thought as she climbed the uneven stone stairs leading to Dragon Tower, is that she gave Cressida the slip without having to come up with any excuses. They'd have to avoid the baker for a time, of course. That man could put the sour in rhubarb. Ever since Telyn could remember, whenever he saw them, the baker would glower. They'd never given him any reason, always been polite. "Hello Mr. Todd." "Good evening, Mr. Todd."

Today, the baker's man had offered them the gooseberry acorn fair and square, without ever saying anything about buying it. *Fie on the baker and his man, too! We did nothing wrong.* Telyn hoped the falling mud had ruined every last billycan.

The arrow slits in Dragon Tower revealed different views as she mounted: the Chaos Woods; the Elbus River and the smokestacks of Harlech; the cart trek north to the lumber mill. The pattern continued as she spiraled upward. Rumors said this had once been a human fortification, but Telyn didn't know the truth of it. These musty ruins, located on the opposite side of the river from Harlech, had been her playground since forever—and her refuge.

The stairs spiraled through a trapdoor to the fourth and final floor. This area had larger windows, perhaps for dropping stones or hot oil on invader's heads. The extravagance of light made this a better meeting spot than the lower floors. Theoretically, they could climb onto the roof through another trapdoor in the ceiling, but the ladder had long since disintegrated.

Hosh and Caitlin, sitting shoulder to shoulder, nodded when Telyn emerged from the stairwell. Hosh had a thing for Caitlin, but he would never admit to it. He and Caitlin had been friends too long. A shame, really; the two would be good together. Telyn wondered if the Dating Circle had put Hosh and Caitlin as a possible match, and what the odds were of them dancing the Promise Dance.

No, she was not at all curious. She didn't care about the Dating Chart. She didn't, not even a smidgen.

"Why are you chewing your cheek, Telyn?" Caitlin adjusted her blue checkered headscarf. "It looks like you're trying to memorize the Philosopher's Codex."

"Wha—? No, nothing." No way was she going to mention the Dating Chart. "I, um, Cressida and I just had a run-in with Archie Todd." Her friends shifted expectantly.

Telyn smiled, pleased to have a story. Briefly, she recounted the unruly trappers, the demands to reopen the Sable Head, the baker unfairly trying to get the twins to pay for the acorn, and the chase. She exaggerated the chase a little, doubling or tripling its length, and adding a couple of goons trying to grab her for good measure. She showed them the split in her dress where the belt had torn it. A welt was beginning to form on her leg.

"Good thing your mom is a seamstress," Caitlin said, fingering the split in the cotton fabric.

"Cressida can fix it," Telyn replied.

The story told, silence fell upon the three friends. Caitlin and Hosh waited for Telyn to say what had brought them here. If she chose to withhold it, they would respect that too. They had been friends a long time.

Telyn had been so excited to share the magical forehead with her friends, but now she felt a certain reluctance.

Why *should* she tell them about it?

Neither of these two had helped Dagger fend off the trogo. Neither had faced down a penumbra daemon, nor had they saved Harlech from a ghost, nor crossed to the flack side of Harlech in the middle of the night to get the pattern witch.

If she told them about it, her friends would want to see the forehead. They would want to touch it, play with it. Telyn's stomach soured.

Hosh scratched his ear and stared at the far wall. Caitlin's brown eyes flicked from Telyn's face to the ground and back again.

Finally, reluctantly, Telyn touched the rear of her temple where the mask met the skin, and she worried her fingers under the edge. "I, uh, I found something in the Sable Head, after the funeral. Don't be alarmed." Little by little, ignoring Caitlin's gasp, Telyn peeled the pliable ceramic away from her skin. "It doesn't hurt," she said, feeling the skin of her forehead bulge. "It just...pulls the eyelids a bit...no reason to worry." The forehead squelched free.

Hosh's hand fell limp at his side.

"Mother of Squirrels," Caitlin said. "You are so dead."

"This is what the flacks were bidding on." The forehead changed from Telyn-color—sort of a pinkish, tea-touched parchment color—to ceramic with gold and bronze plate on its ornamentation. She set it on the stone floor between them. "Well, part of it. Most of the mask went to Enshede with the mind wizard, Yona."

As Telyn recounted the story of what had happened at the Sable Head—the real story this time, leaving nothing out—her friends' faces took on that mixture of fear, excitement, and anticipation you might see on someone about to leap from a cliff into a swimming hole of uncertain depth.

When she finished, Hosh reached forward.

Telyn had to restrain herself from slapping his hand away. She felt quite possessive of the artifact. Quite...defensive.

Hosh tapped the pliable ceramic with the tip of his finger. He grunted and withdrew his hand. "Wicked. Does it give you superpowers or something?"

"No, nothing like that." The muscles in Telyn's back relaxed. "It's not the entire mask. I used it to...well, I wished that Minister Svemas would reopen the Sable Head, and today there's a near-riot at the Prefecture. I think I—the forehead—may have caused that."

Hosh ogled the artifact.

Caitlin, on the other hand, looked increasingly sour. In the tone of a healer asking how often you'd been scratching a rash, she asked, "How long have you been wearing it?"

Telyn didn't like her tone at all. "I don't. I keep it in a tree. I can't let the cornics find it, obviously."

"You were wearing it just now."

"That's different! I just put it on down below to surprise you. I've only worn it once since I found it." This wasn't true. She'd brought it down days before. She loved watching the sunlight sparkle in its material, feeling it mold delightfully to her skin.

Caitlin prodded the forehead with her finger. "When you try to sell it, there'll be questions."

"Sell it?"

"Of course. Like, where did you get this? Where is the rest of the mask? How come a human has something magic?"

"Maybe I won't be selling it."

"You aren't planning on keeping it—" Caitlin said.

At the same time, Hosh exclaimed, "What's that on your wrist?"

On Caitlin's outstretched arm, her sleeve had risen to reveal a black-and-gold lanyard.

"That? Oh, nothing." Red splotches appeared on Caitlin's neck. She snatched the forehead and examined it intensely. "Okay, fine. Joram."

"Joram!" Hosh exclaimed.

"We do live in the same town, in case you hadn't noticed," Caitlin said. "Joram has big plans for his life. He's going somewhere."

"Is that a boyfriend bracelet?" Hosh asked.

"It's something he's doing for the Widow's Club." Which wasn't a real answer.

"Joram is in the Widow's Club? He makes lanyards?" Hosh acted like this was far more shocking than finding out Telyn had the forehead from the Ever-Guise. "I'd rather empty a necessary with a fork than wear his stupid lanyard."

"Good thing he didn't give you one, then."

Telyn cringed. "Guys, guys, I think you should be careful what you say around the mask. It seems to listen to our conversations."

That stopped them with mouths half-open. They readjusted their hips to create a gap between them.

Caitlin spun the forehead in her hands a couple of times. "What do you mean, Telyn? 'Listens to our conversations'?"

"Let's just, um, put that down while we talk." Once the artifact was safely on the stone floor, Telyn exhaled. "Earlier today, I said something like Hosh just now: I told Esther her malt smelled like—" She eyed the forehead suspiciously to see if it would react. "—like the back-end of a brakdaw."

Nothing seemed to happen.

Hosh chuckled.

"The mask sort of popped. Like, sparks came out. I told Esther the fire had popped, but I'm sure the mask sent out sparks."

Hosh could barely contain his excitement. "Imagine!"

Telyn nodded. "We could save the Sable Head."

"That dive? You're not thinking big enough. We could become popular. We could take over Harlech, drive the cornics from the mountains. Bring all the magical creatures on the List to us without having to hunt. We could be rich! Bu-ha-ha-ha-ha!" He gave a fake evil-overlord laugh, snatched the forehead piece, and said, "Give me a thousand hurons."

Nothing happened—at least, nothing that Telyn could sense.

"Did you feel anything? Hear anything?"

"I felt something—a blizzard of stupid running between your empty ears," Caitlin grumbled.

Hosh shrugged and placed the forehead back on the floor. "Maybe some relative will die and I'll be receiving a thousand hurons by mail."

Telyn laughed and pulled her feet underneath her. "You shouldn't look so excited by the prospect."

Caitlin's cute button-nose wrinkled with concern, and she tapped the stone floor with her fingertips. "Telyn, I don't think you should keep this."

"Of course she should keep this! Does that stupid lanyard make you boneless?"

"We don't know what it does. Your relative story, Hosh...that's the way magic always works for humans. You wish for a thousand hurons—your uncle dies. Magic always comes with a big price for humans. We aren't meant to have it, not in this lifetime."

"That's what the flacks want us to think." Hosh rolled his eyes. "Those are baby stories. 'There's always a cost.'" He quoted *Curious Walt and the Fairy*, a story they all had to read in school. "That's how the flacks keep us down—that and their Rules."

"Yes," said Caitlin, "what about the Rules? Have you forgotten them?"

Hosh tsked.

"If we get caught," Telyn conceded, "we will be in a lot of trouble—more trouble than we can imagine. Like...slaver trouble."

"Have you told Cressida?" Caitlin asked.

Telyn nearly coughed. "We do *not* want to tell Cressida. She would make us get rid of it, like, yesterday."

"We need rules," Hosh said. "Who is going to carry it. Who gets to wish, and how many times. What the wishes can be."

"It's not a wish machine," Telyn said.

"I pretty much think it is. We just have to figure out what kinds of wishes work and which don't. The one you said to your mom, about the malt and the brakdaw, that worked." He reached out to touch it again. "I wish to have the biggest muscles in Harlech."

"Hosh! Don't be stupid!" Caitlin said. "What if it takes you literally and gives you horse muscles...or turns you into a dragon? First rule: Don't use the wish to change body parts."

Hiding a smile, Telyn nodded, though in truth she would have paid a dozen birds to see Hosh with giant muscles. "I can agree to that."

"Agreed?" Caitlin insisted.

"It didn't work anyway. I think it's broken," Hosh said, with tremendous disappointment. "Maybe it's run out of magic, or it can only do one wish every full moon or something." He shot out his good foot and kicked it across the floor.

Telyn could have slapped him.

"You have to wear it, dummy," Caitlin said, retrieving the forehead and putting it back in the shaft of light that fell between them. "No body parts. What else?"

Telyn couldn't believe he had treated the mask that way all because he wanted stupid big muscles. She wanted to tell Hosh to get out of the tower and never come back! She wanted to scream and pull his hair. She wanted to stomp on his bum leg—

Was the wish for muscles just a test to see if it worked so he could heal his bum leg?

They all had reasons for wishing certain things, didn't they? Telyn had the Sable Head, not to mention her mother. Hosh had his bum leg. Caitlin must have something, too—Joram's bracelet was proof enough of that. No decent girl would want a lanyard from someone in Tabbard's gang, no matter how cute, unless he offered something.

Still, Caitlin was right. What if the mask did take the wish literally? Best to be careful and to use it for influence, as Dagger advised in the Sable Head.

Telyn cleared her throat to be sure her voice was steady. "No showing it to Cressida, or Joram, or anyone else. And no talking about it outside of this circle. Just the three of us."

"Deal. Good. Next?" Caitlin looked to Hosh. "We keep going until we are all satisfied."

Hosh rolled his eyes. "How about you don't wear that stupid lanyard when you make a wish."

She took it off. "That's your rule, then."

"Hey, wait!"

Caitlin said, "My turn. I say...er...we always make the wishes in front of each other. No secret wishes. Nothing hidden."

"I was going to say we all get to keep it in turns," Hosh complained. "Each of us takes it home for a night and brings it back here to trade."

"But it's not your turn to make a rule," Caitlin said sensibly, looking to Telyn.

"The mask is mine. I found it." Both friends had the good sense to keep quiet. But Caitlin *was* making sense. Hosh couldn't be trusted with it. The question was...could she? Might she become addicted to the mask's power the way Esther was addicted to alcohol?

No way. She would never allow herself to become dependent on anything but her own two hands.

"My rule is—" She took a deep breath to gather her courage. "—none of us takes it home. We hide it someplace. We only use it when we get together, and only when all three of us can be there."

"Where?" Hosh asked.

"I have a place in mind. No one will find it."

"Done." Caitlin squeezed Telyn's foot to show she liked the rule. "Hosh?"

"My rule is—I get first dibs."

Caitlin rolled her eyes.

"Well, that's what I want, okay? Am I right? My stupid wish didn't work anyway." He looked despairingly at his arms. They weren't bad arms, actually. He had strong fingers from conditioning leather at the cobblers, though he had neither a lumberman's frame nor a trapper's hardiness.

"Fine," Caitlin said. "Anything else?"

"It's your turn, Caitlin" Telyn reminded her. "Last one. We don't need too many rules, just good ones."

"Okay, here goes." Caitlin gulped, as if this were the hardest rule of all. "If two of the three of us say to get rid of the mask, we do it. No questions asked."

The blood drained from Telyn's head. She felt dizzy. How dare Caitlin say that? How dare she—? The mask was hers; she'd risked everything to watch the auction. She'd thrown the statuette to the thief and braved the penumbra daemon. She'd summoned the pattern witch and given her own blood to seal the Sepulcher.

"I don't want to get rid of it," Caitlin said in a rush. "Not now. You've convinced me we can do good with it. With the help of this, ah, forehead, we might do something...something significant. Something they'll remember after we're gone. It's not good here now with the cornics, the brakdaw fight—"

Hosh scoffed, "You *would* bring that up."

"It's not fair! The animals don't even know what they're doing."

"You tell that to one that's grabbed onto your legs and started to gnaw them off, or your head."

"The point is, if two of us want to get rid of it, it's probably a good idea. The mind wizard is going to come looking for this. So is whoever Dagger stole it from—cool name, by the way. It's going to get really hot around here when they figure out what happened. Besides, we *are* breaking the Rules—"

"Okay, okay." Hosh waved his hands in surrender. "We get the picture."

Looking at Hosh's face, Telyn realized he would never want to give the mask up. Caitlin, on the other hand, would give it up at the first sign of danger. Her parents chose to work at the Prefecture for the cornics, after all. Some humans considered that treason. Telyn knew different: the Nest family was cautious and practical in equal measure. They'd helped many humans get out of a jam with the authorities, but they did it from a place of relative safety.

One vote to keep the mask, and one to give it up.

That put the forehead's fate in Telyn's hands. Agreeing to this rule would make Caitlin happy, and it wouldn't change anything. "I can agree to that," she said, slowly, "on one condition: I'm the one who gets rid of it."

"That's weird," Hosh said, "but fine."

Caitlin nodded.

"So." Hosh grinned. "What are we wishing for?"

"First," Caitlin said, "we seal the rules. Put out your hands, touch the edge of the mask." With all of them touching one side of the fore-head, Caitlin continued. "The Ever-Guise as our witness, we three take these oaths:

"No wishes to change body parts.

"No showing it to anyone else—especially Cressida.

"No wearing the lanyard when I make a wish. The *stupid* lanyard.

"No secret wishes—we make all wishes in front of the other two.

"No one takes the mask home. We hide it between meetings."

I hide it, thought Telyn.

"If two of us say to get rid of the mask, we do it. No questions asked. Is that it?"

"I'm the one who gets rid of it," Telyn said.

"And I get first dibs," Hosh added.

"Our oaths are our own—" Caitlin invoked the traditional words to seal them. "—to keep or to break on our own honor."

"On our honor," everyone chanted.

They stared down at the forehead, expecting something to happen—sparkles, a vibration, a disembodied voice...

Nothing.

Telyn looked into the expectant, slightly disappointed faces of her friends and understood what the lack of a magical sign meant: They would have to rely upon their own strength of will to keep their oaths.

CHAPTER SIXTEEN

"You can go, Hosh." Caitlin said. "Just be careful. This thing's dangerous."

"Of course it's dangerous; it's magic." Hosh fit the forehead to his face.

The last part of the mask to disappear was the third eye and the prongs for the missing gem. The eye stared mournfully at Telyn as it faded from view, the way a child looked from the back of a wagon on its final departure from Harlech to the lowlands. She couldn't help but reach forward and run her fingers across Hosh's forehead. Every bony ridge, every blemish of skin felt perfectly normal; she couldn't discern any trace of the mask except at the edge by Hosh's temples.

Hosh grinned sheepishly. "That tickles, Tey."

Telyn withdrew her hand.

"All right Hosh," Caitlin said, "make your wish."

Hosh sat there on the tower floor, one leg pulled under him, the other out straight, his lips pursed. Telyn let him have a moment, counted time to the slow pulse of a vein on his neck, and then said, "We agreed, no secret wishes. You have to say your wish out loud."

Caitlin smacked his foot with her hand.

"Would wishing for my leg to heal...to have a normal walk...break the body part rule?" Hosh asked.

Telyn hesitated only a second. She didn't really think it would work; the Ever-Guise wasn't for physical things. But she couldn't deny her friend. "No, of course not," Telyn said, and looked to Caitlin.

"Yes!" Caitlin disagreed. "A 'normal walk.' What is that? Normal for what, a llama?"

"If not 'normal,' then what? The same as my other leg?"

"No! Do you want two right legs?"

Telyn burst out laughing.

"What? It's not funny. Hosh gets along fine. If he follows in his father's footsteps—I mean, well, you know what I mean—he'll be a fine cobbler. It's not like Hosh wants to be a trapper or logger or anything."

"No. I want to be a cobbler with a bum leg."

"What's wrong with that? At least you have a respectable trade. My parents work in the Prefecture. You think that's easy to live down? Everybody hates them. Everywhere I go, I hear 'traitor' whispered in my shadow."

As Hosh started to respond; Telyn put her palm out in warning. "Wait! You're wearing the forehead, remember? Be careful."

"*Careful* would be to lose this thing in the woods." Caitlin crossed her arms under her chest.

"Not *that* careful."

The girls smiled at each other. Caitlin's grin looked a little forced.

Hosh took a deep breath. "What I really want, what I wish for on the Ever-Guise, is to walk like a normal person, without a limp."

"I say it's against the rule we just made," Caitlin said. "No wishing about body parts."

Reaching up near his ears, Hosh peeled the forehead from his face. He blinked away a couple of tears that may or may not have been caused by the mask's sucker-like pull on his eyelids. "Doesn't matter. I've been wishing it the whole time. It didn't work."

The girls leaned in and gave Hosh a hug, the three friends sharing warmth. Hosh trembled slightly.

Caitlin was the first to break the hug. She fit the forehead to her face, and once again it molded perfectly and invisibly. She blinked a couple of times. "Come on," she said, standing. "This place feels cold and stuffy at the same time. Let's take a walk."

"If we're doing this, can I borrow your headscarf...and your jacket?" Telyn asked. "I can't risk Archie Todd recognizing me."

As the girls exchanged clothes, Caitlin confided, "I really don't feel comfortable about this. We only just made the rules, and Hosh has already broken them."

"Then why are you wearing it?"

To this, Caitlin bit her lip and frowned.

The three friends exited the castle ruins and crossed the stone bridge to Harlech. Caitlin tiptoed around, clearly unable to think of anything to wish for, while Telyn thought of something every three steps. She had no end of helpful suggestions, from mandatory tips for cooks to encouraging people that ankle bones really weren't all that titillating, and long skirts dragged in the mud and snow, anyway, so why couldn't people wear anything they wanted?

She acknowledged this last wish might get a little out of hand.

Hosh started throwing out ideas of his own, such as, "Tell everyone to have chickamee stains on their overalls like that guy." Or "Hey, the one-toothed look is all the rage this year."

Fortunately, Caitlin ignored him, or the Ever-Guise might have convinced the townsfolk to knock out their own teeth with rocks or something.

A caravan had gathered under the market hall, the party members displaying solidarity by sporting yellow neckerchiefs. A steep, shingled roof held up by poles, the market hall was the only place in Harlech completely paved with cobblestones. At least twenty individuals, mostly men, took advantage to lay out their packs and dry-load their llamas.

Undoubtedly, they would have preferred to use the short, long-maned horses native to this region, except that humans could not own horses. That being the first Rule of the Cornic Empire:

Humans shall not own horses.
Humans shall not own magic.
Humans shall not own wheels.

Telyn's lips had gone dry from licking them; thinking of the Three Rules made her nervous.

The kids wandered among the members of the caravan, examining the strange breed of human known as "trapper." A rough bunch of men and women both with long hair, they were ever ready with a boast of what this year would bring. Talk of gamble flies, star moles, and tamatins seemed in vogue, though they couldn't know for sure what would be rewarded until the List was posted—the official stuff the Order of Magic was willing to pay for at specific prices with *no haggling*. Of course, such things as dragon eggs and demon gizzards would always be highly prized, whether officially on the List or not.

This particular caravan resembled brigands more than trappers, but that didn't stop Hosh from ogling a red-haired woman with a tattoo around her right eye who struggled to heft packsaddles over the back of a llama. Not because she couldn't lift the pack; it looked as if she could lift the llama if she'd had a mind. No, the llama itself was the problem. Each time she hefted her load, the animal spun away, snorting and stamping and bobbing its neck in something like a derisive laugh.

Telyn gave it an admiring wink.

The kids watched for a while—until Hosh finally approached and placed his body against the llama's side so it couldn't spin in that direction.

"Thanks, hun." The woman hefted the pack over the llama's back and began adjusting the straps. Her loose cotton top emphasized her chest, and her tight leather pants accented the rest of her. For strolling down the streets of Harlech, this attire would be considered a bold choice, but decorum could be overlooked in folks preparing to depart —especially in members of a twenty-person caravan.

Telyn wished *she* could overlook fashion. Pants didn't interfere with climbing the way a long skirt did. Hose stretched even better.

The trapper buckled the belt under the llama's belly.

"Rolled leather," Hosh commented, running his fingers down the bridle. "Was this made at Henricks?"

"Conde Teif," the woman said, causing Hosh's eyebrows to rise. "In Enshede."

"Calfskin?"

"Deer," she replied with obvious pride.

Hosh nodded. "Not the best for durability, but it should hold up well enough. The stitching is very fine. My dad taught me."

On the sidelines with Telyn, Caitlin crossed her arms firmly across her chest.

The trapper snorted. "Humidity isn't a problem. It'll all be frozen beyond Kings Pass. If your beard were a few years longer, hun, you could come along and warm my furs."

Hosh blushed and coughed.

"Pathetic," Caitlin grumbled.

Telyn hid a smile behind her hand.

"Good, er, ah, good to practice with a full load before the exodus—"

"Hands off, gimpy." A big man with a blond ponytail tucked into his belt pushed Hosh away from the llama with enormous, bear-sized hands.

Hosh stumbled back as the big man passed the female trapper a handful of metal 'take' tags.

"Leaving?" Hosh tried to catch the woman's eyes around the massive man. "What about the List? Aren't you going to wait for it?"

"Hosh," Caitlin urged, her tone shifting from sarcasm to concern for his safety. "We better go."

"Eh, I agree," Telyn added, although she greatly enjoyed watching the redheaded trapper flirt Hosh into a fluster.

"Getting a jump on things, hun." The woman hung the tags around her neck on a thong.

"She don't need your help," Ponytail said, laying one of his arms across the llama. "She's just about to walk away, in fact. I suggest you follow her lead."

"Sure," Hosh said. "No harm meant. Good equipment. I'd pull

the strap in tighter here, place more weight on the rear hips and relieve its back."

"I think she'll leave it."

"If the llama can't keep up, try what I said." Hosh took a step away, limping on his bum leg. "I know back pain. I'm an expert in it."

In a small act of defiance, the female trapper adjusted the strap as Hosh suggested. Ponytail shoved her away from the animal. They began arguing.

Curious at the rising voices near its flank, the llama turned its head to stare. Its muzzle thumped the side of Ponytail's enormous head. Enraged, the man pulled a short whip and began striking it across its long nose. The llama began braying and bucking, which further enraged Ponytail. The redhead tried to intervene, but one push and she tumbled backwards over a pile of supplies.

The whipping grew angrier, more frenetic, and the llama bucked and kicked to escape. Its hindquarters hit another llama, which lashed out with its hoof. Chaos ensued. Pounded by the animal kicks and the whip, with the heavy pack pulling it sideways, the redhead's llama tripped over stray equipment and fell. It began to emit a desperate, closed-mouth screech, a screech all too reminiscent of the noises Tums had made when possessed.

The screech reached into Telyn's brain and turned it to gelatin.

Ponytail continued to strike.

Caitlin and Hosh began yelling at the man to stop. Other trappers swarmed in and managed to wrestle the whip from the man.

Dagger, the mind wizard, phantom soot, and wailing eehoos danced behind Telyn's eyes. She stood dumbly, mouth agape, unable to focus.

Slipping between the struggling men, Caitlin reached the llama and gently coaxed it to its feet and away from the chaos. It nickered and stamped and flicked its ears nervously against her hands. But little by little, the twitch in its flanks subsided. It lost that wild look.

Taking a handkerchief from her sash, Caitlin wiped blood from a cut on its muzzle.

As it stopped twitching, Caitlin turned to address the enraged Ponytail, who struggled against the hold of a half dozen men. "What you need is a gentle touch. It works so much better than being rough. Like this."

Turning to the now-passive llama, Caitlin demonstrated a certain scratching of the ears, and then a vigorous back rub, followed by a chin tickle, all of this accompanied with cooing noises. A look of contentment spread over the llama, and it brought its front legs together cutely, like a young girl receiving praise from her parents.

Gradually, Ponytail's snarl was replaced by a head tilt of contemplation.

The trappers released the big man. His cheeks had gone slack. Rather than raging, he approached Caitlin curiously and even asked her to demonstrate her technique again. Soon, he was rubbing the llama's back with vigor.

A circle of trappers gathered, all nodding and smiling, even scratching each other's bearded chins for practice.

Telyn had never seen anything like it. Ridiculous!

Still, it did seem a wiser method than the whip. It would probably work better, too. *She* would respond better to scratching than whipping, that's for sure. Maybe Caitlin was onto—

The mask. Of course! Caitlin used the mask on the trappers.

Telyn wanted to dance a jig.

It had so worked.

After Caitlin showed two more groups her llama-soothing technique and shook everyone's hand, the three friends continued about town. In a little-used alley, Caitlin began to pull the forehead from her face.

"Don't you want to use it?" Hosh said.

Caitlin turned her head this way and that, struggling. "What? Didn't you feel it when I told that possum-breath to be gentle with the llama?" Her breath was starting to come out in rasps.

"Huh?"

"Use the tips of your fingers by the temples," Telyn suggested. "Hang on, let me help..."

Caitlin struggled a bit more until, guided by Telyn, her fingers found the forehead's edge and pulled it away from her skin with a sticky sound.

"Incredible," Hosh said. "I had no idea I was being gulled. Did you, Tey?"

"Not at first," Telyn admitted. She bit her cheek for a second. "I only figured it out when everyone started scratching each other's chins."

"Incredible," Hosh repeated.

"Not really. You were besotted by Leather-Pants. A herd of llamas could have stampeded, and you wouldn't have noticed." While Hosh rolled the term 'besotted' over his tongue, Caitlin handed Telyn the mask. "We need to learn more about how this works. Tey, this could be the key to—you know—something really big. I just tripped into it. If we could access the Library, we could look up the Ever-Guise, find out what it does and how."

"The Library is for flacks and flacks only. Don't you remember Quid's lecture?"

"What about that Rayvn girl from the funeral? She seems friendly," Caitlin said, trying to rub circulation back into her temples.

"Er...no. I don't want to get close to a flack; it's not good policy. You don't have an equal relationship."

"You don't need a relationship. You need information."

"I want even less to ask a flack for a favor."

"Also good policy," Hosh affirmed.

"What if it's got some weird side effect, like it makes your—I don't know—your ears ring or something? Or it makes you besotted by barrel-shaped trapper ladies?"

"I'll think about it," Telyn allowed, fitting the forehead to her temples. The forehead weighed significantly more since this morning, enough that the back of her neck twinged in protest.

The acorn fiasco had been eating at Telyn's insides since the morning. She and her sister had been tricked into taking it in the first place! If Archie Todd had asked nicely—if he'd been honest—the twins would've gone home, gotten the birds, and paid. No problem. That's the way things worked in Harlech. But his employee had tricked them, and Archie Todd had tried to whip them. Literally. With his belt.

Just like Ponytail and the llama.

Telyn's hand found the split hem of her dress and began to rub it.

There had to be a way to use the Ever-Guise against such people—against the Ouzeleys and Archie Todds and Ponytails of the world. Against all the world's bullies.

"Well?" Hosh and Caitlin asked.

"We keep walking."

It didn't take long before they arrived back at the market hall. Harlech had only so many places to visit.

Surprisingly, the caravan had already departed, leaving behind the musty smell of llama, the earthy smell of droppings, and the lanolin of conditioning oil. Only a few people remained—Telyn's least favorite.

Tabbard Ouzeley, the town's chief bully, sat on one of the pillar footings, surrounded by younger kids. He regaled them with some stupid story about his personal glory. Tell-tale crumbs littered the ground around the kids' feet, proof positive he'd purchased them with pastries.

Tabbard was tall (*Something not to be mocked in men*, Telyn thought, dryly), with a round, red face that couldn't grow facial hair apart from a couple of lonely stragglers begging to be tweezed. He wore a deep blue jacket that had been tailored to conceal his girth.

He wore it year-round, as if married to it.

Lanky Joram Lycurgus and the rest of Tabbard's cronies leaned on hitching posts nearby, watching the younger kids with a mixture of scorn and conceit.

Joram gave a little wave to Caitlin, who smiled back. He might have been handsome if he accessorized with different friends.

"Drew," Hosh said, gesturing sharply to his second-youngest brother, one of Tabbard's listeners. The nine-year-old scampered to Hosh's side and tried to wipe the crumbs from his lips without appearing to wipe crumbs from his lips.

"Sorry, Hosh," he mumbled.

A small sense of betrayal hung about the brothers.

Telyn's mind, already overloaded from trying to figure out what use to put the Ever-Guise, became a whirlpool of numbness. The baker, Ouzeley, Tabbard, the mind wizard, the trogo. How in the world could she use the forehead to get justice in this world?

One foot in front of the other. Keep your eyes averted. Hunch your shoulders. Ignore the snide remarks. Telyn's mind seethed with the effort of playing meek.

Telyn, Caitlin, Hosh, and Drew—also known as Mini-Hosh—had almost made it through the market hall when Tabbard called out, "Hey, get a load of Gimpers. He's found someone to play with."

Hosh ignored the taunt and the laughter—and even the stone thrown wide by one of Tabbard's friends.

Telyn knew she should let it go as well, but she'd had enough of letting things go. She put her arm around Hosh. "I'd rather spend my time with Hosh than you any day."

Tabbard started to rise. "Oh, Too-tall comes to Gimpers's defense. Can't stand up for yourself, Hosh baby? Oh, I forgot, you can't even stand straight. You know, just this morning I saw a piece of paper lying in the gutter. Hosh Gamage, it said. His name was so far off the Dating Chart they wrote it on a scrap and floated it down the gutter."

"That's enough!" Telyn said. "Hosh will be more popular than you someday. He's a better man now—"

Power flooded Telyn's mind. The forehead became heavy, almost unbearably so. Her neck bent forward, forward, the weight of it yanking her down, and she pitched face-forward to the cobblestones, dragging startled Hosh to his knees.

Tabbard and his friends roared with laughter.

CHAPTER SEVENTEEN

Customers spilled onto the Sable Head porch. Telyn had to squeeze past several men and women to get inside, and she let out a gasp of surprise to see the number of people—moreover, the number of women. Evidently Raz had suspended the "No ladies after supper" rule. She stood in the doorway gaping until someone pushed her aside with a grunted apology.

Near the bar, Cressida carried a fresh tray of angel water bladders, holding the tray over her head to navigate the crowd. Sucking on the straw-end of the bladders, the patrons looked like chicks tilting their beaks for mother hens to offer them worms—but instead worms from a beak, they suckled from smelly, brown pouches.

They'd be better off with worms, Telyn thought.

As if to punctuate the point, a skinny blonde woman at Telyn's elbow let out an enormous belch.

Before Telyn could retire to the quiet kitchen and her stewpot, Cressida spotted her and mimed over the clients' heads a buttoned mouth and a pitcher of malt. Translation: *No food tonight. Get busy serving.*

Not for the first time, this made Telyn think they should modify their hand-talk language into a visual-only language so it could work across distances. It would be useful to be able to say actual words in a situation like this.

It soon became apparent that many people had come to view the eerie shapes painted by Dagger's ghost: a cityscape of multi-storied buildings topped with onion-domes; pack of hunting dogs chasing a couple holding hands and wearing bedclothes; a conda-like creature with two heads on a throne much too big for him; a knife plunging into a var's neck... Many of the drawings had been smeared by curious fingers. Telyn herself had visited earlier in the week and smeared the image of her own face beyond recognition, the copy of which Minister Svemas had revealed during her inter-rogation.

She'd also used the forehead several times while enthusiastically describing the drawings, and the Sable Head in general, to anyone who would listen. Her face had nearly fallen off from the weight of the mask, and her neck had a perpetual crick in it, but she couldn't be more pleased with the results.

The cornics had finally given in to the populace's demands to allow the Sable Head to open. Second Gajos himself came by to commemorate the occasion with a little speech, and while he didn't look happy about it, he made sure to scratch Tums' chin before departing.

Telyn curtsied to him as she passed him at the bar, the forehead piece firmly in place, and the cornic none the wiser.

Even better, with the kitchen closed, Telyn got to make tips of her own. Not that Cressida ever failed to share fifty-fifty, but the clink of eggs—even a full huron or two—felt great in her pockets.

Tums hung by one paw and foot from the banister on the second floor, dangling the other limbs to give his benediction. Just about everyone reached up to give paw or foot a squeeze before staggering home.

"Don't get cocky," Telyn told the cooing eehoo. "Fame is fickle."

"Hey darlin', you see the revenant?" one of the men asked.

Telyn felt her heart skip—and not because he'd called her darlin'. "Um, no. I wasn't here."

"Where'd he get offed?"

Several patrons leaned forward. A cornic soldier in the corner turned his horned head the other way, pretending not to listen.

"I don't know, really." Telyn pressed a full bladder into the man's hand even though he hadn't ordered. "Must have been in here with all the pretty pictures," she said, taking a vacuous tone and moving on.

She added a sway of her hips for good measure. "Idiot," she muttered under her breath.

That conversation was repeated a dozen times with different partners. It became a sort of a dance for Telyn—a toe-smashing dance with too many inebriated partners and clouds of foul breath.

And a cornic chaperone keeping a lookout for any funny business...or magical masks.

Most of the patrons had cleared out by the time Raz let the twins take a breather over by the long bar. He also took the opportunity to ask them to come in early the next day to scrub the walls. Of course.

The door opened, and in waltzed blue-coated Tabbard with his older sister Medi, followed by their dad, Wulstan, with his silver-handled cane, and their mom, Grebiana. The woman had always struck Telyn as a harpy, leering at everything around her. She had elegant, black- and silver-lined clothes and a foxtail stole.

Tabbard met Telyn's eyes, and he pretended to swoon. He must have practiced for days.

Ignore it, Cressida flashed with her fingers. She often advised that regarding Esther, and Telyn had as much difficulty following the advice there as here. A muscle in her jaw twitched.

Razenbock seemed delighted. "Wulstan, you old chipper. Care for a malt?" He poured a mug and carried it over.

Mr. Ouzeley sniffed it. "Malt? How gauche." He handed the mug to Tabbard—who guzzled eagerly.

"No wonder he's so fat," Telyn muttered, and Cressida hid her laugh with a fake cough.

No way would Esther let them drink malt in front of her. First, they would have to pry it out of Esther's greedy fingers. Second, despite all her other shortcomings, Esther didn't think too highly of inebriated teenagers.

Grebiana sauntered over, her spine rod-straight, and eyed each twin in turn, from floor-length hems to earlobes. Grebiana played the vamp well; she had long legs and wide hips, prominent cheeks, and high, V-shaped eyebrows. Despite the wrinkles lining her mouth and eyes, she was striking. Even though Telyn stood far taller, Grebiana made her feel small. Telyn shifted sideways on the barstool.

"This one could be good for cleaning cobwebs—" Grebiana nodded at Telyn. "—with her hair."

Tabbard laughed so hard, he spewed malt all over the floor.

"They say you killed your first husband," Telyn replied, ignoring Cressida's urgent squeezing of her hand. "Why don't you try for a repeat performance?"

Grebiana could have split walnuts between her scowling eyebrows.

Raz's bright smile may have risen a tad. "Ya come here for something, Wulstan? The loan isn't due until the List is posted. That was the deal."

Mr. Ouzeley leaned on his cane, the head of which depicted a hunting dog. "A week or two won't make any difference, and I happened to be passing by."

Quiet had fallen. Everyone in the tavern had turned to watch the drama. Mr. Ouzeley certainly counted on this; he wanted to make a grand show before many witnesses. From the corner of her eye, Telyn noticed the cornic soldier shift for a better view.

Raz gestured to an open table.

While the Ouzeleys seated themselves, wiping the stools with white handkerchiefs first, Razenbock tromped upstairs to his quarters.

Mr. Ouzeley's frown was epic when Razenbock returned with a cash box and upended it all over the tabletop. Silver and copper coins spilled over the wood. Raz arranged them by tens, making sure the cornic soldier had a clear view. "Since it was a busy evening, I figured you might stop by, Wulstan, so I counted it all out for you. Every bird plus interest. And a receipt for you to sign."

At a gesture from Mr. Ouzeley, Grebiana swept forward to count Raz's bounty. At last, she nodded, and Mr. Ouzeley announced, "That's one year."

Raz spread his arms wide. "You aren't accelerating the loan, are you? That isn't part of the bargain. We are, after all, part of the Cornic Empire, a land of the rule of law."

The cornic soldier may have nodded, but Telyn's gaze was fixed on the unfolding scene..

Mr. Ouzeley clearly struggled with conflicting emotions. "Our oaths are our own," he said, carefully and clearly. "To keep or to break, on our honor."

Raz repeated the same words back at Ouzeley, the traditional binding oath, but substituted "on our lives" instead of "on our honor."

"No repossession tonight, I see. I'll do better placing my coin with Heledd." Medi walked out, probably disgusted at her father's failure. Meanwhile, Grebiana scraped the coins into a large purse.

Telyn felt a burning delight. It wasn't often the Ouzeleys got one-upped—and never had Raz managed to do it. This meant their jobs were safe. Dagger, that wonderful scoundrel, had saved the Sable Head. For Razenbock must have used Dagger's birds to pay off the loan—the birds the thief had paid Raz to clear out the Sable Head in order to hold the auction.

Sure, the clients Telyn helped bring in certainly didn't hurt, but a few days hadn't been nearly long enough to assemble this many hurons.

"The curiosity effect will wear off soon," said Grebiana. If her eyebrows drew any closer together, they'd have to get married.

Mr. Ouzeley banged his cane twice on the wooden floor. "And if you keep serving this malt, your clients won't live long enough to spend any more coins."

"Your son likes it well enough." Raz gestured, and the twins moved behind the long bar. Cressida drew another mug from the barrel. With their backs to the public room, Telyn squeezed in a long shot of angel water.

Tabbard took the proffered mug and drank it with even more gusto than the previous one.

Telyn laughed to herself as Tabbard's face ran pink. *Soon his fake swoon won't be fake.*

"Son," Mr. Ouzeley said, standing, "you're embarrassing yourself."

"When else are we getting anything free in here?" Tabbard punctuated the rhetorical question with a wet burp, dropped the mug to shatter on the floor, and staggered outside.

The parents followed.

Conversation gradually returned to the public room. Raz leaned against the table the Ouzeleys had just vacated and stared at the door. Stroking his short beard, his fingers trembled. The confrontation had clearly taken a lot out of him.

By morning, the Ouzeleys' humiliation would be known to everyone in Harlech.

Well, good. With the Ever-Guise, we can handle anything the Ouzeleys throw at us. I think.

The twins didn't neglect to squeeze Tum's paw before leaving for home.

CHAPTER EIGHTEEN

Crowds packed the market hall like clusters of black currants buffeted by a heavy wind, dense in some areas, scattered in others, never staying still, a heaving mass of sweat and anticipation, all eager to read the List. It was impossible to find anybody.

Just where is Cressida?

Telyn patted Tums' feet. She'd brought Tums on her shoulders, figuring that today the three of them could spend the day together like old times.

Trapper or townsman, flack or human, the entire town had gathered to the market hall to read the List. Written on velum in block letters and decorated with a star-eyed fox in each corner, the List was posted on each of the pillars holding up the market hall roof. As was custom, it described the magical components which the Academy of Enshede's Order of Magic would purchase at the Spring Sale.

Several orders operated at Enshede's great Academy, schools of various disciplines, but the Order of Magic was the most important. It garnered things from the Chaos Woods because of the strange effects the forest had on magic. And since flacks feared to tread where their magic might fail, they relied on humans to do the prospecting.

This explained the relative prosperity and freedom of Harlech compared with human settlements elsewhere.

The Academy of Enshede set their prices ahead of time, making it by far the most desirable buyer at the Spring Sale, but all manner of flacks came there to purchase: freelancers, collectors, foreign agents, mercenaries, eccentrics—and murderers like the trogo and the mind wizard. Telyn had been thinking about that a lot recently. If a market existed, then a black market existed to undercut it—especially for high-priced, highly regulated goods. Which meant that a market existed for the forehead piece, should Telyn ever desire to sell it.

She'd start with Dagger's buyer. If he turned her down or offered a pittance, she'd go elsewhere. She'd just have to do it smarter than Dagger and not get killed.

Telyn spotted a tangle of orange hair and waved, excited to recognize a friendly face. Several girls and women surrounded Hosh—was that Mrs. Leatherby? Hosh waved distractedly, and the crowd swept him away. Telyn felt a pang of jealousy. Mrs. Leatherby, really! She was old enough to be his grandmother.

Telyn fought back the urge to follow. Hosh always knew the best maroon sellers; always found the best deals; always knew just how to stand with the sun behind him so the light shone in his hair... But no, she wanted to find Cressida; this had always been their day together. Telyn had even brought enough coin to buy a gooseberry acorn to share.

They'd have to ask someone to buy it for them, though. Archie Todd was still angry, even though Cressida had insisted on dropping off the money with his helper. There was something unnatural about the way the baker hated her and Cressida. Since Telyn hated him right back, she really didn't care about the *why* of it, but it was unnatural.

She needed to stop trying to stare over the crowd for Hosh's red mop. She would see Hosh later—and tell him what she thought of those groupies, remind him they only pursued him because of the Ever-Guise's influence. They hadn't been friends with him forever like Telyn had.

Telyn spun in a slow circle, scanning the crowd. Telyn had worn the heeled boots Hosh's dad had made for her last year when she'd shot up past most of the other folk in town. At the time, she'd thought it the most thoughtless gift she'd ever received—typical for a Gamage. Lately, Telyn had come to appreciate the heels. No slouching would ever make her normal. She either had to own her height or spend the rest of her days in misery. These boots made a statement: *Accept me and my height or buzz off.*

Yes, Hosh had a bit of his dad's quiet fire in him as well. It showed in his lovely hair. If only she could catch a glimpse of him...

No—she wanted to find Cressida, right?

Right?

The cacophony of exclamations, curses, and banter continued to swell. All the trappers had their take on the coming year: what they knew they could get, what they hoped they could find, and where they thought they could find it. Those who claimed they knew the whereabouts of one or more of the 5,000-huron bounties quickly signed up to lead groups.

A normal fur, say a mink, would sell for one to two hurons, while the least of the List items sold for fifty. So naturally all the trappers sought the List items.

The whole thing reminded Telyn of Dagger's funeral but with even more maroons, more gawking, and more tall tales. As always, Telyn couldn't entirely forget that her dad had carried a List, had set off with the same enthusiasm as these trappers, and had died, as some of them would surely die.

Razenbock, Archie Todd, and Dad set off together; only Raz and the baker had returned. Dad...dead.

Who would these men be leaving widowed and orphaned?

I've got to find Cressida, get my mind off...things.

Traditionally, they'd read the List together and discuss what they would do if they found one of the 5,000-huron items. It wasn't impossible. Why, just two years ago, a pair of gamble-flies had settled on Stan Wellin's llama. He'd captured both and earned enough to move his family to Enshede. Rumor had it he'd set up a restaurant there and lived like a king.

With that much money, we could change things. Set up our family for life. Help Razenbock pay off his debts. Convince the cornics to pass some laws about the treatment of animals. Free a couple of slaves...

Listen to me. Telyn rubbed her forehead subconsciously. *Caitlin and her significance are rubbing off. My wishes are much more modest: save the Sable Head, take a sprinkling of revenge on the town bullies. I'm not asking a lot. In the spring, I'll sell the forehead and make enough to live a decent life here in Harlech or move to Enshede like the Wellin family. What girl doesn't deserve that? Hosh might even come with me, if I had that much coin.*

Now where is my sister?

The crowds had grown denser than she'd ever seen. More elbowing, more "Excuse me, ma'ams" and toes trod. More and more cornic solders gathered around the periphery, either sensing or causing the shift in the mood. Tums' paws tugged her hair nervously. She'd have to take her back to the Sable Head if she didn't find Cressida soon...

Telyn spotted Rayvn and waved. She didn't really know why; her arm seemed to shoot up of its own volition. As the flack drew near, Telyn donned a fake smile.

"Hi-ya," Rayvn said, eyes vacant as usual. "Curious, the way the soldiers have surrounded us."

"No, of course—They what?"

"Didn't you notice?"

"I, well, yes. Not really." Sure enough, the soldiers had formed a complete cordon around the market hall. There were maybe a hundred—more than usually were stationed in Harlech. Telyn had never seen this many soldiers at once in her life. She didn't like it, not one bit.

Rayvn split open a maroon, scooped out the interior with her bumpy tongue, and flipped the shell over her shoulder.

Telyn couldn't help but touch the edge of her forehead just to be sure she hadn't left the Ever-Guise on by mistake. No, no, of course not. She'd left it in the tree. She was safe, and the forehead was safe, no matter what happened here.

She rubbed the sweat off her brow. "What do you think they want?"

"A manhunt, of course. Why else would they bring a slave wagon?

They must be looking for a criminal." Rayvn's tail ears flicked. "Exciting, isn't it? The List, the soldiers—maybe they figured out who murdered Mr. Unknown. Quite a day."

"What? No! Slavers are never a good thing. *You* don't have to worry about them, you're a—" Telyn almost said "flack," but she stopped herself just in time. It wasn't the nicest word to say to a person's face. Rayvn waited with raised, cat-whisker eyebrows. "A pattern witch, a thauma. They wouldn't dare touch you."

Rayvn shrugged.

Telyn stood on tiptoes.

Sure enough, beyond the wall of cornic soldiers she spotted six draft horses hitched to a heavy wagon with a cage instead of a flatbed.

"A single cart," Telyn said. "Do you see any more?"

"Just the one. It can hold twenty or so standing." Rayvn's tone was nonchalant. "Of course, the ones in the middle might suffocate."

Telyn's stomach just about dropped out. Twenty slaves! This wasn't supposed to happen in Harlech. The Chaos Woods put flacks and humans on equal footing, didn't it?

Didn't it?

"Have you seen my sister?"

"Cressida? Yes, she looks much like you."

"I mean, have you seen her this morning?"

"It is noon."

"Rayvn! Where is Cressida?"

They were interrupted by a young voice calling from around her midriff. "Too-tall. Too-tall!" Telyn frowned down to see about the only person she didn't mind calling her that: Mini-Hosh. The boy's eyes lit up at the sight of Tums on her shoulders, and he reached up to give the eehoo a sticky high-five.

"What's up?" Telyn tried to keep the quaver from her voice— soldiers *and* a slave wagon! There was no need to scare Mini-Hosh.

"Come on, I need your height," the boy said, taking her hand and dragging her toward the nearest pole. Rayvn drifted in their wake.

"Having trouble squeezing through?"

"I'm likely to get strangled in one of these beards before I get close enough. What did you read?"

"I haven't read it either. Waiting on Cressida. But—all right."

They waded past trappers to within a half dozen paces of the nearest pole before the crowd got too thick to continue. Telyn squinted at the List. She'd always liked the Academy symbol that graced the corners, a silver fox with a star for an eye.

"I've never seen so many things for five thousand hurons," Telyn said, turning away. "Wow, that was really great."

"Come on, you going to tell me?"

"Oh, you want me to read it aloud?"

Mini-Hosh sort of growled.

Several other trappers leaned closer.

"You want to guess what's on it? You get it wrong, I muss your hair. You get it right—"

"Telyn!"

"Ah, you *do* know my name? I thought I was Too-tall."

"Fifty hurons; start there and read down."

She laughed. Drew was almost as fun to tease as Hosh. She mussed his hair. "Here goes: The Order of Magic of the Academy of Enshede agrees to pay fifty hurons for:

    abyssin cat whiskers
    aria macao (live)
    boreal oleander feathers
    colobe moustac brain (pickled)
    flying jaguarondi fur
    gamble-fly wings (units of seven)
    giant ibjau gills
    pantere nebuleuse (live)
    phauk (stuffed, whole)
    sunflower monkey fur
    tana (live)
    three-toed shambler toes and lips (pickled)."

Several of the entries Telyn had to spell, not being entirely sure what they were, let alone how the words were pronounced.

"You ever wonder what they use this stuff for? *Three-toed sham-*

bler—pickled toes and lips. 'Would you like a nail with your toe? Rough or manicured, Madame?'" Telyn affected a snobbish voice to reply to herself. "'Athlete's Foot, please, hold the cheese.'"

Mini-Hosh laughed, while Rayvn looked concerned about Telyn's sanity.

Waving them both off, Telyn continued reading. "The Order of Magic of the Academy of Enshede agrees to pay agrees to pay five hundred hurons for:

almiqui (stuffed)
armor of pinegolin
galago eyelashes (full set)
gamble fly wings (units of eight)
gamble fly wings (units of six)
harpy eggs
kerivoule peint (stuffed)
phosofomotoad urine (per pint)
rousette (live)
spots from couscous wings
star mole (live)
tamatin fur
tarsier (live)
tenrec soyeux spines
thylogale pouch
white dung from lepilemur."

Telyn looked down at Mini-Hosh. "It looks like gamble flies are the things to get. Maybe we should all leave out rotten fruit to try to attract them."

"And the bottom? The good stuff?"

"Trying." Craning, she finally read: "The Order of Magic of the Academy of Enshede agrees to pay agrees to pay five thousand hurons for:

cobra-gnat venom (per pint)
demon (dead only)

gamble fly wings (units of two)
kraken skull
turquoise dragon skin
voice of aye-aye."

"You going to trap the voice of the aye-aye?" she asked her small companion.

"No one ever gets those things," Mini-Hosh replied in his all-knowing voice. "The Order just puts that there to make people hope. What they really want is for people to bring back the stuff for fifty hurons so they don't have to pay so much. See, cobra-gnat venom, you know what that is? The cobra-gnat is like a flea that lives on dragons. So even if you found one, and the dragon didn't kill you, it would take ages to squeeze enough of them to make a pint."

Telyn smiled at how similarly Hosh and his brother spoke. "Redbeard said that some of the stuff on the List wasn't even real. It's based on rumors and fairy tales."

Mini-Hosh nodded. "They put cobra-gnat venom on the List so people go high up the Cairn where the dragons live, and there they find lots of things like three-toed shamblers and sunflower monkeys, which is what the Academy really wants. They don't have to pay so much, and they get lots of it. While the trappers keep thinking 'Someday I'll get cobra-gnat venom, someday I'll get cobra-gnat venom,' and all they ever get is phauks. Razenbock told Hosh, and Hosh told me, that Raz used to trap, then he gave it up when he found out what really was up."

Telyn tried to keep her smile in place.

That's not why he gave it up. Raz gave up trapping because he and Dad went into the Cairn Range...and my dad never came home.

"That's downright crooked," a young trapper said, who had been listening. "Hey Vernon, did you hear that?" He looked at the piece of paper he had in his hand, copied from the List. He balled it up and threw it to the ground, muttering to himself.

"Certain spells can capture voices," Rayvn said, "but I don't know how they expect a human to do it, unless you find an elemental sponge. They can absorb almost anything."

"Voices are air," Telyn replied. "You can't absorb air."

"Your lungs do it all the time."

Telyn just rolled her eyes.

"Still," said Mini-Hosh, retrieving the young trapper's crumpled list with the reverence of a found coin. "I'd like to have fifty hurons. That's more than...it's...I don't know how long it takes to earn that."

Telyn mussed his hair again. For some reason, she could hardly resist touching the spiky red mop. "You seen my sister?"

"Nope. Didn't see her, don't care," Mini-Hosh said, beginning to wander off. "Oh, Hosh had a message for you."

"What is that?"

"He says he has it."

Telyn's stomach nearly dropped through her bottom. "No."

"Yes. He has it, that's what he said," Mini-Hosh said. "I think it's a love note, because he's been getting a lot of those lately."

"Do you know where to find him?"

Mini-Hosh shrugged. "Yeah."

"Tell him to get rid of it. Right now."

"Tell him yourself. He's right behind you."

Just as Telyn turned to see Hosh with Cressida and four other women trailing behind him, their hands on each other's shoulders as if they were playing wagon-train.

"Oh look," said the pattern witch, all happy anticipation. "I think Minister Svemas is going to announce something."

"Hi ya, Telyn," Cressida said, without taking her eyes from Hosh's back.

All too clearly, everything came together.

Somehow, impossibly, Hosh had climbed the tree and taken the forehead piece for himself. He'd been using it, putting the girls and women of Harlech under his spell. Cressida was besotted.

Why, realized Telyn, *it started affecting me as well! How many times has Hosh used it on the sly without telling us?*

I've got to tell Caitlin. Unless...unless she's in on it?

Mother of Squirrels, he's wearing it right now. He must be. He has it.

From atop a small podium, Minister Svemas' voice boomed from magical amplification. "Good people of Harlech. The List has been posted. It is a grand day, a beautiful day—the beginning of a new trapping season. Fortunes will be made this year, and I am happy to say that the Academy of Enshede has been most generous in its bounties. In fact, there are more artifacts on the list at five thousand hurons than ever in the school's history."

The trappers cheered.

"Come on." Telyn grabbed the pattern witch with her left hand and Hosh with her right and pulled them through the tide of humanity, deeper under the market hall. She didn't know why she wanted the pattern witch at her side, but it seemed the right thing to do. If she'd had time to analyze, she might have said that having a flack ally offered some protection, a certain immunity to suspicion, but really, she acted on instinct. Cressida, unfortunately, stayed right with them like a llama following a handful of clover.

"It is my honor to represent her royal highness, Empress Zhalia, in all matters, including the most high matter of justice." Magically amplified, the word JUSTICE vibrated the very poles of the market hall. Dust fell from the rafters.

Behind Svemas' podium, the six draft horses drew the slave wagon into plain sight.

Human and flack jabbering fell. The denizens of Harlech were tough, independent-minded folks, living in the danger all winter, unaccustomed to many rules of any kind, and chafing against the concept. Threatening them with slavery didn't sit well.

The flacks who lived in Harlech weren't much different. Some of them—most, according to Hosh—were here to escape some crime they committed back home. Why else live where your spit froze before it hit the ground in winter and mosquitoes stole small children in the summer?

The slave wagon drew slowly past the market hall, its massive wheels thunking over the cobblestones, across Main Street, and onto the bridge across the Elbus River and Defiance Falls.

Svemas continued, though few eyes remained on him. "As minister of Harlech, it is my duty to deter crime, to administer justice, and to root out criminals—whoever and wherever they might be. It is my duty as minister to inform you that a very dangerous criminal is on the loose, and we have reason to believe that he or she is among us."

People shrugged into this new information, eyes turned uneasily at one another. Trapper caravans had formed this very morning and would share the winter in the Cairn Range—isolated, freezing, and often hungry, with no hope for succor. In the freezing, white winters, paranoia could turn ordinary men into psychopaths. If they couldn't trust one another, they wouldn't survive.

Two more flacks stepped onto the podium beside Minister Svemas. At his right shoulder was the representative of the Second House of the Cornic Empire, Second Jaromir Gagos; at his left was Corporal Velky. Other cornic officers stood nearby, and behind them, a diminutive schmook sat atop a black mare.

Taito-Vaiana! Dear High Father, no.

Minister Svemas continued speaking. "This fugitive murdered a human and a trogo in the Sable Head and stole a powerful artifact. We have reason to believe that the artifact—and the criminal—may be in disguise." As he spoke, the cordon of soldiers pushed the trappers closer together. "This disguise may be magical in nature."

"I'm going to die," Hosh moaned.

Rayvn looked at him curiously. "Is your chest hurting?"

"Yes! It's about to burst open."

"We should brew you a relaxing infusion—"

Cressida flicked her hair to one side and put her ear to his chest. "Oh Hosh, your heart beats so quickly."

"Never mind that," Telyn said. "Give it to me."

When Hosh raised a hand to his face, Telyn hissed, "Not here, you cretin! Hosh, kneel down."

"Are you trying to remove his heart?" Rayvn asked.

"Something like that. Cressida, take your ear off Hosh so he can kneel—good—now stand at your full height. Hosh is in trouble. Do you understand, Cressida?"

"Of course?"

Why were all of Cressida's answers sounding like questions?

Caitlin had the right of it: they *really* needed to find out more about the Ever-Guise's use...and overuse. Telyn didn't want her twin turning into some mindless worm-head.

"Cressida, just, turn your back on Hosh. It's...er...his hose. Snag. Ew, bad. Pretend to be listening to Minister Svemas as if Hosh's life depended on hearing every word."

"It does!" Hosh wailed from his kneeling posture.

"His life, or his dignity?" Cressida giggled and turned her back, but she kept trying to peek over her shoulder.

Telyn moved Rayvn to the left, and the three girls screened Hosh's crouching form. With so many people around, he practically disappeared; he could be tying his shoe or...or whatever Cressida imagined he might be doing.

"We ask your cooperation in this matter," the minister continued. "If we don't catch the criminal soon, more lives will be lost. When the roads close for winter, we do not want the criminal running loose in the Chaos Woods—or in Harlech."

A ripple passed through the humans as the cornic soldiers began shoving them toward the Elbus River.

"How did you get it?" Telyn hissed.

"I climbed."

"I know you climbed. But you're lame—in both ways. Did Caitlin help you?" A flash or jealousy blossomed on her neck.

"No. I have my lame ways."

Telyn let that stand. She didn't really want to bring up his lameness—not his physical lameness, anyway. He must have followed her to the tree, which meant the cornics could have done, also. She hadn't been nearly as sneaky as she'd thought.

"We have a lot of talking to do. You broke our rules."

"I know. I'm sorry."

"What rules, Hosh?" Cressida said, over her shoulder. "Are you seeing Telyn without me?"

"Hosh isn't seeing anyone!" Telyn snapped. "Keep watching Minister Svemas." She lowered her voice and spoke to Hosh again. "Why didn't you come to me earlier, as soon as the soldiers appeared?"

"I couldn't—get—away—from—the—groupies," Hosh said, struggling to get his fingers under the edges of the forehead piece.

Rayvn leaned toward Hosh. "Is your heart doing okay?"

"That's what I want to know?" Cressida said, dreamily.

"Don't look, you two," Telyn said. "This is private."

"Why do *you* get to look?" Cressida asked.

"Trust me, it's no—Why are we moving?"

"I wasn't listening."

"That was your job!"

"Something about cooperation," Rayvn said, airily. "They are searching for a criminal in disguise. It looks like they are going to run us over the bridge. We all get to take a walk together."

CHAPTER NINETEEN

Taking advantage of her height, Telyn squinted to see what was happening. The cornics shaped the crowd into a funnel pointing at the bridge. They parked the slaver wagon underneath the gate tower about a third of the way across, so that you had to scrunch together to pass through the archway. About a dozen soldiers there squeezed the crowd further into a single-file line.

They moved at the pace of a banana slug. The trappers refused to leave their packs or their animals for fear light fingers would lighten them, and they carried everything. The bridge crossing became the sort of exodus you might expect before an invading army: jangling, creaking, cursing, muttering, and animal baying competed with shouted orders from the cornics. Hosh moved along on his knees, struggling to get his fingernails under the corners of the—

"Got it!"

Telyn reached down to help Hosh up before he got trampled—*slowly*—and he pressed the fascia-textured ceramic into her palm.

"Oh, Hosh, thank goodness you're alright." Cressida turned to give him a tight hug as Telyn hid the forehead behind her back.

The knife of sunlight marking the edge of the market hall approached. Telyn saw three possibilities: ditch the forehead right now and come back for it later; pitch it from the bridge and hope no one noticed; or take her chances with the soldiers.

Which was no choice at all, really. She needed to keep it.

Her future depended on it.

About ten minutes later, her feet made the bridge. Only about a hundred feet downriver, Defiance Falls pounded. The force of it vibrated the stone construction and threw up a fine, cool mist that settled on skin and flattened hair to skull.

Tums pulled on Telyn's ear and made a burp-like noise. Craning her neck, Telyn saw what concerned the eehoo. The poor little marsupial trembled at the sight of the schmook ahead, directing the cornics like a general, the schmook from the Sable Head auction, the mind wizard's ally.

Of course, Tums would remember. She'd been possessed by Dagger's ghost, Taito-Vaiana's sworn enemy.

Telyn squeezed Tum's foot to indicate that she'd noticed, too.

"Oh, look!" Rayvn clapped with delight. "Do you see? A feathered hind, most highly valued. Mom will have to come see."

No longer mounted, the schmook held the leash of a deer-looking thing with a great rack of antlers. Instead of brown and white fur, it sported mottled brown and black feathers with white accents around its ankles, belly and buns.

"Yes, very pretty," Telyn said through gritted teeth. "But what does it do? I'm getting really bad vibes."

"It reflects magical energies."

"Can you be more specific?"

"When you cast spells on it, its feathers form all kinds of beautiful patterns and colors. Scholars have been stu—"

"Why are the soldiers running everyone by it? Would the patterns change if you walked by with something magical? Say a magical...I don't know...a wand or something?"

Rayvn shrugged. "In Vool, it is a sport to see what colors get frozen onto their feathers when they die from a magical attack. The whole country comes to the Feather Festival in summer. Unique patterns are incredibly valuable. The prize winners are taken every year to make the royal headdresses."

So brutal for such a cute-sounding event. Sort of like the brakdaw fight.

"Oh, don't tell Caitlin about that," Cressida said dreamily. "Caitlin has very particular thoughts about animals. She thinks angel water should be served out of pottery instead of bladders. Imagine that!"

"Rayvn, do you trust me?" Telyn asked.

The flack smiled at her. "No."

"Good answer," Cressida said. "Tey's been acting weird lately."

Acting weird? You still have one arm around Hosh's shoulder! A fine thing to talk about acting weird.

Telyn cleared her throat to keep from voicing her thoughts out loud. "Will you do what I ask?"

The flack shrugged.

Cressida shrugged.

"It will be really exciting," Telyn said. "It will break a pattern."

Rayvn's ears wiggled. Hopefully, a good sign.

"I need you to create a distraction."

"What sort of distraction?"

"I don't know. You're the pattern girl, do something with fabric."

"I could give someone a wedgie. That's always—"

Cressida started giggling.

Telyn pulled Tums around to her front. "We need more than wedgies. The hind's harness, that's fabric, right?"

The crowd continued to push. Step by step they drew closer to the tower, the slaver wagon, the schmook. Forty feet, thirty feet, twenty...

"I suppose; it's made of" —The pattern girl closed her eyes— "leather strips, buckles, a woven, hemp collar—"

"Just do it!"

"Now?"

"Yes, now!"

Rayvn gestured vaguely with her hands. The hind's collar swelled. It drooped. The hind shied a couple of steps...and stepped its front hooves right out of the harness.

After a momentary shock, Taito-Vaiana leaned in to cinch things back up.

"Now," Hosh said.

Telyn slipped the forehead into Tums' belly pouch.

The schmook leaned forward; the hind backed clear out of the harness, and the fabric snagged on its antlers.

"Look at that hind, it's getting away!" Hosh shouted.

"Go, hind, go!" encouraged Cressida.

Telyn hefted Tums onto the side of the gate tower. The creature's sucker-paws connected with the stone and stuck. Tums gave Telyn a wounded look and extended her arm. Telyn pivoted away, hoping against hope that the eehoo would climb out of sight. Tums could ruin things in a million different ways: climb down from the tower; toss the forehead into the river; pull it from her pouch and gnaw on it; wail for attention...

Telyn sent calming thoughts in Tums' direction and pulled her companions forward. The mounting chaos helped her ignored the eehoo's accusing croaks.

Rayvn's distraction was working big time. With the harness stuck to its antlers, the hind spooked, dodged this way and that, bellowed, and flung its head. The antlers smacked Taito-Vaiana to the ground then knocked a pair of cornic soldiers aside like a child's wooden blocks. Now, released from the schmook's hold, when the hind shook its head, the tether snapped like a whip.

Soldiers rushed in to cordon it off. They knocked the milling trappers aside with blows and head-butts, but they had a harder time with the pack animals. The llamas bit and kicked back or stood stock-still and stared dumbly ahead. A few spit well-aimed loogies at the cornics' eyes.

Meanwhile, the trappers already on the bridge used the confusion to scamper forward without being searched. Some of them spit loogies of their own.

Rayvn clapped. Cressida shouted encouragement to the hind.

They weren't the only ones. The whole crowd began cheering the animal into a frenzy.

Meanwhile, on the Harlech side of the bridge, the soldiers

continued to shove more humans and pack animals forward until all was a tight-packed mass of leather, hair, animal hide and hooves, bad breath, underarm stench, and fear.

A lot of fear.

After a good deal of knocking, banging, and cursing, the soldiers formed a circle around the hind. The animal clomped around and around, ears forward, eyes wide. Little by little, it slowed. Shivers ran over its body, lifting its feathers in waves along its flanks.

Taito-Vaiana had gathered himself and approached the beast cautiously, hands forward.

The hind shook its rack. "No," it seemed to be saying, "leave me alone. I've found freedom, and I'm going to keep it."

A true resident of Harlech, Telyn thought fiercely.

Cautiously, the schmook reached for the tether. As his hand curled around it, Rayvn twiddled her fingers. The collar frayed. The hind snorted and, with a powerful burst from its legs, sprang toward the Chaos Woods.

The leash broke free of the collar with a sharp snap.

Up, up the animal soared. Llamas croaked. Humans cried out in alarm. Telyn caught a clear view of the hind's muscular rear legs, the ribs straining to gain an extra inch towards freedom, the determination glinting in its eye. The whole picture brushed onto her mind like an oil painting.

The hind seemed to hang there, frozen on a static canvas.

But it didn't actually hang there. It sailed in motion, and the world continued to move around it.

The crowd parted to create space to land. A burly soldier dove and managed to half-tackle the hind in midair. His momentum knocked the animal to the stone rail at the edge of the bridge; its back legs scrambled on the slick stone and, finding no purchase, it slipped over the edge and plummeted toward the Elbus River.

A splash and it disappeared.

Everyone gasped.

The hind's antlers reappeared in the frothy water, glistening and spinning like tree branches as it was carried downriver as bellowing flotsam. Then the current swept the hind over Defiance Falls.

Against the thrum of the waterfall, they heard the hind's final bay. Wide as twin moons, Telyn's eyes began to go dry before she remembered to blink. Remembering to breathe came later.

"Caitlin is going to kill me," she whispered. "Don't tell her I had anything to do with that, okay? I didn't really, did I? No, of course not. It was all..." Telyn gulped a breath of air. "...a big..." Another breath. Everything moved at the speed of fog. "...mistake. A mistake, I swear. I didn't mean it. I didn't want it to fall."

"Do you think it's dead?" Hosh asked.

"It didn't know how to swim very well," Rayvn said, stroking her whiskers. "Too bad; it was very noble."

Back on the bridge, the cornic soldier picked himself off the rail. He smoothed the sleeves of his uniform and turned to face Taito-Vaiana. He looked diffident. Scared, even. None of the other cornics moved to his aid.

He bowed, deeply.

The schmook's posture radiated anger, firm lines, herky-jerky movement, shoulders drawn toward head, spine stiff but bent. Telyn couldn't see exactly what he did. He opened his little, dark hands in supplication—only, it definitely wasn't supplication.

Something that looked like floating black worms swarmed from Taito-Vaiana's fingers. They appeared to greet the soldier like maggots greeting a corpse; they burrowed under the skin, into the nose, through the iris and the ear holes. With a scream to wake the dead, the soldier dropped to the bridge and thrashed.

The schmook's magic left a tingly, peachy taste on Telyn's tongue.

"Oh, Mother of...of..." Hosh couldn't spit out the rest.

Second Gajos came forward to examine the convulsing victim. Telyn couldn't tell what emotion the officer was feeling, if any.

He gestured, and four soldiers bore the casualty away on their shoulders. The soldier's convulsions continued, slowing gradually.

Telyn stared in amazement. The second did nothing; he *allowed* Taito-Vaiana to torture one of his own soldiers.

She dared a look at the tower. Tums was nowhere to be seen; the eehoo must have climbed out of sight.

That easily, in a fit of anger, Taito-Vaiana had tortured the soldier. And they let him. No question asked. No punishment.

Telyn had no doubt that when the convulsions stopped, the soldier would be dead. And Second Gajos did *nothing*.

The line began to move again.

What power Yona and Taito-Vaiana must possess to murder cornic soldiers—soldiers!—with such impunity. Mother of Squirrels, I've got to ditch that mask.

She turned to whisper to her friends. "Keep your mouths shut, all of you. Don't do anything to draw attention to yourselves."

"Ohhhhh," Hosh moaned. "I'm never going to be able to eat peach cobbler again."

Cressida sighed, and Rayvn asked if they needed another distraction. Telyn shushed her.

A few minutes later, the soldiers again had the humans marching forward. Instead of the feathered hind detecting magic, the soldiers did a physical search of bodies, pockets, satchels, and packs. Burly cornic slavers slouched around the slave wagon wearing malignantly bored expressions.

Telyn submitted to the search with head bowed and lips pursed. Most trappers protested loudly, and more than a few got themselves arrested. Men and women who braved the Chaos Woods did not submit easily. All of this suited Telyn, who preferred they got the attention and not her.

Finally, she crossed the gauntlet of soldiers and slavers and had to pass Taito-Vaiana. He made her kneel, bringing them face-to-face— and what a face it was. She wondered how she had ever thought schmooks resembled chipmunks! He had enormous, bright-orange lips, as if he'd let his younger sister practice putting lipstick on them. A veneer of white fuzz surrounded the lips, over which hung a stubby, pipe-like nose. Black eyes sat to the sides of his head on little stalks where his ears should have been, and they blinked at Telyn slowly.

Taito-Vaiana pressed his pudgy fingers around her forehead and cheeks, seeking the edge of a mask that wasn't there. His left eye, right eye, and nose all quested independently, quivering and searching her with multiple senses.

Telyn could not help trembling. Being scrutinized by such an alien was terrifying—a powerful alien, with cornic soldiers and slavers at beck and call.

Sweat trickled down Telyn's neck.

The schmook paused. Had he felt her tremors? Had he smelled her sweat over the condensation of waterfall mist?

No. He was looking behind Telyn; he had focused on someone in line.

He released Telyn's head and gestured for Cressida to kneel. Now the twins knelt side-by-side, the stones hard against their knees.

"Sable Head?" he asked, moving over to take Cressida's face in his hands.

"What?"

"Sable Head!"

"Oh, yeah. I work there with my sister." Cressida nodded at Telyn, who gave a fake smile. "We're twins. She has the frizzy hair."

"Were you there when the thief died?"

"What? No. Raz sent us away." Cressida reached a dreamy hand back towards Hosh, who was held up along with everyone else while Taito-Vaiana considered the twins.

The schmook's fingers pressed into Cressida's temples, and she let out an annoyed "Ouch!"

"A dangerous place to work," he hissed.

Next to them, a bored soldier searched Hosh for a third time. Hosh babbled something incoherent. The delay had caused him to nearly go apoplectic. Sensing a confession, two other soldiers stepped up grabbed his arms to restrain him—but they seemed to have trouble doing that and keeping their trousers on at the same time. The garments kept trying to fall around their ankles. Rayvn's fingers twitched subtly at her sides.

"Stop it. You're hurting him," Cressida exclaimed.

Releasing Cressida's face, Taito-Vaiana joined the soldiers, who had decided to trip Hosh and sit on him—thus keeping both boy and pants under control. They kept asking him questions, but he was too frightened to do anything but babble. Finally, they stripped him to his underwear. Hosh practically passed out, and the schmook had plenty of time to poke the edges of his face for the missing forehead piece.

Telyn took Cressida and Rayvn's elbows and propelled them toward the safety of the woods. *Thank the High Father the mind wizard didn't come in person; he could have read our minds and learned the truth in an instant!*

The moment the cornics allowed Hosh to rise, a rush of women streamed from the Chaos Woods, gathered Hosh into their concerned arms, and hustled him the rest of the way across the bridge. Telyn could hear Second Gajos berating his soldiers for their sloppy uniforms.

Rayvn rejoined them soon after, making a funny, saw-like noise and trying to catch her eyes.

Why, she's purring!

The air-headed, fur-ball-coughing flack actually thinks this is funny. Funny! We nearly get killed, and she's twitching her whiskers and ears like someone's rubbing her back.

Something cracked inside of Telyn—a wall she hadn't realized she'd built—and a bit of warmth trickled through her ribs.

I'll bet her blasted tail is wagging beneath her skirt!

Telyn's attitude toward Rayvn shifted, not much, just a smidgen, but not one she could easily deny.

So, the flack is a prankster, huh. Well, it is sort of funny, isn't it?

Not without misgivings, Telyn offered Rayvn a conspiratorial wink.

CHAPTER TWENTY

Technically, Telyn, Cressida, Caitlin and Hosh didn't have to attend school, having taken all the required classes. But in winter, with the trappers gone and Harlech all but shut down, it was better than staring at knot holes...and *way* better than passing the long, dark days listening to Esther complain, watching her drink herself to death, and inhaling her smelly angel water farts.

Oh yes, after a brief period of sobriety that sparked in Telyn ever-green-scented optimism (She should have known better!), Esther had simply switched her drink of choice from malt to angel water—just as drunk, twice as fast.

Thaumas went to school in the cozy Prefecture, but the human school was a ramshackle building tacked onto the Prefecture's stables. The contrast between the stables and the human school couldn't have been greater. The stables had a stone foundation, airtight tongue-and-groove walls, and a slate roof. Its construction rivaled that of the best human buildings. Many families dreamed of spending the icy, winter nights in the stables with the horses for warmth and company, but those who tried ended up in the Prefecture dungeon in cells too small to stand in—without blankets.

Horses were important. They were made for work and for war. They needed pampering.

Humans only qualified for one of those two occupations. International treaty banned them from combat on account of the ghosts, which was a blessing of sorts.

The one-room human school invited the Marrow Wind in for breakfast, snow for lunch, and rain for afternoon tea. Thankfully, the Dating Circle had built the school a plank floor when Telyn was little, using some of the coin from bets on the Dating Chart. So that wasn't all bad.

Threadbare rugs strewn across one another substituted for desks where the kids sat crisscross or lounged on their sides, with the older kids, now including Telyn and her friends, claiming the warmer common wall between the school and the stables. Periodically, one of the horses would get kick the wall from the other side; anyone careless enough to be leaning against it would be jolted painfully. Two years ago, little Danny Zane had fallen asleep with his head tipped back against the wall, got knocked unconscious, and missed half the school year. He claimed it was the best year he'd ever had.

Telyn disagreed. School didn't teach a whole lot, but the headmaster, Leutric Quid, provided much unintentional entertainment. Quid had been known to sing ribald songs in class and conduct fun experiments involving fire or dung, fish guts or wax—or all four together. One morning, well before Telyn was born, Quid appeared on the steps of the Prefecture standing on his head and spouting the entire Philosopher's Codex—backwards. The Dating Circle concluded that he had gone insane because he'd found a magic book; and they hired him as schoolmaster on the spot.

So they said.

Occasionally, in class, he would read backwards, or spout gibberish that sounded like a magic spell of some sort, and that gave some credence to the story.

Telyn, Cressida, Hosh, and Caitlin sat together. Rayvn, of course, went to the flack school in the cozy Prefecture. Odd that Telyn had thought about Rayvn. She needed to keep her distance from the flack, mental as well as physical.

A girl Telyn hadn't met before crawled over and tugged on Hosh's sleeve. "Hi Hosh, nice hose. Is that a hole in your right calf?"

Hosh wore blue pants that tied just below his knees with white hose under that.

"Er...yeah, I guess."

"Oh, right." She blinked at him adoringly. "See you after class." The girl returned to her spot of carpet, plopped down, and set about ripping a hole in the calf of her hose right there in front of the whole world.

It set Telyn's teeth on edge.

"What's up with her?" Cressida asked, turning to watch the girl and placing her hand on Hosh's knee in the process. "Oh, sorry." She pulled the hand back reluctantly and tucked her perfectly straight hair behind her ear.

Hosh grinned stupidly. "Come on, Cressida, can't you see my fashion genius?"

"Uh, no, she can't," Telyn said, before Cressida could open her besotted mouth. "Those are the same trousers you wore last year—about two inches shorter in the knees since you've grown." Though she had to admit, seeing his calves with nothing to cover them but thin, stretchy, soft material gave her a little thrill. She found herself trying to see his bare skin through that hole in his hose.

She shouldn't have poked fun at his parents' reluctance to buy new trousers. As if *she* could talk about poverty. The Gamage family had far more coin than the Browers ever would, what with their successful cobbler business.

About the only thing she and Cressida *did* have was pretty clothes, thanks to Meander and Mohair, their clothing business—and that only stayed in business by a narrow margin, thanks to Cressida's heroic efforts.

"So, Telyn," Hosh asked. "How's *Tums*?"

"How nice of you to ask," Cressida replied, leaning in front of Telyn. "Why don't you come over to the Sable Head and scratch the eehoo's belly? She likes that, and I can make you something to eat."

Telyn glared around her sister. That was one of the rules—Cressida was not to know about the Ever-Guise—and here Hosh was, talking about it openly! They had decided to call the forehead piece "Tums" in case anyone overheard them, but Hosh shouldn't be that obvious about it. Cressida was no dummy.

"*Tums* is feeling heavy," Telyn said, significantly. "She's been eating too much lately. And she doesn't like to be talked about behind her back."

"I need to see her."

"Well, why don't you walk Cressida to the Sable Head after school? You can make both of them happy."

Cressida took hold of Hosh's arm and sighed. "Wonderful."

We've clearly used the Ever-Guise too much. We need to lay low and let our wishes play out a little bit. The road to Enshede isn't even closed! The changes are getting way too obvious. Taito-Vaiana may be gone, but he could come back if he got word the Ever-Guise had been spotted. Or if the effects of the mask had been spotted. There are many ways to send information: fast riders, pigeons, maybe crystal balls. Who knows?

Hosh's egocentric *suggestions* had brought him more popularity than he could deal with. Half the girls in Harlech had started competing with each other for how besotted they could act—and that included the moms—while the boys and men had become dangerously jealous. Hosh was too blind to see it, but if he didn't watch out, he was going to get his teeth knocked in.

And Caitlin was worse!

Squirrels, mice, pack rats, and skunks lived like spoiled mistresses. People had taken to leaving handfuls of food on their porches, as if their good fortune depended on how many droppings appeared on their stoops overnight. Just the other day, a lumber wagon had run over a possum—a complete accident—and the hangers-about nearly caused a riot!

Caitlin thought she was making a difference. *Yeah, in the amount of dung people stepped in, maybe!*

Every wish brought new problems.

Of the three, only Telyn had been careful. Her wishes—her *suggestions*—appeared the result of careful business decisions. The Sable Head rocked, hurons flew as fast as the patrons could swill angel water, and Razenbock talked about keeping the twins on all winter while the Ouzeley's tavern, the Copcut Ash, languished. They'd already let go all but one bouncer, one serving maid, and one cook.

Of course, the Ouzeleys had plenty of money since they also owned the lumber mill. Telyn's suggestions caused no permanent harm.

Sure, cornic soldiers had taken to hanging out at the Sable Head every evening, but that was to be expected. Telyn's influence extended to flacks as well. They *wanted* to be there. Tastes and preferences had changed, that was all. No one could guess that magic was involved.

All was going according to plan.

The door opened a final time, and bow-legged Leutric Quid strode to the front of the class, blowing a tune on a set of reed pipes. For once, the tune was melodious, and Telyn was disappointed when he stopped mid-song to blow three ear-splitting notes. Quid's wide eyes rolled into focus, with one pointing a little to the side. "Welcome, numbskulls! Welcome, numb skills! Today, I'm announcing that this will be a day of announcements. Learning will be kept to a minimum. Three cheers!"

One of the younger kids actually gave him three cheers, each quieter than the last.

"What a beauticious day to be alive! So much to learn, eh?" Quid stared at one of the younger kids until the girl replied, "Yes, sir."

"You learn, and then you die. Or you stop learning, and then you are the walking dead."

Hosh leaned over to Telyn. "And *then* you die."

"What's that, Gamage?"

Hosh cleared his throat and replied in a surprisingly steady voice: "I said, 'Quid is on his death kick.'"

Telyn felt a thrill of pride for Hosh's bravery, and Cressida gave a thumbs up.

"Gamage is a poet." Quid grinned, revealing a full set of brilliant yellow teeth. "The Sable Head ghost has put me in the mood. Unknown ghosts and unknown knowledge. A metaphor. Without learning, you drift, ghost-like, through life's dreary doldrums. How many of you brought chalk-and-slates?"

Two of the littler kids raised their hands.

Everyone said, "You won't need them."

Quid walked over to the fireplace, stuck his finger in the cold ashes, and licked it thoughtfully. "The winter cometh." He paused and stared out over their heads. Maybe he'd finally lost it for real and good....

He shot his hands out to the sides to embrace all of them. Quid always moved in bursts, like a startled bird.

"Firewood, week three. Sugaring and salting, week two. Brower twins, week one—?"

Cressida replied, "Necessaries." The first week was *always* the necessaries—what some people called "outhouses."

"Correct! The cornics have supplied brand new shovels...iron shovels three." He gestured to the long-handled shovels leaning against the cold, stone fireplace. "Three at a time, you dig until the handles break, and then you will dig with sticks until the handles get fixed. Younger children sharpen the shovels, carry buckets, and provide assistance as needed. Five new necessaries by the market hall, five here, five by the cabins near, and five far." Those were the closest to Telyn's home, and the ones she was most grateful for.

"Youngest students, stay here and learn about—?"

"The bells!" the class replied.

"Correct."

Telyn hated the back-breaking work of digging necessaries. Sugaring and salting wasn't so bad. Every household did their own, of course, but for widows and orphans without other providence, the Dating Circle gathered food supplies and conscripted schoolchildren to preserve them.

A useful skill, sugaring and salting. As was filching a jar of peaches now and then.

"Afternoons—after the community service—I will be teaching the littles. Oldies will tutor or play hooky. You will not lounge here without helping." He blew a few disapproving notes on his pipes. "After community service weeks, the guilds cometh. The merchant guild will present cobblering; lumbering; brewing and distilling; trapping and taxidermy."

Several students cheered at this.

"Not all at the same time, mind; one after the other. There will be no blacksmithing again this year, as the blacksmith got himself eaten." He glared at one of the kids who snickered. "The domestic guild will also be presenting their specialties: reading and writing; sums, statistics and affairs of the heart" —Nearly everyone groaned— "sewing, buttoning and dressmaking" —Telyn groaned. Esther presented this—"midwifing"—The groans cut short, and Hosh's eyes nearly popped out of his head—"tallow, candles and soap; and a special workshop on infusioning and medicine by Heledd Glines.

"Listen, numbskulls and numb skills, you will be required to try all of the merchants and women's guild thingys, and to join two through year's-end. I will be receiving reports regular, and if you fail to participate, you know what that means. Anyone? Mini-Hosh?"

Mini-Hosh raised his hand to the sky, and Quid pointed to him

"Execution?"

Everyone chuckled.

"A noble idea. I'm afraid we do not value education enough in Harlech to consider that. A monetary fine. One egg per skipped class, payable to the headmaster himself. Math lesson one: how many skipped classes until you owe the headmaster a full bird?"

"Ten!" One of the littles shouted.

Quid's yellow teeth gleamed. "Attendance shall be discouraged."

Caitlin raised her hand.

"Ah yes, before the shovels callus your hands, Miss Caitlin Nest wishes to present."

Caitlin stood, and everyone turned to eye her curiously. She unfolded a parchment, flashed it so everyone could see the silver foxes on the corners, then began. "Abyssin cat whiskers. Colobe moustac brain. Gills from a giant ibjau, a type of eel that is perfectly peaceful! A stuffed phauk. The toes—and the lips!—cut from a shambler." The corners of Caitlin's eyes moistened. "The eyelashes—with the lids, no doubt—plucked from the head of a galago; wings pulled from gamble flies' poor little bodies—"

"Don't forget white dung from lepilemurs," Mini-Hosh added, bouncing on the rugs in excitement.

"That one's okay," Caitlin said, dabbing her eyes with a handkerchief. "If you can find white lepilemur dung, bag it, sell it, I don't care. But for the rest, it is time to stop these barbaric practices of killing animals to fuel magic. Magic! Humans don't even use magic. *Can't* use magic. And yet we slavishly scour the Chaos Woods for animals and slaughter them for their parts so the flacks can cast spells."

Quid thrilled a warning on his pipes.

Telyn could see where this was going, and it wasn't good. She tried desperately to signal to Caitlin to lay off. What if Caitlin turned all these kids into little rebels? What if someone reported her? What would the cornics do?

"What about killing animals for food?" asked Sheri Woods.

Caitlin licked her lips awkwardly. "Well, if you can, prefer tubers and...and bread and stuff. But eating meat is...well...normal and necessary, if you have to."

"And tasty!" someone chimed in.

"If you don't have your own fur, wearing leathers and furs is necessary, although spun wool is better if you can get it. And meat...is required to survive." Caitlin didn't look happy about it. She held up a jar in which floated insects. She must have borrowed it from the infusionary. The younger kids ooed appreciatively. "But slaughtering animals so that the Academy can cast spells on us makes no sense."

Telyn's sorrow lurched. Part of her realized Caitlin had just activated the Ever-Guise, but the realization made no difference. Sadness reached out and tried to strangle her. Gagging noises from around the room told her she wasn't the only one.

What were the trappers thinking, going after animals on the Academy's List? It's cruel. It's practically treacherous. They betray the animals, hurt them, skin them, pluck out their parts. They betray their own people. This is war—animals and humans together against flacks....

Telyn stretched out on her side, staring at nothing. The rugs felt so comfortable, better than her bed at home, without question. She lay her head on her arm.

Calm yourself, Telyn, she told herself. *The Ever-Guise has taken hold of you, that is all. You can fight this.*

"Now, you kids know I care about all of you," Quid said, voice uncertain, face working through the furrows of a deep dilemma. "Miss Nest has some good points.

> Sort of fun
> Is white dung.
> Hurts to think
> Of plucked lashes and wings.
> Tis a pickle
> To contemplate
> The hurons, the bugs,
> The empty plate?"

Telyn joined in the applause for Quid's spontaneous composition.

"Ah, but the Academy pays well for these things. Without metal birds, the freedom of Harlech would be in peril. Humanity would—"

"Pays well? Pays well, you say?" Caitlin shouted, indignantly. "The List fuels magic that we can't even use. It gives the, the flacks even more power, even more control over humans." Caitlin stamped her foot. "Worse yet, the taking tortures the poor woodland creatures. It hurts them. Can't you understand that?"

Caitlin's working herself up to another casting. The room will be in an uproar. I've got to do something—now!

But what?

Quid rubbed his hand across his sweaty forehead. "Miss Nest, ah, has a valid point..."

Telyn picked herself off the floor, crossed the room, mostly avoiding the sprawled legs and bodies. She may have stepped on Nina Shelby a little; the girl squealed, which helped attract everyone's attention.

Quid looked slightly relieved. "Yes, Miss, ah, Miss Brower?"

Telyn grabbed a shovel from the corner and put it over her shoulder. "Headmaster, hadn't we start digging those necessaries? The time is getting late."

Leutric Quid swallowed and blinked. "Yes, yes, quite right. I think, I think we need some necessary shoveling to clear our minds. Littles, ten-minute break. Oldies, to the market square for some righteous digging. Telyn, pass out the shovels three and follow me. Everyone else follow her. Last one out, close the door."

Already standing, Caitlin was first in line.

"What were you thinking?" Caitlin snarled, tearing a shovel from Telyn's grasp.

"One of us has to," Telyn replied to her friend's departing back.

Telyn's boots crunched on the frozen ground as she hurried after Caitlin, determined to give her a piece of her mind. What had Caitlin been thinking, calling everyone's attention to herself like a carnival barker, then using the mask to modify their thoughts? Already the parents would wonder why their kids came back with such bizarre ideas. *Let's not eat meat unless we have to, Mommy. Caitlin told us it was wrong.*

Caitlin would have a target on her back from this point on, mask or no mask.

The mask just made the stakes so much higher.

Icicles hung from the eves and golden leaves blew through the streets; the day couldn't decide whether it was fall or winter. The air was almost warm enough for short sleeves, but the ground remained frozen from the night before.

The hour bell rang ten times. "The bell rings every hour from six a.m. until ten p.m.," Quid would be teaching the youngest. Using funny rhymes and sock puppets, the headmaster taught about Harlech's three bells. The hour bell helped people keep time. The funeral bell, which doubled as the call to assembly, and the warning bell, which announced you'd better get inside and bolt the door because some monster had crossed the bridge, or worse yet, the river, from the Chaos Woods.

Run.

Hide.

Die.

Telyn dodged through the clump of kids and fell in alongside Caitlin.

"That was risky," she hissed.

Caitlin eyed her sideways.

"What if the chaos lumber had made the mask misfire? If sparks shot out of your face, even Quid might have noticed."

"The school isn't made of chaos wood. Flacks like to keep chaos lumber as far away from themselves as possible, or hadn't you noticed?"

"Of course I noticed."

She hadn't, but now that Caitlin mentioned it, the school's wood didn't have the picturesque stains characteristic of chaos lumber, nor the red highlights that gave it its distinctive color.

"It was still a stupid risk."

"Stupid, was it?"

"Yeah, stupid."

They walked side-by-side, shovel-to-shovel, Caitlin's vibes colder than the air by far. They both glanced over at the bas relief above the Prefecture:

Humans shall not own horses.
Humans shall not own magic.
Humans shall not own wheels.

The Three Rules.

If anything, Caitlin's scowl became even deeper. "I couldn't help it."

"Oh, you had no choice?"

"No, I don't think I did. Tey, I'm starting to think we should get rid of it. Now. I know I'm doing good with it; I know the work is just getting started, but I don't like this...this need I feel, right here." She rapped knuckles over her heart. "It's like being in love with the wrong boy. You know it's stupid, but you can't help it. No, it's not really like that, but I can't think of anything else. I hadn't meant to use the, ah, the Tums today. I hadn't meant to put it on, or carry it to school, or any of it. But I found myself doing all of that, as if it were someone else doing and me just watching. Do you understand?" Caitlin's eyes sought hers, pleading for understanding. "Tey, I'm scared."

A brief vision of Esther drinking came to Telyn's mind—her mother's absolute need to poison her liver with alcohol no matter the consequences—and she shook it away. She didn't need the distraction just now. "We agreed we had the winter, Caitlin. The road to Enshede will close any day now. One storm, that's all it'll take, and we'll be safe for months. Think of all we can do, Caitlin—just think of it."

They emerged into the square and started to pass under the shade of the market hall. Unsurprisingly, Tabbard and his gang slouched around the pillars and jeered. "Going to dig the necessaries, Too-tall?" Tabbard called. "Don't faint in there and get buried. Or maybe you should; at least you'd have enough to eat." His friends laughed sycophantically.

It irked Telyn to see Joram Lycurgus give a secret little wave—and Caitlin return it. Whatever sense Caitlin may have been making about the Ever-Guise just blew up.

Caitlin's judgment can't be trusted, that's for sure. She's love-struck and besotted. The girl has no sense at all.

Joram Lycargus. How could she?

Tabbard and his cronies fell silent.

An uneven pitter-patter signaled Hosh catching up from behind, accompanied by the girls who always trailed him these days. His first words were, "That was brilliant, Caitlin. Heledd Glines may never sell another infusion. If she had any idea what you would use her bugs for, she would never let you back in the Rusty Shackles."

Glines was Tabbard's cousin, and whether he understood Hosh's comment, he had surely heard it. Tabbard and his friends glared dangerously, but they said nothing at all.

Telyn felt a chill that had nothing to do with fall or winter. Jeers and insults would be fine. A thrown stone could be dodged.

Silence was a bad sign. A very bad sign.

She would trust Hosh with her life, but in a fight, she'd wager on Tabbard any day. He had experience; he'd been bulling people as long as he lived. And he outweighed Hosh by thirty, maybe forty pounds.

Not to mention, he didn't fight fair. Tabbard's gang was known for jumping people three- or four-to-one and beating them to a bloody heap. Then Tabbard would go around bragging that he'd done it all by his lonesome. Anyone who disputed his version would be next on the target list.

And so it went.

Nearby, little Nina Shelby asked, "What's up with them?" Then she turned an adoring look on Hosh. "Hi Hosh. I'm putting a hole in all my stockings as soon as I get home."

"Er...okay. Cool."

Telyn could almost hear the chisel etching *Hosh Gamage* into the Sepulcher.

"Think about what I said, Tey," Caitlin warned. "Think about how much you want to use Tums right now. Ask yourself if that is rational."

Hosh looked from Caitlin to Telyn in something between surprise and shock. "You don't seriously want to get rid of Tums? We're just starting to understand it, ah, her. Think of what we can do. Besides, it's my—"

"Shut your trap, Hosh," both girls said.

Telyn took a deep breath. "We just have to play with Tums a bit less. She's getting spoiled by all this attention. That's all it is. We can control the situation. We can."

CHAPTER TWENTY-ONE

About three feet into the final necessary, week one of school nearly over, the North Wind answered Telyn's prayer. Snow, heavy, soft flakes that wouldn't be melting anytime soon. Flakes so cold the kids couldn't pack snowballs no matter how hard they pressed. They resorted to flinging handfuls of powder at each other, turning their hair snowy and their eyelashes sparkly.

And so it begins.

A big pile-up today, a couple more heavy snowfalls—three at the outside—and the pass will be closed. No more caravans until spring. No more mind wizard or schmook to worry about. Just a few cornics keeping an eye on the Sable Head, and they don't know what they're looking for.

Telyn smiled to herself.

This town will be ours.

Two by two, the kids abandoned the work. Telyn would have left an hour ago, but Cressida insist they keep digging. First off because, as the oldest kids, they had an example to set. Second, this necessary was the closest to their house.

"If we don't get this deep enough," Cressida grunted, stomping the blade into the earth, "we'll pay for it come spring—every time we breathe through our noses."

For now, Cressida and Hosh dug, Telyn and Caitlin carried buckets. They switched every foot of depth or so. Telyn felt a burn in every muscle and sinew in her back. Her arms and legs weren't much better, and if that blister on her palm popped, she was going to scream.

"By springtime, we may all be dead," Telyn commented, grunting as she hefted the bucket to her shoulder. "You'll have worked us to death." She knew Cressida was right about the smell, that they wanted the hole as deep as possible, but in this situation, complaining felt like the proper response to encouragement.

On the low side of the trail, she dumped the damp earth, making the trail a tad wider with each bucket. She stomped the clods a few times for good measure—anything to avoid carrying another load for a few more seconds.

Giving his shovel a good swing, Hosh said, "I'd rather keep digging all winter than go back to class and face—" he made a dramatic ding-dang sound, "—the Dating Circle."

"What's the matter, Hosh," Cressida said, "don't want to plot your name on the Chart?"

Everyone laughed except for Caitlin, who blew a raspberry at Hosh—the forehead's influence, no doubt. If Hosh's name ended up on the Dating Chart, almost every woman in Harlech would be clamoring to get within Hosh's circle.

Not me. No way, no how. I'm not falling for Hosh. Telyn whispered as much under her breath, and Cressida grinned at her.

Telyn couldn't imagine all those busybody Dating Circle women poking around in her private life more than they already did, placing bets on her crushes, on the success or failure of her dates, on whom she would return a promise dance to....

The old busybodies!

Loneliness sucks, she allowed, grabbing another bucket handle and pulling it up, *but I will scratch that itch on my own terms without people placing bets on the outcome...with Hosh or without him.*

Wait, where did that thought come from? Treacherous mind! I don't have a thing for Hosh. I don't.

Little by little, bucket by bucket, the pit sank. The thickly-falling flakes added weight and mass to each shovel- and bucket-full, making the work even more difficult. If Telyn didn't have the insulated gloves Cressida had sewed for her, her hands would be screaming from the cold and the blisters.

Finally, the blister long-since popped, when Telyn had to stand on tiptoes to see over the edge of the pit, she sank her shovel into the floor one final time and sat wearily next to Caitlin, who had given out moments before. Cressida and Hosh climbed down and joined them. Together, side by side, they enjoyed the heavy silence of the snowfall, the rhythmic puffs of their breathing. Periodically, Hosh would turn his head to lick the snow-mound on his shoulder.

"I need an infusion," announced Caitlin.

"Mm," replied Cressida, then added without conviction, "We really should go back to school."

"Steam bath," suggested Hosh.

"Bed," Telyn added.

They considered for a few minutes. The time to crawl out of the pit had come. Hosh had dropped a wooden ladder down the side, but the top looked a long way up.

"Apple-mint tea," Caitlin added. "With a salmon-berry scone."

Hosh rose first, knocked the snow from his head with a vigorous rub. "Steam bath, then?" he asked, hopefully.

"Sorry to disappoint you, but I am not going to the mixed area," Telyn said, "and we can't afford the private rooms."

"Besides," Cressida added, thumping Hosh's boot, "if we *could* afford the private rooms, we ladies would be together and you would be all alone. What fun would that be?"

This whole steam bath business sounded way too suggestive for Telyn's liking. They simply had to stop using the Ever-Guise for a while. Or, better yet, stop Hosh from using it for a while.

"Here's an idea, Hosh," Caitlin said. "Why don't you go home and drop a hot brick in a bucket of cold water."

They all laughed. Everyone in Harlech had tried that at least once. If you heated the brick for a really long time and didn't hesitate before plopping it into the water, it created just enough steam to get your skin damp before the cold air closed back in. Then you were shivering *and* damp.

Only Betty Yarwood knew how to make steam right.

They agreed to check back in with Quid after an infusion, hurried to Caitlin's place so she could grab some birds, then strolled down Main Street because Caitlin wanted to see what might be happening—even though nothing ever did, especially not during a heavy snowfall. Then they turned into the alley behind the Copcut Ash which led up the hill and across the street to the Rusty Shackles infusionary.

The alley, unnamed as far as Telyn knew, zig-zagged between the tall buildings like one of Harlech's purple veins. Shadow-filled at the best of times, four-legged scavengers often startled away from the piles of rubbish or the dank corners.

The friends stepped into the alley, and the wind died. Here, the snow plummeted straight down instead of drifting. In the gloom, the alley seemed darker, stiller than usual, as if holding its breath.

Out of the corner of her eyes, Telyn noticed folks on the log benches behind the Copcut Ash. Considering the snowfall, it seemed odd, but not overly so. She didn't register who they were until they'd already passed them, already ventured from Main Street into the dark, narrow lane, already taken a dozen steps into the artificial night.

The figures rose like wraiths and blocked the way forward. Two goons stepped from the side and took each of Hosh's arms. Tabbard, Joram, and their gang—the last group of people you wanted to turn your back on.

Paralyzing fear ran down Telyn's spine.

Caitlin seemed to fade behind the line of boys as if she belonged to them, as if she had known this was going to happen.

Did Caitlin lead us here on purpose? The thought jumped unbidden and unwelcome into Telyn's mind. *She led us here, didn't she? She suggested the infusionary, Main Street, this particular shortcut...*

Telyn couldn't remember for sure. Her mind seized up along with her spine.

They weren't all boys. Cheryle Uren was there, and Tristam

Harries, and another, older girl, Isla Yarwood, Steamy Betty's niece, who should have known better than to hang around these losers.

If anything, the girls looked more eager to see violence than the boys.

Tabbard advanced his ugly flat nose to within inches of Hosh's face.

This loosened the glue on Telyn's vertebrae. She blinked once. "Oh, hi-ya, Tabbard," Telyn said, and squeezed between him and Hosh. She didn't think even Tabbard would stoop to assaulting a woman—not in front of witnesses, anyway. "Bored now that no one is visiting the Ash, hmm? You should've joined us in Quid's class. We could've used help digging the privies." She tried to smile congenially.

With one massive arm, Tabbard leveraged Telyn to the side, out of the way. *Mother of Squirrels, how's he gotten so big? He has the girth of Razenbock!*

"Now listen," Telyn said, trying to scoot back between them. "We don't want trouble."

"Telyn, stay out of this," Caitlin said from behind the wall of boys.

The goon circle cinched tighter around Hosh. Cressida had already been pushed outside.

"Tabbard!" Cressida said over the heads of the boys, sounding worried and desperate. "What would your parents say?"

To his credit, Hosh didn't try to run, didn't beg for mercy. He stood scarecrow-like, awaiting his pummeling.

"My parents?" Tabbard said. "My mom's been telling me what a nice boy Hosh seems to be. Why can't I wear hose the way Hosh wears it? Why do my leather pants look so baggy around my buttocks? Not like sweet Hosh's buttocks." Tabbard's neck held so much anger that the muscles pulled his head to the side. His hands balled into fists. "My dad, he thinks you've made a deal with the flacks for some sex-appeal spell. Is that so, Hosh? You bribe some flack to give you magic to make women dig your deformity?"

"No," Hosh mumbled.

"What's that?"

"No, sir."

Tabbard's gang chuckled.

"You're a disgusting, crippled freak, barely able to drag your club-foot in front of the other."

"It's not a clubfoot," Hosh said, staring at the ground.

"Wrong answer, Hosh-pucky," Tabbard said. "You're supposed to say, 'May I lick the dirt from your boots, sir?'" He gave Hosh a quick jab to the ribs. Hosh grunted but refused to buckle.

"Leave him alone!" Cressida shouted, hopping on tiptoes to see past the burly boys, as if by keeping her gaze on Hosh she could keep him safe.

I led him to this, Telyn realized. *Me and the Ever-Guise. I showed it to Hosh. I practically encouraged him to wish on it in the beginning. I let him wish as much as he wanted because we were taking turns—because the more he used it, the more I could use it.* Telyn's mind seemed to be working over-fast. Her thoughts darted like fireflies; the snowflakes fell slower than they ever had; the goons moved at a crawl. *Even the Ouzeleys, stupid as they are, have been manipulated by Ever-Guise.*

Even Tabbard isn't responsible for what he is doing—not fully.

"Listen, Tabbard, you don't know what you're doing. You don't want to do this—" Telyn began.

Another jab landed in Hosh's ribs in the same spot as before. Again, Hosh did his best to not react, to not give Tabbard what he wanted. But he didn't try to fight back, either. That would have been futile. That would have guaranteed he'd be crushed.

Maybe killed.

The phantom screen of snow, looming buildings, and nightmare ally contributed to the kind of otherworldly day when someone could get murdered while surrounded by folks staring, whispering, licking lips, clenching fists, wishing they could be the one to do it, to be the one who snuffed out a life—or wishing they could look away.

Look away and forget.

"I kind of think I do want to do this." Tabbard grinned. "Let's see how long before he cries for his mama."

Could the Ever-Guise save him? A well-crafted wish? Like, "I propose that people who attack cripples will be pariahs." No, Tabbard wouldn't know the word. Make it simple. "*People who attack cripples will never know the forbidden dance.*"

Such a wish might have indeed saved her friend, but the Ever-Guise hung in the crown of a tree in the Chaos Woods. It might as well have been on the other side of the world.

"Tabbard, please, leave him alone..." Desperation caused Telyn's voice to waiver.

Would Tabbard respond to begging? Should she drop to her knees—

Four hands grabbed her and dragged her back. In a kind of daze, she looked from the hands to the arms, to the people with the arms, realized they belonged to Caitlin and Joram.

"Tabbard—" Cressida's voice was devoid of hope.

Another jab, then three in quick succession. Hosh's knees buckled. The two boys holding his arms kept him standing.

"Leave him alone!" Telyn shouted, and Cressida wailed.

"Let it alone," Caitlin cautioned. "You'll only make it worse."

"You filthy traitor," Telyn said, ripping an arm free and grabbing Caitlin's hair. She wretched Caitlin's head to the side.

A third boy grappled Telyn's legs, and they dragged her to the ground. Cressida landed beside her, senseless. Someone must have clocked her.

"Hosh has been going too far," Caitlin whispered in Telyn's ear.

Fists were flying. Telyn couldn't see Hosh in the writhing mass of boys and punches and kicks, but she refused to release Caitlin's hair. "We tried to warn him, but he wouldn't listen. Quiet now, or I'll tell them about the thing, about Tums. This has to happen...release the steam...keep the pressure from exploding."

Joram cocked an eye at the word *thing*, and Telyn ceased struggling. Would Caitlin really betray the Ever-Guise to these thugs? Imagine what they would do with such an artifact! If Hosh's wishes had been self-centered, imagine what Tabbard Ouzely would wish!

Each time Caitlin exhaled, her minty breath landed on Telyn's face, and she hated it. Someone was prying her fingers off Caitlin's hair—might have been Caitlin, might have been another. One by one, they twisted her fingers backwards, strained her hand nearly to the breaking, and freed the traitor's hair. The numbers of Tabbard's goons seemed to be endless. Telyn could only growl and writhe. No matter how hard she fought, no matter how much bare skin she scratched, she could not pull free.

"This is your initiation, isn't it? This is what it cost you to join Tabbard's gang?"

"Shush," Caitlin urged. "No. Quiet, now."

Eventually, the sheer weight of her attackers pinned Telyn to the ground. Each breath took enormous effort. She turned her head to look at Hosh. She didn't want to, but she owed him that much.

Amazingly, when the boys parted, Hosh had not fallen. He sagged against the two boys holding him, but he hadn't fallen. Panting, Tabbard put a hand under Hosh's chin and lifted his face. "I've been thinking, Hosh-pucky, I need a new pair of boots." He slammed his massive knee into Hosh's thigh. "Get your old man to make me a pair and bring 'em here tomorrow." He drove his knee into Hosh's thigh again, and again, and again. Hosh's legs gave out, and he dropped to his knees; his arms were twisted upward, behind his back.

"A new pair of boots, Gamage, capiche?"

Tabbard might have let it go then, might have walked away, but another boy—Adda Swansea—handed him a two-foot-long club. Tabbard hefted it, tested its weight, and bounced it against his other palm. "Haven't marked your face, yet, have I? D'you think you'd get away that easy?"

With a wooden club in his hands, of course Tabbard would have to use it. He couldn't *not* use it; that would make him a coward.

Arms twisted behind his back, head hanging limp, Hosh couldn't protect himself or even move to soften the blow. The club would either shatter his jaw or strike him right across the temples. He could be killed—

Telyn gave a wild twist and pulled one arm free. She balled a fist and swung, catching Joram on the side of the head. Joram gave up trying to catch the arm and threw himself atop her. He outweighed her by half, and Caitlin helped pin her down. Telyn managed to pull one leg free, but another assailant grabbed it—Tristam Harries—and Telyn's struggles just succeeded in grinding the snow under her into a muddy wallow. She screamed against the horrible feeling, against being at the mercy of these thugs. They could do anything—beat her; shave her head; strip off her boots, or worse—and she could do nothing.

Nothing.

Her best hope was—

"Help! Help! Cornics, to me!"

If Redbeard or Razenbock heard her, or a cornic, or any men with a shred of honor, they would be come looking.

Tabbard poked the fat end of the club into Hosh's eyes, prodding and testing, dragging out the inevitable. Hosh moaned and rolled his head from side to side. "Shut the prat up." He meant Telyn. "I need to line up my swing just so."

Telyn screamed more, called for cornics, called for help. Anyone would do: Leutric Quid, a trio of moms, even a flack, someone to put fear or shame into Tabbard and his goons.

Caitlin, Joram, Tristam and the other boy flipped Telyn onto her stomach. A knee ground her neck into the ground; rough hands regained control of her limbs. Slush and mud pushed their way into her mouth. Telyn turned her face to the side and tried to push the gunk out with her tongue. She inhaled some and began hacking.

She managed a burbling shout between coughs. "Cornics, help! Help me!"

Tabbard's voice again, more forcefully, more confident, "Caitlin, tell your friend to shut it or I'm going to break her skull—right after I do her boyfriend here."

More weight pressed against her neck. Dirt pushed past her lips and teeth; slush abrased her face and neck and ground into her earhole, but Telyn didn't waver.

She screamed, and she wouldn't stop.

A door in the alleyway banged open. She was sure of it. Salvation.

She kept screaming.

Tabbard cursed. The weight lifted from her neck; the goons released her arms and legs took off running as multiple footsteps descended a short, wooden stairway.

It was all Telyn could do to breathe.

A pair of shiny black shoes stopped next to her, and one of them toed her in the ribs none-too-gently. Telyn rolled onto her back and groaned. Peering with dirt-filled, teary eyes, she recognized the scowl of Wulstan Ouzeley. He'd come to investigate the screaming—along with a bouncer and cook.

Hosh had fallen to his face, but he breathed. The club lay next to his head. It must have been unused, because he lived.

He lived.

Mr. Ouzeley contemplated the scene for a moment. "Someone left their garbage in my alley. See that it cleans itself up. Bad for business, leaving trash lying around." He stepped on Telyn's hand while walking away. With all she'd been through, she barely noticed.

The door to the Copcut Ash slammed again.

Telyn managed to rise to her elbows and gazed blearily around. Caitlin had vanished with Tabbard, Joram, Tristam, and the others. The impassive bouncer had returned to the stoop, arms folded, as if the kids might try to break into the Copcut Ash through the rear entrance. The cook, a rotund woman named Ebby, was helping Hosh sit up.

Feeling as if she had taken Tabbard's beating herself, Telyn crawled over to cradle her sister's head in her lap.

"You need some broth, dears?" the cook asked. "Ouzeley needn't hear *nothin'* about it." She glared at the bouncer, who stopped his protest mid-syllable.

Hosh shook his head, and Telyn managed a grunt that passed for "No."

"Anything broken?" the cook asked Hosh.

"Just my thighs bruised, and my belly," he patted it and tried to grin through his pain. "Could've been worse."

"You need to see Corporal Tomkin in flacktown," the cook said. "He'll take care of you."

"Flacktown?"

"The cornic medic, ask for 'im at the barracks. I've sent people over to 'im for many things: fever, fights, tomfoolery. He don't mind that we're human. Mind, he won't ask nothin' for it, but it's bad form not to give 'im what you can."

"My sister—" Telyn tried to peel Cressida's eyes open. "—she's been knocked cold."

Cressida's eyelids fluttered, revealing more white than green.

"I don't want...dad...to see me like this," Hosh said haltingly. "Might try...do something..."

Cressida managed to moan.

"I'll explain everything," Telyn said, patting her affectionately. "You and Hosh are going to see a medic."

"Wha' that?"

"Come on," the cook said. "We don't got no customers. Business's been as dismal as Ouzeley's personality. I'll take an arm." She scowled as the bouncer tried to protest again. "Ouzeley can stoke the fires 'imself 'till I get back."

Telyn took Cressida's other arm, and the foursome wobbled towards flacktown.

She glanced down the alley, thoughts turning toward Caitlin. *I hope Joram's worth it, 'cause you are so going to pay.*

CHAPTER TWENTY-TWO

Physical pain fueled Telyn's climb. Each shout from an aching joint, each twinge from a bruised muscle, each stretch that pulled on her scabs and scrapes meant another successful hold, another rung of tree limbs ascended.

Telyn hadn't waited a single day. Just as soon as she'd left Cressida in her bed and Hosh at the foot of his stairs—promising to go home herself—she had instead crossed the bridge and entered the Chaos Woods, intent on revenge. The fact that she had told yet another small lie didn't bother her in the least.

She didn't want to worry Hosh.

She didn't want him to try to talk her down or moderate her wish.

Or worse yet, to follow.

Her cloak hung on a low branch. After blousing her long skirt into her belt to free her legs, she had begun climbing. Before winter was over, Tabbard and his buddies would wish they had taken that last caravan to Enshede. Especially Caitlin, who had earned a special sort of revenge.

She didn't know the details yet, but a plan had begun to form in Telyn's mind—a plan seasoned by Caitlin's minty, treacherous breath, cooked by the pain of Joram's knee on her neck, and garnished with the Marrow Wind that buffeted the treetops and made her ears ache from cold.

No matter. The wish had to be done today. She wanted the timing between the bullying and the consequences to be clear in everybody's mind. Attack Telyn and her friends, suffer ten times the consequences. Caitlin would understand the why and how, but even if she told the cornics about the Ever-Guise, the forehead piece was too well-hidden for them to find it.

Besides, after tonight, no one would listen to Caitlin ever again.

The sun fell behind the Sepulcher; the three-quarter moon took over. Resting every few feet and nursing bruises atop bruises, Telyn climbed by touch as much as by sight.

Interminable minutes later, in an angry, moon-fueled daze, Telyn reached the apex of the tree, pulled the forehead piece from the leather bag she had affixed to the trunk, and slipped it on. Right as she got her hair lifted out of the way and the eyeholes positioned above her real eyes, a particularly strong breath of Marrow Wind shook the tree.

Her shoes slipped, one to the right and one to the left, and she fell. Her crotch landed heavily on the branch. The Ever-Guise peeled halfway off her forehead.

A warning, an omen.

She almost never slipped, nor had the forehead ever peeled from her face. Usually, it was rather difficult to remove.

On any other day, Telyn might have heeded the sign—but not this day. Nothing was going to stop her now. She leaned her head against the trunk, grit her teeth against this new ache in her groin, and strove to keep her muscles from spasming uncontrollably. She needed food and water. A hot, honey-laden infusion would be nice, and a cozy sleep beside her twin. At full strength, she never would have slipped.

The day's events replayed in Telyn's mind.

Had Caitlin led them to the alley deliberately?

She *had* suggested an infusion, which naturally took them to the shortcut behind the Copcut Ash. Then again, Caitlin always wanted an infusion—and could afford them—being as her parents worked for the cornics.

The traitors!

But she couldn't have known they would be traveling down Main Street at that exact time, nor had she actually attacked them. She and Joram held Telyn back to keep her away from Tabbard, to keep her from getting pummeled alongside Hosh.

At least, that's what Caitlin said.

Telyn wanted to believe her.

She wanted to hate her.

The wind picked up. It wasn't a random gust that had knocked her off the branch, it was the Marrow Wind itself, the screaming, moaning, crushing soul of the Cairn Range. Fed by a million souls who had perished of cold, starvation, and loneliness, the Marrow stole hope as it stole heat, without timidity or mercy.

The treetop swung back and forth, the branch chafing Telyn's inner thighs as her thoughts swirled.

Caitlin wasn't the real enemy. Caitlin had been blinded by her crush on Joram. It was only speculation that Caitlin had set them up. Hard to imagine otherwise...but not impossible. They'd taken that shortcut hundreds of times without incident.

Telyn couldn't remember who had wanted to walk down Main instead of Middle Street. All of them, likely, being as things happened on Main. So that proved nothing.

Don't be naïve. Of course Caitlin set us up.

Of course.

She held my arms, her and Tristam and some idiot on my legs, while Joram put his knee on my neck. My neck! I won't soon forget that.

She said she was trying to protect me.

She's a liar!

She said she wanted to save Hosh before he went too far.

She's the Princess of Lies. How can I trust her?

My name is Telyn Brower. I am strong. Strong! Nobody messes with me and gets away with it. I'll start with my former friend and make it worse from there, ending with the biggest loser of all: Tabbard Ouzeley.

He's going down.

Her suggestion-wishes had saved the Sable Head—and nearly caused a riot. Her accidental suggestion to Esther about brakdaw-smells had soured malt all across the town and changed the drinking habits of hundreds of trappers: angel water up, malt out.

Mentally modeling her suggestion on the one that had spoiled malt, Telyn stood, balanced, and donned the Ever-Guise again. It felt warm as it molded against her skin.

Picturing Caitlin firmly in her mind, Telyn took a deep breath and projected her voice over the creak of branches. "I propose that Caitlin Siana Nest become hideous—"

She got no further.

An explosion of light blinded her. Stars, emeralds, sapphires, and jagged topaz swirled in her eyes—in her mind—and she fell backwards, tipping away from the tree trunk. This chaos tree was not one of the giants of the deep woods, not one that towered above the crags and took hours to climb. Still, she must be two hundred feet up.

If she didn't halt the fall immediately, she would die.

She spread arms and legs and slammed back-first across the branch. Her head whipped sideways, and the Ever-Guise peeled off.

Her body tilted to the left. Reaching for handholds, trying desperately to save her life, Telyn made no attempt to catch the falling mask. Still sparkling, it plunged out of sight.

She slid sideways. It took a long time and no time at all, but her forearms scraped against a small, nearby branch, and her hands managed to hook it as she plunged. The branch bowed but held. Telyn hung there by the tips of her fingers, her thoughts as wobbly as the branch, wondering if she could gather the strength to pull herself up—or if her finger-strength would give out first.

She tried to blink away the blinding stars. She had seen an explosion like this before...somewhere, some *when*. Her memory flung back to that night in the Sable Head, that explosion of light when the trogo Kulon had tried to use the mask; and then again when he attacked the two schmooks, and they cast a spell to defend themselves.

"The chaos wood," Yona had said. "The magic will not work properly here."

She hadn't bothered to take the Ever-Guise to Dragon Tower; she'd used it in the chaos tree. *The mask backfired because of the chaos wood.*

A bell clanged.

Not *a* bell, *the* bell. The Warning Bell, snapping Telyn to attention.

Telyn's first reaction was fear.

A monster is coming from the woods!

Her second reaction, as her logical mind analyzed the situation, was dread.

The Warning Bell isn't for a monster. It's for me. *They've seen the explosion. The cornics will come to investigate.*

I've got to get out of this tree, get the Ever-Guise, and hide. Fast.

Trying to pull herself up with her arms gained Telyn about three inches before her strength failed. It had been a long climb up, she'd taken a beating from Tabbard's gang, and she hurt just about everywhere. Strength wouldn't get her out of this. She needed to use her brain.

She began swinging. Each swing threatened to pull her frozen grip from the little branch, and the little branch from the trunk, but her legs found what she was looking for: a nearby branch she could wrap her thighs around.

She pulled herself across and, without hesitation, began to descend. A strange scent followed her, like rotten onions topped by a spoiled egg. Perhaps the Ever-Guise's backfire had attracted some monster which, at this very moment, stalked her on the reverse of the tree trunk.

She felt that hopeless feeling when you are racing and you know you are going to lose—but your lungs just can't catch any more air and you can't push your legs any faster and you know you are going to lose....

Across the Elbus River, the peek-a-boo lights of torches and lanterns gathered—a search party coming to see what caused the explosion in the top of the tree.

They'll be armed and jittery, bows and axes at the ready. Shoot first and ask questions later. Me or the monster, they'll kill us both.

Telyn dropped the last few feet into a pillow of snow. She began digging around for the forehead, the *white* ceramic, flinging snow in every direction.

Come on, come on.

Whatever caused that reek didn't show itself. Thank goodness. A curious monster, but perhaps not a deadly one.

The twinkling lights began to cross the bridge. The townsfolk or the cornics or both, come to investigate, come to rid the forest of a potential menace.

Have to get out of here. Have to go, to run.

Run.

Telyn flung herself around several other trunks, made as much mess as possible so the search party wouldn't investigate this particular tree too closely. Then she snagged her long cloak from where it hung and dashed into the woods as fast as her battered body would allow.

Over her right shoulder, a fist-sized hunk of bark shattered, sending grit into her eye, and confirming her fear. Cornic soldiers or frightened hunters pursued her—the kind who shot first and asked questions after. They'd shot at her with an arrow or a crossbow; she didn't know which, and she didn't care.

Another projectile passed overhead, silent and white in the moon-light. It might have been an owl—if owls flew dead straight.

The wind made projectiles iffy—the Marrow Wind may have saved her life

Blinking the grit from her eye, she dodged and swerved toward the thicker, deeper, blacker woods. Now she could hear excited shouts, individual words about *beast, explosion, magic, monster...*

She probably could have called out, surrendered, let the pursuers know they chased a human—but she didn't want to explain herself, didn't want them asking questions.

The mask—lost! How could she have been so stupid?

The hunters would figure out what they pursued soon enough from her all-too-human boot-tracks. And, since she started running, they would figure her for an outlaw. They'd wonder how a human girl caused such an explosion, and she'd end up being questioned in the basement of the Prefecture—questioned with tongs and white-hot metal.

They can't learn my name, or I'll never be able to go home. Got to stay ahead, keep running.

Running.

Run.

Another mess of bark shattered, this one far overhead, and she knew her long legs had given her a lead. If she kept ahead and alive for another mile or so, they'd give up. Turn back. Close the gate over the bridge, tell the townsfolk to keep watch, and—

Her legs zipped sideways. She tilted, crashed her shoulder into something rock-hard, and slid into a bank of snow.

Her lungs pumped; her heart pattered. She must have been hit by an arrow or a sling…but everything hurt alike. There was no sharp pain in any one place, but more of an even, battered feeling all over. She tried to rise, but her hands and feet slipped again.

It dawned on her than she had slipped on a frozen surface, a pond or a stream.

Everything sloped. A stream, then.

Her pursuers shouted at each other and approached from three directions, their lights appearing and disappearing like will-o'-the-wisps among the trees.

In the gloam, she could just make out the churn of her footsteps ending on the bank. The wind had blown the stream clear of snow, so her tracks disappeared. All she had to do was go upstream or down, and fast, and they wouldn't know which way to go.

She chose upstream, not wanting to accidentally slide over an unseen waterfall. That smelly monster stayed with her, and she began to suspect it wasn't a monster at all.

Hideous, indeed!

No time for that. Stop thinking, keep moving.

They'll track me by the smell!

Brain off, worm-head, keep moving.

Her scampering feet sounded incredibly loud in her ears, but she kept them pedaling, back hunched, bear-crawling as often as running. When the lights and voices faded behind her, she continued at a brisk walk. She kept it up for hours, until she didn't think she could go any further even if a brakdaw chased her. She kept going until strength died and fear faded, and only blind will kept her legs moving.

The sun had risen when, finally, she gave out, having fled for nearly nine hours. Using all fours, she climbed up the stream-bank to get away from the cold, hard ice and collapsed with her back against a nearby tree. With the Marrow Wind still whipping, she should be warmer here than in the open, and the leaves and snow piled around the base of the tree made a sort of cushion. She closed her eyes. The flight had kept her warm enough, but now, her skin slick with sweat and cooling fast, Telyn knew enough not to fall asleep. To survive she had two choices: keep moving or to build a shelter, neither of which appealed to her just now.

Not just now. Later.

Soon...

Her eyes slipped shut, the pain from her bruises faded, and she shrugged deeper into the comfortable leaves and warm snow. She drifted languidly on the edge of the long, dark sleep, prepared to add her voice to the Marrow Wind, when another voice whispered:

Telyn Brower has been a bad, bad girl.

CHAPTER TWENTY-THREE

Insistent with knowledge yet lilting with questions, as judgmental as Esther yet as false as a particularly weak lie, the voice sounded a lot like the voice in Telyn's own head—if her guilty conscious had downed shot of angel water.

What have you been up to, Miss Brower? Questioned by the cornic Minister? Deceiving the pattern witch? Pledging yourself to revenge...

How positively juicy!

Telyn's eyes popped open. Night had fallen while she slept; the moon cast trees into shadowy outlines. A slight breeze tickled her frozen cheeks; the snow-laced leaves beneath her back crunched as she shifted; an errant lock of hair itched against her nose. Had she dreamed that voice? No, someone must have sneaked up on her while she slept. She didn't dare make any sudden moves until she had a better idea *who* and *how many*.

The slightly tipsy feminine voice paused while Telyn gathered her wits. Then it spoke again.

Did you hear about the girl who hung the thief on the Sepulcher over her father? Into granite, they chiseled "Unknown," but she knows more than she lets on.

A rough arm draped over Telyn's shoulder, and she nearly jumped out of her skin. She batted the weird arm-thing away. In her scramble to get away and turn around and put up her hands to protect her head she tripped, landed hard on her side. The frozen ground beat the wind out of her, and Telyn lay still, sucking air.

Telyn's furry flack friend freed the feathered hind and doesn't always appreciate annoying alliteration and assonance.

That sounded like something Quid would come up with, but the voice was all wrong. What kind of a weirdo was this?

"Wh-who are you?" Telyn said, rising to her elbows and peering around the dark woods. "How do you know all...all these things that aren't true?"

Telyn is a liar, liar, stockings a-fire. She tells Cressida—

A small tickle on her ankle alerted her, like an ant crawling into her sock. Telyn ripped her foot backwards, snapping the small root or vine that had snagged her, and the voice cut off abruptly. She unwound the vine from her ankle and held it against the moon.

Little branches tipped with round leaves grew on opposite sides all along its length. Even in the dim light light, she knew what this was.

"A rumor tree," groaned Telyn. "Of course! If only I had an ax."

One of the smaller trees in the vicinity, the rumor tree resembled a willow, its branches drooping like the tresses of a shaggy-haired busy-body. Now that she stared hard, Telyn could make out rustling that wasn't justified by the wind. Round leaves scratched and rubbed together, sounding for all the world like words, for the tree was anxious to spread the latest gab.

And gab it would.

By sleeping against its trunk for as long as she had, Telyn had given the tree the juiciest morsels it'd likely ever heard. It'd be talking about "that Brower girl" for ages. The *face stealer*, *thief hanger*, and *friend to feathered hind-freer*. Her entire confession was indexed and cataloged, conveniently located only a few hours from Harlech for anyone to come listen to.

Telyn hated the things.

Quid used to keep a potted rumor tree on his desk at school. If you were particularly naughty, he'd make you hold onto its trunk, and the tree would spread all kinds of rumors about you. Worst of all, the rumors had their basis in truth. Somehow, the magical trees skimmed your mind and took the so-embarrassing-you-could-die things, jumbled them all up, and whispered them to anyone willing to touch it. This led to a game of truth-or-dare at school, because the price for acquiring another's secrets was that the tree would skim your own.

Only a nutter like Quid would happily feed the tree with his own mental drivel. One day, when Quid got to school late, Tabbard had dumped the tree outside and run it through with a shovel—one of the few things he'd ever done which Telyn approved of.

Rumor trees were rare. Trappers used them as location markers, and for leaving messages to those who followed. You could touch the bark and think something real hard, and for several months, the tree would repeat the information to anyone who passed by. Of course, to leave or collect information, you had to be willing to touch the tree and start a whole series of rumors about yourself.

A costly way to send a message: lay your soul bare to any and all. Talk to the tree long enough, and even the squirrels would know the color of your underthings.

And yet, she'd already paid the price. The rumor tree had swiped her most intimate secrets, distorted and jumbled though they might be, and no way could Telyn take them back short of chopping the tree down at the roots. These rumors were so wild and amazing that only someone intimately familiar with her story would be able to decipher them. Hanging a thief at the Sepulcher? Stealing a face? Who under Aumerhem's midden would have any idea what that meant?

Someone like Taito-Vaiana or Yona Unega—or Minister Svemas, that's who.

Yeah right. They'd just happen to be traipsing through the woods in this particular place, following the frozen creek, no doubt. Then they'd reach out a finger and touch the rumor tree just for giggles. They'd learn everything about Telyn and the Ever-Guise and all—and give the tree the opportunity to skim all their own secrets.

No, disaster had become opportunity.

The tree might have useful information—such as how to get back to Harlech. Telyn wasn't entirely sure she could retrace her steps. She could start down the frozen creek easily enough, but when would she turn east and cut across the forest to town?

Was it even east?

If she chose wrong, she could arrive at the Elbus River miles off course with no idea whether she should turn up- or downriver. Guess wrong, and she might travel for days in the wrong direction. She had no food, no way to make a fire, and no bedroll. Her situation was rather dire—one of those situations the trapper Redbeard warned schoolkids about. The Chaos Woods had swallowed armies of people before her. It could swallow one more without even a burp.

The rumor tree's branches writhed like watergrass in a current. Telyn took a deep breath, reached out, and took hold of the offered twigs.

Embarrassed by her body is Brower, legs too long for her torso, chest as flat as a potato-cake, and hairy armpits that collect malodorous smell like—

"My armpits do not collect smell!" she countered hotly. Then she sniffed, just to be sure, and winced. "Is your bole a nose that you care?"

She reeks, she sneaks, the Too-tall girl is kind of a freak—thinks about the Ouzeley boy all the time. Hot on her mind is Tabbard.

"I do not!"

How can she get back at him? How can she attack Tabbard and his family? How can she grab his attention? A kiss, or a stab?

Twins who don't want to follow the footsteps of their boozing mother, each fighting in her own way. One mother-smothers; one sips power. Just a nip, a lick of the Ever-Guise, and the pain slips away.

Telyn nearly choked on the direct reference to the mask.

Lied to Cressida, lies of omission, lies of deception. Broke their own Dragon Tower rules like fools...

What about Caitlin? Why did she betray them? Was it Joram, or the forum of girls around Hosh? Or was she trying to protect Telyn so she wouldn't get hurt?

A dozen voices spoke over each other now, many of them gossiping near-truths from Telyn's life, while others whispered about earlier travelers: a raccoon that didn't wash its food; a vole that plucked out its own whiskers to see what it felt like; a buzzard with indigestion; a trapper named Masha who lost her nose to frostbite and improved her looks in the process; a feathered hind that spent three nights under the rumor tree's branches and just missed a *herd* of feathered hinds.

She wondered about that for a second. Could this be the hind Rayvn had freed on the bridge? What was this about a whole herd of hinds?

Then she caught Redbeard's name.

No big surprise there. *Everyone* knew Redbeard, the short, stocky trapper who taught children the basics of woodland survival, the man with a story for every hour of the day, and the only one who could deliver mail to Enshede and back in the dead of winter.

"Redbeard!" Telyn said excitedly. "Does Redbeard come here? Is he close?"

Several voices took up the chant:

> *Redbeard passed here.*
> *Redbeard lives near and drinks beer.*
> *Left a turd. Lost the herd.*
> *Lost. Telyn is lost. Abandoned. Father dead,*
>   *died in the mountains with the baker*
>   *and Raz.*
> *Hunters will kill both of you.*
> *Telyn loves Redbeard...*

"What's that you said?" Telyn asked. "What did you say about the hunters killing both of us?"

The hunters are circling, closing. Danger on all sides. They're right behind you.

Hot crush, that's what her friends say, hot for Joram.

"That's it, love, just don't be moving. You're in a pickle jar, and you don't even know it." A woman's voice came from the direction of the frozen creek. It was a real voice, not one in her head like the rumor tree. "Careful now, no quick moves."

Telyn had been so absorbed in the tree's gossip she hadn't been paying attention to the woods. It could've been a fatal mistake. She'd been lucky a predator hadn't sprung an ambush. But depending on who stood behind her, this could be worse.

She turned slowly.

Redbeard stood behind her, his hands up in a cautionary gesture. "You're talking loud enough to attract all the rakasuras for a dozen miles around. Lucky we found you first. Now, a little to your right, careful," Redbeard said, gesturing with his fingers—only, he didn't have Redbeard's voice. His was the woman's voice.

Telyn screwed her fists into her eyes. *Yup, still Redbeard, I'm sure of it.* "Are you...Redbeard's sister?"

Climbing into view from the frozen creek, seven or eight wolves flanked the bearded woman on either side. These were *big* wolves, their heads easily reaching Telyn's waist. They glared at Telyn with hungry, yellow eyes. Tongues lolled and fangs glistened in the moonlight. The largest, a brownish-black beast with white cheeks and alert ears, growled deep in its throat.

Telyn took an involuntary step back. This couldn't be the real Redbeard. He would never travel with wolves.

"Not that right," the woman cautioned, "your other right. Step easy, now."

Ignoring the advice, Telyn turned and sprinted. If she could make it to a chaos tree, she could climb out of the wolves' reach.

Redbeard's doppelganger called, "No, don't!"

A snake slithered under the leaves. She bound over it.

Run. Escape. Thought melted to fear to action. *Run. Climb. Escape.*

The wolves leapt into motion. They wouldn't stop now that Telyn had marked herself the prey. She had to escape or die. Some of them yipped; one of them howled.

The hunt was on.

She took another step, then something grabbed hold of her legs and drew them tightly together. Telyn fell, and her skull cracked on a stone while the thing jerked her ankles backwards and up, up, up like a javelin. She caught a brief glimpse of the wolves leaping, snapping, and then she was dangling far above them, spinning on the rope as the pack gathered and yipped in frustration.

She'd been caught in a snare!

Staring up at her, the false Redbeard's face split in a wide grin then began to guffaw.

As Telyn watched, the wolves melted, shimmering and straightening their backs as they each rose to stand on two feet. The howls of frustration became howls of laughter.

Werewolves!

Then she realized that each of them looked like Redbeard—short, rotund, naked Redbeards. They stood below her in a semicircle, laughing and pointing. Blood rushed to her head; her vision blurred. Blood migrated down her hair from the split in her head to drip, drip, drip onto the ground. As the cord twisted her around, black dots crawled over her vision and pulled Telyn unconscious.

CHAPTER TWENTY-FOUR

When Telyn came to her senses, she found herself in a large clearing surrounded by tight, thorny vegetation. All around sat the bearded and hairy Redbeards. Each was now fully clothed, thankfully, in boots, blue overalls, and woolen plaid of various patterns and colors, red and yellow and blue and everything between. Her feet sweated, her shoes lay close to a crackling campfire—the source of light and heat.

She pulled her feet under herself and sat up, crisscross. They'd removed her jacket and boots, but she didn't need them. The bushes reflected the campfire's heat back at them.

One of the few plants that could compete with chaos trees for ground, camp bushes grew outward in concentric rings year by year and died in the middle. Eventually, they formed a protective circle with a clearing inside. One had to shimmy under the three-inch spines to get to the center, typically tearing their clothes and skin in the process, but it kept the largest predators away.

The bearded female she'd encountered first shuffled over until their shoulders touched. "We cleaned your boots, but it turns out you didn't step in scat after all, did you?"

"Er…"

The Ever-Guise's magic backfiring must have infected her with some kind of noxious smell, but Telyn couldn't very well say that, could she?

Caitlin...hideous.

"No mind. A person's smell is her own business, I always say." The woman held out some kind of smoked meat. Fat dribbled from her fingers to the dirt. "Travel here often?"

Telyn accepted the greasy meat and chewed it gladly. She'd had mystery meat in the Sable Head since she could walk; this couldn't be any worse. It rewarded with a gamey flavor like smoked venison, much better than the marmot Razenbock used for speck.

The scabs and scrapes on Telyn's face felt tight as she chewed, and even tighter when she remarked, "You have a beard."

"Aye. You first."

A little blood trickled into Telyn's mouth from her cut lip. She took a second to clear her teeth with tongue and fingernail—and to think about how to respond. These creatures may have saved her life, and they certainly held her life in their hands. They might guide her back to Harlech or drop her into the stewpot, for all she knew. Were-wolves weren't known for hospitality.

Snared like a curious animal. What a fool I am.

Conversation among the bearded creatures had stopped. They made no pretense of doing anything except listening.

"I got lost."

The female raised bushy eyebrows for Telyn to continue.

"I, ah, was running. I was outside of Harlech when there was this explosion, some kind of magic. It frightened me, and I ran until I didn't know how to find my way home. I, ah, found the creek and followed it. I figured it would help me find the way back. And...and I figured I wouldn't leave any tracks in case something was following me."

"Did you see what caused the explosion?"

The werewolves must had seen it too, otherwise they'd have disbelieved her or acted surprised. These folks were judging Telyn, trying to decide what to do with her.

Out here in the Chaos Wood, cornic law didn't apply. Out here, people and creatures made their own law.

She had to tread very carefully, skate as close to the truth as possible without breaking through the ice. No matter what, they couldn't learn about the Ever-Guise.

No matter what.

"It, er, the explosion was in the top of a tree, way up high. It boomed like a star had fallen to earth. I could hardly see for the light in my eyes."

It took tremendous effort not to squirm under the werewolves' scrutiny.

"Why were you in the woods?"

Telyn swallowed. She didn't have the equipment, nor the look, of a trapper. "Climbing. I-I like to climb. And I was mad. Angry mad, not rabid-squirrel mad. My best friend back-stabbed me. She, she went out with someone I don't like." Some of the creatures chuckled. "And they beat up my friend, hurt him bad. I didn't know what to do. And when I don't know what to do, I climb. I was out in the woods looking for a tree to climb, then there was that explosion, and I ran. It was a total accident that I found the rumor tree."

"You wanted to climb a tree, and then there happened to be an explosion in the top of a tree."

"Yeah."

"Hmm." The werewolf woman stared at her with black, soulless eyes for a long time. It was a soul-piercing stare, a secret-sifting stare. Finally, she reached toward her companion, who passed her a drink-bladder, and handed it to Telyn. Telyn pulled the cork and put it to her lips. The contents were deliciously warm—hot spiced cider.

Telyn had almost been hoping for angel water.

"Dried rakasura tends to stick in the throat," the woman said.

"So do half-truths," one of the men added.

Telyn nearly choked.

"I have a beard," the woman said, ignoring the comment, "because I am a gnome. We are hairier than humans—and better looking."

"And fatter," another woman said. She jiggled her gigantic belly to demonstrate.

"Are you going to eat me?"

They all laughed. They seemed a jovial lot for werewolves—gnomes—were-gnomes?

"No, girl," the first woman said between guffaws. She seemed to be the leader of the group. "We have enough rakasura meat for today. I am called Kiiptk. Kiiptk of the Boiling Spring."

"I am Telyn Brower."

"Of Harlech, sister of Cressida, friend of Redbeard."

"Yes."

Had they been listening to the rumor tree? Mother of Squirrels, what else had they heard? Her goose might be cooked in its own fat if they understood even a fraction of the tales that blasted tree would tell.

Keeping her gaze downward, Telyn savored the spiced cider one sip at a time, tasting apples, cloves, cinnamon, and brown sugar. She'd better enjoy it since it might be the last drink she ever had. The air didn't feel quite as warm as it had a moment before.

Kiiptk reached out and wrapped Telyn's wrist in meaty fingers with a grip like a blacksmith. "We thought you might be one we've been looking for, a murderer with many crimes to answer for. Calls himself Mantle." Kiiptk's face rippled, flowed, *changed*, and Telyn was looking at a fair imitation of her own face, if Telyn wore a red beard to her waist. "But I think the rumor tree refers to a kind of mask. Am I right?"

Telyn swallowed and nodded.

"Mind wizards, pattern witches, hanging thieves... A heavy load for a young woman to carry, I think." With a squelch, Kiiptk's face snapped back into shape. She proceeded to slap herself several times, tug on her ears, and tweak her bulbous nose energetically. "By the Sacred Armadillo, that hurts! Too dang old for shifting." She glanced sideways at Telyn's wide-eyed stare. "You try it, why don't you? Want me to pull your ears and smear your nose?"

"Er...no thank you."

"Ah, nevermind. Skin don't stretch the way it used to—like

squeezing molasses through a pinhole. If I'd tried stretching my old bones to your height, you'd have thought a glacier done melted with the crackling and popping. Blast it, what a fool for showing off. No, nevermind, Telyn of Harlech, you have nothing to fear from the Boiling Springers. A friend of Redbeard is a friend of ours."

Kiiptk gave her face two more slaps, then glared around. The other gnomes wiped the grins from their faces and began doing their own things: mending clothes, polishing boots, packing rucksacks—as mundane as mundane could get. Occasionally, one of them glanced back at Kiiptk and snickered when they thought she wasn't paying attention.

They sat there a while, Kiiptk and Telyn side-by-side, Kiiptk massaging her cheeks and nose and glaring at anyone who dared smile, and Telyn enjoying the hot spiced cider warming her belly. Her hair felt like a sticky glob on her head, but she'd deal with that later. Finally, she worked up the courage to ask what she really wanted to know.

"Is Redbeard one of you? A gnome, I mean. He looks a lot—"

Kiiptk shifted and stood. "You'll be wanting to get back to Harlech, now, won't you?"

Oops, wrong question.

Telyn nodded.

"Doggha and Elandspad will take you back to town after the sun rises. Won't be long now, three hours." The gnome chief peered into the treetops as if able to read the time in the starless sky.

"Thank you for saving me." Telyn rose to stand beside Kiiptk.

The gnome smiled kindly at Telyn. "It gets lonely out here in the woods. Sooner or later, everyone ends up at a rumor tree. Feels comforting, hearing stories about yourself, about others. Makes you feel important to know someone is talking about you, no matter what they're saying. No matter that it's just a silly tree, sooner or later you don't even care if the rumors are true, positive or negative. Always snares around rumor trees—and predators looking for an easy meal. This time, we gnomes set 'em. Next time, it could be something more sinister, so be careful.

"There's been a pack of rakasuras running this area, and the cornics pay for every set of ears. Never thought our traps'd catch a girl." Kiiptk reached up to tug on Telyn's ear. She practically had to stand on tiptoe to reach that high.

It felt oddly agreeable. Telyn liked it.

"All the way here, you were mumbling in your sleep. Something about Tabbard, a hot crush, and a forehead. He your boyfriend?"

Telyn's stomach lurched. "Tabbard? I do not have a crush!"

"Easy, girl, I believe you. Never been into foreheads, myself. Now, a strong bicep, yes. Or a broad chest." Kiiptk licked her lips, then barked, "Elandspad! Bring a rag and warm water for the girl. Her hair's a mess.

"The shape you're in, Telyn, it'll take a full day to walk you back to Harlech. And, no offense, but we'll have to blindfold you. This is our bush, see, and if we show up and find others camped inside, things could get ugly."

"I, ah, I understand."

"Good, good. Having a camp bush to sleep inside can mean life or death here in the woods."

Telyn made the gesture for buttoning her mouth.

CHAPTER TWENTY-FIVE

At the pattern witch's house, a rainbow of fabrics billowed in a vivacious welcome—completely in contrast with Telyn's mood. Fabric trembled before her glare; the beaded front door parted like a shimmering waterfall.

The elder pattern witch arrived at the foyer at the same time as Telyn, holding a ball of some kind of dough, flour up to her elbows. She twitched her eyebrow and mouth whiskers in a smile—a distinctly un-flack-like reaction to Telyn. The ears had something to do with it too, the way they swiveled forward gaily.

Her countenance drooped as she registered Telyn's state. "What happened to you?"

"I slipped."

Mrs. de Galati touched Telyn's face gently. Five days had passed since the gnomes had escorted her home, but she still looked like she'd been trampled by a herd of mamocks.

"And rolled a few times," Telyn explained, wincing at Mrs. de Galati's touch to the knot on her skull. "A cliff."

"The cornics have a healer, a medic named Findor Rusk. He's even willing to work on injured humans."

"Er...thanks. I met him."

"You will go see him immediately."

"I'll go see him...after I speak with Rayvn. It's, ah, important. Please, Mrs. de Galati—"

"She's in her room. Through here, up the stairs, first opening on the right. Shoes off. Spinosa infusion?"

"No, thanks."

A corridor of blues and purples offered several curtained entries— *A perfect match for my bruises* and *my mood*—and Telyn found herself spiraling up a wooden staircase.

Step by step, she reviewed what had brought her to this place. She was curious like she'd never been curious before. She wanted to know what the Ever-Guise was. She wanted to know how it worked and who made it. How old was it?

Naturally, there were practical reasons. Who would be coming after it? Who had Dagger stolen it from? Who else did she have to fear?

And the big one: *What else could it do?*

She had some idea of the forehead's powers, but what about the rest? How powerful would it be if completely assembled? Had Dagger separated the forehead because of greed, or did he fear the consequences of transferring that much power to Yona and Taito-Vaiana?

These were the thoughts that had driven her to the pattern witches' house—to Rayvn—despite a lifetime of prejudice.

On the second floor, a shag rug covered the structure's wooden bones; Telyn's toes fell in love. The fabric walls became even more magnificent, now ornamented with sylvan scenes in gold and silver thread, an entire storybook spun on the walls and ceiling.

Telyn wanted to be mad at the wealth, irritated that all this magnificence came at no work at all, crafted through birth magic, or race magic, whatever you wanted to call it. The pattern witches hardly had to practice at all—not like Cressida with thread and needle. All the witches had to do was think it, and they could make it.

At least, so Telyn presumed.

She slowed to run her fingers over the stitching, a silver stag and doe, and discovered reluctant admiration.

The corridor stirred.

It would be something to be in this house during a lightning storm—a storm such as I intend to bring down on Tabbard and his goons.

At the first opening on the right, Telyn brushed aside strands of colorful beads and entered the first flack bedroom she had ever seen. Rather than the greens, silvers and golds of the corridor, the weaves of Rayvn's bedroom showed a cityscape: tiled roofs; horse-drawn carts and chariots; vistas of red, yellow, and orange populated by members of every race from cornic to conda to human. All seemed to coexist peacefully, which made Telyn cluck her tongue in disbelief. The ceiling reflected the same scene upside down, producing a feeling of vertigo.

She pulled her eyes back to Rayvn, who sat on a three-legged stool that seemed to be made of glass and studied a shabby green doily. The flack didn't bother to look up.

A baby could have made a better doily than that. Maybe Esther made it after a bender. Clearly, Mrs. de Galati is the talent in this duo.

"Rayvn," she said, "you and I have to talk."

After a long moment, Rayvn said airily, "Oh, hello Telyn Brower. You stink." Her attention never left the doily.

"Yeah. Foot infection."

Time passed. Telyn tapped her foot a few times on the carpet. She cleared her throat.

Rayvn's white skirt barely covered her knees. Guest or no guest, she had no compunction about showing her furry ankles. Her tail swished left and right, its tip as white as if dipped in whipped cream.

Typical flack, ignoring the human as if she didn't exist. I should have known better than to expect anything different. No matter how friendly they seem—no matter how ostracized from other flacks and needful of companionship—they all consider themselves superior to humans. If I hadn't come asking a favor, I'd walk right out of here. Telyn had picked up an ear infection in the woods, and she began to count the painful throbs to see if they matched her heartbeat. *One, two...*

...seventeen, eighteen...

At *thirty*, Rayvn's doily sprang apart. Apparently, the whole thing had been made using just one string.

"Well done," Telyn conceded.

Rayvn balled it in her palm and blew it down to join other discarded string-balls. "I was trying to fix it."

"Well, if you had an eehoo, it would prefer balls to a doily," Telyn said.

"Any more ghost trouble?"

"No, no. Tums is fine."

Finally, Rayvn lifted her gaze. "The side of your face is turning yellow, Telyn Brower. You should put ice on it. If only we had a tylwig. They can turn water into ice in their bellies. Unfortunately, I don't have that ability. Tylwig babies require freezing temperatures to mature properly."

"My face has met its share of ice recently—and slush, and mud—thank you very much." Telyn touched her cheek gingerly then raised her eyebrows in horrified understanding. "These tylwig-thing-ys make ice in some sort of, like, birth canal?"

"It's very prized by the bartenders of Vool. They are quite fond of exotic cocktails, the Vools. My friend was killed by a cocktail called Skinny Sipping with Nereids," Rayvn said without inflection. "She shouldn't have eaten the gallbladder."

As easy as breathing, Rayvn switched subjects. "Mom says your blood has been helping the spell hold better than she expected. It is strong blood, if a bit erratic, slippery around the edges but deep red in the heart notch."

"That is just...weird."

Rayvn began humming. Despite her high, airy voice, the tune vibrated Telyn's diaphragm.

It came to Telyn that asking Rayvn for help was a terrible idea for so many reasons.

A cocktail gallbladder killed her best friend? Is she joking?

Who knows? Who cares? The flack is a first-class airhead. You never know what nonsense will come out of her mouth. True, that would be some protection in that no one takes her seriously, but still—Rayvn would likely blab to the wrong person and give everything away.

Besides, if Rayvn goes around asking about the Ever-Guise, it will draw attention. The cornics may not know much, but they know they are looking for a magical artifact. The cordon is closing in, and too many people know about the forehead piece already: Hosh, Caitlin, the mind wizard, the schmook, the daemon, whoever Dagger stole it from....

At least Cressida doesn't know anything; I've managed to keep my sister out of it.

As if that was why I didn't tell her anything.

Just thinking about the forehead piece made her want to see it, make sure it was safe, use it to bring misery on Tabbard for bullying Hosh, use it to teach that traitor Caitlin a lesson she'd never forget.

I need to find it. It must be in the snow beneath the chaos tree.

It must.

Why am I wasting my time here? I need to look again; I need to use the Ever-Guise!

Telyn spun on her heel, determined to go to the Chaos Woods right this second and search until she found the forehead or frostbite made searching impossible.

Gauze slid over the beaded curtain.

"Sorry for wasting your time. Got to go." Telyn brushed aside the fabric—and found another layer. Through the semi-transparent material, the hanging crystal beads mocked her.

"Curtains don't interest me, Rayvn. Please open the door."

She moved the fabric aside, only to find yet another layer. Every time Telyn moved a stole, a muslin, a gauze, another layer wiggled behind it. She tried shoving her body by the edge, but she got all twisted up.

Still humming, the pattern girl retrieved a handful of colorful string-balls from the carpet and straightened them over her palm.

"A—little—help—here," Telyn said, pushing and twisting, getting further and further wrapped up until cloth enveloped her feet, her legs, her body. The fabric wriggled like river eels, and she struggled harder. Now she knew what a mouse felt like when wrestling a snake. Red linen pinned her arms to her sides, yellow silk covered her eyes, slippery satin constricted her mouth, her nose.

Finally, blind and huffing, Telyn sagged into the doorway, her breath puffing silk in and out, her legs no longer carrying her weight. She might just die here, a chiffon-entombed mummy.

The fabric smothered the fight right out of her, leaving only help-lessness and fatigue. It might have been funny if she stood on the outside looking in.

Tabbard would have loved it.

"Let me out now, flack." With cloth constricting her mouth, it came out as "Le ee ow now, ffaa."

A tear opened in the yellow silk, allowing Telyn to see but unhelp-fully leaving her otherwise bound. "Watch closely." The threads in Rayvn's hand spun, wove, tightened, formed a lanyard. Five strings dangled from one end. "Pick."

The lanyard reminded Telyn of the one Caitlin wore on her wrist, the one Joram Lycurgus had given her. "String doesn't interest me." ('Sing don in-est ee.') Telyn tried to turn away, but that caused her to bob like a cork in a pond. Sweat began to slick her armpits—all these layers of fabric trapped body heat like a sauna.

Her magic-induced stink became particularly ripe.

"Le ee go, Ra-n."

"You're looking for a pattern. Why else would you have come to a pattern girl?" Rayvn nodded again at the five dangling strings in her hand.

More fabric split, freeing Telyn's hand. Unable to escape, Telyn pinched a pink string between index and thumb. She tugged. The thread pulled free.

"One of them doesn't belong with the others. Pick again."

"Don ew ow it in oli..."

"Eh?"

The satin loosened enough for Telyn to enunciate. "Don't you know it isn't polite to tangle a guest in your dirty laundry?"

"Dangle or pick, your choice."

Telyn examined the lanyard with annoyance. The knots—or what-ever you called them—weren't identical. There were minute differ-ences. Some were square, others bumpy, and others looked incomplete. Not all of them had every color...at least visibly.

She almost picked the blue thread, but the way it appeared always on the outside of the knots seemed too obvious. A trap.

"Will you let me go if I play?"

Rayvn cocked her head like a cat looking at a mouse, waiting for it to make a move.

Telyn sighed. *So much for bargaining when you have no leverage.*

She pulled yellow because it dove straight into the lanyard's heart and didn't show itself again until the other end. The string slipped a bit, and suddenly, the whole lanyard opened into a fantastic, multicolored doily depicting a chaos tree. Little ovals in each of three corners containing white squirrels.

Telyn widened her eyes in reluctant admiration. But there was a flaw: The fourth corner had completely unraveled.

"I picked the right one. Now un-spell this door and let me go."

"My mother would say they are all right, but only one leads to a beautiful doily. The others unravel it—which is a pattern too, of sorts."

Trying to keep her patience, Telyn asked again. "Please let me go."

"To make the full tree with all four squirrels, we would have to restart from the beginning." The fabric imprisoning Telyn loosened, and she thrust her arms out. She had half a mind to try ripping the fabric along its seams, tearing herself free and tearing the whole dang house down—and half a mind to lure Rayvn close enough to slap her silly.

A pair of fabric shears would do nicely for this house!

But that beautiful doily demonstrated something. A friend like Rayvn would be nearly as useful as the Ever-Guise. That fight with Tabbard and his goons would have gone very differently if Rayvn had been on their side. Think if Rayvn had sewn their pant legs together!

Telyn wiped the sweat from her forehead. "All right, Rayvn. I'll stay." *As if I have any choice.* "I have a favor to ask."

"What is your favor, Telyn Brower?"

She needed to phrase this carefully, diplomatically, and definitely not desperately. "I need to make an inquiry at the Library. But, as a human, I'm not allowed."

"Is it something dangerous?" That sparkle returned to her eyes. *Rayvn hoped it was dangerous!*

"Not too dangerous, but, well, yes, a little." *That's so crazy! Why in the world...*

But it made sense. Telyn liked her climbs to be dangerous—not impossible, but with a little danger, a little risk. Yes, she got it.

A claw protruded from Rayvn's index finger, and she clink, clink, clinked it against her glass stool. "Philosopher Aled said, 'Two cleaved with love split kingdoms forged with iron; webs forged from love trap better than a spider. Iron decays to rust and buildings to dust, but love remains.' Love is the great mystery, Telyn Brower."

"You quote human philosophers? I'm more of a Gruffud the Irreverent fan." Something tugged at Telyn's mind, and it flew back to her first conversation with Rayvn. "Love? You're talking about the Dating Chart. Look, I've spent my life entire trying to avoid it. I don't look at it; I don't think about it; I hope those busybodies forget to put me on it."

"Oh, you're on it, in the very corner, along with Widow Vinta."

Widow Vinta—she's about a hundred years old. Telyn was horrified. *Do they really think I'm that unmatchable?* She tried to force a smile. "If you want help placing a bet, I can—"

"Not placing a bet, Telyn Brower, being placed with bets on."

"Huh?"

"Bets on me." Rayvn's whiskers twitched. "I want to get onto the Dating Chart. And you are going to help me."

Half a dozen gamble flies could have flown in and out of Telyn's mouth before she snapped it closed. "*You're kidding*. You're not kidding. Rayvn! No way will the Circle let you onto the Dating Chart. That's a human thing, the oldest, most human thing of all— besides the Sepulcher, of course." Before Rayvn could retort, Telyn added quickly, "And who would *want* to get on it? Love shouldn't be written on circles and charts for everyone to bet on!

"The Dating Chart isn't about love, it's about money! Hurons, capiche? That's all the Dating Chart is—people getting into your affairs so they can bet on them. For the love of ground squirrels, it's run by Grebiana Ouzeley."

"No one loves ground squirrels."

"Exactly."

"Tree squirrels and chipmunks, yes. They are cuddly. But not foundation-undermining, pear-stealing ground squirrels."

Telyn nodded.

"But you and I, Telyn, we sit outside the patterns."

"Fie on your patterns." Telyn had finally had enough—enough of flacks, enough of Rayvn, enough of being trussed up like a foot inside of three pairs of stockings. "Let me out of this...this sackcloth...and I'll show you what I think."

"You want to break the patterns. You are going to break them. And I am going to help you figure out how."

The fabric around Telyn split. She fell against the wall, bounced back, and shoved Rayvn as hard as she could. The feline barely shifted. She was a lot heavier than she appeared.

"What is wrong with you, Rayvn? What is your problem?"

"Not with me, Telyn Brower—with us. What is wrong with us?"

"Tell me why you want so badly to be on the Chart."

"You first. Why do you want to inquire at the Library?"

That did it. Telyn's throat contracted; her glutes tightened; her eyes became dry as ribbon candy. "I...er...I found something. I need to know more about it."

Rayvn's white-tipped tail twitched. "Something magical. You found what the mind wizard is searching for."

Am I that transparent? "The less you know, the better. You can send in the inquiry—"

"Study," Rayvn interrupted. "I must present original research to the Temple if I am ever to be allowed into the Order of Farseers. This Dating Chart blends the mathematics of gambling and the unpredictability of love. What could be a better field of study for a Pattern Master?"

The order of whats?

Telyn shook her head and decided she really didn't want to hear a long-winded explanation that she would only half-understand. She went to the heart of things. "You don't intend to date a human?"

"Date a human? Telyn Brower, that would be strange."

Relief flooded through her, and Telyn burst out laughing. "Order of Farseers, like a degree from the Academy of Enshede or something?" The whole idea struck her as hilarious. She could just picture

Rayvn scribbling tight-looped notes on endless scrolls about human dating. Too rich.

Besides, she really wasn't risking anything. The Dating Circle women would never, ever let a flack onto the Dating Chart. That would ruin everything. If nothing else, it would break hundreds of years of tradition.

The Dating Circle would be the bad guy. She didn't have to do anything.

"Rayvn, I think we might just have a deal."

Rayvn offered her a bare palm; Telyn pressed her hand against it. A hooked, cat's claw extended from Rayvn's pinkie. "I will send your inquiry after you get me on the Dating Chart."

"What? No! I can't guarantee—"

Rayvn's ears flattened on her skull. The glass beads in the doorway rattled menacingly. "You have sworn on naked palms, Telyn Brower."

"I can't guarantee anything. I'm not in charge. I—I'll do my best—"

"You will get me on it, and then I will send the inquiry, or else I will tell Minister Svemas you found the missing mask." A human might have puffed out her chest at such a declaration, but the pattern witch rounded into her shoulders and sank her hips: a cat preparing to leap onto a table, a feline preparing to explode. It might have been subconscious—but then again, maybe not. Either way, Rayvn appeared doubly dangerous. "Do I make myself clear?"

You have never *sounded clear until just now.* Telyn nodded.

CHAPTER TWENTY-SIX

A few evenings later, as a sunset painted the rooftops pink and shadows stretched from one edge of Middle Street to the other, Telyn and Rayvn moved down the dirt lane together, Telyn unconsciously balling her fists, Rayvn with wide-eyed pleasure.

The pattern girl's nearness brought back their previous conversation, and Telyn couldn't help muttering to herself.

"What is *wrong* with us!"

"What is wrong with *us*?"

"*What is* wrong with us..."

Telyn kept repeating this under her breath, accenting different words to create different meanings, making it an exclamation or a question—but always hearing it in Rayvn's airy voice, as if the pattern girl abided in Telyn's head like a furry brain tumor.

The only thing wrong with me, Telyn thought with a sideways glance at Rayvn—who had just skipped like a little girl—*is that I spend too much time with flacks.*

Not really a house at all, the 'public house' occupied the second floor of a townhouse opposite Rusty Shackles infusionary. Anyone could use it on sufficient notice, but it was primarily known as the meeting place of various women's groups, especially that most important women's group, the Dating Circle.

A brass knocker in the shape of a heart marked the entrance. A sign above the door read, "Wear your heart in your hand, all ye who enter here." Telyn cringed every time she read it. The meaning was obvious: You were supposed to tell these busybodies all your hush-hush so they could calculate odds and place bets on your love life. As if it were any of their business!

Just because they used the proceeds—some of them, anyway—for widows and orphans... It was a likely excuse, a guilty-conscience bribe so the town didn't rise up in arms.

It didn't help when a furry finger gently tickled her wrist, followed by Rayvn's purring voice. "You humans are so romantic." It all made Telyn want to spew. But there was nothing for it. She'd made that naked palm promise.

And she needed information from the Library, blast it.

She rapped the knocker a couple of times. The door opened, Hosh's mother on the other side, smiling and bowing and greeting Rayvn like visiting royalty. Hosh stood behind her, wringing his hands and probably embarrassed at his mother's obsequiousness.

"Hello, Mrs. Gamage."

"Ravyn de Galati. Welcome, welcome." Mrs. Gamage's voice quavered. "This is a real privilege. We have been trying to interest fla... er...thaumas in betting for years. It could be a real boon to...ah...to everyone. I have been authorized to assist you to some degree— nothing out of the public eye, so to speak. Now, the Scurloch girl, she might look like a haggard spinster, but I can tell you she and Nathan Hawk have practically reserved the barn stall—"

"A bet?" Rayvn's tail darted from under her long skirt and gave Telyn three sharp taps in her calf.

"Um." Telyn cleared her throat. "We are here for the Dating Circle meeting, Mrs. Gamage."

She'd told Hosh that Rayvn wanted to learn something about betting—which was the truth! But Telyn would rather die than admit that both she and Rayvn planned on joining the Dating Circle.

And here she was—dying.

She avoided Hosh's eyes.

"You are?" Mrs. Gamage blinked a couple of times. "Well, they've already started. You've missed the introductions. Why are you late?"

Relief flooded through Telyn at missing the introductions. "Work. Washing dishes." Telyn displayed the dry skin on the back of her hands as proof, though in truth she'd delayed deliberately, hoping they could slip into the meeting unnoticed.

"Well, go on up then. But don't be surprised if you're made an example of."

Mrs. Gamage waved Telyn up the stairs. But as the pair began to move, she blocked Rayvn. "And where are you going, young, ah, pattern person?"

"She's with me." Telyn reached back, grabbed Rayvn's hand, and pulled her along. Hosh followed.

The stair's treads creaked as they ascended.

"Here, you'll be wanting to fill this out." Hosh handed Telyn a parchment. "There'll be ink and quills in the meeting room."

"Why aren't you inside?"

"I've been through it every year since I was five. I'm now a Dating Assistant," Hosh said with pride.

"And you haven't told me?"

"'What happens in the meetings stays in the meetings.' My mom is Mistress of Romance, remember."

Telyn couldn't think of anyone less equipped to be a Dating Assistant than Hosh, but seeing his pride, she kept that to herself.

In the light of a hanging lantern halfway up the stairs, Telyn paused to look at the questionnaire. The heading of page one read, "A slug line about me." Followed by questions about height, hair and eye color, and a list of "My favorite things."

Telyn couldn't believe anyone would voluntarily give all this information to a bunch of rumor-tree wannabes. "Everything is so twisted. Love is—should be—I don't know, sacred. Pure. Private. But this" — Telyn smacked the sheets against her palm—"this is pure gold."

"Wait until you see the Intimate Intimacies questionnaire," Hosh said. "Come on, they haven't done much yet. You can still get in on the beginning."

They resumed climbing.

"Hosh, you fail to see the opportunity here."

"You keep that idea to yourself, or your membership will be record-short. The questionnaires are more closely guarded than Minister Svemas's horns. No one in the Dating Circle gets to see all of them, and the ones they do see have the names removed."

Telyn didn't really see how that could work. Names had to be associated with questionnaires, didn't they? Otherwise, how could folks place odds and take bets? *Someone* had all that information, no matter what Hosh thought.

She filed that away for future contemplation.

"You get all of this from everyone involved in the Dating Circle?"

"Don't even think about it, Telyn. There are other ways to get back at Caitlin than sneaking her questionnaire and spreading rumors."

"Remember our agreement, Telyn Brower," said Rayvn, sounding a lot less airy than usual. "You promised to get me on the Dating Chart as a member. A full member."

Hosh missed a step.

Telyn propelled him up with a hand on the small of his back. "That's right, Hosh, we are both joining." And more quietly, "Sorry I lied."

At the second-floor landing, Hosh grabbed the doorhandle and turned. "Everyone lies about this," he said, and pulled the door open.

A few candles dimly illuminated the interior, and a table manned by a chubby woman blocked the way. Scattered behind the woman, more people—mostly young people—sat on rugs arranged across the floor. The room stretched the entire length of the building. Just about everyone under the age of twenty-five seemed to be there, including several who had told Telyn they'd rather die than join the Dating Circle.

Telyn crinkled the bridge of her nose. *Stinking traitors.*

"Telyn Brower, sister to Cressida Brower," Hosh announced.

The chubby woman looked up from her list. She wore eyeglasses, the first Telyn had ever seen. They made the woman's eyes look crossed.

"I, uh, didn't sign up. I'm sorry."

Clearly, coming in late hadn't been the best plan to avoid notice. A man and woman, holding hands in front of the room, had been giving a testimony of some kind. Now they, and everyone else, stared at the interrupters.

And Rayvn started purring.

Purring!

"You're twenty minutes late."

"Yeah, uh, sorry. I didn't really expect to be here today."

The woman scratched a wart on her cheek. "I can smell that. Your foot infection, still? Shoes in the cubbies, socks most definitely on. Grab a quill and ink pot from the sideboard."

The people nearby snickered.

This story about a smelly foot infection must have spread all the way across the sea by now. The hideous Ever-Guise backfire *had* diminished over the preceding days, at least. It no longer made babies cry.

"Most understandable that you're nervous. Judging from your pimply cheeks, your hormones have hormones. The dry fire of loneliness tickles even the coldest heart. You are welcome here, Telyn Brower, sister of Cressida Brower, daughter of Esther and Dorian Brower."

My what have what? The nerve! Telyn touched her bumpy cheeks. Sure enough, she'd grown the mother-load. *Aled's rump, the pattern girl will pay for making me come here.*

Her cheeks on fire with the desire to itch, Telyn pushed Rayvn in front of her. "I brought a guest. This is Rayvn, uh, Rayvn..." Telyn's mind went completely blank. "Um..."

"Zamfir de Galati," Rayvn said, and thrust out her furry paw.

"You are most welcome, Miss de Galati. I am Mrs. Pembroke, sergeant at arms." The rotund woman touched Rayvn's fingertips and withdrew quickly—as if Rayvn's fur might carry mange. "We are so happy you came. As you can see, we conduct the meetings with utmost thoroughness and integrity. A clean line from information to compatibility, from compatibility to love, and from love to jackpot. You won't find a more exciting...er...more exciting *stakes* anywhere. A lifetime of happiness and contentment on the line, versus the dry misery of loneliness or worse—a bad match. A measly brakdaw fight is fiddlesticks in comparison. Thank you for coming. Bets can be placed downstairs with Mrs. Gamage. Close the door on the way out."

"Well, that's it, then," Telyn said, trying to turn Rayvn towards the door. "I did my part. Nice try." It was like trying to turn a skinny bear.

"I'm here to join the meeting," Rayvn said, ignoring Telyn's efforts.

The woman set her eyeglasses on the table. "This is a human meeting. No flacks allowed."

The conversations that had erupted all over died as quickly as they'd started.

Oh, Aled's rump, not more attention. Telyn swallowed, gathered her courage, and with as much confidence as she could project, said, "She's with me."

"She's. *With*. You." Again, Mrs. Pembroke scratched the wart. "We'll see. Sit. Shoes off." She pointed to an empty spot on the floor. As they moved to obey, she sent a young boy—who may have been her son—running out of the room with a whispered message. Hosh returned downstairs in case any more teenagers, driven by the dry fires of loneliness, showed up against their better judgment.

Telyn made room for Rayvn at her side, amazed that they'd gotten in this easily. She hadn't noticed Tristam Harries sitting right there next to Cheryle Uren when they sat down, but as the Tristam started whispering and pointing, Telyn extended her stocking foot at them.

The pair tripped all over themselves to get away.

Rayvn took Telyn's arm and purred softly. If felt nice—sort of like Tums holding her arm—and Telyn scowled. She didn't want it to feel nice. She hoped Mrs. Pembroke's son would fetch the full Dating Circle, and the Dating Circle would tell Rayvn once and for all that she couldn't join.

That must be where he's gone. All I have to do is wait. I've done my part; I kept my word. Rayvn will have to send the inquiry no matter what happens here.

In the front of the room, the couple resumed their presentation about how they thought they would be single forever but found true love through the Chart. Batted eyelashes, tilted heads, and cutesy talk ensued.

Bile tried to climb out of Telyn's throat.

"It is so romantic, don't you think?" Rayvn said.

"What happened to slaying a dragon to win your damsel?"

"They did that? How—"

"Explanations are not part of the bargain. You're here, you owe me."

People seated nearby stared at the pattern girl, Caitlin among them. Caitlin had her back pressed against Joram's back.

Traitor!

Telyn turned her head away from her former friend, only to notice a shiny-new pair of knee-high boots next to Tabbard. Her heart fell. Hosh had caved to Tabbard's ransom demand. She understood, but it felt like a betrayal nonetheless.

A betrayal to decency and courage.

Further across the room sat Cressida, eyes wide as dinner plates to see that Telyn had showed up at all...and with the pattern girl in tow!

Telyn gave her sister a brief smile.

The Dating Chart covered much of the wall behind Cressida. It showed a top-down view of Harlech, from the Sable Head in the east to flacktown in the west. The map had been painted directly on— Telyn squinted—rectangular slates fitted together to make a giant writing board. The ladies had chalked little circles all over. Inside the circles were names and equations, ratios of some kind. Right away, Telyn spotted Joram Lycargus, and she sought around until she spotted Caitlin Nest's circle nearby.

The two circles overlapped.

"Pst, fur-ball," Cheryle Uren whispered. "How do you get your fur so shiny? Do you lick yourself clean?" She mimed licking her forearm like a cat.

"Ignore her," Telyn advised. "This is not the place."

No more attention. No more attention, please.

"Go on, we want to see." Cheryle continued fake licking. "How about your tail, can you lick that?"

"How about under your tail?" Adda Swansea asked, causing the boys around him to laugh.

Rayvn's ears flattened.

"Leave the thauma alone," Caitlin said, unexpectedly.

"Yeah, leave her alone," Tristam Harries added. "No one would ever date her anyway, flack or human."

"Understatement of the year," Cheryl said. She seemed about to add something further when a button popped off her top and pinged Joram in the back of the head.

"Rayvn," Telyn warned under her breath.

No more attention, please, please...

The man in front of the room said something about sunshine and rainbows, and his wife put both arms around his head in what was sure to become some sort of icky smooch—

The door opened. Lantern-carrying women charged in and took up positions around the walls, assaulting the room with commotion and blinding light. A black curtain unrolled over the Dating Chart, concealing it.

"What is *she* doing here?" a shrill voice asked, punishing their eardrums with its pitch as much as its volume.

"That's what I want to know," exclaimed Mrs. Pembroke.

Feeling the pressure of all those disapproving ladies, those one-eyed glaring lanterns, Telyn stood. "You said this was for everyone, right?" She shielded her eyes as best she could, but the light attacked from several directions at once. "Even people who have no interest in dating? Well, we're here."

"They know you're here in the next town over with that stench," Cheryle commented.

"Dearest girl, follow my lead unless told to do otherwise," said the shrill one.

Cheryle snapped her mouth closed.

"Telyn Brower, I know your head is literally in the clouds, but what on earth are you talking about? Sit down and be quiet."

Telyn now recognized the shrill one: Tabbard's mom, Grebiana Ouzeley. Naturally. But the nasty woman did not mean to question

Telyn's presence, but Rayvn's. Telyn had the chance—the miraculous opportunity—to sit down, to take the heat off herself for a change.

No more attention—especially from the Ouzeleys, which is nearly as bad as attention from the cornics and not far from Taito-Vaiana or Yona.

She *so* wanted to sit down.

With a drunkard mom and a disappeared dad, Telyn was already considered a pariah by many—practically un-marriageable, a kitchen scullion at the Sable Head dive, a too-tall girl with a surly personality besides.

Telyn's knees bent but refused to go to the floor. Something in her spine wouldn't bend that far. "Her name is Rayvn," Telyn said, with as much clarity as she could muster, "and she is with me."

"You mean she's *with* you?" said Tabbard, and his buddies chuckled. But the Dating Circle lantern-holders didn't chuckle at all. They broke into angry bluster.

"Flacks are not allowed here, Ms. Brower. This is intimate human business."

"The most intimate."

"Oh, dear."

"You should know better."

"We have been profaned, Telyn Brower, profaned. Your mother will hear about this."

"I say!"

"Spying on the ratios, cheating on the Chart. The fur-ball's birds should be off-limits for life!"

"Some nerve, bringing that hairy thing here to human business."

Telyn had never heard such a stream of bigotry in her life—and it cooled her belly to realize she had expressed many of these same sentiments herself. It felt so wrong to have brought Rayvn here, all alone, surrounded by angry humans.

Telyn had never felt such empathy for a flack in all her life. She decided that she would not bow or sit before these women—no way, no how.

Eventually, the tirade burned itself out. Mrs. Ouzeley smoothed her long, gray hair until the last woman had vented. "Let's hear from the pattern girl herself. Why are you here—eh, Rayvn, is it?"

"Yeah, flack," agreed Cherle. "Speak for yourself."

At any other time, Telyn might have sided with the ladies. This was a human affair. Flacks had no business coming here and trying to butt in. Humans had so little to call their own—no horses, no wheels, no magic, and little enough freedom. But at least they had this...this Dating Chart.

No matter how ridiculous, it was a human thing.

But since the pattern girl had proved her loyalty at the bridge—oh yes, she'd saved Telyn's bacon there—Telyn owed her. And they'd made that...that naked palm promise, whatever that was. Telyn always repaid her debts and kept her promises.

"Rayvn de Galati has a good reason for being here," she said.

"*Zamfir* de Galati," corrected Rayvn, standing beside Telyn. "De Galati simply tells where the breeding temple is located."

That caused a stir. Even Telyn couldn't keep her jaw from dropping.

Mrs. Ouzeley quieted the murmurs, laughter, and catcalls with a lip-puckering, eardrum-sundering whistle. "I'm sure we're all interested to hear about your breeding temples" —She pointed a long, slender finger at the door—"outside. The Dating Chart is for humans only.

"Ms. Brower, sit down and shut up before you make it worse for yourself. We will deal with you once the air has cleared."

The wart-faced Pembroke woman opened the door to shoo Rayvn out.

Cressida stepped over a few legs to join them. "We call on the privilege of a hearing."

Telyn didn't know what a hearing was, but it didn't sound good. It sounded all too much like some cornic thing. Telyn leaned over to her sister and whispered, "Wait, I do?"

Cressida took her hand and signed, *Trust me.*

Pressing her nails into Cressida's palm more than necessary, Telyn signed, *No!*

"There is no need for theatrics." Grebiana forced a smile. "A quorum is here, and the quorum doesn't accept non-humans, right ladies?"

Into the muttered agreement, Cressida said, "There is a procedure. Without procedure, the integrity of the Dating Circle fails, and without integrity, respect for the Dating Chart will fail. Which means no more gambling. Am I right?"

"I'm afraid not, Ms. Brower. You need—"

"I second the motion," said a familiar voice, and Caitlin rose to join them.

Telyn couldn't believe it. *Caitlin...standing beside us? What is she playing at? Does she think this will erase everything she has done?*

She resisted the urge to stomp on Caitlin's stockinged foot.

Cressida cleared her throat. "My sister, along with Rayvn Zamfir de Galati, request a formal hearing in front of the full Dating Circle in order to petition the acceptance of Rayvn Zamfir de Galati into the Dating Circle."

"The motion had been made and seconded," said Mrs. Pembroke, formally.

Mrs. Ouzeley glanced round at the gathered women. Enough of them were nodding to overrule her. With a haughty sniff, she announced, "Very well, Telyn Brower and Rayvn de Breeding Temple, consider yourselves on the docket. We shall look forward to it. Now, everyone—"

"Ah, when will that be?" Caitlin asked, raising her hand. "We don't want to miss the hearing by mistake."

"You will receive a summons when we can fit you on the agenda. Our schedule is tight. Very tight."

"But—" Cressida tried to say.

"Your membership on the Dating Circle is provisional, Ms. Cressida Brower, and may be revoked at any time. Remember that." Mrs. Ouzeley glared around the room. "This session is adjourned. Everyone but the permanent members of the Dating Circle, out. You may thank the Brower twins as you exit."

The gathered youth groaned, and Telyn sighed; they'd managed to alienate just about all of them.

CHAPTER TWENTY-SEVEN

It would be so nice to climb. A tall, smooth-barked tree with only a few branches, a tree with the smell of cedar and the height of a chaos tree, one that would take all my concentration. I wish Rayvn would leave me alone so I could go climb.

I wish she would let go of my arm. It feels like a nest of ants is climbing up and down the nerves.

But Rayvn did not leave her alone. After they descended the stairs into the now-dark town, Telyn still reeling from all that had happened, the pattern girl clung to Telyn as if they were best friends on a scare night. Telyn didn't know who led, her or Rayvn; there was some struggle with the direction through that arm connection, with the result that they ended up in Elin Llyweln park seated on a bench, staring up at the silhouette of the chaos tree against the night sky instead of climbing it.

Four oil lamps hung around the park, four whispers of illumination. From the smell, these lamps burned rendered pork fat instead of quality oil. *Or that could be what Rayvn smells like when she's happy,* Telyn thought, darkly.

Telyn figured the rest of the teens from the Dating Circle would go home—or to the Copcut Ash, in the case of Tabbard and his buddies. She decided to wait here silently until Rayvn got tired of holding on. *I won't talk. I won't encourage her friendship. I did what I promised, I took her to the meeting—it was a disaster. What more does she want? What else did she expect?*

Her sister found them soon after. She halted behind the bench, near a bronze statue of a woman holding dice in one hand and an arrow in the other. Telyn didn't have to look; she recognized her sister from her gait in the crunching snow.

"Where did you come up with the 'hearing' business?" Telyn asked without turning around. She wasn't sure she *could* turn more than her head with Rayvn clinging to her.

"While you were climbing and carrying on—and doing whatever it is you've been doing—I've been attending the meetings."

They let that hang between them for a moment.

"Are you a board member?"

"You have to be eighteen to be a full board member. I am a provisional member, as Grebiana made plain. You are eligible to join when you turn fifteen and a half," she said significantly, as if Telyn should consider joining also.

Telyn huffed. *Just because we share the same birthday doesn't mean we share the same interests. Mother of Squirrels, how did we draw so far apart?*

"Oh, hi, Cressida Brower, care to join us?" Rayvn said, as if noticing Cressida for the first time. She extended her free arm for Cressida to take. "We are enjoying the silence. Your sister is good at silence. It is a gift rarely given."

She likes silence? I should have been a chatterbox.

"I've already learned so much about human dating," Rayvn said, "the dry fire of loneliness—so interesting. Are pimples the first sign of loneliness? Does your face smooth out when you get married, or only if you marry for true love? I may have to make a Library inquiry of my own."

"Er...I've got to go work at the Sable Head in a minute," Cressida replied. "Thanks anyway, Rayvn."

Telyn pulled her arm free and straddled the bench so that she could regard her twin. "What now?"

"Now you wait until the Dating Circle summons you." The nearby lamp gave Cressida's brunette hair an angelic glow. "You will present your case on why a flack—sorry Rayvn—should be allowed into the meetings. One of the women will present the opposing side, if that is necessary."

"What do you think?"

"I would like to know why my sister has suddenly decided a flack —sorry Rayvn—should join the Dating Circle. And don't tell me 'the dry fire of loneliness.' That's why *you* joined, Tey, not why you want Rayvn to join."

"There's no dry fire here," Telyn said, pointing at her own breast. "Speak for yourself."

"Maybe I am."

Telyn took a deep breath and let it out slowly. She'd decided to tell the truth as much as possible, especially to her sister. "Rayvn and I have a deal. She will give me access to the Library if I get her into the Dating Circle."

Cressida crossed her arms across her chest.

"She promised to make inquiries for me. I...I want to know stuff about the world outside of Harlech."

"Really."

"Yeah."

"Brower twins, I will sweeten the deal," Rayvn said, sitting up straighter. "I can inquire at the Library for both of you. Since you are with the Dating Circle, Cressida Brower, that should help our chances of getting me accepted. I noticed some reticence today with Mrs. Ouzeley."

"Thank you, Rayvn, but I'm afraid you have no chance. They have already decided against you. Unless you can bring some, er, thauma influence of your own on the Dating Circle. Maybe you should talk to your mother—or Minister Svemas. I'm just a provisional member." Cressida started to walk away. "See you at the Sable Head, sis? Lots of pots to scrub this evening."

"Ah, sure. Be there in a minute."

Once Cressida was out of earshot, Telyn whispered, "You heard her. You have no chance of getting on. They've already decided.

There's just too much prejudice to have any hope. This is considered a human thing—the most human thing."

"I am sticking with our bargain, Telyn Brower. Until I get accepted, no inquiries."

"Then you'd better come up with some influence, because I certainly have none."

"Don't be so sure. You could threaten them with your foot infection."

"The last caravan will—Wait, Rayvn, did you make a joke? Intentionally?"

"Do you like it?"

"No!"

Rayvn's whiskers and ears drooped.

"I...like that you made one, though. It was...okay, it was a little funny. Next time, make one about Tabbard, or Joram."

"Caitlin?"

"Yes, about Caitlin."

Rayvn took hold of her arm again, and it didn't feel so awkward this time.

"Hosh?"

"Yes, Hosh, too."

The Dating Circle met at the public room at five p.m., after the sun set. Telyn and Rayvn tried attending the first week after the debacle and found the stairway blocked by four grown men.

Men!

That was probably as close as men were ever allowed to get to Dating Circle business. And as close as they ever wanted to get.

The men didn't throw Rayvn out, but managed to form an impenetrable wall with their bodies, sliding in front of the flack every time she tried to push past. It helped that Rayvn was on the downstairs trying to come up, and that each man outweighed her by two or three times.

They would probably notice that their stitches had frayed the next time they did their laundry, but Rayvn kept her retaliation to that.

"Get into that meeting, Telyn Brower, and tell me everything they say." The quick flick of her tail spoke volumes. "And get me that hearing."

"Send my inquiry!" Telyn retorted to the flack's retreating form.

The flack just wouldn't take no for an answer.

Unfortunately, the men parted to let Telyn in.

She had been attending ever since—and reporting the proceedings in agonizing detail to Rayvn.

In the front of the public room, Mrs. Pembroke mimed grand flourishes of her quill on an imaginary parchment. Meanwhile, Hosh stepped over crisscrossed legs, random feet, and out-flung arms to distribute the questionnaire in question.

On this, the seventh meeting, the class gathered to fill out the dreaded Intimate Intimacies questionnaire.

"You must be as honest with your answers, as you wish your future spouse to be honest with you," Mrs. Pembroke said.

The other board members present—Mrs. Gamage, Mrs. Bedo, and Mrs. Ouzeley—all nodded solemnly.

As if an Ouzeley knows anything about honesty.

"Bare yourselves," Mrs. Pembroke continued. "No holding back. No keeping anything to yourselves. Your mothers won't be reading these; you needn't worry about indiscretions. Mr. Lycurgus, what is our cardinal rule?"

"No holding back," Joram replied.

"The *other* rule, Mr. Lycurgus."

Joram and Caitlin exchanged a look and shrugged. "Ma'am?"

"No peeking. If I suspect that you have been peeking or—Tabbard Ouzeley?—telling your friends to peek for you, I will read every line you put down to the entire group. Is that understood?"

"Oh, great," Cressida whispered to Telyn. "That will promote openness and honesty."

"*Bare* openness," Telyn whispered back.

"*Naked* honesty," Cressida replied.

"The more openness and honesty you exhibit, Brower twins" — Mrs. Pembroke shot them a glare—"the more accurate the Dating Chart will be. Which, in turn, makes it more likely you will find a suitable spouse."

Telyn caught Tabbard whispering, "A troll."

Since Mrs. Pembroke continued to stare at her, Telyn didn't respond in kind.

Telyn rubbed her face. The skin of her temples felt smoother, haler, and not just because her acne had cleared up a bit. The forehead piece hadn't pressed there in some time. Her skin felt, well, more like her own.

She also felt weaker, less powerful, and less in control. More *human*.

For a brief period of time, she'd tasted power, felt the allure of using magic and the elevated sense of self-worth that came with it. She missed the power. She trembled to think how much she missed it.

But she'd gone back to that tree many times and found nothing. The faux ceramic forehead had disappeared. It was a big forest, after all, and that terrible wind could have blown it for miles...

The Sable Head's business slumped; gaggles of girls no longer followed Hosh around or snickered at the curve of his bottom; random ladies no longer debated the ethics of pinning wigglums to the bottom of their infusions or cheering at the brakdaw fights.

Daily, the Ever-Guise's influence waned.

Which might just be a good thing.

Excepting, of course, that Telyn would have to craft a more mundane plan for revenge against Tabbard and his gang.

With that thought, Telyn's face hardened.

A pair of legs planted themselves in front of her, and Telyn looked up at Mrs. Pembroke. The woman placed her hands on her hips, glaring down at her and Cressida.

"We wives and mothers know more than you think. We hear more than you think, and no matter how much we like or dislike you, we will encourage appropriate pairings—introvert with extrovert;

woodsman with homemaker; taxidermist with barmaid—but we do not know everything. We do not know your secret thoughts. Nor, I may add, do you. Your subconscious is a field filled with clover, wild-flowers, and weeds, and the Intimate Intimacies questionnaire is designed to expose both prickles and blossoms above the concealing viridity.

"I will remind you that eighty-nine percent of the people who marry in Harlech marry one of the primary circle matches. And that holds true to people who answer honestly or dishonestly—Tabbard Ouzeley." Her head swiveled. "If you want the Chart to match you with a compatible woman, someone you may even be happy with despite decades of marriage, the same conversation morning after morning, the same terrible morning breath, the same flabby arms and unwashed—"

Mrs. Gamage cleared her throat, and Mrs. Pembroke seemed to reign herself back. "Well then, answer honestly, or suffer the conse-quences of a lifetime of mismatch. A lifetime of" —Her nostrils quiv-ered—"marital loneliness."

It all sounded so ominous, but these women knew as much about love as a bunion. Sitting here on the hard floor, listening to these bitter souls, Telyn began to feel some sympathy for Esther's alco-holism. Who wouldn't want to hide from such a bleak future?

Not that her dad would have caused such bitterness. She never remembered him as anything but kind and quietly optimistic. His only sin was to die young.

Sure, Telyn would like to find the right man—someone who understood her, earned plenty of birds, loved eehoos, and adored the silence of the deep woods. Maybe she could find a man who liked climbing, too. Someday. When she was ready, which would be, like, in her thirties. She was in no hurry. Particularly when the Ever-Guise would make life in Harlech so much more bearable.

If she ever found it.

Once again, she rubbed her bare forehead.

Hefin Lloyd raised a tentative hand, and Mrs. Pembroke called on him. "Er, we don't have to date the people in the primary circle, do we?"

"No, dear. You can marry a feral llama if you so choose." Tabbard let out a convincing bray, and Mrs. Pembroke glared at him. "The questionnaire and the initiates from Sums, Statistics, and Affairs of the Heart simply chart probabilities and encourage right pairings. It is completely up to you what you do with the information."

Cressida raised her hand. "If people see the Dating Chart and then act on that information, doesn't that actually change the odds of a pairing? As Aled the Wise said, 'When we stare at someone, they stare back. When we test someone, they test back.'"

Mrs. Ouzeley stepped away from the wall, clapping her hands into the quiet room. "Very good. The heart creates the Chart. The Chart informs the betting. The betting informs the odds. The odds inform behavior, and behavior informs the heart. A circle influencing itself over and around. The math becomes very complex. The fact that you grasped this much, Miss Brower, is impressive."

Cressida beamed.

Telyn hadn't grasped a thing—except that she wanted no part of it.

Hosh finally made it to their side of the room. He handed Telyn and Cressida each a piece of parchment. Then he gave an extra page to Cressida from the bottom of the stack, for some reason.

No, he's given me not one, but three sheets, with questions and space for answers front and back. Who would do that? You'd have to leave it face up for a long time for the ink to dry, then as you flip it over, everyone will try to read what's written on the back. Rayvn be bothered —no way will I fill this out here in front of everyone.

"Start at the top," Mrs. Gamage advised. "No peeking, and no collaborating. You don't want to end up with your sister's intended, do you?" This last with a giggle.

"No way," Cressida said. "Do you see these questions?"

Telyn's eye immediately fell to the word "SEX" about halfway down the first page. "If your boyfriend's mom wants to talk with you about sex before the Dead Winter Dance, do you: 1) eagerly engage with her, 2) tell her you don't know what the word means, 3) draw one of the forbidden dances, or 4) stick your fingers in your ears and chant la-la-la-la-la...."

Mrs. Gamage droned on. "There should be no talking once the questionnaires have been passed out. This is individual work, not group work. After all, you don't marry into a group. Life is complicated enough trying to keep one spouse happy."

Telyn read on. The heading of page one read "All About Me," followed by about a hundred nosy questions. Page two was titled "All About My Future Husband;" page three was "My All-time, Never-tell-anyone Secrets;" while page four offered a variety of what-ifs, including "If I could cast any spell on my spouse;" "If frostbite takes his nose...and other amputations;" and "What would I do if his mother dies and inhabits our chimney?" It was a comprehensive list of meddlesome inquiry, the kind of stuff girls whispered about when camping in the woods—after sharing a bag of angel water.

Cressida's hand shot up.

"Do you really want us to answer in front of the class?" Mrs. Gamage said. "Think carefully before you speak."

"Ah, yes, Mrs. Gamage. What is page five?"

"Page five?" Hosh's mom blinked in confusion.

"Demonstrate how you would set up a running differential where Grunts represent the density of eligible males in generation Green, Lovesicks represent the density of single, child-bearing females, Loneliness is multiplied by both Grunts and Lovesicks with an unknown fraction of single Grunts, and Fooltacky representing the Lovesicks' desperation rate..." Cressida's voice trailed off, but her eyes continued scanning the page with interest.

Mrs. Gamage bustled over. "Differences, dear? Of course you have differences. What in the world are you reading?"

"Those are called parts," Tabbard called, predictably. "Or don't you have any?"

"Differentials," Cressida insisted without looking up, "not differences."

Hosh's mom snatched the parchment in question. "Oh, Sums, Statistics, and Affairs of the Heart. This is, um, I'm sorry..."

From the front of the room came an insistent clearing of the throat.

"Yes, Mrs. Ouzeley?"

"I asked Hosh to give that page to Miss Brower on purpose."

"Oh?"

"Unlike the majority of young women and men," —Mrs. Ouzeley's dismissive gaze swung to her own son, who looked away—"Miss Brower understands rudimentary math and might be taught more."

Telyn craned her neck to peer at the parchment, now held by Mrs. Gamage. What Mrs. Ouzeley called 'rudimentary math' looked to her a random jumble of letters, lines, and magic symbols. Or bird droppings.

"We have need of women with mathematical aptitude to calculate and compile the Dating Chart."

"Is that wise?" Mrs. Pembroke asked, thumbing her wart with particular vigor.

"Mrs. Brower is honest."

"Honest, but is she discreet?"

"She is not her sister."

Telyn blushed.

"Funeral-fainter," Cherle fake-whispered.

"Go ahead, dear, start with that page," Mrs. Ouzeley encouraged. "The Dating Circle will make a determination on your eligibility for the Sums, Statistics, and Affairs of the Heart committee based on your answers" —Mrs. Ouzeley glanced sideways at Mrs. Pembroke—"and other factors."

Cressida bent to work with her tongue in the side of her cheek and a gleam in her eyes. Telyn just shook her head, relieved she didn't have the added embarrassment of filling out the sums page.

The room quieted but for the scratching of quill on paper, the tinkle of the quill on the glass ink bottles, and the occasional stifled giggle or rustle of clothes.

Feeling eyes upon her, Telyn looked to her left and caught Caitlin staring. She nudged Cressida. Her sister looked up, narrowed her eyes, and bent back over the parchment. Caitlin gave a tentative smile, then looked away.

Around the room, people twisted themselves in various poses to keep others from reading over their shoulders.

This could turn out to be a contortionist class.

So far, Telyn had managed to answer the top half of the first page.

Question one: In one word, how would you describe yourself?

Various nicknames came to her: *Too-tall; Funeral-Fainter....* She wrote "Spunky" then wished she had written "Rebel."

Question two: In one word, how would your best friends describe you?

Poser came unbidden and unwanted, but she couldn't shake it. *I'm a poser and a liar. I manipulate people with magic.* In the end, she chose the word "Influencer," which fit nicely between the two.

Question three: Circle the word below that best describe your perfect match:

    Steadfast   *Reliable*   *Rebellious*
    Rough   *Refined*   *Hairy*

"Are they matching us or writing a rosy romance?" she whispered to Cressida. She hesitated between characteristics from the opposite ends of the spectrum: *Protective* and *Rebellious.*

The next moment, the pages were yanked from Telyn's hands. She had failed to see Mrs. Ouzeley slink up beside her.

"What's with you?" Telyn sputtered. "Give that back." If she hadn't been startled, Telyn never would have dared address the woman that way. But she didn't regret it, not one hairy bit.

The hideous woman turned the pages in her hands, scanning like a vulture over a carcass.

Telyn though furiously. What had she answered thus far? Not much, thank goodness. She'd skipped over anything to do with boys. Still, having Tabbard's mom read that her secret pleasure was to "eat spicy wigglums head-first" and that her favorite song was "The Heartsick Squire" made her cringe.

"Go on, then, read it!" Tabbard said, sitting up eagerly. "That's what you said, if someone talks in class, their questionnaire gets read in front of everyone."

"Make her fill it all out first," Tristam added, and Cherle squealed.

Telyn blushed into the room's laughter.

"This is the wrong parchment," Mrs. Ouzeley said after a moment. "Hosh, bring me the abbreviated version on the table. That's it, the one with brown ink."

"But they're all the same," Caitlin said, but Hosh scurried to retrieve the other document. "Otherwise, the betting wouldn't be fair."

"How would you know the questionnaires are all the same, Caitlin Nest? Have you been peeking?"

Caitlin blanched, gaped, and finally managed an indignant, "No!"

"Whether or not you all are answering the same questions is a matter for the Dating Circle and the Dating Circle alone," Mrs. Ouzeley said in her gargoyle quaver. "The integrity of the Chart relies on your discretion. Do not share what you are asked or what you answered, for peril of being ejected and ending life dry and alone. Without procedure, the integrity of the Circle fails, and without integrity, respect for the Dating Chart will fail."

"Telyn Brower needs the 'old spinster' parchment," said Tabbard.

"The taaaaall one," Dylan Jones added.

Isla Yarwood laughed harder than the joke deserved and lay her hand on Dylan's shoulder as if needing his help to stay erect.

Those two will share a circle before the day is out, Telyn thought bitterly. She unrolled the parchment Hosh brought. On it was a single, multiple-choice question:

In a single word, how would you describe someone who invites a flack to the Dating Circle:

Fink
Traitor
Quisling
Turncoat
Double-Crosser
Sellout
Backstabber
Telyn Brower

Telyn scowled. *That's two words, you numskulls.*

Everyone had to turn in their parchments at the end. Mrs. Ouzeley unrolled Telyn's, noted that nothing had been written, and rolled it back up without comment. In ones and twos, the teens filed downstairs and outside. Crunching down the street on the frozen ruts came a few younger kids, brothers and sisters of those in the Circle, full of curiosity and questions and not yet plagued with pimples and hormones.

Cressida left to work on her latest design, something Celine Baggers had ordered from Cressida for the Dead Winter Dance. Celine hadn't even bothered to pretend Esther would do the work.

"Infusion?" Hosh proposed, appearing at her elbow.

Telyn shrugged, not in the mood for chit-chat but not in the mood to be alone either. Then a long, broad hand settled on her shoulder. She turned and was surprised to see that the hand belonged to Joram.

"I saw what Mrs. Ouzeley did to you in there," he said.

"You and everyone else."

Hosh, scowling, seemed to fade into the shadows. Telyn crossed her arms.

"I was watching Mrs. Ouzeley talk with you."

"You already said that."

What kind of set-up is this?

"That was really unfair. They could refuse to let the pattern girl in without taking it out on you. Asking isn't a crime. Mrs. Gamage thinks so too—otherwise, why would she have told Hosh to give you the regular parchment?"

Teens continued to exit the public house. Many shot curious glances at her and Joram, since everyone in town knew what happened in the alley behind the Copcut Ash by now.

I do not want to be talking about this here. Not here, and certainly not with Joram Lycargus, not ever. Stress started to tighten the muscles in her neck. Telyn had to tilt her head from one side to the other to fight off a cramp.

Completely oblivious, Joram continued talking. "Frankly, I'm surprised they said no. The pattern witches keep this place from being overrun with ghosts, and who would want that? We need to keep Rayvn and her mom happy."

"They haven't said no yet. Rayvn might be allowed to join. We're awaiting a hearing."

Joram hesitated a bit. He obviously thought her chances were slim to llama puckies. His large hand squeezed her shoulder one final time in a friendly way. "Good luck, then, Tey."

"Thanks," she mumbled, as Joram moved away to join Tristam, Cherle, Dylan, and yes, Caitlin, who gave a little wave.

"I'll just go home," Hosh said from the shadows, turning and limping away before Telyn could reply.

And Telyn stood there as the people she had grown up with—friends, enemies, and in-betweens—moved away from her in either direction. She felt so awash with loneliness that she nearly stumbled. All her childhood friends had someone to be with and something to do except her. Caitlin had Joram; Joram had Tabbard and his gang. Hosh had his family and his role as 'Dating Assistant.' Cressida ran Meander and Mohair, she taught sewing, and half the men in Harlech called her by name. She might even be appointed to Sums, Statistics, and Affairs of the Heart.

Telyn hardly even had Tums anymore. Since the eehoo had become a celebrity, the clients demanded her presence in the public room. Telyn worked the kitchens alone, making terrible spec stew and inedible bide tuber mash. She couldn't even fill out the stupid dating questionnaire without it being taken from her.

A stooped and bearded old man paused next to her. "Girly, was that the Dating Circle meeting?" The words whistled through the gap of a missing tooth.

Telyn nodded, blinking the moisture from her eyes.

The man wore a trapper's outfit, complete with fringed leather jacket and coonskin cap. He would have been handsome thirty years ago. She half-hoped he'd ask her to join him for a malt...at least she'd have the ego boost of turning someone down.

"Any sure things?" the trapper asked, winking.

Telyn nodded again, and the trapper leaned in, listening intently.

"A newbie named Telyn Brower," she said. "Just joined. That one will end up alone, eleven-to-one odds."

He gripped her hand in thanks and rushed off to place his bet.

The dike broke, and tears flooded her cheeks.

CHAPTER TWENTY-EIGHT

In the Sable Head kitchen, robed in filthy aprons and surrounded by food aromas and humidity, Telyn and Cressida stuffed sausages and practiced for the hearing. They hadn't been told when the hearing would take place, only that it would be before the Dead Winter Dance.

In a bucket of warm water, Telyn washed the small intestine skin, tied one end, and fit the open end over a metal funnel. Meanwhile, she conjured reasons a nonhuman should be allowed into the Dating Circle. Cressida stuffed the sausage mush through the funnel with her finger, filling the casings as she poked holes in Telyn's arguments.

Practicing was Cressida's idea; Telyn had always favored improvisation.

Most unusually, two other people shared the kitchen with them: Razenbock, polishing water gourds with oil and commenting from time to time, and Rayvn, examining the fire as though it were the most interesting thing in the world, keeping her thoughts to herself.

"Is not getting to know one another step one in friendship? We have a chance here; the daughter of an important person, er, thauma, wants to get to know humans better. It can only mean improvement in human-nonhuman relationships. Let's seize this opportunity."

Telyn had lost count of how many times she'd tried this argument. The little tweaks she did to language didn't seem to help much at all. Bother all this practice! She didn't want to be a barrister.

"Friendship cannot exist with such irreconcilable differences," Cressida replied. "Rayvn is nonhuman. We are human. One is a magical being, the other spiritual. There is nothing in common. If you want to call what you two have 'friendship,' do not bring the Dating Circle into it."

Telyn bit her lip. Leave it to Cressida to come up with another compelling argument. "The point is, we both use language. We both have thoughts and dreams. We have families. How about we stop seeing each other as flack and human, and start seeing each other as, well..." —She couldn't think of the right word, and ended her sentence lamely—"...beings."

"Beings?"

"Well, yes." She tied the end of her casing so hard it split.

"Why on earth would you want to bring our two races closer together when humans are decidedly nonmagical? This can only lead to a dominant-subservient relationship. A cultural separation is required—for our own protection."

"Irreconcilable?" "Decidedly?" Where on earth did Cressida get these words? Next, she'll start talking about differential math or whatever. In the face of her confident, intelligent twin, Telyn felt like a total dunce.

She threw the empty casing to Tums, who tried to stretch it over her face.

Telyn's pitch rose. "The pattern witches have a special relationship with humans. I wouldn't be asking for a-a trogo, for example, to join the Circle. Trogos enslave humans. Pattern witches—"

"Humans enslave humans," Raz commented. "That's not an argument either way."

"Not in Harlech, they don't," Telyn snapped.

Raz tossed her an onion. "Chop this, why don't you, and cool down."

Cressida pressed on. "I call for a vote. All joining me in opposition to letting Rayvn into the Dating Circle?"

Raz raised his hand. So did Rayvn. Even Tums lifted a sucker paw.

Reluctantly, Telyn raised the onion as well. Her sister had talked circles around her.

"I'm just no good at this," Telyn admitted. It was *decidedly* harder to argue for something you didn't believe in. Although, the more she practiced, the more the words grew on her. She had begun to find grains of truth in her arguments. Maybe they *should* make allowances for certain flacks.

"How about you focus on the smaller picture?" Cressida suggested, mirroring Telyn's own thoughts. "Why the Dating Circle should admit this one person rather than accepting that all humans and all flacks have something in common. Take their minds away from some momentous change that will destroy human culture forever, and focus on what makes Rayvn de Galati different."

"Rayvn Zamfir de Galati," Rayvn corrected.

After some thought (long enough to mince the entire onion), Telyn tried again. "My friend, Rayvn Zamfir de Galati, may be the only thing that stands between Harlech and an army of ghosts."

"An army?" Cressida raised her eyebrows.

"If there's an avalanche or something." Telyn waved her arms. "It's happened. Stay with me. I'm onto something. Rayvn Zamfir de Galati, my friend, needs to study complex human interactions in order to, ah, to improve her spells that keep ghosts at bay. And what better place for her to learn than the Dating Circle? Don't we want to keep those nasty old ghosts behind the Sepulcher? Harlech could be overrun. All your old relatives could come knocking" —She rapped her head—"and try to possess you. If she doesn't learn our love patterns, we'd be overrun with vengeful spirits!"

Razenbock chuckled. "At least you'll entertain them."

Rayvn started humming.

"The flack's mother is the town's pattern witch," Cressida replied with shrill condescension. Whether purposefully or subconsciously, as the afternoon wore on, she had started sounding more and more like Mrs. Ouzeley. "The daughter can learn about ghosts and Sepulcher stone from her. Meanwhile, you would smash human tradition like a fallen icicle. What for? So the witch can study our intimate lives the way an entomologist studies insects in a jar?"

Entomologize my backside.

Rayvn's humming grew louder.

It wasn't tuneless humming. No, it had a melody. Telyn just knew it would replay in her mind for hours before she found sleep.

She took a deep breath. "We should let her in so that Rayvn can develop an appreciation for humans. Pattern witch magic relies on patterns. P-A-T-T-E-R-N-S," Telyn spelled, helpfully. "She's trying to learn them."

"Will she be taking our blood as well?"

Raz grunted appreciatively. He seemed to be rooting for the "nay" arguments to carry the day.

Cressida held up a finger. "A name," —Another finger—"a few drops of blood, that's all the pattern witch has ever needed. No, Miss Brower, this is one of your impetuous whimsies, and the Dating Circle will not humor you."

The hum's volume increased another notch.

Telyn stabbed her knife handle-up in the table and turned to face Rayvn. "Do you have something to add?"

"Me? No."

"Because I get the distinct impression you are trying to get our attention."

"Is it time to vote?"

"No! I have more to say."

Just as Telyn started again, Rayvn said, "The Dating Circle revolves around love, hmm?"

"Betting, more like." Raz rubbed his fingers together as if they held coins. "It's all about the birds. Gossip's the best sauce, but without all the betting, they wouldn't bother with a Dating Circle."

Rayvn's ears twitched excitedly. "Somehow, Harlech has married the two most unlikely spouses: Love and Gambling. As a seeker of patterns, I would study the mysterious pathways of human love and how they intersect statistical gambling. My insights could increase the accuracy of the Dating Chart. Logical."

The twins looked at each other.

"Really?" Telyn said. "You could do that?"

The flack's tail made a question mark.

Raz had stopped polishing the gourd. "The flack's onto somethin'."

"Hmm," Rayvn agreed.

"And if you learn more about it, your betting'll get more accurate?" Raz asked, a greedy glint under his bushy eyebrows.

"If Telyn's arguments carry, we will find out."

Razenbock placed the shiny water-gourd on a shelf next to a dozen others. "Listen to the pattern witch, Telyn. She wants in; let her make her own arguments." He made to leave but paused in the doorway and held the door open. "Someone here to see ya."

Telyn expected Hosh or Mini-Hosh, or some irate trapper who had found a bug in his stew. Never in a thousand years would she have expected Caitlin. Yet here she was, bundled in a long coat with snowflakes on the shoulders.

Caitlin thanked Raz for holding the door, strode in, planted her feet, and crossed her arms. Raz traded places with her and stepped into the public room.

Cressida's mouth opened. Then she closed it, grabbed another handful of meat-mush, and began poking it through the funnel with her finger.

Finally, Telyn said, "If you want malt, it's on the other side of the door. If you want sausages, you'll have to wait. Outside."

"Why are you trying to get Rayvn into the Dating Circle?"

A thousand things flew through Telyn's mind. She really, really wanted to wind Caitlin up—say something so ridiculous that Caitlin would be telling her friends about it for days. But nothing snarky came to mind, not even anything halfway funny. So, she told a half-truth. "She asked me to."

Rayvn watched with head tilted and tail twitching.

Caitlin scoffed. "Are you besties now?"

"What of it? Rayvn doesn't run with Tabbard's crowd, at least. She knows something about loyalty."

Caitlin's arms remained crossed. Her foot tapped a steady beat on the greasy wooden floorboards. Despite the heat and dripping humidity, she hadn't removed her coat.

She doesn't plan on staying long. Good.

"What are you doing here, Caitlin?"

"I'm asking you a question."

"For yourself? Or for Joram?"

Caitlin's face seemed to soften. "You wouldn't understand about Joram. Unlike most of this cloistered town, he's going places—" She took a deep breath. "This isn't like you. You hate flacks."

Rayvn's head tilted the other way.

"Why would you get all of Harlech in a stitch about this? Everyone's yacking about it; they say you've sold out, gone over to the cornics. I know that isn't true—my parents would've heard. So, what is it?"

Telyn's eyes flicked to her sister, who stuffed sausages as if that were the most interesting job in the world. How wrong this all was, that her frienemy knew about the Ever-Guise when her best friend—her twin sister—had to be kept in the dark.

She *so* wanted to tell Cressida, to have her twin on her side, to let this whole thing drop and go back to the way things were before the Ever-Guise.

A vision of it popped in her mind, and her stomach tightened.

"Only flacks can inquire at the Library. And I...I want information. Rayvn told me she could send inquiries to the Library if I got her into the Dating Circle."

Caitlin stared until understanding clicked into place behind her brown eyes. "That's the first sensible thing you've done in months."

Telyn bit her lip, nodded.

"She's not getting in. You know that right?"

Telyn refused to rise to the bait. She wiggled the knife free from the table and sought around for something to chop.

Rayvn hummed a new tune.

Caitlin stared a bit longer before turning to go. "Oh yeah, the hearing is tonight, eighth bell."

Telyn felt like dumping the bucket of casing-water on Caitlin's retreating head. "You mean you weren't going to tell me that unless I said something you liked? This was a test?"

"That's about right," Caitlin replied as the door swung shut behind her.

A growl escaped from between Telyn's gritted teeth, a growl that sent Tums crawling for the ceiling.

She hadn't been paying attention, but they must have rung seventh bell already.

CHAPTER TWENTY-NINE

azenbock returned the minute Caitlin departed. "So, the relationship experts planned to hold the hearing without the star defendant," he said, stroking his beard and nodding. "Where did you say they would have it?"

"Ah, Caitlin didn't say."

"Twisted her crank, did yah?" Raz said.

Telyn scowled. "No! She deserved it. It'll be at the public house."

Raz continued to nod annoyingly.

"Won't it?"

"Could be in the Copcut Ash for all I know. Sounds like half of Harlech'll be there."

"They wouldn't."

"Grebiana Ouzeley's chair; she'll want to put on a show. I'm afraid that in her twisted mind, taking down Telyn Brower will serve as substitute for taking down Razenbock Cauthom. 'Sides," he added, winking, "they'll have plenty of space. No one goes to the Copcut Ash these days. Better get moving, girls."

Cressida and Telyn shared a look, removed their aprons, and sprinted outside. Rayvn followed.

The girls raced through town, stopping at all the major gathering places. The Lucky H held its usual assortment of heavy drinkers, the Copcut Ash occupied their wealthier cousins, and the public house was locked up tight. So was the human school. The Prefecture rang the first of eight bells.

Panic began to overtake them.

"We have to think logically about this," Cressida said.

Telyn gave up wringing her hands and kicked the school door, hurting her toe more than the door. "Caitin made it up, the prat. She has us running around in circles for her own personal amusement."

"Has she ever done that to you before?"

"Well, no."

Cressida tapped her lips, deep in thought. "All the Dating Circle board members will be there, right?"

"So?"

"So, we don't need to find the meeting," Cressida said. "All we have to do is find one of the board members."

And both girls said, "Mrs. Gamage."

Fourth bell rang before they'd reached the Gamage door. From the sod rooftop, Hosh's younger brothers peered down at them. One of them called, "What you want?"

"Mini-Hosh," Telyn shouted back. She didn't have separate nicknames for the younger Gamage boys, they were both "Mini-Hosh" to her. The brothers' real names were Brax and Drew. "Where's your mom?"

"How should I know?"

"Think. Did she tell you anything?"

"No." Drew pulled away from the edge of the roof, but Brax stayed. "She got all dressed up, said something about impressing the cornics." He pointed west.

"Thanks."

The boy returned her smile. He was cute in an annoying sort of way, always trying to flirt as if he stood higher than an ankle.

"Cornics" and "dress-up" could only mean one thing: the Prefecture. Which explained how Caitlin knew all about it, being as her parents worked there.

They caught Mr. Nest, Caitlin's dad, leaving his post by the

Prefecture entrance, and he directed them to a room on the second floor.

"Oh, bother it," he said. "I'll take you myself. We didn't think it right not inviting you and all, the missus and I." He huffed each word between breaths. He looked fit enough, but the stairs took the wind from him. "Would've told you myself, but we figured you would find out. Half the town's here already. Quite the turnout."

They exited on the second floor and moved the opposite direction from Minister Svemas' office. "Glad you made it in time. How did you find out?" He opened one side of a double door.

"A little bird told us," Cressida replied.

Manning her usual place by the entry, Mrs. Pembroke intercepted them in the foyer. She directed Cressida to sit in the audience and stood aside to allow Telyn and Rayvn to proceed to the center of the room.

The sisters faced each other. In her twin's green eyes, Telyn saw love and worry and questions repressed. Telyn smiled with as much confidence as she could muster. "I'll be fine, thanks to you. No need to worry."

"You're doing the right thing," Cressida said. "Knock 'em dead."

She gave Cressida's hand a squeeze. "Knocks away." Then she entered the room to argue against everything she'd always believed.

Lonely and exposed, two simple, hard-backed chairs sat in the middle of the room. A slender woman in a red bonnet whirled to see who had arrived late. She had obviously been addressing the gathered humans and clammed up mid-argument.

"Ah, the petitioners. Thank you for being on time," she said sarcastically. It was Mrs. Dragan, and whatever she had been saying, it couldn't be good. Telyn had once played a trick on her and her daughter, and Mrs. Dragan had never forgiven her. An innocent trick, really, Telyn'd just swiped a pair of the Dragan girl's pants, stuffed them with straw, and placed them under a fallen tree as if the girl had been crushed.

Now that Telyn considered it, it hadn't been all that funny. But she'd been twelve; how was she to know how seriously parents take that sort of thing?

Mrs. Dragan moved to the end of the room and climbed three steps to take a seat, her mouth pinched like she was sucking on lemons.

Only now, emerging into the light of a dozen lamps, did Telyn realize they were in a real courtroom. On a low dais at the end of the room, high-backed chairs sat in a semi-circle, and each was occupied by a severe-faced woman of the Dating Circle board. They all sat as stiff as their chairs. Some, like Mrs. Gamage, acknowledged Telyn with little nods or brief smiles. Most stared stonily.

"I apologize. We were waiting in Minister Svemas' office and didn't hear the bells." Telyn had meant it as a power move, but she realized as soon as the lie left her mouth that she'd miscalculated. She'd just reinforced that this was an "us versus them" situation, and Telyn Brower was squarely in the "them" category.

Telyn placed her hand on Rayvn's back and urged her forward, into the lamplight.

Above and to the right of the circle of women sat a chair—almost a throne—upholstered with bright red felt. A gilded star insignia crowned its back. *This must be where Minister Svemas sits in a real trial, Telyn thought.* This evening, Second Gajos Jaromir occupied the seat. She didn't let her eyes linger on the cornic lest he catch her eyes. She never got a good feeling from him.

To her right and left, the residents of Harlech occupied row after row of bleachers. Their eyes roved between Telyn, Rayvn, and the Dating Circle.

Telyn's belly grew cold. *Everyone over the age of twelve must be here!*

"Mrs. Dragan," Mrs. Ouzeley said, obviously presiding over the hearing, "now that the Brower girl has arrived, do you wish to continue your argument?"

The slender, bonnet-wearing woman shook her head curtly and folded red-gloved hands over her knees.

"Very well. With the human present, the Dating Circle acknowledges that the petitioners have standing. No need to sit, Miss Brower, we have been waiting for you. Please, state your case."

As the floor was surrendered to Telyn, she became aware of how they must look. Rayvn wore a long dress in the Harlech fashion, emerald green in color. A felt hood covered her ears. The long, white ribbon that encircled the hood trailed to Rayvn's waist. The outfit managed to look both unusual and rather elegant and—thank goodness—covered ankles, ears and tail.

Much better than Telyn's stained dress, which smelled strongly of sausage.

The disapproving gaze of all those people weighed down on them. Telyn could hardly draw enough breath to say, "We ask that Rayvn de Galati be allowed to join the Dating Circle."

"Join, as a member?" Telyn didn't know the Dating Circle woman who spoke. "Not simply observe?"

Telyn hadn't considered asking for anything less than full membership. Her heart sped up. She hadn't counted on making decisions here, only in presenting her case. "Full member."

If only she had the Ever-Guise, she'd have made quick work of the ladies' objections. A few suggestions, and *they* would be petitioning the pattern witch to apply for membership, not the other way around.

"Why are you speaking on Rayvn's behalf?" asked another woman.

Good question. Why am I sticking my neck out in front of the whole world?

Because I'm a fool, that's why.

"As a human, and an eligible girl" —The crowd snickered—"of the Dating Chart, I am petitioning on her behalf."

"We know that, dear," Mrs. Gamage said, gently. "Can you be specific? Harlech breeds rumors like a rooster breeds chickens. We'd like to hear the truth from your own mouth."

"I, ah, I know…am getting to know Rayvn de Galati." She could hear Tabbard snicker from somewhere in the audience. "But she, ah, is not familiar with human customs. As her friend, I am petitioning."

Mrs. Pembroke leaned forward. "What could this de Galati possibly contribute? You don't mean for this—this Rayvn de Breeding Temple to have relationships with humans, do you?"

The crowd broke into excited muttering. Even Mrs. Gamage looked scandalized. Some of the men stroked their facial hair thoughtfully. Too bad the men didn't decide these things. Rayvn could flash her ankles a couple of times–done!

"Well, Miss Brower?"

Heat flooded Telyn's face. All the logical arguments Cressida had encouraged her to use fled from between her ears. "No, of course not. She just wants to understand us."

"Understand us? Like pulling apart a bug?" Mrs. Pembroke asked.

"Dissecting, dear," said someone in the audience.

"Pinning it to a board and pulling off its wings? Why on earth would she want to?"

"That's not what entomologists—oh, never mind."

"The point is," said another of the women seated on the dais. It was Betty Yarwood, "Steamy Betty" herself. "This is a human ritual. It's got nothing to do with nonhumans. I've known your mother and father for years, Miss Brower. Your ancestors populate the Sepulcher behind the sand. Does human integrity and tradition mean nothing to you?"

Oh yes, yes it does.

Telyn wanted to spill her heart out, confess how conflicted she was, and all she could do was utter the stale argument she'd rehearsed. "Pattern witches keep ghosts from overrunning Harlech, and all the other places. There could be an avalanche of ghosts, ah, too many, if a lot of people died at once, and she needs to study dating patterns to learn, um, to keep spirits away better."

Cressida gave her a thumbs-up, but her cringe betrayed her real assessment: Telyn had bungled an already lame argument.

Mrs. Pembroke sniffed, which seemed a rather appropriate reaction. Telyn's throat went completely dry, unwilling to utter any more inanities.

All this time, Mrs. Ouzeley had remained standing at the edge of the dais, watching the proceedings with her arrogant smirk as Telyn sunk deeper into misery. Now she raised a white-gloved finger. "I think we need to hear from the petitioner herself."

"The pattern girl?" Mrs. Pembroke asked, scandalized, "speak here, in a Dating Circle proceeding?"

"She's standing right in front of us. Why not? I'm sure it will be... enlightening."

"Before we start," Mrs. Gamage said, "I would like to say that we thank you and your mother" —She looked down to read from a scrap of paper—"Anicuta de Galati, for all your work at the Sepulcher. Do not think we aren't grateful—"

"Very well, very well, we are not here for that," Mrs. Ouzeley interrupted. "I see that your mother is not among us, which tells me, Rayvn, that you are doing this of your own initiative, hmm? Tell us, Miss Pattern Witch, why do you want to join the Dating Circle?"

Rayvn straightened her dress unnecessarily. "The intersection between love and gambling is a pattern both within and without the natural world. Humans have a worldly body but a heavenly spirit that can manifest here as a ghost, and similarly, love and gambling breed that most rock solid of natural laws, mathematics, with that most ephemeral, love. As the Philosopher Aled the Wise said, 'Love is the greatest pattern breaker and the greatest pattern maker.' Or, as Gruffud the Irreverent said, 'Love yourself as you would love an eehoo. Love each other as an eehoo loves you back.'"

Mrs. Ouzeley's eyes narrowed. "Are you in love, Miss de Galati? With a human?"

The surrounding crowd broke out into excited chatter. Scattered voices said "Unnatural" and "Sorcery," and Telyn was pretty sure she heard something about kittens from Tabbard.

When things quieted, Mrs. Ouzeley gestured to Mrs. Pembroke, who stood. "We have now heard from Miss Brower and this de Galati —quite unusual, but better done than not. Does anyone want to change their vote?"

Telyn blinked. *They already voted?*

Mrs. Gamage half-raised her hand.

Mrs. Pembroke scowled. "What is it, Sylva? Are you up or down?"

Mrs. Gamage turned her thumb down.

Mrs. Yates actually tittered behind a gloved hand, and Mrs. Pembroke had to raise her voice over the whispers.

"Very well. Mrs. Gamage has changed her vote." The ladies stood, and Mrs. Ouzeley smiled coldly. "Thank you for your most persuasive argument, Telyn Brower. And for yours, de Galati. It's unanimous, then. Petition for Rayvn Zamfir de Galati to join the Dating Circle has been denied."

Telyn could hardly breathe.

They voted before we got here? All of this has been a farce? And, after my arguments, Mrs. Gamage changed her vote...against us?

"I protest," she managed with barely a mouthful of air.

Mrs. Ouzeley tilted her head. "To whom?"

"To...to the cornics. To Minister Svemas."

Grebiana turned to the gilded chair where Second Gajos sat. "Thankfully, we have the Empire's representative right here. No need to delay."

The second burped with his mouth closed and began chewing his cud. "The Dating Circle's judgment is upheld." He slapped his hairy hand on the arm of the chair.

Everyone started talking at once, and the babble bounced around Telyn's head like the buzz of a beehive. She found herself holding onto the back of the chair so as not to collapse. She'd never even been given the opportunity to sit down; she'd failed too quickly. Her knees held the strength of potato dumplings.

"I'm sorry," she managed. "Sorry Rayvn, truly." She discovered from the knot in her belly that she really was sorry.

Rayvn patted Telyn's shoulder. "You just have to get me in the Dating Circle some other way."

The words took a few seconds to sink in. Telyn thought she had misheard.

"Er...even if that *is* possible...it's not..." Did the pattern girl understand what just happened? They'd been refused by the Dating Circle and Second Gajos both. Everyone was against them! "Even if I could —and I can't—we can't—it's too late to get an answer from the Library in Enshede. The roads will be closed. You can't keep your end of the, ah, agreement. Our deal is off, Rayvn. Kaput."

"I sent your inquiry already."

"You did?"

"I will give the reply to you once you get me on the Dating Circle."

Telyn goggled. If even a feather had landed on her shoulder her knees would have given out. Did the pattern witch think Telyn could spin clouds into yarn?

"Bye, then." Humming, Raven wandered out of the room, seeming oblivious to the storm of indignant, scornful, salacious, and even hateful chatter of the gathered humans.

Outside, around the corner and out of sight so the exiting crowds wouldn't get any satisfaction, Telyn wept on Cressida's shoulder. She hadn't realized how devastating it would feel to put herself out there in front of all her brethren—and lose. She hadn't realized how visceral the anger against flacks could be, nor what it felt like to absorb that prejudice first-hand.

Flacks are not all *evil. They do not all lord it over humans. Rayvn doesn't deserve this hatred. She hasn't owned any slaves. She doesn't exploit anyone.*

She's ditsy, but she and her mother keep the ghosts away.

And so her thoughts continued for a long time.

When she'd cried herself out, Cressida pushed Telyn to arms' length. Her face was compassionate but stern. "Are you going to tell me what this is really about?"

Telyn swallowed but could not reply.

"You've been keeping secrets from me. You've been lying to me— me!—your twin. This is about that magic mask, isn't it, the one the cornics have been searching for."

Telyn wiped the snot from her face with her sleeve before it could freeze there. "It doesn't matter now."

Cressida's eyebrows raised. "We're sisters, remember? We share things."

Biting her lip didn't provide any answers. No matter how much she wanted to share, she had gone too far. She had kept too many secrets. Couldn't it just blow over? Couldn't things go back to the way they were before? If she told Cressida the depth of her lies, forgiveness would come, but trust would never return completely.

I've already lost the Ever-Guise. No need to burden Cressida with the truth, not now.

"It's nothing. I just wanted information."

What a strange thing, Telyn thought, *to know you're lying to yourself and to do it anyway. Of course, this has nothing to do with burdening Cressida and everything to do with my own shame—and the hope that I can find the forehead piece again.*

I hope it with all my heart and soul. I will find it again, and I will learn how to use it, Library inquiry or no.

"Do you have the mask, or don't you?"

Telyn shook her head, and Cressida dropped her arms.

"Do you know who has it?"

"No. No...I don't have any mask...or whatever they're looking for. Promise. Pinky promise, hope to die."

"I'd tell you to be careful, to be sure you know what you're doing, but you won't, and you don't, so I won't bother." Cressida's understanding face had been replaced with the one usually reserved for drunks just before Raz threw them out. "Do me a favor: when you leave, read what's engraved over the Prefecture door.

"Oh, and come to the Sable Head. All these folks will be hungry with gossip."

The twins turned in different directions, Cressida heading towards the Sable Head and Telyn towards the Elbus River. She didn't have the strength to face the Sable Head just then. She wandered back across the bridge into the woods.

Of course, she took this direction. This was where she'd lost the mask. Yes, she recognized the same addiction Esther had for alcohol in her need of the Ever-Guise. Always, Telyn thought about the slippery, not-ceramic artifact, the way it fit so perfectly over her skin, the way it grew heavy when you made a successful proposal.

The way it made you feel important.

Powerful.

Telyn was willing to stand before all of Harlech and humiliate herself for it. She would befriend a flack just to get information about it....

And when Telyn tried to not think about the mask, that put it squarely in her brain. *A circle influencing itself over and around.* Mrs. Ouzeley's mocking voice floated back to her. *The math becomes very complex.*

Fink
Traitor
Quisling
Turncoat

The full moon and reflecting snow made a lantern unnecessary.

It's just as well that I lost it. The Marrow Wind did me a favor. Now I can stop lying to Cressida and start healing so we can be a team again. The Brower twins together again.

Together against the world.

She intended to go deep, find a new tree to climb—at least a two-hundred-footer—but her feet led her past the one she had nearly fallen from, where the magical misfire had covered her with stink and ripped the Ever-Guise from her life. Her eyes couldn't help but dart around the snow to see if enough of it had melted to warrant another search. Her feet couldn't help but circle the trunk one more time.

She'd looked everywhere, all around, multiple times. She no longer cared that the cornics could easily follow her trail; the forehead piece couldn't be here. She'd searched too many times.

With the way the Marrow Wind howled that day, it could have blown far, landed in another tree, and no one would find it in a thousand years. It might have blown straight into the river for all she knew.

She looked up at that ill-fated perch—and saw the gilded ceramic. About ten feet up, just out of reach for any normal human, the stubborn forehead had wedged in the crook of a dead branch.

I should leave it here; pretend I've never seen it. Maybe someone else would find it, maybe not. Who cares? I've nearly broken the addiction. I think of it fifty times a day instead of every second.

Do I really want to end up like Esther? Really?

But these thoughts came from a distant part of her mind—a weak, girly part that she hadn't listened to in a while.

A grin walked from one side of her lips to the other.

Telyn Brower needs no ladder.

She sprinted toward the chaos tree, kicked her foot off the trunk into a flying leap, and snatched the forehead. When she landed, she twisted her ankle. Pain shot through her shin, made her stumble, made her cry out.

And it didn't matter. No, it didn't matter at all.

She had the forehead again.

CHAPTER THIRTY

A clump of snow sloughed off the Sable Head's roof and plopped onto the three-foot drift which had blown against the porch overnight. Sitting side by side on the bench to the left of the door, Telyn pulled her long parka tighter and leaned against Hosh a bit more. From the center of town drifted the sounds of buckles clanging, leather creaking, and the nickers of horses anxious to be away, the final caravan leaving Harlech for the winter.

The bench to their right held four younger kids, the one to their left Razenbock and two other men. Most of the other porches and benches in town were likewise occupied.

Watching the final caravan depart was a favorite spectator sport in Harlech.

Hosh said, "My dad tells the story of one of these caravans, before we were born, which got caught in an avalanche at Gopher Pass. They got stuck there for weeks until some mages from Enshede got them out. Ended up eating the ones who froze to death. That's why they call it 'Gopher Pass:' too much snow fell to clear it, so the mages used fireballs to dig a tunnel through like gophers. So much snow fell that the Spring Sale wasn't held until five years later."

Telyn had heard this story many times. While mostly true,

everyone added their own twist. Five years? Exaggeration, pure and clear. The Academy wouldn't wait five years for their components and creatures.

But fireballs? That was a new one. Wouldn't they have roasted the survivors? Not to mention melting the snow and causing more avalanches?

Avalanches could kill armies of people, Telyn thought, wryly, remembering her hearing rehearsal.

She wished Cressida had joined them on the bench, but her twin had decided to spend the morning sewing. *I hope Cressida takes the time to watch the departure and doesn't work straight through the day. She works too hard, trying to make up for Esther.*

Trying to take care of her rebellious sister.

"The worst part is," Hosh continued, "when the mages came, the people didn't stop eating each other. They just asked if the flacks could supply a bit of vinegar sauce to liven it up."

Telyn plopped a handful of snow on Hosh's head. "Stop talking about cannibals."

"Why? Does it make you hungry?"

"No. It makes me...I'm feeling...lonely." Telyn blushed at her honesty. She'd meant to say "ill," but the word that had come out more correctly identified her feelings.

Lonely?

Yes, I am. It is better with a friend sitting next to me. But still, I wish I had someone like...well, not like Joram...like a nice Joram.

Hosh looked at her, wide-eyed. "You, lonely?"

Might as well own it.

"Yes, Hosh. Does it surprise you that I have feelings?"

Hosh rubbed his nose vigorously. He looked a tad guilty.

"You have the same hormones." Telyn touched her face, scowling. "It's that stupid Dating Circle thing. I'd never bothered thinking about boyfriends and all of that. Now we talk about it all the time. Well, you all do. I get to look at my 'fink, traitor, quisling' questionnaire."

"Why don't you just answer it?" Hosh said. "Give them what they want, and you can get your name on the Chart. You might enjoy—"

"No! I am not a quisling, whatever that is."

Proceeded by steam from the animals' breath, the draft horses of the final caravan rounded the corner. Six cornic riders plowed through the fresh snow, clearing paths for the wagons to follow. The lead wagon resembled a wheeled armadillo. It looked strong enough to withstand a battering ram—because it was. The wagon was designed as an avalanche shelter. If a roar started on the cliffs above, you abandoned everything and took shelter inside. Within, you could survive for several days. It had food and water, blankets and digging gear. Hatches could be opened from the inside, and the occupants could dig their way out.

In theory.

It also provided shelter in case of a rakasura attack. It didn't work too well with brakdaw-sized monsters and larger; the thick walls just slowed the beasts down and prolonged the inevitable. But those were rare this side of the Elbus River.

Behind the shelter wagon came a dozen or so wagons and sleighs. And another figure, a feminine figure, with her coat flaring over her hips.

"Uh, Telyn—"

"You invited Caitlin?" she asked, incredulous.

"Listen, you don't understand."

Caitlin caught Telyn's eyes and hurried faster, as if Telyn might actually want to see her!

"We need more information, right?" Telyn didn't deign to answer, but Hosh pressed on. "We've been wishing on Rayvn, and she hasn't budged."

"A few times—we've only wished a few times."

"And the mask gets too heavy to use. It seems to get heavier faster with fewer people using it."

"Hold on, Hosh. What are you saying?"

Caitlin was almost within hearing distance. Only the creak-clomp-clang of the horse-drawn wagons covered their conversation now.

"We need someone else to share the burden. We'll get thirty-three percent more wishes if we bring her on."

"No. Way."

"She already knows about the mask. She hasn't betrayed us to Joram, or...or Tabbard, or the cornics..."

Telyn had to admit, if Caitlin had betrayed them, Tabbard would have set up a second ambush—or finked to the cornics.

Too late to ponder much. She put on a fake smile, returned Caitlin's stiff, arms-outstretched hug, and plopped back onto the bench as quickly as possible. Caitlin settled on the other side of Hosh. Telyn put an arm around Hosh and pulled him close.

My friend, she thought, fiercely. *You quisling.*

A tall wagon-wheel passed close enough to throw slush on their boots. The hated CE stamp whirled by their faces, marking it as authorized by the Cornic Empire.

One of the Three Rules: *Humans shall not own wheels.*

Never had Telyn enjoyed watching the last caravan less, and yet she dreaded it coming to an end. When the caravan ended, she'd have no excuse to remain silent.

Mother of Squirrels, when did talking become more difficult than climbing? Hosh is right. We need—

A deep breath.

We need Caitlin. Two people isn't enough to carry the Ever-Guise's weight. I can barely make a wish every other day without cricking my neck.

She glanced left and right to be sure the folks on the other benches weren't listening, then leaned over Hosh. "Caitlin, I respect you for telling me about the hearing, even though it turned out the way it did. And for not telling Joram or Tabbard about the Ever-Guise. Especially the, ah, the fact we still have the forehead piece."

"I didn't."

"That's what I just said."

"Well, in that case," Caitlin said, without looking Telyn in the eyes, "I respect you for not using the forehead on me...or Joram or the others...these past weeks. I would have known if you had."

"You think so?"

"Yes. And Tabbard might have, too. You aren't nearly as sneaky as you think. The Ouzeleys were growing suspicious that magic was involved in driving all the business from the Copcut Ash to the Sable

Head. I had to throw them off by saying it was the shift from malt—which Raz waters down—to angel water, which he doesn't. Yet."

"That is so insulting."

"I just told you I respected you."

"Insulting to Raz."

"Has he tried watering down angel water?"

Telyn crossed her arms defensively. "Well, yes."

"Isn't anyone going to respect me?" Hosh asked.

Caitlin said, "No!" as Telyn said, "Be quiet."

"Thing is," Telyn admitted after a moment, "I didn't use the forehead on Tabbard because I didn't have it. I hid it in a tree, and the Marrow Wind blew it away. So, you don't have to respect me for that."

Caitlin's face went pale—the same pale as Esther when she ran out of angel water. The semblance disturbed Telyn a great deal.

Hosh enthused, "But we have it again. Bing-bong!"

"You found it!" Brightening immediately, Caitin began patting Hosh's face with her gloves. "Are you wearing it? I need to see it."

Hosh slapped away Caitlin's hands playfully.

Telyn lurched to her feet. "We had rules, we three. From day one, we started breaking them." The nearest cornic rider, a solder in a fur-lined coat, glanced at them curiously. Telyn waited until the soldier had resumed watching the road before continuing. "The lure of making suggestions outweighed our loyalty to each other, our rules, our common sense, everything. Using its magic became the most important thing in our lives. We're addicted."

"What? Telyn, you've got to be kidding." Hosh pulled off his glove and held his hand flat. "Am I trembling? Are purple veins showing up on my nose? When you lost it, I didn't lie around in bed, moaning."

"I live with an alcoholic. I know the signs."

"That sounds far-fetched," Caitlin said. "Sure, I think about it—a lot—but I managed to stay away from you even though I thought you had it. I didn't even climb the tree to try to find it."

"Listen to yourself. 'Managed.' 'Didn't even.' 'A lot.' You had to try really hard to stay away, didn't you? Really hard?"

Hosh snorted. "I'm sure the creators wouldn't have made it addictive. The problem could be that we don't have the other parts. Or because we're humans. Or, I don't know, a million other things. Why would they make something that hooks the wearer?"

"Exactly!" Telyn agreed. "We need more information. Caitlin, I wanted Rayvn in the Dating Circle because that was her condition—she would send an inquiry to the Library about the Ever-Guise if we got her into the Dating Circle. The Library is sure to have information on it. There are branch libraries in every major city in the world. Master Quid called it the 'world repository of knowledge.'"

"Huh." Caitlin made a helpless gesture towards the passing caravan. "One problem, in case you hadn't noticed: this is the last caravan until spring."

Four human shepherds riding llamas and their flock of black-haired goats trudged past, accompanied by the pungent scent of mohair. Thankfully, Telyn's 'foot infection' had almost completely healed, so the friends could appreciate the goats' aroma.

Telyn allowed a grin to spread over her lips. "Rayvn told me she put the inquiry in, and that it would go out in this caravan if not before."

"You aren't seriously telling us we can't use the mask until spring, are you?"

"You forget, who always comes to the Sable Head to tell stories?"

As one, Caitlin and Hosh shouted, "Redbeard!"

One of the younger kids on the nearby bench responded by throwing a well-aimed snowball. It knocked Hosh's head sideways.

Hosh fired two back, awkwardly. One of them veered completely off-course and struck the flank of a llama, causing it to start. The rider cursed at both Hosh and the llama.

The kids laughed. So did Telyn.

The caravan neared its end. Up by the Lucky H, they could see the townsfolk falling in behind the final wagon. Many would pile into the Sable Head. Razenbock, Telyn, and Cressida would work themselves to the bone this evening. Tomorrow, Harlech would seem darker and duller; the sun would rise later and set earlier; the cold air would bite harder.

"Redbeard will bring the Library's answer, and Rayvn said she'd pay for it with her own money."

"And she'll give it to us," Hosh enthused.

The kid threw another snowball. Hosh just couldn't keep his voice down.

"That's what she said...after we get her into the Dating Circle."

Caitlin's face drooped. "You've made the Ouzeleys your personal enemies. You're never getting Rayvn on the Dating Circle now. Even if we all use the Ever-Guise to pressure them, I don't believe the Circle will change its mind. Minister Svemas might have forced the issue, but he seems to have left this to Second Gajos, and Second Gajos is in the Ouzeley camp. He invites the Ouzeleys to dinner in his house in flacktown."

Turning to hide her body from the caravan and the townsfolk following along behind, Telyn unbuttoned her coat. From an inner pocket, she lifted the pliable ceramic just enough so her friends could see. It felt good to show them—and to share the addiction. "We have to convince Rayvn to want to give us the information."

"You want to use this on..." Caitlin leaned across Hosh as if drawn by the mask. "...on your friend?"

Telyn wanted to deny this. She wanted to deny that she had been using this to bend her friend to her will. She wanted to deny that a flack could even be her friend.

Pattern witches are flacks, not humans. How could a human be friends with a flack? One has their magic in life and the other in death. That whole petition to get Rayvn on the Dating Circle was a farce, a means to an end...

But she had to admit, Rayvn was growing on her—the flack's quirky sense of humor, her stubbornness, the strange way she looked at the world.

Telyn could not in good conscience deny the one nor the other, and so she did not reply.

"We need to make that one of the rules. We don't use the mask on a friend," Caitlin said. "Not on purpose, I mean, not directly."

"I don't know how you keep the effect confined to strangers, but there may be a way." Telyn buttoned up her coat. "That's one of the things we can try to learn from the Library."

Caitlin's breath came in little gasps; she seemed to be fighting an internal struggle. "It's not...not ethical...to use...on a friend." She wet her lips with her tongue between phrases.

Telyn closed her top coat button. Ordinarily she didn't do that, but she didn't like the greedy way that Caitlin had stared at the forehead.

Caitlin is right. It is never okay to coerce a friend into doing something they wouldn't have done on their own—not with alcohol, not with lies, and not with the Ever-Guise.

Especially not with the Ever-Guise.

The final vehicle, another shelter-wagon, trundled past their bench, its tall wheels spitting slush. Many in the following crowd had taken up a song, "A candle in the window," a desperate song about winter and loneliness. A song that, ironically had a jaunty, syncopated beat. Many folks quit following, tromped up the porch, and ducked into the Sable Head. Despite her winter layers, each footfall passed through the wooden bench to vibrate Telyn's bones.

"No showing the mask to Cressida or anyone else. Just the three of us." For some reason, Telyn felt the need to restate the rules. She cleared her throat. "We all make wishes in front of one another, no secret wishes. None of us takes it home. We hide it someplace."

"No wishing to change body parts," Hosh said.

"Don't wear the stupid lanyard when I wish," Caitlin added, making a show of removing the black-and-gold lanyard from her wrist and putting it in her pocket. "If two of the three of us say to get rid of the mask, we do it. *Tey* does it. No questions asked."

Telyn had been hoping the others had forgotten that one, but she nodded. "So, we add, 'No using the mask on friends.' Okay?"

"That's getting to be a lot," Hosh complained.

"That's eight," Caitlin said. "That shouldn't be too hard since you still have two unassigned fingers—"

Hosh dropped a fistful of snow down the back of Caitlin's jacket. She squealed.

Almost like old times. Almost. Can't trust her completely while she's with Joram.

Telyn removed the glove from her right hand and held out her pinkie. As the others hooked their pinkies over hers, Hosh said, "You're forgetting my rule: Hosh gets first dibs."

"Nine rules. Room for one more before you have to count on your toes," Caitlin said.

After the gloves were back on, Hosh sighed. "So, what now? Our new rule stops us from doing anything useful."

"We'll think of something," Telyn replied. "We always do."

"Actually, it is possible our new rule doesn't apply here," Caitlin allowed, slipping the black-and-gold lanyard back on her wrist before donning her glove. "A true friend wouldn't make conditions on the Library inquiry. She would share all the information with her friends voluntarily."

Hosh popped to his feet. "You're right. A friend would *want* to share anything she learned from the Library," he added, with a twinkle in his eyes. "Besides, she's a flack. The rule does not apply to Rayvn."

He beckoned the two girls to follow him into the alley behind the Sable Head. Both girls did so, but for some reason, Telyn's chest felt distinctly empty.

CHAPTER THIRTY-ONE

A week later, in Rayvn's billowy, second-story room—a room that reminded Telyn of living inside of someone's petticoat —the gang gathered to see if their wishes had moved Rayvn to give them the Library's answer. The four of them sat on square poufs in a circle.

Being fur-covered has some advantages, Telyn thought, pulling her hands into the sleeves of her cloak. The fabric walls did little to keep the cold at bay.

Rayvn wore a thin, white blouse and a cobalt-blue, split skirt that would have raised eyebrows to the roof of the Sable Head but allowed her tail to flit around without exposing anything underneath. The fact that she showed her tail openly seemed to indicate that she was growing increasingly comfortable with them.

Hosh certainly appreciated the skirt. Every time his eyes landed on it, they darted around like a frightened fish, knowing the struggling worm was hooked but unable to stay away.

Telyn grit her teeth and wished she'd worn something more provocative than her gray work dress.

The conversation had gone 'round and 'round, Telyn's friends trying to get Rayvn to agree to give them the Library's response, and Rayvn insisting she be let into the Dating Circle first.

Obviously, they hadn't used enough wishes. *Or maybe, directing wishes at a specific person just didn't work. They needed more information!*

"You don't know those Circle women," Telyn argued. "Once they've made up their mind, you might as well try to dig out a tree with a spoon. Especially that Mrs. Pembroke. If anything, she's worse than Mrs. Ouzeley."

"If you dug in the dirt with a spoon, the spoon would bend," Rayvn said, "and if you didn't have a long handle, you would scrape your knuckles. Why would you choose such an inappropriate instrument?"

"What I mean is there is nothing I can do. We went to the hearing; we were turned down. You are not getting in. Nor am I." Telyn was surprised by her own bitterness, given that she'd had no intention of joining the Dating Circle in the first place.

Telyn had stopped going to the meetings. Why bother, when every time they simply handed you a paper that asked if you were a traitor or a quisling (whatever that was)? "We tried. We really tried, which is all you can ask of us. So why don't you just agree to give us the Library's response when it comes? We'll even pay for it."

"There's still a way," Rayvn said. "Isn't there, Hosh?"

Hosh sort of squeaked. His shoulders had climbed up to his ears, and he was blushing. Telyn goggled when she realized why: Rayvn's tail snaked from under her skirt to tickle his ribs.

Caitlin gasped. "Are you flirting with Hosh?"

Rayvn smiled and tilted her head.

"He doesn't have any experience with flirting!"

"He seems to be adapting well. And I need the practice if I'm getting into the Dating Circle."

"That's not natural," Caitlin said, beginning to rise from her pouf. "You're furry! He's just skin."

"Ah, ladies, I'm right here," Hosh said.

Telyn felt a thrill spin down her legs. With the other two fighting, she'd have Hosh all to herself...

Wait, what? I'm not thinking clearly. I don't care about Hosh, not in that *way. What's wrong with me?*

"Hosh, what have you been thinking?" Caitlin wagged a finger first in Hosh's face, then in Rayvn's. "Leading the flack on like you might be interested, letting her touch you with her tail. The thing is disgusting, dirty. When Rayvn walks, it drags in the dirt like…er…just like—"

"Not 'What has Hosh been thinking?'" Telyn interrupted. "But what has he been *wishing*?"

Caitin blinked a couple of times until understanding dawned. She then punched Hosh's shoulder with a resounding *whap*, and his guilty head-duck was confession enough for a blind judge.

Telyn glared at her two friends.

Hosh has been using the mask to get popular again. No wonder we can't persuade Rayvn to give us the Library's answer. Caitlin is probably trying to save bugs with her wishes, too.

That also explains why it never seemed to get lighter…

"I really, really want to give you the information, Hosh," Rayvn said. "Really, I do. But Telyn and I had an agreement. Breaking an agreement is like breaking a pattern."

"So, what do we do?" Telyn asked, trying to keep her composure. She recognized the beginning of a negotiation. "If we put aside the impossible, we still have a dictionary to explore," she quoted Gruffud the Irreverent.

"Hmm, what can you offer me?"

"No, pattern girl. Your turn. We are asking the reasonable; you are asking the impossible."

Rayvn paced the room a couple of times, her annoyingly beautiful legs exposed with each stride, and that annoyingly cute tail nearly brushing Hosh on each pass.

Toying with a person's emotions this way is absolutely wrong, she decided. *If Hosh ever uses the Ever-Guise for popularity again, I'm going to sit on him while Caitlin shaves his eyebrows.*

"Your mom is part of the Dating Circle, Hosh. Your mom, Caitlin, works at the Prefecture where the Dating Chart is kept. Your mom" —Rayvn turned to face Telyn—"is a drunk."

"Thank you for that reminder," Telyn said impatiently. "So what?"

"Between Hosh's mom and Caitlin's mom, you have access to the Chart and the questionnaires and the book of calculations. I would give you the Library's answer for a full and complete copy of all of them."

Telyn gaped. "Is that all? How about the crown of the Cornic Emperor while we're at it?"

"In addition, I want your sister to make me a dress, Telyn, and Hosh can teach me the Promise Dance."

"HE WILL NOT!" Caitlin roared, pulling Hosh protectively into her arms.

If Hosh could have climbed the fabric walls to get away, he would have.

"This is ridiculous." She really had to give Hosh a piece of her mind. A spanking would be fun, too. "The Dating Chart and calculation book—if such a thing exists—is the most highly guarded artifact in Harlech. I'd have a better chance sneaking into Minister Svemas' office to steal his chair—with the Minister sitting on the chair and a fist of cornics guarding the door."

"That's my final offer," Rayvn said, sweetly.

Hosh peeked through the arms Caitlin had wrapped over his head. She'd actually climbed onto his lap! "Even if we got you the Chart," Hosh said, "it's like a, a snowflake, frozen in the moment. It gets updated every week. The Dating Circle has spotters all over town. The observations come in, and weight—I mean, importance—gets assigned to them. Somehow the ladies in Sums, Statistics, and Affairs of the Heart take this information to create models and make predictions. I don't know exactly what they mean by 'models.' What I do know is the Chart changes daily. Like the icicle getting warmed into water, if it freezes again, it will be a different shape."

"Could we, like, find out where they store these models? It must be a cellar or something." Telyn imagined a giant room filled with pink dolls and pin-cushion hearts.

"Um, not that kind of model. It's just paper, Telyn," Hosh said. "They fit in a few drawers and file cabinets in the Prefecture."

"Oh."

"This is serious business. The names are removed before the Sums ladies see the papers, and the calculations are never shown to the rest of the board. It's as blind as blind can get. The money is held by the cornic exchequer."

"Someone knows the whole picture," Telyn mused.

"If anyone does, it would be Mrs. Ouzeley and Mrs. Pembroke. Those two draw the chart and announce winners and losers. So, we're back to square one."

"I don't care about the money," Rayvn said. "I plan to write a treatise on emotional love connections and mathematical—"

"This is all stupid," Telyn said, "*emotional love connections.* Why don't you make your own observations at the Rusty Shackles, the taverns, the Mirror Pond, hide out in the stable after dark? You'll see plenty. The Dating Chart isn't about real love, it's about bets and odds and artificial stuff."

Rayvn turned to her with interest. "Do people marry outside of their primary Dating Circle?"

"It happens. Sometimes."

"Like, less than five percent. That's why you win big if you bet on those," Hosh said, mournfully. "Dad is always thinking he has a line on the next long-shotter."

Rayvn nodded sympathetically. "If I could get a look at the patterns, I could increase your dad's chances of winning."

They all returned to their individual poufs. Caitlin scratched an ankle absently—probably hoping Hosh would look.

"What do we do?" Telyn asked. All she could think of was using the Ever-Guise on Rayvn and trying again in a few days.

Caitlin hummed. "Could Cressida help us? She's on Sums, Statis—"

"Absolutely not," Telyn cut in. "We are not bringing my twin into this. This started with getting Rayvn into the Dating Circle as a legitimate member, and now you want to us to steal a-a calculation book. Some people would kill for this; they can make or lose a fortune based on the results. No involving Cressida, and no stealing. That's final."

"Beca Evans," Hosh said randomly.

The name tickled something in Telyn's mind, but she didn't remember what. "Who?"

"Beca Evans. She came up with the first Dating Chart. There is a statue to her in Elin Lleweln Park."

The bronze woman with the dice!

"Was she some kind of genius?" Caitlin asked.

Telyn snorted. "More like a busybody."

Silence embraced them. Time passed. Rayvn started humming. Caitlin started tying the beaded door into knots. Hosh picked at the skin on the back of his hand.

But Telyn kept thinking about charts and questionnaires, and about what Rayvn said earlier about their access: Hosh's mom on the Dating Circle, Caitlin's mom working in the Prefecture, Hosh gathering questionnaires, Cressida understanding differential equators, whatever they were.

Their little group had a lot of resources.

And then it came to her: Hosh's melted icicle could reform in a different shape, a shape that they controlled. "Let's make our own Dating Chart."

There was a brief pause as they all considered it.

"Like, from scratch?" Hosh asked.

"That's not what we agreed to," said Rayvn.

"That would take a lot of work," Caitlin observed.

"Think about it. If you really want to know how it works, Rayvn, you can be involved from the beginning. You can interview humans. Create tables. Learn how log rhymes work. If Beca Evans came up with the math, we can too." Telyn smiled. "After all, Beca didn't have a pattern witch helping her."

Hosh nodded. "Yeah. Love connections are all about geometry."

"Geometry?" Caitlin scoffed.

"Angles, odds," —He grinned—"triangles and cones. I like cones."

Caitlin smacked him. "How about feelings and love? Commitment and selflessness?"

"Math isn't my strong suit," Rayvn admitted. "I'm more of an intuitive pattern witch."

"We can work that out together," Hosh enthused. "I'll help you."

"He just wants your tail on his side," Caitlin said.

"Really?" Rayvn put her tail there.

Hosh smiled and blushed.

"Don't do it!" Caitlin said. "He's had an unfair...influence."

"Does that mean you have a crush for Hosh also?"

"Of course not."

No wonder Rayvn's lonely; come to think of it, with no other pattern witches in town. A little nudge from the Ever-Guise, and of course she develops a crush on Hosh. After all, he does have nice calves...

"Well, Rayvn, what do you say? We four create our own dating chart."

"How do we get people to answer our questionnaire?" Rayvn asked, sensibly.

"Let us take care of that," Telyn replied.

Caitlin and Hosh gave little nods.

CHAPTER THIRTY-TWO

They decided to call their circle *Kiss, Kindle, and Flame* and, Telyn had to admit, Rayvn worked the Sable Head like a first-class huckster. She would sit with the drinkers, chat them up, tease them with snippets of the questionnaire until they practically begged to see it, then feign reluctance to let them fill it out.

If that didn't work, Cressida 'mistakenly' served the drinkers another round, paid for. "Yes, I'm sure it's paid for—anyways, in this crowd, I honestly don't remember who to give it to. You have to take it." Rayvn would accidentally tickle their ribs with her tail, and the patrons would practically exhale their answers all over the parchment. It was disgustingly efficient.

Women seemed equally vulnerable to Rayvn's charm as men. Telyn decided it was the incisors. Two inches long, sharp as toothpicks and whiter than snow, their bobbing had a hypnotic effect.

To make them seem even more appealing, Rayvn started charging an egg for each questionnaire she handed out—more than enough to pay for the parchment and ink.

Standing in the swinging door to the kitchen, Telyn watched with arms folded, using her nose to warn her when to flip the sausages. No one seemed to care if they were a little black on one side. Or two.

Crowds jammed the public room cheek to jowl, and it had nothing to do with magic; tonight, Redbeard would auction off the mail. Among many other tricks, the old trapper could navigate Gopher Pass in winter. Either that, or he knew another route. Speculation ran high regarding Redbeard's secret pass, but he never let on one way or the other.

A small voice in the back of Telyn's mind wondered whether Redbeard was a gnome—or a gnome-human hybrid. Was such a thing even possible? Kiiptk had turned downright cagey when she'd asked about it. Shape-shifting would certainly help with winter survival.

As Rayvn handed out yet another kit—a loaner ink bottle with brilliant green ink, a silver-painted quill, and parchment—her inquisitive, violet eyes caught Telyn's for a moment.

A muscle in Telyn's jaw twinged. She wanted to be annoyed at the flack's smug little expression, but the annoyance came halfheartedly. First of all, Rayvn didn't have a smug little expression. In fact, Telyn had begun to realize, her face didn't have as much mobility as a human face. She couldn't really sneer or smile or pout—not with her lips. She showed pleasure in her posture, in the swivel of her ears, the wiggle of her whiskers and the swish and swoop of her tail—which she seemed more and more comfortable showing in public.

The annoyance came as part of the seesaw feelings Telyn felt for this one particular...girl.

Am I coming around to flacks?

No way. Not a chance.

Maybe just this one, a little.

A true friend would have made the inquiry to the Library without asking for anything back. If we didn't need to learn more about the Ever-Guise's powers, learn how to use it more efficiently and without addiction, and discover who would be coming after it come springtime, I never would have agreed to all this.

Telyn gave Rayvn an encouraging wave.

She's actually chatting up Raz. Wait, did he really—he did! Raz took a parchment.

"What are you goggling about?" Cressida returned with the latest stack of filled-out questionnaires. Once she had learned that Telyn had no intention of initiating gambling to go with her little experiment, she'd taken to the task with a smile. So much for not involving her.

"Huh? Oh, Raz just took a questionnaire. Can you believe it?"

Cressida joined her in the doorway. "Rayvn could sell venison to a deer."

"Yeah, who knew?"

"Seven more," Cressida passed across the rolled-up parchments. "A few spills, but readable. Tabbard actually filled one out."

Telyn pulled herself out of her thoughts. "What?"

"They're here. The oppression of winter has got to the Ouzeley's, too."

More like the oppression of the Ever-Guise. Telyn smiled wryly. All three of them—Telyn, Caitin and Hosh—had been using their wishes to convince people to fill out *Kiss, Kindle, and Flame* questionnaires. Things had been going much more smoothly since Telyn had insisted that "No secret wishes" meant that from now on, the three of them had to wish out loud.

Now the Ouzeleys, that is interesting. They'll lie, since lying is in their nature, but still...

Telyn almost felt sorry for the people with how much she and her friends would know about them. *But they fill out the questionnaires willingly, which makes it alright, right? The Ever-Guise just nudges them in that direction; it doesn't tell them what to put down or how much to bare.*

"Well, what kind of person is Tabbard looking for? Brains can't be any part of it."

"I know enough not to unroll it in that crowd. Don't you dare peek. Someone will catch you, sure as snowballs. This is supposed to be anonymous."

"I wouldn't think of it."

"You just did."

Telyn shrugged.

"This is anonymous, right?" Cressida asked.

"Of course. The names will be removed before odds get calculated, just like for the Dating Circle." Telyn turned back to the milling crowd. "I don't see Rayvn."

"Probably working the porch. The crowd spills clear across the porch to the street. I hope Redbeard has brought a lot of mail, or there is going to be a riot."

"Well, if he doesn't have enough, we can just give him some of these questionnaires to read."

They both laughed.

Wearing a bewildering assortment of leather straps, metal buckles, and knitted wool, his hair poking out of a coonskin cap in all directions, Redbeard set up near the fireplace in such a way to attract everyone's attention, with much shoving of tables, banging of benches, and mutters of "excuse me." He was short, stocky, hairy, and loud. The most remarkable thing about him were his eyes. Under unreasonably bushy eyebrows, surrounded by more wrinkles than a dried chamois, Redbeard's golden eyes reflected the firelight like a wishing well to another world.

Once he had created enough space, he cleared his throat to get the last few die-hard chatterers to turn his way. Then, with dramatic flair, he extracted a wax-sealed letter from his leather pack. The crowd roared in approval and began shouting the names of people who tended to receive the most entertaining correspondence: Fanny Flume-Bottom; Captain Dungfallow; Ellie Belly...

El-lie Bel-ly
El-lie Bel-ly
El-lie Bel-ly

Some of these were nicknames, some made up whole cloth. Kind relatives in Enshede or beyond sent fake letters for Redbeard to read to keep the snow-bound residents of Harlech entertained, and kinder relatives in Harlech paid to have them read.

Redbeard squinted at the writing. "Quackly Ducks?" Then he

said it again, louder. "Quackly Ducks?" The room quieted. When no one responded, he held the letter over the fire dramatically.

Telyn figured Mr. Ducks had never existed. This must've been one of the made-up ones, always entertaining. Telyn and Cressida had taken stools along the bar, and Telyn rocked back and forth, eager for someone to come forward.

"I'm Quackly Ducks," a trapper yelled, finally, and blew a raspberry on his forearm. The crowd chuckled.

"Two eggs buys you the letter," Redbeard called. "Three for me to read it aloud."

"How much for you to stuff it?"

"Already done; that's why the bargain price."

The crowd chanted "Read it, read it, read it..."

The theatrics continued for some time, until finally, "Mr. Quackly Ducks" went forward with three eggs held high. Redbeard accepted payment graciously, climbed from the bench onto a table—which made him just above average height—and broke the seal with flair. "Mrs. Quackly Ducks, I write to you with grave news. Your gizzard has been arrested for offensive indigestion..."

After the hilarity of the made-up letter ended, Redbeard descended from the table and again put his hand high in the air, wiggled his fingers, and plunged it into his leather pouch. Telyn had always wondered if he shuffled the letters randomly or if he carefully organized everything for best dramatic effect. More likely the later, she decided, seeing as how the whole evening appeared to be a well-choreographed improvisation—if that wasn't an oxymoron.

The next letter was more serious, to one Mrs. Wynne—a real person—and labeled *confidential* in red. Mrs. Wynne produced two eggs for the letter, but sensing the gravity of the woman's countenance, bidding started immediately. Mr. Pembroke won with a bid of three birds and two eggs—and this *was* entertainment, after all. Returning to his perch on the table, Redbeard read the letter aloud, an announcement that Mrs. Wynne's husband had died of swine fever and left them with debts, and would they kindly send payment plus interest to so-and-so esquire or face the seizure of their property. If they had no property, then her servitude would suffice for a period of one year per hundred-huron debt, that portion allocated to the debt minus upkeep and rounded to the nearest full year.

It was the kind of disaster everyone dreaded—a debt you inherited without even being responsible for—and Mr. Pembroke looked well pleased to have paid the birds to have it read aloud. It would feed the town's gossip for many a moon. With pats and handshakes, the Ouzeley's and several other men congratulated Mr. Pembroke on choosing well.

Redbeard apologized to Mrs. Wynne upon presenting her the letter, and he handed her all three birds, two eggs at the same time. She turned away with a mixture of sadness, embarrassment, and gratitude.

Several other folks in town began a collection in her name.

Yes, public humiliation hurt, but it also engendered sympathy. In a small town like Harlech, sharing your sorrows could be the best way to get help—as long as someone like the Ouzeleys didn't figure out how to take advantage of you in the process.

Telyn narrowed her eyes at the Ouzeley and Pembroke families sitting together near the stairs. They'd pointedly brought their own bladders of angel water, loudly stamped with the stylized green symbol of the Copcut Ash.

Razenbock didn't complain, probably because he owed them money.

Gruffydd the potter received news of his daughter's marriage, and Hari Uren got accepted into the guild of shipbuilders. In bogus news, Oopsie Sneezalot got his face shaved off in a freak barbershop accident, and Afon Puffylips won Vool's annual jellyfish-kissing competition.

Telyn had to wipe the tears of laughter from her eyes with that one. She was sure Hosh and Caitlin must've been somewhere in the crowd, but she couldn't spot them. A barrel of fish couldn't have fit in more beings than the Sable Head on letter day. No matter. She and Cressida enjoyed themselves immensely. Even Esther showed, nodding a greeting at her daughters and finding room near the fireplace with some of her Sewing Circle friends from way back. This might possibly be the best evening of the year. It felt like times past, before the auction and the Ever-Guise had made life so dramatic.

"Rayvn Zamfir de Galati," Redbeard announced. "Billowy fabric house in the town of Harlech, daughter of Anicuta Zamfir de Galati, Pattern Witch. Inquiry response from the Library at Enshede. Rayvn Zamfir de Galati?"

Rayvn glided forward, bronze eggs in hand. Telyn's heart beat a little bit faster.

Telyn felt something, some pressure of attention, and she made the mistake of taking her eyes off Redbeard—and found them drawn to Tabbard. He stared at her from across the room. He'd noticed something in her posture.

"Miss de Galati?" Redbeard asked. "Aloud?"

Rayvn extended the hand holding her coins. "Private, thank you."

Redbeard began to pass her the letter, when Tabbard stood and shouted, "Ten birds, right here!"

"No thank you," Rayvn said, her arm extended.

"I'm calling it. Ten birds to have the inquiry read."

The crowd murmured. Flack letters didn't get read in public. It wasn't done. If they took advantage of Redbeard's services at all— which flacks rarely did—they paid their money, and that was that.

Telyn's heart could have stopped. It felt like it *had* stopped. Pain moved from her chest through her limbs.

No, no, no no. Why in the world did I have to meet Tabbard's eyes at that precise moment? Sneaky skunk, he's been watching me this whole time, looking for a clue. And like a complete idiot, I gave it to him.

"I don't want it read, please," Rayvn said, as forcefully as her airy voice would allow.

Redbeard hesitated, the inquiry poised between finger and thumb. Ten birds was a lot of money; upsetting flacks wasn't the best plan. The two thoughts must've been warring in his mind.

Wulstan Ouzeley rose dramatically and smacked his silver-handled cane on the floor. "Come now, Redbeard, are we making different rules for flacks here, in the free city of Harlech? All are equal here on mail day, aren't we? Humans and nonhumans are both eager to be free of winter's oppression for a brief period."

"I'll give you five birds if you don't read it," Rayvn said, fishing around at her skirts for a pocket.

Telyn squeezed her eyes tightly shut.

Rayvn couldn't have made a worse move. Now *everyone* wanted to know what the Library had to say.

"Twelve birds to read it," Tabbard announced immediately.

Conversation broke out all over.

Slowly, reluctantly, Telyn opened her eyes again, wishing to find herself in bed, just waking from a nightmare. Tabbard divided his attention from Redbeard to launch evil sneers at Telyn, and her pulse quickened. She wanted to burst forward, grab the letter and chuck it into the fire.

Could she reach it before Tabbard did?

Cressida grabbed her hand. "Is this bad?"

Telyn nodded.

Cressida pursed her lips. When they were young, Cressida used to don that exact expression when she prepared to take the punishment for something Telyn had done. Their father trained them to be a team, and so they never ratted each other out, never complained about sharing each other's punishments—until the Ever-Guise, that is.

Too many secrets. Telyn felt a twinge of guilt for the umpteenth time. *I have to tell Cressida the truth one of these days. Soon.*

The mask is making me keep secrets. It's tearing me and Cressida apart. Is it...could it be...evil?

Patrons began pooling their resources, and several other bids were offered. Four members of the Dating Circle offered fifteen birds. Leutric Quid offered sixteen.

"Sixteen whole birds—from Quid!" Cressida whispered. "Must be half his life savings."

Telyn could only moan in despair. She didn't have that kind of money. None of them did.

Evidently, Rayvn hadn't brought more than five birds, for she stood there stupidly in the middle of the room. For all the world, it looked like she had started humming.

Redbeard's grin grew wider. "How much for the mysterious inquiry from the Library at Enshede, the world repository of knowledge, the guardian of the world's most heavily guarded secrets?"

Telyn couldn't let this happen. She couldn't! "Five birds to give it to the pattern girl, unread," she said, "or Minister Svemas will hear about it."

Redbeard held the letter to the lamplight, squinted at it with one eye. "Ah, the Minister himself, is it? I'm trembling in my boots."

"We'll give you twenty, Mr. Redbeard, courtesy of the Ouzeley family." Wulstan put his hand on Tabbard's shoulder. "For the good of all residents of Harlech. Let's hear what our pattern girl is trying to hide. Is it something to do with ghosts? Murders?" He pointed his cane at Tums suckered to the wall. "Vengeful spirits possessing eehoos?" He swung the cane to point at a figure sitting in the rear of his own table. Telyn hadn't noticed him before.

"Second Gajos is here as my personal guest. He will take the information to the Minister, won't you?" The cornic raised a C.A.-stamped bladder of angel water in agreement.

Sensing the end of the game, the crowd quieted.

In the flickering firelight, Redbeard accepted the Ouzeley's birds with a formal bow, broke the important-looking seal on the letter, and scanned it. His expressive eyes didn't travel all that far. He raised his chin, set his long beard at a jaunty angle, and cleared his throat.

"It says here, the letterhead, 'Great World Library, global repository of books and scrolls, trans-species distiller of true information, Magical Inquiries Division. Inquiries numbered one through eight regarding the Ever-Guise: denied. Entries represent security concern or misinformation.

"Inquiry number nine regarding Galati Breeding Temple: Pekrul, Ivantie." He spelled the name letter-by-letter.

Looking rather perplexed, Redbeard refolded the letter and extended it toward Second Gajos. When the sheep-headed cornic waived it off as unimportant, Rayvn accepted the letter, tucked it into her belt sash, and regained her seat. Wulstan Ouzeley blushed and sat, having just surrendered twenty birds for nothing.

Tabbard glared back and forth from Rayvn to Telyn, until both Telyn and Cressida stuck out their tongues at him.

The rest of the evening passed in a blur. Yes, the remainder of the letters contained some good drama, entertainment and gossip, but Telyn couldn't appreciate it. They'd learned nothing.

Nothing at all.

And it wouldn't take a genius to guess that their interest in the Ever-Guise went beyond ordinary curiosity.

"What a nice evening," Rayvn said, joining the twins at the bar as the last of the patrons filed outside. She looked as happy as an eehoo in a barrel of tubers. "We have a hundred thirteen questionnaires filled out, and I learned the name of my fiancé."

CHAPTER THIRTY-THREE

They hadn't met at Dragon Tower in ages. The place seemed ageless, the light slanting in from the window slits frozen in time, the damp air un-stirring, the woody, powdery scent of moss suspended in place. Not for the first time, Telyn wondered how long the ruins had stood and what they must have been like in their heyday, and why the fortifications were built on the Chaos Woods side of the Elbus River when danger generally emerged from within the Chaos Woods. Had there once been a civilization on the forest side of the river, one that feared the denizens of the coast more than the beasts of the forest?

It was almost a shame—almost—to bring out the devotion bugs. Telyn smiled as she placed the striped, bulbous bugs in the windowsill. Sprinkle a little alcohol on them, and *whiff*—they'd thank you with a floral potpourri that could melt women's hearts and drive the most recalcitrant men to perform the promise dance. Ironically, they laid their eggs in dung—preferably llama. She'd found these bugs not far from the human school.

Telyn dripped angel water on the first brown-and-white striped bug and inhaled the resulting sweet spice. She intended to donate the bugs for the Dead Winter Dance—after she'd inhaled her fill.

Unusually, Caitlin's footsteps on the stairway preceded Hosh's shuffle.

"Well, you're early," Telyn said coldly. She placed the bugs in the windowsill so any breeze would blow the scent throughout the room.

Rather than greeting her, Caitiln rushed over for a hug and sobbed. This hadn't happened in ages, and Telyn hardly knew what to do with her arms—especially the hand holding the bladder of angel water. She'd never been super affectionate except with Tums, and she didn't know if she wanted this with Caitlin. Finally deciding not to over-think it, Telyn simply draped her arms around her friend's back until Caitlin pulled away.

Not knowing what expression was appropriate, Telyn frowned with her eyes and gave a half-smile. "All better?"

Caitlin wiped a string of snot from her nose. She looked around for where to put it.

Telyn retreated a step.

"What's that smell?" Caitlin said, finally, using a clump of moss as a kerchief. "S'nice."

Telyn presented the devotion bugs with a wave of her hand.

"Tell me your troubles," Telyn said, half quoting the Gruffud the Irreverent. The other half of the phrase was "and I'll show you my snore," But she didn't think that would be appreciated.

"Joram isn't loving to me anymore."

Telyn tried to hide the satisfaction that rose like the morning sunshine on her face. "How so?"

"When we used to go to Rusty Shackles, he'd touch my calf with his ankle. When we walked in under the market hall, he'd hold my hand. He used to brush my hair out of my face," —She demonstrated —"and touch my chin with his finger before he kissed me."

Telyn felt an involuntary thrill. Having never kissed a boyfriend herself, she wondered what it felt like, how well she would do. Would she crack her teeth against the guy's teeth? Drool like a fool? Could she hide any awkwardness without appearing to have too much experience? Some guys didn't want a woman of experience. Others—

Well, those others she didn't want. She'd never been attracted to bad boys.

Unexpectedly, Dagger's face popped into Telyn's mind. She cleared her throat. "He's just getting the pre-dance jitters, that's all. What does the Dating Chart show?"

Almost mournfully, Caitlin replied, "We are in the innermost circle. Joram's closest secondary match is Isla Yarwood."

"Hmm. How close?"

"Their circles aren't even touching."

"There, you have nothing to worry about."

Another sob burbled from Caitlin's toes through her shoulders to exit her mouth in a wail. "What if I'm a long-shotter?"

"You won't be. What's not to love?" Telyn touched Caitlin's wavy, brown hair, looked at her dimpled chin and wide, kissable lips, and meant every word. "Jordan would be a silly goose not to love this."

Caitlin wiped the few remaining tears from her cheeks. "I need to make it true."

Coming up the stairs, Hosh's uneven footfalls broke the moment. His head emerged moments later.

"You two didn't start wishing without me, I hope," he said. Then he looked at Caitlin as if noticing her for the first time. "What's with her?"

"She thinks she and Joram are long-shotters."

"Really?" Hosh's eyes got a calculating squint.

"You are *not* betting against your friend," Telyn said.

"I didn't say anything."

She glared until Hosh hobbled to the windowsill and sat, not meeting her gaze. Singles weren't allowed to place bets through the Dating Circle, lest they form pretend relationships and rig the system, but side wagers and surrogate betting happened all the time.

"So," he said finally, "you aren't wasting wishes on llamas and bugs, are you?"

Caitlin withdrew a little and sat beside Hosh. Both friends gazed at Telyn expectantly. Each had that sallow, haunted look you got if you didn't use the Ever-Guise's magic often enough.

Telyn had seen that look in her own reflection that very morning. They hadn't touched the forehead since Redbeard had read the mail.

It was too hot now. Rayvn's inquiry may have come up empty, but it mentioned the Ever-Guise specifically.

That wannabe minstrel Corporal Velky shadowed Telyn quite openly now. Another soldier kept an eye on Rayvn, and Tabbard and his gang seemed to be watching them as well.

Telyn had moved the mask from the top of the tree to the chute that passed under the Lucky H, part of a sewage labyrinth that drained rainfall away from Harlech. Kids used the tunnels all the time as shortcuts (when they weren't traversing the sod-roofed homes), so it wasn't unusual to duck into one. This way, any of the three could retrieve the forehead, confusing any observers. Or so their theory went.

Hosh had come up with the plan, and it seemed sound.

Telyn avoided the chute and even the nearby ally, lest her traitorous feet bring her there on their own. She hated to admit how hard it had been to stay away. In her struggle to resist the Ever-Guise, Telyn had acquired a new appreciation for Esther's addiction.

She swallowed noisily, as if her mouth were full of doubts. "We need to be careful."

"Everyone thinks Rayvn has the mask. We have nothing to worry about." Hosh's confidence looked forced.

"That's not good, either."

"She's a flack!"

"So?"

"So—who cares what happens to her? Flacks enslave humans all the time."

"Not in Harlech."

"Doesn't matter. They could if they wanted to. Rayvn will be fine. She's not just any flack, she's a pattern witch." Hosh wiggled his fingers. "Untouchable. The cornics would never risk her mother leaving the Sepulcher unguarded."

Telyn found herself shaking her head. "It's not right to shift suspicion to her; she never did anything to hurt us."

"We didn't do that on purpose. Besides, her inquiry at the Library turned up zilch. What did you get for your pain, huh? Nobody likes you, *and* you found out nothing."

"Hosh, your mouth," Caitlin warned.

Telyn picked up a devotion bug and inhaled its stock-and-roses aroma, trying to fill the emptiness Hosh's indelicate words spawned in her belly. The musky sweetness that came—er, from its rear, probably—helped clear the rattles from her brain. *"Nobody likes you." Mother of Squirrels, does Hosh have it right?* Despite her best efforts, she hadn't been able to ignore the Dating Chart entirely.

She'd found Cressida's name alone in a circle on the corner of the map. But Telyn's own name had not been added—and never would be. Not unless she admitted to being a *fink, traitor, quisling*...

Telyn Brower was outside the odds, outside the calculations, doomed to be alone.

Not even a long-shotter; a no-shotter.

For a second time that morning, Dagger's face flashed in her brain.

How weird. Why would the thief's mug appear when I'm pondering the dry fire of loneliness?

"Come on, Tey. The Dead Winter Dance is in three days. You might not plan to go—"

"Fine, fine. One wish each. We have to be very careful not to be seen going into the tunnel. I can scout—"

"Way ahead of you." Caitlin pulled the forehead piece from her coat pocket. "Should have asked, but no one was around; I got in and out without being seen." Wasting no time, Caitlin slipped it on and, the second the ceramic had melded against her skin, said, "I propose that the men of Harlech find me attractive."

"You don't need that, Caitlin." Over the past couple of years, Caitlin had developed the bosom of an adult while retaining the smooth vitality of youth, eyes wide and intelligent, posture confident, brown hair glossy as silk. "All you need is your dress, Caitlin, your smile. Any man would be fool not to offer you a promise dance."

Shyly, Caitlin peeled off the forehead piece and handed it to Hosh. He repeated the same wish, substituting only the word *women* for *men*. Neither Caitlin nor Hosh looked at the other this whole time.

Receiving the now warm-and-heavy ceramic, Telyn grinned. "Look out, or you'll end up together."

Her friends booed—and spent a lot of energy not catching each other's eyes.

"What are you going to wish?" Caitlin asked.

Telyn had thought about a thousand different wishes, and a million phrasings of the thousand, and finally, she had decided to not make any choice at all. She'd just let her gut tell her at this very moment—or her heart. Whichever spoke first.

She recalled a conversation she'd had with her sister a few evenings before. Back in their cabin, when Esther had gone to the privy before bed, Cressida took Telyn aside. "Swear to me you aren't doing anything with the mask and that pattern flack."

This was one oath Telyn could take, since the pattern girl didn't have anything to do with the mask...directly.

She swore.

"Swear to me you aren't still keeping secrets from me."

Telyn shook her head. This was an oath she most definitely could not make.

Even though they were the same age, even though Telyn towered over her sister by three inches, Cressida's intensity intimidated her.

Cressida squeezed Telyn's arm until it hurt, and she thought they might actually come to blows. She'd never seen her sister so angry. No, angry wasn't the word for it. *Fearful*.

Concerned.

Seeing the hurt she caused her twin, Telyn had teared up.

"Watch your back," Cressida had forced through clenched teeth. She released Telyn's arm and began stripping down for bed.

They didn't speak the rest of the night. Cressida refused to acknowledge Telyn's hand-talk and departed before dawn.

Telyn had never felt so isolated from her twin in all her life. If only she could tell Cressida why she was keeping secrets—to protect her!

Right now, Cressida was completely safe. If she knew anything, anything at all, she'd be as exposed to arrest or retribution as Telyn and her friends. And now, with the Library inquiry read aloud in the Sable Head, they were all as exposed as Rayvn.

She had to keep Cressida safe—even if it tore them apart.

Telyn took a deep breath. "I'm going to wish that...that the flacks look elsewhere than Rayvn for the Ever-Guise." To her friends' surprise, she added, "She saved our skins when she made those cornics' pants fall off on the bridge, remember, Hosh? She owed us nothing, and she saved us."

Telyn fitted the ceramic to her forehead and let the words come. The tension in her neck and back relaxed. She felt as warmly comfortable as if wrapped in a blanket, as if the wish had been preordained.

CHAPTER THIRTY-FOUR

For obvious reasons, Telyn avoided the Copcut Ash—except on dance day, the one day of the year when curiosity overwhelmed her dislike of the Ouzeleys. *Probably that dry fire of loneliness thing. It's brought my cold heart out of hibernation.*

She'd found three excuses to visit already: donating the devotion bugs to the decorators; helping Raz cart over barrels of malt from the Sable Head (his donation); and stringing evergreen garlands from the crown molding with Cressida. Her twin took the opportunity to ask again if she and Rayvn were in any kind of trouble. Cressida even asked if this had something to do with the ghost from the Sable Head.

Way too close for comfort.

Telyn pretended she had forgotten the ghost and lamely redirected the conversation to the transformation of the Copcut Ash into an enchanted wonderland. Soft textures, twinkling lights, and layers of shadow turned the already-beautiful public room into a fairyland. Silken garlands were strung from the ceiling, and innumerable candles hung like will-o'-the-wisps on the crystal chandeliers.

Like a centerpiece along the north wall, the Dating Chart had been festooned with red-berried holly. Over its bird's-eye view of

Harlech the names had been penned in glowing silver ink to appear to hover above the town.

As a child, Telyn had conjured up all kinds of unlikely contortions for the promise dance. The reality was entirely different.

On the woman's part, it involved a certain amount hip swaying, eye-batting, and suggestive looks over your shoulder. But most symbolically, as the music closed, the woman would extend her right foot, pointed, if possible. The man would spin around and around, sort of like the combatants in the brakdaw fight, bow to the proffered foot as if it were some kind of divinity, and offer a ribbon.

If all went well, the man would drop to one knee and proceed with a symbolic tearing of the stocking. He then would tie the ribbon around the bare ankle.

Marriage would come later, presumably.

If the man was a particular cad, he would swap the red ribbon for the black breakup ribbon, tie that around the ankle, and whirl away to leave the woman looking the fool.

Half the crowd would then storm to the betting table to collect their winnings.

The suspense was terribly exciting.

On dance night, a crush of people waited outside the Ash, from the elderly down to swaddled babes in their mothers' arms. At first, waiting in line with all the others, Telyn told herself she just wanted to see everyone's pretty clothes. If she had worn her best dress beneath her cloak, the green one that buttoned up the back with fancy, porcelain buttons and left a bit of cleavage in the front., well, it felt good to dress up now and then.

After she'd been waiting in line for fifteen minutes, Telyn managed to convince herself that she just wanted to have a peek inside, just a quick peek at the decorations.

It took another fifteen minutes to file past the bouncers and devotion bug-scented festoons above the front door. By this time, Telyn admitted to herself that she really was going to the dance, but she would only stay for a few songs.

And she wouldn't dance.

She recognized her bug hanging upside down on the ribbon festoon, the one whose leg she'd broken upon picking him up. It was a nice touch, having the smell of roses and stock greet the guests. She mouthed an apology to the bug for breaking its leg, removed her cloak, and handed it to the bouncer as she stepped inside.

Several heads turned.

She felt...beautiful

She may be Too-tall, but her legs could make an entrance, and this dress showed them nearly to her knees. Only the thin layer of her white stockings hid her ankles.

Remembering the night when she'd acquired the forehead piece, she wondered what that pickled trapper would say if he could see her now. *If I recognize him, I'll slap him—or dance with him. I'll decide on the moment.*

Telyn laughed as if drunk. It was that kind of night.

The band had already begun to play. They had been relegated to the corner. This night belonged to the dancers...

...and the betting.

On the Chart, she found Caitlin-Joram penned above the Prefecture and smiled wistfully. Joram's name was strong and angular, Caitlin's swirly and feminine. She'd gotten over the fact that Joram ran with Tabbard, hadn't she? After all, there weren't that many boys their age in Harlech. Why shouldn't Caitlin be happy?

Hosh's name hung over Mirror Lake surrounded by a constellation of women. Further east, Cressida Brower sat alone. Had Cressida calculated her own odds? What an equation that would have been: a dividend of beauty and generosity over a poverty divisor, carry the remainder of a Too-tall sister, resulting in a quotient of inescapable loneliness.

Refusing to dwell on the fact that her own name would never be inscribed here no matter how many bugs she found and donated, Telyn moved on. She didn't care. Not a bit.

The Dating Chart isn't real love; it's betting, odds and math and hurons. Stupid.

A new song began, first with kettle drums, which were joined by strummed lyres, playful recorders, and a pair of bass voices bopping out nonsense words. The crowd surged onto the wooden floor, but Telyn refused to be rushed.

Cressida manned a table displaying lovely ribbons. Each green ribbon was embroidered with a different number of red hearts, one through four, depending on the level of interest you might want to show—publicly—to your date. Even the black and silver breakup ribbon was beautiful in a way. The ribbons cost three eggs; you were required to buy a whole set so as not to influence the betting. Some couples would tie the ribbon to the lady's ankle right away; others waited until the final dance of the evening.

Unused ribbons would be burned in a public bonfire at the close of the dance, and the Dating Chart would be wiped clean.

Joram and Caitlin brushed past Telyn with barely a nod. Joram purchased his set of ribbons. He conspicuously shuffled the four-heart ribbon to the top, and while Caitlin smiled gratefully at him, the girl's eyes were puffy.

They've been fighting again. Which makes me sad, and...hopeful?

Past the Dating Chart and ribbons, Mrs. Gamage and Mrs. Pembroke manned the betting table, guarded by four cornic soldiers. Four! As if brigands would dare break in and steal the strongbox on a night like tonight. Betting proceeded briskly, with well-clad people coming and going, dropping coins as fast as they could clink.

Telyn approached the table and tugged Mrs. Gamage's sleeve. "I'd like to place a bet, please."

Mrs. Gamage stared at her oddly. "But you're single, Telyn dear. That isn't allowed. Unmarried couples could try to rig the outcome."

"You won't find my name anywhere on the Dating Chart, will you? It is literally impossible for me to rig anything."

Mrs. Gamage looked to Mrs. Pembroke, who shrugged.

"I almost envy you, dear," Mrs. Gamage said conspiratorially, gesturing toward the iron-bound strongbox. "All of this takes the zing out of the sparkle. Love should be spontaneous, not scrutinized and converted to probabilities." Mrs. Pembroke cleared her throat, and Mrs. Gamage focused. "Well, Telyn dear, who do you want to bet for?"

"Not for," Telyn said, pulling out the entirety of her purse. "Against—Joram and Caitlin. One bird, three eggs." Not that she wanted them to fail, exactly, but the mismatch between those puffy eyes and their position on the Chart didn't make sense.

"Wishful thinking makes for poor betting," Mrs. Gamage said, taking Telyn's money and handing her a receipt. "You will learn in time, dear."

Mrs. Pembroke straightened her crocheted shawl and jotted the bet down in a book.

A beefy hand wrapped around her own, and Raz's gruff voice asked, "You dancin'?"

Telyn smiled gratefully and allowed the big man to sweep her into a square dance alongside Redbeard, two widows, and several strangers.

Altogether, it turned into an enchanting evening. Several men asked her to dance, and in the group dances, they didn't have much of a choice. It amused Telyn more than a little that Tabbard, Dylan, and Hefin left a square rather than take a spin with her, and she ended up with Hosh for the do-si-do. She hardly minded that she didn't have money for hot spiced cider, meatballs, or sweet pastries, having bet everything on Caitlin getting the black and silver breakup ribbon.

And the best part?

As the name Telyn Brower didn't appear on the Dating Chart, no married men cut in for the express purpose of asking nosy questions, nor did ladies take her aside to encourage her to bare her soul.

Since they couldn't bet for or against her, they didn't care.

The Dating Circle may just have granted Telyn her freedom.

Every hour on the hour, the ladies redrew the circles based on the ribbon exchanges they'd managed to spot. The midnight hour proffered the most amorous turmoil, as evidenced by the profuse turpentine smell from the solvent used to erase and redraw. Heledd Glines even arrived with a strongbox from the Rusty Shackles to place her own sizable bets, which caused still more redrawing.

About this time, Telyn noticed Heath Robinson standing alone. She crossed the room and held out her hand. "A dance?" She enjoyed his look of surprise. He turned out to be as good a dancer as a brawler, and he didn't mind that she had a couple inches on him. They danced four or five songs, until he asked if she was interested in taking a walk in the moonlight. Telyn declined politely, and Heath became surly in response, snagging a mug of malt and downing it in one long gulp. Since he seemed more interested in malt than in dancing, she left him with thank you and a peck on the cheek.

He was too old for her, anyway.

Later in the evening, in a break between songs, Caitlin sought Telyn out. A stain blemished the waist of her blue dress, and her breath smelled like mulled wine.

"How are things?" Telyn asked, a little disingenuously given that she had bet her whole savings on her friend's love life collapsing.

"Awful. Never mind that. They know you have the mask. Tabbard, Joram, Mr. Ouzeley, they all know. Their tongues are loose with drink, and they've been talking in front of me."

Telyn pulled Caitlin out of the lamplight to a corner table. They pressed their heads close together, just two friends commiserating. Nothing could be more natural.

Telyn spread their hair over their faces to hide their lips from lookers. She felt eyes upon them—though they were probably watching Caitlin. No bets had been placed on Telyn, so there was nothing to see there. She felt surprisingly calm. "They think Rayvn has the mask."

"I don't know how they know, but they know."

"Caitlin, they're using you." She could see it all now. This whole dance, the whole courtship of Joram and Caitlin, was just to get information.

"It's time to get rid of it. Now, tonight. Pitch it into the river like we said."

"But we're almost there," Telyn reasoned. "The Sable Head is doing well; the Prefecture issued an edict about llama abuse; Hosh hasn't stopped dancing all night—"

"Tey, I'm scared. I can't get caught. My parents work at the Prefecture! Imagine what the cornics would do to them."

"That won't happen."

"It's against the Rules."

"Caitlin, they are baiting you, trying to see if we have it or not. They made a couple of guesses after Redbeard read the Library inquiry. They are just digging around like badgers to see if they can uproot some silly voles. We can't be the voles, Caitlin, we have to be the wolves."

Telyn tried to sound confident, but she wondered how much the Ouzeleys really knew. *As dumb as Tabbard is, he can be maliciously clever, too—like when he set up that ambush for Hosh. He might be smart enough to puzzle things out.*

He might just be smart enough to enlist Caitlin's help.

She hated to think that, but Caitlin had betrayed them before in the alley. What if her allegiance had always been to Tabbard and Joram?

Some of Caitlin's panic infected her. She wanted to check on the forehead piece. *Has someone already taken it from its hiding place? I should have left it in a tall tree rather than the sewer; it's too easy for someone to find it by accident there.*

Caitlin held out her hand. "Touch it." When Telyn hesitated, she insisted again.

Telyn touched Caitlin's hand and felt tremors shooting up and down, as if every little muscle was spasming.

"I think about the Ever-Guise all the time. I can't stay away. Even if they are—baiting me—it won't be long before I lead them to it. Me, or Hosh, or even you. It's stronger than we are. It will ruin us all. I'm begging you, Tey, get rid of it."

Telyn leaned her forehead against Caitlin's and squeezed her friend's shoulders to transmit some of her own strength. "This will pass. I'm sorry if Joram isn't what you thought, but you will be fine. We'll think of better wishes—"

At this, Caitlins teeth clenched, and with a hiss, she said, "Get rid of it, now—tonight—or we're all lost." In a whirl of blue satin, Caitlin spun back onto the dance floor. The band played a reel, the dancers placed hands on each other's shoulders, and the beautiful dress and brown hair blended into the crowd instantly.

"Well, that just spoiled the mood," Telyn muttered. On a nearby table sat a mug half-full of mulled wine; she took it and downed it in a few swallows, not worried about whom it might belong to. The mellow, clove-flavored wine calmed her nerves, but she couldn't pretend she wasn't shaken.

Of course they are playing Caitlin. Naturally. And Caitlin fell for it, carrying her fear straight to me, and now her fear infects my mind like subterranean termites in a sod roof.

Well, it isn't going to work. I can resist. I'm tough, a survivor. I managed when Dad passed away; I'm stronger than anyone knows. I didn't break then, and I won't break now. Which reminded Telyn that she hadn't visited her dad's name at the Sepulcher in oh-so-long. She made a mental note to do that soon.

I've still got to avenge Hosh against Tabbard—and ensure my future at the Sable Head. Hosh isn't capable of the one—he hardly seems interested!—and Raz isn't capable of the other. Without me and the Ever-Guise, Ouzeley would own the Sable Head already.

I've got this one winter to do it all. In spring, before the roads open, I'll pitch the forehead piece into the Elbus River. Caitlin's right; it has to be done before Yona comes for it. But not now, not while the Ouzeleys are goading us. Not until I have my revenge.

She surveyed the public room until she spotted Tabbard, Hefin Lloyd, and Joram seated together in a dark corner. Hefin actually raised his mug at her.

Oh yes, they want me to do something stupid. I won't fall for it. I won't visit the Ever-Guise. I'll leave and go straight home. All will be well. No need to check on things. No one will find the forehead piece unless I lead them to it—which I'm not going to do.

She made her way to the exit, snagging another half-full mulled wine for good measure.

Cressida's desk was unmanned. *She must figure that everyone who needed a ribbon has already bought one. She's probably out dancing. Good for her.*

The betting booth was doing a riotous business. Mrs. Gamage,

Mrs. Pembroke and Mrs. Ouzeley had all they could do with a constant stream of men and women placing bets. A couple of cornics waited in line, too.

Coat wrapped tightly around her, scarf knotted at the side of her throat, Telyn drifted outside. A surprising number of people braved the cold: couples kissing, threesomes chatting, groups telling tales, and individuals enjoying icicles broken from a nearby eave. It was easy to avoid being noticed—but impossible to avoid being seen. People stared just enough to be sure one of their bets wasn't making an early exit, then they went back to whatever they were doing.

Telyn passed the nearby mercantile several times, backtracking and making sure she wasn't followed. Then she made for the sewer. Stone-lined and neat as any bridge, the passage under Main was tall enough to stand in. Telyn leapt down into it and waited a few seconds to see if anyone followed. Crowd noises continued above, muffled by the stone.

She walked forward casually, letting her eyes adjust to the dim tunnel. *Just a girl taking a shortcut out of the wind. In a fancy dress. At one in the morning. Nothing out of the ordinary.*

I don't need to see it. Not really. It must be the wine; I never should have drunk that wine. Making me paranoid. Still, won't hurt to go by it just once.

It was nearly pitch-black in the tunnel. She didn't need light; she could practically navigate the sewer blindfolded—and had once, from the Sable Head to the Prefecture on a dare. But what if Caitlin was right? What if Tabbard and the others really were onto them? Whispers of air moved against her bare cheeks.

A couple tunnel intersections later, Telyn arrived at the hiding place. She walked three steps beyond the loose stone just in case, paused to listen...then returned quickly. Still, no one behind her. Normally, she came down here without a care, but tonight her heart raced as at the end of a long sprint.

Coming here was stupid. Stupid! I did exactly what Tabbard and the others wanted me to do. If they're following me, they have a really good idea where to start looking. I should just go on, pretend I don't know the forehead piece is right behind this loose stone...

Her eyes had strayed to the stone, which sat a little askew.

She glanced in either direction, knelt. The stone had been replaced sloppily, as if the person didn't know quite how to do it or had done it in a hurry.

Panic built inside her.

I should go back to the dance. All alone in this tunnel things could happen, things that no one would ever find out about. Tabbard, Joram, and Hefin set up Hosh just like this behind the Copcut Ash. In these tunnels, they'll be no one to hear me if I scream.

Or go home, pull the covers over my head, pretend this nightmare never happened. I could cross Middle Street and exit by the potter's...

But Telyn couldn't stop herself. She had to know.

She pulled the stone, rocking it to get it out of the tight fit. She had to use two hands because it was wedged in there improperly. Finally, after much grunting and cursing and scraped fingers, it came free.

The forehead piece had been taken. Instead of white, flexible ceramic, behind the stone lay a folded piece of paper, nothing more. She placed the stone on the floor and removed the note, unfolded it square by square. She couldn't read it until she moved near a stone grate where bars of light beamed down from a streetlamp on the road above.

On the paper, in Cressida's neat handwriting, were the Cornic Empire's Three Rules:

Humans shall not own horses.
Humans shall not own magic.
Humans shall not own wheels.

CHAPTER THIRTY-FIVE

Telyn read the note again and again. Her face flushed in a confusing mix of anger and embarrassment.

Anger: *Cressida took the forehead. My twin! She hasn't done anything to earn it! She didn't survive Kulon or the penumbra daemon. She didn't hide the thing in the top of the chaos trees, or befriend a pattern witch, or, or lose her place on the Dating Chart, or face interrogation by the cornic minister himself, or inquire at the Library.*

Embarrassment: *The lies I've told, the sneaking around, the distance I've put between myself and my sister...*

I've been found out. She found me out!

The whole conversation with Cressida took on a new meaning. "Swear to me you aren't doing anything with the mask and that pattern flack." Asking if she and Rayvn had been in any kind of trouble, asking about the ghost in the Sable Head, asking if she was still keeping secrets.

"Watch your back," Cressida had said, at the end.

She'd been testing her, offering her an opportunity to fess up.

How dare she!

Cressida must have been planning this for so long—just this morning acting so sweet, so nice, and all the while knowing about the Ever-Guise.

Cressida left this stupid note just to rub it in. I'll show her a fink, traitor, quisling!

She'd better not have pitched it over the falls. If so, I'll make her swim for it.

Telyn would get the Ever-Guise back.

She'd get *her twin* back—

The tunnel suddenly brightened, casting Telyn's shadow across the floor. Telyn whirled, thinking it must be Cressida come to taunt her. She readied to give her sister a piece of her mind. But in the tunnel stood not her twin, but a burly cornic holding a lantern. She recognized him, the soldier who had searched her when she entered Minister Svemas's office. The soldier who kept hanging out at the Sable Head. He sang:

"Snared in Farmer Rob's field

Refused to lay down and yield

The quick and bushy-tailed hare."

Before Telyn could think of running away, a curse and the sounds of threads ripping came from the other direction.

Tabbard!

Tabbard tried to drop into the tunnel, but his fancy blue coat had caught on a sharp stone and hung him a few inches from the ground. His arms and legs gyrated. With a final tear, the coat ripped up the back and Tabbard staggered into a wall that dripped with moisture.

Telyn knew she would pay for that.

Just after Tabbard followed Hefin Lloyd, who jumped down and landed without incident. Hefin crossed his arms and grinned evilly. They looked bulkier than ever. There would be no way Telyn could dart past those two, and still less past the cornic soldier.

"Told you she was up to something," Tabbard said.

"You'll be giving that to me, now," the cornic said, stepping closer, eyes darting from the note, to her face, and down to the stone on the floor. One large hand fingered a dagger in his belt.

Corporal Velky.

Telyn lowered her eyes and extended the note. "'Course you'll want to read it."

Corporal Velky snatched the note from her hand. "What are you hiding in here for?"

"I-I came in here to cry. My name's been removed from the Dating Chart."

At this, Tabbard belched and Hefin chuckled.

"What's this?" the soldier asked, turning the paper over and over as if secret words might appear.

"Quid's going to give a test, the teacher. I'm having trouble learning the Rules," Telyn said, trying to sound as thick as she could.

Tabbard came up quickly and peered at the note. "That's a lie. She can remember just fine—except to keep her place."

"What's that stone doing out of place?"

"What stone?"

Corporal Velky shoved Telyn against the wall. His great strength made it feel like she was pressed there by an ox. He forced her to put her hands above her head—and keep them there—with two fierce kicks he made her spread her legs.

"Search her," the cornic bade to the two boys.

They started with her belt sash, but didn't stop there. Tabbard checked beneath her hair, her lower back, her armpits and belly, while Hefin probed her legs and wrenched off her shoes. They thoroughly groped her, taking every advantage, cruelly pinching when they came up empty.

Tabbard turned her leather purse inside out, scoffed at its emptiness, and kicked it to the far end of the tunnel.

By now, Telyn was weeping for real.

The warning bell sounded above them.

"They got someone," Corporal Velky said. "If you've led me to the wrong prey..."

"Telyn has it. I'm sure of it! Her or her stupid flack friend." Tabbard seemed oblivious to the look of hatred that crossed the cornic's muzzled face at the word *flack*. "She's been attacking our family, making strange things happen, and making that Hosh popular. The only thing could've done it's magic."

Again, the bell pealed.

"You're coming with us," the cornic said. When Telyn began to protest, he put his cud-breath next to her ear. "Unless you want to be left in the sewer with those two. No telling what they'll do to you."

Telyn gave a brief shake of her head.

"That's what I thought."

And so, with as little effort as it took Telyn to pitch a mouse off a smooth counter, the cornic pulled Telyn to the lower exit of the sewer and up to the brightly lit street. Deliberately, she was sure, he paraded her in front of the Copcut Ash where everyone would see her.

Tabbard and Hefin trailed behind, hooting, in case anyone might have missed it. As if.

But all thoughts of her own discomfort, anger, tears, embarrassment, all of that disappeared in an instant as she saw the main attraction: a dozen cornics surrounding a single female prisoner.

Her sister.

The two groups merged, and Telyn pretended to stumble to fall in next to her sister.

Cressida's hands were bound behind her. Telyn's were free, and she pushed them against Cressida's hands.

I'm sorry, she signed.

Don't say anything, Cressida signed back, awkward from the binding ropes.

My fault. I will take the blame.

No! Cressida signed hard enough to scratch. *Don't be stupid.*

You will get punished.

They didn't have a word for slavery or execution, though those were very real possibilities.

Better one than two, Cressida signed. *If you confess, two punished.*

I'm sorry!

It's okay.

No. Not *okay.*

Don't admit anything. Pretend you know nothing.

Before they could sign anything more, one of the cornics yanked Telyn's hands behind her and bound them so tightly the rope chafed her wrists every time she took a step.

She recalled that silly, stupid wish she'd made in Dragon Tower—that the cornics search elsewhere than Rayvn for the mask. She was a such a fool!

CHAPTER THIRTY-SIX

The cornics separated the twins immediately upon entering the Prefecture. Most of the soldiers went up the narrow stairs with Cressida, presumably to an interrogation room, while the remaining soldiers took Telyn down two flights of stairs into the dungeon. They tossed her into a small cell near several other empty cells.

The ceiling was low, deliberately so. The corridor had a normal ceiling, but this cell, chiseled out of native bedrock, rose half that height. Even a short person could not stand upright without banging her head. The stout wooden door had metal hinges. This Telyn registered before the soldiers left, taking with them her shoes, her jacket, and the lamp.

Telyn was left alone in darkness with her worst enemy, her own thoughts.

She rehashed everything in her mind. Again. And again.

All her wishes. The silly, shallow wishes.

Make me popular.

Treat the animals better.

While all over the Empire, humans get sold into slavery, we wished about popularity and animals. Where's our significance now, Caitlin?

Save the Sable Head—the silliest wish of all. Hard work would have done the same. Hard work and something other than dried, salted marmot for speck.

My petty need for revenge on the Ouzeleys.

"He who worships feelings will end up numb...or wishing he were so," the philosopher said. She couldn't remember which one.

If only she'd read more philosophy and spent less time on her own feelings! She'd put her sister in peril—more than peril. Certain slavery or death. Which would Minister Svemas choose? Was the trial taking place now?

Cressida had signed, *Don't say anything. Don't confess.*

Because the cornics don't have the forehead piece yet? Or because Cressida and I don't both need to take the fall? Is Cressida protecting me even now?

I need to confess. I need to be the one punished.

Is that selfish? Foolish?

What if the cornics don't have the mask? What if they are only guessing?

Cressida may very well have simply moved the forehead piece to a different hiding place...or...or pitched it into the river. Does the note that Cressida left tell the cornics anything? Will they interrogate Caitlin? Hosh? Rayvn?

Will they use thumb screws? Fire?

Telyn wanted to confess. She absolutely needed to confess.

For whom?

Cressida told me not to.

All this time, if I'd just listened to Cressida, told her the truth...

I should start now. She told me not to say anything, and I won't...

No, I should confess. This isn't Cressida's fall to take. Maybe they'll be lenient if I confess...

Round and round, Telyn's thoughts attacked her soul. After a time, they all said the same thing over and over:

Guilty
Guilty
Guilty

Liar
Liar
Liar

Shame
Shame
Shame

When Telyn couldn't stand the deafening sound of her own thoughts any longer, she called out, at first quietly, and then louder, hoping for some company other than her guilt.

No one.

All the nearby cells appeared to be empty.

Wherever they held Cressida, she was unable, or unwilling, to respond.

Her throat grew hoarse. Time passed with the alacrity of a banana slug; her thoughts did not.

Her nose helped her discover a disgusting metal bowl, one she had to use before long—and then again. Cold water leaked down one of the walls. Swallowing all sense of pride and hygiene, she licked it against the burn in her throat.

No one visited.

They might have forgotten her.

Time passed. Days, she thought, as her hunger grew, waned, grew again, became a gnawing in her belly. The temperature was cool but not cold, but there was nothing between her and the floor except her dress, the one that showed a bit of cleavage and didn't cover past her knees. Its fancy porcelain buttons dug into her back when she lay down.

Her fingers and toes had lost all feeling long ago. If they warmed up now, they would be screaming.

She begged the air to bring food; to take the stinky metal bowl away and dump it; to leave some light....

Her lovely green dress was soiled beyond any hope of washing. She wanted to burn it to ashes along with the Prefecture and this whole, stinking, unfair system that made humans lawbreakers just for possessing magic—when all the world possessed magic. All the world *was* magic, except for humans. Except for her.

Time passed.

Shame and guilt remained.

She swore to herself: no matter what price she paid, no matter how she did it, she would get her sister free.

They brought her to Minister Svemas's office and sat her in the same chair as before. The minister's office did not have a window, but the diffuse light in the hallways indicated morning—the first indication of time she'd had since being thrown in the dungeon. But which day?

Second Gajos sat to the minister's right, and Corporal Velky stood behind her. The minister reached across his desk and, lifting a little crystalline decanter, sprinkled alcohol on the devotion bugs to either side of his desk, partially covering Telyn's stink with their spicy sweetness.

He patted the black velvet bag on his desk. "We found something—"

Before he could finish his thought, Telyn reached for the bag. Corporal Velky would have stopped her, but Minister Svemas nodded, and Telyn fished inside the bag and removed the familiar faux ceramic.

She tried to feign surprise.

Minister Svemas nodded vigorously. His curved ram's horns seemed to spiral as his head bobbed. "This is, as you might well imagine, what everyone's been looking for."

"You found it," Telyn said, turning it over and over in her hands. She touched the prongs that might have once held a gem for the third eye. "It is beautiful. What does this have to do with me?"

Second Gajos leaned his large fists on the minister's desk. "There are ways of knowing who used an object's magic, cocotte."

"No need for that language," Minister Svemas said. "We have the guilty party already. Miss Brower just happens to be the culprit's sister."

Telyn didn't have to fake the pallor that crept over her face and down her long arms and fingers.

"Thieves never work alone," Second Gajos growled.

"Whatever the Brower twins are, they are not thieves," Minister Svemas said. "You learn things working in Harlech for twenty... twenty-three years, longer than the twins have been alive. You know the thieves, the murderers, the people to watch. However this artifact came into their hands, it wasn't through thievery. Murder, possibly" —A smile split his muzzle—"but not thievery."

"You let the thief get away," Second Gajos murmured.

For a second Telyn felt a thrill. The thief got away... Did Cressida get away?

"Did I? We have the mask and a new slave for the Cornic Empire. The original thief hangs on the Sepulcher. Anonymous, yes, but he won't be stealing any more artifacts. I would say this has been a productive few days."

"We don't know he was the thief. An anonymous ghost, that is all, and not even a body to identify."

Dagger hanging on the Sepulcher. And a new slave...that would be Cressida, my twin, the innocent one.

It should have been me. She's protecting me again, like she always has.

I don't deserve it. I don't deserve her.

All this time, as the self-condemning thoughts clanged in her head like bells, Telyn stared at the forehead piece. The desire to put it over her face nearly overwhelmed caution. She began to argue with herself:

Could I wish my way out of this?

No, it's too slow. It makes suggestions only.

It might just work. What do I have to lose?

Everything.

"In House Gajos, we would execute the entire family and return the mask to its proper owner."

"House Gajos is not in charge," Minister Svemas said. "We are in the Cornic Empire, and we have procedures and rules for our citizens. If you are *not* a citizen, Second Gajos, then other rules apply." He looked pointedly at the other cornic, who removed his fists from the desk and sank into his chair.

A glance passed between the second and Corporal Velky. They seemed to be communicating silently, conspiring together, much as Telyn and Cressida used to do. Telyn wondered if Minister Svemas noticed it.

My only chance of survival rests with Minister Svemas. The others actively hate humans. I have to appeal to his sense of justice.

"My sister couldn't have stolen this. From who? How? What would she have done with this, this piece of ceramic?"

The minister gently removed the forehead piece from Telyn's hands and returned it to the black bag. Her fingers trembled from the loss of contact.

You missed your chance, idiot.

"No, I don't believe she stole it."

"Of course she did!" Second Gajos said. "She and her twin murdered the man in the Sable Head and took the artifact off his body."

"You just implied that the thief might still be alive," Minister Svemas said, gently. "We are letting emotions get away with us."

Dagger. The thief's name roared back into her mind.

"You see!" The second jumped up from his chair and waggled a finger at Telyn. "She knows more than she is letting on."

"Corporal Velky, please remove Second Gajos from the building," Minister Svemas sighed. "He is disrupting my interrogation."

The corporal looked from one to the other, wide-eyed.

"Give me the mask," the second hissed in fury. "House Gajos will not be pleased if you do not."

"It seems to me the ownership of the artifact is in some dispute."

"We brought you proof."

"I received quite another story with the mail." Minister Svemas leaned back and folded his hands over his belly. "One Glas Courier of Barmouth, she claims it was stolen from the Temple of Peristeri. Given her station, the claim must be taken seriously."

"A lie!"

"We must establish ownership before I can release the artifact.

Rest assured; it will go to House Gajos if the proof favors that outcome. In any case, you aren't going anywhere until spring, Second Gajos. You might as well learn to enjoy Harlech while you are here. I hear the steam baths are invigorating. I can't partake, unfortunately; makes my wool all staticky."

Corporal Velky hesitated, paw-like hands twitching, torn between the need to obey Minister Svemas's orders and fear of the cornic second.

Finally, with a sheep-like gurgle, Gajos departed. Corporal Velky bowed and trotted after.

Minister Svemas poured a little more angel water on the devotion bugs then closed the office door himself. "We'll get you out of that horrible cell soon," he said, in a grandfatherly voice.

"Minister, sir, my sister didn't do anything. She couldn't have done anything."

Returning to his chair, he smiled at her and waited.

Waited.

Cressida's finger talk wouldn't let her continue.

Don't admit anything. Pretend you know nothing.

A long silence passed. Telyn practiced deep breathing. Finally, "Why do they want this so bad?"

"Good," Minister Svemas said. "You know when to keep quiet."

"Cressida, she's innocent. I can testify. I can say whatever it takes. I can...I can take the blame." There, that was as close as she could come to confessing without breaking her word to Cressida.

"Who else knows about this?" Minister Svemas said.

Don't admit anything. Pretend you know nothing.

"About this, ah, this thing? Is it a mask, is that what it is?" The minister's scowl told Telyn she'd laid it on a bit thick. "Just you, the second, the soldier who was in here. Me."

The minister nodded.

"The...ah...the mind wizard at the unknown man's funeral, he sort of told everyone...in general...with his mind thingy, you know. Please, sir, if one of us has to go...go down, I'd assume it'd be me."

"I'm afraid it is too late for that. The trial was mercifully short. We did not even have to interrogate the prisoner. Cressida was found with a magical artifact on her person. There were no mitigating circumstances. I found her guilty of breaking the second Rule and sentenced her."

"She's already been sentenced?" Telyn's world fell to the bottom of Defiance Falls and lay there, crushed by the weight of the minister's words.

"She will live a life of slavery for her crime. If she is fortunate, she will get picked up by a merchant house in Enshede as a domestic. I will use what influence I have. The quick trial saves me from opening a full investigation."

Saving Caitlin. Saving Hosh. Saving herself. Maybe even saving Rayvn.

Seeming to notice that Telyn had difficulty swallowing, Minister Svemas took a pitcher from a sideboard, poured something into a ceramic cup, and handed it to her. It turned out to be mulled wine, just above room temperature.

She lubricated her mouth and throat and took a second swallow for good measure.

"Do you have any questions for me?" Minister Svemas asked.

Feeling rather small for once, Telyn asked, "How can I get Cressida back?"

"You can visit her starting tomorrow. Until the slavers come for the Spring Sale, Cressida will be our guest here at the Prefecture. I have arranged special accommodations."

"How can I get her...free?"

"Ah. Now, that is more difficult. You see, I wrote up her sentence without a bond price, but one could be added." Telyn's eyes widened, and he continued. "I do not trust Second Jaromir Gajos, and less still the Mistress of House Gajos. In my opinion, they do not have the best interests of the Cornic Empire at heart. We live in an empire divided, Telyn Brower, and I fear you have landed between the lines.

"Do you know how the Empire works?"

"Er, I have Schoolmaster Quid." As good as saying, 'No.'

"There are two officers for every major post. One from the ruling family, the Svemas family—may Empress Zhalia Svemas reign in peace —and one from the second-most-powerful house, the Gajos family.

This system has kept outright civil war from happening for hundreds of years. But the ranking of the houses changes from time to time. If this artifact is as powerful as it seems—given the interested parties—it might be enough to sway the balance."

From what Telyn had seen, she absolutely did not want the Gajos family in charge. "What can I do?"

"Be my eyes and ears here in Harlech. Tell me what the humans are doing. Tell me what the thaumas are doing. As a cornic, people with a...say...a rebellious bent...won't talk to me. But as the sister of a slave girl, you will have their sympathy."

"Done," Telyn said. In the back of her mind, voices whispered, *Traitor, turncoat, quisling...*

She pushed those voices down.

Minister Svemas moved a parchment in front of him. While it had been sitting on the edge of his desk the whole time, Telyn hadn't noticed it. He dipped a quill in ink and penned something at the bottom. He then turned it for her to see.

She scanned quickly. The top had gold foil and fancy calligraphy from the Empress of the Cornic Empire, Writ of Justice...Guilty...No contest...Cressida Lynn Brower, Born: Year 399; Height: five feet nine inches; Sex: female; Wool: brunette; Eyes: green; Scars: none; Tattoos: none. It also bore Cressida's likeness drawn by a skilled hand.

To the bottom right: Sentence: slavery, life. Next to that, wet and shiny with new ink there was a bond price: 4,000 hurons.

"Four thousand!"

"That is the lowest I am allowed to set for such a grave infraction. Your sister broke the second Rule."

"It would take me years to earn that. The Sable Head itself isn't worth that." Nor did she imagine that Razenbock would sell the place just to rescue her sister....

Would he?

"Years," Minister Svemas said. "Years, you have."

"No. No, I don't. I have to get Cressida free now, this winter, before the slavers come and take her to Enshede." Her lips trembled. Tears overflowed her eyes. "Only the top things on the List are valued over 4,000." She remembered Little Hosh saying that those things didn't really exist in the first place.

"If you want to trap your way out of this, you have all winter, although I've always preferred the slow, sure way," the minister said in his steady rumble. "In the meantime, remember our bargain. You will be my eyes and ears. Check in with your sister regularly and come to see me at the same time. We will have things to talk about. Avoid Second Jaromir Gajos if you can, and at all costs, do not tell him you are watching for me.

"Now, I've asked your mother here to pick you up. She is waiting downstairs."

Esther waiting downstairs... Mother of squirrels.

I am so dead.

CHAPTER THIRTY-SEVEN

Esther met her in the lobby wearing her long maroon dress with black sable around the neckline and wrists—the one she wore to funerals, which did seem appropriate. Eyes lowered, face unreadable, Esther mumbled some sort of greeting. Telyn took her arm as they had done in years past, and side-by-side, they walked swiftly past the stables, the road to the Sepulcher, and the stares of the townsfolk.

Telyn must have looked quite a sight with several days of prison grime caked to her dress. And, of course, gossip flowed swifter than the Elbus River in flood, so everyone from here to Enshede would know she and her sister had been arrested, and why.

Oh, they might not know exactly why. But everyone knew the cornics had been searching for a stolen magical artifact. They would know Cressida was being sold into slavery, and two plus two made four. Even Schoolmaster Quid could calculate that far.

As soon as Gopher Pass opened, Yona would know, too. It wouldn't take a genius to figure out the rest. He would be coming for them like a hungry brakdaw—or a blizzard.

Unless he sent the rabid ferret Taito-Vaiana after them.

The Sepulcher's granite face frowned down from above the treetops. Telyn thought about how Dagger rested there behind the flimsy Unknown spell, and her dad as well, even though he had died somewhere in the distant Chaos Woods, and again she remembered that she ought to visit them both. And then the trees near her cabin obscured her view of the stone.

Inside her home, these cozy walls and cozy bed where she could stretch out full-length, Telyn wanted to flop down and sleep to gather enough energy for a bath. Maybe—yes—a steam bath. If she won the bet against Caitlin and Joram (she'd have to check with the Mrs. Gamage), she had enough for that, get the grime from her pores. And then visit Cressida—

Esther had another idea. She lifted Telyn's chin and stared into her eyes with a rare sober and sobering intensity. "Swear you had nothing to do with this."

Telyn stared back as long as she could and finally gave a little shake of her head. Her greasy, dirty hair clung to her head. "No, Mother. I cannot, I will not...swear."

Esther hauled back her open hand.

Telyn could have blocked it, could have pushed her mother away or stepped out of reach. Instead, knowing she deserved this and more, Telyn simply closed her eyes and waited for the blow to come.

It came with a resounding slap and more sting than she'd imagined possible from her mother's hand.

"I knew it! She's protecting you, ain't she?"

Weeping tears of shame, Telyn nodded.

She didn't feel taller than Esther. She felt oh-so-small—and wished she were smaller still. She wished she could fit under the bed and hide there until this all went away.

Instead, she took Aled the Wise's advice, "Thank the hand that disciplines you justly," and stood up taller. She practically invited the second slap.

It nearly knocked her jaw loose.

She wanted to tell Esther the whole story, from that night in the Sable Head until now, and explain exactly what happened and why Cressida was in jail when it should have been her.

"If I confess, we'll both get hauled to slavery," Telyn explained, when Esther stopped at two. *And no chance to rescue her if we are both slaves.* "Cressida got caught dead-to-rights."

"Of course she did. The good ones always get caught. Too bad it wasn't you," Esther said, "then I'd be rid of you."

You don't mean that! Telyn wanted to shout. *Or does she?*

Telyn had gotten Cressida arrested. The bad twin had gotten the good twin arrested, sentenced to slavery. Cressida would be hauled away in chains, lost to Esther forever.

The good twin—gone.

The bad twin hanging around like a tumor, like malignant cancer.

Yes, Esther probably did mean it. And Telyn deserved it.

"Thank the hand that disciplines you justly."

How many times, in the black of night, had Telyn hoped the drink would simply take Esther away so she wouldn't have to deal with her? Each time, she regretted the thought, disavowed it, refused to believe it was more than passing emotion.

Whenever Esther drank herself to sleep, the dark thought returned: *Maybe my mother will just die.*

Telyn deserved the slap and so much more.

"I am sorry...mother."

She didn't use "mother" instead of "Esther" to engender sympathy. It just came out. In this time of confession, this baring of the souls, she could not deny their relationship by using "Esther." Her soul wouldn't let her.

Esther's glower darkened further. "Take your things and go."

"Go...where?"

"I don't care." Esther dropped onto Telyn and Cressida's bed as if denying Telyn the occupancy. She shifted slightly towards the wall, away from her daughter. The air seemed to cool significantly.

Telyn made a few choking noises. Whatever she wanted to say, her mind wouldn't form the words, and she didn't think her throat would let them out if they came. Tears again dripped from her chin. After the deprivation of her prison, she didn't think she had that much salt-water left. Her heart must've been dehydrating into a dry husk to shed all these tears.

And so, exhausted beyond belief, sad beyond measure, Telyn gathered her few possessions in her rucksack, tied a few baubles that wouldn't fit on the outside, and, still wearing her Dead Winter Dance dress, took the upper road to the Sable Head.

Razenbock gave her an empty room, and, when she awoke, a room-temperature bath awaited at the foot of her bed. He must have filled it with buckets without waking her.

It was good enough. She soaked off the prison grime and fleas, then crawled back into bed where the fleas found her again.

The treatment was too good for her. She didn't deserve it. Cressida, the good twin, would have no such bed and no such bath ever again. She would be a slave forever.

Unless Telyn could free her before spring—before Yona Unega came looking with his own form of justice.

CHAPTER THIRTY-EIGHT

Razenbock put Telyn to work immediately, and as a favor, offered to let her board for only one huron per day. Which meant she'd have to work five hours just to pay her room. She accepted immediately, having no choice.

As soon as she could, she sat him down one evening after the last patron departed. Razenbock had warmed mugs of malt infused with cardamom for both of them; in Telyn's opinion, it tasted like running week-old bath water strained through old stockings. But she took it and pretended to enjoy it.

Hot spiced cider would have been so much better.

"I knew you'd be comin' for help," he said, pulling a cashbox from behind the bar. "I got it all right here. Everything I've been able to save. It won't free Cressida, but it's a start. I'll keep it safe for you."

Telyn dearly wanted to count it but held her peace for now. "Her bond price is high."

Raz grinned and patted the box. "Seventy-five hurons. Bet you ain't seen that much money in your whole life."

She looked into his eyes to see if he was joking.

Nope.

"I was thinking, maybe, the Sable Head..."

"Yes?"

"Could we borrow against it? I could work real hard. I have some ideas on how to make it better, bring in more customers. Like the bread soup—"

"Bread soup what? Everyone likes the bread soup."

"We could make it with real speck from pork. I've got a recipe from the butcher—"

Razenbock's head started shaking before she even finished her sentence. "Business is falling off again. You don't make money by spending it. Oh, look, don't cry. I'd borrow against the Sable Head if I could, but I don't own it, see? Wulstan Ouzeley owns it, leastaways until I pay off my debt. That's the way it works when you borrow money. You give a deed to your land, and, for all practical whatchamacallits, the other fella owns it until you pay the last thing-y. That ain't going away any time soon."

"I thought you paid him off past spring. I was there; I saw him come in..."

"Nah, I paid him what I owed him. Really twisted him off, too. He thought he had me. He's been wanting this place for years 'cause it's the first thing you come to in Harlech. But business jumped, and I got him paid off for the year and made this besides," he patted the cash box, and slid it back behind the counter. "For your sister. It ain't easy makin' a profit, real speck or no."

Telyn nodded glumly.

"Ah, listen, the Spring Sale's coming up, and I'll pledge everything I make. I'll even put a collection box here for her. She's real popular; people've been asking how they can help...and they ain't real happy about her being sold into slavery 'n all. That's not a popular concept in Harlech.

"When I was growin' up, there was a movement to declare this a free land where runaway slaves could go for sanctuary, but 'course that went nowhere. I know who was involved. They'll be the first to pledge. How much more do we have to raise?"

"About four thousand."

Raz's choking sprayed the counter with malt. He spent a good deal of time wiping his beard clean and avoiding her eyes. Eventually, he managed, "That's an awful big number. Ouzeley himself would have trouble coming up with that."

"How much you think you can raise with the pledge box?"

"A few hundred, maybe, if I call in some favors. Four thousand —!" He shook his head in dismay. "No wonder they don't want no free zone if slaves bring in so much."

They sat side by side for a time, staring at the kitchen fireplace and watching the glowing coals crackle, flare, darken. Their malt cooled into an even more disgusting brew.

Finally, Telyn slid off the stool. "I'll take the hurons now, if that is okay."

Raz hesitated. "This is for your sister, not for you to go spending—"

"I'm going to invest it to make more."

"You ain't going to go gambling them on the Dating Chart, are you? Gambling's a fool's way, especially with love. Long shots and all —you can never know who'll date or get married."

"I want to go trapping. There are things worth thousands on the List."

Raz leaned back, appraised her. "Come to think on it, gambling ain't such a bad idea. Don't shake your head at me. What experience do you have at trapping?"

"Redbeard taught me enough."

Like every other kid in Harlech, Telyn had taken the survival class he taught at school. Plus, Redbeard had taken her and Cressida out a few times on their own. They'd even caught a ferret. Well, it was Redbeard's trap, but they helped set it.

Raz thrummed his fingers on the counter. "If he taught you a thing, it was not to be a fool. The woods are crawling with experienced trappers, and I can count on my wartless fingers how many come back with those things at the bottom of the List. Lots of other beasties crawling in those woods—things you wouldn't want to meet with a fist of cornic soldiers by your side. You won't do your sister any good dead."

"I only have this winter," Telyn replied. "Once Cressida gets taken to Enshede, how will I even find her? What if she becomes a galley slave? She won't last a month."

As if unable to listen to any more nonsense, Raz stood, walked outside, and returned with an armload of wood. Two logs he put on the fire, and three he piled nearby. He took the time to stir some cardamom into a fresh cup of malt and handed it to her.

She managed to thank him, although she couldn't help grimacing.

"It broke Esther when your father died."

Telyn snorted. "She won't break if I die, trust me."

"Dorian was one of my best friends. Called him Dori, I did. Growin' up, we spent many winters trapping near Harlech, me 'n Dori. Helped plenty of ladies line their cloaks with fur, 'n picked up a couple of awards for rakasura ears from the cornics as well. Thought we knew what we were doing. Even stayed a few overnights in the woods just to prove we didn't have to come home to our warm beds at night. Real tough men we were." He took a long draught. Setting the mug down, he wrapped it in both hands and leaned on his elbows.

"Dori was the leader, 'n I followed 'im. He was after the questing armadillo. The Academy of Enshede put a price of three thousand hurons on it, 'n a guy by name of Skinny Dee said he'd been tracking one, lost her near Aumerhem, the demon peak. Your dad thought he could pick up the trail along the Bubbling Baseline."

Telyn had heard much of this, but never from Raz. She half-returned to her stool, sipped her malt, wondered where the big man was going with this.

"Bubbling Baseline?"

"What trappers call the edge of the Chaos Woods, where the Cairn Ridge begins to climb steep. Lots of heat vents, mud pots and hot springs along that line. Some of 'em are poison, some hot enough to scald you in winter, or cook your food in. But, if you need it, you can find running water in winter all along that baseline—'n lots of animals looking for fresh water.

"Was a good plan, we thought. We equipped a half dozen llamas."

The name reminded Telyn of Kiiptk's tribe, Boiling Springs, but she blinked away the thought so as to not lose the story-thread.

"We?"

"Me, your dad, half a dozen others. Archie Todd, the baker, was one. Dori planned 'n led the expedition. Seemed a sure thing until we set foot across the bridge. From the beginning, the woods were against us. Your dad's llama dropped his leg in a hole. Broke it bad; we had to butcher her. We split the gear 'n buried what we couldn't carry.

"Wasn't all bad. We caught some good furs, mink 'n white fox, mostly, valuable enough. But from the first, a pack of rakasuras harried us, ripped into our stores in the night. They can climb, the blighters, 'n took what meat we hung from trees. Lost a lot of sleep to keep watch. We killed a few." He shook his head, his eyes seeming to view the past in the fireplace.

"Every day, we battled the rakasuras until our rations disappeared. There was no end to them. Course, we could've guessed they'd come for the llama meat.

"Had a big fight, lots of shouting. There's a strong superstition among trappers that if you don't cross the mountains before winter solstice, the night of the Dead Winter Dance, bad luck will follow you. All the trappers I know try to get through before then. What with that superstition 'n gettin' harried by rakasuras—'n your dad was stubborn, don't you doubt it.

"Well, I thought knives would be pulled before it was done. In the end, the majority gave off 'n went home, counting their blessings to be alive with enough mink 'n fox to turn a good profit. We started out with eight, ended up with three: me, your dad, and Archie Todd. Not a day goes by I don't wish we hadn't turned back with 'em."

Razenbock sighed, drank, and wiped the foam from his beard thoughtfully.

"If all the trappers try to get through the pass by winter solstice," Telyn said, "it means the near woods are empty of trappers, don't it?" She felt a twinge of hope in her belly, like the first ray of sunshine striking your boots on an ice-cold morning. "The animals must have figured that out. Once solstice is over, I'll bet they come out of hiding. Even a...even a not-so-experienced trapper might have a chance."

Raz retrieved the cash box and set it between them. "I see a lot of Dori in you. Stubbornness, responsibility, 'n recklessness all in one. Nothing I can say'll stop you, so I ain't gonna try." He opened the lid and began stacking the copper hurons by fives. "This'll get you the proper gear. Take plenty of warmth and plenty of food. 'N don't go alone. Take someone with experience, if you can. Ask Redbeard; he's still in town. The cold, getting lost—those're your biggest dangers."

"What happened to my dad?"

Razenbock kept his gaze firmly on the coins he continued to stack on the wooden counter. "Some other time."

"Raz, you were just about to tell me."

"Mistake."

"Raz! I need to know."

"It won't do you no good."

"Raz…"

He swallowed. Thrummed a copper huron edgewise on the counter. Whether for Telyn's sake or Cressida, he finally decided he'd better tell her. "There's more 'n one pass over the Cairn Range. There's King's Pass, the one everyone takes. 'N there's another further north, Aumerhem Pass. Higher, more dangerous, closer to Harlech but rarely used, with a glacier you have to skirt around…or cross. We made to cross it. We'd lost so much stores, see, we had to get there and back in a hurry.

"Dori, he kept pushing, pushing. Archie 'n me, we told him we should go back, sell our share of the furs and the rakasura ears, come back 'n try for the questing armadillo another year. But old Dori, he had a way about him. Got people to do what they didn't really want to do. Gave 'em courage when they hadn't none. 'N like you, he never backed down.

"But it was a warm winter, which ain't good around glaciers. Ice'd never really settled in. Leastaways, that's how I figure it. But you never know on a glacier. It's living ice, always moving and changing—just like them mountains, just like them woods. We came to a crevasse. We could see it to the right and to the left, bottomless, straight-down vertical, with that beautiful light blue color fading to *nothin'*, as if when you stared down the crevasse, you were lookin' across a horizon of white 'n blue. I stared down it a long time, a bad feelin' buildin' with each thump of my heart.

"But there were tracks ahead of us, two lines straight as a bow-shot across a snow bridge. Someone had passed with a sled. Someone had gone before us, so we knew it had to be safe. We poled it, too—stuck poles into the snow to be sure it would hold. Didn't want to take no chances. The poles showed it was deep and firm."

"What happened?"

"Your dad insisted on crossing first. He'd been the one insistin' on keeping on, you see, so he said crossin' first was his responsibility. When he was halfway across, we heard a little crack, no more than me popping my neck." He twisted his big head to demonstrate. Four pops sounded from his vertebrae. "The bridge collapsed. Heard Dori scream all the way down."

No one had ever told Telyn the story in such vivid detail. Always before it had been, 'Your dad went out and never came back. Lots of trappers do. I'm sorry.' She'd never even known that the baker, Archie Todd, had been on that expedition. It struck her suddenly that this was why the baker hated her so much. Every time he saw her or Cressida it reminded him of Dori Brower.

With difficulty, she moved her lips. "What happened?"

"I'll tell you what happened. We left him."

A chill dropped to Telyn's belly, wiping out that ray of sunshine and hope. "You left him?"

"Left him cold." Raz wiped his eyes on his long, white sleeve. "We didn't hear nothing. We affixed a rope to the sled, and the sled to a couple of stakes, and Archie climbed into the hole, went clear to the end of the rope. I was bigger, so I helped hold above. Dori was probably dead. He probably was. We didn't hear nothin'."

"You said the crevasse was really deep. You did what you could."

Razenbock stroked his beard some more. Clearly, he wanted to leave the story at that, and just as clearly, he wanted to tell her everything, get the burden he'd been carrying off his enormous chest.

Finally, he sighed and wiped his nose on his plaid sleeve. His voice trembled. "No. No, if we had, I could sleep with myself at night. Archie never reached the bottom—we ran out of rope—but Dori didn't neither. Archie saw your dad lying on a shelf about twenty feet below the end of the rope. Archie called to him, shouted himself hoarse. Nothing. All of this I heard but couldn't see from up top. Eventually, when Archie's voice gave out, I pulled him up. We debated what to do. Finally decided to just leave him there."

Telyn could picture her dad on the little shelf of ice, lying on his back, sprawled with one leg dangling into darkness, an arm flung above his head, and his other across his heart, a dusting of snow as funeral blanket. His brown eyes were open and staring... No, in her mind, she closed his eyes, imagined a serene expression on his face.

She preferred him that way.

"You did what you could."

"No. We could've reached him. We could've cut up our furs 'n extended the rope. Wouldn't have been no trick. We had plenty, 'n we knew how to weave 'em strong enough to hold a man. I could have dropped Archie back down, tied your dad to the rope, and hauled him out."

"Raz, he was dead. He'd fallen into a crevasse."

How backwards that I have to comfort Raz! My dad died. MY DAD...

...and yet Raz was shaking his head and weeping, and Telyn felt the need to reach out and put an arm across his large back. Uneven shudders passed through his powerful muscles.

"No, Tey. No. We decided the furs were too valuable to cut into strips. We'd get home with nothing but debt. But with the furs, I could make a down payment on this place, and Archie could buy his bakery. We figured your dad'd pushed everyone past his limit; he'd sort of asked for it, and Aumerhem delivered."

"Raz, you don't have to explain. He died. You did all you could. And now I'm able to make a living here thanks to you and the Sable Head." *And Cressida, once I get her out of jail.*

"No, Tey. We left him there. Alive."

The chill in her belly turned to ice. She must have misheard. "What?"

"We left him there, alive."

"You said he wasn't moving."

"Nor talking. But Tey, I know he was alive. We could've saved him but for greed."

Telyn stared until the moisture dried in her eyes. She refused to blink.

She'd forgotten how.

"We, ah, we stayed for twenty-four hours. We listened and we called down. Thought I heard him once, but Archie said it was just an echo. I accepted that...'cause I wanted it to be true. I wanted them furs. I'd wanted to buy this Sable Head for the longest time. It'd been my dream from forever. 'N with the furs...with Dori's share of the furs...I could finally afford it. After twenty-four hours, we left him... alive...alone...to freeze to death." He buried his massive head in his hands.

"You don't know that."

No. No, this can't be true. I refuse to believe this. Raz has been carrying this around too long. Guilt and sadness have gotten hold of his mind, of his voice. Raz has always been good to me.

Raz would never leave someone to die.

He never would.

She pulled the barkeep tighter into her hug. "Raz, my dad had fallen eighty, maybe a hundred feet. He wasn't moving. He wasn't talking."

She said it as much for herself as for the barkeep. She wanted, needed to believe in Razenbock's goodness. She didn't have any other men in her life. He was the last.

"Raz, he was dead. You did what you could. I'm sure you did. He fell down a crevasse and he died on impact."

He shook his head and sobbed out the words: "No, that's not true. I know it's not true."

"How do you know?"

"No ghost, Tey. No ghost."

CHAPTER THIRTY-NINE

So much fell into perspective after that conversation—Esther's ambivalence toward Raz; Raz going out of his way to help their family; the baker's dislike of the twins. Each of her dad's partners faced their demons in their own way.

Just as Telyn had to face hers.

No ghost.

Left alive in the bottom of a crevasse, ice and cold and the dark for company, slowly dying, knowing your friends abandoned you... If Dad had woken up, that would have been terrible. Mother of squirrels— High Father—I pray he stayed unconscious.

It had been a long time since she had thought of the High Father, the One who created everything, the One who seemed to have set the world spinning and then walked away.

Probably Dad would have died anyway. Broken back, broken head, internal bleeding; you can get so many injuries from a fall like that. You can't accuse Raz and Archie of murder.

Not murder.

Greed, selfishness, putting the value of the furs above the skin of their friend Dori. My dad. They took away the slim-to-nothing chance that Dad might have made it back to Harlech alive. They took it upon them-

selves to make that determination rather than letting Dad fight for his life.

"Just leave him there. He's too hurt, anyway. He'll never make it."

How could they know that?!

What if he hadn't been as hurt as they thought? What if he wasn't as hurt as Raz said at all? Maybe they murdered him!

No, mustn't go there. Mustn't start thinking in conspiracies, or I'll go wacko.

Maybe it worked out the way the High Father wanted: Raz can help Dori's daughters earn their keep; Esther had an excuse to drink away her life; and the baker could be the slug he was always meant to be.

Knowing how her dad died certainly didn't make her grief any easier. Nor did it change the facts. Four thousand hurons—the price for Cressida's freedom, the price of a few stupid wishes from the Ever-Guise, the cost of Telyn's stupidity and lies.

Only one way to make that kind of money in Harlech in a short time...short of stealing the Ouzeleys blind, which Telyn wasn't about to try.

Two days after Raz had told her the truth about her dad, Telyn visited the Prefecture to tell Cressida her plan. Well, not the entire plan. That she had a pretty good idea what she intended to trap, and where to find it, she kept to herself. Going up the stairs, her feet burdened with what might be a last goodbye, each lifting of the knee took a force of will. Twice she had to pause to gather...not breath, but courage.

In forever and no time she stood before a solid wooden door with a small, barred window.

Cressida had indeed been moved to a nice cell in the top of the Prefecture, a room beautifully paneled in the swirls and shades of chaos lumber. If it weren't for the expletives scratched here and there, and a wide, shallow hollow in one corner where someone tried to claw their way out, the room would have made a stately bedroom. Minister Svemas was indeed showing mercy. Greenish light came from a jar of millipede glowers, of which a third lay legs-up on the bottom.

At first, Telyn didn't understand why a cell would be made this way, but she had come to understand this was intended to be a flack cell, and the magic-bending wood would ensure that their spells would misfire.

On one of her visits, since Cressida habitually declined to converse, Telyn had knocked around the walls with her knuckles. Everything sounded solid and thick as a tree trunk. The lumber must have been set into brick or stone, so even if you pried the boards away, you would be stuck.

The only weakness was that door.

Today, Cressida sat on one end of her bed hugging her knees. Telyn sat on the rug and related Raz's story. In all the visits Telyn had made since the arrest and conviction, Cressida had hardly spoken a word. So it surprised her when, Cressida spoke in a choked-up voice. "Thank you for telling me."

Telyn rolled some lint between her fingers. She did her best to ignore Cressida's cracked and irregular toenails. She'd always taken such care of them, even giving herself pedicures! "Mom must have known. You know how she felt about Raz. She sort of hates him, you know? Likes him for helping us and hates him at the same time."

Cressida nodded.

"Did...did you know?"

A little, hair-jiggling head-shake. Only clean locks could jiggle that freely. Minister Svemas had let Cressida bathe and clean her clothes— and use an outhouse. The bedpan sat under the bed, unused.

Telyn reached out and felt the bed's wool blanket with the palm of her hand. It was rough and serviceable—better than the one in Raz's guest room. "No fleas?"

"Less than the Sable Head."

Telyn smiled. "Truth is, I'm better off there. Esther and I...we wouldn't have much to say."

"And the fleas were hungry—only so much of Tums to go around."

Telyn laughed. "She won't even sleep with me. She prefers to snore from the ceiling all night."

Something moved in front of the barred window, and the door opened. There stood Rayvn with a giant armload of parchments. "Dating questionnaires," she announced, dropping them on the bed.

It took several moments before Telyn managed to use her gaping mouth. "What are you doing here?" *My sister is finally opening up. We are finally, finally having a real conversation, and you show up!*

"We need someone to calculate the odds. Cressida can write on the verso—saves money on parchment—and I brought a pencil." This she proceeded to pull from behind her triangular ear.

Pulling her legs up, crisscrossed, to allow Rayvn to sit next to her, Cressida surveyed the first parchment. "Did my sister get you in on her mad scheme as well?"

"Oh, yes. If we are forbidden from the Dating Circle, then *Kiss, Kindle, and Flame* must continue. We have a deal."

"Cressida is talking about my plan to go into the Chaos Woods and trap something from the List so that we can pay her bond price."

The pattern girl nodded. "Ah, yes, I see." She turned to Cressida. "Your sister, Hosh, and Caitlin came to my house. They pretended to like the infusion my mother gave them. And then, when mother left the kitchen, Telyn said, 'Rayvn, you're my friend, right?' I said, 'You sound unsure.' She said, 'Yes, well, you are. I thought about it, and despite our differences'—and she named fur and ears, tail and whiskers, magic and breeding temples—'despite our differences, you are my friend.' 'Okay,' I said. 'Do we take a bath together now?'"

Cressida nearly choked.

"'Or should we get a tattoo on our necks like the Ghetti?' Your sister said, 'Rayvn, focus, no baths or tattoos. You know those stories where the hero leaves his friends so they won't get involved or hurt? He goes off on the quest on his own and leaves everyone behind?' I agreed that this happened in many stories. Your sister said, 'Those heroes are stupid. I need my friends. I need their help. I need *your* help, Rayvn, and Hosh's, and, ah, Caitlin's. My stupidity got us all into this, and I need all of you to get my sister out of it. I can't do it alone. I can't.' And then she started bawling like a donkey when you separate it from its mother."

When it became apparent that Rayvn had finished her ridiculously long rendition, Telyn opened her eyes. Cressida scrutinized the pattern girl oddly.

Telyn cleared her throat. "Raz donated seventy-five hurons, enough to buy proper equipment."

"Huh," Cressida commented.

"His collection is going well. The folks don't like your sentence, don't like the idea of slavery. They'd rather see you scourged."

"Or hung," Rayvn added, helpfully. "The citizens of Harlech truly dislike slavery."

"Not helpful," Cressida scowled.

Telyn continued, "Raz calls it his Freedom Bucket, passes it around in the evening. And Hosh asked for donations to put up for sale in your name. Lots of people gave. That little section by the front door where no one sits has become the C-store, for 'Cressida.' I donated my Dead Winter dress." Cressida raised her eyebrows. "Oh, come on. It was nothing but rags! When you get out, you'll make me another."

"Tabbard bought it," Rayvn said. "He dressed up a stick figure and hung it in the Copcut Ash as his 'Slave doll.'"

"She did *not* have to know that."

"After that, he and his friends pranced it around town on the back of a llama—"

"Rayvn, enough!" Telyn said.

Cressida stood and began pacing. "Rayvn, my sister is too dumb to listen to reason, but you do not have to die for me. Freezing to death in the Chaos Woods won't do anyone any good."

"Come on," Telyn said. "You must have a teensy desire to see me freeze to death in the woods."

"You..." Cressida pinched her fingers close together. "Not Hosh, not Caitlin, not Rayvn."

Rayvn painted a big smile with her tail.

"You are always protecting me," Telyn said.

"You got the stupid, stubborn, and tall," Cressida said. "I got the motherly instinct, the responsible itch, the practical bone."

"And the straight teeth. Don't forget the straight teeth."

"I have nicer boobs, too."

"She does," Rayvn agreed.

"What?!" Telyn pulled her blouse tight against her belly and pretended to examine her curves. "Now I'm going to have body image issues."

"I have a mirror outside if you want to check," Rayvn said. "They wouldn't let me bring in my purse—"

"Thank you. I'll think about it."

Rayvn's absolute sincerity was enough for both twins to crack a smile.

"I see." Cressida's pacing came to a standstill, and she tugged on the hem of her sweater. "I see that you two *have* become friends. So, the impossible really can happen. However, I meant what I said. Rayvn...and Tey...you must not go into the Chaos Woods for me. Remember what happened to our dad. What chance do you have to trap anything worth four thousand hurons? None at all. The woods are crawling with experienced trappers, which you are not. It's also crawling with brakdaws, and ice spiders, bears and rakasuras, and creepies we don't even have names for. Did you ask Redbeard to go?"

"Yes. He's busy."

"Busy?"

She almost said he was headed back to Enshede with the return mail, but she remembered that lies got her into this mess, or at least compounded it, and she wasn't going to lie to her twin again if she could help it. So she told the truth.

Telyn had asked him, and Redbeard told her not to be a sap-headed fool. When she'd pressed him, he told her the only reason he'd go into the woods with her is to haul her back and tie her to her bedframe until she learned sense. And whatever they trapped, before or after he pulled their rashers from the fire, he got fifty percent of the take. More than fair, he said, for keeping them alive.

She'd politely declined.

"Rayvn, listen," Cressida said, "Telyn is stubborn as...as that donkey you were talking about. She brays like one when she cries, right?"

"Right."

"So don't listen to her. She's just being stubborn to be stubborn. But if you don't join her in the woods, she won't go. She needs you and Caitlin and Hosh. Even Telyn won't go alone."

Rayvn nodded, and Telyn thought she'd been converted. Cressida's expression grew hopeful, and Telyn's heart dropped through her toes.

But as usual, Rayvn surprised them. "Now you are taking the role of the loner hero who goes off on his own, leaving his friends behind, Cressida. Your adventure is to go off into slavery by yourself."

"Mother of Squirrels!" Cressida exclaimed.

"That's my line," Telyn said.

"You plan to become a martyr. I will think on this pattern as we pass boring nights in the Chaos Woods, too cold to fall asleep."

Cressida slumped against the wooden wall. "Just go. Get me out of my misery...your misery...all our miseries."

She did return Telyn's hug, limply.

"Don't get lost," Cressida murmured as Telyn and Rayvn left.

Rayvn descended to the ground floor. Telyn exited one floor above; she had one last visit to make. Corporal Velky patted her down before letting her into Minister Svemas's office. She made her final report, telling the minister all she had seen and heard, from the Freedom Bucket Raz passed around, to Tabbard buying her Dead Winter dress and prancing it around Harlech, to the three cornic soldiers who had taken to playing senet in the Sable Head, the ones who seemed to report to Corporal Velky—who might've been listening at the door right then.

The minister asked probing questions that revealed that he knew much of this already. He seemed unconcerned, in control.

Steady.

The fact that Corporal Velky broke into "Eyes Like Pools of Lies" next door did not help matters.

Finally, when Telyn's silence indicated she had nothing to add, the minister asked, "When are you leaving?"

"Tomorrow." She was unable to keep the waver out of her voice. The waver came from both the import of her decision, and from the fact that she knew—she felt—that Minister Svemas kept the forehead piece in his desk, practically within reach.

Mother of squirrels, did she ever want to put it on.

"You pledged to be my eyes and ears in Harlech."

She'd been waiting for an objection and had a response ready. "You will have me the rest of my life. My eyes and ears are yours. But my sister only has this winter. Once the slavers come for her...."

"Telyn, terrible things are afoot in Harlech. Much more is at stake than your twin's freedom, hard as that may be to believe at your age. If you stay in Harlech, you can help me stave it off."

What forces could possibly challenge the minister? He has the whole Cornic Empire behind him.

She didn't know what "it" referred to, but she knew bargaining, knew she had some leverage at this moment that she hadn't had until now.

"Can you pardon Cressida?"

"I can do many things, but the law is out of my hands. If authorities do not follow the law, then chaos follows. In the absence of law, there is but one rule: Power wins."

Easily said by the one who has the power, Telyn thought. But this was a time for bargaining, not philosophy. "Can you switch our places—write my name in place of Cressida's?"

"Cressida Brower was caught with forbidden magic, not you."

"She confessed to spare me."

"Are you confessing to a crime?" the minister asked, slipping back into his judicial persona. And Telyn knew without question that if she confessed right now, she would be sold into slavery alongside her sister, and the minister wouldn't even blink. He saw himself as the blind arbiter of justice. Circumstances didn't matter; love and reasons didn't matter, only the facts.

It sure made life simple.

"Minister Svemas, I have to try. When I come back with the bond price for my sister, I will be your eyes and ears the rest of my days."

He folded his massive hands on the desk. "That attitude will make you a valuable spy one day. Of course, you have to try."

"Well, then. I've got to prepare." Telyn stood, and with great reluctance pulled her eyes from the wide desk where the mask sat, almost within reach.

She could practically feel it calling to her.

Put me on.

Put. Me. On.

Make a proposition. Make the world a better place, Telyn. All you have to do is wear me and wish.

As she shrugged into her coat, Telyn added, "They will be coming for it. The mind wizard, and the schmook...and whoever killed the man in the Sable Head."

"Yes? Do you have information for me?"

"Be careful, Minister. We both have only this winter to...to get this right."

"In that case," he said to her back, "don't get lost."

In the foyer, Corporal Velky scratched out some kind of report on a roll-up scroll. He continued to hum, "Eyes Like Pools of Lies," but she could tell his mind wasn't on it. Pretending to fiddle with her coat buttons, she hummed one of Quid's catchier tunes, "I'm a Fool and This Fool Loves You Too." When Corporal Velky modulated his humming to this new tune, even tapping the beat on the desk, she grinned to herself.

Taking even that small measure of control made her feel better. She descended to the ground floor with almost a skip in her step.

CHAPTER FORTY

Their feet thudded dully on the dirty snow covering the stone bridge that led from Harlech into the Chaos Woods. The sun's glare off the snow and the frozen Elbus River stung their eyeballs. The Marrow Wind skimmed over the ice and threw cold at their faces.

All four wore shapeless leather pants over woolen stockings, scarves over nose and mouth, and hoods pulled over their heads. Even the llama, Biscuit, wore a face scarf.

The guard tower provided momentary relief from the wind.

"Be careful out there," a cornic soldier called from the window. "We spotted a rakasura in the trees. Where there's one…"

"How long?" Hosh shouted back.

"Two, three hours ago. Nab one, it's one huron per pair of ears."

The other cornic said something about the rakasura nabbing them, but the wind snatched every other word.

They kept plodding. Telyn had Biscuit's right flank, Caitlin the reins and head. Hosh and Rayvn walked on the left.

Rakasuras only three hours gone? Not reassuring at all, thought Telyn.

The furry, bird-quick bipeds hunted in packs and could climb better than eehoos. Sure, they were cowardly, too. They'd wait to ambush a lone traveler who wandered off to tinkle in the woods, or harry a group until they could separate them, or come for you while you slept.

When it comes to pack predators, "cowardly" seems a synonym for "clever." Little wonder the cornics place a bounty on them.

"Did he say two or three hours?" Caitlin asked. "Do you know how much meat a rakasura has to eat to last the winter?"

"If it comes to that, we leave the llama," Hosh replied.

"Biscuit can outrun you."

"Not if I cut her throat first." Hosh patted the long knife in his belt, a gift from his parents for this specific journey.

Caitlin scoffed.

He's probably been preparing that line all morning in order to look manly. Telyn grinned to herself.

Leaving Biscuit as bait *would* be the smart move, but Telyn doubted any of them had enough ruthlessness to do such a thing—especially not Hosh. He'd get heartburn squashing anything that wouldn't fit in his infusion mug. And Biscuit had been in the Gamage family for years. His brothers would never forgive him if he came back without Biscuit.

Already rakasuras, and we haven't even crossed the bridge. What are we getting ourselves into? The heinous creatures harried Dad's expedition until it fell apart. Rakasuras doomed him, come to think of it. If his party had all stuck together, Dad would never have died. Even if he had fallen into the crevasse, the whole group would have had enough rope—and courage—to rescue him...or retrieve his body.

Midway across the bridge, Telyn brought them to a halt. The low clouds obscured the Cairn Range, but she peered intently anyway, trying to memorize the flow of the treetops. If she climbed high enough, she could use the forest's contours as a rough directional guide.

She pointed with her entire arm. "This is our direction. Any time you see moss on a tree, let me know. Moss always grows on the northern side."

"Usually," Hosh amended.

"Look for patterns. There might be a contrarian, Hosh-like moss that grows on the south side, but the regular moss grows on the north. We take our bearings whenever possible: when the clouds lift, and we can see the Aumerhem gap; when smoke from town is visible. Any time we can we double-check our position, we do so."

It felt good to be executing a plan, to have some control over destiny. Telyn had come to realize that the Ever-Guise had given her a false sense of control, but virtually everything she touched with its magic had gone wrong. She'd spoiled Esther's malt, so her mom turned to even stiffer drink. She'd attacked the Ouzeleys and provoked Tabbard into beating Hosh. Hosh had made himself popular and lost any chance of wooing Caitlin.

Had the magic backfired because their plans were all selfish in some way? Or were unintended consequences an inherent part of the magic?

"Plan wisely," Aled the Wise advised, "and trust the future to bring chaos."

Their plodding footsteps bore them under the tallest of trees where a thin trail led into the dusk-lands. Short daylight would limit their progress, but the heaviness on Telyn's legs told her it wouldn't make much difference. Four or five hours with these heavy packs, the uneven terrain, and the snow, and they would be more than ready to make camp.

Everything worked to dampen their senses. The snow and crowded evergreens deadened sound. Their thick hoods rubbed against their ears, causing audio interference even as they hampered peripheral vision. The cold numbed their sense of smell and touch.

When they'd started out, Telyn could feel the take permit—a bronze tag on a thong—jangling between her breasts. Now she couldn't even feel that. They could probably walk right underneath the rakasuras without noticing the monsters. Their best hope lay with Biscuit the llama. His senses probably outmatched their own, and he would give warning if a predator approached.

Or so Telyn hoped. Biscuit's egg-shaped head didn't look all that alert, but it *was* cute.

She rubbed his nose, and he clucked, a happy sound like clucking your tongue against the roof of your mouth.

They needed him for cargo, anyway. With just their backs, the four friends wouldn't have been able to carry supplies for more than five or six days. With Biscuit's help, they could stay comfortably in the mountains for four weeks—longer, if their traps were successful.

That first night, upon Telyn's insistence, they strung a trap line. It seemed necessary to begin the survival routine right away, even though they hoped to find the hind and go home long before their rations gave out. By the time nine traps had been put out, it was dark indeed. In the winter, daylight lasted all of eight hours.

The feathered hind—oh yes, this was Telyn's plan. She'd had to share it with Rayvn, Hosh and Caitlin before they agreed to come—and she didn't blame them. Without a plan, might as well gamble on a long-shotter on the Dating Chart. But she'd seen the feathered hind by the rumor tree. It was a domesticated animal, lost and alone, and probably relied on the rumor tree for company.

So she reasoned; so she hoped.

If it hadn't been eaten yet.

If they caught the feathered hind, they could pay Cressida's bond debt and go back to leading normal lives. They didn't even have to worry about the mind wizard or schmook anymore; the Ever-Guise was Minister Svemas's responsibility now.

Hosh's clay firepot came through—the coal he'd stored within still sparked, and they found enough pine needles and dead branches to make a campfire. Redbeard said that fire separated men from beasts, and hope from despair, that being its primary purpose. Warmth was only secondary. Its protection, of course, was mostly psychological; the beasts a fire kept at bay numbered approximately as many as it attracted.

The friends huddled around it. The light dazzled their eyes and made it less likely they'd see danger approaching, and they didn't mind. The real danger came from within. Already, on day one, doubts began to breed. Nobody spoke their doubts aloud, but they showed in the hunch of their shoulders and the downward cast of their eyes.

Telyn turned to Caitlin. "I can't believe your parents let you come."

I can't believe you wanted *to come.*

"I told them it was a lark, a camping trip with friends."

"It is," Hosh said, holding a pine needle and letting it burn until he had to drop it. "I'm going to grow a mustache. When it gets long enough, I'm going to oil and curl it."

"They don't care about me as much as you think." Caitlin leaned over to retrieve a little evergreen cone that had fallen atop the snow. Half had a perfect shape, and half had been gnawed to pieces. With gloved fingers, she cracked apart its scales and a couple of seeds fell out. "Mom and Dad've raised and seen off four other girls, each of whom made their way to Enshede to be married. All they want is to finish raising me and move seaward. That's all they talk about.." She tossed the cone atop their crackling fire. "Their hearts have always been in the city. If it weren't for me and their plum job in the Prefecture, they would've picked up stakes long ago. If I get lost here, it would simply move up their schedule."

"Wow, Caitlin, why don't you just say what you feel?" Telyn said.

"That's harsh," Hosh added.

Caitlin shrugged.

"Is that why the, ah" —Telyn shifted on the little rock she'd procured for a chair—"Joram, animals...*quest for significance*?"

"What's wrong with significance? Or animals?"

"Okay, okay, just—"

"How do you naked things survive?" Rayvn blurted. "I'm shivering to the tip of my tail."

They all stared.

"No fur, naked?"

"Can't you, like, grow us some fur with your pattern magic?" Caitlin asked.

"A mustache!" Hosh added, rising to his knees in eagerness.

"No."

"Aren't people patterns? We have blood vessels in patterns, lungs, spleens..."

"What is a spleen, anyway?" Telyn muttered, neither expecting an answer nor getting one.

"Living patterns must not be altered," Rayvn said, staring straight into the fire.

"Dating patterns are living patterns, aren't they?" Hosh insisted, "and you are very interested in those."

He's probably thinking about his leg again. Rayvn would end this conversation one way or another—possibly with a wedgie for Hosh if he didn't shut his mouth—and Telyn tried to redirect the conversation. "What about your fiancé, Rayvn? You said in the Sable Head that the Library supplied his name."

"You were not interested in my personal life before, Telyn Brower."

"Ah, well, I was surprised the Library refused the other answers. I'm interested now, promise." She was, she really was. Just because she hadn't thought of it until now didn't mean she wasn't curious. "Do pattern witches have arranged marriages?"

"And can you grow me a mustache?" Hosh added.

Rayvn scowled. "That is not something to talk about." She stood and wandered into the trees.

After several seconds, Telyn also rose. "Should I go after her?"

Caitlin said, "She is probably just beyond our sight, watching us."

"I was just asking questions," Hosh muttered.

"I wanted to hear the answer to Telyn's question," Caitlin said, hands on hips.

Telyn peered but could not see far; the light from the fire ruined her night vision. Finally, she elected to call out rather than wander blindly in the dark.

"Don't go far, Rayvn. Holler if you get lost."

At daybreak, as Hosh and Caitlin loaded Biscuit, Telyn walked their string line and recovered the various traps. She found Rayvn awaiting her at the final one.

"All empty," Rayvn announced, smiling broadly.

"You look happy about it."

Telyn dropped her load onto the ground so she could undo the final trap from its stake and pull the stake from the ground. Her hands ached from touching icy metal.

"We all help break camp and load the llama—every time," Telyn said irritably. "Your tail doesn't get you out of it."

"But it does help me climb, and I found the perfect tree to climb," Rayvn said, unperturbed. "Come on, I'll show you."

Telyn bundled the traps together to make them easier to carry and followed. A fair distance away was a tall tree, well situated, true, but with no low branches whatsoever. Rayvn had somehow attached a rope a good eighty feet above, a rope with ladder-like knots and hoops.

Telyn reached up to the first hoop and pulled. It held firm. "Did you do this with magic?"

Rayvn nodded. "I threw it over the branch and used magic to tie it in place. I wasn't sure my magic had the range. There are limits."

Good to know in case I ever make her mad at me.

"Unless this is the tallest tree around; I'm not sure this will be any use. The mountains might not be visible."

"No, but you might be able to see the smoke above Harlech; and the dip of the frozen creek which passes the rumor tree."

Telyn held out her hand, palm outward, and after staring at it, Rayvn gave it a smack. She smiled.

Telyn began to climb. She didn't want to waste too much energy on this, but Rayvn was right—in these woods, from ground level, they could pass within a hundred feet of the rumor tree and never see it. Their best hope lay in finding that frozen creek. But would they arrive upstream or downstream from the rumor tree?

If they guessed wrong, they could travel for miles in the wrong direction. The low odds of success were worth the energy it took to scale the tree.

Telyn scrambled up the rope with ease. "Rayvn," she shouted down.

"Hum?"

"We were worried about you last night. Don't wander off like that again."

"Thank you for your concern, Telyn Brower."

The rumor trees had vine-like branches with light green leaves, and yellow streaked the bark. If Telyn could get clean view, she could probably recognize it.

I wonder if it has a name. "*Miss Eliza Gossip, at your service. Pleased to meet you.*"

She remembered Redbeard's lessons. "If you're lost—truly lost— begin again. Begin a new map in your head. If you have paper, then draw one, startin' now. Don't try to fill it with what you think you know. Shed the past; begin from here and now. Then, like magic, you're no longer lost. You know right where you are on this new map. You've less chance of wandering in circles or panickin' and runnin' headlong into a brakdaw. You won't lose hope because you ain't lost on this new map."

Sort of an Aled-the-Wise saying for trappers.

Well, we're not lost, but it certainly wouldn't hurt to verify the landmarks.

Her mind thus occupied, it didn't take long to reach the apex. Rayvn had chosen well; this was one of the tallest trees around. She stopped around fifteen feet from the top, enough to get a panoramic view if she stepped around the central trunk.

Each step caused the chaos tree to rock like a ship in a storm. She exaggerated her weight-shifts, pulling on the trunk, bouncing on her toes. She loved the trunk's wobble and trusted its thin strength.

The clouds had blown away, and the Cairn Range rose breath-taking in the distance, seven piles of stone and ice. Legends blossomed in her mind—the three kings and three queens buried beneath the heaps of stone, and the demon Aumerhem who ruled them all. Telyn stared until her tears dried in the icy wind. She brushed her hair from her face and began to draw her mental map.

First, the seven cairns. The road which ran between King and Queen Two was called King's Pass. Come fall, most of the trappers traveled that way to get into the Hinterland Mesa. If Telyn failed to get Cressida's bond price and she had to break her sister out of prison, this would be their route of escape, there to live like dryad vagabonds. Hopefully they would find rogues to marry or bandits to join.

Telyn let a wry smile cross her lips at the impossible fantasy.

Between Queen Three and Aumerhem Peak lay another pass, glacier-filled, nearer and more dangerous—the pass that had claimed her dad.

She stepped around the trunk on thin branches.

Southeasterly, a haze of woodsmoke hovered over Harlech. A sheen of sunlight reflected from the Sepulcher. She could discern neither the town nor the mighty Elbus River, so tall were the trees and so deceptive the folds of topography.

Mentally, she drew the triangle to navigate by: The seven Cairn peaks, the town-smoke, and the Sepulcher. That, with a little help from the sun, should keep them on track.

The sun was already higher in the sky than she'd like. She'd have to move quickly, or they wouldn't get anywhere today. She could only hope her friends wouldn't be mad at her for taking so long.

Peering for any sign of the rumor tree, she realized that spotting it from above was hopeless. The forest was not a sea of green, but a palette of hues. The short rumor tree could be obscured in one of countless dips which could indicate camp bushes, a hidden pond, or shallow soil. If the Elbus River itself disappeared from this vantage, how likely was she to spot the frozen creek she had followed the night the Ever-Guise had exploded in stink?

On the way down, she noticed chocolate-brown forms dangling in a neighboring tree like brown-leafed mistletoe. She could have ignored the innocuous shapes—and nearly did—but something about them raised the hair on the back of her neck.

"We spotted a rakasura in the trees," the cornic soldier had warned them.

So had Raz. "They can climb, the blighters..."

Rakasuras.

Her heart beat faster.

If I had climbed that tree instead of this one, would I have awakened them? Would my friends have heard my scream, or would the rakasuras have killed me too fast?

Telyn's pants tore on the way down, but a word from Rayvn fixed them. When they rejoined the group, Telyn communicated her findings, suggested a direction change, and didn't have to suffer much more than cross looks from Hosh for her tardiness.

"We've got to get as far from here as fast as possible," Telyn said. "No cooking until nightfall. We don't want to do anything to attract them. With luck, they will follow someone else."

Caitlin, surprisingly enough, looked chipper and told her it wasn't a problem. She'd make dinner when the time came, and she'd be sure it didn't smell. "Boiled bidy tubers?" she suggested, to which Hosh made fake barfing noises. "Better bidy tubers than a rakasura attack."

She actually pinched his cheek, which seemed to please Hosh.

They tucked stockings around the traps and metal bits of their gear to keep them from rattling and led Biscuit deeper into the woods.

CHAPTER FORTY-ONE

Caitlin really stepped up. Always first up, she took care of Biscuit, fed and groomed him, stowed the blankets and gear, then loaded the packs on his back while Telyn and Rayvn scouted.

Hosh left more and more of the chores to Caitlin. And, if she were honest with herself, Telyn did as well. It felt good to be taken care of, and to have time to do what she really liked to do: climb.

Climb in the cold.

Climb in the wind.

Climb in the snow, the fog, and the dry mornings where branches crackled like old skeletons.

Hosh picked up the empty trap lines and hung them on the outside of Biscuit's pack saddles. Caitlin tied strips of cloth between them so they didn't jangle.

They learned a little about Rayvn's fiancé. He hailed from the same breeding temple as Rayvn, although she had never met him; he was seventeen years old and had all his claws and whiskers. That's about all Rayvn knew. The farseers felt his pattern and Rayvn's meshed well, which should be good enough for any witch, even though their predictions had failed Rayvn's mother.

Yes, Rayvn intended to travel to the temple to meet Ivantie in person, which made Telyn feel surprisingly melancholy, although she couldn't understand why. She hardly knew Rayvn.

They started traveling in circles on purpose.

They figured that they must have passed the rumor tree and fanned out to improve the odds of finding it. Telyn knew the topography, knew she couldn't be more than a few miles from the gossipy stump, and yet it eluded her. Even the creek she'd followed that fateful night couldn't be found.

Six oppressive days passed; each day felt shorter than the last, each night colder and darker. One early morning, Hosh asked to accompany Rayvn and Telyn as they scouted for a climbing tree. This was unusual because looking for taller trees generally meant going uphill, and Hosh tried to keep his walking to a minimum.

Caitlin, happily rubbing Biscuit down, waved them on. The llama hummed contentedly, as he often did around Caitlin. She certainly had a way with animals.

As soon as they were beyond Caitlin's earshot, Hosh asked if they thought the Ever-Guise had addled Caitlin's brain.

Telyn looked sideways at him. Rayvn's cat-ears shot forward.

"She keeps doing all this work for me, Tey. We agreed that I would saddle and groom the llama—Biscuit is my family llama, after all—but Caitlin insists on doing it. Oh, I know she likes animals, but she loads the pack saddle by herself, ties on the traps...I don't understand it. Unless...unless I used the mask too often. I think she's besotted."

All Telyn could do was glare at Hosh—which she did with all the intensity she could muster. What she couldn't figure out was why Hosh's hair didn't catch on fire.

"When a girl does all your chores for you and won't even let you help, that's got to mean more than friendship, right?"

Right in front of Rayvn!

"Now is not a good time, Hosh. We are looking for a tree to climb."

"Did Cressida let you three use the Ever-Guise, then?" Rayvn's head tilted just like a cat looking at a dust bunny that she might investigate. "If so, then you all should be up for slavery, not just Cressida."

"Oh," Hosh said, his face going ashen.

"Yeah, 'Oh,'" Telyn repeated sarcastically.

"This would explain why you asked me to inquire at the Library, rather than your sister asking me."

"Yes, guilty as charged," Telyn said. "What are you going to do about it?"

"I will continue to ask questions."

"I mean about the cornics. Are you going to turn us in?"

Rayvn shrugged. "The law should be applied equally to all."

"Do you believe that? Really? What if the law is unjust?" She wanted to say 'I thought you were my friend!' but knew that was absurd. Flacks and humans couldn't be friends—not when it counted.

"Is it a human concept to believe it fine that the law is applied unevenly, so long as the law is unjust?"

"Don't try to confuse me with complicated logic," Telyn warned, and poked Rayvn's chest with her finger.

Hosh gasped, and no wonder. Neither of them would have dared poke a flack a few months ago. But they'd become familiar with Rayvn, and Telyn just didn't care at the moment. "What if the law is written to hurt your race specifically, to make sure you don't have any rights?"

"Well, then the law would have to be changed."

"You can't change the law. You don't have any rights! You can't even join the military."

"Uh, Tey, you're making a lot of noise," Hosh said, and tugged on her sleeve.

"Do you want to join the military, Telyn Brower? I do not advise this. Humans do not have the fortitude of cornic shock troops—"

"Listen, Rayvn, we did use the Ever-Guise. A part of it. And why not? If a-a pattern witch, or a schmook, or a whatever had used it, it wouldn't have been a crime. How is that—"

"Telyn," Hosh said, his sleeve-tugging growing more insistent. "I think you should quiet down."

She followed his pointing finger.

There, a rakasura peeked from the gloom of a tree-trunk. It looked a little guilty at being seen, like a grandfather caught sticking his finger in a pie before dinner. It rubbed its face with a clawed hand.

Standing on muscular, rear legs, it resembled a cross between a bird and a badger: a raptor's forelegs, claws, and beak; a badger's fur and musculature. Rakasura fur changed color with the season, and this one's was white with dapples of brown and slate, very difficult to see against the bark, leaves, and snow.

Telyn immediately looked up—she'd heard many stories of people being ambushed from above. She saw only branches, needles, leaves, shadows.

The rakasura stopped rubbing its face to clack its claws together. The hollow sound resounded in the forest.

"It's calling the others," Hosh whispered. "What do we do?"

"Attack," Telyn replied.

"Attack?" Hosh said, meekly.

"'In battle, unlike in marriage, the unexpected is generally best,'" Telyn quoted Gruffud the Irreverent. She freed her ice ax from her back, raised it high above her head, and ran screaming at the rakasura.

Despite its small size, the rakasura could have shredded her, but Telyn had never heard of one attacking by itself. They always, *always* attacked as a group.

She heard Rayvn growling right behind her, and Hosh followed a moment later.

The rakasura allowed them to get to within about five feet, realized they weren't bluffing, and leapt to the side. Powered by those strong rear legs, it easily evaded the charge then rabbit-hopped into the trees. The three friends shouted after it to make sure it kept going.

"Back to camp," Telyn said, breathless. "Caitlin is alone."

They traveled as fast as Hosh could hobble, which meant that Telyn couldn't quite break into a run. Their panting, the crackle of leaves, and the clang of gear on their belts kept them company, until Rayvn decided to fill the silence.

"In Harlech, if I did your chores, that would mean that I wanted you in my debt. Or I might be demonstrating my affection for you. Is that correct from a human perspective?"

"Er," Hosh said, thrown by the return to the earlier subject of conversation.

"Here in the woods, where we are forced together most of the time, I surmise a reversal in the pattern." Rayvn's breathing hardly changed, despite their near-run. "If I did your chores, that would mean that I didn't want you around me. By my actions, I would be encouraging you to go elsewhere. Therefore, Hosh," Rayvn concluded, triumphantly, "I believe that Caitlin does not like you."

"Oh."

A couple of steps further, and Telyn's footsteps came to an end. *The flack and her patterns...she's hit it straight on.*

"Mother of Squirrels!"

"Telyn?"

"Caitlin obviously likes you, Hosh. That's been obvious for ages. So why else do you think she is doing your chores?"

"Ah, excess energy?"

"Of course not. She's hiding something." Hot indignity made Telyn flush. "I'll bet she wants to make sure we never capture the feathered hind! I'll bet she goes around each morning sabotaging our string line."

"Telyn, get a hold of yourself," Hosh said. "Caitlin is not sabotaging us. And we have more important problems, like, rakasura problems."

"Right. Come on. Caitlin is alone."

When they arrived, Caitlin looked just a little uncomfortable. While Hosh related the rakasura story, Telyn poked around. She found the clue with Biscuit, whose jaw worked a little too vigorously to be cud chewing. She extracted a long stalk of alfalfa from the side of his mouth and waved it accusingly at Caitlin.

"What in the Philosophers Tomes is this? Did a farmer plant a hay-field nearby?"

"He needs food! He can't live on forage alone."

"Yes. He. Can. That's why we brought him."

"He doesn't like digging," Caitlin pouted, flicking guilt-ridden eyes towards the saddle-packs. Telyn stalked to where they rested against a tree and began removing gear. Below the spare clothes, ropes, and tools, Telyn found oil-paper wrapped food.

Telyn added those to the pile.

Caitlin shuffled her feet.

Telyn reached the bottom of the pack without finding any alfalfa. She stared at the pile for a while, then started massaging the various oil-paper packages. Some felt awfully light.

"I just brought him a little snack to keep his spirits up."

Telyn split one open...and found a tightly bound bundle of alfalfa. She tore through the rest, paying little heed to the wrapping.

About half contained human food; the other half alfalfa.

"Look," Caitlin said, tapping her foot and crossing her arms, her face a mixture of embarrassment and defiance. "You didn't really expect me to camp in the woods for a month without even a necessary or anything, did you?"

"That's what we agreed to. A month of camping to save my sister from a lifetime of slavery, is that too much to ask?"

"Look, Tey, this isn't going to work. We don't know what we are doing. Just because we live in Harlech, we think we're trappers, but that isn't true. We know nothing. We haven't caught anything—not a rabbit, not a coyote, nor a fox or squirrel. Nothing! We need to go home." She sounded so pouty that Telyn wanted to slap her.

The other packs remained closed, and Telyn didn't want to tear them apart just now. After all, the rakasuras might be coming.

"How long?"

Caitlin swallowed noisily.

"How long until we run out of food?"

You are such a traitor.

"Two weeks. If we're careful."

"Two—! We go on half-rations starting tonight." Telyn started shoving the packages roughly into the saddlebag. "You can eat straw, since that's what you packed."

"That isn't fair. You're the one who got your sister in trouble. You refused to give up the Ever-Guise when I warned you—"

"We," Hosh said tentatively. "We got Cressida in trouble. It was all three of us." He refused to meet Caitlin's eyes, but Telyn was proud of him for speaking up. "Maybe we got scared a little earlier than Telyn, but that doesn't, eh, doesn't mean we're not guilty."

Rayvn watched all this with round eyes. Probably calculating how they all should have been sold as slaves months ago.

"I say we go home now," Caitlin said, "find some other way to help Cressida. My parents have pull at the Prefecture. They can probably influence who buys her—"

Telyn really, really wanted to slap her. "If you want to go, Caitlin Nest, just go. And good luck with the rakasuras." When it became clear Caitlin would neither leave nor say any more, Telyn added, "Half-rations starting tonight, and no lunch." She was in the mood for punishing them.

All of them, including herself.

Redbeard's first rule of trapping: lay everything out before you go and check inventory—no matter how much experience you have, no matter how much you trust your partners.

I neglected a basic rule. Stupid, stupid, stupid. And stupider still to trust Caitlin.

"Any other secrets I need to know about?"

"No," Caitlin responded sullenly.

Biscuit brayed.

They marked the trees and headed out. They did not fan out as before; they stayed close together.

Fear followed on silent claws.

The sounds of things: sleeves brushing against jackets; footfalls on snow-covered leaves; Biscuit's hoarse breathing; clumps of snow sloughing off branches.

When no one was looking, Telyn checked the straps holding her ice ax to her back. It was the sharpest tool she owned, and she knew how to swing it into ice. It would work against a rakasura skull if needed—if she swung true. She didn't think they would stand still for her; she'd have to swing fast.

A knotted thong kept the pick snug on her back, but she could pull one string and loosen it. With that undone, she could jiggle the bottom free of its ties....

She could have the ax in her hands in seconds. Re-affixing it was another matter.

She noticed Hosh fingering the hilt of his long knife. She suggested he practice drawing it.

At noon, when they paused to melt some snow for water, Rayvn affixed a blanket to her back as a sort of cape. It didn't look particularly warm.

"Hosh," she purred, catching his attention immediately. Then she shouted—and caused the cape to billow up like a gigantic hood.

Hosh was so startled he fell backwards, and Rayvn laughed in delight.

Telyn nodded.

They couldn't actually fight a pack of rakasuras; but they could frighten them.

"Can you do that for all of us?"

"At once?"

"Or whoever is in front. But yes, if necessary."

"When it's calm and I'm not under pressure, I think so. If we are under attack" —Rayvn smiled airily—"that would be difficult."

"We can do difficult," Telyn said. *We have to.*

Using her pattern magic, Rayvn split blankets and fashioned capes for all of them and practiced dividing her magic five different ways— since Caitlin insisted Biscuit wear a cape of his own.

The capes did not inflate nearly as well with the pattern girl's attention divided multiple ways. She could do three just fine, but more than that, and they floundered.

Later, as they walked, Telyn whispered to Rayvn, "If we are attacked, forget Biscuit. He can take care of himself. We need to scare the rakasuras, not make them laugh."

"Yes, Telyn Brower, you are correct. Too bad it isn't summer. We could walk through a stream to wash off our scent."

Something clicked in Telyn's mind: wind, leaves, frozen creek....

"We've been walking over it all this time! Not literally, but I'll bet we crossed it two or three times without noticing. There must have been wind; of course there's been wind, and the leaves just blew to the low place and covered it."

Within a few hours, feeling relieved and stupid, they located the ice-ribbon creek under a foot of blown debris.

Telyn pointed upstream. "Thirty feet apart. Look for round, yellowish leaves and drooping branches; the rumor tree looks like a weeping willow. And don't listen to it. Whatever it says is lies. Except about the hind; if it says anything about the feathered hind, pay attention."

"The tree lies about humans, but tells the truth about feathered hinds?" Rayvn said. "That doesn't make any sense."

Hosh snickered.

"It'll talk about you, too, Rayvn, don't think it won't," Telyn warned. *That breeding temple thing should be interesting.*

"I could use some of that," Hosh said. "The more they talk about you, the more popular you are."

"You have issues, you know that?"

CHAPTER FORTY-TWO

Caitlin spotted the rumor tree first. Telyn walked right past; it looked so different in the daylight with most of its leaves fallen than when she'd stumbled upon it in the dark weeks ago. If an oak stump sprouted a thousand grape vines, it would look something like the rumor tree—except its branches waved like algae in a stream.

A bit of searching located the tree the gnomes had bent to catch Telyn, but all of their efforts couldn't get it to do more than sway. To bend it double to make a spring-trap, the gnomes had either used magic or were incredibly strong.

When Hosh suggested Rayvn try pattern magic to bend it, she growled menacingly.

"Surely trees don't count as living things?" Hosh protested. "We cut them down all the time for lumber, kindling, furniture, flooring—"

Caitlin smacked the back of his head.

And so they decided to make simpler traps, ones Lutric Quid had unwittingly prepared them for—pit traps.

Side by side, shovels in hand, the friends gathered the courage to approach the tree.

"Look at us," Telyn said, laughing aloud, "four wallflowers working up the courage to ask someone to dance, afraid of a little embarrassment."

"A little! Remember when Quid had that rumor tree?" Hosh shivered.

"Don't remind me," Caitlin said. "It told everyone I'd started my cycle! And it wasn't even true yet."

Four steam-filled breaths later, still they had not moved.

Caitlin shifted her grip on the shovel handle. "Do we really have to do this?"

"The closer we set the traps, the more likely they'll catch something," Telyn replied. "Kiiptk said that sooner or later, everyone approaches a rumor tree. The feathered hind is a pet. It might enjoy freedom, but it misses companionship." *I hope. High Father, please let that be true.*

She began to close the distance, her vision taken up by the invitingly treacherous branches. "Careful what you think. Quid's potted tree might come from this one's acorn."

"Seriously?" Hosh scoffed.

"Just sayin', keep your thoughts on the job."

"On the hind, you mean?" Hosh snickered. "I always do."

Behind Telyn, Caitlin smacked Hosh again with a muffled *thwack*.

Rayvn asked something about rumor tree dating, but Telyn tuned her out. The nearest vine settled across her shoulder in a familiar way.

Welcome back, Telyn; you brought friends. Or are they? Secrets from you, secrets from each other they keep. How can friends keep secrets from one another unless they aren't really friends?

"Tell it to the knot-hole," Telyn replied, which sent its many vines to jiggling, as if they enjoyed being talked back to.

"You don't mind if we dig around here, do you?" She plunged the metal spade into the ground, found it softer than the dirt in Harlech, and booted it to the handle. "This is going to work, guys."

The tree didn't protest when her movements snapped a vine; another would take its place, or a thin root would climb her ankle. She'd shoveled a neat outline of a square, about six feet on each side, before her friends joined her.

The rumor tree badgered them collectively.

Listen, Caitlin, listen to the bole. Hosh has secret feelings for some-one, someone with soft auburn curls and a soft derriere. They've been taking picnics at the pond...

The voice descended to suggestive murmurs that Telyn could almost, but not quite, make out. She looked over and noted that Hosh and Rayvn both had stopped digging in order to listen better. Only Caitlin continued, jabbing the metal tip into the soil and stamping it with her boot, nodding occasionally, smiling a bit. *She* could hear just fine.

Telyn shook herself free of the spell. "Don't listen; it's all lies anyway. We're here for the feathered hind."

"I have never used my tail to clean Hosh's ears," Rayvn blurted.

"You kind of did," Telyn said, laughing.

"Not the wax-filled part; just the, what do you call it, the part that gets pierced."

"It looked like the icky, wax-filled part to me."

"I was trying to duplicate how humans flirt. Observation is not as good as empirical practice."

"Practice on Hosh's nose, why don't you?" Caitlin said. When Rayvn glared at her, she added, "That was a joke. No, do not practice on his nose—or anyone's nose, for that matter."

"I do not exaggerate my limp so Mummy will take care of me!" Hosh burst out.

Ah, I sort of think you do, Telyn thought, then amended, *sometimes.*

They kept working.

One shovel handle broke, and they only succeeded in getting one pit to a satisfactory depth the first day. That didn't matter much. They had plenty of time to dig, dig, dig until their backs ached and their arms felt like they would fall off. They'd forgotten buckets to carry the dirt away, so that had to be done one shovel at a time.

While they dug, they couldn't wait to be finished. Three days and four pit traps later, the gigantic piles of the loose dirt cleared from the area and a camouflage of thin branches laid over the top, they had altogether too much time to kill. They sniped at each other until they had run out of snipes, absorbed the tree's rumors until they began to believe, and suffered the hunger and cold in sullen irritation. Telyn just knew Caitlin was counting the days until they ran out of food and had to go home. She didn't need the rumor tree to tell her that, although it did—gleefully.

Only Rayvn seemed immune. She studied them all with wide eyes, waiting for them to crack so she could log the weakness of the human psyche in her over-analytical brain.

Over-analytical and yet ditsy, what an odd combination.

Aloud, Telyn worried that they had left so much human smell in the area that the feathered hind would never come. Caitlin disagreed. In fact, she said, as a domesticated animal, their scent might attract it. The disagreement turned into an argument, into hurled insults, and finally into a vote, which went to Telyn three-to-one.

Therefore, they moved the camp to the far side of the frozen, leaf-covered stream—reluctantly. The rumor tree comforted like a nagging aunt who lit the fire every evening before you came home, criticized your appearance while serving you tea, and warned you to get your act together while tucking you into bed.

Now they had to live with the forest's silences and sounds: frozen branches crackling, snow accumulating overhead, leaves rustling in the wind, owls hooting, undefinable scratching in the dark, the snow, now over-heavy, plopping onto the ground.

Two or three more days passed; Telyn began to lose track. Every day that passed, Telyn's sister grew further away, and the reality of her impending slavery grew nearer. The luxury prison of Harlech's Prefecture would give way to the stark reality of forced labor—or worse. Possibly much, much worse. Telyn couldn't bear to think on it. Lying down at night, far too early to sleep but with little light and less to do, she forced her mind down brighter paths: the Spring Sale; gooseberry acorns; snowball fights on the lake; climbing; bringing the hind in, collecting the reward and freeing Cressida; a steam bath celebration as everything turned out right...

Their bellies grumbled; they never got completely warm. They could have posted a guard. They could have, but they'd seen no sign of rakasuras or any other predators, and the cold boredom made it practically impossible to stay awake, and Hosh assured them Biscuit would awaken them if any danger approached.

Still, they could have taken shifts.

CHAPTER FORTY-THREE

A boot to the foot woke Telyn up.

"We caught something."

Hosh's voice.

Telyn grunted, sat up, and attempted to appear wide-awake and clear-headed. She strained her ears. Over the noise of the others rising and dressing, she heard animal sounds. She accepted Hosh's help to rise, threw her cloak over her shoulders, pulled on her boots.

She didn't allow herself to hope. Hoping would lead to disappointment. Too much smashed hope would lead to despair.

We caught something.

Mother of Squirrels, what if we caught the hind? What if I can free my sister?

The other three awaited her.

"Light or no light?" Caitlin whispered.

Light would show their approach from far away. No light, and they wouldn't be able to see until they were right on top of the pit traps.

"Light," Telyn decided, grabbing her ice ax. "Whatever it is, it's caught. It can't run away, nor can it ambush us."

Rayvn lit a hooded lantern and, leaving Biscuit tethered to a sapling, they crept toward the rumor tree.

No question about it, the sounds came from one of the pit traps, snorting and huffing from beneath the level of the ground, hooves pacing narrow confines. They'd dug the pits about ten feet deep and narrow, so the hind couldn't get a running start. No telling how high a hind could jump given enough room.

In Harlech, the holes would have made super-deluxe necessaries.

Don't hope. Don't hope. Wait and see. A regular deer would be good too. Even if we haven't trapped the hind, we need food. With food, we can stay longer.

Mother of Squirrels, just let me free my sister, catch the hind, get the reward, and end this nightmare.

The cone of light from Rayvn's hooded lantern pushed into the clearing and, as one, the four friends halted. A dozen or more rakasuras surrounded one of the pit traps, the first and deepest they had dug. The furry beasts quivered, hopped over each other, and nipped on each other's flanks the way puppies do when dog-piling on a runt.

From the pit came grunts and snorts, and antlers appeared and fell back down as the animal attempted to jump free, antlers and a soupçon of myriad colors.

The feathered hind—they had caught it.

But the rakasuras had gotten here first.

The hooded lantern's light reflected off several pair of eyes as the rakasuras looked their way. Whether or not they could see the friends through the glare was an open question. The predators acted neither afraid nor particularly interested. They had the perfect quarry—alone, isolated, and trapped. They gave a series of warning clicks with their foreclaws and turned away.

The larger rakasuras crowded around the pit, jostling each other for a better view. One leaned far over the edge. Dirt sloughed in, and the monster put its jaw as low as it could. A blow from a soaring antler knocked the monster's head up and back; the others chirped and yapped. One took the opportunity to attack the wounded rakasura, and they rolled on the ground, whistling and chittering. Dirt flew, and blood, and the clacking and yapping from the pack of rakasuras swelled.

Scrambling back and forth, the combatants attacked with beaks and claws and placed their back legs on each other's bellies, swiping to disembowel.

As the wounds multiplied, a fishy sort of blood-smell emerged. One of those swipes would split Telyn from chin to groin, yet the creatures' hides held stronger than well-cured leather. Their strength far outstripped a human's.

No contest.

No chance.

Any one of these beasts could take any two of us—except maybe Rayvn; she might be a match for one. Maybe.

Telyn's eyes could not have grown wider nor her breath shallower.

The two fighters finally separated, bloodied but not crippled. Then both turned and shoved back to the edge of the pit, wagging their thick, furry tails in excitement.

"Mother of Squirrels," Telyn breathed. The blood-fish reek dizzied her. Animal blood didn't normally affect her the way human blood did, but that...that horrible, fishy-blood smell was horrible. Blackness threatened to blot out consciousness.

"Let's get out of here," Hosh whispered. He had drawn his knife.

Much good that would do, barely scratch their hide. Telyn tried to breathe deeply, clear her mind. *If Hosh keeps trembling like that, he's going to drop it* and *lose the knife in these leaves.*

What a stupid, crazy thought. Got to focus. Focus on the important, the now.

"That's my sister's freedom in there," Telyn said, as Caitlin said, "I can't believe it. We did it."

"If we let those rakasuras kill it, we won't have done anything."

"Telyn, the hind can defend itself," Hosh said, shielding his eyes, for Rayvn had turned to listen better, and the lantern had swung with her attention. "They won't climb into the pit where they will get trapped also."

"Yes, they will. You know they will. They'll work themselves into a frenzy and they won't even—Rayvn, turn the light back that way."

The hooded lantern swung back toward the rakasuras—and revealed that in the absence of the glare, three of the little monsters had crept towards the humans. The predators looked at each other as if wondering whether to pursue this new prey or return to the pit.

"They'll kill the hind, Hosh." The ax felt leaden in Telyn's gloved hands. "My sister...she's counting on us."

"We can't fight them, Telyn, there are too many." Frozen leaves crackled as Hosh took a careful step back.

Teyln now made the apex of a triangle—Hosh to her right, Caitlin and Rayvn to her left. Her friends wore their capes; Telyn had forgotten hers.

"This is for Cressida. I am not leaving without that feathered hind." Telyn cast about for a suitable stone. In her experience, animals tended to be more afraid of projectiles than weapons. Flying objects impressed and confused them since animals couldn't throw things.

The streambank had many suitable stones, but they were all frozen in place. Each time she bent to pry one out with the ice ax, the rakasuras took a cautious step in her direction. Their long heads swiveled from side to side; they called to each other and clicked hollow claws.

Telyn filled her pockets as quickly as she could, and her friends loaded theirs as well.

Most of the rakasuras remained around the snorting hind, but six now advanced on the friends. They closed about half the distance.

They won't go back to the hind now. They've passed the point of no return.

"This is not about getting your sister free," Hosh argued, trying to dig stones with one hand while brandishing his knife in the other. "This is about you feeling guilty for putting her into slavery."

Ouch. It must be true—or partly true—because even in the heat of action, the accusation hurt too much to be otherwise.

She didn't have time to discuss it. "Grab a rock or go back to the llama, but don't get in my way."

"Tey, one of them will be the dominant male," Caitlin said. "Make him run, and the rest will—" The large, bloodied male hopped into the pit. A great, grunting fury arose as hind battled rakasura. "That would be him. Never mind."

"What do you mean, never mind?"

"They won't run now, not unless the leader is killed. They are just going to—There they go."

The second, bloodied rakasura dove jaw-first into the pit, and a great many more crowded the lip. Giving off a series of reluctant whistles, the six that had been stalking the friends scurried back to join those surrounding the pit.

"Now's our chance," Hosh said. "Back away slowly. Go back to camp, get Biscuit—"

"Run? You want to run?"

"Yes," he hissed. "As soon as we're out of their sight, we run."

"Hosh Gamage makes sense," Rayvn added. "Although I think he won't be able to run very fast."

Telyn tuned them out. They'd become a distraction. *Got to save my sister. Got to save the feathered hind to save my sister.* She took two huffing breaths, gathering her courage, and rocked back and forth on her toes like a runner preparing for a sprint.

"If the leader is in the pit and can't get out...I don't know what they'll do. They may jump in. They may leave off and—" Caitlin broke off, staring wide-eyed at Telyn. "Tey, don't do it. You can't outrun them, and once they start after you, they aren't going to—"

Her friends' voices sounded indistinct and far away.

"Wait! Take the cape," Rayvn said, untying her own and throwing it at her.

With the ice ax in one hand, Telyn fumbled to even get the cape near her throat, but it slithered forward and tied itself (*Thank you, Rayvn!*). Then she was ran straight at the rakasuras.

"And there she goes," Caitlin sighed behind her.

Hosh's quiet "No, no, no, no" faded behind her.

Get their attention.

Divide them.

The pits, use the pits.

Swing the ice ax like a mad-woman, split sculls.

Kill the monsters.

Scream.

She started with the screaming.

"She's brave!"

Rayvn's compliment bolstered her as Telyn sprinted across the open area, swerved as near as she dared to the gaggle of rakasuras, and shouted at the top of her lungs. She beaned one with a thrown rock and kept moving.

Other than a glance from the smallish beast who'd been hit by the rock, they paid her no mind whatsoever.

If she had had a spear, she could have run one of them through. Focused entirely on the fight between the leaders and the feathered hind, their skinny butts quivered, their heads danced side to side, and their clawed back feet threw dirt ten feet behind them.

The fight was really going in the pit now, with antlers crashing, rakasuras grunting, and dirt flipping out. The hind seemed to be holding its own. But if they all piled in, there was no way it would survive; it wouldn't be able to move trapped beneath a pile of beaks, jaws and claws. The survivors would simply walk out on the backs of the others.

Telyn approached close enough to kick dirt on them—way closer than she would've liked. Two small rakasuras, maybe two feet tall each, finally glanced backwards and made eye contact.

Telyn waved the ax. "Look, I'm running. I'm turning my back on you. Come and get me, you cowards. Come and get this lanky piece of jerky." She turned and made it about three steps before several rakasuras peeled off and followed.

Telyn accelerated, taking full advantage of her long legs.

The predators gained fast.

A volley of rocks sailed past her shoulder; her friends giving her a fighting chance. If she could just lead the monsters to the other pit traps...

She didn't look back.

A few steps further, and her friends' shouts joined the rakasura grunts. It sounded like they were encouraging the rakasuras to catch her, though she guessed they wanted to distract them.

It didn't work; Telyn's long legs were just too enticing. She was like a fleeing blood-sausage. She nearly pulled a complete blunder as she curved around the rumor tree, and her foot plunged through a pile of leaves into nothing.

Pit trap.

She'd misjudged the location, stepped through the branches concealing one corner...

Her shin slammed against the far wall. She fell face-first, barely avoided driving the ice ax through her own belly as she planted it into the far side and rolled sideways.

Rakasura claws raked her calf as the lead beast caught her—and then lost its grip as it plunged into the hole. The other rakasuras skidded to a halt, peered down at their fallen comrade, and clacked their beaks.

Using the ax, Telyn levered herself to her feet, turned, and, with half-an-eye behind her, picked up speed again. After some chittering discussion, the three remaining rakasuras rounded the now-visible trap and followed.

Too dang fast!

Monstrous shadows stretched past her as a jiggling light came from behind—Rayvn with the hooded lantern, sprinting to catch up.

There—the mess of branches indicated the third trap. She would go to the far side, lead these two right into it—

More rakasuras rounded the rumor tree on the far side, spilled around the corner like a stampede of beaks and belly-ripping claws, coming right at her. Eyes flashing in the wobbling lamplight.

Voices exploded in Teyln's head.

Ooohh, Telyn's last stand, ice ax in hand, the rumor tree narrated. *A hundred rakasuras she felled before they dragged her to her death...*

"Shut it," Telyn said, between heaving breaths.

She couldn't climb; she couldn't run; she could only fight. The Ever-Guise she'd given up in fright.

And left Cressida to galley rows

While drunken Esther mourns.

Ooohhhh, the rumor tree tittered, thrilled into lyrical rhyme.

Telyn tried to reverse direction; her boots skidded on wet leaves, and she barely managed to spin without falling.

Three rakasuras were almost on her, and Rayvn was right behind them.

"Stop!" Telyn shouted in desperation.

Over her back, her cape lifted and spread like giant wings.

Two of the rakasuras veered off, frightened by the apparition. The third came straight on.

She managed a quarter-swing; the tip of her ice ax bit, stuck in bone, twisted against the creature's thick diaphragm, and Telyn landed hard on her back with the fighting beast going for her throat. Her ax turned sideways between their bodies; she had no distance to swing, and she dropped it, put both hands against the snapping jaws to keep them away. The other two rakasuras returned, snipping at her flailing limbs. One of them bit a boot and dragged it off. The next bite would be her foot or ankle.

"Use the cape!" Rayvn called.

Telyn had all she could do to protect her throat. Her hands were slick with rakasura spit and blood...hers, likely, though in the struggle she didn't feel any pain.

The rakasura was lighter than she thought. She should be able to throw it off, but it was sinew-strong and twisted like a river-eel.

Rayvn kept shouting about the *cape* and *face* and *smother him*, and the cape struggled against Telyn's throat, one second protecting her, the next trying to crawl away like a living thing.

Which didn't help at all!

She could barely breathe; she didn't have time to worry about a stupid cape. She had to squeeze her chin to her chest to avoid getting her throat ripped out.

The rakasura kept trying to curl its back claws against her belly so it could tear out her intestines. Then the creature leaned its torso back, preparing for one final death lunge, and Telyn pulled the cape around to cover her face and head.

When the rakasura's head snapped forward, the cape leapt from her hands, wrapped around the creature's muzzle, and clamped its mouth closed.

Pattern witch magic!

The beast went crazy.

Telyn managed to roll away, taking damage to her calf from a random, flailing claw.

She staggered upright. Right away she saw why the other rakasuras hadn't pulled her apart: Several wore their own cape headgear.

One had given up fighting completely and lay on its back, twitching, while several rakasuras began to tear into it. They had no compunction about cannibalism.

Two others moved slower and slower as the fabric tightened around their throats.

"Do I kill them?" Rayvn asked.

Telyn leaned over with her hands on her knees, catching her breath, thinking. Caitlin and Hosh had arrived also, Hosh with knife in hand, and Caitlin gripping a shovel in both fists.

"Obviously," Hosh said.

"Yes," Telyn said, looking to her friends. "We've no other choice."

Caitlin swallowed hard and nodded.

The capes tightened until the rakasuras stopped struggling.

Shaking from adrenaline, Telyn, Hosh, and Caitlin made their way back to the first pit, each holding a cape. Rayvn followed with the lantern. Dirt and antlers, feathers and blood flipped over the rim, accompanied by a cacophony of grunts, clacks, snorts, and the deep bellow that Telyn recognized as coming from the feathered hind. Only four rakasuras, runty ones, padded around the outside. The others must have joined the fray inside.

"The blankets are on Biscuit," Caitlin said. "We only have three capes, and we don't have time..."

Before she'd finished the sentence, the cape she held divided neatly down the middle.

"Now four," Rayvn said.

Hosh said, "Can't you just, like—they have patterns, right? Our organs are patterns, blood vessels are patterns. Bones are patterns. Can't you tie their blood vessels in knots or something?"

The pattern of life
Scales blown on a fife
The pattern witch keys
Major to minor a breeze

Whether it was Hosh's comment, or some taunting from the rumor tree, Raven curled a fist at Hosh, outrage evident from the set of her ears and the baring of her incisors.

Hosh straightened suddenly and toppled over, his clothes stiff as dried leather.

Rayvn's voice choked as she said, "We are *not* to interfere with living patterns. That is forbidden. Absolutely forbidden." The cape began to writhe in Telyn's hands. "You must never say such a thing. To even have suggested it...if I told mother what you asked for..." The cape wrapped around Telyn's hands and began to tie itself into a knot. Caitlin managed to drop hers, but Telyn's stayed on like a determined snake—a snake that wanted to crush her fingers.

"Rayvn," Telyn said. "Rayvn, stop!"

She didn't.

Telyn's knuckles cracked. The blankets twisted cruelly.

Hosh squeaked.

"If you ever ask such a thing again—! I will not even finish my thought, you, you humans!"

The cape suddenly released Telyn's hands. It slithered across the ground faster than any serpent and ascended one of the runty rakasuras. When the monster bit at the invading wool, the cape crawled inside its mouth. Its eyes bulged.

Telyn had to turn away, but she couldn't tune out the burbling and gagging sounds that followed.

In minutes, all four rakasuras around the rim died, and the sopping wet capes wriggled into the pit.

Shakily, the friends approached the edge. None of them dared look Rayvn in the eyes. None of the dared glance at her.

Rayvn shone the hooded lantern downward.

All is not lost.

All is not lost!

Cressida, yes!

Half-buried under rakasura bodies—some killed by antlers, some by cape strangulation—the feathered hind blinked up at them. Bloodied, torn, winded...but alive.

It gave a mournful bellow.

And Telyn reminded herself to never, ever make Rayvn mad at her.

"Well?" Rayvn demanded, looking at each of them in turn.

"Ah, looks like, er," Hosh trailed off as he received the fiercest of Rayvn's glares. "Looks like, er, ah, I'm going to need a new cape."

CHAPTER FORTY-FOUR

The good news was that they had plenty of meat, and with the outdoor temperature well below freezing, it would keep indefinitely. Food was no longer a problem.

The bad news was that lacerations covered the feathered hind from muzzle to haunches. The skin over its belly had been shredded; a thin membrane barely kept the guts from spilling like a bucket of worms in gelatin. A few more seconds, the rakasura's back claws would have pierced that, and Telyn couldn't see any way they would have saved the hind's life.

Even now, a vigorous jump, such as if he tried to leap out of the pit, might tear the animal's belly beyond healing.

The hind, a male, lay on his side among the pile of rakasuras, trembling slightly. He seemed to understand that they wanted to help. He did his best to keep those sharp antlers from scoring them as Rayvn magicked ropes under his back. They tied these to Biscuit (Telyn wished silently that he was a mule instead of a llama), and with a lot of coaxing and false starts, they convinced Biscuit to back up and heft the heavy animal out of the pit.

One of the hind's ridiculous wings had nearly been torn off. They probably should have amputated, it but they couldn't bring themselves to do it. Instead, they wrapped it tightly to his side with strips of blanket.

Hosh had brought a flask of angel water—which gave Telyn an angry, queasy feeling—but they poured most of it on the wounds. So, it came in handy, and it meant Hosh wouldn't be nipping drinks at night.

She'd have a talk with Hosh later about the evils of alcohol and what it had done to her family. If he brought up her hypocrisy of opposing alcohol consumption while working in the tavern, why, she'd smack him upside the head.

Caitlin with her hay and Hosh with his angel water—I will definitely require everyone to lay out their gear next time we made an expedition, Telyn thought, grumpily. *I should have paid more attention to Redbeard's first rule of trapping.*

The rumor tree began making things up immediately. *Tired of his three-female harem,* young *Mr. Hosh has taken a feathered hind as a bride. He plans to name the children Down and Velvet.*

"But the hind is a male!" Rayvn said. "How can they have fawns?"

"Oh, shut it, you barren, acornless bush," Caitlin muttered. "If I had time, I'd chop you down myself."

Caitlin gets grumpy on her cycle, the tree announced, earning curses from all three of them—even Rayvn.

Pattern witches have cycles? Hmm. It had never occurred to Telyn that a flack might have to deal with something as mundane as a menstrual cycle when she could magick a weapon out of a wool cape. It made the fla—er, *thauma* more relatable.

Once the obvious had been accomplished: hind removed from the pit; wounds assessed, cleaned, and bandaged; wing immobilized; gear packed...the group looked to Telyn for instructions. Since she had organized the expedition, this was not entirely unexpected, but the weight of it did make her heart thump.

This adventure felt more and more like one of Redbeard's stories: when the hero got close to what she desired, more and more obstacles threw themselves in her way. The closer she got, the more difficult the obstacles were to overcome.

Except that in the stories, the heroes always seemed to have a mentor or adviser telling them what to do next.

All Telyn had was the rumor tree.

Telyn has been talking about Rayvn behind her back. Again. Nasty words she uses, like 'flack.' Nasty rumors she spreads...

"We have to get the hind back to Harlech in one piece. That's number one."

The others looked puzzled.

Telyn thought she'd spoken aloud, but with all the adrenaline and confusion of the last hour, she wasn't entirely sure. She reclined on her haunches and, remembering Redbeard's lessons, tried to make a plan—and ignore the gossipy bole.

"We'll need a stretcher. Two long poles with some cross braces and a blanket between should suffice. We can chop the branches from the rumor tree; they are flexible and the right diameter."

The tree's yapping abruptly stopped.

"Rayvn can bind them in place. We can use our ropes to attach the long poles to Biscuit's packsaddle." Hosh limped to the pack and began rummaging for the hand ax. He took his time about it, as if less than eager to carry out this...what...suggestion? Order?

Am I giving orders now? Me, the one who got us all into this mess?

How messed up is that?

She pictured her dad Dorian, how he should have been lifted from the crevasse and hauled back to Harlech. If Redbeard and Archie Todd had made a stretcher, maybe he'd be with her now, and this whole mess wouldn't have happened. Cressida wouldn't be in prison awaiting slavery. Her friends wouldn't be beat up and freezing in the forest. Even the hind wouldn't have been nearly disemboweled by rakasuras.

If only Raz and the baker had tried just a little harder...

No ghost, Tey. No ghost.

"Wait, Hosh, don't take the branches from the rumor tree," Telyn said, "unless its rumors get particularly nasty. I was kidding."

Slapping the ax against a gloved hand, Hosh surveyed the blackness outside the glow of the lamp.

"I'll go too," Rayvn said, draping three blanket-stoles over her arm and smiling at Hosh's grateful nod. They left together.

> *A simple little tail*
> *Creeping up Hosh's hair,*
> *The pattern girl has a crush*
> *On the gimping boy's tush—*

"You don't even rhyme!" Caitlin complained. "Shut it with the poetry."

The tree stayed silent a second, then, *Are you going to let the hind die?*

"Of course not. We're taking it away from you, and we're never coming back. You know, I happen to like animals—a lot more than humans—but I can make an exception in your case." Caitlin stuck her tongue out at the tree.

Telyn cocked her head. The rumor tree had never asked a question before. It had always mixed and mashed their thoughts into despicable —or funny—rumors. How much did the tree actually understand about what it was talking about? Was this tree actually *sentient*?

"Rumor Tree, Ma'am, we're taking the hind back to Harlech, to the human town, to be healed," Telyn said.

The golden pond can heal it.

"The golden what?"

In the mountains, a bubbling spring: new flight for the bucks and love galore for bitter Caitlin.

"Idiot," Caitlin muttered. She lifted the hind's head and cradled it in her lap, the antlers flanking her like giant branches. The hind closed his large, black eyes. "We need a healer. With magic, preferably. Oh, Telynnn." Caitlin's half-suppressed wail drew out Telyn's name. "Oh Tey, Tey, the hind is never going to make it back to Harlech. I am so sorry."

"We will! We'll haul him back, and the cornics will heal him and pay us the reward money. We didn't catch the hind just to lose. Imagine the odds of us finding him here. I can't believe we would get this close just to have him die."

The High Father wouldn't tease us so, would he? I can't believe that. I won't believe that.

Caitlin shook her head. Tears edged their way from the corners of her eyes.

Bouncing over rocks and roots to Harlech is Telyn's plan. I'd bet on long-shotter Caitlin and Joram dancing the promise dance before the hind surviving.

"So, give me something, rumor tree," Telyn growled. "You seem to like the hind. I suppose he has been keeping you company—too scared to go back to Harlech, too used to voices and companions to strike out alone."

The golden pool can heal all but death.

This sounded a lot like fairy stories she'd heard. Starving, frostbitten travelers who stumbled across a glowing, silver spring would walk out ten years younger. Bald pates grew hair, crooked teeth straightened, and frostbitten fingers healed.

Return a day later, the spring would be dry or frozen or simply a mundane spring—no silver color, no magic.

Which was rather convenient for tall tales, wasn't it?

"Caitlin, what if the golden pond is real?"

Caitlin stroked the hind's muzzle. "Magical ponds that only appear to people in need?" She sniffed. "You're grasping at clouds."

"We're in the Chaos Woods, remember? Anything can happen."

"Tey, you're listening to a tree."

"Remember Jess Bryant? When he left Harlech, he had an underbite so bad he could hardly chew. When he came back..."

Caitlin wiped her nose on her sleeve. "His teeth were straight as an abacus."

"And practically glowed. His smile was so fine he became a prince in Enshede."

"I saw. He was kinda cute."

"Exactly! We've captured a winged deer-thing that can detect magic, and we're talking to a tree. Anything can happen in the Chaos Woods."

Here in the Chaos Woods, someone like me can redeem myself and save my sister.

Caitlin frowned. "My parents said a flack dentist yanked some of Jess's teeth and used magic to straighten the others."

The golden pool is real, insisted the rumor tree. *As real and hot as Rayvn and Hosh kissing. What else do you think they've been doing? They've been gone a long time, tee-dee....*

The sun had begun to light up the sky enough to form shadows. Rainbows ran along the hind's feathers. His eyelids rested half-open over filmy eyes. His nostrils barely moved with the in- and exhales. Something wet rattled in his lungs.

"He's not going to make it, Caitlin. We have to take the chance. This is for my sister."

Caitlin shifted under the animal's weight, twisting her torso to face the rumor tree. "Tree... Ms. Rumor—may I call you that? Please tell us the truth. No rhymes, no teasing. Is the golden pond real? Can it heal the feathered hind? If you don't give us a straight answer, we will take the hind straight back to Harlech, and the hind will die and, and Tey's sister will become a slave. If you give us an honest answer, one that we can understand, we'll, ah..."

"We'll bring you gossip every chance we get," Telyn promised enthusiastically. "Every chance from here on out. The juiciest gossip you've ever heard."

Yes.

"Yes—Yes you want gossip? Or yes, the golden pond is real?"

The golden pond is as real and hot as Rayvn and Hosh kissing...

"Where is the golden pond? Where is this magical hot spring? I promise we will go there and bring you back everything we see. News. Gossip. You can have it all; we promise."

Telyn likes Lutric Quid, icky sticky love poems from the schoolmaster...

"Mother of Squirrels! Not this again."

> *The hind herd tramps*
> *Sonnets on a snowy page*
> *To the Aumerhem Pass*
> *Where the baker and Raz*
> *left your dad*

to freeze
to die

The hind's intact wing gave a couple of weak flaps, as if confirming the direction.

The Aumerhem Pass, of course. It had to be.

"Where is the Aumerhem Pass?" Caitlin asked. "How do we find it? Tey—"

"I know. Mother of Squirrels, I know where that is. The hind will never last that long. It's steep—and bound to be rougher than going through the Chaos Woods. Better to drag him to Harlech and hope the cornic medic can do something."

"I hear your words," Caitlin said, "But I sense hesitation."

Telyn wrung the hem of her cloak between her hands. "If it's on the near side, where the trail begins to climb, then yes, the golden pond is closer than Harlech. That, well, that would make sense. There's a whole mess of hot springs called the Bubbling Baseline where the Kings and Queens begin to rise." *So I've been told, at least.* "If the pond is at the top, or-or beyond the glacier, there's no way. The hind would die before we made it halfway."

You could visit your father's ghost, Telyn. Tell him how much you miss him. Tell him you love him. He awaits in the crevasse.

Was that the rumor tree or her own thoughts?

"So, Harlech is, ah, a better bet," Caitlin said.

"Yes. Yes, we go home. Back to Harlech. We've already had one miracle."

Will the cornics even pay the reward to humans? the rumor tree whispered. *Will they accept the feathered hind as it is, beat up and near death? Or will they blame you for its wounds? Do you trust them?*

"Minister Svemas wouldn't do that!" Caitlin replied. The tree must have been speaking to both of them. "My parents work in the Prefecture. They know him."

The minister's loyalty is to the Empire. What wouldn't he do to save the Empress four thousand hurons?

Hosh and Rayvn returned before the discussion could continue.

Telyn berated herself for actually looking to see if the two looked like they had been kissing, whatever *that* might look like: disheveled hair, blushing cheeks, furtive glances at each other...

The rumor tree tittered in her head.

"What've you been talking about?" Hosh asked suspiciously.

"We're taking the feathered hind to the Aumerhem Pass to be healed by a magical spring," Caitlin said.

Telyn nodded.

Rayvn's ears swiveled forward.

A golden pond, corrected the tree.

Hosh drew his knife dramatically. He was starting to get the hang of both the knife-drawing and the serious face that went with it. Too bad he couldn't grow more than a lichen of a beard.

"Well then, we'd best start butchering these rakasuras. There's a reward on the ears, and we can take as much meat as we can carry. If we hang it at night, it'll freeze and keep for as long as we're out here."

Caitlin gaped. "That's it? We decide to haul the hind to the Aumerhem Pass and you don't ask any questions? Do you realize that the Peak is named after a demon? A demon who may still live there?"

"Rayvn and I have been talking," Hosh said. "If we take the hind back wounded, the cornics won't pay the full reward. In fact, they might decide to jail us for wounding it. And if he dies...." He sliced off a rakasura ear with a single, precise stroke. Cobblery had trained him well. "Best to bring the feathered hind home whole or not at all, that's what I say. Besides, the rumor tree talks to me too."

He looked from Caitlin to Telyn and back, and a sly smile creased his face.

"What? What did it say?"

Hosh's grin widened as he continued slicing ears.

"What did the tree say, Hosh?"

"Oh, my? Really?" Rayvn exclaimed.

"Can you pack up, Tey?" Caitlin lay a hand on Telyn's shoulder and winked. "I've done enough of that; keep the meat well separated from the alfalfa and oat hay."

"What are you going to do?"

"I'm going to keep talking to Ms. Rumor—see if I can get more details in exchange for some of my gossip about Joram and Tabbard." She bent and kissed Telyn on the cheek.

The rumor tree tittered.

CHAPTER FORTY-FIVE

Telyn climbed a chaos tree and took a sighting. Barely visible in the clear morning air, the smoke of Harlech beckoned her with its warmth and familiarity, while in the other direction, between Queen Three and Aumerhem Peak, water from the Aumerhem glacier promised a miracle.

It felt like a game of senet when your pieces were far from the end—but if you tossed the dice just right, you could block your opponent, and with a second perfect toss, you could win. The longer the odds, the more your belly tied itself in knots as you rattled the die in the cup.

By the time she descended the tree, Rayvn was making the final adjustments to the ropes which connected the stretcher to Biscuit's saddle. The stretcher was essentially two long poles with a blanket between them, rigged in such a way that the front was elevated and the rear dragged on the ground. The feathered hind had been strapped into it with head and antlers cushioned by what clothes they could spare.

They paralleled the frozen creek for several hours, until they had to veer around some fallen trees and couldn't navigate back. Here, they turned more directly toward the pass. Periodically, the stretcher would bounce over some fallen log or rock under the mulch or snow, and Telyn would wince. Once, the hind's antlers tangled in a bush, and Telyn thought the poor animal's neck would break what with the bush dragging to the side and Biscuit pulling forward.

Only quick blows from Hosh's ax to the bush saved him.

Each step took them further from Cressida and closer to Dad—not that she would ever reach him. The glacier where he'd fallen lay thousands of feet above their destination.

They left him to die.

She ground her teeth.

"No ghost, Tey, no ghost."

They left him to die.

A few steps later, she shook her head. *No, no, they hadn't. It was a terrible fall, broken bones, probably brain damage, internal bleeding.*

Raz has been good to me; I can't hate him.

I won't hate him.

What a terrible, terrible weight that must have been for Raz—blaming himself, second-guessing their decision, wondering if anything could have saved Dori even if he and Archie Todd had been able to haul him out.

And no matter what Raz had said about cutting the skins and weaving them to make a rope, they hadn't been traveling with a pattern witch. Dorian Brower was tall. He probably weighed as much as the feathered hind.

"Tey, you okay?" Hosh asked, limping back to her.

She'd stopped without knowing it. Biscuit had pulled the stretcher out of sight. Her thoughts had trouble finding the present. Her mind was full of glaciers, crevasses, ghosts...

"Tey? It's not safe to be away from the group. Rayvn found tracks. I think they're brakdaw."

"Right, I'm coming."

"We can take a rest."

Telyn realized she'd been wringing her hands. She dropped them. "How's the brakdaw doing? I mean the hind...the feathered hind."

Hosh halted, obviously wondering whether he should give her a hug, put a reassuring hand on her shoulder, or stand there awkwardly.

He chose the latter. "Caitlin fed him some alfalfa. He swallowed a little. Good thing she brought it—the alfalfa."

"Yeah, good thing."

"I named him Taffy. What do you think? Caitlin hates it."

Telyn took a deep breath. "Are we doing the right thing, Hosh, chasing after this golden pond?"

Hosh shrugged. "This is all crazy. I tell myself we're really on a camping trip, just traveling the woods on a lark, and it doesn't matter so much. Puts my mind at ease..." He trailed off. "Sorry."

"No, it's okay. I know what you mean. If we pretend it doesn't matter, the pressure is off."

"Right. No pressure—except for rakasuras and brakdaws" —He started counting on his fingers—"starvation, Rayvn turning us in for having magic, getting lost, getting lost and then starving..."

Telyn managed to crack a smile and began walking again. "Don't forget frostbite."

"Right, frostbite. Nose or fingers?"

"Nose, definitely."

Caitlin appeared in the distance. "Everything okay? What are you two talking about?"

"Noses!" Hosh replied.

They plodded past the onset of a pale, colorless sunset. What with the dense and denser woods, the stretcher, and legs as heavy as millstones, they covered fewer miles than they'd hoped. The weight they carried, their general exhaustion, and the elevation gain forced them to take two or three breaths for every weary step. Breathing itself became a chore, as if their lungs were billows they had to consciously pump to keep the forge at temperature.

It didn't help that nighttime came so early this time of year. When the dark became thick as velvet, they finally stopped. A half-hearted search for dry wood came up empty. They abandoned hope for a fire, huddled together around Taffy, and tried to sleep.

Dense foliage hid the stars, and so, despite waking several times during the night, Telyn didn't realize fog had arisen until the next morning, when she could see no further than Hosh's outline on the other side of the hind. No use climbing trees; they'd have to rely on their memory and sense of direction as guide.

She rummaged around in the saddle pack until she found Caitlin's smuggled alfalfa, knelt at Taffy's head, and tried to feed him.

He refused.

"Come on now, have to keep your strength up," she said, trying to slip a single stalk between the animal's black lips. Eventually, he pulled the blade into his mouth and chewed a bit. Telyn touched the blanket-bandage on his belly.

Tight. Tight and hot, like a bed warmer.

"Rayvn? Rayvn, come here."

From out of the fog came grumpy waking sounds. Eventually, Rayvn crawled over, smacking the bad taste from her morning mouth and looking altogether human.

"The bandage must have shrunk in the fog. It's really tight."

Rayvn touched the wool, closed her eyes, and stilled her breathing. The weave of the bandage twisted, and a little moisture dripped from the sides. "It's stuck to the wound. I can't do anything without peeling it off—which isn't a good idea."

"But it's so tight."

"It's infected, Telyn Brower. The wound has bloated like an overfull skin."

"Can you do anything?"

"I am a pattern witch. Fabric or Sepulcher-stone I can work with, not flesh. Taffy needs a healer."

"We need to get going. We've wasted too much of the day."

Rayvn looked up into the white. "How can you know?"

"Because I'm awake, and we're not walking." Telyn grabbed her ice ax. Rayvn helped secure it to her back. Hosh and Caitlin finished packing quickly.

"Let's go."

Taffy groaned as they hooked the stretcher to Biscuit's saddle, as if he wanted them to leave him to die. He caught Telyn's eyes, and his one healthy wing curled like a beckoning finger.

"Not on your life," Telyn said, cinching the rope and smacking Biscuit's haunch into motion.

Fog. The jangle of traps against Biscuit's flanks.

In the white blindness, roots reached out to trip them; branches stooped to slap them; spiderwebs clung to their eyebrows and tried to infiltrate their lips. Hosh took to holding his knife vertically before him.

Rayvn was delighted. She collected all the webs she could find with a stick. She even separated the sticky webs from what she called the "walking webs," where the spiders could walk without getting stuck in their own traps. These she treasured especially.

They found tracks. With all their woodcraft—and Redbeard taught the children of Harlech well—they could not be sure if they were feathered hind tracks, but they *were* hoofprints. At first a few, then dozens converged on the same game-path the friends followed.

Then Hosh found a feather in a bramble, and Caitlin spotted another. These they pocketed.

So, Ms. Rumor may have been telling the truth. A whole herd of feathered hinds traveled this way, going to the golden pond.

Or at least a partial truth, at least. Most rumors have enough truth to believe. That's why they are so insidious, sort of like the most effective suggestions on the Ever-Guise.

A herd of feathered hinds going somewhere.

If only she hadn't taken that stupid forehead piece, or hadn't used it, or a thousand other things. If her dad had been around to keep her straight. He would have known what to do. He wouldn't have let her get so deep into the Ever-Guise's spell she'd become dependent.

Addicted, like Esther to her booze.

Again, lost in thought, Telyn fell behind.

The slope steepened, and the footing grew more treacherous. Biscuit's clomping changed from the thud of feet on dirt to the staccato of nails on stone. The wooden skids of the stretcher, no longer insulated by mulch, scraped and shrieked on the rock path, announcing their presence to anything for miles around.

We've made the mountain trail, they said. *We've left the cover of the forest. Prey here! Prey for the taking.*

Prey with nowhere to run, nowhere to hide.

Taffy moaned.

The trail narrowed. Onward and upwards they climbed.

With the suffocating fog, Telyn couldn't see more than three feet in either direction—couldn't count her fingers if she held her hand at arm's length—but from the strain in her ribs and the labor of her lungs, she surmised they'd passed the tree-line.

They might pass within a hundred paces of the golden pond and never see it.

Telyn felt exposed. Naked.

If the fog lifted, every predator for miles around would be able to see them on the exposed path. There were no trees to shield them, nothing to burn at night for warmth or protection. Switchbacks bore them towards Aumerhem Peak, the glacier, and her father's tomb.

Would his ghost still be there, haunting the crevasse?

If they had thought that camping in the forest was difficult, camping on steep rock was ten times worse. No matter how thick their coats, a bump always managed to rub directly on a rib, a hip, an anklebone (the worst), or a skull. And nothing—nothing at all—lay flat. Gravity urged them to start rolling towards, well, who could say? They'd ascended into the clouds.

Weather came that Telyn had never seen: monster hail fell from the fog, each frozen stone an inch in diameter, shattering against the granite, rattling down the precipice, knocking their skulls.

They threw up their arms to protect themselves. Hail beat their heads and bodies, and it would have killed the feathered hind if Caitlin hadn't shouted for them to help it. They untied the stretcher from the llama, let Biscuit huddle against the rock face they had been paralleling, and shifted Taffy as close to the wall as possible. Then they shielded the poor hind with their bodies, simultaneously protecting their heads with gloves and scarves.

So loud came the rattle of hail that they gave up trying to shout at each other. If the woods had made them feel alone, and the mountains made them feel small, the hail made them feel insignificant—mites that the world could wipe away as easily as a human might brush away a mosquito.

It felt like Tabbard's gang pummeling them in the alley, over and over, never-ending jabs that especially hurt the little bones of their hands, which they couldn't conceal because the blows to their skulls could kill them.

When the hail finally slowed, when the roar faded to a rattle-a-tat-tat, Caitlin dropped to the ground and curled into a ball. The hail stopped a few minutes later, and Rayvn knelt beside Caitlin, her furry head bowed. Hosh put his hands under his armpits and whimpered.

Taffy's head lay flat like a sick llama-calf; the bend was gone from his neck. Their party looked beaten, defeated. Even Rayvn's perky ears lay flat.

From her experience climbing, Telyn knew that look.

They had reached the place most people turned back. She'd felt this when nearing the lip of the frozen waterfall, fingers numb and muscles aching, hardly able to swing the ax or kick her foot spikes into the hard ice, only to discover that the top leaned outward beyond vertical, and she'd have to rely on upper body strength to heave herself beyond it. That's when most contestants tugged the cord to let the men above know to haul them up, over the top. That's when they forfeited. Those last few feet divided the winners from everyone else.

That's when Telyn performed best, why she placed in the top ice climbers of Harlech the past three years. That's why she would save Cressida when others would fail.

When others predicted *she* would fail.

She lifted her chin and shouted at the demon on Aumerhem Peak. "Is that the best you can do, Aumerhem? Is that your best shot—a little ice? We eat ice for dinner."

Telyn grabbed the stretcher poles herself and tucked them under her arms. "Come on," she said. "You bring Biscuit. Daylight is wasting."

CHAPTER FORTY-SIX

Into the fog Telyn pulled the hind, over the balls of slippery, frozen hail, leaving her friends behind. One step—another, and another. She focused on breathing and breathing alone, lost in the expansion-contraction of her lungs. Later, as she rounded a switchback, uneven footfalls caught up to her. Hosh took one of the stretcher poles, and, despite his limp, he bore it well.

She nodded thanks. Maybe he could see her, maybe not. Two things mattered: to continue forward, and to stay on the path. She could sense tremendous depth yawning to her right like a malevolent invitation.

Rayvn, Caitlin, and Biscuit soon caught up. The four friends took turns with the poles. One of them led, calling out a warning if the trail suddenly narrowed or changed direction.

The fog probably is helping. If my friends could see how far the fall would be, and how treacherous the hail makes the path, they might freeze like a rabbit in a wolf's glare.

Telyn bore the right pole and Hosh bore the left when they finally crested the canyon rim. The trail, followed more by feel than by sight, turned to the left. Rayvn and Caitlin scouted ahead to be sure, but no other direction made sense. As they passed over the rim and descended in a long curve, they felt the walls open around them; the fog stirred more freely. Visibility increased from an arm's length to three, even five feet. Ahead, ice crackled—forming or melting, they couldn't be sure. It smelled different here, less moss and forest and mulch, less granite and dampness, more springtime and button flowers. More fur and manure—more animal.

"It smells like a stable," Hosh remarked.

Telyn plowed ahead with renewed energy, and Hosh stumbled to keep up.

The fog shifted from white to warm gold.

The sun must finally be breaking through. Above them, though, the fog seemed to go on forever. *We walk within a cloud like the High Father—*

Her feet sloshed into water.

"Tey?" Hosh asked, halting beside her. "Is this—?"

The stretcher pole jerked out of their hands and clattered to the rocks beneath their feet. Taffy began kicking. Caitlin tried to calm him, whispered soothing words so that he wouldn't tear his belly open.

He kicked harder.

"Telyn Brower?" Rayvn said, her usually airy voice pitched higher with worry. "I think we're not alone."

Taffy spun his head and clipped Caitlin with his antlers, knocking her rag doll-limp.

Telyn cried out, grabbed Caitlin's arm, and dragged her away from the pool and the thrashing animal. "Caitlin, Caitlin, wake up." Telyn gently slapped her friend's cheeks.

Snorting, Biscuit spun his hindquarters, muscles twitching, and kicked blindly.

Hosh and Rayvn backed into a defensive circle, each with a cape in hand. Telyn fumbled with the straps holding the ice ax to her back. The loops had twisted, and the pick snagged, its handle within reach but useless.

Through the fog came broad shapes.

Already, an ugly purple bruise had begun to spread across Caitlin's temple.

"Caitlin, come on, wake up." Telyn shoved Biscuit sideways with her shoulder so he wouldn't trample her friend.

Just as Caitlin's eyelids fluttered, the fog parted enough to reveal a half dozen feathered hinds, each larger than the last, encircling them on silent hooves. One of them nuzzled Taffy curiously. The others brandished three-foot-long antlers at the friends and snorted. Their oval eyes seemed to spark with fury.

Hosh gasped. "We can catch...so many...think of it. We'll be rich! Be ready, Rayvn."

The lead buck sprung forward, snagged Hosh' cape with an antler, and flung it away.

Pedaling backwards, Hosh tripped on a loose stone and fell onto his hip with a grunt.

"We're trying to help!" Telyn cried, holding her hands out defensively.

The buck pawed the ground.

Angry animal sounds came from everywhere, dozens and dozens of snorts and bellows. This wasn't a family group; this was the entire herd, just as the rumor tree had promised.

"Telyn Brower?" Rayvn's cape danced before her like a snake. The nearby hinds shied away from it. But how much use would that be against the whole herd?

"Just, ah, stay calm. Don't make any sudden moves."

Caitlin moaned, and Telyn knelt at her side. "Caitlin, what should we do? We've found the herd. They don't like us very much."

Caitlin licked her lips, lifted her head, blinked.

Two of the bucks pawed the rocky ground, as if preparing to charge. Now three.

"Are you there?" Telyn asked. "We could use some advice."

After a long moment, Caitlin finally responded in a dull, flat voice. "Release Taffy."

Rayvn looked askance, and Telyn nodded.

The binds keeping Taffy on the stretcher unraveled; his agitation ceased. He rolled to his side. Slowly, with great difficulty, he stood.

A breeze rose; the fog lifted more.

They had arrived at the edge of a hot spring in a cirque maybe two hundred feet across, a round, flat valley on one of the many shoulders of Aumerhem Peak. Golden light radiated from the spring itself.

No, not from the entire spring. On second glance, Telyn discerned that the light came from a golden orb in the middle of the pool, just beneath the surface. The herd gathered on all sides of the beautiful pool, a hundred or more feathered hinds as silent on their hooves as mountain goats and as majestic as dragons. Even their puny, useless wings seemed somehow wondrous. The orb's golden light turned their plumage into fireworks. They all seemed to be staring at the four friends, their llama, and the wounded hind.

The breeze pushed the fog still further, until it arched into a cathedral ceiling. Steam rose from the golden pool, white fingers that wanted to drag the cloud back down to obscure the secret hind-ritual.

A mound at the pool's exit, as fabulously unreal as icicles on the edge of a frozen waterfall, explained the crackling they'd heard earlier. The hot water exiting the pool froze within a few feet, growing and snap-crackling into awesome shapes, a horde of semi-transparent monsters clamoring to plunge downstream.

"The golden pond," Hosh breathed. "I don't believe it."

One of the bucks ululated.

Although they had heard all kinds of hind-calls, this one sounded unreal, ghost-like. It echoed from the walls and sent ripples over the water. It hurt their eardrums—and caressed them.

As one, the herd lost interest in Telyn and her friends. The bucks menacing them turned and trotted to join the others around the edge of the water.

Taffy sagged back onto the stretcher.

Hosh helped Caitlin sit up. He had to steady her so she didn't tip over sideways.

Please let her not have brain damage. Mother of Squirrels, keep her mind intact.

"A chrysalis," Caitlin said.

Telyn and Hosh shared a worried glance.

"A what-a-lis?" Hosh asked.

Caitlin licked her lips and did not reply.

Telyn tapped her head and whispered, "She's lost it."

Hosh nodded.

The bruise on Caitlin's temple had grown from ear to eyebrow, the ugly blue turning sickly green. It hurt just to look at.

"Chrysalis, like when a caterpillar turns into a butterfly," Rayvn explained. "One of the strangest patterns in nature: the caterpillar builds a cocoon around itself, transforms itself into jelly, and the jelly grows wings, transforming from helpless worm-thing to agile butterfly."

"Huh," Hosh replied.

"A jelly?" Telyn said.

"Certainly. The Princess of Sindok, a graduate cum laude from the Academy of Enshede, created a spell that would do the same to trogos. Unfortunately, she choked on a grape while performing the spell. Her entire court ended up preserved in glass jars. Thus ended the Confederacy of Sindok and began the Age of—"

"What are you talking about?" Telyn scowled.

"The history of Sindok, of course."

Just great. Rayvn is talking nonsense, and Caitlin has lost her marbles. We've made it all this way, and now Taffy is going to die!

My sister will be lost to slavery, and it'll be all my fault. I failed again. Now I will be alone. Esther will drink herself to death, and I'll have to marry some drunken lout who works in the lumber mill for the Ouzeleys.

Caitlin pointed to the middle of the pool. "The queen."

Telyn looked again, eager for anything to keep from thinking about her failure.

Some of the hinds were larger than Taffy, some smaller; some had blue feathers on their rears, others red. Some had racks with as many as five points, others as few as two.

"They're all males," Hosh remarked. "All bucks."

"It's a...a breeding temple," Rayvn said. "Oh...the chrysalis holds the queen, and these are her husbands. This is so romantic."

Heat pulsed from the chrysalis in increasing waves. The golden pool began to bubble.

Sweat pooled over Telyn's eyebrows and slid down her jaw, dripping from her chin. A spot of red appeared on the tip of the chrysalis and spread down one side jaggedly. The water sizzled around it. The bucks pushed to the water's edge and began to ululate. They sounded like perfect brass horns, each warbling the same notes, as if the trumpeters, while talented, were raving drunk.

Then they commenced a cascade of scales and intervals that made hair rise from arms and napes of neck.

The egg—chrysalis—turned rose gold.

More and more heat radiated from it.

The pool bubbled furiously. The magic came not just from the egg—from the queen—but from the males as well, the whole together. Ice on nearby cliffs crashed free. All around the cirque, water began to flow with noisy, gurgling abandon.

Telyn removed her cloak without taking her eyes from the unfolding ritual.

A crack started at the egg's crown, then spider-webbed over sides —then the chrysalis shattered. A magnificent creature appeared, as much feathered dragon as hind, sleek and long, with wings that unfurled above the water a dozen paces across. Of all hue and variation of red shone her feathers: rose, crimson, blood, blush, and wine didn't even begin to describe the feathers along her long, sinewy neck.

Steam poured from those unfolding wings.

Rather than antlers, the queen had two spiraling horns that lay flat against her skull. She swiveled her magnificent head at Telyn and her friends, judged them deserving of a respectful nod, and leapt clear of the pool.

The wind from those flapping wings ruffled Telyn's chestnut hair.

The queen soared into the vaulted cloud and disappeared.

The brassy, horn-like music faded. Only the largest bucks remained at the water's edge; while Telyn's attention had been absorbed entirely by the queen, most of the herd had backed away from the boiling pool. These larger males stomped their feet, shook their heads at each other, and snorted. Little by little, the less confident males backed away until only one remained, a huge buck with five points and the nub of a sixth. With a triumphant bellow, the victor charged into the pool. He disappeared entirely from sight.

The pool must be far deeper than it looks, Telyn thought.

The second strongest plunged in after.

Then the third, fourth, and fifth.

Little by little—with a lot of antler clashing, shoving, and snorting—the smaller hinds gathered on the shoreline again.

Watched. Witnessed. Waited.

Minutes passed.

Caitlin wobbled to her feet to get a better look. She had to cling to Hosh to steady herself.

The shattered pieces of chrysalis shell continued to glow on the bottom like the interior of a flame. Occasionally, a hind-shaped silhouette passed over them.

Finally, the strongest buck burst from the surface. But he was *transformed*.

While he retained his antlers, in all other respects he resembled a dragon—the length of his neck, the sleekness of his body, the swoop of his wings. His color was darker than the queen's, slate gray instead of bright red, but he was no less magnificent. Into the cloud-ceiling he flew, followed shortly by another, and another.

All the dominant bucks pursued the queen.

Now the entire herd charged into the water with a mad crashing of antlers and skulls, flanks and feathers, hooves and bubbling water.

Caitlin bent to take hold of the stretcher pole, wobbled, and sat down. "Put Taffy into the water. It might heal him. I'm sorry...I don't have the strength."

"You're fine, we've got this," Telyn said, taking the right front pole. Hosh grabbed the other side, and Rayvn managed to lift the stretcher's two rear poles by herself.

It took a few steps before they coordinated their movement and made any progress. A sense of urgency made Telyn want to sprint. She wanted to be done with this before that whole herd emerged as little hind-dragons—and she feared that when the final hind emerged, the magic would end.

"This will heal Taffy, right Rayvn?"

"A transformation of this magnitude takes a lot of energy. I think it more likely—"

"Does it matter?" Hosh interrupted. "We've got to try."

They advanced step by wobbly step. Telyn turned her ankle on a loose rock, of course, and fought through the pain.

A little further, just a little more...

As Hosh and Telyn were about to step into the shallows, Caitlin cried, "Wait, don't get wet! You might change!"

Telyn managed to stop.

Hosh's foot hovered over the water; he would have fallen in, except he held onto his pole, and Rayvn secured the other end. Two hinds burst from the pond, splattering them. Hosh dropped his pole and frantically wiped droplets from himself. The stretcher tipped, and Telyn and Rayvn tried to lower their ends to compensate and level it back out, but Taffy rolled off and bounced on the rocks.

Blood began to leak from the belly bandage.

"You worm head!" Telyn said, all fear and stress. "You complete, squirrel-brained idiot!"

"I can't help it. I don't want to be a dragon-thing."

"Help us get Taffy back on. The water isn't doing anything to you."

They positioned the stretcher next to the now-moaning Taffy. They dragged him partway onto the stretcher using his forelegs, unmindful of the belly wound.

Too late to worry about that, now. Got to move fast.

"Hang on, Taffy. Hang on," Telyn breathed.

Wet, sticky-slippery blood made the task difficult and unpleasant, and Telyn felt the familiar spin of her brain within her skull...

Blood...going to pass out...

She tried to distract herself by imagining herself like the queen, and the mental image was not unpleasant: flying away, loose among the clouds.

Freedom. Strength.

Rescuing Cressida with brute force.

Breathing fire?

"Do you really think we could become...dragons? With feathers?"

"I think it won't do anything to a non-hind," Rayvn said. "But you never know about patterns until you enter a new one. You and the feathered hinds are different species. Humans are distinctly nonmagical, and feathered hinds can detect magic. There are many variables to contemplate."

"Look at the bright side: if you become a dragon, you wouldn't need to be on the Dating Chart," Hosh said. He grunted as he helped Rayvn heave Taffy's rear end onto the stretcher.

They took their places again, lifted the poles, and paused. None of them much wanted to chance putting a toe into the golden pond.

The water sloshed and churned; hinds emerged as feathered, winged creatures. The water's golden color started to fade to silver. The chrysalis-shell pieces dimmed, and they could more easily distinguish the maelstrom of hinds transmuting to dragon-shapes.

"Not here," Telyn said, "too shallow. We have to get Taffy completely submerged without touching the water ourselves."

"It'll be steeper on the Aumerhem side of the pool," Hosh said.

"Right. Come on."

It was rough going with just the three of them, but they managed to carry Taffy to the mountain side of the pool where, indeed, the edge dropped far more steeply. They lined the stretcher up sideways to the deepest part.

The pool had become entirely silver.

"On three," Telyn said. "One, two..." and on "three," Hosh and Rayvn dropped their poles, which were nearest the water, and the stretcher tipped. A stray hoof clipped Telyn's right thumb, tearing the skin from nail to base. As Taffy tumbled away, the sudden lightness of her load made Telyn stagger. A hail of bubbles lifted from Taffy's feathers as he sank.

Into the depths he vanished.

Clutching her thumb to her chest, Telyn sank to her knees on the edge of the pool. She had never felt such a combined feeling of satisfaction and loss. She knew—knew!—that she would never see the hind again, and her only chance to make the bond price for Cressida was gone forever.

She also felt pride that they had all done the very best they could, pushed themselves to the absolute limit, and succeeded in doing the right thing. She prayed to the High Father that their efforts would be enough, that they had saved Taffy's life, and somehow, impossibly, this would help save Cressida.

From across the pool's silver glow, Caitlin beamed at them. Telyn smiled back. There would be time enough to worry about the loss, to worry about...everything. Rayvn rubbed Telyn's arm in a comforting gesture, and on impulse, Telyn hugged her, fuzzy ears and all.

"Thank you."

As the stragglers broke the surface and flew, the three friends picked their way across the rough, rock-strewn valley, occasionally getting pelted by water droplets from the departing hinds. Telyn's thumb throbbed, but only a little disgusting blood leaked down her wrist. As long as she kept her mind firmly on the magnificent, dragon-like hinds, she could ignore it.

They returned to recline beside Caitlin.

"Do you think we're the first humans to ever see this?" Caitlin asked.

"No," said Rayvn. "The first humans *and* pattern witch."

"We should have caught one of them—one of scrawny ones," Hosh said. "We were so focused on saving Taffy that we didn't even think of trapping another." Hosh pulled a biscuit from a pocket of his jacket, tore it in two, and handed Caitlin half.

Of course! What fools!

Like snapdragons, a few final hinds popped from the water in ones and twos. The shapes in the pool grew fewer and fewer still. Then there were none left—only Taffy remained beneath the surface. The four friends stood and approached the water's edge, took each other's hands, and counted breaths, trying to see deep enough to know if the transformation would save Taffy or finish him.

The bubbling slowed. Less and less steam rose from the pool; winter began to reclaim its dominion over the cirque. Telyn watched the surface carefully, expecting at any moment to see her hind—Cressida's hind—rise and roll on its belly, drowned and bloated. Her stomach began to sour, and her throat closed as fear became certainty.

And so, when Taffy burst from the surface as a magnificent, feathered dragon-thing, Telyn slipped and fell backwards onto her bottom.

Taffy appeared to have fully healed. His feathers shone. Rather than flying into the clouds, he landed nearby and shook, splattering them. He issued a series of snorts and grunts.

Was Taffy trying to thank them for fighting off the rakasuras and bringing him here, or was he angry that they had dug the pit in the first place? Both had merit.

He might not know we dug the pit, Telyn hoped.

The dragon-hind's elongated face gave no clue; it didn't move the way a human face could move. It neither smiled nor frowned, but from Telyn's seated perspective, the parted lips and chattering teeth looked rather frightening—as did the wings extending ten feet or more to either side.

Telyn was so shocked she didn't even think to try to trap it until, having said what he wanted to say, Taffy backed up and gathered himself.

"Rayvn, help. I'll throw it..." She pulled at her cloak, freed one arm, but the other snagged, and she couldn't—

Taffy hurled himself into the sky, bellowing. A trail of droplets wet a line across Telyn's upturned face.

"It thanked us," Caitlin said.

"Well, Aled's sacred rump. I lost him. He was right here, offering himself to me, and I goggled like a blithering idiot."

"He will never catch the queen now. The others have too much of a lead," Rayvn added. "I wonder what will happen to him."

"It's my sister's life I'm talking about!"

Caitlin and Hosh knelt to put their arms around Telyn.

"Don't you ever tell Cressida I let him go," Telyn said, tears beginning to pour down her cheeks. "You promise, okay? We failed utterly. We never saw the hind. We got lost in the woods, and, and—"

Another lie. Another stinking lie.

"There will be other ways," Caitlin said, rubbing Telyn's back. "No matter what happens, we won't stop until your sister is free. But not this way. Taffy is with his herd where he belongs. He is, ah, free."

Telyn's head jerked up as a sudden thought came to her. *Biscuit! Where—?* Then she relaxed. Biscuit browsed contentedly on some foliage nearby.

Hosh limped to the pool and scooped up a handful of water. He didn't die, shrivel up, or sprout wings, even when he took a cautious sip. "We need to get that shell," he declared, pointing into the center of the pool. "That's worth something. We can swim to it."

Pity it didn't transform him. I could use wings about now.

"Don't just wade in there like an idiot with your clothes on," Caitlin barked, alarmed. "It's going to be freezing in an hour or less. The water is cooling off fast. Hosh, you gather firewood—a lot of it. We'll need to dry off. Build the fire near the cliff-face in case the wind comes up. The rest of us will strip down and swim for the egg. We can't afford to get our clothes wet."

Hosh stared wide-eyed at Caitlin, then at the others. "Sure thing," he said, beginning to grin. "Only...what wood?"

Caitlin nodded toward the creek tumbling down from the pass. "Break off some willow branches for kindling and chop up the stretcher. We won't be needing it anymore"

Hosh limped toward Biscuit to get his ax.

Caitlin dropped her cloak and undid her belt. "And don't look this way," she called after Hosh. "Don't you dare!"

He waved over his shoulder.

"Are you up to this, Caitlin? Your head."

"This is for your sister. We can do this, together."

Pulling herself to her feet to disrobe was one of the hardest things Telyn had had to do. Telyn envied Rayvn then. Even without clothes, the flack didn't look much more naked than an eehoo, except, well, she had breasts. Two of them, Telyn was relieved to see. She didn't know what she would have done if pattern women had litters—or eggs.

The last thing Telyn removed was the take permit. One side of the permit showed a fearsome brakdaw, and the other a lowly gamble fly. The thong snagged for a second on her matted, frizzy hair; the bronze glinted as she placed it on her clothes pile, brakdaw side up.

On impulse, she kissed her fingertips and brushed them against the metal.

The girls nodded at each other, gathered their courage, and started diving. The pool's depth made Telyn's eardrums hurt, and the air want to climb out of her throat. At best, they could only snag one or two chrysalis shell pieces at a time before having to resurface, making the collection an exhausting process.

At least the water made her thumb feel better.

Little by little, piece by painstaking piece, the pile on the shore grew. It was a race against time, for the magical heat faded quickly. The bottom part of the chrysalis shell was irretrievably cemented to stone, but they retrieved three quarters of it, maybe more. Each piece was beautiful in its own right, a work of abstract art, and Rayvn thought she might be able to spell it together once she had studied its pattern. Red and gold light crawled along the broken edges of each shard, leaving no doubt about the chrysalis's magical nature.

Once they'd finished and dressed, they sat shoulder-to-shoulder before the little fire to share warmth. The ends of her matted hair began to freeze in place—she just couldn't wring enough water out to prevent that. It became stiff and unwieldy.

Telyn tested the sharpness of a shell edge against her skin—about like broken pottery. *It's not what we came for, but it should fetch a good price at the Spring Sale. Better than we could've hoped for, really. We are going to do this, Cressida. We will do this.*

CHAPTER FORTY-SEVEN

The temperature had dropped far below zero overnight, and though the morning brought clear skies, the sun's rays brought little comfort at this altitude. As they descended back toward the valley, the uncertain, wobbly footing sapped their energy. Their boots jarred against the bone-bruising stone of the mountain path, and the snow piled atop mulch over slippery soil made each step treacherous. Even Biscuit fell multiple times, once skidding a dozen yards before slamming into one of the rare chaos trees sprouting from the crook of a switchback with a bleat.

They didn't have the heart to unpack the chrysalis pieces from his saddlebags to see what damage the crash had done.

You would have thought that traveling downhill, without the weight of the sled, would have made their trip faster, but exhaustion had overtaken them. If their feet didn't know how to plod of their own volition, their conscious minds would never have been able to puzzle it out.

"Mom's gonna kill me if I lose my fingers," Hosh said, clenching and un-clenching his gloved hands.

"Or your nose," said Caitlin.

"Nah, I can still work without a nose."

Telyn's head weighed a hundred pounds, her feet a thousand. The thought of climbing a tree to get their bearings didn't occur to her. Either they'd picked the right game trail—the one that lead back to the rumor tree—or they'd wander the Chaos Woods until death. She hardly cared. If she thought at all, she wondered how many toes and fingers she would end up with; she'd lost feeling in all of them, which added to the difficulty in walking without tripping.

The meager fire made from willow sticks and stretcher poles hadn't been enough to thaw the girls out after emerging from their swim. They'd been cold ever since—the kind of bone-snapping cold that layers of clothes could do nothing about, only hot drink and hot air could aid, and only a steam bath could really cure.

Between the cold and the awe and heartbreak of their adventure at the golden pool, Telyn hadn't slept at all that first night, and she'd only gotten a few hours the four nights since. Yes, they knew it'd taken only three days to travel uphill, and going down should have been far faster, but they could only plod on and hope.

Hopefully, they hadn't missed the tr —

Hosh cried out, and his cry cut off mid-breath, as if an ambush predator had dropped onto his back and knocked the wind from him.

Telyn lifted her gaze in time to see him pitch headlong into a hole. Telyn, Rayvn and Caitlin trudged to the edge and peered down.

"I'm okay, I'm okay," he called up.

She could smell the loam wafting from the hole; it must be warmer there than on the surface. The ladies lay down at the edge, reached down, and, between the three of them, they hauled Hosh out. They half-lay and half-sat there, panting.

In a daze, Telyn examined her surroundings.

They had reached the rumor tree. Hosh had fallen into one of their own traps.

"Aled's rump," Telyn remarked. "We'll survive after all."

"Never doubted it," Hosh said, popping some frozen meat into his mouth and chewing contentedly. He'd been eating meat-icicles nonstop since morning. They'd cooked it in the coals of their last fire, of course, but it froze soon after unless packed right against a body's warmth.

The Fellowship of the Feathered Hind, the rumor tree said, its tendrils snaking around their various limbs. *You have returned from your quest to the golden pond to stop at your friend Chisme's for a respite.*

Numbly, Telyn climbed to her feet and secured Biscuit to a nearby tree—but not the rumor tree. There was no telling how Biscuit would react to whatever it would tell him. It'd probably say something awful about the llama's traveling companions, like how they wore llama-skin cloaks and ate llama meat...

"We camp here until we've regained our strength," Telyn said, returning to the group. "As long as it takes. We don't press on until... until we're ready."

"You sure?" Hosh frowned and looked around. "This is like the public room of the forest. All sorts of creatures come to hear the latest gossip: feathered hinds, brakdaws, rakasuras, trappers. Who knows what might show up?"

The Fellowship of the Feathered Hind is frightened of the dark, the rumor tree said.

Telyn was too tired to see how the rumor tree had connected to her this time: root, branch? She couldn't care less.

Damsels of the Fellowship: the animal lover, the pattern seeker, and Princess Grumpy.

Rayvn giggled.

"Caitlin, are we safe here?"

"Safe?" Caitlin was already stripping the packs off Biscuit. "At least if we stay here, we know where we are. Camp more than a few paces away, we could get lost. Come on, Hosh, give me a hand."

"It's decided then. Before night falls, we gather wood and build a fire. Come on, now, a little more effort and we'll all be warm. And you, Chisme, if that's your name." Telyn wagged a finger at the rumor tree. She didn't know if the tree could see it or not, but it felt right. "Be nice, and we'll stay close and keep you company."

They gathered wood, made camp, and even roasted a little rakasura meat. With their backs to the rumor tree and the fire between their feet and the open woods, Telyn allowed her eyes to close...and when she opened them a moment later, she was back at the golden pool. The bull hinds surrounded and bowed toward the chrysalis in the middle of the pool. The place smelled of steam, sulfur, and animal manure—not altogether unpleasant—as if someone built a stable on the back of a chemist's.

Not bothering to remove her emerald Dead Winter Dance dress, Telyn waded into the warm water. The chrysalis shell pulsed with light and heat. Cracks webbed down the shell, and a thump resonated through the water and through Telyn's diaphragm. The thump indicated that the queen was trying to break free, but the resultant fissures were too small for the shell to lose integrity. The sides of the shell bulged, and little worms of vermilion light darted around the cracks with each thump, but the shell returned to its original shape.

Around the pond's edges, the bucks pawed the earth nervously.

Telyn waded further. The floor dropped away, and she struggled to tread water in her soaked dress without swallowing too much of the golden liquid.

More thumps, more cracks, and yet the shell held.

The queen will be trapped forever...

Feeling a growing sense of urgency, Telyn dog-paddled toward the chrysalis, determined to set the queen free, but her heavy clothes and water-filled boots dragged her down. Finally, knowing her time was short, she shed her clothes, only realizing at the last moment that the only tool she had to open the egg had been the ice ax strapped to her back.

The ax now rested on the bottom of the pool, far below.

Forward she paddled.

The chrysalis was far, farther than she had imagined; the pond stretched away from her, and fog began to descend. The bull hinds disappeared in the whiteness. Now and then, one of them bellowed mournfully.

Telyn could see no further than the tips of her fingers. Only the chrysalis's golden light pierced the fog. Without that glow, Telyn would have been completely lost.

And on the pond stretched.

And on.

Finally, out of breath, strength failing, Telyn arrived. She threw her arms over the chrysalis to rest. Her right thigh had begun to cramp. Her belly pressed against the hard shell with each breath.

No thumps; no pulses.

The queen had stopped struggling.

Telyn tried to force her fingernails into the fissures to pry it open. Why had she dropped her ax? Why didn't she think before shedding her clothes, before acting?

Her nails tore painfully. Blood colored the water around her hands.

The pool began to cool as the golden light dimmed. Crackles came from all around. At first, these puzzled her; Telyn heard the noises, but the eggshell had not sundered. Then she recognized the sound of water freezing quickly; the edges of the pool turned to ice and closed in on her.

Shivering, Telyn's limbs began to slow.

I have to dive down and get the ax, feel around with my fingers and toes. I hope it landed in an easy place to find.

Can I hold my breath that long?

Can I find it in the dark?

If I emerge with wet hair, will I freeze to death before I can bring the ax to bear?

How can I swing when I'm treading water? I have to try. Have to—

She took a deep breath and plunged underwater. Very quickly, she ran out of light.

She kicked and groped downward until, chest burning, her hands discovered softness. The clothes she had discarded. Yes! She groped around, trying to find the handle of the ice ax.

Convulsively, she swallowed the saliva in her throat, then swallowed again. This gave some relief to the pain in her chest, but not enough. The pain in her lungs grew and grew until she had to release some of the air.

Her head began to throb. Her brain needed oxygen.

She couldn't think straight.

Swallow the spit; don't open your mouth, no matter what. Don't open...

Slowly, she awoke and found her hands buried in Rayvn's coat.

They'd been spooning, and Telyn rolled away with mild embarrassment.

I spooned with a flack to keep warm. Who would have thought? Certainly not me.

Never me.

Everyone else slept. Biscuit snored nearby. Chisme mumbled something about rapacious gophers.

Something had awakened her—some noise from outside their camp. It approached.

Listening intently, Telyn couldn't decide what manner of beast to expect. It seemed to slither over the dry leaves, crushing them in fits and spurts, but then she distinctly heard footfalls, then more slithering. Stutter-steps now, like a newborn babe learning to walk.

Telyn jiggled Rayvn, but the pattern girl simply smacked her lips and continued sleeping.

While her friends sleep, Telyn receives a visitor in the night, a secret friend.

How romantic.

A friend!

She only knew one person likely to find her here.

"Kiiptk," Telyn called. "Kiiptk, is that you? I'm here with my friends."

The noises grew louder, more footfalls now, less slithering.

Chisme had sent multiple roots and vines over Telyn while she slept, and these snapped like thick spiderwebs as she threw off her blanket and stood.

Hoping to wake her friends, Telyn called louder. "Kiiptk, over here. Did you bring Redbeard?"

Gnome-friends haven't returned, but another brings good news, the best kind of news for a girl with a sister-slave.

Caitlin and Hosh began to grumble. For some reason, Telyn didn't feel afraid. She managed to trim the hooded lantern and light it with the flint. She shone the light to where the sounds came from.

From the deep woods emerged the feathered hind. From his back hoof dragged a sort of skin, similar to what a snake might shed, though goopy instead of dry and covered in feathers. This Taffy kicked free and trotted forward.

Telyn Brower wants to trap the feathered hind, the rumor tree said. *Trade it for her sister.*

"Darn right, I do," she said. "Taffy is a tame hind, and wants to be with people—er, cornics. And thank the High Father for it."

She held out her hand, and Taffy nuzzled it. Then she knelt down, threw her arms around the hind, and like a lunatic, laughed while tears streamed down her cheeks.

CHAPTER FORTY-EIGHT

They decided to bury the chrysalis shell in the bottom of one of their pits, hiding all but two little pieces, which Rayvn took to practice her binding on. They then filled all the pits in and covered them with leaves. How else could they keep the booty safe? The Spring Sale wouldn't be here for months, and anything could happen: the shell could get stolen; their parents could confiscate it; or Biscuit could roll over his saddlebags again and crush the pieces even smaller.

Besides, they'd only purchased one take permit, and they needed that for the feathered hind. Telyn was taking no chances with the cornics' sense of fairness or generosity. She would buy a second take permit for the chrysalis shell.

Rayvn harvested the feathers from Taffy's discarded skin because she thought they looked pretty, and no one argued with her.

They took the return trip slowly, stopping each night well before dark. They talked of steam baths and food, which infusion would taste the best, and how their families might react to their homecoming. Hosh's family would roast maroons and drink mulled wine until his dad gave a lengthy toast. And if he'd had too much wine, he would try to recite the Lynette Epic, and Hosh's mom would have to read the end because he never could remember past when Prince Kyffin looked into his silver chamber pot and fell in love with his own reflection.

Caitlin's parents would interrogate her like inquisitors, wanting to know every detail of their adventure, asking the same question half a dozen different ways, until the telling of it became such a chore, she would never want to speak of it again.

It sounded like Caitlin looked forward to the process.

The pattern witch, Mrs. de Galati, would have an infusion brewing when Rayvn arrived, some rare variety of wigglum that could only be found a certain time of year in a certain type of loam under a certain type of log. They would sit quietly together, Rayvn's mom waiting for her to speak, and Rayvn weaving and unweaving a lanyard.

"Are you going to tell her about our adventures?" Hosh asked.

"Only if she asks."

"You just said she wouldn't ask. So why don't you just go ahead and tell her? I'll bet you want to tell her almost as bad as she wants to know."

Rayvn shrugged and smiled with her eyes. She never mentioned the "justice" that Telyn and her friends should be sold as slaves for using the Ever-Guise, and the humans didn't ask. It amazed Telyn that she trusted Rayvn not to say a word—and not because she had no other choice, either.

They had become friends.

Telyn wasn't sure when it had happened. It probably began back in Harlech when they had begun working to get Rayvn into the Dating Circle. Why else would Rayvn have accompanied her on this mad adventure? Why else would Telyn have bothered to ask her to come?

Whenever their friendship started, the pieces came together here, on this forest adventure, glued like fine furniture by, well, love, and held in place by the clamps of adversity.

How impossibly odd. Telyn had come to love Rayvn as much as she loved Caitlin and Hosh.

And trust her far more than Caitlin.

As for Telyn, nothing much would happen until she paid Cressida's bond price. Then, Raz might host a party in the Sable Head to celebrate Cressida's homecoming, in which case they'd all be invited, with their families too. Telyn would make bread soup with extra garlic and real rakasura speck.

Hosh groaned at that, and they laughed.

Mostly, Telyn thought about freeing her sister.

She didn't expect a warm reception; that would be too much to hope for. Nor did she deserve it. All of this was Telyn's fault. She patted Taffy's side, and the buck rubbed his neck against her ribs as they walked. In a short time, the two had become fast friends, hind and human. Caitlin might be the animal expert, but Taffy preferred Telyn.

Telyn sent silent thanks to the High Father, the Mother of Squirrels, Aled's rump, and any other powers that might be listening for her friends and for the creatures who had helped her: Biscuit, Chisme, and especially this amazing hind.

And for the way this all came out.

She would never, ever screw up this badly again. No more masks. No more magic. No more lies. From now on, she would live in the Truth with a capital T.

"And when I can finally get away from my family," Hosh was saying, as they came to familiar trees, a human path, and the welcoming smell of woodsmoke, "mind, it might take a few days. Dad'll have a bunch of chores he's kept aside especially for me, and Mom won't want to let me out of her sight; she'll expect me to take off into the woods again at the drop of a hat. Drew will have a carving he'll want me to finish...

"Anyway, soon as I can break free, I'll collect the reward from those rakasura ears and treat all of us to a private room at Steamy Betty's."

"*You'll* collect the reward?" Caitlin said, pushing him sideways and laughing. "Why you?"

"You didn't think to cut them off. They'd be in a brakdaw belly if you had been in charge."

"The five of us caught the rakasuras together. We share the reward." Caitlin always counted Biscuit as a full member of their crew, which Telyn now found more endearing than irksome. "We can use Biscuit's share to buy him some hay."

Hosh shrugged, but his voice whined as he said, "Fine. Can we agree to the steam?"

"A steam—fine. But if you want to treat us to a *private* room, that comes from your share," Caitlin said, trying to keep the quirk from her lips.

Through the tree trunks, they caught a glimpse of Dragon Tower —and then more than a glimpse, which gave them pause. The stone tower came into plain sight long before it should have.

Telyn thought her eyes must have been playing tricks on her. She pinched herself to be sure she wasn't dreaming. Had they been gone so long that she'd forgotten the view of Harlech from this side of the river? She wanted to climb a tree to scout ahead, but knew her friends were too eager to spare the time.

Step by step, her sense of unease grew. They emerged into a new clearing. A swath of stumps spread to the north and south where Telyn had spent hundreds of hours climbing, where the Ever-Guise had misfired on that fateful night. Saws worked against frozen trunks in the distance like monster teeth grinding against boulders.

The friends fell silent.

Never had Ouzeley logged this close to Harlech. Always before, they'd felled trees upriver and floated them to the lumber mill. Minister Svemas strictly enforced this rule.

Things had changed in the short time they'd been away, and Telyn didn't like what she saw. She reached out to touch Caitlin's wrist, to tell her silently to tread carefully, then reminded herself that Caitlin didn't know the secret hand-talk; only Cressida knew it, and she was still in jail and headed for a life of slavery.

My fault.

No, not anymore. I've fixed this. All we have to do is get the hind to the Prefecture and trade him for Cressida's bond price.

They'd all pulled up short at the edge of the woods, staring across the stump-littered field to the stone bridge and the shingles and sod roofs beyond.

"You think one of us should stay here with Taffy?" Hosh asked.

"I don't like the looks of this," Caitlin agreed. "We could wait until evening, then cross upriver on the ice. I can wait that long for a good meal." Her mouth tightened. "I can."

"Me too, Telyn Brower," Rayvn added.

They all waited for Telyn to make a decision. They all understood that she had the biggest stake in this.

"We go on," she decided. "Let's get this done. My sister has been waiting in prison too long."

They hadn't taken three steps when one of the bridge guards exited the tower and sprinted back toward Harlech—gone to tell the minister they'd brought back the feathered hind, no doubt. Telyn breathed easier. Once she was under Minister Svemas's protection, all would be well.

The remaining bridge guard stared through the window as they passed. They were shocked to see the solder wasn't a cornic at all.

"Mr. Thomas?" Hosh asked, giving a nod.

The human stared back with hollow eyes.

"Who is Mr. Thomas?" Rayvn asked.

"One of Mr. Ouzeley's relatives," Hosh said. "He's...not the worst."

Town seemed to be deserted. There was no foot traffic on Main Street nor any animals tied up in front of the Copcut Ash or Lucky H.

Telyn wished she had taken her friends' advice, both to keep Taffy hidden back in the woods and to cross the frozen river at night in secret.

Just get to the Prefecture, turn the hind over to Minister Svemas, collect the reward, pay the bond price, and free Cressida. That's all that matters.

The bond price for my sister.

Nothing else matters.

Telyn fingered the take permit around her neck with one hand and tightened her grip on Taffy's harness with the other. Biscuit grunted every few steps; his flanks quivered nervously.

The sounds made by their footfalls changed as they advanced: stone bridge to dirt road to cobblestones in the market square.

Rounding the market hall, several new, wooden structures came into view—six, to be exact. Telyn counted them.

One, two, three, four, five, six.

With loud flaps of their wings, a murder of crows broke from the unlucky structures. Annoyed at being disturbed at their meal, they flew directly over the friends, landed on nearby rooftops, and cawed. Many had taken strips of meat with them.

Now closer, Telyn could see more clearly.

They weren't six individual structures, but one long, elevated platform with six frames rising from it—with a body hanging from each.

Six bodies.

Three human, three cornic, hanging by the necks.

She knew the humans: Heath Robinson, Tyre Flint, Arvel Grummore. Three young cornic soldiers wearing uniforms and burnished medals hung beside them.

Telyn's legs became leaden; she tasted bile in the back of her throat.

"Tey, Tey, I know you're in a hurry, but I don't think this is a good idea." Caitlin's voice cracked twice in that little sentence. "Can we find out what's going on before going to the Prefecture?"

"Yes, yes, I think you're right."

Telyn had never seen an execution. She didn't think they did them in Harlech—and now six at once?

They turned aside, trying hard to not look at the scaffoldings, to not look like they were in a hurry.

"There aren't any ghosts," Rayvn said. "My mother must have already engraved their names on the Sepulcher."

No ghost, Tey. No ghost.

"I will inquire with her." Rayvn broke from the group, heading east toward flacktown at an easy lope towards, and Telyn felt their fellowship splinter.

"Just a little further," Telyn said, as much to herself as her friends.

They didn't get far before two cornic soldiers intercepted them. One planted his spear vertically. The other fingered the hilt of his short sword. They wore scarves over their faces, though with the cold the stench of bodies was disturbingly slight, almost as if the condemned were carved of wax.

"Your business?"

"We brought back the feathered hind," Telyn said, trying to sound confident. It wasn't easy with the wind pushing the condemned from side to side; their ropes creaked in morbid rhythm. "We're claiming the reward."

"If they wanted the reward," said the soldier with the spear to the one with the sword, "then where are they headed?"

Trying hard to appear nonchalant, Telyn answered. "Wanted to put up the hind in the stable before we claimed the reward. You don't want us to bring it into Minister Svemas's office, do you?"

The one with the sword smiled with half his muzzle. "Wouldn't want them to bring it to Minister Svemas's office directly, now, would we?"

"What happened? Why the hanging?" Hosh said.

"Friends of yours?" the spear-solder asked.

Hosh shrugged.

"They used to drink too much in the Sable Head," Telyn said, covering for him. "Got in fights."

"You, boy?"

"It's a small town."

"Friends?"

"I knew them."

"See that you didn't know them too well. That could be dangerous to your health."

Telyn and Hosh both gave little shakes of their heads.

"We will be relieving you of the hind." The grinning soldier fingered his sword hilt with his right hand, while his left reached for Taffy's lead rope.

With a nauseous, vacuous feeling—the kind you get when you lend someone a tool, a dress, or coin you know you'll never see again—Telyn let Taffy go.

I let him go without a fight.

I let him go.

A fight with cornic soldiers was not something they could win, not something they could survive.

I have to get to Minister Svemas and explain the situation fast, claim the reward before these soldiers make up some story about how they managed to catch Taffy themselves.

Minister Svemas is fair-minded. He will believe me.

He will.

Taffy tried to stay with Telyn and her friends, but the cornic dragged him toward the stable the way one might muscle an unruly dog.

Taffy bellowed. Biscuit answered with a screech. Telyn wanted to screech right along with him.

Within minutes, Telyn, Hosh and Caitlin were alone with their llama. Alone, but not unobserved. It felt as though people watched them from every doorway and every knothole, including the bank of windows in the nearby Prefecture.

"What now?" Caitlin asked.

"There's no time to lose," Telyn replied. "I've got to see Minister Svemas and get the bond price before those cornics make Taffy disappear—or claim they caught it themselves."

"I'm coming with you," Hosh said, "in case you need a witness."

"Me too," Caitlin said. "My parents can help. They work there."

They kept as much distance between themselves and the scaffoldings as possible. The slave wagon was no longer parked in front of the Prefecture. Ordinarily, this would be good news, but Telyn didn't think so—not this time.

The entrance hall of the Prefecture was uncharacteristically quiet. No one sat on the benches lining the hall, waited in lines, or chatted with each other. The door to the hallway and stairs had always stood closed but unguarded, but no longer. Before it stood a cornic soldier at attention, and as Telyn and Hosh approached, he knocked Hosh back with an outstretched palm. Nothing malevolent, just a stern interdiction.

Telyn stopped short. She had no desire to experience any blows from cornic hands. "We're here to see the minister. My name is Telyn Brower. I have a standing pass."

The soldier took in their disheveled appearance. "You been in the Chaos Woods long?"

"What's it to you?" Hosh asked, trying to square his shoulders after the blow to his diaphragm.

"You'll have to renew your pass at the counter." The soldier nodded at the window where Caitlin's parents worked.

"Well, okay. Thank you," Hosh said, and the friends moved over there, happy that something was going their way for once.

Only, it wasn't.

Caitlin's parents were not there. Instead, a cornic female manned the counter. At least she didn't wear a uniform.

"Hello...er...Miss... I'm Telyn Brower, I have a standing pass. We're here to see Minister Svemas."

The cornic's head tilted to the side.

"Telyn is here to see the minister. We are here to collect the reward on the feathered hind." Hosh upended the leather bag he'd been carrying and dumped the rakasura ears on the counter. Frozen, they landed stiffly, like dice. "And on these. That's fifteen pairs."

The cornic's pinched cheeks indicated she didn't believe a word. "And who did you steal these from?"

Hosh blanched.

"He brought you fifteen pairs of ears. The reward is one huron a pair; says so right behind you." Caitlin pointed to the sign on the wall. "And these are clean, not halves or anything to dispute. Full, beautiful ears. Or have things changed since we went into the woods?"

The female smiled wryly, exposing the yellowed ivory of her teeth. "Oh, things have changed—for the better. We don't accept stolen goods, for one thing."

Hosh choked on his own surprise.

"Hosh has never stolen from anybody in his life," Caitlin said.

"A gimp barely into his whiskers took all these ears by himself?"

"With his friends."

Telyn just wanted to get upstairs to see the minister. She wanted so much to sweep the ears back into the bag, onto the floor, anywhere, and get on with it.

Get on with it already!

I need to renew my pass. I need to see my sister. No, first see Minister Svemas, then my sister.

Cressida, I love you. I'll be there soon.

"I might believe you took one pair." The tall, burly cornic leaned forward on the counter, exposing altogether too much woolly cleavage. "But with fifteen, I'm asking myself what happened to the trapper? Is he missing a sack, or did you bleed him out? Fifteen, I'm wondering how you broke into the Prefecture and took the ears we've already paid for."

"There are fifteen pairs of ears in front of you because we killed fifteen rakasuras."

"Minister Svemas could settle this," Telyn broke in. "Why don't we call him? He knows me. Besides, we need to tell him about the feathered hind."

Now, finally, the cornic female glanced in her direction. Appraising...no, gloating. "He could settle this *if* he could spit the lye out of his mouth."

"The lie?" Hosh said, fear and anxiety expanding his outrage. "The lie?!"

Telyn's hand shot out and she pinched Hosh's arm, stifling whatever he'd been about to add. She heard the word "lie" as well, but she knew that wasn't it, that wasn't it at all.

Those men outside, executed. The changes, the guards, the arrogance. Not a lie, but the white powder they poured on bodies so they wouldn't smell.

The *lye* pit where they dumped the bodies after the funerals.

The ears sat between the three humans and the cornic, and Telyn realized there was a great possibility of the ears disappearing behind that counter.

If that happened, they would get nothing.

"I think you miscounted, Hosh," Telyn said urgently. "These thirteen...er...twelve pairs of ears we got legitimately in a pit trap. We got lucky, that's all. The rakasuras fell in one-by-one, and we waited until they starved. Everyone deserves a bit of luck, don't they?"

The cornic eyed them a bit longer. Then she pulled all fifteen pairs of ears over. Twelve went into a bin, and three disappeared elsewhere.

"A bit of luck, then." She laid twelve copper hurons on the counter and Hosh took them up. Then, thinking quickly, he returned a one huron. "For your time."

The cornic made the coin disappear too. She leaned forward and whispered, "We're instructed to be lenient for those trappers who've been absent, who haven't heard about the changes. Minister Svemas, he's no longer with us, see. There's been an uprising. The perps decorate the square outside."

Telyn's heart beat faster and faster. "We brought back the feathered hind."

"Maybe you did, and maybe you didn't. Since I haven't seen it, I don't need to report you. Maybe you're just talking. Too much time in the Chaos Woods, especially with your youth, can do things to a human mind. Make them see things that aren't real."

"We turned the hind over to soldiers. They took it to the stable."

The cornic female's squint tightened; she was obviously at the end of her patience. "If you insist on seeing the minister, I'll give you an appointment with Second Gajos. He has authority in Harlech until a new minister arrives. You won't like it much; he tends to hold his meetings in the dungeon.

"I paid you generously for the ears and didn't even ask you for the take permit, though that has changed as well. Nothing gets removed from the Chaos Woods without a permit, including ears. It's all Empire goods, now. If the feathered hind's really returned, that should put Second Gajos in a good mood. But if you insist on a reward" —She shook her horned head slowly—"it's likely to be found at the end of a rope."

Treacherous tears leaked down Telyn's cheeks. "I need those hurons to free my sister. She's to be sold as a slave come spring."

The cornic's eyes softened—but only a little. "You won't get nothing by returning stolen goods—not unless you bring back the thief as well."

"The hind wasn't stolen," Telyn said in a whimper. "It escaped on the bridge. It jumped on its own."

"You have three seconds more."

In a squeak, Telyn said, "May I see my sister?"

"Name?"

"Cressida Brower."

The cornic looked down a list; Telyn counted around a dozen names, each assigned to a cell.

"You are the sister?"

Telyn nodded.

"You can visit Miss Brower just as soon as she returns this evening; your pass is acceptable. Your sister is not going to become a slave come springtime—she has already begun working off her debt for the good of the Empire."

Telyn felt like she just stepped off a branch into thin air and she was falling, falling, falling with nothing to grab onto, nothing to slow her, nothing to crash into and end the sense of bottomless loss.

Ever.

The three friends stumbled from the Prefecture into the deserted plaza, deserted but for six bodies and about a hundred crows.

CHAPTER FORTY-NINE

"It must be...it must be Ouzeley. He's using them in the lumber mill," Hosh said.

By unspoken agreement, they'd walked to Elin Llyweln Park. There they stood, facing each other, each with one foot on a wooden bench, feeling the townsfolk staring from darkened windows. The slushy, muddy mess that had been a grass field around the chaos tree in the middle of the park reflected their mood.

"How are we going to rescue Taffy?" When Telyn turned a sharp eye toward her, Caitlin continued. "Y'know, to save Cressida? We have to get the bond price one way or another, and the hind is the only thing that has any chance. I mean, the chrysalis shell is pretty and all, and if it keeps its glow, it's bound to sell for something at the Spring Sale, but it isn't even on the List. We'd have to find a buyer—a buyer willing to pay a fair price. Even then, well, it won't touch four thousand hurons. You know it won't."

It was the longest speech Caitlin had said in some time, likely a reflection of the pent-up emotion of the road and its tragic conclusion here in Harlech.

"Taffy is on his own," Telyn said with finality, "same as we are."

A long silence indicated better than any speech that none of them had any ideas about how to get out of this mess. "I need to get home," Hosh announced, finally. "Mum'll be worried."

"Don't say anything about Taffy, or about rescuing Cressida, or anything else about our adventures." Telyn disliked the lecturing tone she'd taken. However, she was unable to change it. "When they ask about our 'camping trip,' make it as bland as bread soup. No one is to know about the herd of hinds, or the chrysalis shell, or the glowing golden light, or even Chisme. We don't want anyone going out there and digging around. The rumor tree and the chrysalis shell—they're still ours. Before we can figure out what to do, we have to find out what's been going on since we left."

"Minister Svemas was murdered, and Second Gajos is in charge, that's what's been going on," Hosh replied.

"You don't know that," Caitlin said.

"That cornic woman said as much. Heath and his crew are hanging for it, along with those three cornics. And I've got to get home before Mum skins me." He hobbled off.

Caitlin give Telyn a big hug, tears in her eyes. "We'll figure this out."

Telyn nodded. "Heads down, eyes open."

As soon as her friends disappeared, immense loneliness swept over Telyn. All her plans had been for nothing. Minister Svemas was dead. Heath Robinson, Tyre Flint, Arven Grummore were all dead—along with three cornics who were probably just as innocent as the humans.

She didn't believe Heath and the others had been so stupid as to murder the cornic minister. She couldn't believe it. No way; they got blamed for someone else's doing and were hanged for it.

Minister Svemas enlisted me to keep an eye on things. 'We live in an empire divided, Telyn Brower,' he said, 'and I fear you have landed between the lines.'

A lousy spy I made. I didn't see any of this coming; I certainly didn't see any threat to the minister.

She may have spent an hour standing there, one foot on the park bench, staring pensively at the muddy footprints of the square. Time passed slowly in this place of what-ifs and if-onlys. She'd become so still a blurry fox scurried past; the creature projected a simulacrum of three tails from its rump to confuse predators. It paused near an entrance to the sewers, wrinkled its nose at Telyn, and darted inside.

Later, Telyn found herself in the public room of the Sable Head, rather unsure as to how she'd moved from Elin Llyweln Park to here. As a cool breeze followed her inside and caused the firelight to flicker, about five patrons lifted their gazes indifferently from their mugs, and Razenbock stopped rubbing the counter long enough to notice her. Despite her fatigue, she would have liked to talk to him, to find out what the barkeep knew of Heath Robinson and Minister Svemas and the others, to ask "What in Gruffud's irreverent name had been happening around here?" as Raz would. But another head raised from the long bar to see who stood in the open door, this one framed with sheep horns and rather more alert than the humans. Telyn let the door swing shut behind her, nodded at Raz—he raised the rag in greeting— and climbed the stairs to her room. It wouldn't have surprised her to find it occupied, but Raz had kept it vacant for her. She looked around at the sparse furnishings, the bed with a lumpy straw mattress, one wooden chair, a cow-hide rug, a pewter pitcher of stale water— nope, it'd dried and left a white rung about halfway up—and the candle, long burned out.

I can't do this alone. I can't.

Telyn returned to the public room, retrieved Tums from the walls, and brought her upstairs. She shed her clothes and climbed into bed, pulling the blankets over her and Tums's heads. Tums played with her hair for a while, then they eventually fell asleep, snoring softly.

She dreamed, and it was one of those dreams where you observe but do not participate. She looked down into the stone prison cell where she'd spent three nights, the one too small to stand up in. Cressida slept on the floor in Telyn's place.

Despite the fact that she lay on her side in the fetal position, the single blanket only covered to her knees, and Cressida trembled uncontrollably. Human guards wearing the red tunic and bronze buttons of cornic uniforms came in the morning, banging on the iron bars and calling, "Wake up, lovely, you've got interest to pay." They escorted Cressida from the cell and led her outside, across the stone bridge, to where Tabbard waited with his gang.

The guards turned back there, leaving Cressida with the hoodlums.

As a watcher, Telyn could not participate in the dream, and her jaw tightened at what they might have planned, but the hoodlums simply patted Cressida on the head like a favorite animal and bade her follow.

With hollows under her eyes, scruffy hair, and a bent back, Cressida looked the part of an animal, too—an animal eager to please its masters.

Telyn felt the edges of her own mouth turn up. She'd imagined the worst, but this—this wasn't bad. This made sense. Cressida had broken the second Rule, after all. A beating would've been deserved.

Humans shall not own horses.
Humans shall not own magic.
Humans shall not own wheels.

They all walked together, Cressida leading the gang through the wasteland of chaos tree stumps, Tabbard, Joram, Dylan, Hefin, Marc, with the girls trailing behind, Cherle, Tristam, Isla, and Caitlin. They sang a ballad that could only have been composed by Leutric Quid: "Nine ways to butter your toast."

Now and then Cressida skipped.

Why has Caitlin joined Tabbard's crew again? Is she back together with Joram?

Well, the ballad is catchy, and Cressida has a spring in her step, so everything will be all right.

They arrived at the lumber mill, and Cressida took up one of the long, single-man saws. With the gang's encouragement, she lifted up her long skirt all the way to her hip, giving the boys a wink.

Mr. Ouzeley appeared. "Work is behind schedule," he said. "We need to feed the Cornic Empire. Do you understand?"

"Work is behind schedule," Cressida repeated with a throaty voice, tossing her sandy brown hair.

The boys laughed at the ridiculous way she flirted with her grimy skirt and greasy hair.

As if anyone can be attracted to a slave!

Telyn laughed, too.

Cressida didn't seem to mind. She put her leg onto a sawhorse, placed the saw-teeth between her second and third toes and, with grunts and moans, began to saw her foot down the middle. Sweat beaded on her brow, her body trembled, but she didn't slow.

"No sacrifice is too large," Mr. Ouzeley said, "for the good of the Empire."

"No...sac...rifice," Cressida mimicked, sweat pouring from her face, a face quickly turning from red to ashen.

On a nearby stump, Leutric Quid strummed a lute to the rhythmic squelch of the saw's teeth. He sang:

> "Left and right, deft with a knife
> Mrs. Peady spreads yellow tallow
> Her daughter cries, 'That's unseemly!'
> Melted and dripped
> the butter goes best..."

Telyn woke up feeling refreshed and a spell better about losing the feathered hind. It was truly a shame that Cressida had become a slave for Telyn's sin. Her sister hadn't anything to do with the Ever-Guise, after all, but Cressida's labor did benefit the Cornic Empire. She'd never have to worry about food or lodging, or a mother who drank herself into a grave.

The Cornic Empire was Cressida's mother now. One could almost envy her.

Tums held out her arms and cooed, asking to climb Telyn. Cats needed sand, dogs liked to be walked, and eehoos needed to climb, so you learned quickly not to stand below their morning tree.

Cressida usually did this, as the more responsible twin, while

Telyn climbed, explored, used the Ever-Guise, or otherwise got into mischief.

Tums'll be missing her. Too bad Cressida's in the lumber mill, slaving away.

An uneasy feeling that she couldn't quite place settled in the pit of Telyn's belly. But Tums was insistent, and she had chores to do, so she shrugged aside her unease and started her day. She'd visit Cressida later, after the work was done, in a day or three.

She assumed her sister's role as best she could, serving bags of angel water and mugs of malt, which had made something of a comeback. Raz asked little about the trip and seemed unconcerned that they had failed to bring back the feathered hind.

Telyn blinked.

We brought it back.

"Hum?" Raz said, half listening as he sought to maneuver a log onto the fire without burning himself.

Had she spoken aloud? Everything felt fuzzy.

"We brought back the feathered hind...from the Chaos Woods. The cornics took it away."

Raz spared a glance at Telyn over his shoulder. "Took it away? How so?"

She blinked into the tabletop. In the polished wood, a sad girl stared back at her. Her sharp cheekbones looked bone-gaunt; her frizzy hair stood like the cords of a mop that had been used to clean a dirty floor and then left to dry unevenly; her eyes were puffy.

As one of Quid's ballads went:

> Three malts in the chamber-pot
> and two in the belly.
> One more in your fist
> to make you be merry
> Singing tra-la-la Lady
> of Mercy
> of Mercy.
> Tra-la-la Lady
> of head-pounding

Mercy. Have mercy.
Have mercy.

Telyn's reflection blinked slowly back up at her.

They're using the Ever-Guise on us. That dream I had last night— Cressida working for Ouzeley. I've only been here for one night, and look what it's done to me.

She felt thick of tongue, lethargic of thought, double of vision, like the worst hangover she'd ever had times five—a Heath Robinson level of hangover.

Mother of Squirrels, I was almost okay with Cressida being a slave. Someone powerful is using the mask. Someone who knows how to cast spells, not some Too-tall Harlech girl. This person knows what they're doing.

Could it be they'd returned the forehead piece to the mind wizard?

No, Yona can't be here. Winter will keep him away. And why would he bother helping Ouzeley? He'd take his revenge on me, and then he'd leave this town that stinks of humans.

It must be Second Gajos' doing. He's teamed up with Ouzeley.

Just knowing her thoughts were not entirely her own—and admitting it to herself—loosened the Ever-Guise's grip. Telyn vowed to visit Cressida that same evening, and to meet Hosh, Caitlin, and Rayvn as quickly as possible. Once on their guard, the four of them could resist the mask's effects more easily.

We need to come clean to Rayvn about everything. We need to marshal our forces. We need the thauma on our side, along with as many of the townsfolk as possible.

I'll start right here, with Razenbock.

A few hours later, she cornered him upstairs as, on both knees, he ran a brush down the floorboard seams in the largest of the guest rooms, the one most prone to after-hours imbibing and its aftermath. The previous night had been no exception. He'd broken out the cider vinegar to kill the smell of vomit.

"What're you blocking the doorway for?" he asked.

"Just wondering about my job, is all. You ain't put in an order for slaves from Enshede, have you?"

He stopped scrubbing and rubbed his nose. "What? Nah, don't you worry none. You're always welcome here."

"You can take out rent for the weeks I was away in the Chaos Woods. You can take it from my salary. I don't want anyone thinking I'm a freeloader."

"Telyn, what is this talk about? You're welcome here, I said. You'll always be welcome."

Telyn moved into the room, sat on one of the rumpled beds. With the blankets strewn about, it looked as though three men had slept there—and six had been sick.

She watched the barkeep's back muscles ripple as he bent back to work. She had to see how far the Ever-Guise had penetrated his way of thinking, had to know how far she could trust him, if at all.

"Things have turned; men are hanging in the square by the neck, slaves working for Ouzeley."

Raz shook his head. "You shouldn't've had to see that. I'm sorry. They should've taken them down the moment they stopped kicking."

"Heath Robinson? Raz, what did he do?"

"He killed Minister Svemas is what."

"Heath Robinson?"

"Along with three cornics."

"You believe that?"

"They caught 'em dead to rights. The cornics talked 'em into it, no doubt. Heath wouldn't have dared on his own. Talk, and a lot of birds, no telling how it works a man's mind." Raz sounded as if he were trying to convince himself of something he didn't believe. "A man'll do almost anything for a few birds."

Such as leave my dad in a crevasse? The skin around Telyn's forehead tightened.

Raz flinched away from her stare. "They should've taken them down. S'not something for a young woman to see, men hanging, crows feasting."

"So, you're okay with the executions? And the slave-taking, are you okay with that?"

Raz poured a little more vinegar on the floor and scrubbed with the bristle brush. "This oughta be your job, Telyn," he muttered.

"Cressida would've volunteered to clean up here, but she's working... for the good of the Empire."

Telyn moved right next to the big man and sat so her knee would poke his ribs with each scrub and hamper his elbow, too.

He sighed in exasperation and sat on his heels. "What do you want me to say? Things change. Slavery is wrong...but it might be okay for those who could not do otherwise. Take your mother. What has freedom gotten her? Daily self-destruction and misery. Tell me your mother wouldn't be better off under the Ouzeleys' care."

"Ouzeley's *care*?"

"She'd eat regular. She'd exercise those stiff limbs. By wise Aled's rump, she'd get out of bed once in a while. If your father were still alive, he'd agree. Freedom just ain't good for some folk. They can't handle it."

With a snowbank in her belly and an ice-cave around her heart, Telyn stood. "I gotta go for a walk."

Raz nodded, looking as confused at the words that had spewed from his own mouth as a child who spontaneously answers Quid's most difficult question and has no idea what he's just said.

As Telyn descended the stairs, the whish-whish of the brush began again. Raz had dumped so much vinegar on the floor that a drip came through the ceiling.

CHAPTER FIFTY

The standing pass still worked, and to Telyn's relief, her sister hadn't been moved to the cells in the dungeon. According to Cressida, it hadn't worked out too well when Second Gajos had tried it on the new slaves. Sleep all night bent like a pretzel, and your work suffered. Pulling a saw or a plane over frozen lumber required a strong and flexible back, and a good night's sleep facilitated that. So, for Ouzeley's new slaves, they got the wood-paneled flack cells.

Other things had changed, however. Visiting hours were severely restricted; guards seemed to be everywhere; and no one got into the Prefecture without passing by Taffy. The hind had tried to nuzzle Telyn when he saw her, which earned Telyn a cuff and strong words from its handler. Her upper lip had started to swell from it.

No more than I deserve, she thought, touching the lip tenderly. *I'm responsible for all of this.*

"Eight," Cressida replied to Telyn's question.

"Eight? I can't believe Ouzeley bought eight slaves!" In the back of Telyn's mind, she corrected herself: *Not slaves. Free people.*

A song un-spooled in her mind, not one of Quid's but something

much more ancient called Hornblower or unofficially, the Freedom
Song:

> A white kerchief polishes brass
> Until buttons shone
> In the golden shaft
>
> Kisses wife and children goodbye
> Leaves family and home
> For freedom he fights
>
> Hornblower, how much does it weigh?
> Heavy as gold
> lighter than chains
>
> The horn that plays the one-note tune.
>
> Hornblower, how long shall we pay?
> Till tyranny's gone
> The High Father reigns
>
> Hornblower glances left and right
> Sees soldiers ready
> To die or to smite
>
> Mothers don't weep, fathers don't groan
> As free men they
> Choose to fight for home
>
> Hornblower, how much does it weigh?
> Heavy as gold
> lighter than chains
>
> The horn that plays the one-note tune.
>
> Hornblower, how long shall we pay?

Till tyranny's gone
The High Father reigns

As wind-blown snow they charge ahead
Temporary and
Gloriously free

Into the sun and testing heat
Following the peal
Of freedom's conceit

Hornblower, how much does it weigh?
Heavy as gold
lighter than chains

The horn that plays the one-note tune.

Hornblower, how long shall we pay?
Till tyranny's gone
The High Father reigns

"Didn't buy; rented," Cressida mumbled around mouthfuls of gooseberry acorn. The prison guards—cornics—had let Telyn bring in an acorn, so long as she brought them two. Cressida shoveled the food in without balancing it on her tongue, without taking care to separate the sour and sweet, jelly and fruit, crumble and crust, without any apparent pleasure at all—except that of filling a starving belly.

"Ouzeley couldn't afford this many slaves, especially not old folks like Mr. and Mrs. Parry. They hardly work; we have to cover for them. No, he rents us. Come the Spring Sale, I reckon we'll be sold down-river. This is just a side gig...for the good of the Empire," she added, licking the last of the crumbs from her fingers.

The cell's vibrant wood paneling mocked Cressida's gaunt, sunburned face. She looked part-beast, her hair knotted and wild, strands poking out in every direction like deranged sunflower petals.

Her skin was scabbed from wind and sun, her eyes were bloodshot, and her ear...

"What happened to your ear?" Telyn asked.

With shaking fingers, Cressida reached up and touched its curve; the top part of her right ear had blackened. "It's called frostbite. Do you like it?"

Telyn's legs buckled, and she lowered herself to the wooden floor.

The silence between them stretched long enough for Telyn to contemplate more than she'd like. How she got her sister into this mess. How it really should be *her* in prison and not Cressida.

Why did Cressida protect me? She should have turned in the Ever-Guise and me at the same time, for the good of the Empire.

No, this is me blaming my sister again.

Telyn bowed and rested her head in both hands, trying to think clearly.

If I had come forth immediately, well, Minister Svemas was as reasonable as cornics come. If I had explained everything from day one, starting with the auction and the thief, and Yona, Taito-Vaiana, and the penumbra daemon, the minister might have swapped Cressida for me without question. What is one human life for another in the eyes of a cornic, anyway?

Justice is what cornics care about. Justice and information.

With Minister Svemas dead, any sort of confession is impossible. Second Gajos would throw me into prison next to my sister and add our friends for good measure. The more slaves the better, so far as he is concerned. It is all revenue—for the good of the Empire.

No, we have to raise the bond price or break Cressida out of here before the Spring Sale. Before it is too late.

"Where exactly does Ouzeley have you working?"

"The lumber mill."

"Where in the lumber mill?"

"We aren't going to run into the Chaos Woods, Tey. I know that look."

Telyn sighed. "It wasn't so bad. We managed to kill fifteen raka-suras. Fifteen of them! We could survive, you and I. Especially if we team up with other trappers. We get over King's Pass to the plateau where the weather isn't so brutal, we'll be okay. The Fae live there year-round. We could trade with them for food and tools. They've been known to take in strangers."

"They've been known to skin people alive, too."

"Better take our chances there than staying here and being sold downriver. *Better to fight and die than to live a coward*" —She quoted Gruffud—"*or read bad poetry, which is a fate worse than death.*"

In the back of her mind, Telyn had been steeling herself for failure, preparing to see Cressida taken to Enshede as a slave. Failure was always a possibility—failure to come up with the bond price, to trap anything at all in the Chaos Woods...

In fact, failure was the most likely outcome.

She didn't know it until this moment, but unconsciously, she had accepted that fact from the very beginning.

But not now. Not after seeing Cressida's blackened ear, the skin peeling from her wind-burned nose, the sullen look in her eyes.

Telyn would succeed...or die.

No less effort would suffice; she owed her sister everything, all her effort, unto death.

With a more choked-up and yet more resolute voice, Telyn said, "Tell me what they did to you."

Cressida noted the change. Though her head did not turn, her eyes met Telyn's from the side. "My ears? That's nothing. They did nothing *to* me. I'm not worth anything special. They are as indifferent as the cold. Gave me a taste of life to come, is all. Since the river isn't flowing and we can't float trees down from upriver, some slaves are cutting nearby trees. I'm getting the lumber mill ready for the spring thaw, cleaning, lubricating, planing new sawhorses and such where old ones have worn out."

"How do the other workers tolerate it?"

"Tolerate it? I'm a slave now, Telyn. I broke the Rules. I knew you were up to something, and I let you do it. You, Caitlin, and Hosh aren't nearly as sneaky as you suppose. I'd even guessed you'd got hold of something magical. So, I'm just as guilty as you; I deserve what I got. The only injustice is that you three got away with it."

The blood rushed away from Telyn's face. "That's the Ever-Guise talking," she croaked.

"That's the High Father's truth."

"The cornic second is using the Ever-Guise. They've planted that idea in your head, Cressida. They're trying to turn Harlech into a slave town. At night, the dreams—you've had them?" Telyn had trouble swallowing as her throat tightened, remembering the dream about Cressida sawing through her own foot. "They're sending people awful dreams so we think slavery is okay. I know them, because I used the mask too. I sent dreams, too."

"So, you been manipulated the people of Harlech because, what, you wanted to be famous?"

"That was Hosh." Telyn cleared her throat. "I'm not proud of it. I tried to help Raz make the Sable Head popular. I thought that would guarantee our future and help Raz pay Ouzeley back as well. Raz did better, and the Copcut Ash suffered. For the first time in my life, I had power. People listened to me. I-I didn't feel helpless. All our lives, we've been at the mercy of...well...like leaves in the wind. One gust, and we'd be blown away. One spark, and poof. No money. No future. At the edge, last pick on anyone's Dating Chart, no dad, no mom— not really—life a dirty tavern and filthy rags to wipe it with." Cressida nodded once, acknowledging the sentiment. "But over time, I tried to punish the Ouzeleys for the way they treated people, for their rich- ness, wealth, arrogance. Whatever."

"Telyn Brower, minister of all justice."

"I may not know justice, but I can see injustice when it happens!"

"'Envy a neighbor, and you will end up with his debts and burdens tenfold,'" Cressida quoted Aled the Wise.

"I see it now. I see it in you taking the blame for me. I see it in people taking advantage of slaves to get wealthy. Since when was slavery accepted in Harlech? That's because of Ouzeley and Second Gajos, and the filthy Ever-Guise robbing people of free will. I did that, too, with my selfish wishes. I'm no better than they are.

"Listen, Cressida, the bond price is still in place. That hasn't changed; Second Gajos can't change the Empire's rules, just twist them in his favor. But we can't get that many hurons—I mean, we can't execute the plan—until the Spring Sale. We've got..." Telyn took a breath and clenched her fists. "We're working on things to sell. If that doesn't work, you working at the lumber mill will make the backup plan easier."

Cressida stared a long moment, reading the plan in Telyn's heart. "So, we're going to run free in the Chaos Woods, tra-la-la? You don't think I haven't thought of that?" It sounded even more outlandish coming from Cressida's weather-beaten lips. "Don't you remember what happened to our dad?"

"Trappers make it through King's Pass every single year. Cressida, listen, we survived a blizzard and rakasura attack."

"From what I heard, you had a flack helping you. I would be alone."

"Never alone. I would stay with you forever."

"Like you did this past year?"

"That's different. I didn't know what...how this would end up. I thought that by keeping it secret from you, I was protecting you, that I was taking the risk onto myself."

"We'd be fugitives."

"If we find enough things from the List then, over time, we could pay the bond price—and the fine for escaping. It wouldn't have to be forever. Freedom has a price in the Cornic Empire. We get enough things from the List, we could return and pay all our debts." Telyn raised one coquettish eyebrow. "Put our names back on the Dating Chart before we're old maids?"

Cressida turned to stare at the wall. "You think Ouzeley and Second Gajos are working together?"

"Minister Svemas thought so. He wanted me to be his eyes and ears. If I hadn't run off to get the feathered hind, well, I might have seen something, warned him in time." *Was this yet another bad decision on my part, or something I couldn't have foreseen?* "It's obvious, isn't it? Mr. Ouzeley provides the market, the cornic second provides the labor." *And probably assassinated Minister Svemas himself. Heath Robinson would never have acted so boldly.*

"And you, Too-tall Telyn Brower, are going to bring the traitor down."

"No. I'm not all that ambitious. But I *am* going to rescue my sister, whatever it takes."

Cressida wet her finger and used that to pick up the remaining crumbs that had dropped on her shirt. "How is Esther doing?"

"I-I haven't visited her."

Cressida's eyes tightened. "She's come every day to see me."

Telyn swallowed. "I will go...after this. I will see how she's doing. What can I do for you? Besides visiting Esther, I mean."

"She's our mother."

"I am not calling her that."

"Until when?"

Telyn didn't have an answer. "Until never" came to mind. But it wasn't what Cressida wanted to hear, so she kept it to herself.

Cressida rose and padded to the door. "You know the worst of it? Besides the cold and the hunger, I mean? The boredom. There is absolutely nothing to do here."

"I'll visit, I promise. Now that we're back—"

Cressida banged on the door and called for the guard. "My sister is ready to go. She has a visit to make."

As the key turned in the lock, Cressida said, "Bring me more of your Kiss, Kindle and Flame questionnaires. Aled's rump, the things people put down when they think they are writing anonymously!"

Telyn stood. "Seriously? That's what you're concerned about, the Dating Chart?"

"This infernal place is driving me mad. Yes, I'm serious." Cressida threw her scarecrow-thin arms around Telyn, hugged her to bony ribs, and buried her face in Telyn's brunette mop. "I need something, ah, to get my mind off the future. Ask Redbeard, Quid, anyone you can find... I want to compare you all—mathematically, of course."

Ah, now I understand. Of course, sis. "We'll bring you the good ones, I promise."

"Bring me the challenging ones."

The door swung open, and a sheep-headed guard made a stiff gesture for Telyn to leave.

Telyn extracted herself from her sister's embrace. "Rayvn will be glad to hear it. When we started into the woods, the Dating Chart was all she talked about." Cressida could lose herself in a scroll-length equation for hours, the way Telyn lost herself in a challenging climb.

Good. Maybe this will put a little fire in Cressida's belly. We are going to need that before this is done.

"This isn't going to make you lonely, is it?"

"Give your sister a little credit. And more gooseberry. Gooseberry acorns, plea—" The cell door slammed shut, cutting off her last word.

CHAPTER FIFTY-ONE

Cressida and Telyn agreed to a sort of routine: Telyn would visit three evenings in a row and skip the fourth, when Esther would visit, and the seventh, which Telyn promised to spend with Esther in the cabin. Hosh, Caitlin, or Rayvn would visit Cressida on that evening. Telyn made her friends promise to also visit Cressida each fourth evening, since she had no faith that Esther would remember.

They brought Cressida as many questionnaires as they could gather, although Telyn stubbornly refused to fill out one for herself.

And yes, Telyn would make sure Esther ate, keep her woodpile well-stocked, the sheets washed, the wash-basin full, and the chamber pot emptied.

Cressida liked routines, and Telyn began to appreciate them as well. Routines helped keep life manageable, helped the twins pretend they had a modicum of control.

But Ice Climbing Day was no ordinary day.

As last year's champion, they would have let Telyn compete as a walk-on whether or not she bothered to register, which is why she'd hung her cloak over the ice ax, so as not to be reminded. She had no interest in climbing. None. At all.

How could she have fun, how could she compete, while her twin languished in prison—because of her?

All night before the competition, nervous ants crawled up and down Telyn's spine; she flopped and turned and awakened—if you can call it that when you hadn't properly fallen asleep—well before dawn.

She needed something to do, but the Sable Head wouldn't open until after the contests, and she had absolutely, positively no interest in those. In the morning, competitors would climb Defiance Falls. At noon, they'd have snowball wars on Mirror Lake. In the afternoon, there'd be frozen fowl bowling on Main. Ah, the snowball wars. The Dating Circle ladies had recruited townsfolk to cut through the ice on the lake last night, removing thick blocks and setting them in random patterns to make barriers for the combatants to hide behind. Better still, a thin sheet of ice reformed where they'd removed the blocks. With the glare of the sun and the heat of the action, the difference in thickness could easily be missed. If you stepped on the thin layers, you'd crash through into the icy water.

Great fun!

Strong swimmers stood ready to pull out the unfortunates, offer them spiced wine and dry robes, and a pass to Steamy Betty's. Some folks had been known to fall through on purpose.

Raz was one of those swimmers ready to rescue people. Raz, strong in so many ways. Raz, who'd left her dad to freeze to death for the price of a few skins.

Telyn closed her eyes and tried to smother her anger. Anger served nothing. *Dad had almost certainly broken his back. He wouldn't have made it. Nothing could've been done...*

I believe that. I do.

Telyn's head buzzed like she'd conked it on a low ceiling and disturbed a beehive between her ears. She dressed, went downstairs, and started scrubbing. Tums ogled as if Telyn had grown a pouch and carried a baby eehoo.

"What?" Telyn demanded, as she set stools on tabletops in preparation for the wet mop. "I've scrubbed before. This is not that unusual."

Tums moved higher up the wall and gave a fearful meowl.

"I'm not giving you a bath, if that's what you're worried about." *Though that isn't the worst idea.*

When the sunbeams stopped coming through the small windows at an angle and she judged the townsfolk must be at Mirror Lake, Telyn donned her layers and stepped outside.

Harlech was not entirely deserted. Smoke rose from several chimneys. Men hauled barrels into the Lucky H. But the lumber mill would be closed for sure.

Would they let the slaves out to view the competition? I'll bet not. Ouzeley and that cornic second wouldn't know mercy if it bit them in the undershorts. I'll go visit Cressida. That will make us both feel better.

She ran into Leutric Quid at the public fountain. Apparently, he was composing a new ballad, and he clanged giant cymbals when he'd successfully imagined a new line. She grinned and nodded a greeting at him, and the lyrics changed from:

> *The were-beast howls,*
> *Rending ivory talons*
> *Devours*
> *The predators cower...*

To:

> *The Brower girls flower*
> *ribbon candy towers*
> *Growls*
> *Single men turn cowards...*

That will amuse Cressida, she thought, rolling shoulders stiff from all the scrubbing.

Cressida didn't much like talking about her work at the lumber mill, and Telyn was tired of hearing about Kiss, Kindle and Flame. And not the good stuff, either—her sister had become infatuated with statistics; the names and drama behind the numbers mattered to her not at all. The personalities, the quirks, the breakup tears or the successful marriages—that sort of thing Telyn could understand. It even intrigued her a little. But the odds—who cares?

She tugged the wooden handle of the Prefecture—made of cedar, not chaos wood.

Locked.

Of course. Even the Prefecture would be closed today. Cressida and the other...slaves...would be well and truly alone.

Telyn checked the other doors just to be sure. All locked. If any cornic soldiers remained on guard, they stayed inside, out of sight.

At least the bodies of the traitors have been taken down and buried: Heath Robinson, Tyre Flint, Arvel Grummore. Telyn reminded herself of their names. *Human beings, not traitors. People.*

They probably were framed by Second Gajos.

I can visit them. That will keep me busy. I'll climb the scaffolding, visit my dad and the three humans who'd been falsely executed.

A course decided, she set off with purpose—but a set of unusual tracks stopped her cold.

Cat tracks. Big ones.

She squatted to get a closer look and brushed a bit of loose snow out of the print. Not a cat, she decided. The prints were longer, and the claws didn't retract. Could be a black bear, they were about the right size, but these tracks were deep and precise, almost as if the paws had melted the snow—as if each individual print had been cut out with a scalpel.

She didn't like this, not one bit.

The distance between these prints told her the animal, whatever it was, had been trotting, and yet no snow had been flipped out by the heel, nor had the edges blurred or caved in; they'd been cut in the snow the way a biscuit cutter carves dough.

These were recent and angled directly across her path. Telyn removed her glove and tapped the print; a sheet of ice covered the bottom.

The tracks crossed the road and dodged through the trees, keeping close to the road but out of sight.

Telyn wanted to run in the worst way—run to Mirror Lake where people gathered, beg for whatever protection a crowd would afford. Instead, she gathered her courage and followed. The weird, ice-prints skirted the necessaries and headed straight toward the shacks. There, the distance between the prints lessened as the creature slowed. There, the tracks systematically, deliberately circled each shack—like a hound seeking a scent.

Telyn didn't bother to follow the track's exact course. She returned to the road and sprinted toward her cabin. *Mother of Squirrels, let Esther be at the lake, let Esther be safe.*

Please, High Father, keep my mother safe.

Redbeard taught that tracking involved more than just following tracks; it required the hunter to put himself in the mind of the animal he followed. Indeed, many times Redbeard recounted that he had followed prey for miles and miles without seeing any sign at all because he taught himself how to think the way the prey thought. Then, long after most hunters would have abandoned the chase, he'd spot a bent leaf; some turned earth a bit darker than the stuff around it, indicating newly exposed moisture; a bit of scat; a squashed bug. And from this small sign, he could discern the prey's direction for many more miles or guess where it would hide or turn to attack.

Telyn knew what these remarkable prints meant, and who their intended quarry was.

The pass to the coast is snowed closed. No one can travel from Enshede to Harlech until spring. No one—except for Redbeard.

And Kiiptk's gnomes.

And the penumbra daemon.

The daemon.

Unable to pay a visit himself, Yona Unega must have sent the creature after the forehead piece.

Telyn closed her eyes and tried to remember the statuette's name. A-G-O-R-N-I-C, or A-F-O-R-N-T-A-K?

Why couldn't she remember it?

It was something like that, but neither word sounded right. She was close to remembering. The true name would pop into her mind in a day or two, when climbing, or walking, or when sitting in a luke-warm bath.

She was too nervous to recall it.

She made for the tree behind her shack where she'd first learned to climb, and, squatting on her heels, she stared at the tracks.

They made a beeline to her cabin door—and went inside.

Listening intently, Telyn could just make out human noises from downtown. No help from there. Even if she could get someone's attention by screaming, what could they do against the nebulous daemon?

No help from the Prefecture, either. Anyone who might have enough innate power to fight such a monster—a fist of cornic soldiers, for example—would be watching the competitions or staying warm in flacktown.

The sounds from her cabin...she couldn't be sure. Slippers on a wooden floor? The soft pad of bear-like paws? It could be Esther, or something else.

The sounds could be her imagination.

High Father, grant that my mother went to Mirror Lake, please.

One set of daemon tracks went in, and nothing came out. Too many human prints to know for sure if Esther was home or not. Redbeard might be able to read the signs, but Telyn couldn't be sure. Either it had already killed Esther and awaited Telyn, or Esther hadn't been home.

Telyn realized that she cared—deeply.

My fault or not, it doesn't matter. I do not want my mother to die.

No weapon I possess can harm the daemon. Even if I return to the Sable Head for my ice ax, if I stab it into the daemon, the iron will simply dissolve the way Dagger's knife dissolved.

If I bring anyone else into this, I'll be leading them to their doom.

Maybe the cornics can do something, but they'd have a ton of questions for me and my friends. Hosh and Caitlin would end up in chains —maybe Rayvn, too.

And some of the cornics would die.

This is my problem. I started all of this. I brought on Yona's wraith, and I've got to pay the price, now, before anyone else gets hurt.

Now, before I lose courage.
She rose from her haunches and marched to the door.
I'm sorry Cressida; I'm sorry Esther. I love you.
She flung it open.

CHAPTER FIFTY-TWO

In a million years, Telyn wouldn't have expected to have found the tableau before her: not the penumbra daemon ready to pounce, not the room in a shambles from a life-and-death struggle, not a mess of blood, nor a hole where the daemon had dissolved a corner of the bed where he'd absorbed, where he'd killed…

…No, Esther was fine, whistling as she lifted a kettle from its hook over the fire and poured boiling water into her favorite ceramic cup. She looked as if she hadn't slept in days—nothing unusual there. Her hair was like a packrat's nest, she had travelling bags under her eyes, and her breath could knock a bear into hibernation. Telyn could smell that breath from the door.

On Cressida's empty bed, looking as if he hadn't a care in the world, sat the mind wizard himself, Yona. His thin lips pressed together in a line, and his throat tentacles offered no clues, but Telyn could have sworn he looked pleased.

The penumbra daemon was nowhere in sight.

"There you are, girl," Esther said, sprinkling a few precious dried hibiscus flowers into the steaming water. "I told your guest he could find you at the Sable Head, but he insisted on waiting." She handed the cup to Yona with a stiff curtsy and an unpracticed, "If you please." Then she waited, hands tucked behind her back, for his approval.

Yona nodded a polite thanks.

Something looked off about the mind wizard. His edges blurred as if seen through a heavy fog. He wore a formal black suit with red trim and three-quarter sleeves, and a white, long-sleeved shirt underneath. No, the suit was more slate than black, and the trim was gold rather than red. The colors washed from one to another before Telyn's eyes.

On the off-chance she was dreaming—*High Father let this be a dream!*—Telyn pinched herself.

The pain felt real enough.

Then, as if the mind wizard could not see, Esther sidled up to Telyn, hooked her wrist, and yanked on it to draw her down to her height. "You ain't danced the forbiddens for him yet, have you?" she whispered.

Telyn looked with alarm at the cereb, realized that no matter what Esther thought of her, Esther would *never* believe that Telyn and the cereb—this flack—could have danced....

"He is *not* my boyfriend!"

Yona plunged his throat tentacles into the steaming mug and slurped loudly.

Esther's grip tightened on Telyn's wrist until it hurt. "He ain't said more than three words since he got here: Telyn; Brower; wait. I was beginning to think you'd hitched up with some kind of feeble-mind. His head ain't got stepped on, has it?" She paused to turn and smile at the cereb, as if he hadn't been listening to every word.

The cereb lifted the mug in a salute.

Esther must be seeing some kind of illusion. Telyn looked past Esther to meet Yona's eyes. "Should I be scared?"

The cereb's form wobbled a little, took a moment to compose itself, then spoke. "You can turn around and run out. I will not stop you." The movement of the mouth and the sound of the words didn't seem entirely in sync.

Esther's eyes narrowed, appraising the situation anew. "Just enjoy your infusion a minute. I have something to say to my daughter." She pulled Telyn outside. The door banged shut behind them.

"Is he mistreating you?" Esther asked, staring deep into Telyn's eyes.

Telyn wanted to tell Esther to run, run far away. Her pulse stammered, as uncertain as her brain. What could they do to get away from the mind wizard? Where could they go? Who would protect them?

How had he found her?

"You're scared of him, I can see that."

"No, Esther—Mother. I'm surprised, that's all. I thought he wouldn't come back until...until the Spring Sale. He's a trapper. Last I knew, he'd hiked into the Chaos Woods for the winter."

"You could have told me you were hitched."

"Uh, sorry. I wanted to be sure...ah...that he'd come back for me."

"I *knew* you didn't really go camping in the Chaos Woods," Esther scoffed with self-satisfaction. "That's what the ladies are saying—you, Hosh, Caitlin and that furry—and I told myself, not my Telyn. She's too lazy to pull a stunt like that. Why would she go in the cold? She'd have to walk; she'd have to set trap lines and build fires to stay warm. My Telyn's got no survival skills—besides the obvious ones of getting others to take care of her. She'd freeze to death in the first half hour. And that Hosh, he can barely hobble three yards without pausing for breath! So, I told myself, those kids are lying, but why? What kind of trouble has Telyn got them into?

"Where were you and your beau hiding out—the Lucky H? Or has Raz stooped that low—"

"We were not together, Esther."

"You dance a Promise Dance with him without it official-like on the Dating Chart, in front of witnesses and everything, he'll leave you so fast—"

"No, Esther. The Dating Circle doesn't want me. You never showed me the Promise Dance, and Quid is a little rusty." She yanked her wrist free. "Our guest is waiting. Esther—Mother. Let me talk to him alone. *Please*. Go...go to the Sable Head. I'll join you there in just a moment."

"I'm not going anywhere." Esther planted herself next to the door with her arms crossed. "I'm going to wait right here."

"I've got a tab at the Sable Head, Esther. You can help yourself, as much malt or angel water as you want, on me."

There, that should do it.

A longing came over Esther, and it broke Telyn's heart. Esther's lips parted slightly; the skin around her eyes softened. When she swallowed, Telyn knew she had her.

"It's not like I need it or anything."

Telyn shrugged.

"You're a wicked girl. You don't want me protecting your back, fine. It's your back; it's on you if it gets strapped or worse."

"Yes, Esth...Mother."

Esther straightened her vest. "It's cold, I should get my cloak." She reached for the door handle, and Telyn put her hand on top of Esther's.

"Just go, Esth...Mother. Raz got a special distillation, the best stone berries, fresh bags and everything. I'll be fine."

Esther's eyes darted toward the Sable Head and back. "I'll not be far when you come runnin'."

"Yes, Mother. Say, ah, say 'hi' to Raz for me."

As Esther strode quickly downhill, Telyn took a moment to compose herself. Her mother's concern and awkward attempt to defend her touched Telyn more than she would have imagined. If anything, it twisted the knot in her belly even further. But she didn't have time to process; more lives than her own depended on what happened here. Wiping as much of the fear from her posture and face as possible, she ducked into the small cabin alone.

Yona had not moved. "You do not look surprised to see me."

"But I am. The roads are still closed, and the tracks don't exactly match your boots."

The hand that held the infusion became blurry, and with the telltale sucking-mud-sound, the cup dissolved. A little liquid dribbled onto the floor.

"Ah yes, I am not really here. The roads are indeed blocked to caravans and foot traffic—and even to mind wizards—but that is no barrier to my penumbra daemon. The daemon has shaped itself to look bipedal, and I am able to offer suggestions across long distances through it with the Ever-Guise. As your mind tries to make sense of what it is seeing, it fills in the gaps.

"Your mother, for example, supplied the *boyfriend* explanation on her own." He wiggled his tentacles. "The idea that a mind wizard came calling on Telyn was too much for her; she decided to see a trapper with a beard instead of these handsome appendages."

"Why are you telling me this?"

"Bragging. I see it is wasted on you," he replied matter-of-factly, then waved a hand in dismissal. One of his hands passed disturbingly close to Telyn's face, and she flinched.

"Telyn Brower, we have a mutual problem."

"I, ah" —She took a half-step back—"what would that be?"

"Ms. Brower, I have learned much of what you have been doing since the auction in the Sable Head. Do not try to deny it. I can appreciate a good lie—reward it, even, if it amuses me. But treat me as a fool —" A hand, really the daemon's tentacle, sliced Esther's spinning wheel neatly in two. The pieces clattered to the floor; the cut wood smelled of varnish and the daemon's telltale burnt breadcrumbs. "I have spent the past several hours gathering information using my own particular form of persuasion, and I can surmise much by the changes that have befallen your fair village. You have been very active this past year, very active indeed, along with your friends Hosh Gamage and Caitlin Nest. Your twin sister Cressida, unfortunately, got caught in the middle, didn't she?"

"I don't have it," Telyn blurted, adding, "I don't have it anymore."

"No, unfortunately, or this could end here." His expression, albeit indistinct, made it clear he knew as much about the forehead's whereabouts as she did.

He doesn't know about Rayvn; he didn't mention her by name. He doesn't know everything.

"Can't you just" —Telyn waved her hand vaguely—"make Second Gajos do what you want the way you did with my, ah, with Esther?"

"I didn't make your mother do anything. She sees what she wants to see and acts accordingly. But the cornic second is a different story. Cornics are notoriously resistant to magic and mental persuasion in particular. That is why they are used the world over as bodyguards and mercenaries. Their physical prowess is only a secondary, albeit useful, species trait. No, we need another way into the Prefecture."

"If you can't get the forehead piece with all your power and resources, I certainly don't have any way to do it. It's not like before, when Minister Svemas was around. Second Gajos has guards at all the entrances, and they're using Taffy to check for magic."

"Taffy?"

"The feathered hind."

"Ah, that does complicate things. Should I just kill you now?" As Telyn stammered, the daemon-cereb continued. "I think you are quite a resourceful girl. Over the years, I have found it useful to cultivate relationships with resourceful people."

"Even humans?" Her voice came in a dry, fearful rasp. She wanted to swallow, but she had no saliva left.

The daemon-cereb rose and began poking around the house, turning over stacks of fabric, opening drawers. Apparently, the daemon could control its powers of absorption.

"Especially useful are those who move without being seen: humans, servants, eunuchs, females, slaves. Telyn Brower, you have access to the Prefecture to visit your sister. I need you to find out where the Ever-Guise fragment is being held. I need you to determine any weaknesses in the Prefecture's defenses, the routines of its inhabitants, who is susceptible to bribery and who is honest, what other thaumas frequent the place, and what areas are off limits even to them. I need you to draw me a map of the interior. When the time is right, you will get me inside."

This reminded her disturbingly of how Minister Svemas had wanted to use her. Was this how the powerful used the weak? Was this normal?

The last thing Telyn wanted to do was to become Yona's spy, but it crossed her mind that she had some of this information already; she knew at least one cornic functionary who took bribes. She could keep herself alive by feeding information to him little by little.

If only she could remember the activation word of the daemon, she might have power the cereb wouldn't expect; she might be able to turn him off.

If Minister Svemas were still alive, she might consider going to him, confessing everything, and begging for mercy. But with Second Gajos in charge? No way. She trusted him less than Tabbard.

"What about my mother? You will leave her alone?"

"Ah yes, Ether has access too. Thank you for reminding me that I don't really need you. But your mother is a poor backup plan, Telyn Brower. Her diet of angel water and malt makes her unreliable."

That sounded right. A poor backup plan, but a valuable hostage. "And if I help you, you will free Cressida?"

"If you manage to retrieve the missing piece for me before I take things into my own appendages, I will free your sister. It is a small matter to have an intermediary purchase her and set her free. If you merely *help* me with information, and I have to retrieve the piece myself, I will allow you to live for as long as you are useful to me."

"Promise me you will free Cressida, no matter what you do to me."

"We will establish a permanent relationship which will be far more valuable to you in the long run than the bond price for your sister..." He let that hang.

"All I care about is setting Cressida free."

"We both know that is a lie. Many people you care about: your mother, the bartender, Hosh, Caitlin, the witch Rayvn, each one just a thread from disaster. And yes, your sister, already available for purchase. So easy to make Cressida my personal property where I can do with her what I like: set her free, lease her to the galleys...or the brothels...all within the boundary of the law. Telyn Brower, see that you find a way to retrieve the missing piece of the Ever-Guise for me."

The apparition dissolved back into the shape of the penumbra daemon, the black-within-black bear that sucked half the light from the room. A tentacle reached out, lifted the latch, and pushed the door open.

Telyn followed to the threshold to see in which direction the daemon headed and started upon seeing Esther leaning against the side of the house—eavesdropping, of course. She slurped from a fresh bag of angel water, her expression puzzled.

"You didn't tell me your boyfriend had a dog."

How in the world could she answer that? How in the world could she keep her mother out of this? *Sarcasm, that might help. It usually helps keep people distant.* She suddenly recalled Quid's lyrics.

"He doesn't have a dog, Esther. My boyfriend is a werewolf," she quipped. "Do you like him?"

CHAPTER FIFTY-THREE

Telyn stayed long enough to believe that Esther had only heard the final bits of the conversation and didn't know much beyond the fact that Telyn's "boyfriend" was bad news. She gave Telyn the "All men are evil and will leave you to die cold and alone" lecture and the "Save the forbidden dance for the man you intend to marry—unless you intend to end up cold and alone." These not only seemed like complete contradictions, but they embarrassed Telyn to no end and prompted her to go straight to Hosh and tell him what had happened.

"That's not the worst of it." Hosh paced from one end of his room to the other, picking up random objects (split-shoe molds, scissors, a cloth measuring tape..) and setting them down absently.

Telyn's eyes widened, trying to imagine what could be worse than the cereb nominating her as his personal informant. She took a swig of salmonberry juice before she dared ask.

"Caitlin didn't show up for Preserving and Pickling."

"Ah, that's the worst of it?"

"Not that, but the *why* of it."

"Well? I'm dying here."

"Joram just gave Tristam Harries the four-heart promise ribbon just this morning."

"Wha—?" Telyn started so hard, she spilled half her juice on the floor. She could only imagine Caitlin's fury—and wondered how much of it would be directed at her for taking them into the Chaos Woods right when Tristam was making her move. "But the Dating Chart didn't even have Joram and Tristam in the same circle! There's, like, a zero chance of that happening. Mother of Squirrels, this puts Joram squarely in the enemy camp."

"Was there ever any doubt?"

"Yes, actually, there was. Joram wasn't the same as Tabbard. He may have been helping Caitlin keep the...ah...the attack behind the Ash to a minimum."

He may *have been. Joram had certainly convinced Caitlin that keeping us out of the fight would reduce the beating Tabbard inflicted on Hosh.*

In years past, Telyn been attracted to Joram in a general, from-a-distance sort of way. He'd said some kind things, and well, who wouldn't find Joram attractive? If things had turned out differently, and Caitlin hadn't put the moves on him, and a whole lot of other 'ifs,' Telyn might have danced with him herself.

"Caitlin must be off somewhere crying, or plotting revenge. Training some chinchillas to rip Joram's head off—or Tristam's."

"Really? They can do that?" Hosh asked excitedly.

"We need to find her and talk her down."

"No good. I already looked. She's gone underground."

Telyn had her happy places: Dragon Tower or the top of a tree. Hosh liked his room, where he would pick up random objects and stare at them as if he'd never seen them before. Rayvn made complicated doilies out of spider silk.

Caitlin?

"Steam bath," Telyn said, confidently. "We need to gather a few things, then we'll get Rayvn. She's part of this now. We have an intervention to make."

Black ice covered the stoop in front of Steamy Betty's virtually all winter, as the warm air from inside melted the layer covering the doormat whenever the door opened, and the cold air from outside froze it again as soon as the door closed. As such, it was the only building in Harlech that had handrails on the front porch.

Hosh hung on the rail for dear life and inched his way to the door. The door handle was carved to resemble a troll, and he sighed with relief as his hand closed over it. Telyn and Rayvn pushed off from the porch's edge and glided to join him, arms over each other's shoulders to stay upright.

As the door opened, a puff of humid air blew in their faces and painted the stoop with a fresh coat of water. The smell of cedar incense greeted them, as did Betty, the proprietor. About as wide as the door, with flaming red hair and welcoming smile, Betty Yarwood was known throughout Harlech as the most discreet woman ever born. Her reputation made her very popular among the men and persona non grata among the Dating Circle—not that a few of the women didn't appreciate discretion also, but officially, they disapproved.

"Would that be a public or a private," Betty asked, appraising the unlikely threesome. "Or will the pattern girl be wanting a private room?"

Rayvn put an arm around Telyn and her tail around Hosh. "We're all together."

She's really gotten flagrant about displaying her tail; she wore a split skirt for that very purpose!

Betty's head tilted. Hosh's face could make a radish look pale.

"Ah, what she means" —Telyn stifled a laugh—"is we are looking for someone who may have gotten lost here. She's probably a prune by now. We're her friends."

Betty maintained her wide, disinterested smile. "That would be the public room." Betty waved off Hosh's money when he offered it. "You're welcome to go in. She's been scaring off all the customers with her blubbering and carrying on. She's normally such a cheery soul. Do you know what's the matter?"

Telyn shrugged, not wanting to share their business, but Rayvn said, "It's the Dating Chart."

At that, Betty lost her smile and hawked a most un-ladylike loogie through the narrow gap between Telyn and Hosh. It landed on the stoop and froze immediately. "The world is turned inside out. We should bet on ice climbing and pugilism and brakdaw fights, that which is outward. The inner life—love, hate, grief, prejudice—that should be as private as hemorrhoids.

"Well, come in and close the door, unless you intend to bring a cord of wood with you. You're letting out all the heat." She turned her wide back on them. "Leave your clothes in the changing room. For an egg, I'll get them washed while you wait."

"We're to go in naked?" Telyn asked in dismay.

Betty laughed. "In the private rooms, you do what you want. In the public, you wrap yourself. We can't have your bottoms getting too friendly with the benches, now, can we? Don't worry, we wash the towels every season." She eyed Rayvn's thick fur and long tail, now sticking rigidly upward and twitching at the end. "You'll have to figure it out."

They entered separate dressing rooms. Telyn was beginning to think her luck had turned. Her first time in Steamy Betty's—comped? She half hoped Caitlin would be a long time in finding consolation and then berated herself for the thought.

She found two piles in the dressing room, one of robes and one of towels. She took a voluminous robe, turned her back to Rayvn and, with only a little hesitation, and began shedding her clothes. These she folded and placed in one of the empty cubbies. Stripping off hadn't seemed like a big deal at the golden pond, but here in her hometown, inside a public space...

Telyn didn't want the pattern girl to see how uncomfortable it made her. Rayvn didn't seem to have any trouble with it; she was purring! Well, with all her fur, she didn't reveal as much as Telyn would.

"Ready," Rayvn bubbled.

Glancing over her shoulder, Telyn started. "Put on a robe! You don't want—I mean—Hosh!"

The pattern girl had simply fastened a towel around her waist. She looked at her naked breasts curiously. "Are they so different from yours?"

"No! I mean… They're the same—apart from the obvious. The fur, I mean. There's fur."

Rayvn's luxurious white, gray and brown fur pretty much concealed everything…but not really.

Not exactly.

"You can't do that to Hosh."

Rayvn raised one eyebrow—complete with four-inch whiskers. "You don't like the sound of my purr?"

"No! I mean, yes. Don't you expose yourself to Hosh, I mean. It isn't fair. Put on a robe. Or tuck the towel under your arms and over your breasts, like this. It'll make a sort of dress." A very short dress.

What a zany town this is, Telyn thought, *that didn't want girls to show their ankles, and then expected you to prance around nude in the steam bath.* Telyn huffed.

Rayvn fastened her towel higher. It seemed to shape itself around her contours, tightening around the waist and flaring over the hips.

Rayvn winked. No question about it; she'd enhanced the shape with magic.

Telyn's robe, on the other hand, hung off her like a rain-soaked drapery yet barely covered what needed to be covered. Another drawback to being *Too-tall*.

She grabbed a towel and the care package she'd brought for Caitlin, and the two stepped back into the corridor.

Hosh awaited, towel around his waist, looking anywhere but directly at them. His chest glistened. Telyn glared sideways at him as they moved to the public room, but Hosh pretended not to notice.

He doesn't look so bad; a lot more muscular than I thought. If he trained in pugilism, he might defend himself pretty well. What I wouldn't give to see Hosh give Tabbard a drubbing.

They entered the public room and stepped into a wall of heat and humidity. A master carpenter must have designed it, for the room had been shaped into a butterbean-shape; there were no angles anywhere, except where walls met floor. Even the doors were curved. Telyn found it amazing that the wood retained its shape with all the humidity and heat.

A massive stove on one side heated a flat tub of water. Hosh drew a ladle from the tub and poured it into a small hole in the stove. Steam billowed out.

Three ascending rows of curved benches rose against the walls. The lower benches would be the cooler; those closer to the ceiling hotter.

Caitlin lay on the top row, face-down and cradling her head in her hands. She peeked to see who had arrived.

"Go. Away."

Then she started to sob loudly. Deliberately loudly—or so it seemed—to drive everyone out.

They each found their places: Hosh on the bottom, coolest level, Telyn on the bench just below Caitlin, and Rayvn at Caitlin's feet. Telyn's hair plastered to her shoulders and neck. Water droplets wept from Rayvn's whiskers.

"Let me see your fingers," Telyn said, taking Caitlin's hand. "Very prune-like, nearing critical."

Caitlin turned her head toward Telyn and scowled. "I said, go away."

Telyn removed a bladder from the care package.

"Drink something. You need it." Telyn dribbled a few drops onto Caitlin's lips, and Caitlin's tongue flicked out.

She frowned. "This is malt!"

"Sable Head malt, which makes it half water. Drink."

Rising to her elbows, Caitlin upended the bladder and drank it flat.

"The odds were fifteen to one," Caitlin said, wiping her mouth on her forearm.

"Affairs of the heart, who can discern their pattern?" Rayvn said. "It is folly to try to understand."

They all nodded sagely.

What an odd thing for Rayvn to say, Telyn thought, nodding with the rest. *Here she was, trying to figure out human love, and yet she thinks it is impossible to figure out. Unless she said that just to make Caitlin feel better. Or maybe she's thinking about her mom and dad.*

"He was a jerk anyway," Hosh said. "I always knew—"

"Don't. Just don't," Caitlin said.

"I won't. Sorry."

They sat in silence for a long time.

"Thanks for coming."

"Sure."

"I have to pee."

Nobody moved. The heat stole their ambition. After a time, Hosh dipped water from the metal pan and poured it into the stove's hole. Steam gushed forth to caress them.

Caitlin sat the rest of the way up.

"I really have to pee."

"Why don't you?"

"Have you seen the floor in the necessary?"

Telyn rummaged around in her care package and produced a pair of clogs with a "Ta-da!" She made a face. "I've heard about this place. We can all share."

They waited for Caitlin to return from the necessary—chamber pots only—before beginning the official meeting. Telyn began by telling the others about her encounter with the daemon-cereb.

Even through its steam-induced pinkish glow, Caitlin's face paled as Telyn recounted the story. "Mother of Squirrels, Tey, a cereb *and* a daemon? What're we gonna do?"

"The prudent thing is to give him what he wants," Rayvn suggested.

"Do you trust him? Will he buy Cressida's freedom if you help him get the forehead piece?" Caitlin asked. "This all started when his penumbra daemon betrayed the thief and the trogo."

"No, of course I don't trust him."

"Nor can we fight him," Rayvn said. "The penumbra daemon will simply absorb any material I use to try to bind him. This is not a simple pack of rakasuras."

Simple pack of rakasuras. Telyn smiled to herself. *How we've changed.*

"We need to stall him." Hosh smacked a fist into his free palm.

"Stall him? What good will that do?" Caitlin cried. "If the passes open, Yona himself will come to Harlech. Then he can make us do whatever he wants just by thinking about it. Is that what you want— to be a mind wizard's puppet?"

"Shh!" Telyn warned. Voices came from the hallway, along with the clomp-clomping of clogs on the wooden floor. She patted Caitlin's shin, which hung near her ear. "Start blubbering. Put some snot into it!"

When three curious women poked their heads in, Caitlin let out a convincing wail, Hosh started fake-crying, and all four friends huddled in a shoulder-shaking hug, as if unaware anyone stood in the doorway looking in. The women scuttled further on.

"We don't have much time," Telyn said, once the intruders had left. She quickly explained to Caitlin how they had entered for free. "Sooner or later, Betty'll make you weep outside."

Caitlin wiped her nose with the back of her hand. "I wasn't weeping for that jerk. Not really."

"Okay, okay." Telyn turned to the rest of the group. "Who has another idea?"

From the care package, Rayvn removed the two pieces of chrysalis shell she'd practiced on. "This is the best I could do. I can bind the pieces, but I cannot erase the cracks entirely." A red line ran between the fused halves. Every now and then, vermilion light transversed the zig-zag crack.

"Imagine having the whole thing in a dark room at night," Hosh said. "It would be like having a permanent fireworks display in your bedroom. Betty could charge a fortune if she had the shell in here."

"It *is* beautiful and unique and magic," Rayvn agreed.

"So...we can sell it at the Spring Sale and use the money toward the bond price of my sister." Telyn looked at each of her friends in turn, trying to read their faces. "You all worked just as hard as me getting it." She swallowed. "It would be okay if you...if you wanted your share. I wouldn't be mad. I can come up with the money some other way."

Hosh elbowed Telyn sharply, and Caitlin rolled her eyes.

"We all agreed before going into the Chaos Woods," Rayvn said, looking more confused than usual, "the reward money is for Cressida's bond price, right?"

"Sorry," Telyn said. "I had to make the offer. I've done everything else wrong so far."

"Everyone betraying everyone..." Hosh's eyes grew wide. "It's like the Ever-Guise is cursed."

"People will do anything for money, power, or fame—and the mask offers all three."

"So don't free your sister," Hosh suggested, shifting his shoulders back and forth. "She broke the Rule, after all."

"*We* broke the Rules," Telyn mumbled, fighting the dreamlike ease that threatened to dull her senses like a wet blanket. "All three of us. We all deserve to be slaves."

"Cressida took responsibility for it; let her live the life of slavery," Hosh continued. "It's her choice—for the good of the Empire."

Telyn couldn't believe what she was hearing. "Do you really mean that?"

"She got caught. Let her pay the price."

"Hosh is right." Caitlin said dryly as she lay back down on the bench and sighed contentedly. "Freedom is overrated."

"It's not for everyone," Rayvn agreed, beginning to purr. "Humans don't do well without a leash."

Telyn nodded, appeased, savoring the heat and steam. "Certain people are better off managed. For the good of the Empire."

After an awkward pause, Hosh said, "Caitlin, I'll dance you the promise dance—if you don't want to be free."

Caitlin closed her eyes. Glistening sweat slid from her jawline down her throat. Telyn had to admit, even with swollen, bloodshot eyes and a red, just-been-sobbing nose, the girl was beautiful. No wonder Hosh had a crush on her.

Why in the world Joram would have chosen Tristam over Cait—

Caitlin's eyes popped open. "Why did we say that?"

They blinked around at each other, at the steam-filled room, at the bubbling water atop the stove. Red, worm-like lights zipped along the crack between the chrysalis pieces in Rayvn's hands.

"Second Gajos is using the mask," Telyn surmised. "Right now, at this moment. What time is it?"

"About an hour since we got here," Rayvn said.

Telyn considered everything she had seen of late: Cressida resigned to her fate; Mrs. Gamage no longer visiting the prison nor baking freedom pasties; Raz talking about the cost advantage the Lucky H had from using slaves, and how many birds he had to give Telyn—not that he'd ever ask her to leave or nothin'; even Caitlin, good-ol' animal-loving Caitlin, mentioning the feathered hind might be better off in the safety of the Prefecture's stables than running free.

"He's using the mask to weaken our resistance to slavery. And you know who'll profit most from that?"

"Ouzeley," Hosh growled. "They're in league!"

"If Harlech's resistance to slavery dissolves, all kinds of people will profit," Rayvn said, "at least in the short term."

"Short term?"

"In the long term, slave-based economies tend to perform poorer than free societies, which have to develop efficiencies to make up for the price of labor."

"Whatever," Telyn said.

"She means," Caitlin explained, "that the rich will be okay, but for everyone else, things will stink, and common commoners will suffer even more."

"Oh, duh. Isn't that always the way?"

Rayvn cocked her head quizzically.

"The cereb will want to know this," Telyn added. "Cornics are creatures of habit, a military society organized around timetables and marches and drills. I'd be willing to bet Second Gajos uses the mask at the same time every day. This could be valuable information. Guys, keep track of whenever you feel, like, overly comfortable with slavery, or when you think or say things you wouldn't have a few weeks ago. Mark down the time for me. We'll develop a schedule—"

The first mistake of a dead general, according to Aled the Wise, is to underestimate his enemies. The second? Trusting the untrustworthy.

They considered this plan of action.

Hosh asked, "Are you actually going to help the mind wizard get the mask?"

"We can't let the second keep it. He would make all of us slaves before the second winter."

"You didn't answer the question."

"I am wondering if it's even ethical to keep," Telyn said, rolling the hem of her towel between her fingers. "Everything we've done has turned sour as vinegar. What if—what if we're meant to destroy it?"

"Aled the Wise said, 'If you don't have the luxury to consider universal goodness, consider being kind to a stranger,'" Rayvn quoted. To Hosh's evident confusion, she added, "We must think of Cressida as the stranger, and let the rest of the patterns work themselves out."

"Not everything went sour," Caitlin said. "They changed the brakdaw fight to a game of tag, and that's a lot more dangerous for the people than the brakdaw. I say the mask is a tool. It can be used for good or ill."

They hesitated. Hosh had time to add another scoop of water to the stove.

"So...are we really doing this?" Caitlin asked.

"I talked to Redbeard," Telyn said. "The chrysalis shell will fetch a good price. He himself offered a hundred hurons, which means it's worth about triple that to the right buyer. It's a good price; any trapper would be proud to have recovered it."

"Not enough to free your sister," Hosh said.

"Not enough," Telyn agreed. "If we want to free her—"

"We want to!" Caitlin cried. "Don't let the mask convince you otherwise."

"—we will need to steal the forehead piece and sell it."

"Or break Cressida free," said Rayvn.

"Or break her free."

"And live forever in the Chaos Woods with the rakasuras, rumor trees, feathered hinds..."

"A short life, but glorious!" Hosh quoted from the *Lynette Epic*.

"Either way, we need to learn as much about Second Gajos's habits and the Prefecture's defenses as we can. And we need to find the fence that Dagger wanted to sell the forehead piece to. Rayvn, we'll need your mom's sketchbook to see if he appeared on the walls of the Sable Head. That's the only way I can figure to identify him without exposing us too much. It's a long shot, but it's the best we've got."

CHAPTER FIFTY-FOUR

Arriving at the de Galatis' home, Rayvn and Telyn removed their shoes. Rayvn led the way into the foyer then stopped cold. And no wonder—her mom blocked the way with arms crossed, hackles raised, and ears flattened. Mrs. de Galati wore a loose, baby-blue dressing gown held shut with a wide sash. It should have looked like a rich person's loungewear, but on her, it looked more like combat garb.

The older witch ignored Rayvn completely.

"Telyn Brower, months have passed, and Rayvn remains at your side."

Telyn started to reply but found her jaw unable to move, for the pattern witch had crossed the space and seized her chin between thumb and finger. "Curious. Very curious."

"Grrfuf?" Telyn managed.

"You wish to involve my daughter in a crime, no? 'Lawbreaker' is written all over your face."

Telyn jerked her head back and, thankfully, the thauma let her go. She resisted the urge to rub the hurt away, though she did work her jaw a few times. She'd come to ask Mrs. de Galati for her sketchpad, but the meeting had started on the wrong foot—or paw.

Rayvn licked the side of her hand and used the saliva to wipe down the fur behind her ears. This seemed to irritate her mother. "She is only guessing. Mother takes the worst of our nature, multiplies it by ten, then formulates her hypotheses."

The pattern witch turned and padded down the hall, throwing a "Come" over her shoulder. Unlike human feet, hers seemed to hinge in the middle; her heels never touched the floor.

They arrived at a turn in the hallway, but instead of following it, the pattern witch crooked a finger, and the fabric ahead split down the middle.

"The inner sanctum," Rayvn whispered as they entered a circular room.

The pattern witch sat on a pile of embroidered cushions and gestured for Telyn to do the same.

Rayvn remained standing.

"As a child in the city of Galati, Rayvn 'befriended' some street urchins. She thought they were going to show her the turtle they had caught. They coaxed her into approaching a wooden crate, and convinced her to peer inside, closer and closer still. As my daughter leaned over, they flipped her inside the crate, nailed the lid closed, and carried her halfway to the slave market before I caught them."

Telyn tried to picture the scene and wondered why Mrs. de Galati had chosen to tell that particular story. "But couldn't Rayvn have strangled them with their shirts or something? She...ah...handled herself against rakasuras."

Mrs. de Galati's whiskers wiggled in what might have been irritation—or a smile. It was hard to tell. "It is difficult to use pattern magic when you cannot see the pattern, and more difficult still through the walls of a chaos wood crate. Also, my daughter is so naive, she probably thought the children were taking her to a better place from which to see the turtle."

Rayvn sighed, looking embarrassed. "Mother's hypotheses are usually correct."

"And?"

"And mine wrong."

The pattern witch stared at Rayvn for a long moment. "I would speak to Telyn a moment, daughter. Be useful and wait in your room. I'll judge whether your friend is capable of extracting honey without disturbing the bees. From the looks of things" —She sniffed—"I very much doubt it."

After Rayvn left, and the fabric wall wove itself back together, Telyn looked anywhere rather than the pattern witch's geode-sharp eyes. The inner sanctum was...a lot. Over-decorated to Telyn's mind, enough to give a simple girl a headache, with gold and purple, silver and pink everywhere. And the pillows! Pillows of every size and shape —flat, puffy, square, cylindrical and round, with and without tassels, with and without fringes—covered every surface, all embroidered with elaborate animals, plants, beasts of all kinds. There were even images Telyn had only heard about, like the palm trees with hammocks and swinging monkeys on a square pillow by her foot. If Esther had worked for three weeks straight, she couldn't have sewn a hundredth part of the designs.

Embroidered centipedes populated the pillow under Mrs. de Galati's right hand, and every time her fingers tapped, they shifted a little, the silver threads lifting and re-tying in new places.

"So, you took my Rayvn on an adventure, yes? Nearly got yourselves killed from frostbite and rakasura attacks."

"Actually" —Telyn swallowed past the dry lump in her throat— "she insisted on coming."

"You did not want her?"

Did one of the thread-ipedes actually migrate from one pillow to another, to a pillow closer to Telyn? She was sure of it.

"Tell me, daughter of Dorian and Esther Brower, what makes you different?"

"Er..." Telyn crossed and uncrossed her legs under her long skirt. "I get in trouble. A lot."

"My daughter has never found friends here in Harlech. The cornics despise us because of our connection to ghosts. The humans despise us because of our connection with cornics."

"*Despise* is sort of a strong word," Telyn said.

"Fear, then." The pattern witch flicked her hand dismissively. "Cornics fear that which they do not understand—ghosts—and humans fear that which suppresses and enslaves them—flacks." She emphasized that derogatory word. "You, Telyn Brower, you are thinking about stealing the mask."

"What? No. It was just a passing thought."

"Your passing thoughts appear on your face as clearly as your triangular nose."

Telyn's left hand reached to fondle her nose before she'd even thought about it. No question about it: this woman *did* make her as nervous as the penumbra daemon.

"Let us play prophet's wheel." Without awaiting a reply, Mrs. de Galati produced a circular weaving frame holding layers of colored thread, so many and so tight that the threads formed a tambourine-like surface. "The temple where I was born—the breeding temple in Galati—raises a lot of money from these games. What makes the Galati prophet's wheels unique is that each wheel is as individual as one pattern witch from another."

Telyn brushed her fingertips over the surface as the wheel was extended to her. Taut as harp strings, the nearly-invisible threads produced musical notes.

"Does that mean each witch can only make one?"

"Oh no, they are influenced by our experience but do not represent its entirety. That would take a weaving as large as our lives. If you create a game, Miss Brower—a climbing game, for example—it would also be influenced by your experiences, hmm?"

Telyn took the tiny, hooked knife Mrs. de Galati handed to her.

"The goal is to predict the images hidden in the wheel. Every thread you cut, every choice you make, holds the potential to create a different, recognizable image. The man smoking a pipe becomes a woman blowing a kiss; the standing bear becomes an eehoo climbing a tree."

Yes, among the threads, Telyn could almost discern the things the witch described. Almost, but not exactly. She was sure Mrs. de Galati wouldn't reveal the hidden patterns so easily.

"As one tries to create an image, the other tries to destroy that and replace it with one of her own. Cutting from the edge, I will demonstrate." As Mrs. de Galati's knife passed around the edge of the wheel, each individual thread glowed. When she hooked a thread and sliced, the little string rang pleasingly. "The nice thing about being a pattern witch is that after the game, I can reset it. If everyone could do that, it wouldn't make much of a fundraiser."

Thus, the game began, and Mrs. de Galati passed the wheel back and forth with Telyn. After about ten cuts each, neither player had made discernible progress. Telyn squinted at the pattern before her and predicted, "A tree."

The trunk showed plainly, along with a knot. All she had to do was reveal the branches.

The pattern witch took one glance at the wheel and countered. "A face, with a particularly bulbous nose."

Her tongue between her teeth, Telyn cut. The pattern witch countered. Three cuts later, the almost-tree dissolved into the face.

"The point goes to me," the pattern witch said.

They continued, and frustration creased Telyn's brow. This sort of game irritated her like a mattress infected with fleas—especially when the other player was a ringer, if not an outright cheat.

The witch said, "A ship at sea, full sails." Telyn didn't see anything like that, but had no doubt it would appear momentarily. Mrs. de Galati looked up at her. "You do not look happy?"

Telyn struggled to smooth the frown from her lips as she accepted the wheel back from the witch. "You know this wheel so well. Did you make it?"

"Is it not for us to walk in patterns made by others?"

Telyn cut two strings by mistake.

"You lose your next turn. A tall ship."

Telyn exhaled and handed the wheel back to Mrs. de Galati. "You didn't answer me."

Again, that quirking to the pattern witch's whiskers.

The ship appeared, three masts with triangular sails and a mermaid carved into the prow. "Point number two. The images will become simpler as threads disappear."

Pressure built in Telyn's breast. She didn't like to be made fun of, and it definitely felt like Mrs. de Galati was making fun of her. If they'd been out ice climbing, Telyn could show her a thing or two.

The pattern witch probably wouldn't make it past the first overhang before she'd be begging to be let down by rope.

Aled's sacred rump, this isn't helping my sister go free. Mrs. de Galati can take me or leave me as far as I care, just as long as she helps me identify Dagger's fence.

"In professional games, a timer keeps the players from stalling too long, Miss Brower."

"I'm thinking," Telyn growled, but squint as she might, she couldn't see any pattern to create from the sailing ship other than a ship with holes.

"Rayvn, you can stop spying."

Once again, the wall behind Telyn split down the middle. Holding a tray with both hands, her tail wrapped around one ankle, Rayvn looked rather abashed. She had changed into a pink dressing gown with a lilac sash.

Telyn took the opportunity to stab her hooked knife through the Prophet's Wheel and run it in a circle. *I'm tired of this stupid game, and I'm tired of people judging me.*

She intended to carve all the threads at once, end this stupid game for good, but it didn't work out that way. With a cacophony of high-pitched twangs, the hooked knife twisted, and the whole thing sprang apart.

"Just thought that you two might like a spot—" Rayvn cut off in mid-sentence.

"A spot of what, daughter? Did you interrupt just—" Then Mrs. de Galati did a double-take at the Prophet's Wheel. "You have lost the next—one, two, three, four...two hundred and ninety-three turns, Telyn Brower." Then she looked up, and those geode eyes met Telyn's with something like respect. "And you have created something entirely new."

The surface had divided into five distinct segments. In the middle was an iridescent, unblinking eye, very reminiscent of the empty setting in the middle of the Ever-Guise's forehead.

"Sorry, I just, ah, I have more important things to do. I need to save my sister." Telyn didn't like that eye staring at her from the prophet's wheel at all. She wiped her suddenly sweaty hands on her skirts.

The pattern witch held out her hand, and Telyn put the hooked knife into it, handle first. "Set the tray down, Rayvn. You look ridiculous. If you want to spy on us, spy and be done with it."

"I was spying the normal way!" Rayvn replied indignantly. "Through the hole in the ceiling."

"Don't dignify her by looking up," Mrs. de Galati said flatly. "There is no hole in the ceiling."

But Telyn looked anyway. She didn't see any hole—but then again, it would have been hidden by the hanging gauze.

Telyn worked her mouth silently, trying to decide how much to tell Mrs. de Galati, then finally decided she'd better tell most everything. She reasoned that Rayvn had become involved deeply enough that the pattern witch wouldn't go running to the cornics. Rayvn wouldn't be sold off as a slave just for possessing magic, but she'd be in trouble, nonetheless.

"I want the illustrations," Telyn said. "The ones you sketched inside the Sable Head."

"The memories of the ghost?"

Telyn nodded.

"Earlier, you admitted you wanted to commit a crime."

"Not true." Telyn did not remember admitting to anything. "I want to recover something that belongs to me." Her tone held more vehemence than she'd intended. She felt hugely possessive remembering the allure of the forehead piece, how powerful she'd felt wielding it, how natural it felt melded onto her own forehead.

She liked that feeling, liked it very much, and feared it. That must be how Esther felt about alcohol before she'd surrendered herself to it entirely.

Mrs. de Galati watched the emotions flit across Telyn's face.

Telyn added more quietly, "I want to recover something that used to belong to me...to free my sister."

"Why the illustrations?"

"I need to..." Telyn sighed, knowing how absurdly improbable this must sound. "The thief, the dead person at the Sable Head, intended to sell a magical artifact to someone during the Spring Sale. I need to find out who the buyer is so I can make contact with him."

"You intend to steal the mask from Second Gajos and sell it to this buyer."

Telyn gasped.

Rayvn cringed at Telyn's reaction. "Mother's only guessing."

Mrs. de Galati gestured for Telyn to continue.

"The ghost was—I think—a thief. He stole something valuable, a mask called the Ever-Guise, like you said, and he sold it in an auction at the Sable Head. I saw what happened; I saw him get murdered. The thief sold the Ever-Guise to a mind wizard named Yona, but he didn't sell all of it. One part he hid in his boot."

And Telyn told the whole story, just as she had told Caitlin and Hosh, and, she realized, no one else. She'd never told Cressida the whole story, nor had she told Rayvn, despite the fact that the pattern girl had saved her at the bridge, followed her into the Chaos Woods, fought rakasuras and frostbite, and helped drag Taffy all over creation.

I make a lousy friend. By rights, I should be completely alone. What do these people see in me? Hosh, Rayvn, Caitlin...Cressida? They'd be better off without me.

Aled's rump, Cressida found that out in a big way.

They'd be better off without me.

Everyone would.

Esther was right to kick me out.

Her thoughts grew drowsy. Her shoulders slumped; she felt like nodding off.

Rayvn looked around vaguely. "The mask is being used. I can feel it. It always makes me imagine having a human grooming my back with a bristle brush, particularly now that the weather has started to warm up. I shed terribly on my clothes and bedsheets, and loose fur doesn't respond to pattern magic at all. I've started giving myself allergies. It does help to view the sky and smell the fresh air. Do you mind, mother?"

Yes, that's it. Telyn clutched the sides of her pouf dizzily. *When someone uses the mask I feel comfortable, relaxed, as if all is right in the world—even in the middle of a foot-sawing nightmare.* She stifled a yawn. *It's insidious.*

A rip appeared in the wall somewhere near the ceiling. Through it, she glimpsed blue sky and the tip of a cloud. Telyn inhaled deeply through her nose, taking in the cedar-rich air, and her thoughts brightened a little.

"Well, the Ever-Guise, that which so many are seeking, a relic from the Dawn of Champions, and" —The pattern witch examined Telyn carefully—"that for which your sister was sentenced to slavery."

Telyn continued to stare at the diamond of blue sky, drawing strength from it. "I want to save my sister, nothing else. I've learned enough to not want to wear the mask, nor let any of my friends wear it, either. But Mrs. de Galati, I have only one chance to free Cressida, and that is to raise the bond price before she gets shipped to Enshede. If she goes to the slave markets, the chances of ever finding her again…" She shook her head in the anticipation of failure and despair. "I need to discover the buyer's identity. The fence won't turn me over to the cornics."

I hope. Mother of Squirrels, I have no idea if that is true. Dagger he knew, respected, maybe even feared, but a teenaged Too-tall and her friends?

"Do you think you will find him with just a charcoal sketch?"

"Pretty much everyone who traffics in magic comes to the Spring Sale. It's my best idea." *My only idea, other than breaking Cressida free and running until the cold or the cornics catch us.* "If I can sell the forehead piece, the fence might give us enough money to pay the bond price. I need to get Cressida back; she knew nothing of what I was doing. Your daughter didn't, either. That was all before we became…" It was difficult to say the word with respect to a flack, but Telyn had warmed considerably to Rayvn in the past couple months. "…before we became friends."

There it was again, that whisker-twitch. It didn't bother Telyn too much anymore.

"Telyn Brower, you are a remarkable young human. I am pleased to hear that Rayvn didn't know about your violation of the Rules before today. If I go to Second Gajos with your confession, she will be exonerated."

"Yes, ma'am."

"I *will* protect my daughter."

"Yes, ma'am."

"I will protect my daughter with every whisker and hair on my body. I will choose the best course for Rayvn and myself, whether that includes helping you or turning you into the cornics or drowning you in the Elbus River so no one will find your body."

"Yes, ma'am."

"You may go."

"But—"

"The sketchbook was taken by Minister Svemas for his investigation. I can only imagine the investigation has been closed since your sister has been arrested and the mask—the forehead piece of mask—has been found." She lay her hand across the wooden frame of the prophet's wheel. The threads began weaving themselves back into the original non-pattern.

"Can you help us?" Telyn said.

"I will raise the issue with the Prefecture. But if I must draw from memory, it will be difficult. A few monuments I recognized from major cities; those would be easy. The faces," she shook her head, slowly. "They held the symbolism of dreams. A king with a sword over his head. A scholar tearing pages from a book and feeding them to a dragon. No one stood out to me as a fence for stolen goods."

"Thank you, Mother," Rayvn said, helping Telyn to her feet and steering her through the hall and foyer and out the front curtain. When they were outside, she clapped her paws together once. "That went well."

"Will you tell me what she decides?"

"Oh no, you will be the first to know. If your sheets strangle you, she has decided that our friendship puts me in too much danger. If the cornics come for you, she has decided to turn you in."

Telyn swallowed on a tightening throat. "Any other possibilities?"

"Of course. In that case, I will bring you the illustrations."

"What do you think, Rayvn?"

The pattern girl smiled vaguely. "With or without the sketchpad, I think you need to create something entirely new."

CHAPTER FIFTY-FIVE

As the date of the Spring Sale approached, Rayvn announced she was going into the Chaos Woods to retrieve the chrysalis shell. She needed time to fuse all those shell pieces together. She told them not to worry, either; with all the trappers wandering in from their season of exile, the rakasuras and other predators would make scarce. Hosh and Caitlin volunteered to accompany her while Telyn continued her vigil for the daemon-cereb.

In fact, they *insisted* Telyn continue her vigil.

They probably want to get away from my waspish mood. Well, can you blame me? I've heard nothing from the cereb about stealing the mask from second Gajos—nothing! How could she make a counter-move if she didn't know his move?

Or might his plan actually include freeing Cressida as he'd indicated?

Besides snapping at her friends and innocent Sable Head customers, all the stress had caused Telyn to start arguing with herself.

The moon had gone through two full cycles since she had encountered the daemon-cereb in her cabin; barefoot weather had returned, and much of the snowpack had melted. The pass was open—and still no news.

It drove her to distraction!

A perfectly normal reaction—for a lunatic.

If Telyn could have escaped herself, she would have. Today, she did the next best thing: she climbed the Sepulcher.

From the ground up, wildflowers had been wedged into the great stone's cracks: poppies, bluebells, and daisies being popular. Visitors who had once lived in Harlech, or who had ancestors from here, came to pay their respects. Since they couldn't talk with the ghosts once the pattern witch had done her job, they left flowers.

The pass is open, people are swarming into Harlech like bite-mes, and what have we accomplished? Diddly-squat, that's what.

We're still alive. As long as we stay alive, there's hope.

We might be better off dead when Yona gets here.

Telyn's negative inner-voice seemed to be gaining ground.

She paused at her dad's name, Dorian Garrett Brower, pulled out the handful of fireweed she'd tucked into her belt, and fit it into the nearest crack. She pointed the sprigs toward his name, as if he could enjoy the little flame that kindled at night.

They had made *some* progress, she allowed. Rayvn, Hosh, and Caitlin were on their way to get the chrysalis shell at this very moment, and they had Mrs. de Galati's sketchbook.

The pattern witch had brought it to Telyn in the Sable Head. "The news from beyond the mountains compels me to share this with you, Telyn Brower," she had explained in Telyn's room. "Although I am not without misgivings. The march of history has taken a dark turn; the Cornic Empire prepares for war, and I feel you and your sister—and my Rayvn"—She spared a sorrowful glance for her daughter, who covered her mouth and yawned—"—have roles to play."

They reviewed the sketchbook together. Mrs. de Galati helped identify some of the places: the orange porticoes of Academy's Order of Magic; seemingly endless wharfs in Vool; blue onion domes over the Barmouth; an austere breeding temple—

When she mentioned this, Telyn couldn't help herself. "Why do you call them 'breeding temples?' What goes on there? Not like I care or anything..."

Sitting on the edge of Telyn's bed, Caitlin and Hosh widened their eyes. Rayvn's expression didn't change in the least.

The witch smiled with ears and whiskers. "Shocking, isn't it? The term is a translation from a dead language. Today, you would say this is where weddings are performed, like a chapel, but it is much more than that. Matches are made; futures are considered. A match for my Rayvn has been selected, has she told you?"

Telyn nodded.

Mrs. de Galati flipped the pages to show a castle straddling a river with walled towns to either side. "This is the Temple of Galati, an important place for your thief, evidently, and where Rayvn will go to meet her fiancé."

"If you were married at this, ah, temple," Telyn asked, "then what happened to Rayvn's dad?"

"We were not compatible." Mrs. de Galati's voice hitched. "That was many years ago, now."

Rayvn's father, gone, just like mine, Telyn flipped pages to hide the awkwardness of the moment. *We share so much, after all.*

"Rayvn cannot remember him," Mrs. de Galati added.

Rayvn began humming.

The pages clearly identified several participants in the Sable Head auction: Yona the cereb; Kulon the trogo; the conda with the glowing lure sprouting from his forehead; and a frightening shadow that represented Dagger's actual killer—the penumbra daemon. The schmooks all looked alike to Telyn.

But Dagger wouldn't have been planning to sell the forehead piece to a participant in the original auction—that was highly unlikely. They'd be furious Dagger pocketed part of the mask in the first place. They would refuse to trust him a second time. No, it was more likely the fence was someone else entirely.

The sketchpad memories recorded a dozen other recognizable human and fla—er, thauma faces: an aged cornic female in white bedclothes with a scar down the middle of her forehead and one missing horn, the other horn nearly completing a full circle; a pair of full-cheeked, jovial humans that must be brother and sister, both wearing expensive-looking, long-sleeved shirts with frilly cuffs; a feathered var holding a foil in an en garde position; a smiling trogo female —likely an innkeeper—holding bouquets of foaming mugs in each hand. None displayed coins or scales or anything that screamed "fence," but it was a start.

Over the intervening weeks, Telyn and her friends spent much time poring over the drawings. If they saw any of these folks at the Spring Sale, they had a good chance of identifying them.

One of them must be Dagger's fence.

He must be!

Hosh was rooting for the happy brother and sister, but owning magic would be against the Empire's rules for them just like for Telyn and her friends. Telyn figured the fence must be a thauma—and they'd find him or her in the Hall of Magic.

Aled's sacred rump, it's been two full moons since I talked with the daemon-cereb, and half a moon since the pass to Enshede has been cleared. Why hasn't the daemon come? Does Yona intend to return to Harlech in person?

That would mean disaster.

He'd probably just kill me. Or make me a mindless puppet—and then kill me.

The vacant cabins were all full—the rooms at the Sable Head as well. Folks poured into Harlech from all over to see the marvels of the brakdaw fight (now the brakdaw *game of tag*), the Hall of Magic, and aberrations of the Chaos Woods. Most visitors regarded Telyn and the other locals as aberrations as well, living in the wilds all year long, snowed-in for the winter. Who would *choose* such a hard life?

They're not wrong. Telyn's inner voice nagged her as she arrived at the apex of the Sepulcher's wooden scaffolding. From here, she could only progress by swinging out over empty space, then up and over the catwalk—the only challenging part for an experienced climber, the part she enjoyed the most. For a few breathless seconds, her fingers clinging to splintery wood and legs cantilevering out-up-over, Telyn's mind went completely, blessedly blank.

The balance between relaxing, swinging, pulling, and pushing came naturally from her subconsciousness, as much improvisation as muscle memory. Move and flex, relax and swing just right, and it would feel effortless.

And—

There she was, pulling herself onto the top. She hadn't even held her breath.

She lay on the catwalk panting, enjoying the warmth of the sun that the wooden planks had absorbed through her thin blouse and long skirt.

When she looked over the edge, a beautiful view of Harlech stretched before her, from the Sable Head to flacktown and the pattern witch's home. People thronged the market square, Elin Llyweln park, the roads. She sat up and squinted at a large group walking down Main Street. Those in the middle appeared to be human women wearing the peaked headgear of rich merchants. The men surrounding them—she was sure of it—the men surrounding them wore manacles.

Slaves.

No one would have dared bring slaves to Harlech in years past—not even flacks. There would have been an uproar. An uprising. A good chance the owners would have been killed and the slaves freed.

Already they knew—everybody knew, somehow—that the score had changed. Harlech now embraced slavery. The Chaos Woods no longer made this place special and different and free, a sanctuary of sorts to the downtrodden humans of the Cornic Empire. The Ever-Guise—even a small piece of it—had already perverted the order of things.

How could Telyn Brower, a too-tall teenager from Harlech, do anything about that?

Keep going as if you have a plan. Keep going as if your plan is going to work. Never give up. Fight them with your sinew and your blood.

Elin Llyweln, a legendary human wueen, had won a battle just this way. Grievously wounded on her arm, the battle-maiden had dropped her sword. As the demon spawn Paimon closed in for the kill, Elin dipped the fingers of her left hand into the wound and flicked her own blood at her enemy.

Paimon paused to wipe its eyes, and in that brief lapse, Elin removed her helmet, swung it from the chin strap, and bashed in the demon spawn's head.

It must have been quite a helmet.

A gust of wind made the colorful banners around town snap. Telyn blinked, drawing her mind back to the present. Today, the Hall of Magic would go up, and this was the best view in the house. But that was not the primary reason she came.

She stood, strode to the end of the platform, and found UNKNOWN on the broad face of the Sepulcher. There, she placed the last of her flowers—a thistle, which seemed appropriate for Dagger. As she twisted the prickly stem into the crack over which UNKNOWN had been chiseled, she examined the granite closely. The name lay on a slab that might be loosened with a few blows of a chisel. Much like Dagger himself, the stone that held his name (his *non-name*) was separated from the Sepulcher, a part but apart.

A few hard blows, here and here... She ran her fingers over the rough stone. *And the whole slab should come crashing down. Exactly the places you would* never *anchor a belay.*

She memorized the topography, felt the warmth of the sun on her back, and sent well-wishes to the silent ghosts.

You will help me, won't you? We're all in this together. If I fail, if I don't get the forehead piece away from Second Gajos and keep it away from Yona the mind wizard, your ancestors may end up in chains.

You don't want that, do you?

Aled's sacred rump, I must be going mad, talking to the ghosts who've been laid to rest as if they could hear me...

...as if they could help me.

Three other names had been carved onto this delicate shelf of stone: Heath Robinson; Tyre Flint; Arven Grummore, the three who'd been hung for murdering Minister Svemas.

Those three would become vengeful spirits if anyone would. Especially Heath; he'd fight for any reason and no reason at all.

Telyn and her friends had come up with a plan. A good plan, she thought, one that put much of the risk on the cereb himself and didn't endanger many human lives. But it required one thing beyond their control: the daemon.

She patted UNKNOWN one final time then turned away. In the square before the Prefecture, workers buzzed around a two-story frame laying ropes, pulleys, stakes, and folds of white cloth. Tent poles rose high overhead. Men began to pry up cobblestones where stakes would be driven in.

Nearly time.

Sitting on the edge of the scaffolding, Telyn could see most of the square, although the Prefecture blocked a portion. Around noon, the call went out, a shout, and six pattern witches stepped forward.

One of them must be Mrs. de Galati.

Telyn had never watched from this vantage point. She swung her legs in anticipation. The town quieted down. The snapping of the flags became the loudest sound.

A high-pitched call from one of the pattern witches carried to the Sepulcher. They raised their arms.

With a whoosh, the white canvas that had been sitting on the cobblestones launched itself, flowing like a flood up, high up, over the platform and the tips of the tent poles, then back down, relentless and purposeful, to crash into the cobblestones of the far side. Air filled the interior, puffing the walls and roof before the men placed any stakes or tightened any ropes. The shapeless cloth became a gigantic structure, the Hall of Magic, with its steeply pitched apex nearly as tall as the Prefecture itself.

The six pattern witches dropped their arms.

Even though you couldn't see a whisper between the cobblestones and the fabric, men carefully staked the canvas down every couple of feet, tight as a drum.

Telyn didn't have to be close to know that; every kid in Harlech had tried to sneak into the hall at least once, but the tent was closed up tight and sealed with more than human strength.

The pattern witches began to spell it, dipping their fingers in a golden urn and dancing fingers over the surface, painting it with complicated symbols, symbols which un-moored and floated across the canvas beyond their reach, swirling like toy boats in a whirlpool before fading. They worked together, slowly and methodically, a foot at a time.

How am I going to get in?

That's where she would find Dagger's buyer. Try to sell the forehead piece anywhere else, she'd be bundled up and sold as a slave before you could write UNKNOWN with a quill.

Or executed on the spot.

Second Gajos would enjoy that.

Transactions involving magic could not take place anywhere but within the Hall of Magic. That was a rule as hard and fast as the Three Rules. Even flacks complied.

A foyer faced the town center where security would screen the trappers and take permits. Soldiers stationed all around the tent would make sure no one went in or out but through the front—as if the spell-work wasn't enough. The hurons that changed hands in the Hall of Magic each year could hire a thousand mercenaries, according to Razenbock. Disruption there, from children trying to sneak in to outright thievery, was taken very seriously.

Telyn unconsciously rubbed her back, remembering the beating she had received when she had tried to crawl inside at the age of ten. She'd managed to get an arm under the canvas, and half an ear, when a cornic soldier dragged her outside and gave her a beating to end all beatings—a beating so hard she couldn't muster the strength to sob. If she hadn't hobbled away when the soldier gave her the chance, the beating might have commenced again, and she didn't think she'd have survived it.

Young Telyn hadn't left her bed for days. She'd contracted a fever. In her times of lucidity, she'd seen Esther muttering with the herbalist.

The second time she tried to get in, she'd been more careful—

A flash of sunlight flickered across her face. It was Rayvn's idea: use a mirror to bounce the sun to each other. It wasn't really necessary today, but they'd taken the opportunity to try it out.

Taking hold of the edge of the platform, Telyn swung her long legs over the side. Her body followed, and last of all, her hands released their hold on the wood as her feet connected with the crisscrossed scaffolding supports.

Just the way Telyn liked it: one fluid motion.

Swiftly, she descended while her mind pondered the enigma of

Rayvn. That girl had some of Mrs. de Galati's steel, after all; she had proved her mettle in the Chaos Woods time and again. And the mirror signals idea demonstrated her resourcefulness yet again.

And yet—that vacant look! You wouldn't think Rayvn had more between the ears than an eehoo. Perhaps that was her secret weapon.

They met near the Hall of Magic. Ordinarily, a pattern girl and human conversing would be remarkable, but nobody gave them a second glance today.

"Did you see the signal?" Rayvn asked with enthusiasm, trying to flash her with the mirror again.

"I'm here, aren't I?" Telyn shielded her eyes. "It's, ah, good. A good idea, really, in daylight. If we have a lantern, it might work at night, too. Can you knock it off?"

"Oh, sorry."

"Did you see what you needed?" Telyn asked. While Telyn had been surveying things from the Sepulcher, Rayvn had been spying on the pattern witches below. They didn't believe for a minute they would be able to waltz into the Hall of Magic through the front. Security was tight. The cornics would search anyone who came in to be sure they brought only those things they'd paid taxes on.

And they would be using Taffy.

"I need to go talk to my mom," Rayvn said. "What they're doing doesn't look all that complicated. If only I knew what was in that urn... Not blood, I think. If I tell her I want to help next year, she might let enough slip for us to get in."

Telyn gave her friend's arm a squeeze and tried not to think about an urn full of blood. "You did well, Rayvn."

They spoke a bit more, then Rayvn jogged off, and Telyn turned the other way and circled the tent. It had always fascinated her, this Hall of Magic. Their entire town depended on it. The hall put Harlech on the map, made it famous the world over, and guaranteed that humans maintained some level of freedom.

Someone had to hunt the creatures of the Chaos Woods, and none of the flacks wanted to do it. Ergo, human trappers could earn a living, and Harlech lived off the trappers.

The hall and the woods—strange keys to freedom.

As she rounded the corner, she nearly ran into a cornic soldier. She murmured an apology—best to stay humble and quiet around authority—and tried to bypass him, but he stepped in front of her.

"Ah, yes sir?" she asked, avoiding direct eye contact. "I was just moving along."

"Telyn Brower," the soldier rumbled. "How convenient to find you here."

Her gaze lifted. The soldier's face looked off; the nostrils of his muzzle didn't quite line up, and his eyes were wider than expected. Most telling, the creature's exhales smelled more like burnt crumbs than a sheep's sour cud.

Telyn looked around wildly. Yes, several people stood within screaming distance, but no one paid them any mind. "Where have you been? I've been waiting for you."

"I had a nice visit with your mother. If Esther continues to drink, she will sleep all day and night and never wake up."

Telyn swallowed against her fear. "You promised not to hurt her."

"One," he said, raising a blurry finger, "I made no such promise. Two, you do not have the forehead."

"Not yet. But I know how to get it. How *you* can get it for yourself."

"If *I* am going to get it, of what use are you? Or your mother?"

"I can get you into the Prefecture, to the room where the mask is kept." Telyn gestured to the daemon's form. "With this daemon body and what it can do, once you have the mask, you can get out, no problem."

"That was not the bargain." The daemon-cereb lay his fingertips against the hall's canvas. Runes appeared and rushed toward his touch. They gathered there and began to vibrate.

"I have a plan," Telyn said, desperate, and trying desperately not to show it. She could *not* lose this deal. She had to free her sister within the next few days, or she would never get another chance. "It won't work until the Hall of Magic opens. Right now, there are too many soldiers in the Prefecture. If you'd come a few weeks ago, maybe, but they've brought in a fist or more, and they have nothing to do but hang around the Prefecture all day." There, put some of the guilt on the buyer, just enough to keep them off balance. "Once the Spring Sale starts, most of them will be patrolling the town, breaking up fights, or guarding the Hall of Magic. The Prefecture will have a skeleton crew, and I won't have trouble getting you inside—or you getting out.

"All you have to do is become the little statuette, and I can get you inside. Then, at the proper time, you can revert to the daemon form, grab the forehead piece, and dissolve your way out, home-free."

The false soldier appeared to draw his sword with his free hand, but by squinting, Telyn could discern that it was no sword at all, but a tentacle.

Her voice quavered. "Second Gajos keeps the forehead in a vault —a metal vault. Can you get into it?"

Mrs. Nest had learned that much, now that she'd been demoted to mopping floors and dumping chamber pots. Caitlin's mom had joined the ranks of the invisible, which had its uses.

The daemon-cereb spread his fingers on the hall's wall, and the runes scattered up the steep canvas. He appeared to be toying with them.

Mother of Squirrels., Telyn thought, becoming queasy. *Can Yona dominate witch magic the way he dominates minds?*

"Chaos wood is impenetrable to the daemon," the daemon-cereb said. "I believe your sister is being held in a chaos wood cell, is she not?"

Telyn grinned, hoping that would hide her misgivings. "This will work! You've got to trust me."

"Have I? You have an agile mind, but your resources are few."

A massive gong reverberated across the plaza—the warning bell. The hall's protective spells must be linked to the Prefecture in some way.

So, the pattern witches' spells did react—after a fashion. He's not invincible.

"If you had any other plan than using a teenage girl, you would have used it already. I'm invisible, remember? No one even notices me." *Not since Minister Svemas was murdered, anyway.*

People were looking now, looking and pointing. What they saw,

Telyn had no idea. Could the daemon-cereb trick so many minds the way he tricked Esther's? Would they all see a teenage girl talking to a cornic?

With no haste at all, Yona removed his hand from the canvas and spoke again. "Your tenacity amuses me, Telyn Brower. I am willing to take a chance on you. To activate the daemon, spell the letters on the bottom of the statuette."

"Okay, got it. No problem."

Heavy boot-steps came from both sides of the tent.

"One more thing." The daemon-cereb's form began to warble; the voice became tinny and insubstantial. "You must be touching the statuette for the activation to work. Otherwise, you might as well be talking to an echo." The daemon-cereb shrank, collapsed into itself until it formed a statuette suspended about three feet from the ground. The statuette dropped onto the cobblestones, an impenetrable shadow. Telyn concealed it with her bare foot as real cornic solders came into view.

One skidded to a stop directly in front of her. "You there!"

Telyn smiled. "The test worked just fine. Mrs. de Galati told me to poke the fabric to see if the alarm would work."

Several pattern witches rounded the tent, and Telyn waved cheerily at Mrs. de Galati, who waved back.

She looked confused, but she *did* wave.

The soldier gave Telyn a suspicious tilt of the head, but he led the others away and told an underling to run to the Prefecture to stop the warning bell.

Telyn bent casually, picked up the statuette, and tucked it into her belt sash.

A few people regarded her as if not believing their eyes—exactly as she'd hoped.

Chaos wood impenetrable to daemon magic; have to be touching the statuette to activate it. Mother of Squirrels, this changes everything.

CHAPTER FIFTY-SIX

"Your plan," said Hosh, between bites of his sandwich, "is overly complicated. Why not just bribe a cornic guard to get the statuette inside?"

Telyn felt a blush beginning to build. She knew her neck must be turning red, and soon it would spread to her cheeks. Then it would bloom on her forehead. *Mother of Squirrels, bribe a guard? Why didn't I think of that?*

That would have been way simpler.

But how would I know who to approach or what to say without getting arrested? I guess you start with some hints and see how they react, but who does that? Cornics all seem so neat and square. I mean, that female who replaced Mrs. Nest and took the rakasura ears, she's obviously corrupt; maybe I could have asked her.

"It's too late for that. I've already spent all my money getting Quid to compose a song."

Hosh pretended to die. Since he was sitting on his bed, he didn't have far to fall. He made a convincing cadaver, except that he maintained his grip on his sandwich.

Not to mention that he continued chewing.

They'd placed the bear-like daemon statuette on Hosh's desk as a sort of talisman. It sucked some of the light from the room and made Telyn nervous, but it also kept things real.

"Where did *you* spend your hurons, know-it-all?" Caitlin asked. She and Telyn both sat on the floor.

"On this sandwich, and elk jerky, and iced infusions, and sweets. I've been enjoying my rakasura ear money."

"We were to use them to help free Cressida, remember?"

"A few birds won't make any difference." Hosh levered himself upright again. "I'm a growing boy. I get hungry."

"You're seventeen and have the belly of a forty-year-old."

"Not fair! I have a limp."

"Gang, please, this is not helping," Telyn begged. "The plan is in motion. We shouldn't change course mid-stream. Caitlin, did your parents agree?"

"Dad quit when they demoted all the humans. He wouldn't suffer the humiliation of cleaning chamber pots and feeding, and I quote, 'stinking slaves.' The mask has him good. I always thought Dad was a little elitist, and the Ever-Guise has brought that out in an ugly way. Mom's on board."

"Even with the, you know, the..."

"That won't bother her; she used to clean diapers for a few coins. 'Hard work can take you anywhere,' she says, 'even in a town ruled by Second Gajos.' She hates what the cornics have done to your sister, and she hates the way my dad feels less than nothing. She's on board. She has a few ideas of her own, including leaving a note tied to the statuette with the lyrics."

"That's good. That's really good."

Hosh fake-died again.

Telyn hated two parts to her plan: involving Cressida and involving Mrs. Nest. If either of them got caught... Well, she didn't even want to think about what would happen.

If Minister Svemas were still in charge, this would have been easy. She could have asked for an appointment and walked right into his office with the statuette, activated it, and the daemon-cereb could do the rest.

Which may explain why Minister Svemas was dead.

Now, with Second Gajos' new security measures and Taffy checking everyone for magic, things got a lot more complicated.

She exhaled loudly. "Let's review the plan. First, I slip the statuette to Cressida."

"Easy as roasting macaroons," Hosh said, "with Ouzeley's goons watching her."

"Then Cressida takes it inside the Prefecture. The prisoners leave and enter through the back door. There's no scrutiny by Taffy for magical artifacts. However, since cornic guards escort her inside, she'll have to take it to her cell."

"And since the chaos wood lumber holds daemons as well as humans, she can't just activate the statuette in her cell," Caitlin said.

"Right."

"The daemon might just absorb her for sport," Hosh added.

"Which is why she will not activate it. She will, instead, hide it in the chamber pot, under, you know..."

"Just like cleaning diapers," Caitlin said. "Mom can handle it."

"Also, the daemon can't get through chaos lumber, so it has to be removed from Cressida's cell. But because of point, er, two or three..." Telyn had forgotten what point she was on. "The absorbing thing; Mrs. Nest can't activate the daemon herself."

That would be way too dangerous. Telyn would never forget what the daemon had done to the trogo and Dagger.

"Mom will leave it where Corporal Velky can find it. Every time I've seen him, he's humming or singing something or other. He sees the note with the lyrics written out, and then notices the name spelled out on the bottom of the statuette. He won't be able to resist singing Quid's song. Ta-da! The daemon appears, steals the forehead piece from the vault, and escapes."

"Right."

"That's the weakest part of your plan," Hosh said. "How can you be sure Corporal Velky will sing the name?"

"Have you ever tried not to sing a tune that's stuck in your head?" Caitlin asked. "Just try it right now." She started singing, wisely substituting dah-dah for "A-G":

Dah-dah-O-R-M-I-C
That's the name that makes me think
I love you
I love you

Dah-dah-O-R-M-I-C
Naughty boys might think you stink
But they don't know just how I think
I love you
I love you

Hosh scoffed, but Telyn had to smile. It felt great to have Caitlin on their side again.

"Hosh is right, that is the weakest part of my plan. But I've heard Quid's tune, and I think this can work. It's every bit as catchy as Hornblower. Remember, getting the forehead into Yona's hands is just the first step. The most important part happens after, when we take it from him."

"Ah. Good thing we're going over the easy part first," Hosh scoffed.

"Don't you dare die again, Hosh." Caitlin stood and held out a hand to help Telyn to her feet. "Come on, Tey, let's practice the hand-off."

They practiced various versions of transferring the statuette invisibly, from standing next to each other and palming it to hugging and tucking it in each other's sash—from fake falling together to pointing in one direction and throwing it in the other. Telyn *really* hoped she didn't have to try that one; it was about as obvious as her height.

The daemon statuette was about four inches tall and three wide, so concealing it wasn't easy, but it wasn't impossible, either. Its inherent dimness helped.

Hosh told them if he glimpsed the statuette during the hand-off. In the beginning, he called out every time, which was super annoying. But the first time Hosh didn't call out at all was a real thrill. After an hour of practice, he glimpsed it one time in three.

And he knew what he was looking for.

When they heard Hosh begin to mouth *Dah-dah-O-R-M-I-C, Naughty boys...* under his breath, she and Caitlin shared a high-five.

Hosh had no idea what they were celebrating.

This might work. It just might.

And then comes the hard part: getting the forehead from Yona.

She looked over at the coal-black statuette and wondered suddenly if Yona could listen through it in stone form. *If so,* she thought, *losing her grin, then we are all dead.*

CHAPTER FIFTY-SEVEN

Three rumbles converged on the cart-trek leading to the lumber mill. First, as Telyn departed Harlech, the revelry of chatter and song from the approaching Spring Sale rose and fell in pleasant waves. As she crossed the stone bridge, Defiance Falls came to dominate. Swollen from the spring thaw, the pounding waterfall vibrated its banks, the bridge, and Telyn's jawbone. Finally, after she'd crossed the river and made her way northward, the third rumble swallowed the other two: the grinding teeth and whirring machinery of the lumber mill itself.

She was surprised to realize she had never taken this road all the way. The great explorer, the intrepid climber had never investigated the second heart of Harlech. She'd managed to ditch every school field trip to the place, even though the other children enthused about the mill's clever waterwheel and the belts that ran up from the wheel, along the ceiling, and dropped down here and there to power saws, planes, and all manner of tools, distaste for the Ouzeleys had kept her away.

An A-frame building came into view first, an open structure near to but elevated from the river to protect it from floods. A sluice took water from the wild Elbus and brought it inside.

Closer still, and she could see that the sluice divided into two: the largest part fell over a sizable waterwheel; the smaller dropped over a smaller wheel. People moved about in coarse overalls, busy and intent, dwarfed by tree trunks, planks, boards, and machinery.

Amazing that such insignificant creatures as humans could accomplish so much, even without magic.

The beautiful, freshwater smell of the Elbus river, which she hadn't even been conscious of, gave way to the aroma of sawdust. Telyn inhaled deeply. She enjoyed the smell almost as much as she enjoyed the smell of the gooseberry acorn in her hand.

Besides herself, she'd brought two things of utmost importance: the pastry and the penumbra-daemon statuette.

The men working there—she recognized a few—averted their eyes. She was able to ghost inside and wander as she pleased, looking for her sister. Until she nearly walked right into Mr. Ouzeley, that is. Seeing him, she turned quickly, ducked between two machines, and found Tabbard's giant backside blocking the way.

Unaware of the girl standing behind him, Tabbard lined up a board and ran it through a band saw. The cut took a sound eye and steady hands, and the fact that Tabbard executed this well surprised her. She hadn't thought he could do anything well other than lout about.

She waited until he'd finished and walked up to him directly, clearing her throat to get his attention.

"I'm looking for my sister. I've brought her a gooseberry acorn."

He made a show of admiring the smooth cut he'd made. "She eats what I tell her to eat." The board landed atop a pile of similar boards, and he went about selecting another.

"I bring her food every day at the Prefecture. That's my right."

"You're not there now, are you?"

"Tabbard! Why are you talking to it?" Mr. Ouzeley shouted, a looming storm of indignation.

With a swift blow of his cane, he knocked the pastry from Telyn's hand. The blow stung her bones, and she couldn't help feeling nearly as much hurt for the fallen acorn as for her hand. When the money from the rakasura ears ran out, they would become an unaffordable luxury again.

Ouzeley raised the cane again, this time threatening her head. "Who gave you this?"

Tabbard snickered, but he managed to speak. "This is the sister. She brought the slave a treat."

Mr. Ouzeley lowered the cane and managed to look a little embarrassed. "Ah…Telyn, was it?"

Telyn nodded, not sure if she could bend to get the pastry from the floor or if she'd get clobbered again for trying. This wasn't the time for defiance—not when she had to get that statuette into the Prefecture.

"Yes, sir. I am Telyn Brower, daughter of Esther. It is nearly the Spring Sale, and I brought my sister a treat, being as she will be in jail for the whole thing, and then" —It wasn't hard to bring tears—"and then sent to Enshede."

"She shouldn't have broken the Rules. Rules are there for a reason, to keep order. To keep people in their places, for the good of the empire."

Telyn regarded her boots and the splattered pastry. It was still salvageable, though ants were beginning to converge on it.

"Do you see my men eating tarts?"

"I have to feed her. That's my job. I bring—"

"Do you see my men eating tarts?" The silver-tipped cane banged once on the wooden floor.

"No, sir."

"I can't have a slave" —Mr. Ouzeley filled the word with disdain —"eating better than the men I pay." And with that, he ground his boot-heel into the gooseberry pastry. A couple of seeds popped out.

"May I see her? I'll tell her what she almost got. Please, sir, it's the Spring Sale."

"Go. Tabbard, take her. And boy, she's a filthy slave's sister. No touching."

Tabbard spit on the ground.

Having Tabbard along was a complication, but she'd gotten permission, and that was enough.

Beyond the lumber mill, the cart-trek became a footpath which crept through the stumps of trees just above the river's high-water mark, all newly cut since the minister's assassination.

Tabbard led in silence.

Telyn fingered the hem of her apron, wishing that she carried a knife—or better yet, her ice ax. By calling her a "filthy slave's sister," Mr. Ouzeley had been insulting her, sure, but the insult had been part of the warning not to abuse either girl. That meant that Mr. Ouzeley didn't trust his own son to *not* touch them.

It must have happened before.

She'd heard nothing about this from Cressida, and she thought she would have noticed if it had. Therefore, whom had Tabbard assaulted? One of his girlfriends? One of the newly minted slaves?

Probably the later. Tabbard would enjoy having total domination over someone.

Her dislike for the young Ouzeley grew even more.

Although they were the approximately same height, Telyn had no illusions how long she could resist if Tabbard attacked her. Without a weapon, it would be her desperation against his bulk, and desperation can only get you so far.

In the back of her mind, she held onto the name A-G-O-R-M-I-C. If she had no options left, she wouldn't let Tabbard take her; she would spring the penumbra daemon and see what happened.

If it came to that, she would.

She'd rather be absorbed by the daemon than let the lout touch her.

They came to a point of land jutting into the Elbus. "There, with the polers." Tabbard pointed to the water's edge, where several people worked to free logs that had become snagged. It looked like difficult, dangerous work. They stood out in the river on stones, using the fifteen-foot poles as much for balance as much as for moving the floating logs. On the furthest rock, she could distinguish Cressida, the only poler wearing a skirt.

"What happens if they fall?" she asked.

"If they can grab someone's pole, they get out. If not, they get swept either to the waterfall or to the mill where they get dumped over the waterwheel. We only drown a couple that way every year," he said. "Usually, they get crushed by the logs before that happens."

Cressida slipped as Telyn watched, nearly toppling into the water between two logs. At the last second, she caught herself with a shove of the pole.

"Why are you so mean?" Telyn asked.

Tabbard's eyes flicked back toward the mill. He set his teeth, took his time answering. "If it were me, I'd throw her in. It'd hurt less." He turned away, hesitated, as if wanting to say more but unable to bring himself to do it.

Telyn couldn't help asking. "Hurt less than what? Slavery? What are you doing to her?"

"Nothing. We ain't doing nothing," he replied, and departed. His wide shoulders sagged as he picked his way over the rough trail.

Throw her in…it'd hurt less…

Mother of Squirrels, what have your patents put you through?

For just a moment, Telyn saw Tabbard as a hurt, vulnerable young man. For just a moment, she almost wanted to hug him, to tell him it would be all right. Tell him that, if he wanted, he could have a friend.

But it only lasted a moment; she knew he hurt people and enjoyed doing it.

And she had a job to do.

She descended the slippery rocks, cracked some puddle-ice that hadn't realized spring had arrived, and trampled a few intrepid shoots of grass at the water's edge. From there, she hopped from rock to rock until finally, with a precarious leap, she shared the stone with Cressida.

It was the perfect spot; anyone looking would see everything the two of them did, so they wouldn't be looking too closely. At the same time, no one could get close. No one could see precisely what they did.

"Hi," Telyn said upon landing.

Startled, Cressida nearly fell. She did drop the pole, and it slipped sideways and drifted downstream.

"Oops," Telyn offered.

Cressida stared after the pole in dismay, her hands extended and grasping at air.

Thankfully, a man downstream managed to retrieve the pole. He hopped a couple of rocks and extended it to Cressida with a friendly wink. As Cressida reached forward, Telyn grabbed her waist to stabilize her—and slipped the statuette into Cressida's belt sash at the same time.

It was about as sneaky a maneuver as she'd ever pulled off. She and Caitlin had practiced for hours. Telyn almost imagined she could become a street magician with enough practice. The pole drop had been a lucky accident.

"'Oops' is for spilling a malt in the Sable Head," Cressida said, leaning her weight on the flexible wood. "Losing a pole is more like, 'Aled's rump, I'm going to be beaten until I can't stand.'"

Telyn's throat tightened.

"You bring me anything?" Cressida said.

"Yes, a delicious gooseberry acorn. Ouzeley knocked it from my hands and stepped on it."

"You mean you didn't bring me any?"

"I thought about salvaging it," she admitted truthfully, "but with both of them glaring at me, I thought better of it."

"Sounds delicious."

"It was. I took one bite pre-knocking; I was hoping you'd not notice. The mill ants are loving it."

Cressida nodded, moving the pole back into position and heaving on a log to get it moving downstream. She managed to look both emaciated and whip-strong at the same time.

Cressida's built more muscle here than I did hauling Taffy into the Aumerhem Pass on a stretcher. I've got to bring her fewer treats and more speck. We might need her muscles if we fall back on Plan B, the Chaos Wood route.

"You know you have it?"

Cressida nodded. "They're watching us. Always watching here."

"Good. Then they know we haven't done anything suspicious. All you have to do is put that in the chamber pot in three days' time. And, er, hide it there so no one sees it."

"Easy as trampling a gooseberry acorn."

"Exactly."

As Cressida struggled to straighten a wayward log, Telyn dodged the butt end of the pole. Behind them, the Chaos Woods loomed free and immense. They'd have to move far and fast to escape there, but there was always a chance if everything else failed.

Although Aumerhem Peak dominated, she could see the three Kings and three Queens in the distance. Should they run to the safer King's Pass, or to the lesser-used Aumerhem Pass?

Would the slave-catchers be expecting that, since the Browers had a history with Aumerhem Pass?

I'll let Cressida decide if it comes to that. I'll let her decide a whole lot—

The pole whacked her in the ear.

"Sorry, this is a small rock for two," Cressida said.

So...we're not that friendly yet. Or she's afraid of reprisals.

"Yeah, got it. See you soon, back home."

Cressida nodded, and Telyn leapt from stone to stone back to shore.

"Your optimism," Cressida shouted over the river and the saws, "never lose that."

CHAPTER FIFTY-EIGHT

Flowers and more flowers, candles, acorn carvings, colorful leaves, polished stones, bits of cloth, and messages written on paper. Telyn and her friends hadn't counted on all the visitors to the Sepulcher. They had to wait, wait, wait. All day and into the evening, visitors had been leaving little mementos.

Locals left flowers which wouldn't have to be picked up; visitors didn't look that far ahead.

After the last visitor left—an old woman with a bent back and gray hair tied up in a bun—Telyn, Rayvn, Caitlin, and Hosh ascended the scaffolding, carrying their tools in heavy packs.

All had insisted on coming, and Telyn had accepted their company gratefully, with the admonition that they depart the instant the ritual was performed. This was one trial Telyn had to face alone.

Bowl, chisel, spike, unguents, and powders they lay on the wooden planks at the top of the scaffolding, and then they roped themselves in for safety.

The bright glow from the Spring Sale lit Harlech's rooftops like a hundred bonfires. Rayvn set up a waist-high frame several feet long and spread across it a black curtain to shield them from prying eyes. "There," she said, lighting a small oil lamp. "Now we can work."

Telyn blushed, realizing she would never have thought of using the shielding curtain—realizing how much they depended on the thauma.

She dropped her gaze. "Rayvn—" A lot of apology went into that single word.

"Are you well?"

"About our friendship…"

The feline met her eyes. "You were not appropriate when we first met."

Telyn nodded.

"And many times since."

More nods.

"This is a garment long creased and not easily ironed, Telyn Brower. It is also perfectly understandable. Ours, on the other hand, is a matter of arrogance."

"Sit down, you two," interjected Caitlin. "That curtain is only waist high. You look like a firefly on the wall with that lamp."

They sat, legs crossed.

Rayvn laid out her tools neatly and kept adjusting them until they were perfectly aligned…including that blood spike.

Telyn could hardly keep her eyes off the glass pipette. When that jabbed into her hand, blood would spurt. Red, sticky blood bubbling from her palm, dribbling, dribbling, hot and slippery.

She had to put her hands on the planks to keep from swooning.

"On it," Hosh said, bumping her arm with a bladder.

He had brought a cold, floral infusion of some kind. She sipped it gratefully.

Rayvn poured powder into powder, a potpourri of colors, and stirred with a wooden spoon.

"Are we doing the right thing?" Caitlin said suddenly.

Telyn said, "I should be asking that."

"You *never* ask that."

"I should."

"Your job is to break the pattern," Rayvn said, not looking up from her concoction. "You are the face that walks into the spider's web."

"The what?" Hosh asked.

"The face. You are walking in the forest," Rayvn said, "and your face pops through a sticky spiderweb. You get strands in your mouth, across your eyebrows—"

"Ew," Caitlin said.

"—your face smashes through the elegant web, destroying its pattern. The spider must rebuild, but the second web will never be exactly like the first."

"Not the stone that drops into the pond?" Caitlin mimicked the stone dropping, and the subsequent ripples, with her hands.

Rayvn wiggled her mouth whiskers. "But a stone dropped in water creates concentric circles. Why would dropping a stone into water represent a pattern breaker?"

Hosh started to chuckle.

Caitlin just shook her head.

Rayvn shrugged and continued mixing.

"Thank you for that explanation, Rayvn. The way you'd intuited about our friendship, I was beginning to think you'd been replaced by a shape-shifter." Telyn held the infusion-bag under her nose. Was that lavender? Yes, and another flower she could not identify.

Hibiscus?

Elderflower?

"The longer you stay possessed, Telyn Brower, the more difficult it will be to reverse. In any case, we will need my mom. I have never done an exorcism. I have never broken a binding, either, but breaking is always easier than fixing." She smiled at Telyn, and it wasn't a mocking smile. "You have the easy job, Spiderweb Face."

"I, ah, I'm not sure about that nickname."

Hosh laughed. "I dig it, Spiderweb Face."

Caitlin nodded. "I can go with that."

"Aled's sacred rump!" Telyn complained.

"I could go with that, too," Hosh affirmed.

The ingredients were measured, stirred, chanted over, and warmed. Rayvn's clever lamp had a flat attachment that enabled it to double as a burner. Gradually, the friends' chatter died, and they were left with the voices and music carried on the breeze from the Spring Sale.

Telyn rubbed her arms and drew her knees to her chest. She dug some dirt from the cuticle of her pinkie toe.

Barefoot again. Yes! And fie on Hosh ogling my ankles. I don't care, not one bit.

Finally, Rayvn dipped the blood-needle in a glass bottle, rolled its now-wet tip in powder, and held this over the lamp-flame until it produced a smell like burnt walnuts.

"How long do I have?" Telyn said.

"My mother can reverse the possession within a few hours, I am confident of that. But every time the sun sets with Dagger in your head, it will become more difficult to separate the two of you. It is far harder to bind a ghost a second time."

Rayvn touched her gently on the arm. "Try to get the ghost to tell you his name. That will make my mother's binding much easier to do. The first time all we had was Unknown. If you get his name—his true name—we have a chance. But do not make any promises to him. He is a vengeful spirit. He will want to exact his revenge before letting go. Promise the wrong thing and it will bind his goal to yours, his soul to yours, and there will be no way to free you until his vengeance is complete."

"Couldn't we have gone over this before tonight?"

"Then you might have backed down," Rayvn said, "and I would never have had a chance to see if this works, Spiderweb Face."

"If that nickname sticks, I'll have my own vengeance to take."

Hosh chuckled. "You made a pun. Spiderweb Face, nickname sticks. Get it? Spiderweb sticks?"

"I'll stick that spike somewhere dark if you don't shut it."

The powder turned from gray to orange. Rayvn raised the blood-needle and met Telyn's gaze. "Ready."

"Ready," Telyn agreed. She swigged from the infusion bladder—*Roses, that's the other flower*—closed her eyes, and held out her hand. Just in case the pain forced her eyes open, she turned her head away.

She hoped the heat and the glowing, orange chemical baked onto the glass would make the spike go in easier, make the pain less than before.

Wrong.

As the hot glass ripped through her hand, Telyn shrieked and felt no shame for doing so.

The needle seared her, tore her, cleaved skin and muscle, severed blood vessels, sent shock-waves up her wrist. Tears sprang to her eyes; she trembled before she knew she was trembling.

With her feline-strong muscles, Rayvn twisted Telyn's hand downward to ensure the blood spurted into the bowl rather than all over her dress.

A vibration started in Telyn's feet and drove through her teeth. The scaffolding shifted and groaned.

"Wha-What's that?" Caitlin said.

Her life pumped into the bowl with a steady beat. Each throb made Telyn dizzier, as if the blood drained directly from her brain.

"The ghosts, they want to come out," Hosh guessed. "Guys, this isn't rakasuras. This is ghosts. We can't do nothing about ghosts."

The night began whispering.

"You sure you want to go through with this?" Caitlin's breath hot on Telyn's face, urgent and caring. "We could bust Cressida away from the lumber mill. Tey, Cressida would flee into the woods with you if there's no hope for rescue some other way."

Telyn's eyes popped open.

Spirits flit and flickered around them. Rayvn, calm, held a dripping red brush suspended over Unknown. Hosh and Caitin had frozen in a frightened tableau.

This was it—the last chance to turn back. The apex of the climb. The place where she was most likely to give up or fall. Telyn had been there many times, suspended a hundred feet above the ground by the tips of her fingers or the slim metal of her ice ax. And she never hesitated. That's why she won at climbing.

That's why she would win here.

"We wouldn't last in the Chaos Woods," Telyn said.

"You'd last a few years," Caitlin said, "until you got old, or sick, or broke a leg, or a spider bit you."

"Very reassuring," Telyn said.

"The cornics would forget you after a while. You could cut your hair short, disguise yourself…"

"Telyn, Caitlin, you got to hurry it up," Hosh said, trying to wave away the ghosts. His hands went through a man-shaped vapor, which caused Hosh to whimper and crawl away until his back bumped against Caitlin's.

Only Rayvn remained cool.

"Telyn, listen to me," Caitlin said, urgently. "Lots of people die in the Chaos Woods. Your dad died there. My cousins, three of them. It's common, a normal death—an honorable death. This, this isn't normal. You'd be possessed, controlled by some entity, an evil entity. A thief! Your sister would prefer to take her chances with you in the woods. At least you'd be you."

"I don't think Dagger is evil." But Telyn wasn't sure, was she?

Remember Tums?

Remember when he padded out into the public room and howled his piercing, unholy howl?

Would a good ghost have made that noise?

Would a benevolent spirit have nearly shaken the Sable Head to the ground?

Would a good thief have stolen the Ever-Guise in the first place? And held an auction with the mind wizard, the trogo, and all the rest?

I'll keep Dagger under control. I will. Just long enough to free Cressida. Then I'll be done with him. Mrs. de Galati will exorcise him.

I know she can do it.

"You will be possessed by a ghost, Tey," Caitlin said. "People that come out of this are never the same. You'll know all of Dagger's icky thoughts, and he'll know yours! And it's a big risk—that you don't come out of it, I mean. Exorcisms are difficult, and you only have a few hours to get everything done. What if Cressida doesn't get the statuette placed in time? Or Corporal Velky doesn't read your note? It could be days before it's found!"

The brush stopped dripping blood. Rayvn dipped it back in the bowl.

With her clean, bloodless hand, Telyn took hold of Caitlin's hand

and squeezed. "Thank you, Caitlin. You are a true friend. But I don't want a normal death. I don't want a normal anything."

Taking that as permission, Rayvn began painting.

Caitlin leaned forward and kissed Telyn on the cheek.

The scaffolding groaned and swayed. The bowl spilled, spread a crimson puddle on the planks, on Telyn's knees. Rayvn leaned into the rock face to keep her balance and covered Unknown with her new concoction as fast as she could. All the ghosts began screaming. From the town came lamps and torches, bobbing past the stable, past the cabins and the necessaries, rushing along the path to see what the commotion was.

"U-N-K—"

Rayvn spoke each letter of UNKNOWN as she covered them with the unguent.

"Uh, time for us to go," Hosh said, taking hold of the rope ladder. "Bye, then."

He and Caitlin vanished over the lip of the scaffolding. The black curtain collapsed and dropped away.

"N-O—"

The scaffolding pitched sideways. The lamp tipped over, rolled off, and disappeared, leaving them in near total darkness. Rayvn managed to hold onto the slab of rock; Telyn slid away. Her feet pitched off the wooden planks. Her legs flailed and her grip slipped until her toes found an impression, a name to cling to.

"Are you okay?" Telyn shouted. She knew she should abandon the catwalk, stick to the much more permanent stone. Sweat on her fingertips made her grip precarious.

"Yes. Nearly done."

"Can you see it?"

"Yes. Pattern witches can see better in the dark than humans. The bowl fell, but I think there's enough on the brush—"

"Just paint."

"Painting. Now W. Now N."

Orange specks rolled across the letters. They began to smoke. It smelled altogether too much like burned hair.

Coordinated and cat-like, Rayvn crawled nearer. She kissed the top of Telyn's head. "Stay here a moment longer, Spiderweb Face. You must be the nearest soul when Dagger is free." Rayvn's magic drew the rope ladder to her, and she scrambled out of sight.

Telyn heaved herself back onto the precarious catwalk. The scaffolding, it seemed, would not collapse completely. She lay there, panting. The ghosts had quieted.

Human voices approached from Harlech; she could almost make out what they were saying. She wondered if her friends had descended in time or if they would be seen.

Nothing happened.

Nothing except that they'd caused serious damage to the scaffolding. That would earn her a few days in jail—

And then, in a deafening explosion, the Sepulcher shattered.

Blinded by the flash and deafened by the roar, Telyn fell.

CHAPTER FIFTY-NINE

The body of Telyn sat on the bed of her room at the Sable Head. Shoulder to shoulder, Hosh and Caitlin sat to her right, on the trunk. Rayvn stood before the door, hands folded. The shutters were closed. Three tallow candles illuminated the room.

"You let her out," Caitlin said.

"We've been over this. I am Telyn."

No, he isn't. I'm right here.

"If you are Telyn," Caitlin said, putting her chin in her hand, "then tell us the plan."

"That's what I'm asking you. I hit my head rather hard when the Sepulcher exploded. If you could just remind me of the details..."

"Ha," Hosh said. "He doesn't know it. That's the thief talking, not Telyn. What's your real name?"

That seems important. Someone, some-when told me I had to get the ghost's true name. Names are identities. They are keys to locks. Names, like keys, open doors.

The thief crossed his legs, Telyn's legs, in as girly a fashion as he knew how, kicked one foot impatiently, and gave his best teenage eye-roll. He considered it a masterful performance, but from the humans' faces, he could tell they didn't buy it. It might have something to do with what he was wearing.

Most of the women here in Harlech wore long skirts all the time. Something about hiding their ankles, of all things. Surely in her own room, Telyn would be allowed to wear stockings with a long-sleeved shirt.

Or should he grab socks from the drawer?

The pattern girl's face was harder to read than the humans, which made him angry.

Unreasonably angry.

"This isn't getting us anywhere," Caitlin said, and began pacing the room.

We haven't much time. We have to keep moving! But, why? I remember that Cressida is in danger. If I don't hurry...what? What was so important—so urgent—that I let myself get possessed?

Caitlin and Hosh know, but they aren't talking to me. They're talking to...to...

To Dagger.

Telyn wanted to speak, but she didn't control her vocal cords. She could only observe through senses—sight, smell, hearing, touch, taste—senses dimmed by distance, except in the case of pain, that sixth sense, no distance separated Telyn from pain.

None at all.

That felt all too real.

And she hurt. Oh yes, her right shoulder ached, and when the thief did a circle with that arm, it produced a grinding noise that recalled disturbingly the saws in the lumber mill, and caused her enough pain that Telyn blacked out.

But the thief didn't. He kept Telyn's body upright on the bed. He'd grown accustomed to pain; even a broken collarbone didn't slow him down much.

Dagger kicked that foot a little more vigorously, a little more *contentedly*. He had discovered the girl's pain threshold. If he ever needed to be rid of her for a while, he could give this borrowed body a broken-collarbone worth of pain and drive her away.

Strange. This was his second possession, and in many ways, he preferred the eehoo. Much less junk in Tums' brain than Telyn's.

He flexed his new hand, opened and closed it a couple of times. A scar ran the length of the thumb; he wondered how that had happened. He didn't have access to all of Telyn's memories, although something told him—yes—the scar was recent. It must have come from the girl's trip to the Chaos Woods.

Images flitted into his ghost-mind: rakasuras, a wild fight in darkness and trees, animate capes.

'You've been through more than I would have guessed,' he told Telyn, who was in no condition to reply.

Dagger turned the hand over. Examining his new body kept his simmering rage under control, sort of. Such long fingers. He could make great use out of these fingers. Strong...for a woman. He would have to remember that these didn't have his muscle memory. These fingers have never picked a lock, much less a pocket. They probably haven't fought with a knife when the handle was slippery with blood—your own, the other's, it didn't matter. If you dropped the knife, you died.

He examined the short, practical nails and sent a bit of magic down them, making the air hum between the fingers. He smiled, and the straight teeth felt alien to him. Growing up, Dagger always had crooked front teeth—until one got knocked out when Connor Phelps banged his head against the floor of their shared room. Then he'd had a gap.

A knock.

Telyn's head swiveled toward the door, lethargic, and Dagger realized he had let his guard down. He hadn't been listening to the footfalls outside. This body was not ready, not *aware*. It had slow reflexes, too used to the easy ways of honesty.

Inattentive.

The way of the still and the dead.

The door cracked open, and Telyn's body did not react. Dagger rested on Telyn's sit-bones, thinking about how he was sitting on her sit-bones, not reacting. He was focused inward on a teenage brain filled with junk, just thinking about how it was filled with junk.

The knocker was a bearded man with a barrel chest.

Razenbock.

The thief read the name on Telyn's mind. 'We are growing closer, you and I. Good. Let me have it all.'

Telyn—the pent-up spirit of Telyn—groaned into his mind.

The barkeep asked for Rayvn, whispered something to her. Ordinarily, Dagger could have read the man's lips, but Telyn's nerves worked at a quarter of what he was used to. And her ears—it was like Telyn's ears were gummed with molasses. They needed training.

He looked around, noticing details for the first time. The room had no decorations, nothing to say this was home, not even a throw-rug on the floor. A vagabond's dwelling, the thief thought, but the walls had been painted with his own memories. Painted with dust and carbon from the candles.

'That,' he realized, 'is what happens when a ghost appears. When *I* appeared. I will have to erase those drawings, make sure the Yona never sees. He can't guess who I really am.'

Dagger's rage simmered at the thought of the mind wizard, Yona Unega. He clenched the girl's fists until the knuckles turned white and her arms shook.

One of the kids, Hosh, held collection of charcoal sketches in his lap—a collection that needed to be burned.

Telyn's spirit resurfaced slowly from the depths of pain. *I feel like I'm in a fever dream and seeing the world from the outside, like I'm seeing my own fists through Dagger's eyes. No, not his eyes—his mind.* Telyn recognized that they were in her own room at the Sable Head. She had no recollection of how she got there.

Everything is all fuzzy. Dagger's mind covers my own like gauze.

A mental click.

We haven't much time.

We have to get the forehead piece. The forehead...and the buyer. Find the buyer, pay the bond price, redeem Cressida.

I let Dagger into my head so he could help me find the buyer.

Telyn tried to project her thoughts to the thief. *Dagger, who did you plan to sell the forehead piece of the Ever-Guise to? What does the buyer look like?*

The body shifted. Dagger seemed to know that she wanted to communicate, but either he was incapable of responding, or he chose to ignore her.

Hosh patted Caitlin's arm and pointed. "Tey? Telyn, are you there?"

But Telyn's eyes abruptly shifted away from the walls to look at Rayvn and Razenbock.

After whispering with the barkeep, Rayvn turned. "I've got to go. The Sepulcher had been breached; other ghosts have come out, and some of them are causing havoc. My mom needs me."

"Mother of Squirrels," Hosh said after Rayvn and Raz departed. "What have we done?"

"It will be okay. We have the best pattern witch in the world, and the best pattern witch's daughter," Caitlin said.

"What if Harlech burns down? What if it shakes itself apart? What if all the ghosts get out?" Hosh buried his head in his hands.

"We *needed* a ghost out," Caitlin argued. "It's going to be all right. The pattern witches will corner the other ghosts. If the spell hadn't shattered those other names, we wouldn't have had the distraction we needed."

Caitlin focused on Telyn again. "Listen, Dagger, we rescued you from the Sepulcher, and now you need to help us."

"What do you want me to do?"

"Get somebody out."

"I am sensing a theme."

"An all-too human theme," Caitlin said wryly. "Slavery."

"I don't rescue slaves. There's not enough money in it, and there are always more slaves where they came from. You get the idea."

"All we need to do is pay the bond price. That's where you come in."

"Do I have money?"

"Not that I know of. And if you did, there wouldn't be enough time to get it. We have about, eh, an hour, max."

The thief rose in Telyn's body, wobbled, and sank into the bed again. These were just teens, and naive as newborn calves, but it seemed he needed them for the moment.

"What's the plan?"

"We don't know," Caitlin said.

"Brilliant."

"Only Telyn knows the whole plan," added Hosh, straightening his hair with his fingers. "No one else. She did that on purpose, so you'd have to talk to her."

Dagger examined the room again. No weapons within easy reach. No reflexes to use them, anyway. He tried his ghost powers, and the nearest candle flared down to a wax puddle. He experienced a momentary thrill, but more carbon flew from the candle to the walls and painted the ballroom where he'd pulled his first heist.

His burgeoning smile turned to a scowl.

He'd never paid much attention to ghost lore. Would his memories keep appearing everywhere he used magic? Inconvenient, that, especially when you wanted to remain anonymous.

If Yona ever figured out who he was...

Dagger might be beyond Yona Unega's grasp now—How badly could the mind wizard hurt a dead man?—but his family, his beloved Aeres...

He pushed that name from his mind. He didn't want anyone to know that name, didn't want their love story painted on some wall— didn't want the girl he inhabited to learn it, either. He couldn't let Telyn know how much he loved his wife. Couldn't let her know he *had* a wife.

No one could know.

His anxiety smoldered; the Sable Head walls trembled.

Caitlin and Hosh had been speaking, and he hadn't been listening. He pulled his mind back to the present. "So, you want me to pay a slave's bond price with no money and no plan to get any. And we only have an hour."

"Could you, ah, stop that?" the boy Hosh said.

Dust rained from the ceiling and painted more memories on the walls. Dagger smothered his emotions with difficulty.

Normally, his emotions didn't vacillate like a whipit snake. He kept his cool, always. It helped his reputation, his thought process.

The girl Caitlin mouthed something, and this time the thief did manage to read her lips. Two words: "Vengeful spirit."

His eyes narrowed. If that were true, and it *felt* true, he would have even less control over his anger than he thought.

That is to say, none at all.

Hosh tapped his own skull. "Telyn has a plan. You have to wake her up so she can tell you herself."

"Why shouldn't I just walk out of here?"

"Because," Caitlin replied, "if you try that, the pattern witches will lock you in the Sepulcher for good. They are friends of ours, in case you hadn't noticed. You will never get your revenge. You want something, and we want something, so let's deal."

"What if I kill you?"

The girl actually smiled. "We thought of that. There are seven pattern witches in Harlech, and one of them went to Sheol and back with us. You don't want to make her angry."

No, you don't. Absolutely not, Telyn confirmed.

Startled, Dagger turned his mind inward. 'So, you can talk with me?'

Getting the hang of it.

'Don't use that word. It's too close to a pun, and I hate puns. You aren't going to like it, living here with me.' He tapped his temple with a knuckle. 'Go back to sleep.'

He made to swing his arm again.

CHAPTER SIXTY

"Why did you do that?" Hosh asked, leaning forward. "Why'd you tap your head like that? Telyn, is that you?"

This time, when Dagger agitated his broken collarbone with a shrug of his arm, he screamed. He couldn't hold it back. The girl did not pass out; she forced him to holler at the top of her lungs.

Not acceptable!

The bedside table cracked in half; the ceramic pitcher shattered and spewed water all over the floor. The two remaining candles dazzled like shooting stars.

Dagger didn't wait to see what memories they painted. He had to get out of here, had to get moving.

Revenge.

Yona.

'Get ready for a ride, Telyn.'

Dagger propelled the body out of the room onto the landing over the public room. At the balustrade, he paused.

Down below, in the public room, a few patrons sipped malt and angel water or snacked on sticky bangers. Whatever they'd thought of the unnatural earthquakes, it hadn't driven them from the important task of imbibing and eating.

Caitlin and Hosh fell in behind him.

Tell my friends they can't come with us. It's too dangerous. Dagger opened his mouth, but nothing came out. *No, that's no good. They'll want to protect me. Tell them...tell them they have to wait for Yona elsewhere, in case he—Oh, never mind. I'll do it.*

And to Dagger's astonishment, Telyn began using her voice. They were his vocal chords—his!—but she'd taken control of them.

"Caitlin, listen to me. This is Telyn speaking. I need you to wait on the road east of here in case Yona tries to escape to Enshede. If you see him, tell him he has to pay me what he owes me. We did everything he asked, and a deal is a deal."

Dagger scoffed. 'Yona will kill the girl as easily as a fly.'

The point is to get her safely away. Yona is not going east.

"Yeah, okay Tey," Caitlin agreed uncertainly.

"Hosh," Telyn continued, "you wait here in my room in case Yona actually shows up." The boy actually stuttered. "Don't worry. If he comes here, he means to keep his word. Tell him he owes me four thousand hurons for the forehead. Four thousand, not an egg less. Got it? It will be all right."

'Yona never keeps his word,' Dagger thought with a growl. 'But you already know that.'

"When Yona swipes the mask, the cornics will be hot on his trail. He'll leave by the quickest, least-likely route possible: the Chaos Woods. And that's where we'll be waiting. But, in case I'm wrong, you two need to watch my room and the road to Enshede. Agreed?"

After a glance at each other, Caitlin and Hosh shrugged. They looked decidedly uncomfortable, probably balking at the use of "we" instead of "me." Well, it made Telyn uncomfortable as well. She hadn't meant to use the plural; it had just sort of slipped out. But there it was, real and accurate and irrevocable. She and Dagger were together on this.

"What is the password, so we know it's you?" Hosh asked.

Telyn wrinkled her forehead. "Password? We didn't make a password."

The boy nodded.

"I think we should stick together," Caitlin said.

"No! Time is running out. If we don't get to our places soon, Cressida will be in shackles forever." Telyn and the thief started down the stairs.

"Yup, definitely Telyn," Hosh said.

'The forehead piece, do you have it?' Dagger thought.

Why would I say, "We need to get the mask?" if I already had it?

'A good thief lies to everyone.'

Telyn snorted. *I tried that last year, and look what it got me: possessed.*

'I resent that. Some women would love to have me—'

I am not going to banter with you inside my own head. Loser.

This amused the thief, but he stayed silent.

They descended the stairs into the public room. The clientele all sat on one side—the side that didn't house the large puddle of malt. The room smelled ripe; someone had blocked open the wide door to the outside to let in some fresh air.

Raz was mopping pieces of porcelain and malt-foam into a pile.

Telyn didn't remember how her friends had transported her here after she'd fallen from the scaffolding, but clearly Dagger's ghost had begun to manifest before they made it to her room.

She mouthed "I'm sorry" to the big man and vowed to help repair the damage just as soon as she freed her sister.

Outside, Harlech was in an uproar.

Which wasn't all that different from Spring Sale normal: unruly crowds, clashing smells, cacophonous music. But people held more tension, moved a little more like startled birds than the with usual carnival slouch. Their eyes darted rather than staring with wonderment.

Hundreds thronged Main Street; they hadn't taken shelter after the Sepulcher breach. Guests and residents of Harlech didn't scare easily. Ghosts could be dealt with.

You still there, thief?

'Unlike you, I don't need to fill every silence with jabber.'

We're going the wrong way.

'I thought you were controlling the legs.'

Fine.

They wobbled like a rod puppet as each tried to turn the body around, Telyn to the left and Dagger to the right.

'Wait, are you left-handed?' Dagger asked.

Yes.

'This isn't going to work.'

Telyn gritted her teeth so hard she thought they would crack. *So give me control.*

They almost wrenched their back trying to go both ways at once.

Three passing schmooks gave them an exceedingly large birth. Dagger lost interest in the body. He stared. Could one of the schmooks be Yona's ally?

"Taito-Vaiana, betrayer, vengeance.' Mindless anger colored his sight shades of vermilion. The world appeared shadowy and wraith-like, but the shadows were made of fire.

The Sable Head's second-story windows shattered one by one. With cracks and pops, slats spun off shutter-frames.

The schmooks sprinted to the cover of an alleyway. People began screaming—and pointing at Telyn.

'Kill. Vengeance.'

Even when Dagger realized that none of the schmooks was his enemy, he couldn't stop hating.

With a huge effort, Telyn turned their body—*her body!*—to the left. As she gained distance, her puppet-like movements smoothed out; she walked with a near human-like gait again.

Still, everyone stared.

Shutters banged as they passed. Random folks' hair stood on end. Bows in children's hair unraveled.

Telyn began jogging.

'Why are we running?'

Stop doing whatever you're doing.

'I'm not doing anything,' Dagger growled, which wasn't true. He was hating—a good, smoldering hate.

At the Lucky H, the water trough frothed. Three horses tied to the hitching posts began whinnying and kicking. One pulled free, reared, and kicked another. Revelers panicked and tried to force their way through the bar's swinging doors, jamming the entrance.

Dagger made Telyn's mouth grin…until cornic soldiers emerged from between the Lucky H and the next-door tenement, took one look, and gave chase.

Three of them had hands on sword hilts; the other two raised crossbows.

We were supposed to be incognito.

'Run faster!'

His hate dissolved, and she ran.

The girl ran okay, but Dagger didn't like the way she kept eying the eves, the low rooflines. 'What are you thinking? You can't outrun crossbows. Stay in the crowd, and they won't shoot.'

That's a fool's game, putting off the inevitable. She panted between thoughts. *We have to ditch the people. Yona will be leaving town any time now. I need to intercept him. I need to save my sister!*

'Yona!'

Roof sod exploded from the pretzel shop as they passed, raining grass and clumps of dirt. Telyn used distraction to duck into an alley, spring off a barrel, and scramble onto a low roof. She traversed this roof, jumped to the next one, and rolled. She'd done this a hundred times, though never with the whole world after her.

And never with a broken collar bone. Biting pain attacked her; with an audible grinding noise the bones slipped and stabbed into the meat of her chest. She yowled, tripped, and nearly fell off the roof.

'Steady! Steady!' Dagger seemed able to loan her some of his mettle. As though doused with enchanted chickamee, her mind-fog cleared; the pain receded to a dull ache; she regained her balance and looked behind her. Few could have followed her up that steep roof, and the coast was clear in that direction. But they didn't have to follow—ahead, several cornics and a half dozen humans mounted one of the sod roofs.

The cornics meant business.

The humans were laughing, cheering her on, and interfering with the cornics as much as possible

Laughing! The drunken louts, what do they think is happening?

'Everyone can see us. We've got to get down.'

No, they can't.

'This might be a good place to hide at nighttime, but during the day, we're in plain sight.'

Telyn scowled and sprinted harder, accelerating to the eves. She took a flying leap. A couple of projectiles whizzed by, but she landed true and kept running. From all around—the men behind her, the crowds on the streets, and from the rooftops on the street above—came cheering. The town surged after her like this was some kind of sporting event.

The final structure in the row was the Copcut Ash. In order to make the jump, she would have to clear the alley where Tabbard had ambushed them. She'd never attempted this jump. For one thing, she didn't want Ouzeley to catch her on his roof. For another, it was a long way and a steep roof.

No hesitation, do or die.

She gathered herself and jumped with everything she had. Every bit of strength in her thighs, in her calves, in her arms and shoulders reached to bridge the distance.

Time seemed to move in slow motion. Up, up she soared. Wind rushed past her ears. She felt light as a feather. Her knees lifted, her feet relaxed, her chest rose...

...and then gravity caught her and pulled. The Copcut Ash's shingles approached.

Fast.

As she descended, a bolt or arrow ripped through the tangled mat of her hair.

Ow! My hair!

'Could have been—' Dagger began.

Telyn made no effort to soften her landing; she hoped, in fact, that it rattled the ceiling and maybe dislodged a chandelier, both for the distraction and to stick it to the Ouzeleys.

'Could have been your head! Get off the blasted roof.'

Blue lightening crackled over her left shoulder, nearly singeing her.

'Stupid flacks!' Dagger thought. 'They're throwing magic with all this chaos wood around.'

Only way is up. Come on.

Telyn realized that the thief was right. On top, they would stand out like trees atop a ridgeline at sunset.

Easy targets.

No choice; made mine already.

They crested the tall, peaked roof and found the market square chock full of humans, nonhumans, and pack animals. A corral had been set up for the aberrations captured from the Chaos Woods. A possible distraction? Could they free some of the creatures, cause a stampede?

To a man, everyone in the square appeared to be awaiting her. Every face stared at the roof of the Copcut Ash. Every transaction paused, every conversation ceased, and even the babies hushed.

Telyn pumped her fist, and the crowd roared. When a squad of cornic soldiers jogged towards the Copcut Ash, human men and women linked arms with thaumas and blocked them.

Clearly, the cornics' pro-slavery policy had angered a lot of people. Even those who tolerated slavery in their hometowns didn't want to see it spread to Harlech.

'Are we going to posture, or are we going to live?'

Right.

Telyn slid down the final slope, jumped to the ground, and rolled. Humans closed in around her, making it impossible for the cornics to shoot arrows or crossbow bolts without serious collateral damage.

The crowd parted before and closed behind her in an act of defiance toward the pursuing authorities, and Telyn moved quickly. Her gaze fell on the steam bath's entrance.

In there.

'No, bad idea.'

The door opened; an old woman hobbled out. Telyn ducked under the porch's handrail and slid inside.

A small reception area, tile, humidity.

Dagger wouldn't let her continue. He'd frozen her legs. 'This is a trap. They'll be waiting for us at the back door.'

More than one door.

Betty Yarwood set down a load of white towels. "Honey, are you in or out? Pay in advance, its four birds for—"

"I'm coming in," Telyn mumbled, jerking away from the door frame and staggering forward. The thief resisted every step, tried to turn her muscles in the opposite direction.

'Don't do this.'

Let me go. I know Harlech, you don't.

'I scouted escape routes when I set up the auction, and this isn't one of them.'

Betty placed her hands on her hips. "I recognize you, young woman. I let you in for free to help your blubbering friend Caitlin, but today you pay full price. Spring Sale price, dear, four hurons."

Telyn reached into her purse, and to Dagger's surprise but not her own, found only two eggs. She placed them in Betty's hand. Each move cost her tremendous effort. The thief resisted the whole way.

'Have to leave, fool girl.'

No!

Betty stared between the insufficient coin to Telyn's tortured face. "Even though Leutric Quid is schoolmaster, I'm sure you can count better than—Are you okay, honey? Do you need a doctor?"

The door smashed open at Telyn's rear: cornic soldiers and spectators jammed together, all trying to pile in at the same time.

Dagger suddenly stopped resisting and began urging her on, punctuating 'Go, go, go,' with 'I told you so, fool girl.'

But, as Telyn dodged ahead, Betty grabbed hold of Telyn's shirt and spun her to a stop. The wool tore some but held.

"It's four hurons the entry," the proprietor managed between gritted breaths as Telyn struggled to break free.

Telyn hammered her fist on the woman's arm, but it didn't budge.

Dagger growled; he had sent that arm, but Telyn didn't have his fighting skill. She'd missed the nerve.

Don't hit people!

'No choice, fool—'

Always a choice.

Telyn shrugged out of her blouse.

"Keep it!" she shouted, dodging through the door into the steamy, surreal world. Nothing unusual about wearing nothing but an undershirt in Steamy Betty's. In fact, she was overdressed.

A hallway stretched before her, broken by curtains to the left in a long row—changing rooms. Individual chambers were arranged on the right, steam leaking underneath the curtains.

It was crowded with semi-clad folks, men mostly, a few women, and a couple of scaly anaconda who flicked their long tongues at her. Wet footprints covered the tile floor.

"Hey, no street clothes!" someone exclaimed.

To the right, a door hid the room where she, Caitlin and Rayvn had met. That was a dead end.

Telyn knew the spa had at least two exits besides the main one; she just didn't know exactly how to get there. But it couldn't be too complicated, could it? One was upstairs, near the roofs where she felt comfortable.

'We need a disguise,' Dagger said, eying the cubbies. 'Lots of clothes here.'

Betty Yarwood's shrill voice from behind demanded four hurons apiece or *no one* was getting in. Apparently, the woolen shirt was sufficient for Telyn's fare, for Betty seemed to be doing a good job containing the onslaught, but it was only a matter of seconds. The hubbub grew.

Telyn snagged a fuzzy robe from the cubbies and bundled it under her arm.

'A bathrobe?'

It's Spring Sale, anything goes. Telyn also grabbed a man's plaid shirt that might just be her size.

She ran straight, then veered right toward the wealthier, private chambers and stairs—or a back door, she hoped.

A wall-tile shattered in front of her.

Telyn had trouble processing how that could have happened. One minute, a white tile wall stood about head-height; the next, it dissolved into an explosion of little shards.

Are you doing that?

Another explosion. Slivers pierced the skin of Telyn's neck. She ducked right, through a curtain—not where she'd intended to go. Four women lay face-down on benches with stones in rows down their backs. One of them stirred.

'Bolts, crossbow,' the thief thought. 'Don't panic.'

"They're trying to kill us!" Telyn shouted. "The cornics have gone mad."

The women sat up. Two strangers, along with Annalise Dragan, the girl whose trousers Telyn had swiped and stuffed with straw, and her mother.

Of course.

"Who—" Annalise asked.

Telyn reached the door on the far side of the room. Locked.

We are trapped! She wiggled the handle like crazy.

'Kick the door right on the lock. It's old, flimsy; probably dry rot in this place. Try it, now.'

Dry rot?

'Wet rot—just kick!'

"What's happening?" Annalise asked, as all four women stood.

"They're after me," Telyn said, rearing back, "soldiers."

Telyn kicked. Something flared within her foot. Probably just the pain of kicking the door, but the room seemed to grow cold, and the wood old, and the door splintered around the lock. Her ankle didn't break, nor did her foot.

Annalise stared wide-eyed at the shattered door, and then she did something completely unexpected. She picked up the bench she'd been lying on and lay it crossways against the entry. "Come on, help me," she said, and the other women began building a barricade with their benches.

Even Mrs. Dragan helped.

'Stop staring and run!'

"Thanks," Telyn called over her shoulder.

The architecture changed. No longer marked by tile and scummy grout, flagstone and boulders made up the decorations, and the air was heavily laden with cedar. She'd ducked into the expensive thauma side of the spa.

All manner of bodies lounged on the benches, from short, hairy schmooks to glistening trogos and everything in between. Upon seeing Telyn, they all wore the same jolted expression of a person waking up from a nightmare.

Into a nightmare, more like.

A door splintering in your face might just do that to you, Telyn reflected. *Or a human intruding in thauma-land.*

The main difference here was that when these creatures moved, the air crackled with magical energy, not something you'd have on the human side.

The schmooks reacted first, wiggling their little fingers and sending black, creepy worm-things through the air at Telyn's waist.

'Jump!' The thief ordered inside her head.

Instead, Telyn dove. Enough slick covered the floor that she glided forward and plopped right into the wading pool. She ducked underwater and pushed off with her feet. Shattered ceiling tiles told of magic gone awry or crossbow bolts hitting overhead, or both.

Angry shouts told of collateral damage.

All manner of debris began hitting the pool—tiles, towels, drinks —and bodies followed. Not dead bodies, but brawling nonhumans swinging elbows, fists, and horns.

Telyn didn't have time to note who fought whom.

'Good, they all hate each other,' the thief mused. 'They probably hate the cornics worst of all.'

Telyn frog-kicked to the stairs, happy to be barefoot. The water boiled with falling thaumas and churning magic. She pushed up with her hands, emerged on the far side of the pool, gasped in a breath, and climbed out between fighters casting magic and colorful language. The plaid shirt had fallen from her hands, but she managed to maintain her hold on the robe, now soaking wet.

Dagger began laughing while she tried to breathe. They lost body coordination. Her head grew light, and she sagged against the wall, exiting the room and moving around the corner awkwardly.

Keep going...

She pushed toward a spiral stairway leading up.

The thief kept laughing.

You aren't entirely stable, are you?

If anything, his laughter intensified.

Telyn's laughter intensified.

I must look like a lunatic.

No, I am a lunatic. *Holy Mother of Squirrels, a ghost lives inside my head!*

Telyn's mind clicked. This was a similar stairway to the one in the Sable Head, though curved instead of square-cornered.

This should lead to apartments or rooms upstairs.

The laughter ceased. 'We'll be trapped.'

There's a door up here somewhere.

'They will be guarding the doors.'

A window, then. *We haven't any choice, unless you can make an exit in these walls with your magic.*

Riser after riser they climbed, the stairway curving around itself. Coming level with the landing, Telyn met the last person in the world she wanted to see.

Worse than Second Gajos.

Worse even than crossing paths with Yona Unega or Taitl-Vaiana.

"Mrs. de Galati," she breathed.

The pattern witch spread her arms and spoke arcane words, casting some sort of spell.

In Telyn's head, Dagger screamed.

CHAPTER SIXTY-ONE

"Mrs. de Galati," Telyn said again, breathlessly, as the pattern witch stopped chanting for a moment. "What are you doing here?"

She wore a formal-looking kimono with golden-embroidered dragonflies on the cuffs and a knee-length skirt. She might have come to enjoy the spa, but Telyn didn't think so.

The thauma's ears flattened against her head. She bared her incisors. "What have you done with my daughter's friend?"

The thief lurched within but managed not to respond...barely. He cowered somewhere within Telyn's liver—or so she imagined. For the first time since becoming possessed, her thoughts were completely clear, her memory whole. She couldn't believe she had just caused so much havoc within the spa...and half of Harlech. She felt stunned and terrified and exhilarated. And she knew what she had to do.

"Mrs. de Galati, Rayvn helped me free the...the ghost you put away. The one that had possessed the eehoo—"

"I recognize you. You will not possess this girl."

"No, Mrs. de Galati, you don't understand. This is Telyn talking. I need him."

"The ghost is manipulating you, human girl. This is a vengeful spirit. He will do anything to fulfill his obsession—lie, cheat, maim, kill. Nothing will get in his way. You are his vessel. He will use you up and find another body, if that is what it takes. He has no honor and no loyalty; nothing remains to him beyond the obsession for revenge."

"This is me talking, me, daughter of Esther and Dorian Brower."

The pattern witch's violet eyes bore into Telyn's own.

"It won't be. If he can't wrest control from you by force, as time goes on, the spirit will get more and more subtle at manipulating you, until you cannot even tell where the thief ends and you begin. Human girl, I know the seductive power of possession, and I cannot let you fall into it."

All this time, the pattern witch's hands twisted and curled. Her claws extended and retracted as if, beyond Telyn's awareness, she engaged in a wrestling match with Dagger.

"You don't understand."

"*You* don't understand, Telyn Lilith Brower. The way angel water took your mom away from you, the spirit will take you until there isn't anything left but the absolute, burning need for vengeance."

A well of hollowness filled Telyn. Angel water, malt, alcoholism—this she understood, feared, hated, just like the thief's ghost hated Yona Unega.

Inside her liver, the ghost hissed. Whatever remained of Dagger had turned pure animal.

Shouts and wet footfalls sounded nearby. The searchers had nearly found them. Water dripped from Telyn's hair down her back. She shrugged into the robe she'd been carrying. Of course, the robe was as soaked as a drowned llama, but at least it wasn't transparent.

"My sister needs me to do this. Please, Mrs. de Galati, I know what I'm saying. Rayvn trusts me. She helped me do this."

Understanding filled the thauma's eyes. "I know she helped you, human girl. But can you trust Rayvn's judgment?"

"Yes. Yes, I do. She is my friend." Telyn took a deep breath. "The question is, Mrs. de Galati, do you?"

Sympathy softened the pattern witch's eyes. Telyn saw there a touch of humanity. "I can, under one condition."

The thief stirred within Telyn.

"Tell me your true name." A rumble of power accompanied the words.

"No," Telyn replied, without thinking.

Mrs. de Galati smiled by baring her incisors. "You don't have the control you thought, do you, human child?"

Come on, tell her.

'Never,' Dagger replied. 'The pattern witch will hurt me. Hurt *us*. Flacks are evil. You know this. I've seen it within you. You hate them, and with good reason. Flacks enslave us. They manipulate us and keep us down. They will sell your sister to the galleys or worse.'

No, that isn't true. I do not hate them, not all—

The pattern witch twisted her hands, as if wringing out an invisible rag, and not only did Dagger groan, but Telyn did as well. It felt as if her guts had been torqued by those cat claws.

Telyn fell to her knees. Her bowels wanted to explode.

"We are taking you to the Sepulcher, Miss Brower. You are not responsible for what has happened here. We will exorcise this vengeful spirit once and for all and bind him to the eternal stone."

"No, please, Mrs. de Galati," Telyn managed to choke out. The pain in her guts relaxed partway, and she began to cry. "I have to do this. *Please*. Please trust Rayvn's choice. She helped us free the ghost in order to save my sister."

"We must move fast, my dear. The vengeful spirit nearly has you."

'Not true,' the thief thought. 'We are partners, Telyn. We can help each other. We *must* help each other. Only I can take on the penumbra daemon, and only you can give me the time I need. You need to convince the witch to let us go.'

"Give me your true name. Otherwise, we are going now." The pattern witch freed a pouch from within her sash, and Telyn knew this was the end. Whatever was in that pouch would end her choices once and for all.

Tell her.

'No.'

If you don't tell her, you will never get your revenge. Yona Unega will have beaten you.

'No!'

"Dagger," Telyn said, quickly. "His name is Dagger."

"Good," Mrs. de Galati said. "If you lied, I would have had to tear the ghost from you by more violent means, and you might not have survived. Then Rayvn would have to make a new friend, and she doesn't make friends easily." She took a short step forward, until her long, white eyebrow whiskers brushed Telyn's chin.

"Dagger is not a birth name, not a true name. This is your last chance, spirit." She freed the strings of the pouch, dipped her fingers inside. It smelled slightly rotten.

The oil lamps flared, and their smoke began to paint on the walls a cityscape with canals and onion-domed buildings. A high-pitched whine began in Telyn's ears, hurting them.

Whatever you're planning, don't do it.

'She won't take me.'

She is not the only pattern witch in Harlech. There are six more.

The thief growled.

Grout powdered and rained down. Mrs. de Galati's neck shifted, as though she were readying for a brawl.

If you don't tell her your real name, I...I will tell Yona you have a wife, Telyn said, feeling scummy at the lengths she had to go to free her sister—to correct her own original sin. *I will draw a picture of her. I have seen her in your memories. Aeres, isn't it?*

Some of the hate Dagger stored for the mind wizard shifted to Telyn; like a pulsing cancer, the hatred turned on its host.

There was no forgiveness in this entity. The part that had returned from the Sepulcher was partial, incomplete, guileful, and merciless.

The lamp-carbon ceased drawing on the walls. A few final grains from the ceiling grout rained on Mrs. de Galati's head.

A door banged open behind them. Sloshing footfalls approached.

"We are out of time, spirit," Mrs. de Galati said. "Give me the names of your parents, the spellings and pronunciations. You have three seconds."

The name spilled from Telyn's spittle-wet lips.

"No parents, orphan. First name Lindsey, middle Medyn, last Cannock."

"Now the ones who raised you, their hometown, and where you plan to go if you escape from Harlech."

"Raised by Hatchet Nation, section boss Connor Phillips. Going to kill the cereb Yona Unega and the schmook Taito-Vaiana if we...get out of here...alive."

Telyn didn't control her neck. She wanted to turn to look behind her, but her gaze remained locked onto Mrs. de Galati's geode eyes.

"Yona is not in Harlech, not yet," Telyn said. "That's why we're in such a hurry. We have to get Cressida free before the mind wizard comes."

"You will help Telyn free her sister, and then you will come back to me, Lindsey Medyn Cannock. You will not leave Harlech until we have spoken again," the pattern witch said. "And you will not harm any of her friends. Swear to it."

Telyn's neck suddenly relaxed, and she was able to look around. Humans and flacks in various states of dress and nudity had gathered on the lower stairs, watching the exchange with fear. A cornic soldier, armored, holding a crossbow, pushed his way to the front of the crowd.

The soldier pointed his crossbow at Telyn's back. He squeezed the trigger.

Just as the bolt fired, one of the human women stumbled into him. The bolt went wide.

It was Mrs. Dragan, her face fierce and unreadable.

"I swear it, witch," Dagger vowed, with Telyn's voice.

The pattern witch stepped around Teyln, descended the stairs with her hands held up, blocking the cornic's line of sight. In one hand, she held up the pouch.

"I've taken care of the situation. She is no longer possessed. I've got to get this to the Sepulcher before it explodes. The vengeful spirit is inside." The bag began to writhe, pattern witch magic animating the cloth, no doubt.

Mrs. de Galati swept down the stairs, holding the talisman before her, and the mob parted to either side. Even the soldier scrambled out of the way, fear plain on his sheep-like muzzle.

"Beware," the pattern witch continued. "Beware, extremely volatile..."

CHAPTER SIXTY-TWO

Telyn and the thief padded down Steamy Betty's second-floor hallway. Through an open door, she noticed a window and entered the small room. It was a simple matter to lift the window, ascend to the roof, and drop into the crowd on the far side. Their dripping wet bathrobe and stockings weren't the strangest getup at the Spring Sale. They hardly attracted any attention at all.

The pattern witch could have at least wrung out our clothes, Telyn thought petulantly. Her wet underthings began to chafe.

We are going to cross the bridge and wait for the penumbra daemon in the forest.

'Yona will make for Enshede as fast as he can.'

We're not going to meet Yona, but his penumbra daemon. Yona will be inside it, you'll see. If you remember, your ghost powers disrupted the daemon in the Sable Head. That's why, er, why I need you—but we have to wait for the right moment.

'I'm listening.'

The daemon came to Harlech and talked to me—Well, not exactly. Yona talked to me through the daemon. It's complicated. Point is, the daemon-cereb came to Harlech in the dead of winter when all the passes were snowed shut. No one can do that—excepting Redbeard. That tells me the daemon is comfortable in the wilds.

So, here's what I think: When the daemon-cereb steals the mask, Harlech will boil like a cracked beehive. First thing, the cornics will block the road to Enshede. They won't think to block the bridge until later. This bridge is the closest escape route. The daemon-cereb will come here.

'What if he takes the road past the Sepulcher and Mirror Lake?'

Telyn nearly missed a step. *I, ah, I hadn't thought of that. But no, that way is just a round-about route into the Chaos Woods. No, the daemon will pass here.*

'If you're wrong, we miss our chance at the forehead. We won't be able to pay the bond price for Cressida, and once your sister disappears into the slave markets of Enshede, you will never find her again.'

I will not second-guess myself. Telyn didn't like the uncertainty boiling in her belly.

Then, for the second time in twenty-four hours, the warning bell tolled.

"That's it," Telyn said aloud. "The penumbra daemon has taken the forehead."

The thief growled.

While the Spring Sale continued its flurry of activity, another kerfuffle began. Around the Prefecture and along Main Street, cornic soldiers moved, marched, ran, shouted, and executed various combinations of actions that indicated officers in a panic and soldiers without clear orders. Telyn hadn't realized so many soldiers had been in Harlech until they all roiled around like blood-salmon after a wounded otter.

The crowds withdrew from the bridge. In their minds, threats came *from* the Chaos Woods; threats did not flee *to* it. When the warning bell sounded, the locals assumed some monster must have been spotted out in the wilds, and the charging cornic soldiers confirmed their worst fears.

Soon, the bridge was abandoned, leaving only Telyn standing on the Chaos Woods side like a knight awaiting a duel in one of Redbeard's tales. If only she had a sword at her side and fancy, embroidered clothes with wide sleeves and thigh-high boots.

Telyn bare-hands Brower, Knight of the Soaking Bathrobe, she thought.

She brushed a strand of kinky brown hair from her face, feeling exposed and vulnerable—not to mention uncomfortable.

'Pattern witches are dangerous,' the thief growled within. 'In many ways, I think they rival cerebs in sheer power, although they can't take control of your mind.'

Telyn snorted. *You have that in common with Yona.*

'Don't compare me to that monster.'

Then stop trying to take over my mind.

'If I knew what a pain it would be, I never would have possessed a teenager.'

I will not banter with you.

Across the Elbus River, soldiers had cordoned off the Prefecture, and a fist of them proceeded down Main Street towards Enshede.

See, she taunted Dagger, *I guessed correctly. They haven't bothered with the bridge.*

'The daemon could blow right by us,' the thief countered.

If he does, use your power to disrupt him.

'To exert that much power, I will have to seize you completely. I am just learning to control this.' The thief spread Telyn's fingers. The hair on her arm lifted—and that was all.

You'll have to do better than that.

'It seems to be getting harder, not easier. The power is more... contained.'

Great. Just great.

'I gave the witch my name. She took things from me.'

If you want revenge, Telyn thought, deliberately provoking him, *You will have to make it work. Anyway, Yona won't blow by us. He's too arrogant. He'll stop to brag.*

A flicker of shadow seemed to pass under the bridge pillar. If she hadn't been watching, she would have missed it.

Be ready. He's coming.

Faces appeared from the guard post, two human and one cornic. They surveyed the situation briefly, then disappeared back inside. Like the rest of Harlech, they probably associated the warning bell with danger from within the Chaos Woods. They hadn't yet been ordered to prevent people from fleeing Harlech.

Telyn tossed back her hair and stood proudly, challenging, glad of her height.

The penumbra daemon sprinted halfway across the bridge, slowed, and padded the last few feet to pause in front of her. It rose to its back legs, and the shadows coalesced into a flickering version of Yona Unega, the mind wizard.

His eyes took in her appearance from toes to ears. "You should leave fashion design to your sister."

Telyn belted the robe tighter around her middle. "Thank you for bringing me Cressida's bond price."

"You agreed to bring me the mask, human. I had to break it out of the vault—and the building—myself," the daemon-cereb said in his wavering, half-manifest voice.

The thief's control began slipping. 'Revenge.'

Not yet, Telyn urged. Through her bare feet, she felt the bridge begin to tremble. *Not yet.*

To try to keep the thief's rage from showing, Telyn affected a more formal tone. She nearly succeeded. Nearly. "Thank you for admitting you have the forehead piece. My plan got you into the Prefecture and past the guards, and I tricked Corporal Velky into activating the statuette so that you could, ah, recover the forehead. You owe me the bond price, as agreed."

Dagger's mental growl descended into a hiss.

The cereb sent crushing pain into Telyn's mind. Telyn dropped to one knee and clutched her temples with both hands. If Dagger hadn't taken control, she would have curled into a ball there on the bridge.

"You are a clever girl. It is a shame to waste you, but you have become too arrogant, a character flaw you have not earned."

More pain stabbed through her mind—their mind. Dagger refused to drop completely to the ground. Little by little, inch by agonizing inch, he pulled his hands away from his head—*My head!* Telyn thought—rose to stand on two feet, and squared his shoulders with as much dignity as the pain would allow.

'You did well, Telyn. Let me take this from here.'

Telyn gave a mental nod and released her hold on her body. Allowing the ghost to flow over and around her was a relief. He cooled and soothed her, as if her mind had been seared and the thief plunged it into ice water.

Telyn became a spectator through her own eyes.

Will I ever be myself again?

'Sure...whenever I need you to be, Too-tall.'

The thief tossed his head—Telyn's head—in what he hoped was a feminine hair-flick. "You can't crush me, Yona Unega. Pay me, and I will forget we ever met."

"Oh, you *are* a rule-breaker." Yona chuckled with something like admiration. "What other talismans have you collected besides the Ever-Guise's forehead, human girl? No one can resist my mind without magic to help them."

"You are too far away to use your mind-powers effectively, dirty flack, even through your daemon. I got the Ever-Guise piece for you; without me, you would never have recovered it. Now pay me what you owe me." Dagger mentioned the Ever-Guise deliberately. He wanted to plant that idea in Yona's mind that with the mask, his powers would be amplified. The mind wizard *had* to believe that—and act on it.

There followed a silence. The daemon-cereb's smoke-like mouth tentacles weaved in questioning circles. "That may be so. But, through the daemon, I have other powers. I can absorb you. The daemon would enjoy that, and, I admit, it would be interesting to experience for the first time."

No, don't let him do that.

"Go ahead, mind wizard. I dare you."

To Telyn's dismay, Dagger actually grinned. Inwardly, he taunted Telyn. 'Why not? If your body gets absorbed, I can just possess another, more cooperative body—one Yona has never seen. Much easier to sneak up on him if he won't recognize me from a mile away, Too-tall. Much easier to enact my revenge in the time and place of my choosing.'

Telyn thought furiously. She'd given away too much. She couldn't so much as move a finger, though she tried with all her might. It was like trying to grow wings and fly! The muscles and nerves no longer belonged to her.

She had to get Dagger back on her side.

We're alone on a bridge, fool of a thief. Last time, you had to possess an eehoo. What will it be this time, a squirrel? Maybe a dung beetle? Listen, you can't kill Yona now. He isn't here in the flesh.

'Kill!' thought the vengeful spirit.

The bridge vibrated for real. The soldiers exited the guard post, looked both ways, and sprinted toward Harlech. They must've thought an earthquake was beginning. Or a flood.

Which might just be true.

You can't kill Yona, Telyn repeated in her mind, *but you can hurt him. Get him to show you the forehead piece. Stick with the plan, and we hurt him a little now. Later, we'll kill him.*

'Kill!'

"What is wrong with your face?" the daemon-cereb asked. "You keep frowning and smiling, clenching your jaw and winking like a fool."

"As if you can talk, maggot-neck," Telyn managed through clenched jaw and gritted teeth. She retrieved enough control to stop winking. "Give me the bond price or give me the forehead piece so I can redeem my sister."

"You are a clever girl. I suspect your sister is as well—which is why I purchased her this morning." The daemon-cereb pulled the forehead piece from somewhere within himself, shadow blending with ghost-clothes, mind wizard with penumbra daemon, and Telyn gasped. "Since you took your sweet time moving forward with the plan, I sent my associate to Harlech to retrieve the forehead piece in his own, unique way. Purchasing Cressida Brower was an afterthought, a trifle. No, you won't be freeing your sister anytime, soon. With Cressida, I get two slaves for the price of one, isn't that right, Telyn? As long as I command Cressida, I command you as well."

The daemon was living shadow; the forehead piece was real and solid. When placed on the creature's face, the Ever-Guise did not blend completely. It did not mimic the flesh as it had when the humans had worn it; it hung there, suspended on smoke.

With the forehead in place, the power of the mind wizard's attack came much stronger, a howling ache behind the eyes, and both Dagger and Telyn screamed.

"You are not alone, girl," the daemon-cereb said. "What magic is this? What have you done?"

Use your powers, Telyn managed.

Her body tensed, and only a tiny crackle came from between her fingers. A leaf flipped over.

'That pattern-thing took my name,' Dagger rasped. 'I can't do it.'

"You dare threaten my daemon," the cereb said, probing now. The pain spread from her eyes to her ears and tongue. "Now I know how the human dares resist me. She does not control her own body. Who are you in there?"

"I come to you from the grave," Dagger said, pushing to access his ghost magic. "I am your nemesis."

"Give me your name, *nemesis*," the daemon-cereb said, sarcastically, "so I can kill your family and your family's family."

Again, Telyn-thief stretched out her hand, and again, no more than a tiny crackle of power manifested, hardly enough stir the air. The mind wizard's attack turned from Telyn to the ghost, and incredibly, it seemed to be working. The attack drove Dagger from Telyn's mind altogether. Telyn found herself feeling empty, wobbly, like a clay vessel awaiting the blow that would smash it to pieces.

Dagger was gone.

"You want my name?" she mumbled. "Let me spell it for you." Reaching out to touch the daemon (it was slippery but solid enough, and it didn't absorb her), she spelled the one word that had a chance to save her. "A-G-O-R-M-I-C."

Abruptly, the mind wizard's attack ceased. The daemon-shadows sucked together, became solid, and the statuette clattered to the ground. The ceramic forehead dropped to the stone of the bridge, bounced once, and landed upside down.

"Aled's rump, he didn't change the activation word." Telyn reached down and picked up the statuette.

It turned slippery, then spongy, and darkness surrounded it. The daemon was in the process of reforming.

'Maybe it isn't easy to change,' said Dagger, returning from wherever he'd been hiding. 'Maybe he *can't* change it.'

He's changing it now, Telyn thought. *Quick, we have to get rid of it.* 'How?'

What I should have done with the forehead; what Cressida told me to do. From the side of the bridge, Telyn pitched the statuette as far as she could. A shadow surrounded it, but the remaining nugget hit the edge of Defiance Falls. The churning whitewater carried it over.

'Do you really think that will stop it?'

I think so. It won't kill it, but even the daemon runs on land. It needs something solid to hold onto. It will be far downstream before it pulls itself from the water. She squatted to retrieve the forehead. *Then it will have to find a way back, which won't be easy, even for a creature like that. And the cornics will have Harlech cordoned off and watched. They won't forget this bridge for long.*

If they daemon-cereb tries to come back to Harlech, it will have a fight on its hands. That gives us time to sell the forehead and redeem my sister.

With the mask tucked into the breast of her bathrobe, Telyn-thief began walking back across the bridge and toward the rendezvous point with her friends. Before they made it to the town, a cornic squad took up station at the guard house.

The thief began laughing through Telyn's mouth. The soldiers eyed her wryly—not as a threat, but as if she'd had too much angel water.

What's so funny?

'You beat the mind wizard, girl—a teenager.' He gave a mental shake of his head. 'A teenager, Aled's glorious, pimply rump. A teenager!'

Within her own mind, Telyn said, *I knew he would have to show off.*

'And that was enough.'

CHAPTER SIXTY-THREE

Telyn gathered her friends, and they returned to her room. There, she changed into dry clothes: stockings and a long skirt, a white, short-sleeved shirt with a green belt sash, and a frilly white hood as a sort of disguise. After a much-needed glass of sweet salmonberry cordial, they went over the plan one more time; and then, as the sun began to fall, they infiltrated the Spring Sale.

Caitlin and Hosh took the chrysalis shell and joined the line in front of the Hall of Magic, while Telyn and Rayvn took a rolled-up banner and went to the Prefecture.

Per age-old custom, at twilight, all Harlech's bells—funeral, hour, and warning—gonged simultaneously.

A roar went up from every human, every thauma, every mouth that had a voice and some creatures that, well, Telyn wasn't sure how they made their noises. Torches on long poles flared all along the avenues, in a ring around the market square, and along the bridge to the Chaos Woods.

The Hall of Magic was open.

Nothing could have stopped the Spring Sale at this late date—not even Second Gajos losing his prized artifact, nor the fact that the thief remained at large.

The line of trappers wanting to sell their wares snaked all the way across the arched bridge into flacktown, and that line pushed forward eagerly, compressing the space between men and beasts. Their progress stalled right away, for just inside the tent, cornic administrators checked take permits against the goods the trappers wanted to sell, confiscated any unauthorized booty, and administered justice against "poachers."

Telyn and Dagger both hated this term, which implied that everything within the Chaos Woods—mineral, vegetable, animal, and soul—belonged to the Cornic Empire.

Hosh and Caitlin waited in that line with the chrysalis shell and their one take permit.

For the forehead piece was another matter. That was why Telyn and Rayvn scaled the face of the Prefecture in front of cornics, trappers, and the rest of the world. Rayvn wore the garish clothing of a circus performer: sheer orange pants, a pink undershirt with a blue, sleeveless slipover blouse embroidered with centipedes along the seams and a matching belt—*What is it with pattern witches and centipedes?*—topped off with a goblin mask she had purchased at the sale.

Telyn's more traditional attire was supposed to blend in. 'Look at the pattern girl,' it said. 'She's the star. Nothing to see here.' Her bare feet stuck almost like eehoo paws on the building's stone face. She'd been climbing so long that she had a hard time understanding how other folks could not scale even simple surfaces. The Prefecture's stone offered innumerable hand- and footholds to the experienced climber; she'd just never dared scale it before.

The girls hefted a rolled-up banner between them. When they approached the top, they unfurled it.

*Welcome to the Spring Sale
to the Glory of the Empire*

Rayvn flung off her cape, which glided over the crowd like an enormous, tropical bird. Those folks who bothered to watch cheered. By the time anyone thought to look for Telyn, she had slipped over the roof line and into the bell tower. There she waited, curled into a ball, hands clamped firmly over her ears just in case she'd been spotted and someone rang the warning bell.

This part of the plan wasn't strictly necessary, and she wondered if the risk was worth it—but she wanted any advantage she could get.

When Yona had triggered the alarm on the Hall of Magic, the soldiers arrived in seconds. She needed more than seconds.

Telyn had no doubt that a few townsfolk had noticed her climb up here, but likely they would be expecting her to perform some trick, or perhaps they simply thought she would exit down the staircase.

That was her theory.

Dagger hadn't voiced his opinion. He'd gone dark; maybe he was sleeping.

Do vengeful spirits need sleep?

When it became clear her intrusion would not trigger an alarm, she stood inside the warning bell's mouth and began to secure rags around the clapper. (*So much metal! How had they even lifted the bell this high?*) Once she was sure any toll would be muffled, she used a knife to cut most of the way through the rope that descended through a hole in the floor.

If the cornic downstairs grew frustrated that the warning bell didn't ring and pulled really hard, the rope would snap—in theory, at least.

Further delay. Delay is good.

Her work accomplished, she ducked out and put her chin on the balustrade for a moment, captivated by the beauty of her beloved home.

At night, Harlech was usually a silent town, a shadow town. With the Spring Sale in full swing, it had become a torchlight town. In the distance, the Sable Head glowed from lamps within and torches without. The Copcut Ash outshone it, of course, with some sort of yellow and green braziers around the outside twinkling like fireflies, magic that a man like Ouzeley could rent without breaking the second Rule.

Cook fires dotted the streets and the sod roofs, while the torches on the bridge into the Chaos Woods—the way they seemed to draw together in the distance—resembled a path into one's imagination, law into chaos, today into the unknowable future, life into afterlife.

Telyn felt, somehow, that her destiny and those woods were linked. She would, someday, enter the Chaos Woods again, traverse Aumerhem Pass where her dad had fallen, and explore the plateau beyond.

Telyn breathed a deep sigh. If only she had pitched that forehead piece into the river in the beginning, this town would still be hers. If only she had thought before making her wishes, or made none at all, or made stupid wishes like Hosh.

She chuckled a little.

She could have coaxed Joram into liking her, or a dozen Jorams, and experienced attention and popularity until she tired of it—and then flung the forehead piece into the river.

Her eyes teared up. She didn't think she would be able to stay in Harlech after this, not with the rules she had broken and the Ouzeleys hating her, not while she was known as the spirit-possessed girl, the freak with the sister-slave.

'We could blend, your mind with my mind, twice the intellect. All it takes is surrender,' Dagger thought.

Ah, awake at last. How do you know about surrender? You been a ghost before?

The thief gave a mental shrug. 'Yes, with Tums. And no, I don't really know.'

You ruined my musing.

'Then we might as well get off the roof. Or do you want one of the soldiers to glance up here and investigate?'

One more thing.

As she side-stepped around the bell, Telyn removed four shims from her pocket. She didn't dare drive the shims in with a hammer— if anyone remained on the top floor, it would be too loud—but she didn't think it necessary. Instead, she used a pair of pliers to wiggle the triangular pieces of wood in the corners of the trapdoor.

It would slow them down.

Now, for the Hall of Magic. If he's any kind of buyer, he will want to be there from the moment the curtain opens so that he does not miss the best merchandise.

'How did you know the cornics wouldn't post a lookout here? The bell tower has the best view in town.'

Number one, I've been watching. Number two —She climbed over the rail on the flacktown side—*if they rang the bell while anyone was here, he would go deaf.*

They rejoined Rayvn behind the Hall of Magic, counting on the dim lighting, the excessive alcohol use, and the anonymity of the crowd to hide their activities—which consisted of nothing more than waiting at first.

Dagger's impatience built, creating a tremble in her fingers like what Telyn felt before an ice-climbing competition or if she hadn't slept all night and had drunk too much chickamee.

The tip of Rayvn's tail was likewise puffy. It must be terribly obvious that they were up to no good.

Telyn considered telling her friend to ditch the goblin mask then decided it didn't really matter. Lots of people in the crowd wore masks.

They ended up buying maroons so as not to look too suspicious, and they ate the sweet nuts until they felt bloated and gross.

Finally, Little Hosh appeared. "They went in just now."

"Did their take permit work?"

"I couldn't see, but the cornics are only letting people in when someone comes out. I think it's okay."

Telyn held out an egg. "Thank you, Mini-Hosh. You did well."

The coin disappeared into a pocket, but he didn't leave.

"Ah, you're not coming inside."

"Yes, I am!"

Dagger flared inside her.

Mini-Hosh must have seen something in Telyn's eyes, because he shrank back. "Okay, okay, it was worth a shot. When can a kid get into the Hall of Magic?"

Telyn had to stuff Dagger down or he would have said something wholly inappropriate. He *really* didn't like how many people she'd involved.

"That's not what we're doing," Telyn said.

"I want to see."

"Not on your life."

He folded his arms. "I have news Hosh said I should tell you."

"Well? You're not getting another egg, so out with it."

He held out a good thirty seconds. "Okay, okay. Second Gajos is inside the Hall."

Telyn bit her lip, tapped her toe, and finally offered Mini-Hosh a second egg. Making happy sounds, he sped off—presumably to spend the coins as fast as he could.

"What do you think?" She'd intended the question for Dagger, but since she spoke aloud, Rayvn answered.

"It is natural for the second to be within the Hall of Magic. Many important figures will come to regard and bid on the magical aberrations of the Chaos Woods: members of wealthy houses, representatives of the Academy of Enshede, foreign dignitaries.

"It is also natural for the second to be here if he is looking for someone trying to fence the forehead piece. While he may have the cornic army at his disposal, he prefers to find it for himself. He will only trust a few cornics to help him. Did I do well?"

Telyn gave her a one-sided hug. "You did well, my friend."

'We're wasting time,' Dagger interjected.

They squared their shoulders to the tent, and Telyn said, "Once we're inside, no one will know whether we passed through the front or not. Ready? Let's go."

With that, Rayvn ran a claw down the canvas, splitting it asunder as easily as Mrs. de Galati had opened the wall into her home's inner sanctum.

Blue runes appeared and scattered around the hall's canvas, just like when the daemon-cereb had touched it. Rayvn and Telyn stepped through the rent into a warren of stalls and noise. A pass of Rayvn's claws, and the tent stitched closed behind them.

No warning bell: the rags had worked.

"We haven't much time," Telyn said. "Let's go."

She turned to see a pair of vars staring at their dramatic entrance. One of them winked; the other buzzed its tongue.

"He's laughing," Dagger translated through Telyn's voice. "Nothing to worry about. Vars appreciate ingenuity."

CHAPTER SIXTY-FOUR

With Hosh and Caitlin nowhere in sight, Telyn and Rayvn took a direction at random. Lemongrass-colored glow lamps hung overhead and reflected from the tent fabric and gauze-draped ceilings. Aisles branched in every direction, as if a spider had designed the Hall over uneven shrubbery.

The hall's footprint covered an area roughly a hundred paces long and fifty wide, but its blind aisles made it seem to go on forever. *Okay, Dagger, it's time you described your buyer. How can I find him if you won't even show me what he looks like?*

He'd been holding out on her, keeping that valuable piece of information to himself, which didn't seem fair.

Dagger didn't have to name him; he could show him. The ghost could share memories or hold them back at will. Telyn could as well, which made for an interesting game of senet inside her own head.

He finally replied, 'In good time. Act like we belong here.'

They wandered.

Seeing that humans outnumbered thaumas about four to one, Telyn relaxed a little. Hundreds of trappers had collected goods from the Chaos Woods, and they wanted to sell while the flacks still had coin—and while coin could be turned to good entertainment at the Spring Sale.

During the sale, anything could be had for enough hurons; later in the year, all one could buy in Harlech were infusions, alcohol, or a steam at Betty's.

Or a dress from Meander and Mohair and terrible speck stew.

"Oh, there's Tabbard—" Rayvn said, starting to wave.

"What? Don't attract his attention."

"Why not? We have nothing to hide."

Telyn pulled Rayvn down a side aisle. "That family is trouble, that's why." *That family is renting my sister like...like a pack llama!*

Rather than the cacophony outside, the hall was filled with a low murmur, the sound of haggling in dozens of languages. Hanging curtains separated booths of every size and decor. Some of the nonhumans tried to lure Telyn and Rayvn inside like carnival barkers; others waited patiently behind makeshift tables. It could have been a market anywhere in the world—if that market purchased instead of sold; if the goods in question were magical; and if all the buyers were thaumas and the sellers human.

A surprising number of booths had goods for sale, which might have explained Tabbard's presence, but Telyn didn't take anything for granted where that family was concerned.

They gawked at ever-clipping nail cutters; wart wands (for cursing your frenemies); never-dry ink pots; and one-stroke sharpening stones. So many things that would make life more convenient if only humans could possess them legally.

They might get away with keeping some of the living creatures, like meditation frogs and phase-puppies (so cute!). You could always claim you'd captured them in the Chaos Woods and were holding them until the sale—especially if you could afford to keep a spare take permit hanging around. But fire wands, retro-mirrors (which reflected what you looked like before years of worry) and belly-tucking girdles would mean a lifetime in prison for a human to even own.

So unfair! It burned Telyn's hide—and Dagger's.

Where are Hosh and Caitlin, anyway?

They were supposed to meet right where Rayvn and Telyn had

broken in. However, noting the complexity of the layout, Telyn didn't doubt they had gotten lost. She prided herself on her sense of direction, yet *she* could hardly differentiate between the sloping outer wall edge of the tent and just another dividing curtain.

Again, they ran into Tabbard; this time, he was examining cages holding rust-colored, praying mantis-like creatures. Lumps of half-melted ice littered the cage around them. As Telyn turned the other way, she noticed one of the creatures sit up, squawk, and lay a marble-sized egg of ice.

"Wait, was that a tylwig?" Her head whipped back around.

Rayvn nodded. "Highly prizes in Voolian cocktails. Raz should adopt some for the Sable Head."

Maybe Tabbard wanted a tylwig for the Copcut Ash—they could afford it—but Telyn didn't believe it. "He's following us. We need to find Caitlin and Hosh and get this over with. No more dawdling."

"If the cornics question us, we will tell them we have already sold our booty, a rumor tree acorn." Rayvn shook a coin-purse. "I can prove we have the coin. And we know where to find the tree, if necessary."

"Nice thinking. But if it comes down to our word against Tabbard's... Well, yours might count."

The aisle broadened, and soon they stood before the grand staircase to the second floor. Cornic soldiers and bureaucrats regulated traffic up and down the stairs.

'We need to go up there,' Dagger told Telyn. 'The buyer is upstairs.'

Telyn quickly gauged the scene. The symbol of the Academy of Enshede hung over the staircase, and the guards here wore Academy livery. The symbol consisted of a circle of keys laid end-to-end and surrounding three objects: a parchment, a magnifying glass, and a barn owl. On exposed tent-poles to either side of the staircase hung the List.

As they watched, the clerks turned away group of trappers. Clearly, not everyone was welcome upstairs.

"There you are." Caitlin's arm slipped around Telyn's shoulder.

"When we couldn't find you, we decided to wait here. Hosh's idea; all the aisles eventually lead here."

Hosh grinned around the egg-shaped blanket he carried. Rayvn had managed to bond the chrysalis together, although the cracks had not disappeared entirely.

"Where is the buyer?" Caitlin whispered.

Telyn nodded toward the stairs.

"Oh."

"Leave that to me," Rayvn said, taking the shell from Hosh.

"No, wait!" Caitlin and Hosh exclaimed, loud enough that the whole world turned to look. They began babbling about searches and restrictions, and Telyn just knew Hosh would say the wrong thing and give them away.

"Save it," she barked sharply, cutting off their babble. She steered everyone away from the staircase. With purposeful strides, she zigzagged among the crowd and the booths, trying to find anonymity.

"Did you get Tums in without setting off any alarms?" Hosh asked, wheezing in his struggle to catch them. He was referring not to the eehoo, but to the Ever-Guise.

Telyn pulled everyone into the first unmanned booth she encountered. Unmanned, but not empty. In addition to a rectangular wooden table and chair, it held a bookshelf crammed with books, two glow lamps, and shag throw rugs. It was unclear if the absent merchant was selling or buying.

"Yes, we have Tums. And a senseless bozo who doesn't know when to keep quiet."

"Sorry."

"What was the deal back there? The buyer is upstairs."

"How do you know?" Hosh asked.

In reply, Telyn tapped the side of her head.

"Then we're doomed," Hosh said. "You can only go upstairs if you brought something from the List."

'That's not true,' Dagger said in her mind. 'If we have Academy business, they'll let us upstairs. We just have to convince them.'

How do you intend to do that?

'The shell should do the trick. That's unusual enough if you ask for Hootie specifically.'

Hootie—is that our buyer?

Dagger's silence was answer enough for Telyn.

"We can do this. I've got a plan."

"Wait, there's more." Caitlin raised her hands, urging caution. "They're searching everyone who goes upstairs."

"Not the Ouzeleys," Hosh grumbled.

"The Ouzeleys are upstairs?"

"Mister and Missus went up a few minutes ago. But for normal folks, even flacks—sorry Rayvn—they check pockets, bags, sleeves, shoes...everything. They're feeling around people's faces, too."

"Okay. We have a plan for this. Rayvn?" Telyn patted the table, and Rayvn set the egg there, uncovered. "Risks must be taken."

Caitlin pulled the booth's hanging curtain closed.

Except for the bottom of the chrysalis, which remained glued to the bedrock, Rayvn had managed to fuse the collected pieces into an intact shell. Momentarily, a vermilion worm-light crawled along the one of the seams.

"Tip it on its side," Telyn instructed.

This exposed the missing bottom. The pattern girl fished inside and produced a leftover piece. "Ready," Rayvn said.

Slowly, reverently, Telyn removed the Ever-Guise forehead from her belt sash. This she lay onto the piece of shell. The forehead formed itself along the shell, satisfied either by the chrysalis's organic or magical nature. They melded perfectly.

Holding this in her hand, Telyn reached deep inside the chrysalis, glad for her long arms, and sandwiched the forehead between the loose piece and the dome.

She nodded, and Rayvn began to caress the chrysalis. A wet-feather aroma wafted from the hole.

Little by little, the pieces fused, with the Ever-Guise between them. Once Rayvn had finished her magic, it was close to perfect. The sensitive tips of Telyn's fingers could detect a thickness to the dome, but from the outside, the difference was undetectable. You'd have to shatter the chrysalis to find it.

"Good job, everyone." Telyn removed her arm and breathed freely for the first time since fleeing the staircase.

"Are you selling or buying?" came a bored voice from the entrance. "Because I don't want your shell unless the egg is inside of it, alive."

The kids whirled to see a schmook peeking in through the edge of the curtain. One of his two eyes peered at Rayvn, while the second took in the chrysalis. The tar-black nose sniffed, its nostrils winking open and closed.

Dagger rumbled in Telyn's mind, but he quickly decided the chipmonk-like face didn't belong to Yona's ally.

"A feathered hind shell, how unusual." The schmook said, sliding the curtain fully open. "How did you come across it?" The creature wore black academic robes to his ankles. The fox-with-a-star-eye was emblazoned on the left breast of his robes.

He's from the Order of Magic.

'Not our buyer,' Dagger said. 'But he might do.'

"We...We got it in the Chaos Woods," Hosh said. "We have a take permit."

"I should hope so. How much do you want for it?"

As Rayvn scooped up the shell, Caitlin dropped the blanket over it, saying, "Four thousand hurons only."

On the tips of their stalks, the schmook's eyes goggled. "Was that human humor?" he asked, as they edged past him into the aisle.

"Huge human humor," Rayvn offered, emphasizing the alliteration.

'The only thing worse than a bad poet,' Dagger complained as they made their way back to the central staircase, 'is a bad comedic poet.'

I kind of like it, Telyn countered, just to be contrary.

Arriving at the checkpoint to go upstairs, Rayvn took the lead. Whipping the blanket off the egg dramatically, she advanced upon the clerks and guards. With the egg, her garish outfit, and goblin mask, she certainly caught their attention. One of the soldiers half-drew his sword.

"My friends and I wish to go upstairs," Ravyn said from behind the hideously grinning mask.

The guards shifted. The female clerk frowned down at a copy of the List. "Not harpy eggs; too big. What exactly..."

"This isn't on your List," Rayvn said, pleasantly. "If it were, we would have been murdered upon setting foot in Harlech. This is so valuable, it would buy the emperor's palace."

Hosh leaned in. "She's overdoing it."

The girls nodded. Rayvn might be an awesome friend, but bargaining clearly wasn't her strong point. Best case scenario, the cornics would laugh this off and send them away.

'Maybe she'll convince them with her beautiful poetry,' Dagger added sarcastically.

The clerk, who had one horn broken off near the skull, folded up her copy of the List. "I'm sure this, eh, this shell is magnificent. But only the highly valuable or highly unusual—which is generally the same thing—would interest the buyers upstairs. Does your artifact—?"

Before Telyn could say anything about Hootie, the male clerk interrupted.

"Let them through, Gandy." The male's voice rang with high-pitched authority. His eyes seemed to quiver.

"Yes, Norfolk?"

"They will be welcome upstairs. That's an expensive item, ah, and it will be added to the List, ah, now." Norfolk's voice rose as he quickly dipped his quill and wrote "Giant egg shell" on a leather-bound ledger.

"This is highly unusual," Gandy said, drawing her sizable eyebrows together.

"Actually," Rayvn said, "it is a chrysalis."

Sweating down his black muzzle, Norfolk scratched off "shell" and wrote "*chrysalis.*" Next to that, he scratched "+/- 1,000 hurons."

A soldier searched them thoroughly enough to make Hosh stand on tiptoes and squawk. The cornic ran his fingertips through their hair and all around their faces—even Rayvn's. He examined the goblin mask as if a ghost might be hiding there—but allowed her to keep it. He made Telyn remove her belt sash and counted the contents of their coin purses to every huron and egg, jotting this in a ledger next to their names. Clearly, he intended to check this against their inventory upon departure.

Thank goodness we sealed the forehead within the shell before attempting the stairs. Telyn resisted the urge to wipe her brow as she tried to keep the soldier's impartial groping from bothering her.

As the soldier searched, the broken-horned Gandy began a recitation in a tone one adopts when repeating something for the umpteenth time.

"When you set foot on the stairs, you are on Academy ground where—in addition to Cornic Empire law—Academy rules apply." She fluttered her hands at the required admonition about Cornic Empire law—in her mind, it seemed, only Academy rules mattered. "The hall is warded with specific spells to make sure that transactions are recorded and binding. Understand?"

Retying her belt sash, Telyn nodded. "Sure." She just wanted to get on with things, get upstairs, redeem her sister, and be gone.

But Hosh missed Telyn's sideways look and said, "No."

Naturally.

Evidently, one "no" was enough to require another precooked spiel.

Norfolk practically bounced on his toes, and Gandy eh-hemmed in annoyance, but she continued reciting. "In the past, there have been unfortunate incidents where people have disputed transactions, despite the prices clearly labeled on the List, terms and conditions agreed to in front of witnesses, et cetera, and so forth." She removed spectacles from the collar of her vest, breathed on them with her sizable mouth, and wiped them with a cloth. Telyn had only ever seen one other pair of glasses—the ones Mrs. Pembroke wore. When worn, the glasses made Gandy's eyes appear to bulge in odd places.

"Once a negotiation has begun, it cannot be stopped until both parties agree on a price, however high, low, or unlikely, or until both parties agree that they will never come to an agreement. *Both parties.*"

She tapped her wool-covered index finger on the table with the last two words. "The rule is strictly and magically enforced.

"You four look young, so I offer this advice free of charge." She glanced around before continuing, as if imparting free advice was forbidden. "Academy negotiators are especially patient, so I advise caution before beginning anything. They have been known to keep people through multiple changes of chamber pots in order to beat down the price, if you know what I mean."

"They're clear," announced the soldier, jotting the inventory of Hosh's purse in his log.

Giggling nervously, Norfolk waved them upstairs. "Good luck," he called. "Break a leg."

"That was weird," Caitlin said, as they mounted the stairs.

"What just happened?" Hosh asked.

"Gave that guy a little taste of the shrinking bloomers," Rayvn announced proudly. "I am beginning to get the hang of being a rebel, don't you think?"

"Oh, Mother of Aled's rump!" Telyn said, increasing her stride to two risers at a time. She couldn't take the rest of the stairs fast enough.

CHAPTER SIXTY-FIVE

Two by two, the friends emerged from the staircase, and the wooden boards of the second floor flexed under their feet. The stairway opened into a circular great room, perhaps fifty feet across and surrounded by a curtain wall. Openings led away from the great room like spokes on a wheel. Many creatures milled around in pairs or small knots, speaking quietly. Thaumas outnumbered humans at the opposite proportion from downstairs, maybe four or five to one, many of them wearing Academy of Enshede robes.

Absent a ceiling and offering a clear view to the tent's peaked roof, everything felt grander and opener here, and Telyn inhaled deeply, savoring the hint of forest air over the bodies, perfumes, and bizarrerie of the sale.

Periodically, like herds of great, glowing crayfish, runes scuttled across the tent's canvas, presumably sealing official negotiations or performing some other arcane function.

Or maybe they were just bored.

If only I could climb. Get rid of the crawlies in my stomach before meeting this Hootie character.

The few humans present tended to clutch cases, sacks, or jars and keep to themselves. And no wonder, if they had managed to bag one of the things on the bottom of the List. Many cutpurses would murder for a fraction of the value.

Okay, Lindsey, enough waffling. Where to?

'Don't use that name! Forget you ever heard it.'

You must have some idea.

'You've brought my name to the surface. A mind wizard could skim that from your thoughts without even trying.'

No need to worry about how to survive a five-hundred-foot fall; we need to concentrate on climbing.

'Meaning?'

If Yona is here, we're dead anyway.

'Hmm. Not bad as sayings go, but I'm more of a Gruffud the Irreverent fan.'

That's a Telyn original.

The generic Academy symbol—circle of keys surrounding a parchment, a magnifying glass, and a barn owl—was woven with silver thread into the curtains. Many of the thaumas milling about wore medals around their necks designating specific orders. Some seemed obvious—three pomegranates must represent agriculture, and the quiver, spur and shield must be the military—while others were more oblique. What did the goat holding the hammer and chisel represent?

Those who wore the fox with a star for an eye—the Order of Magic's symbol—seemed the haughtiest and, frankly, the most frightening. Three individuals chittering unintelligibly belonged to a species Telyn could not identify, a race of insect-like beings whose bare legs seemed to hinge the wrong way.

She studiously avoided their compound eyes—or so she hoped. It wasn't easy to tell what they were looking at.

Rayvn indicated a heavily-guarded opening. A crest hung above it: a whole orange still attached to a branch, an orange half peeled, and one half-eaten. "The Imperial Bank," she said. "Oranges symbolize prosperity."

This Telyn understood completely. An orange would cost her a week's pay.

"Do you see that, Tey?" Caitlin whispered. "Mrs. Ouzeley in line for the bank, depositing her millions."

Telyn nodded. What could she say? The Ouzeleys had the run of Harlech, and it seemed they had a run of the Hall of Magic as well.

"No need to keep our visit a secret." Telyn lifted her chin and trying to quell the bubblies in her stomach. She didn't like the fact that they kept running into Harlech's new slave-masters, but the Ouzeleys represented the five-hundred-foot fall you couldn't survive and couldn't control, and Telyn needed to think about climbing right now more than ever. "They'll know why we came here soon enough, when we redeem my sister. I'm going to ask after Hootie and get this over with."

'He's with the Order of Magic,' Dagger said, 'Follow the fox with a star for an eye.'

Of course.

She located the designated crest and approached that particular opening. Once again, she faced a cloth-draped table and a plump cornic bureaucrat. This woman reminded Telyn all too much of Mrs. Pembroke registering newcomers to the Dating Circle.

Caitlin gave a nervous giggle, probably thinking the same thing.

"Which List?" the cornic asked, running a quill up and down a parchment as they approached.

"Er," Telyn replied, "not on the List?"

"In that case" —The cornic settled back in her seat and dropped her quill back into its ink-jar—"the Academy cannot help you. All the buyers interested in artifacts off-List are downstairs. Prices are not fixed, and the Academy takes no responsibility for the legitimacy of transactions outside of its control. Who *is* watching the stairs! If someone makes me say that one more time, I'm going to pull out their fingernails or snap their horns, depending on the species."

"I have business with Hootie. It won't take long, but Hootie would hate to miss me. I promise." Telyn straightened her spine and tried to look both confident and reasonable.

The cornic woman considered the four of them, paying special attention to Rayvn.

"I, ah, have business—" Telyn tried again.

"What's under the blanket?"

"Shell," Caitlin said, offering a peek. "We have a take permit."

"Species?"

"Human," Hosh said, "and a pattern witch."

"Of the egg."

"Ah, sorry. Feathered hind."

The cornic poked the nib of her quill on her tongue, which was splotched black—it must be a regular habit—and smacked her lips a couple of times. "Hootie might be interested, at that. Names?"

Telyn gave them, and the bureaucrat jotted them down. Then she piled her papers in a neat stack with the wet ink and their names on top. "I'll take you myself. I need a break from all that sitting. I feel like a tick."

As they skirted the table, a prickle danced along Telyn's spine. She glanced back to see Grebiana Ouzeley, now with her husband Wulstan, staring after them. Mr. Ouzeley twirled his silver-tip cane.

He looked altogether too satisfied.

In the great room, the wooden floor stood bare, but down this corridor a carpet with elaborate scroll-work showing the crests of the various Orders preceded them. White fabric hung for walls, with draw-curtains for doors every ten feet or so.

Telyn smiled a little. Rayvn could turn this entire place into a weapon if she needed to.

Academic-robed people wandered about. None of them seemed in a hurry; many were positively distracted by this or that in their hands, fur, feathers, small cages…. Telyn noted at least two bell jars containing flies: gamble flies, no doubt. Some trapper had scored big.

"Is Master Hootie expecting you?"

"Er, not exactly," Telyn replied. *Master Hootie, indeed.* She'd heard some ridiculous names in her time, but this took the billycan.

Telyn was beginning to wonder if this cornic female was, in fact, the buyer; she kept checking behind curtained doorways as if looking for a private place they could talk, but finally she seemed to have found what she was looking for.

"Master Hootie, you have guests," the cornic announced, gesturing the friends inside. She let the curtain close behind Hosh as he entered last, and they heard her footfalls fade away on the carpet.

'That's your buyer,' the thief said inside Telyn's mind, raising her gaze to indicate the room's sole occupant.

A tall-necked var bent over an ornate desk made of mahogany and topped with yellow marble. He held a magnifying glass in one feathered grip and examined some kind of glass cube. Without bothering to look up, he tweeted out a series of notes that would have made a songbird blush.

Is there some kind of password or something?

'My face was the password. Too bad I'm not wearing it.'

Besides the desk and a single chair occupied by the var, the room did not have any furniture. Another curtained doorway lay to the var's right. The slanted canvas of one wall indicated that this room pressed against the Hall's outer edge. Telyn followed it with her eyes to the tent-pole high overhead.

Indistinct conversation came from all around. Privacy would be relative. They'd have to speak in code or risk attracting unwanted attention.

Dim light emanated from a single, glass-blown lotus on the desk. The glow came from the interior of the flower and scattered through the petals in a soft, pleasingly pink hue.

Telyn stood tall, chest out, hands behind her back, and buzzing with anticipation. This was it—the final act. She had to succeed.

She had to.

Behind her back, her hands wrung.

Telyn was grateful when Caitlin cleared her throat and "Ah-hemed." Her own throat had frozen in place.

Hootie continued to ignore them.

Finally, Rayvn pointed a lazy finger at the var's black robes. From the silver fox on his left breast, a thread pulled free and began to unravel. The fox lost half its head, the thread grew to a several inches in length before, wearily, the var slipped the cube out of sight, rummaged in the desk drawer, and came up with a sort of bag that he fastened around his long neck like a choker.

The bag's shape distorted every which way, and from a hole in its side came words they could understand. "Please do not damage the robe any further, pattern witch. We have to pay for them ourselves, and the Academy does not give price breaks even to full professors."

It was strange to hear the tweeting and the translation simultaneously.

Those nervous bird-eyes darted from one to another and lingered on Hosh, sizing them up like a horse trader. "Females and a lame human. You do me honor, pattern witch," —His tone said Rayvn did no such thing—"but I am not in the market for misfits."

Rayvn's tail swished indignantly. "They would make perfectly good slaves! This one can reach things from the highest shelves, and the lame one travels better than most humans his age—"

"Rayvn, focus!" Caitlin exclaimed. "You are not here to sell slaves."

"Oh, yes, of course."

The exchange loosened something in Telyn's spine. She gestured for Hosh to step forward. "We brought something off-List. I have been told you have an interest in such things."

Squinting at the blanket-covered egg, the var nodded, and Hosh set the chrysalis shell on the marble desk-top and removed the blanket.

"This comes with compliments of Dagger," Telyn said. "A friend of yours, I believe."

While the var's beady bird-eyes did not react the way human eyes would, the stiffening of his posture indicated he recognized the name "Dagger."

Does he need your real name?

'Absolutely not. I told you to forget my name.'

"Beautiful, but I am not in the market for eggs. You should go."

"This chrysalis shell comes directly from the queen of the feathered hinds." She *might* be their queen. They sure treated her like one. "We took it from the Chaos Woods at great peril. It was in a golden pool which steamed and bubbled from the heat the chrysalis produced. A wounded hind—wounded and near death—entered the golden pool and emerged whole. That same hind now stands watch at the entrance to this Hall of Magic. It is possible—probable, even—that this shell retains some of those healing powers."

One of those red worm-lights chose that moment to crawl around the chrysalis' seams. Master Hootie cocked his head and brushed the shell with a scaled digit. Another worm-light crawled.

The var played with the chrysalis shell in this way for several breaths.

"Obviously, the queen is no longer inside."

"She flew away."

"She flew," the bag puffed incredulously, "with those ridiculous wings."

"The golden pool, it—well, it changed her."

"They were magnificent," Rayvn said.

"Yeah," Hosh said. "Really cool, like dragons."

Hootie took in this information with rapid twitches of eyes and head. "The bottom piece is missing."

Although Master Hootie continued to address Rayvn and ignore the humans, Telyn continued to answer.

"Several pieces. We weren't able to retrieve them before the pond began to freeze over again."

The var leaned back in the chair. Seconds passed. "Remove your mask."

Rayvn complied, holding the goblin mask in one hand.

"I do not know you, pattern witch. You travel in strange company."

"These are my friends. How much would you pay for them?"

"Rayvn!" Caitlin said.

"Only joking," Rayvn said. "To me, the shell looks like a blood-shot eyeball, with light flicking down the swollen capillaries when you poke it."

"Can you get the missing pieces?" Hootie asked. "The four missing pieces?"

'Careful,' cautioned the thief. 'He's being too direct.'

Four missing pieces, like the pieces of the Ever-Guise: left and right cheeks, chin, nose. The forehead makes five.

Now we're getting somewhere.

"What you see is what we have: just the one shell. The missing pieces are glued to the bottom of the golden pond," Telyn replied. "Others might be able to retrieve them, but they are lost to us."

"Even in summer?"

"I'm afraid so."

"Pity," said Master Hootie. "I should like to have the complete set."

The curtain to the var's right opened. Telyn caught a brief glimpse of a crowded little alcove on the other side of the opening, but she didn't have time to examine it closely, for two pattern witches, one male and one female, advanced on them like soldiers. Around their necks hung Order of Magic fox medals.

Telyn had just enough time to confirm that the cat-like female wasn't Mrs. de Galati before they flicked their hands, casting some sort of spell. The canvas wall of the Hall of Magic stretched into the room like a fabric tentacle and seized Rayvn. Glowing blue symbols swarmed all over it.

Rayvn's ears twitched, and her whiskers turned upwards in her version of a smile. "Impressive!" she commented as the fabric pinned her arms to her sides. And then the canvas spread over her like tar. The individual threads seemed alive; they wove themselves through Rayvn's clothes, her whiskers, her hair, like the leading edge of a flood. The goblin mask dropped from Rayvn's hand to the floor.

Telyn felt glued in place, frozen in shock, unable even to breathe, let alone speak. Rayvn had seemed so powerful, nearly invincible, their secret champion—but these two pattern witches handled her like a kitten.

When the tent wall snapped back, it had incorporated Rayvn completely. The fabric spit her outside. Telyn could see Rayvn's weight pressing down on the steep tent for a moment, and with a miaul, she slid away. The canvas returned to its former tautness, as flat as if it had just been starched.

The two pattern witches wore expressions that combined amusement and satisfaction, like two boys who had just thrown someone into a lake.

"That will be all," boomed the voice of Second Gajos from behind the witches. "We will handle these other trespassers."

Like well-practiced soldiers, the witches turned on their heels and exited the alcove.

CHAPTER SIXTY-SIX

In walked Second Gajos with Grebiana, Wulstan, and Tabbard Ouzeley, along with two others: Taito-Vaiana, the cereb's schmook ally, and Cressida.

Cressida! In a metal collar....

Her sister's head hung as low as the metal collar would allow. She looked completely beaten. Lumber mill overalls hung on her like so many rags. A leash ran from the collar to Taito-Vaiana's furry little hand.

Anger washed over Dagger while dismay poured over Telyn.

'Enemy! Kill!'

They've my sister collared her like an animal. Even the Ouzeleys didn't do that.

The thief ground Telyn's teeth as tears welled up in her eyes.

My fault. Yona told the truth; he purchased her. He really purchased her.

The thief's rage battled Telyn's dismay and despair.

What can we do? What can we really do?

'Enemy! Kill!' A crack spider-webbed down one of the lotus-lamp's leaves. The curtain over the door twitched.

No, not now! Keep yourself hidden, Dagger. The pattern witches are near. Wait.

"That's her, the troublemaker," Mr. Ouzeley said, pointing to Telyn.

"As you predicted," Second Gajos replied.

Ouzeley bowed slightly. "The credit goes to my son, Tabbard. He guessed what this slave's sister would be up to, and where," he sneered.

And then, incredibly, though her head remained bowed, Cressida's emerald eyes lifted and met Telyn's. A sparkle of defiance shone there.

She has a plan., Telyn realized, her heart leaping. *Cressida has a plan.*

'Let me handle this.' Dagger sent power surging between her fingers. Static electricity lifted Telyn's arm hair.

The glass leaf broke from the lotus-lamp. Hootie chirped as cracks appeared in some flower petals.

No one else seemed to notice.

Stay hidden, Lindsey. My sister has a plan. Trust her.

'Taito-Vaiana must die,' Dagger groaned in her head.

A pretty name for such a vile creature. Telyn clenched her fists against the thief's influence. *We rescue my sister first. We can't kill the schmook here, not with the pattern witches close by. They'll send you back to...er...wherever.*

Dagger's one-word answer twisted her guts. 'Revenge.'

It disturbed Telyn how easily she had connected the word "kill" to Taito-Vaiana. She had never imagined killing someone before. Even Tabbard, no matter how mean, deserved a chance to live. Didn't he?

And if he didn't—if he did something so vile as to deserve death—did she, Telyn Brower, have the right to take his life the way Second Gajos took the lives of Heath Robinson, Tyre Flint, Arvel Grummore? What gave her that right after all the harm she had done to her sister, Harlech, and everything else?

Traitor
Quisling
Turncoat

Double-Crosser

The Dating Circle's accusations were true; Telyn had earned all of that and more, just not in the way the women supposed.

Besides, did Telyn even have the courage to take someone's life? On purpose? Deliberately? Outside of war or self-defense?

Yes. With the vengeful spirit inside of her, she most certainly did. And that scared her—a lot.

Don't drive me to that point, please. I don't want to kill anyone.

'Fool girl...keep your mind...' The effort to form a coherent sentence clearly cost Dagger terribly. "Keep your mind present."

Yes, you're right, Dagger. Sorry for thinking your name earlier. Patience, then revenge. Talk our way through this. If we are successful here, you have kept the forehead away from Yona. You will have won a round. A stone removed from the board.

'Yona. Kill.'

Stay with me.

"What's wrong with her face?" Tabbard asked, frowning at Telyn. "It keeps...twitching."

'Taito-Vaiana must die.'

"Bad malt," Hosh said, quickly. He put both hands on his tummy. "I feel like hurling, myself."

Telyn's ears popped against a sudden change of air pressure. The tent wall shuddered. Whatever Dagger was doing, it was going to be bad.

Dramatically, terribly bad.

Telyn realized that if she and her sister died, it wouldn't thwart the vengeful spirit. The spirit might not even care. Dagger had his pick of bodies to inhabit within the Hall of Magic: cornic, var, human, anaconda, those insect-thingys, even a feathered hind.

She had to calm him down.

Dagger, stay with me. We have a plan. Count with me, five, four, three...

The thief gave a mental shudder.

...two, one and a half, one and a quarter...

Like a shoulder that, with a tremendous wrench, pops back into its socket, Dagger wrested control over his rage, though it burned there still, an orange coal under a veneer of ashes. He smoldered with desire to destroy Taito-Vaiana as the first shot against his real foe, the cereb Yona Unega.

Without warning, Dagger took control of Telyn's voice. "We have begun negotiations for this chrysalis shell. We are on Academy grounds. An interruption would be considered an unfortunate breech of law."

Everyone paused.

With a glance at the curtain where the two pattern witches had disappeared, Second Gajos said, "You will leave off negotiations."

"No," Telyn-thief said. "We are bargaining. We continue until the end."

"Obey your betters," Ouzeley said in a low, dangerous voice. He lifted his silver-handled cane as if to break it over Telyn's head. "Second Gajos gave you a direct order."

On her own, Telyn would have panicked, sprinted for the door, wrestled for the cane, or begun babbling. But Dagger held her steady as a stone and kept her gaze firmly on Hootie. Once he'd mastered his rage, he began to enjoy himself and the uncertainty of Second Gajos and of Taito-Vaiana.

Why doesn't the second have his guards with him? Why in the world is he with the Ouzeleys and the schmook?

'Think about it, Telyn Brower,' Dagger responded in her head. 'The slaves in the lumber mill; Corporal Velky following you underground to where you hid the forehead. Second Gajos did not work alone. The Ouzeleys know about the Ever-Guise—at least, Wulstan and Grebiana do. The second doesn't trust any of the other cornics to keep the secret, so he enlisted allies.'

Telyn bit her cheek, considering. *Corporal Velky knew. He followed me to where I hid the forehead piece in the sewer.*

'Who led him there?'

Tabbard.

'Exactly. What did Minister Svemas say to you—something about terrible things being afoot? More being at stake than Cressida's freedom?

'*Thieves never work alone,*' Telyn remembered. *That's what Second Gajos said.*

'That's right. But trust me, the cornic second does not consider the partnership with the Ouzeleys equal. If knife comes to sword, he will abandon them in an instant. We can use that.'

"The girl is right," Hootie said, at last. "We are negotiating the purchase of this magnificent chrysalis shell. It comes from the Chaos Woods at great peril, I am told, and belonged to the queen of the feathered hinds. I would purchase it for the right price, then you can do what you will with the pattern witch" —He gestured dismissively at the humans—"and these others. With all due respect, sir." He tilted his bird-head slightly at Second Gajos. "We *are* on Academy ground; a transaction must be followed until the end."

At this declaration, a small herd of glowing blue runes manifested in the tent canvas and began spinning slowly on their axes. Telyn didn't know if she and Hootie had really been negotiating before, or if Hootie had decided to cover for them, but they *were* negotiating now, no doubt about it.

"The Cornic Empire is ruled by law," Telyn-thief added, "which includes respecting a slave's bond-price no matter the owner, no matter the slave. Minister Svemas set that bond price at, I believe..." —*Four thousand*—"...four thousand hurons."

Second Gajos inclined his sheep's head. "We are not here to disrupt any transaction."

"Good," said Hootie. "Then we will complete our negotiation and be done with it. And these smelly humans can remove themselves. I do wish you had not ejected the pattern witch. Her, at least, I could respect."

Tabbard made to crack his knuckles; Wulstan popped Tabbard's shin with his cane to warn him to keep still.

'You go. Do your best. She's your sister.'

"You were offering four thousand hurons for the chrysalis," Telyn said.

"I believe that was *your* offer. My counter was considerably lower."

Telyn kept half an eye on the tent's runes in case they punished lying, but it didn't seem to bother them. They looked content to drift slowly around the perimeter of the room.

"The long-term viability of the shell is proved," Telyn said. "Despite being only a partial shell, the magic functions quite well, as you can see." She poked the shell again, and pretty red lights meandered around the seams. "At four thousand hurons, it is a bargain."

"As I was saying before the interruption, where is the broken piece? Or pieces?"

Telyn held her hands out as in supplication. "The bottom remains glued to the bedrock at the bottom of the pond. When winter ends, I might be able to retrieve it, if I assemble a strong team and equip them well. We barely survived an attack by rakasuras as it was, but if you wish to hire us at this time..."

The schmook's eyestalks twisted to stare between Telyn, Caitlin, and Hosh.

He knows we're talking about the Ever-Guise.

'Don't be so sure. He believes his master stole the forehead from under the second's muzzle and escaped to the woods. He is laughing inside at the second's misfortune—and cannot imagine that a human girl outwitted his master.

'He also knows the guards searched us carefully before ascending the stairway—searched us and found nothing illegal. It is the slave he doesn't want to lose. I've had dealings with Taito-Vaiana. He has been imagining such cruelty for your sister, and he doesn't want to miss that opportunity for any price.'

Beginning with Cressida, the var's beady, unreadable eyes regarded each of them in turn, settling on Telyn at the last. With something like regret, he said, "With a missing piece, the shell is not worth nearly as much as if it were whole. My offer stands at three thousand hurons."

This was the first time Hootie had actually put forward a price. Hosh drew a sharp inhale, and Caitlin took his hand.

Three thousand hurons!

Telyn had never hoped to earn so much money in her entire life. She could buy the Sable Head outright, the Rusty Shackles infusionary, and maybe even the Copcut Ash.

With three thousand, she could open a bank account, and she

would never, ever want for anything in her life. If she shared with Caitlin, Hosh, and Rayvn, they would all be rich.

But Cressida was standing right there—her sister, the one who'd carried all Telyn's sins on her yoke. *I deserve to be in chains, not Cressida. Never Cressida.*

"We, ah, we need four thousand," Telyn replied. "You will be the only person, ah, thauma, with a queen's chrysalis shell in the world."

The bag at Hootie's neck puffed in and out rapidly. The hooting it produced sounded disturbingly like laughter.

"The world, really," Wulstan Ouzeley sneered.

Tabbard made to spit on the floor but thought better of it and had to swallow.

"Loser," Hosh whispered.

"For the whole chrysalis, with the queen inside, I would pay four thousand," the var said. "But not an empty shell."

"The queen's magic is still inside," Telyn insisted, "as you can see from the red worm-lights."

'Careful!' Dagger warned. 'You are being too direct.'

"What if I smash it, how much will it be worth then?" Tabbard said.

"You would be arrested," Second Gajos said mildly, "and charged with the difference in value. Isn't that the rule on Academy grounds?"

"Quite right," Hootie agreed. "And I grow weary of negotiations. This is definitely not the only chrysalis shell in the world, but it may be one of the most complete, and one of the freshest. I am willing to offer three thousand two hundred. Not an egg more, so to speak. Since you are unwilling to budge, this negotiation has ended."

"Telyn?" Caitlin urged.

Second Gajos made to step forward.

"No, it hasn't!" Telyn blurted. "It takes two parties to end a negotiation—two parties. I haven't finished."

"If you insist on continuing, I will call in a professional negotiator," Hootie said. "I am old and fatigue easily, especially when dealing with non-thaumas."

Can we raise another eight hundred? Can we? Do you have gold hidden somewhere, Dagger?

'Accept it. This is a good price. We will need this money to go after Yona.' A tremor went down Telyn's arms as Dagger thought the hated name.

True. Trying to exact our revenge would be next to impossible without cash to grease palms, purchase information, hire a team...

Her thoughts began to blend with Dagger's, and she welcomed it. It felt natural.

We could...we could find Yona Unega's enemies, get them to pay us a reward for his head. Yona's head would be worth a thousand, easily—

Okay, you're right, Dagger. We need to accept this and move on.

Things might have ended there, but for some reason, Taito-Vaiana yanked on the chain leading to Cressida's throat. Cressida made a gagging sound.

Indignity stiffened Telyn's spine.

No! We need to redeem Cressida now. As long as she is the schmook's slave, she remains at risk. He could slit her throat, and no one would say a word. You told me yourself, he plans unspeakable cruelty.

'You cannot murder in the Cornic Empire. Even slaves have certain rights.'

He plans to abuse her, at the least. He could put her in the galley, as you said. She wouldn't last a month chained to a bench twenty-four hours a day.

"Is that your final offer?" Second Gajos said. "We grow impatient."

"Yes, yes, please," Hootie twittered, "three thousand two hundred. In the name of the Order of Magic of the Academy of Enshede, let us invoke a contract."

On the tent canvas, the runes became profiles of silver foxes with blue stars for eyes. They spiraled into a ball.

"The Order of Magic offers three thousand two hundred hurons for the chrysalis shell owned by the pattern witch, not present, Telyn Brower, and her friends."

Tabbard looked like a wolf staring through a fence at chickens, planning how he would dig under the wire and eat them one by one. He was obviously counting on forcing Telyn to give him a share of her cash, if not every egg, probably by jumping her in a blind alley.

Grebiana acted as if the whole thing bored her, as if she couldn't care less if the shell sold for three thousand or three million. Only the thin tongue licking her thinner lips betrayed her.

Wulstan Ouzeley's face pinched like a horned toad's. Even for him, that was a lot of money.

Second Gajos appeared reluctantly impressed.

As far as Taito-Vaiana, he could have been deciding what spell to cast to murder them all—and probably was.

The fox runes on the tent wall began to pulse. Telyn wondered if they were visible from the outside, if the people in the market square noticed and wondered what great bargain was being struck.

It was no bargain at all, a loss, the most profitable loss in the history of the world.

Cressida, I'm sorry.

I'm so, so sorry.

'This is it, now or never,' Dagger said. 'Your word will be final and binding. Trust me, if he calls in a professional negotiator, we'll be lucky to get half this amount.'

Can we sell the forehead elsewhere? There must be other buyers willing to pay more!

'Don't be a fool. This is the best offer you will ever get. After this, Telyn Brower, we are going after your real enemies.'

I will not help you get your revenge as long as my sister remains in chains. This I swear; this is my oath. Do you understand, Lindsey?

And then, head bowed, eyes downcast, Cressida flashed hand-talk. Trained as a soldier, Second Gajos noticed the movement. He emitted a deep sort of bleat in his throat, a warning.

Telyn couldn't understand what Cressida had signed. Their hand-talk had been developed in bed, under the covers, and required feel and not sight.

She gave a brief shake of her head to warn Cressida not to sign again, not with Second Gajos watching. She hadn't understood what Cressida had said, but she caught one thing.

She wants me to accept. Mother of Squirrels, Cressida has a plan. Unless...unless she's just looking out for me again.

Which is it?

Nearly gagging with indecision, Telyn-thief replied, "I...I... Let me see it first."

I've taken this as far as I can. Cressida, my sister, I pray that you can take it the rest of the way. Please. Don't protect me any further. Save yourself.

With a scowl, Hootie retrieved a certificate with gold-leaf scrollwork around the edges. He scrawled the number three thousand two hundred on one side with a description of the chrysalis shell on the other.

What is this? Where is the coin?

'You expect them to haul thousands of hurons to and from this village? We have to take this to the Academy Bank in Enshede. Anywhere else will kill us with commissions.'

Academy Bank? What are you talking about?

'Hush. Let me think.'

"Well, yes or no?" Hootie said.

The fox runes had all but faded from the canvas.

"This is enough," Telyn said. *Mother of Squirrels, I hope Cressida knows what she is doing. I sure don't.* "The deal is struck."

The whirling ball of magical symbols lifted away from the tent canvas and spun into their room, star-eyed foxes of power, and infused the certificate like magical watermarks.

Hootie rolled up the parchment, tied it with a red ribbon, and held it towards Telyn.

But before Telyn could take it, Mr. Ouzeley commanded, "Hold!"

Telyn jumped. To her disgust, she didn't just take the certificate. Her muscles just wouldn't move until the drama played out.

"Tell us what you saw, Tabbard," Mr. Ouzeley drawled. "Tell us what you saw on the stairway."

CHAPTER SIXTY-SEVEN

The little, canvas-walled room in the Hall of Magic felt claustrophobic. The cornic second, the schmook Taito-Vaiana, and the Ouzeley family stood in a semi-circle of power and opposition; outnumbered and basically powerless, Telyn, Hosh, and Caitlin faced them.

Telyn really, really wished Rayvn were still here. The pattern girl's presence would provide some comfort, since against the magical might of Second Gajos and the schmook, none of them could do a thing.

Not a thing.

The var and Cressida stood apart, Hootie behind his desk and Cressida bowed and diminished, linked to Taito-Vaiana by a silver choker-and-chain.

Tabbard pulled the hems of his long blue coat straight, a soldier reporting for duty. The gold thread embroidering the cuffs and collar reinforced this image. A lifetime of abusive satisfaction settled into his round, pink face.

"I saw the four of them, these three plus the pattern tramp, bully their way upstairs past the soldiers. They didn't have anything from the List, but somehow, they talked their way past."

"Bully, us? You are the only bully in this place!" Caitlin said, outraged. "I saw that firsthand, I'm ashamed to say. I could tell some stories of you and your stupid friends, and I should. The way you knocked little Lily Vance to the ground just because you could. They way your friends distract the owner while you steal ribbon candy from the mercantile."

Her speech made absolutely no impact. As a unit, the Ouzeley family continued to sneer at Telyn and Telyn alone. They had identified their true adversary. They thought they had her beat.

They might have, at that. Telyn hadn't any plays left. In a game of senet, she'd be short of stones and against the back row.

Taito-Vaiana and Second Gajos regarded the tableau with interest. Cressida remained downcast and docile. Telyn wished her sister would sign something—some instruction on how to handle this, a bit of encouragement, anything.

Even Dagger remained silent in Telyn's head, unwilling to help. This was probably a good thing. With the schmook right there in front of him, the vengeful spirit might explode at any point. As he had warned, if Telyn died, he could simply take another body.

He literally had nothing to lose.

Hootie the var extended the writ towards Telyn, beckoning her to take it, but she couldn't bring herself to move.

The vile triumph on Tabbard's gray eyes equaled the loathing in Mr. and Mrs. Ouzeleys'. They would destroy her if they could—her and Cressida both. They would love that. Not just win, not just beat, but destroy. In their minds, Cressida and Telyn had helped Razenbock keep a prize from their grasp. The Ouzeleys had coveted the Sable Head for years, and if they didn't know how exactly the Ever-Guise had been used against them, they had probably guessed a good deal, and they knew for a fact that the twins had served food and malt, cleaned rooms, scrubbed floors, and greeted customers for Raz.

That alone made the twins the enemy.

Of all the names Telyn would like to call that family, foolish was not among them. The Ouzeleys were as devious and dangerous as rabid coyotes.

"How could these children bully their way past cornic soldiers?"

Second Gajos asked reasonably. His bass voice made Telyn's chest vibrate. "We would make a poor army indeed if our soldiers gave in to children."

"Not the children," Grebiana said, "but the young pattern witch. Wasn't it she, Tabbard dear? She used a little cloth magic, didn't she?"

"She made the soldier dance like he had fire ants in his shorts." Tabbard laughed. "He could hardly wait to wave them upstairs. I'm surprised he didn't report it. He must have been scared."

He did not dance! Telyn wanted to protest. *He screeched like a goose.*

"The pattern witch has a perfect right to be upstairs," Hootie said through his translation bag. "If she wants these non-magical beings to accompany her, what is the harm, Second Gajos? Take them downstairs, throw them out of the Hall of Magic, and be done with it. Trespassing is not a capital crime, and the witch facilitated a profitable transaction. The Empire takes ten percent of every sale, am I right?"

"Quite right." The second nodded.

"Good," Hootie said. "The Academy will not be pleased if the result of a legitimate exchange is a scandal."

"If this is so, then why would the pattern witch bully her way upstairs?" Grebiana said, taking the relay from Tabbard. "It doesn't make sense...unless the children are doing something illegal."

Foxes began to form on the canvas, but rather than the soothing blue color from before, now angry black strokes formed the outlines while wicked orange painted the star-eye. The runes seemed to stare at Grebiana accusingly.

"Consider carefully your next words, human," Hootie warned. "The shell has been purchased, the contract bound by runes, and I will not renege on such a contract. If you try to force me to break my word, a curse shall befall—"

"No one is trying to break any contract," Second Gajos said hurriedly, motioning for Grebiana to be silent. "The shell is yours."

Clearly, rune-sealed contracts and the Academy carried some weight with him.

Wulstan Ouzeley cleared his throat, unwilling to give up. "Why would the children have had to bully their way upstairs? Do you have some idea, dear?"

"They don't have a take permit," Tabbard announced, elated. "They are trying to steal from the empire."

Grebiana frowned at her son. Clearly, she wanted to be the star of the show. "The Cornic Empire rightly claims all of the Chaos Woods for its own, and magical items removed from it without a take permit becomes property of the Empress." Grebiana reached out and smoothly slid the rolled-up parchment from Hootie's feathered fingers. "Those who remove magical artifacts from the woods without a take permit are guilty of poaching. This writ" —Grebiana spun on her heels and extended the certificate toward Second Gajos—"belongs to the Empress."

With a bow, Second Gajos took it.

Tabbard snickered. The schmook did as well, a scratchy, irritating wheeze.

"So, you have not wasted our time after all, humans," Taito-Vaiana said to the Ouzeleys.

The foxes shifted back to silver-blue, drew together, formed a circle. They grew brighter, preparing to grant title of the writ to the Empress of the Cornic Empire.

"A take permit? You mean, like this one?" Hosh said, tugging a lanyard from under his shirt. The triumph melted from the Ouzeleys' faces as Hosh passed the medal to Second Gajos.

The second held it close to the broken lotus light, turning it over to check carefully.

Hosh blushed at Telyn's look of gratitude.

"That's the old design!" Grebiana hissed. "He hasn't replaced it with the new design."

"It's a simple exchange," Hosh said. "I can do it at the Prefecture when it opens."

"You had to do it before coming to the hall," Mr. Ouzeley added.

"Not true!"

Surprisingly, Second Gajos looked torn as to what to do. It almost appeared he wanted to side with Telyn and her friends. Or perhaps he simply loathed the Ouzeleys.

That, Telyn could understand completely.

"This is an older design—" the second allowed.

"I think I can solve this dilemma," Hootie interrupted. "If the runes accept the Empress as titleholder, we must consider the contract binding. Agreed?"

The cornic second and Taito-Vaiana were quick to agree, followed by the Ouzeleys.

What are we going to do?!

'We've been outplayed. We have no choice. Agree to the terms, and you might get out of this with your skin intact.'

Reluctantly, Telyn nodded. Caitlin took her hand on one side, Hosh on the other.

"Good, for I have no wish to sully this room with a curse. They can be messy." Hootie drew another certificate from his desk. "Three thousand, two hundred hurons," he said, dipping his pen in the bottle and filling in the certificate as before. The canvas runes flickered and spun.

Telyn's heart fell through the floor. Now she had truly lost everything. All her work, her planning, her hopes, her chance at redemption.

No, that was about her.

What about her twin? What about Cressida's freedom? How much would she suffer in Taito-Vaiana's black little paws?

Mother of Squirrels, how much?

"Chrysalis shell from the queen of the feathered hinds, taken from the Chaos Woods in the three hundredth Year of the Broken Wing by Vool reckoning," Hootie spoke each word aloud and much more formally than he had previously. Taito-Vaiana peered intently, verifying that the spoken words matched Hootie's neat calligraphy.

The silver and blue fox runes separated from the canvas. They formed a nearly solid sphere in the air.

Telyn wanted to reach out and bat them away, but fear held her in place. Cressida's face, shiny with sweat, reddened more. A drop of sweat stole down her nose and dripped to the floor.

Or was that a tear?

"Pay to the Empress Zhalia," the var wrote on the bottom.

The fox runes shifted to an angry red and screeched away from each other. They flew about the tent, darting at hair, flying between legs, terrorizing everyone like manic, flying crayfish. Where they touched skin, they left a welt—and they seemed to be aiming for the eyes.

Everyone reacted—some badly. Hootie started so hard his chair flipped backward, his translation bag squawked and bounced across the floor, and ink spilled all over the desk.

Cressida dropped to her knees and covered her head in her hands.

Second Gajos pulled a curved knife from somewhere and slashed at the runes, while Mr. Ouzeley brought his cane across his body like a shield. Tabbard and Grebiana struggled to see who could get furthest from the runes, while Caitlin, Telyn, and Hosh pressed back-to-back like soldiers making a last stand. They batted at the runes with their hands and quickly became covered with painful sores. The air reeked of burnt skin, smoldering cotton, and singed wool.

Hootie crawled to his desk and, after a struggle with a rune that tried to infiltrate his beak, managed to withdraw a flint. He struck the second certificate aflame. It flared and burned to ash.

Shifting from red to orange and finally back to tranquil silver-and-blue, the fox runes vanished with a loud bang, like a hundred corks popping at the same time. They left behind an aroma of burnt feathers.

Heart pounding and eyes watering from the smoke, Telyn gradually straightened up. What in the world had happened?

The door curtain opened; the two pattern witches peered inside.

After a series of whistles and hoots, Hootie managed to affix his translation bag to his throat again. "No issue. Nothing wrong. I, ah, made an error on my writ."

Second Gajos sheathed his knife.

"I took care of it. The writ has been burned."

That's when Telyn realized the burnt feather smell was not inherent to the runes. Hootie had several singed spots along his neck and arms.

The pattern witches frowned to the left and right, taking in the various members of the strange menagerie before withdrawing.

"Well, that settles it. The runes do not lie," Hootie huffed, his translation bag puffing in and out between each word. "The writ belongs to the humans."

"My face. My face!" Tabbard moaned.

"Go and get a poultice for your face, dear," Grebiana said. "You are too beautiful to suffer. I will see this ugly business through."

"I wish to redeem my sister," Telyn said, as soon as Tabbard departed. She resisted the urge to stuff her swollen hands under her armpits like Hosh.

Second Gajos bounced the writ in his hand. "You do not have it, Miss Brower. The bond price is four thousand hurons."

Mr. Ouzeley banged his cane on the floor and grinned wickedly.

"Well, then, leave the blanket on the way out, human," Hootie chirped. "You aren't charging for that separately, are you? I find the roving lights of the chrysalis distracting."

Hosh obediently covered the chrysalis shell with the blanket.

"Our business is done here. I have things to do." Hootie removed the translation bag from his neck without further ado.

Telyn still had not physically touched the writ. So much gold—an unimaginable amount to her mind—and yet—

'We need that gold,' rumbled Dagger. 'You cannot fight a war without money.'

The schmook yanked on Cressida's chain. Cressida stumbled against the marble desk. "The show is over, and I've had enough of filthy men. Time to go."

"Minister, er, Second Gajos, sir," Telyn pleaded, "please, I can come up with the rest of it."

'We need this money. We have magistrates to bribe, palms to grease, tongues to loosen.'

That's not what we agreed to.

'Agreed? *Agreed*? You and that filthy pattern witch locked me in Sheol, and then you yank me out again and expect me to make some sort of bargain? I agreed to nothing, girl.'

"She's doing that mouth thing again," Mr. Ouzeley said, stroking his mustache.

"I paid for this slave," Taito-Vaiana said. "Unless you produce the bond price now, I will be taking her back to Enshede with me—today."

We have to do this now, in the Hall of Magic, where his word will be bound.

'As the second pointed out, we do not have the full amount. There is no deal to be struck. Let her go, Telyn, before I force you to say the words.'

"I can come up with the rest of it," Telyn repeated, desperately.

"My parents will lend it to her," Hosh offered.

Grebiana laughed derisively.

Second Gajos spread his thick, furry hands. "There is no urgency, Miss Brower. The bond price has been fixed. If you bring the full bond price—today, tomorrow, ten years from now—the owner is obligated to free the slave."

"In whatever condition she may be in," Taito-Vaiana added, snapping the fingers of his free hand. "Breaking a slave is like breaking a teacup."

"Well, yes. Until that time, the slave remains Master Esera's property."

"And if she dies from a wasting illness in the waterfront brothels, or from scurvy on a galley, or bleeds to death from a flaying, that is my affair as well." The schmook didn't even bother to look at Cressida. "It is no different from breaking a hammer or spilling a glass of wine upon the ground. The loss is a red entry on my ledger, if I bother to record it."

Master Taito-Vaiana Esera. Telyn filed the schmook's name away just in case this failed.

'Now you understand revenge.'

Now I understand. Yes, I understand.

Taito-Vaiana Esera might not be aware that the cereb, in the form of the daemon, had retrieved the forehead from the Prefecture, and that Telyn had stolen it back, but he would learn soon enough. And the nearest target of the schmook's wrath would be close at hand: Cressida.

Once again, Cressida would suffer for Telyn's choices, for Telyn's failures.

She could only imagine what torture Taito-Vaiana would put her through.

And if, by chance, he did not kill Cressida, the mind wizard could leave her body perfectly intact and tear her mind to pieces. Telyn might end up paying the bond price on a husk, or a madwoman, or a merciless child-murderer, whatever the mind wizard wanted to make of her.

Am I wrong? Telyn knew Dagger had been watching her fears roll across her mind like a marionette show. She'd made no effort to conceal them. *Tell me the schmook won't torture Cressida, or place her on the galleys or in a brothel. He bragged as much! Tell me the mind wizard cannot pervert her mind.*

The ghost paused a moment before replying. 'I stand ready. I will do what you ask. If we fail, I will get another body.'

Telyn bit her lip. *I like your spirit, Dagger.*

The floor rumbled slightly.

'I hate puns.'

Dark chaos spun around Telyn's balled fists. Dust rose from the floor and began to draw images from the thief's past.

We can't let them leave Harlech. We have to stop them before they rejoin the mind wizard.

'Revenge, kill,' Dagger agreed.

"This is pointless," Mr. Ouzeley said. He didn't seem to notice the spirit electricity or unnatural vibration in the floorboards. "Does Master Esera look like a bank? Either you bring all the money at once, or this meeting is over. We have better things to do than listen to this girl's sniveling."

"But we have the bond price," Cressida said, unexpectedly. Telyn had practically forgotten that sparkle in Cressida's eyes from earlier. "Right here, in this room. All four thousand hurons."

"What nonsense is this?" Grebiana asked.

Cressida lifted her head toward the hideous woman—and smiled. "I've had a lot of time on my hands in prison. Nothing to do but look at the Dating Chart, and the questionnaires, and I have been calculating the odds behind it all."

"That is not possible. The questionnaires are locked in the Prefecture." Grebiana shot a nervous glance at her husband. "No one looks at them who is not a member of Sums, Statistics, and Affairs of the Heart."

"Did I give you permission to speak?" Taito-Vaiana yanked on Cressida's chain for spite.

Cressida wrapped the thin sliver chain around her hand and squared her back. She stood a good head-and-shoulders taller than Taito-Vaiana. In a bare-handed fight without the benefit of magic, she could probably take him.

But he was a flack.

He had magic.

The schmook's orange lips compressed in a thin line; his eye stalks crooked like scorpion tails. Black, wiggly lines began to form over the creature's head.

"I would hear this," Second Gajos said. He almost sounded amused. "Let the slave speak. The Dating Chart is, as you know, a source of revenue for the empire and a matter of interest to the empress, and what is of interest to the empress is of interest to house Gajos."

Taito-Vaiana growled, but whatever black spell he'd been preparing remained over his head, spinning and wiggling.

Cressida ignored everyone but Grebiana. "When Joram did the promise dance for Tristam Harries, I started to think. The odds were roughly thirty-to-one against, and yet, you managed to guess right, didn't you?"

Grebiana cleared her throat. "Members of the Dating Circle are not allowed to bet, are they?"

"Nor are the unmarried," Mr. Ouzeley added. "This is pointless. Why should we listen to a slave?"

"No, neither members of the Dating Circle nor the unmarried may bet or profit from betting. But I started to ask myself, why are the odds so long? Who has been betting against this match? After all, Tristam and Joram have many of the same interests. They both play reed pipes in the Barmouth style; they both like baby llamas, and getting up before dawn to watch the sunrise, and being the first to try the latest infusions. They both run in the same gang with Tabbard Ouzeley."

Telyn had only known that last fact. *People really do bare their souls on those questionnaires. Mother of Squirrels, how stupid can you be?*

The edges of the second's long mouth began to curl into a frown. Grebiana stood so straight and nervous she could crack walnuts between her buns, and Wulstan had started yanking his mustaches again.

Hootie stopped pretending to analyze his crystal cube and cocked his bird-like head at Cressida.

"Members of the Dating Circle cannot bet; nor can single men or women, but your married employees can. The mill is the largest employer in Harlech; all those lumberjacks and woodworkers race to place coin on the Dating Chart every payday. I observed it for myself. The foreman, Damon Marcus, distributed the eggs, didn't he? I'll bet the maids and cooks at the Copcut Ash got a little help as well."

"Nothing wrong with giving the employees a few extra eggs for hard work," Mr. Ouzeley said. Hosh coughed at Ouzeley's fake generosity. "We never told our men to bet on Joram and Caitlin—or anyone else, for that matter. You can ask any of them—under pain of torture, if you care to."

"No, you wouldn't have. You're too careful for that. You told your men to bet with the odds, and you instructed Joram how to behave toward Caitlin. Once the Dating Circle put Caitlin and Joram in a near-circle, the bets pushed them closer and closer together because of the mathematical confluence of betting and behavior, didn't it?"

"Your word means nothing, slave," Taito-Vaiana said. "You are impugning the reputation of Harlech's most outstanding citizens."

Poke the walls, Telyn thought to Dagger, *just a little*. The thief sent a beam of spirit chaos sideways. The tent wall bulged, and blue symbols swirled across it, maddened. The warning bell gong from the Prefecture boomed across the square—evidently, the cornics had removed the shims and rags.

Because Dagger had used ghost power, dust motes flew every which way, landed on the var's desk, and began painting an onion-domed palace across its top. Mrs. de Galati had identified that place as Barmouth; something important in Dagger's past must have happened there.

"The Academy's spells don't like lying or cheating, Grebiana, Wulstan." Telyn spoke with as much gravitas as she could muster. She hoped no one else would recognize that the "onion dome" drawing meant the runes were reacting to a ghost and not the Ouzeleys' lies.

The Ouzeleys took a half-step away from the dust-mote palace forming on Hootie's desk. Even Second Gajos eyed it uncertainly.

Hootie simply looked surprised. He leaned forward and erased it with a feathered forearm.

"Harlech's population is only a few thousand," Cressida continued, "which means the total number of bets on any given relationship are small. That makes it very easy to change the odds, isn't it Mrs. Ouzeley? A change of behavior, a word whispered here and there, a couple dozen small bets..."

"This is outrageous," Mr. Ouzeley complained, shaking his silver-tipped cane. If not for Second Gajos' insistence, no doubt he would have struck Cressida, and likely Telyn, Caitlin and Hosh as well. "You said yourself, slave, we told our men to bet in favor of the match. But the match failed—"

"Your men bet a few eggs in favor, but Heledd Glines bet against it in the hundreds, didn't she?"

Mr. Ouzeley's mouth snapped closed so hard his molars clacked.

"She bets against all the obvious couples—and she never loses, does she? These are very large bets for the owner of an infusionary."

"I-I have nothing to say," Grebiana said.

"Nor will we" —Telyn nodded at her sister—"if you turn oversight of the Dating Circle over to Mrs. Gamage—for just compensation. She will run it honestly. And if you pay Cressida for all the work it took to audit the chart. Her work will be invaluable to the reputation of the Dating Chart going forward."

The black lines around the schmook fizzled. He released his grip on Cressida's neck chain. It rattled to the floor.

A muscle pulsed on Mr. Ouzeley's jaw. "Pay her," he said.

Grebiana's mouth nearly hit the floor. "I will not!"

Mr. Ouzeley reached for his wife's bulging purse and pulled out a blank certificate.

"Make it a thousand hurons." He spread the certificate on the var's desk.

Trembling with rage, Grebiana used the var's own quill and ink to fill it in for a thousand hurons. The blue, star-eyed fox runes gathered, spun, and watermarked the writ.

Second Gajos nodded. He extended his paw-like hand, and Ouzeley put the writ there.

"Right," Telyn said, eying the cornic second closely. If she judged his ram's face correctly, he was satisfied.

Possibly even amused.

She had no illusions of getting the two hundred surplus hurons back; that would constitute the second's bribe.

"Plus ten," Telyn added, "for working evenings doing the audit... ah...after full days at the lumber mill."

Yes, a smile definitely twitched at the edge of the second's muzzle.

Mr. Ouzeley paused just long enough to lick his lips, then counted out ten more hurons. These he dropped onto the table. Several bounced and rolled onto the floor.

"Come on," he said, and the Ouzeley family departed.

With a hearty "for the good of the empire," Second Gajos retrieved the coins from the table, dropped them in his own pouch, and cinched it tight. "I was right about you, Telyn Brower; you *are* a dangerous girl." He paused at the booth's opening, turned his over-sized head, and added, "I enjoy danger. It makes life interesting."

Seething, Taito-Vaiana touched the silver collar on Cressida's neck. Although Telyn could not see any latch, the collar snapped open. "You will both belong to my master before this is over. Master Unega never forgives, never forgets."

"Yeah, I know the feeling," Telyn replied.

The schmook coiled the chain around his fist. Even in his little hands, the collar and chain would make a formidable weapon. "Master Unega lets me play with his toys before they die, Miss Telyn Lilith Brower. Remember that."

Telyn cocked her head. *Where did he learn my middle name? No one knows that.*

'He's trying to throw you off,' the thief said in her mind. 'Don't give in. The mind wizard probably picked it from your thoughts.'

Why would I have been thinking my middle name?

Telyn didn't like the strange feeling simmering in her gut, like she had missed something obvious, like when you are daydreaming and step in front of a charging horse-carriage without looking left or right.

"I look forward to meeting again." The schmook glared once more and left.

A moment passed.

Cressida and Telyn embraced. Both girls trembled. Second Gajos hadn't bothered to retrieve the hurons from the floor, and Caitlin knelt for those, saying something about, "Infusions and gooseberry acorns all around."

Telyn turned to Hootie, who had been watching the entire exchange with an unreadable expression. Before she, Cressida, and their friends departed, she pitched her voice lower and leaned toward him conspiratorially. "At night, the chrysalis shell is magnificent. But in daylight, if you hold the shell up to the sun, you will see its true beauty."

Hootie trilled in reply.

'Too direct,' Dagger complained in her head. 'Too direct by far.'

CHAPTER SIXTY-EIGHT

Cressida took Telyn's hand, and the friends left the Hall of Magic by the front door. In the square, Caitlin and Hosh gave hugs and said their farewells, giving the sisters space. They said little as they walked, except for Cressida repeating that she would have a bath, and replace the water and have another bath, just as soon as she finished this meat sticker.

And this banger.

And this dumpling....

Telyn only smiled and paid for one more treat. Dagger grumbled some at the waste of coin that they'd need against Yona. But for the most part, he kept quiet—especially when Telyn bought a huckleberry cloud for herself. Dagger enjoyed the taste of huckleberry whipped cream as much as she did, which was creepy if you thought about sharing taste buds and all with some ghost she barely knew.

What if she got a boyfriend? Eww!

In the crowds and the torchlight, they remained relatively anonymous. If a few people recognized Telyn from the destructive pursuit through town, they did no more than give her a wide berth and a sideways glance.

They must assume that the ghost has been put to rest.

'I hate puns.'

That's not a pun. That's real.

Mrs. Pembroke ran into them at the game of darts and cried out in surprise—not from seeing Telyn, but from seeing Cressida. "Free?" The woman exclaimed, looking from one girl to the other. "You broke her out, didn't you, Miss Telyn? I heard the gong. You can't get away with it. I'll go straight—"

Cressida leaned down at her—Mrs. Pembroke was five foot nothing if she was an inch—and blew a raspberry. The toad-like woman shrieked and scurried away.

"She'll be calling the cornics on us," Cressida said, watching her go. "I hope Second Gajos has informed them of my freedom."

There was too much to say for a long apology, so Telyn gripped her sister's arm a little harder and leaned her head on Cressida's shoulder as they walked.

Not long after, when they passed a knot of cornic soldiers, one of them waved. The second must have indeed informed them the bond price had been paid. Cressida said the soldier had played senet with her when he was on duty.

Which seemed very odd. Telyn was sure the second had murdered kind Minister Svemas—and yet he had acted, if not friendly, then at least equitable in the Hall of Magic. And now he kept his word about the bond price. The Academy's magic might have forced him to accept their bargain, of course, but he didn't have to run out and tell all his soldiers to leave Cressida alone.

Cornics are complicated.

The thief snorted. 'Like women.'

Like men, you mean, and grumpy ghosts.

"You're doing the mouth thing," Cressida said.

"Sorry. I'm possessed."

Cressida did a double take.

"How long?"

"Around twenty-four hours."

"Aled's rump. Why aren't we going to see Mrs. de Galati?"

"I don't want to think about it. Let's just enjoy ourselves."

Now and then, Telyn shot a glance at the Sepulcher. Although she had a fingernail moon to see by, and wood smoke gathered against the mountain, she could make out its details reasonably well. Lamps hung from the scaffolding created halos in the haze, and people and thaumas crawled over it, fixing the struts, carving names anew, and putting the escaped ghosts to rest.

Combining the scuttlebutt about town with what she could see with her own eyes, she concluded that (thanks to Rayvn's explosion) a large slab had broken free and shattered on the ground. Somewhere between a dozen and three dozen ghosts had escaped (the number depended largely on the inebriation of the speaker), and had gone storming through Harlech, breaking windows and scaring the folks in the steam bath completely free of their clothes.

"Why, you should have seen..."

They heard the same version of the story a half dozen times, saving Telyn the necessity of explaining exactly how she had become possessed.

Should she turn herself over to the witches?

Mrs. de Galati had Dagger's true name. And if Mrs. de Galati alone didn't have enough power to exorcise the vengeful spirit, with all the pattern witches in town, he didn't stand a chance. Telyn could be completely free to start over with her sister.

The mind wizard would leave her alone now...wouldn't he? Once he got his report from Taito-Vaiana, he would put two and two together and realize she'd sold the Ever-Guise.

'Don't be naive,' Dagger warned her. 'In Yona's mind, you and I have become entangled, which means you stole the forehead piece from him twice—once in the Sable Head, and once on the bridge. He will be coming for you for revenge if nothing else.'

His mental tone said he approved of Yona's sense of justice, at least in theory.

What will he do with Hootie?

'Hootie will be all right," Dagger said. 'He has connections.'

You don't sound convinced.

'You have to learn to keep your concerns to what you can control. Like in that ice climbing you love—all you can control is a little circle described by your arms and legs.'

Yona manipulates things from miles away.

'Hundreds of miles with the help of the Ever-Guise,' the thief corrected. 'Even with my help, you are no mind wizard. Our powers are decidedly limited, especially since that pattern witch took my true name.'

Cressida had paused to examine a game where you tossed a ring at bottles. She wouldn't miss Telyn's undivided attention for the moment—not that Telyn's attention would ever be undivided so long as Dagger resided in her bosom.

Hootie saved us in there. Is he a good friend?

'Let's say he has a sentimental streak. He pretends to hate humans, but he had done much to improve their condition in Enshede.'

How did he trick them? Why did the blue runes turned red and go crazy?

Dagger laughed. 'If I had to guess, and since I don't know for sure, I do have to guess, I would say he over-spent his purse. Both writs existed at the same time. Six thousand, four hundred hurons is more than even a full professor's budget is likely to comprise without approval from above.'

Hootie's writ was no good? He overspent—like me with the gooseberry acorns.

'Yes.'

They shared a laugh at the var's simple trick.

Telyn turned to watch Cressida play the game. Even with her matted hair and filthy clothes, Cressida looked beautiful. Telyn wanted to give her another hug. She wanted to snuggle with her like old times.

Old times. She snorted. *More like last fall. Old times, indeed.*

Lindsey Medyn Cannock, you know I've been thinking about going to the pattern witches. She used his true name deliberately to provoke him. *Why haven't you tried to stop me?*

Silence stretched long enough that Telyn thought he wouldn't answer. Cressida's fifth and final wooden ring bounced over the bottlenecks and landed askew.

"Win!" Cressida shouted.

The carnival barker picked the ring up and handed it back to her. "That's a do-over."

Pursing her lips, Cressida threw the ring again. It bounced once and dropped between the bottles.

"Sorry, that's a miss." The barker offered her a honey-chew. "Looks like you've had a bad day."

"One of the worst ever," Cressida replied, pulling the candy in half to share it with Telyn, "and one of the best. Thank you."

The barker winked.

'Telyn Lilith Brower,' Dagger said, returning the favor of using her full name. 'In this, you have as much choice as I. The Ever-Guise has pulled you into its sphere; you, me, Taito-Vaiana, Second Gajos, and Minister Svemas—even Yona Unega has been caught in it, though he thinks he is the master. There is no escape for you until the Ever-Guise is destroyed. There will be no exorcism. Of pattern witches, I worry not at all.'

No escape. Telyn began to feel miserable again. *For a human, not even death provides escape. At best, you get a half-life in Sheol; at worst, you return to haunt the living.*

Eventually, as morning's pink fingers started to reach from the eastern sky, the twins headed back toward their cabin. Cressida wanted to sleep there rather than at the Sable Head, and Telyn could hardly blame her. The ruckus and hubbub wouldn't stop at the taverns until the Spring Sale ended. And if Raz spotted them, he'd try to put them to work.

To her surprise, Telyn found the small elevation gain from Main Street to the Upper Road cabin tiring. The air became hard to breathe. In all the bustle of the Spring Sale, she hadn't noticed how much smoke had gathered.

But with the dawn, it became obvious; the Sepulcher could hardly be seen. Haze smothered the town; white flakes began to fall. Telyn had to blink to rid her eyelashes of ash. The road began to turn white.

Then they noticed orange flames leaping from between the trees. One of the cabins was burning.

And it was theirs.

The twins sprinted the last hundred yards. A line of men passed buckets from the nearest public fountain up the hill. They threw water on the lower branches of the surrounding trees and on the walls and eves of nearby structures. Men and women with shovels followed drifting embers to keep them from catching fire to dry leaves.

They had given up trying to douse the Brower cabin; the orange flames owned it.

Razenbock, empty bucket in hand, blocked the two sprinting girls from approaching further.

"She's gone." He dropped the bucket and pulled the twins into his embrace. "She didn't make it."

Even here, fifty feet away, with Razenbock's girth between them and the fire, the radiant heat made the air uncomfortably hot.

"The schmook murdered her," Telyn said, vengeance flaring within her. For the first time since her possession, Telyn felt at one with Dagger—one of mind, one of purpose. "I'm going to *kill* him."

'Yes,' Dagger hissed. 'Vengeance. Death. Kill.'

Cressida squeezed her hand. Her fingers danced on Telyn's palm, telling her to say no more in front of Raz and the other firefighters.

'Secrets and vengeance,' the thief's ghost whispered. 'Yes, Taito-Vaiana will die; Yona Unega will die most painfully.'

The vow melted like honey butter on toast, soaking into the deepest recesses of her mind.

'Yona Unega will die most painfully,' Dagger repeated, savoring the thought.

"You'll both be sleeping in the Sable Head tonight," Raz said. "The, ah, the funeral will happen in a few hours. With all the pattern witches in town, they'll take good care of Esther."

Released by the big man, the girls staggered around their cabin, the heat keeping them from approaching too closely. Raz trailed them at a respectful distance, as if unwilling to intrude, but ready to block them if they hurled themselves at the inferno.

"Where's the story?" Cressida asked. "What happened here?"

"If her ghost knew any tales, they're within the flames." Raz shrugged. "She ain't appeared yet."

Had they arrived a few minutes before, Telyn might have tried to dash inside to save what she could.

To save Esther, if she could.

Now—no.

Not only could nothing have survived the blaze; but nothing would remain of a human in such heat but ashes and coals. It would've been a fine funeral pyre if Esther had died a natural death.

Telyn remembered those squiggly worms, the black magic that Taito-Vaiana had used to torment the soldier on the bridge when Taffy fell into the river—the same worms the schmook had summoned in the Hall of Magic before Second Gajos stopped him.

She imagined those magic parasites swarming over her mother, burrowing beneath her skin, digging behind her eyeballs, climbing up the spinal cord to the brain.

She shivered.

Her mother. She hadn't thought of Esther that way in a very long time. *Mother of Squirrels, I hope it went quickly. I hope Esther did not suffer.*

Thankfully, Dagger did not add his own commentary. Telyn did not think she could have stood it if he'd described the effects of that pitiless spell.

"I'm staying here," Cressida announced. "I want to see Mom when she comes back." They all knew what she meant—when Esther came back as a ghost.

Cressida looked tired as death. She could use a few hours of sleep before the funeral; they both could. But what Telyn said was, "I'm staying, too."

Razenbock looked from one determined face to the other. "I'm bringing blankets."

He brought blankets, pillows, and mulled wine, and the twins set up a vigil on the Sepulcher side of the cabin, away from the lookie-loos and foot traffic of the upper road. A chaos tree made a decent enough backing to lean against.

The firefighters managed to keep drifting embers from catching anything else, and as the danger passed, they drifted back to the Spring Sale, leaving a ring of water-filled buckets the twins could throw in case something sparked.

Hours passed.

Cressida's eyes fell closed, and her head dropped against Telyn's shoulder. Her breathing became shallow, even, peaceful.

'She stirs,' Dagger announced.

Telyn's eyes popped open. She'd sworn to herself not to fall asleep.

'There, in the smoke.'

Eddied swirled, but there was no wind. What seemed a blue fire danced above the coals.

"Mother?" Telyn asked.

She'd never seen a blue ghost, but the thief did not feel alarmed. He felt at peace. And she figured that Dagger probably knew ghosts as well as anyone except Mrs. de Galati.

The blue flame came nearer.

"Mother?"

The shimmering blue form, now shaped as a female silhouette, hovered about four feet away. Unlike when Dagger had manifested, this spirit showed no desire to inhabit anyone. Even if invited in, Telyn felt certain Esther would choose to remain in the spirit world. Since her husband died, Esther had spent her energy escaping from this world through alcohol; she certainly wouldn't choose to come back.

She probably couldn't wait for the pattern witches to seal her beyond the grave for good.

"Wake your sister," came Esther's voice from the flames.

Telyn started to shake Cressida then thought better of it. Resentment burgeoned in her breast. They had a moment to themselves, and all her mother wanted to do was talk with Cressida?

This is so like Esther!

"You always loved Cressida more," she accused.

After a long pause, the blue spirit admitted, "Yes."

Nothing more.

No apology, no explanation. No story about how this came to be. They'd been born at the same time and shared the same father, yet Esther had chosen to love one of them more than the other.

Telyn's teeth ground together. She so wanted to leave it at that, to leave Esther without her last wish.

And yet, she shook her twin's shoulder until Cressida opened her eyes and gasped.

They all stared at each other for some time. Telyn wondered if Esther had lost the ability to speak. Already, her vaporous form had lost some cohesion.

"Am I dreaming?" Esther asked. That wisp of smoke may have been her arm trying to reach out and touch Cressida. It fell short. "Or am I in heaven where both my girls are free?"

"We're free, Mother. Telyn freed me."

A small vibration grated on Telyn's jaw, like the annoying whine of a mosquito. Esther, the ghost, showing displeasure. "Telyn's foolery put you in chains."

"No, Mother. She got me out. She found a way to pay the bond price."

The whining grew louder. "Thief!"

"I didn't steal, Mother," Telyn said.

"You mean to say you raised thousands of birds on your own?" The ghost seemed to grow until Esther glared at her like Leutric Quid on a tear. "Or are they tipping extra well at the Sable Head?"

"I didn't steal nothing."

"Swear it."

Telyn rose to her feet and crossed her arms across her chest. She felt like turning her back and walking away—but this was Esther's ghost. After the funeral ceremony, she would never be able to talk to Esther again. No matter how unpleasant the conversation, this was their last one.

"I swear I didn't steal to free my sister. I didn't steal nothing. We found a chrysalis shell in the Chaos Woods and sold it at the Hall of Magic. I swear it."

And we found the mask, too. That wasn't stolen. Well, not by me.

'Finders keepers.' Dagger laughed inside Telyn's head.

You stay out of this.

'What a touching reunion.'

Shut it.

"It's true, Mother," Cressida said. "And I figured out that the Ouzeleys rigged the Dating Chart, and I made them pay the rest."

"I knew it. You freed yourself."

"Telyn did most of it."

"Telyn got you in trouble, and you got yourself out."

"That's not true! Telyn never gave up on me."

"It's okay," Telyn said, wiping a tear from her cheek. "Just let it go. She'll believe what she wants to believe." She took a deep, calming breath. "You're right about me, Esther. I get people in trouble. I'm not responsible like Cressida. I try to fix what I break—I swear that I do—but I break an awful lot. I found something, a magical mask" — Cressida gasped at her confession—"and Cressida got caught with it. She was on her way to throw it in the Elbus River when she got nabbed. So yes, it was all my fault.

"But I went into the woods to find something—anything—that could pay her bond price. And we did it, me and my friends. I couldn't have done it without them: Caitlin, Hosh, and Rayvn, the pattern girl. We found a way."

Telyn toed a half-burned plank that had fallen near her feet. It crackled and flared as she moved it, and the air got underneath. Fire sprouted again, yellow-red and hypnotic. "I got you killed, too, Mother. It was that mask again. Someone came back for it, a schmook, and—it's complicated. They wanted to hurt me, so they killed you." She looked back at the ghost, as close to eye contact as she could when the ghost didn't have any eyes. "It's all my fault. And I'm sorry. I'm not the daughter you wanted."

"Cressida's been taking care of you for years. And she's gonna have to keep doing it for years more the way you're going. No man will put up with you—no man worth his malt."

"Yes, Mother."

"Cressida," Esther said, her tone clearly a dismissal to Telyn. Cressida wiped her tears to listen better. "I'm sorry I ain't been a good mother. If I'd 've been better, you could've had the childhood you deserved. You wouldn't't've had to play mother to this one."

A gong sounded from the Prefecture. The funeral bell. Shutters snapped shut all along the upper road.

"That for me?"

"Yes, Mother," Cressida answered.

"Then I'll be going." But she hovered above the smoldering wreckage a moment longer. "I love you, girls. I love you both."

Telyn gasped.

"Goodbye, Mother," Cressida said, and the blue ghost faded into the wood-smoke.

Cressida pointed to the plank at Telyn's feet. Painted there in soft, charcoal lines was a single picture—Esther bouncing a baby girl on each knee, and a man—their father, Dorian Brower, leaning over Esther's shoulder.

"Goodbye, Mother," Telyn breathed.

CHAPTER SIXTY-NINE

The funeral bell sounded, slamming the doors and shutters shut and calling the townsfolk to follow the death car without urgency. Beginning at the Sable Head, Leutric Quid sang "Ode to the Departed," gathering folks lazily as the four llamas clomped forward. The procession lacked urgency because neither a vengeful spirit nor a howling eehoo spurred it along.

Few people stirred around the Hall of Magic at this early hour; the locals had the funeral to themselves. Telyn retrieved her funeral best from the Sable Head: white blouse, full skirt, blue belt sash, and leather boots—since she knew Esther would have preferred her to wear shoes. All of Cressida's clothes had burned with the cabin, so she borrowed a plain shirt and Telyn's hunting trousers, adding an auburn vest for a touch of class.

Wheeling past the Sable Head, Leutric Quid flicked the llamas' reins and tipped an imaginary hat at Telyn and Cressida, who took the place of honor directly behind the wagon. The death car carried neither body nor ashes; the cabin heat would keep them from recovering anything for hours yet. Nor did Mrs. de Galati need one. The body wasn't important. They had Esther's true name and her next of kin for the blood-spell. Even if the ghost had wanted to stick around, it didn't stand a chance.

The twins followed the death car to the split in the road, where they climbed the stairs to the Sepulcher and the wagon turned left and continued to the lye pit.

At the base of the Sepulcher awaited their friends: Hosh, Caitlin, Rayvn, and Razenbock in his best black duster. Mrs. de Galati, looking formidable in what Telyn called her battle kimono, bowed deeply. This set the strings of pearls around her neck to clicking.

The other pattern witches hadn't bothered to come, nor had the maroon venders, probably under the impression that the crowd would save its appetite for the sale later in the day.

It was a chill, windless morning, and yet the tips of the trees swayed, as if just above their heads, the wind whispered.

"Do you feel anything?" Telyn asked.

"Don't you?" Cressida answered, a little sharply.

"I mean the ghost, worm head."

They'd become familiar enough in the past twelve hours—reacquainted, as it were—that they could jibe without fear of offense.

"No," Cressida replied. "Mom checked off this earth when Daddy fell into the crevasse in Aumerhem Pass."

Razenbock made a sound between throat clearing and gagging and turned away in embarrassment. That's when Telyn noticed Archie Todd—the baker—standing a little behind Raz. He looked anywhere but at the twins, and she didn't know if she should be angry at him for all his wrongs or grateful that he'd come to Esther's funeral, dressed in his black-and-white formals.

"It still hasn't...hasn't set in that I will never hide another one of her bottles, never redo her stitches while she sleeps so she thinks she can still sew straight, never bicker with her again." Cressida sniffed back unshed tears. "She visited me near every day in jail."

Telyn nodded.

"She did the best she could; she really did."

Leutric Quid's singing grew softer in the distance, replaced by the shuffling footsteps of mourners and whispered rumors. Speculation ran of a candle carelessly left among the dressmaker's fabric, or a lamp tipped over by a careless elbow.

A woman too drunk to react in time, died of smoke inhalation before her liver gave out, a mercy, almost.

But what of the twins?

Razenbock will take care of them. He acts like their father. He might be; you never know with a drunk like Esther.

Pity, sorrow, remembrances, and a dash of cruelty carried across the still air, no matter how Telyn tried to ignore it.

"How did Cressida escape the chains, anyway?"

"On the very night her mother's home went up in flames, isn't *that* a coincidence."

"Harmless old Esther. Who would have thought?"

"They say her sister came up with the bond price, no one knows how. But the Ouzeleys are furious."

"They aren't here, are they? They never miss a funeral."

And on the crowd droned. Nobody would have imagined a thauma had murdered Esther; no one would have conceived of such a thing. What would a thauma have to do with the miserable of Harlech?

Telyn hardly noticed when Second Gajos arrived and began to give the speech about ghosts and the dead, replicating Minister Svemas' oratory almost word-for-word.

"I don't feel anything supernatural," Cressida said, abruptly. "Esther stayed back at the cabin. She's not eager to possess anyone."

"Especially not me."

"Hey, I'm the slave. I brought the most shame down on the family."

"She told me she always knew I was responsible. Do you reckon she did?"

"What, Telyn responsible for getting us in trouble? That's always a safe bet." Cressida toed at the soft dirt of a gopher mound. "She could be mean. She was angry at the world, angry at Dad for not coming home, angry at herself for giving up and becoming a...a drunk. She could be cruel with her words."

"Then why is my throat so tight I can barely talk?" Telyn shifted back and forth from one leg to the other.

"This is not your fault, Telyn." Cressida pressed her head against Telyn's, the girls' smoke-scented hair mingling, and whispered urgently. "The alcohol possessed Mother the same way the thief possesses you. It formed a lens over her eyes. Everything she saw was seen through the filter of malt—even us. After a while, she couldn't function without it. Alcohol became her everything: her stew, her speck, her water, her husband."

"I haven't been entirely fair," Telyn allowed. It felt good to be physically close to Cressida; it felt like old times, when they could trust each other. When *Cressida* could trust *her*. "Mom changed when Dad fell into the crevasse. She felt betrayed and alone."

For the first time that morning, Dagger stirred in her mind. 'Razenbock and Archie Todd betrayed your mother. Never forget it; never forgive it.'

"Lots of people lose husbands here in Harlech," Cressida said, "and brothers and sons. They don't all react like Mom. They don't all drown themselves in alcohol. Life is full of tragedy. Your character" — She poked Telyn in the chest—"determines how you react to it."

"Um, okay?"

"The ghost, Dagger, he's going to try to take you the way the alcohol took Mom, a little at a time, until there's nothing left of Telyn —nothing left of my sister."

"Cressida," Telyn whispered, feeling decidedly uncomfortable at this sudden turn of conversation. "Everyone is staring."

"Shut it. Shut it and listen."

"Sorry."

"The Ever-Guise took you once. I saw the changes take you little by little. You became Not-Telyn." Telyn bit her lip and nodded. "You don't even know, Telyn. You think you do, but the changes, they went deep." Cressida hiccupped. "Aled's sacred rump."

'Your sister is going to give us away. She is going to ruin everything,' Dagger warned.

"Maybe we should go," Telyn said. She tried to step away, but Cressida's grip became firm.

"This ghost, he isn't something you can take off and hang on a coat rack," Cressida insisted. "He's buried all the way inside. You won't even know which thoughts are yours and which are his after a while."

"If I try to swap spit with Caitlin, I'll know," Telyn said, trying to make a joke. It came out flat. "Sorry."

"Stop saying that."

"Sorry."

Second Gajos ended his speech. Mrs. de Galati gestured for the twins to join her, but Cressida held Telyn a moment longer. Her green eyes, normally so gentle, took on a hard, pleading edge. "You have a chance to be rid of him. Mrs. de Galati can rid you of Dagger once and for all."

Telyn stiffened. "You think I haven't thought of that? I can't think of anything else. But you heard the schmook: '*Master Unega never forgets, never forgives. He lets me play with his toys before they die.*' And in case we didn't take him seriously, he murdered Esther."

Mrs. Pembroke had sidled close enough to hear, and she gasped at this revelation. Telyn wanted to twist the foul woman's ear until she screamed, but she settled for glowering at the nosy woman until she scuttled away.

When Mrs. Pembroke was out of earshot, Cressida lowered her voice and said, "You once told me we could run off into the Chaos Woods, live our lives there. I'm willing, Telyn. We could go together. There isn't much for me here now that Esther's gone. I'm a former slave. Who in their right mind would want me? I'll be a long-shotter forever."

Telyn had barely considered that, barely thought about how being a former slave would sully Cressida's reputation. She'd been so focused on freeing her sister; what came after didn't make a whole lot of difference. But, of course, it did.

She turned to face the Sepulcher and took Cressida's hand. Together, slowly, they approached the scaffolding.

"We wouldn't last long," Telyn said, remembering their foray into the woods. "One injury, one deer we failed to trap, and we'd starve to death. We tried it for a few weeks, and even with a pattern witch on our side, we barely made it."

"We could join a trapping party. Our odds would be better there than chasing after one of the deadliest flacks in the world—one who knows we are coming."

'Our odds...we are coming,' Mother of Squirrels, Cressida plans to join me on Dagger's quest!

They joined Rayvn and Mrs. de Galati on the lift. The men turned the crank, and with the creak of wood and ropes, the party began to rise.

"We have Dagger to protect us against the mind wizard," Telyn said. "And there's one more thing."

"How did I guess?"

Telyn put her hands on her hips. "Okay, smarty. What?"

"You want to destroy the Ever-Guise."

"Aled's rump! How am I so transparent?"

"*Sacred* rump. And yes."

Atop the catwalk, Mrs. de Galati chalked Esther Dany Brower on a rough section of stone. Rayvn swung her hammer, and the letters took shape. The fresh break on the granite, where the slab had been knocked loose, twinkled in the morning sun, bits of mica reflecting sunlight. Seven or eight new names had been chiseled there already— those ghosts Telyn, Rayvn, Caitlin and Hosh had freed, no doubt.

Unknown was not among them.

Cressida went first. Mrs. de Galati held the bronze bowl and recited with some ritual that Telyn paid no attention to, while Rayvn heated the glass spike over a candle.

Feeling wobbly, she leaned back against the Sepulcher and stared over her valley. Where their cabin used to be, embers glowed softly between the trees. Woodsmoke, pungent with the oily smell of burning fabric, drifted from the wreckage.

"Goodbye, Mother," Telyn said. "I love you."

If there was an answer, it was in the silence of the watching crowd and the singing of the birds. Without taking her eyes from the view, she offered her arm and barely felt the glass shaft penetrate her skin.

She had entered a kind of phantasm of half-perceptions, as if she lay on the bottom of a pool and viewed the world through the rippling surface.

The pattern witch leaned in, her whiskers brushing against Telyn's cheek and nose. Vaguely, Telyn heard Mrs. de Galati offer to exorcise the thief, and she shook her head in reply. Her sight blurred at the movement of her head.

Dagger rumbled but did not speak.

"Are you sure, Telyn Brower?"

Telyn swallowed.

"Sure."

Later, Telyn realized Cressida had descended, Mrs. de Galati held a steadying hand on her arm, and the lift awaited. The pattern witch lifted her whiskers in a sort of smile, baring one incisor.

"Ready," Telyn affirmed. "But not like this. I need to climb."

Mrs. de Galati gave her a peck on the cheek, which somehow felt appropriate.

Telyn climbed. The sunlight hit her back. The scaffolding wood felt familiar on her callused hands. Hand over hand, foot to foot, she descended. She allowed her thoughts to cover the past year.

Why had it all happened? What could she have done better? How many mistakes had she made?

So many.

Starting with using the Ever-Guise to try to influence people. Ending with becoming not-Telyn, someone she hardly recognized, someone who lied and posed and manipulated others as badly as the Ouzeleys.

Telyn paused at her dad's name, kissed her fingertips and pressed them to the "D" in Dorian—"D" for Dad.

At her back, her beloved town of Harlech and the mysterious, wonderful Chaos Woods. To her front, the names and the ghosts. She could practically feel them calling to her, calling to the ghost inside her, probably.

Dagger stirred.

I won't let them take you. We have work to do.

'Revenge,' the vengeful spirit rumbled.

She ran her hands over the indentations one by one. *Dorian Garrett Brower.* She leaned forward and kissed the first letter of each name then pressed her forehead against the Sepulcher and wished peace for her father.

Well, Dagger, what now? Are we headed to Enshede? Beyond? Are we going after Yona?

Telyn did not want to be on a quest for revenge; the whole idea of revenge grated against her idea of morality.

"Judge yourself," Aled the Wise said, "leave the rest to magistrates and the High Father. If you happen to be a magistrate, judge yourself doubly harsh."

This isn't revenge, Telyn tried to tell herself. *This is survival.*

"He lets me play with his toys before they die," the schmook had promised before murdering Esther. "Master Unega never forgives, never forgets."

How much had he toyed with Esther before killing her?

'Think of your gooseberry acorns,' Dagger replied. 'You are not ready for the juicy middle yet. We start around the edges. Taito-Vaiana comes first. He will be the easier target—if we can catch him away from his soldiers.'

Soldiers? Wait, is he a general or something?

'More like a crime lord—and not the highest ranking member of his clan. Which probably explains why he hooked up with Yona Unega. He is either setting up shop on his own, or plans some sort of coup within his family.'

Or something you haven't thought of yet—something hidden like the pictures in a witch's pattern wheel.

'You are beginning to understand my world—trust no one and nothing. Even those closest to you end up betraying you for the right price.' He seemed to be thinking about a specific person or incident, and Telyn remembered how Kulon the trogo had taunted Dagger about someone called Glas Courier, and how the taunts appeared to hurt Dagger every bit as much as Kulon's fists.

How are we going to—to kill Taito-Vaiana if he has soldiers at his back? Telyn still wasn't comfortable with the idea of killing a thauma or human. If felt too much like murder, and who gave her the right to end someone's life, anyway? No matter how justified, she hated the idea.

'Taito-Vaiana is just practice for the bigger prize, child's play beside killing Yona Unega." Telyn's belly tightened when Dagger thought that name. Even when they weren't struggling for control, the vengeful spirit's emotions affected her physical body more and more. 'Besides,' he continued, 'Taito-Vaiana killed your mother. That should help stiffen your spine.'

Telyn swallowed. *I am not afraid. I can do what I have to do.*

Dagger's laughter did not reassure her in the least.

Not in the least.

Reviews sell books! If you enjoyed *Chaos Woods* (or even if you didn't) please consider leaving a review on Amazon, Barnes & Noble, Kobo, or wherever you normally shop for books. Thank you!
—Scott T. Barnes

ABOUT THE AUTHOR

An itinerant coffeehouse writer, Scott T. Barnes started scribbling fantasy and science fiction on the back of napkins at the age of eleven. He has since graduated to a laptop. His story "Insect Sculptor" won the *L. Ron Hubbard Presents Writers of the Future Award. BookLife* by *Publishers Weekly* gave Scott's novel *Memories of Lucinda Eco* a coveted Editors Pick, calling it "a fun, epic adventure."

Western Americana is in Scott's bones and blood and it often finds its way into his stories. Both sides of his family have been farming and ranching in Southern California for several generations. Scott grew up on a farm (specializing in apples, pears, and cut flowers) in the small town of Julian, and later wrangled cows on ranches in Northern California and Oregon, where he spent many happy days breathing dust and learning colorful turns of phrase from the cowboys.

In addition, Scott has spent many years studying Systema with Joseph Stoltman and samurai arts (Nami Ryu Aiki Kenjutsu) with James Williams.

To learn more about Scott and his upcoming projects, check out his website at www.scotttbarnes.com and sign up for his newsletter.

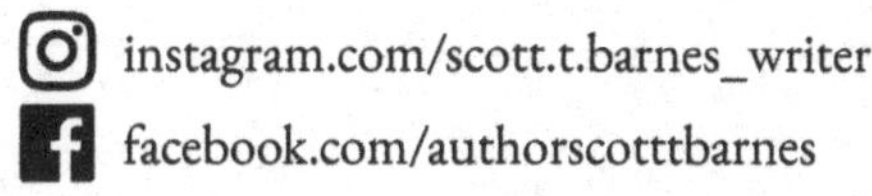

instagram.com/scott.t.barnes_writer

facebook.com/authorscotttbarnes

The gripping adventure continues
in Book II of the Chronicles of the Ever-Guise,
coming Fall 2026.

Turn the page for a sneak peek.

PROLOGUE

Mantle ran his fingers along the rough burnt wood and melted slag that used to be a wall safe. This sort of damage could only have been caused by a daemon, but which one? Only a few daemons had access into the world, and he hadn't heard of any in the area for decades. Unless the barrier into Sheol had weakened....

No, best not to consider such things. Mantle couldn't ponder the imponderable.

Instead, he focused on the task at hand. He was disguised as a cornic Inquisitor and wore a soft blue tunic that draped to his knees with a single red splash embroidered across the heart, as if to remind those who would defy the Cornic Empire what awaited them. A white cape hung from his shoulders to symbolize purity. Like all cornics, the Inquisitor had a ram-like head with a long muzzle, black gums, and horns curling over his ears. The longer the horns, the more venerable the cornic, but also the more probability one was to be recognized, the more likely someone would ask why they hadn't met before. Which is why in his Inquisitor's guise his horns curled only half a turn. Better to let your enemies think you had advanced quickly through the order than raise such questions.

The aroma of mildew permeated the small office—a disagreeable byproduct of fairies. Mantle had brought with him three humanoid females with dragonfly-like wings. When they weren't conversing in singsong whistles in their wicker basket, they flitted about like bees, tasting the air—more specifically, tasting the magic in the air. The three could speak after a fashion, and they confirmed that daemon rot had destroyed the safe. They also confirmed what Mantle's ears had already told him—that the usual occupant of this office was just outside, speaking in a low voice with the corporal who acted as his secretary. Afraid to come in, no doubt, afraid to confront his doom.

Minister Svemas—the cornic in charge of this small, provincial outpost—had been murdered, presumably by the one who hesitated outside the door. Mantle would use this, as he used every stitch of information that passed his way. But he didn't really care about the murder. His focus was on the safe that had been melted out of the wall—and what it must have contained.

The fairy queen had not given him a timeline for returning the Ever-Guise mask or for extracting revenge on its thief. Banrión Tierney, fairy queen of the Chaos Woods, was far too chaotic for deadlines. When Banrión determined too much time had passed, she would assign another assassin, and Mantle would die. Things were clear with Banrión Tierney. Beautifully, chaotically clear.

Nevertheless, Mantle was glad he had the three fairies with him. Fairies existed partly in this world and partly in Sheol, the world of the dead. And this mask—this Ever-Guise—did also.

Before this is through, I, too, will learn something of Sheol, Mantle thought. *I am among humans now and humans have souls...and souls create ghosts and there is no escaping it. Without the fairies I have no power over ghosts. Unless, of course, I ally myself with a pattern witch.*

Mantle chuckled at that preposterous thought. Pattern witches did not ally with assassins.

A fairy fluttered to his ear and confirmed that yes, the Ever-Guise mask had once sat here.

"Why did it take so long to confirm?"

"Incomplete, partial, not entire."

This news sent a thrill up Mantle's furry arms. The mask had been broken into pieces! Finding it would be that much more difficult. That much more *challenging*. Mantle enjoyed a challenge.

There came a hesitant knock. The commander of Harlech had delayed three whole minutes before entering his own office. Five seconds later, the latch opened, and Second Gajos stepped in.

So, Mantle thought, *Second Gajos is indecisive, but given time he gathers courage.*

Mantle continued running his hands over the melted slag that had been the safe's door and the machinery for unlocking it, showing Second Gajos his back. He almost hoped Second Gajos would try to kill him.

He did love a challenge.

The scent of melted steel and burnt wood lingered in the gaping hole. Clear cedar by the looks of it—similar in its straight grain and reddish hue to chaos lumber. But they wouldn't use *that* in the Prefecture. Chaos lumber disrupted magic, altered it in unpredictable ways. Sometimes it worked, sometimes it didn't. And sometimes casting a spell around chaos wood would blow your head clean off. The magic-using races feared it and avoided it.

Not Mantle, of course, for his was an internal kind of magic. Chaos wood did not affect him. In fact, Mantle was a creature of the Chaos Woods. One of the wild beasts. He felt at home there.

Mantle cleared his throat. On cue, the three fairies zipped out of their wicker basket and darted about the room.

Second Gajos threw himself prostrate, landing with a clang. By peering beneath the desk, he would see the Inquisitor's hooflike feet. Certainly not military dress code, but carrying around extra shoes made Mantle's bag far too bulky, so he had decided to forego that part of his disguise. The Cornic Second would either be in awe of what he thought was the Inquisitor's cheek—or Mantle would have to kill him. Best not to let Second Gajos contemplate too long.

Mantle turned.

The clang had come from the sword Second Gajos wore on the belt at his waist; it now twisted awkwardly beneath his torso. He was unusually large; he must have been over six feet tall, and stocky as well.

Maybe three hundred fifty pounds, accustomed to intimidating others.

Not today. Second Gajos' face wore a look of fear and wide-eyed scheming. No doubt his mind raced to think of a series of lies to avoid torture and execution. No doubt he was trying to guess who had betrayed him, wondering if the corporal in the other room had set him up....

Second Gajos burped. He must not have intended to, for he chewed the cud in surprised fits and bursts, a mash so foul its sourgrass reek swam about like odiferous gnats.

Yes, he is terrified. Second Gajos' guilt in Minister Svemas' murder couldn't be clearer.

Mantle flicked out his cape and sat in Second Gajos' own leather chair, smirking at the other's discomfort. "Sit, Gajos. I have no desire to crick my neck staring down at you." He didn't use the honorific "Second," which denoted that Gajos belonged to the second-most powerful house in the Cornic Empire. Such things mattered not to an Inquisitor. Nor to an assassin.

As Second Gajos rose, Mantle added, "If I decide to break you, it will not be here. You will lead me to the dungeon and hand me the tools yourself. If I'm in a generous mood, I may let you choose which to start with."

With tremors in his forearms, Second Gajos removed his sword belt and hung it on a stand. He sank into the red velvet-upholstered visitor's chair, and it rocked. His teeth snapped together; the chair had uneven legs to keep visitors off-balance.

"Your pin, please." Mantle extended his hand until Second Gajos removed the small ruby pin from his breast—the signet from House Second—and handed it over. Mantle pocketed it. "You had something in your possession, a mask. I have been looking for your report to the Empress on this valuable artifact. I'm sure you intended to write one —but it doesn't seem to be among your papers."

Second Gajos set his large, sweaty hands on his thighs. "Minister Svemas, my predecessor here in Harlech, confiscated a magical artifact from a human girl and sentenced her to slavery for it. Her name is Cressida Brower. Doubtless, the Minister wanted to inform the

Empress of his discovery, but Harlech is isolated in winter. No one gets in or out."

No one except for that trapper Redbeard, thought Mantle. He'd been in town long enough to hear about Redbeard and his exploits. He also knew Minister Svemas sent and received reports via Redbeard. Not to mention via pigeon.

"Where can I find this Cressida Brower? Who is her master?"

"She...she was redeemed. By her sister."

"Redeemed! A serving girl managed to pay thousands of hurons for her sister's freedom?"

Something like recognition passed across the Second's face. Inwardly, Mantle cursed. He shouldn't have let slip that he already knew about the Brower twins, Telyn and Cressida.

"I can have her brought in—will have her brought in, sir. These are matters beyond my understanding. I am but a temporary replacement..."

One of the fairies buzzed the second's face, causing him to flinch. Good timing. They really were a lot smarter than anyone gave them credit for.

"You had some fun with the mask, I see, bringing slavery to Harlech where it had never been."

With a clogged-drain sound, Second Gajos managed to swallow his cud. "Ah. The mask was stolen. I no longer have it."

"By whom?"

"A daemon. It dissolved the safe, took the...the mask, and escaped. Three of my soldiers died trying to stop it." Second Gajos shuddered.

Probably a genuine reaction. He would have to be a fool not *to have been afraid.*

Mantle steepled his fingers under his muzzle. "I will ask one final question in this comfortable office, Gajos. Your answer will determine whether or not we head outside...or to the dungeon. A cereb and a schmook came looking for the mask last year." Second Gajos nodded. "They bought the mask off a thief called Dagger. Where is Dagger now?"

Second Gajos stuttered nonsensical syllables, composed himself, and began again. "The—, there was a murder—"

"Another murder?"

"A hu—, human was killed in the Sable Head ta—, tavern. That human must have been your, ah, your Dagger."

"Is there a ghost?"

"The pattern witch held a funeral. No—, no ghost."

"Show me the thief's name."

"I cannot. The Sepulcher shattered."

Mantle slapped his large hands on the desk. The fairies' wings whirred. "A slave redeemed by a serving girl for thousands of hurons." He let his voice drop menacingly, slowed it to a poisonous drip. "A human murdered under your noses without a culprit—not to mention your predecessor, Minister Svemas. And the Sepulcher has been shattered."

"The pattern witches have put it all to rights. All the ghosts have been banished."

"Really. Where is the mask now?"

"I...I don't know. I swear it."

"You swear it on Minister Svemas's life?"

"On my own, Sir. On my own!"

"Yes, of course you do. Gajos, I wish you to consider what implement of torture you wish me to start with if you do not satisfy my curiosity. We so rarely even think about which forms of pain we can stand, and which we cannot, do we? Personally, I enjoy the challenge of using sharp implements for as long as I can . . . without soaking my towel through with blood. It's a little game I play.

"Now, let us start from the beginning. When did you become aware of this magical mask...."

Carrying a duffel bag over his shoulder, Mantle departed the Prefecture by the main entrance. The soldiers flanking the door stood at attention and looked anywhere but at him.

The blue Inquisitor's tunic and white cape tended to elicit that reaction.

Mantle dodged around three humans swaying arm-in-arm and

singing "A Shanty with Mammy." He'd been in Harlech during the Spring Sale before, but this year it had a completely different feel. The white canvas Hall of Magic had gone tan from the smoke and dust; the reek of garbage undercut the roasting meat stickers; the streets felt half-deserted rather than half-full; and the revelers' attempts to drink themselves into a good time felt a little desperate.

Mantle wandered randomly from stall to stall, pausing now and then to pretend to watch jugglers or street magicians to be sure no one tailed him. Then he ducked into the alleys near Steamy Betty's. *So*, he thought, stepping over a languid couple who might have been wrestling or kissing, *the Ever-Guise mask has been broken into pieces, and Second Gajos only touched the Influence part, the forehead. And this forehead has been stolen by a daemon.*

Could it be in Sheol and beyond my reach? No, I mustn't ponder the imponderable, he reminded himself.

He focused instead on what he *could* ponder.

The girl, Cressida Brower, was sentenced to slavery for possessing the mask. Where did she get it? Why did she have only the forehead? Who broke it into pieces? What role did her twin sister, Telyn, play, and how in the Creator's universe did she raise enough hurons to redeem a slave?

Did Second Gajos murder Minister Svemas to take the mask? That seems likely.

Mantle began to piece together a timeline.

Dagger stole the Ever-Guise from Banrión Tierney. *He came to Harlech and died here. The human girl, Cressida Brower, came into possession of the forehead. Probably an accident. Probably she found it or stole it, not knowing what she was getting.*

The cornics caught Cressida with the forehead piece and sentenced her to slavery. Second Gajos, guessing at the mask's value, murdered his boss, Minister Svemas, took his place, and took the mask. He used it to introduce slavery to Harlech and enrich himself. He must have thought its Influence could keep him from being punished.

Months later, a schmook named Taito Vaiana purchased Cressida, the penumbra daemon stole the Ever-Guise forehead from Second Gajos, and Telyn Brower redeemed her sister-slave for four thousand hurons.

The same day that Telyn Brower redeemed her twin sister Cressida, their mother was murdered.

Coincidence?

Mantle laughed out loud.

Second Gajos hasn't seen all these connections—not directly. But they are there, plain as the sun at midday.

But I don't understand everything, not yet.

Three things are certain: the Ever-Guise has been divided; the Brower twins hold at least one of the keys; and my life just got more complicated.

A wide grin split his muzzle. The life of an assassin was always a heady mixture of simple and complicated—as simple as slitting a person's throat, as complicated as Empires collapsing from that same act.

Before interrogating the Browers, Mantle wanted to visit the Sepulcher to verify if Dagger truly had met his end. That would please the fairy queen, at least, and give Mantle more time to locate and return the Ever-Guise before his contract was canceled—and his life. The fairies he carried were more than a useful tool; they were his contract, his reward, his death sentence in case of failure.

In a shadowed alcove, Mantle exchanged the blue Inquisitor robes for the hose, knee-length trousers and loose shirt worn by many of the local humans. Mantle didn't bother with shoes.

With some squelching and popping—and a good deal of pain— he morphed into the form of a young human male, red-haired, stocky, with a flat face and flat-top haircut. Mantle did some stretching to alleviate the pain, and repacked the bag. This form would appear nonthreatening but not overly so; he didn't want to have to deal with cutpurses.

The Sepulcher was a great granite half-dome that dominated the skyline to the northeast of town. The fairies in the wicker basket twitted excitedly as they approached the formation's flat face—they seemed to feel some hum of ghosts and silent magic within. Mantle scaled the scaffolding that rose before it and easily located the twinkle of freshly broken stone that confirmed Second Gajos' tale. There, pattern witches had carved the names of the three humans accused of killing Minister Svemas. They had also carved the word *Unknown*. They hadn't known what to call Dagger.

Someone had managed to shatter it.

The daemon? But why?

Mantle released the fairies, and one after another they landed on the word *Unknown* and tasted its magic. They confirmed the spell had something of Dagger in it, and something of another, which confused them. But this level of fairy didn't speak in full sentences, so Mantle may not have full understanding.

So, Dagger really is dead. I don't know how I feel about that. He would have made a worthy opponent.

Mantle whispered a message, and one of the fairies flew into the Chaos Woods to inform her queen. She would be gone for a week or more, but wherever Mantle went, the fairy would find him.

It frightened him that he didn't know how they tracked him. If he ever had to escape them, he honestly didn't know how he would accomplish that without killing all three.

That would only buy him a little time, until the fairy queen sent more servants.

He descended the scaffolding deep in thought.

"Ho, man, you haven't paid the toll," a voice called as Mantle neared the bottom. It was a cocky voice, the kind Mantle liked to break.

Mantle jumped the final five feet and turned. Three young men regarded him with narrowed eyes. They wore fine coats despite the warm weather.

The local aristocratic bullies, Mantle deduced. Every town has them. He bent his neck in a subservient posture. "Er...toll? Sorry, didn't know about no toll. I'm looking for a friend of mine. Maybe you know her. Cressida, Cressida Brower."

Hearing that name, the largest human advanced to within two paces. "The stinking slave? Yeah, I know her. I beat her a time or two. You got a problem with that? Maybe I'll beat you. We owned her, the tramp. Not that anyone'd be looking at their ankles, they're as dirty as a brakdaw's behind."

Ankles? Ah yes, Harlech has some bizarre ideas about the propriety of revealing a woman's ankles.

"Whoa, I'm a friend of hers, not her boyfriend." Mantle held out his hands in a peaceful gesture. "Maybe she owes me something, too. I went to her cabin to collect, but it looks like it burned down. Where does she live now?"

The bully's cheek twitched. "What does she owe you? Never mind, she's at the Sable Head. She's a tavern wench like her too-tall twin. I'll take you; she and her sister owe me plenty." The three young humans exchanged a look. The leader brushed past Mantle, arrogant and sure of himself. The others hung back.

They've done this before.

Mantle turned and hurried to catch up, and the other two humans fell in behind.

"What's your name?" Mantle asked.

"Tabbard Ouzeley. Remember it."

The fairies became agitated inside their basket, which was tied to the outside of Mantle's duffel. He whispered for them to keep quiet, earning suspicious looks from the humans.

Tabbard led off-trail into the woods, and Mantle's excitement swelled. He didn't let himself look at the followers to see if they held weapons. That would be so much more exciting! He hoped so...but they appeared too arrogant to shank him from behind. They probably would rely on their fists—at least at first.

Too bad. Too easy.

He edged ahead of Tabbard, and pretended to be surprised when Tabbard threw a muscular arm around his neck. The other humans rushed in and began punching Mantle's ribs.

Tabbard pulled Mantle into a decent headlock. He had strength but little skill; his fat arm blocked neither windpipe nor carotid artery sufficiently to induce unconsciousness. Still, he moved quickly for one so large. And his friends landed irritating little jabs.

Mantle morphed. The glands in his skin secreted a resin which hardened almost immediately, creating a bone-like plate across his ribs

—with rows of little spikes as a dainty. The two accomplices shouted in surprise and agony as—driven by the force of their own punches—their knuckles splintered.

"Happy now?" Mantle hissed. He relished this kind of fight. He only wished the humans posed more of a challenge.

He placed his right thigh behind Tabbard's hip, twisted to break the headlock, and dropped the human on his back. Before Tabbard could scramble up, Mantle grew sharp bills in place of his hands, like the bills on the dreaded bladefishes that terrorized the Tatra Sea. He spun these sword-like appendages and slit the other humans' throats. They wobbled a moment, blowing air from the holes in their tracheas as they tried to scream.

Now on his feet, Tabbard froze like a frightened rabbit, probably seeing the futility in running, the danger in turning his back on Mantle. His allies fell. They had died in seconds.

Tabbard weighed the possibilities. "We will kill you. We have friends. You won't be able to hide."

That defiance, how Mantle relished it! He would enjoy breaking this one. Too bad about the ghosts. That was the cost of killing humans—there were *always* witnesses.

Mantle lengthened his tongue, split the end into a V, and licked Tabbard's nose. "This is where I stick my tongue into your ear and lick your eardrum until you go mad—or you tell me exactly what I need to know."

The human's knees began to quake. "What...what do you want to know?"

"Slaves in Harlech? The Sepulcher shattered? A cornic minister assassinated? Tell me what happened here."

"I— I don't know what happened. I don't know nothin' about that stuff."

"Tell me everything you do know, Tabbard Ouzeley, beginning with the slave girl Cressida Brower and her too-tall sister Telyn. And don't waste my time. I have other people to see tonight."

NEW MYTHS PUBLISHING

CRAFTING WONDER
THROUGH STORIES IN TIME

New Myths Publishing specializes in the publication of written works of fantasy, science fiction, and the Old West. We pride ourselves on bringing our readers high-quality stories that will transport them through time and genres.

Best of NewMyths V: The Growers

Whether it's a dystopia after the end of civilization, a distant world with fantastic beings, or a far future with advanced technology, it will need farmers. Thirty-six of the world's best fantasy and science fiction authors celebrate in prose and poetry the few who feed the globe:

- A grieving widow from another world with a struggling desert farm who rescues a strange creature...and must find a way to provide for them both.
- A combat robot at the end of its career escapes to the countryside and must make peace with a sheepdog to find a new home.
- Bickering families at the edge of space who must work together or be destroyed by a terrifying monster.

Join our authors in honoring the fantastic, the uncanny, and the conceivable farmers.

See more quality publications at www.newmythspublishing.com.